APPALACHIA

Love Nestles into Four Mountain Towns

IRENE B. BRAND
GINA FIELDS
JOANN A. GROTE
CATHERINE RUNYON

BARBOUR
PUBLISHING

Afterglow © 1999 by Irene B. Brand
Still Waters © 2000 by Gina Fields
Come Home to My Heart © 2000 by JoAnn A. Grote
Eagles for Anna © 1996 by Catherine Runyon

ISBN 978-1-59310-672-0

Cover art by Getty Images

All scripture quotations are taken from the King James Version of the Bible.

Published by Barbour Publishing, Inc., P.O. Box 719, Uhrichsville, Ohio 44683, www.barbourbooks.com

Our mission is to publish and distribute inspirational products offering exceptional value and biblical encouragement to the masses.

 Member of the
Evangelical Christian
Publishers Association

Printed in the United States of America.
5 4

Afterglow

Irene B. Brand

Prologue

But I've never compiled a history," Hester Lawson protested to her friend, Belle Noffsinger, who had telephoned to warn Hester that she would soon receive an invitation from Mayor Arthur Stepp to write a history of the town of Afterglow.

"There's a first time for everything," Belle laughingly said, echoing the home-spun philosophy of the Appalachian region where she lived. "Besides, you're a journalist," Belle argued. "Writing a history shouldn't be so much different from your newspaper work. Our mayor is determined to hire a professional writer for the job, so Clint and I recommended you, and we do hope you'll consider it."

"I wouldn't have much to write, would I? Haven't you always said that you live in a town where nothing ever happens?"

"It's quiet now, but Afterglow had its moments in the past."

"I don't know," Hester said slowly. "I would love to see you, and now that Mother is gone I intend to travel some, but I hardly had a little Appalachian town in mind. How many people live there. . .five hundred ten?"

"Oh, it's five hundred eleven now," Belle retorted. "We had a birth yesterday. Seriously, I don't want you to feel obligated, but I know you can do it, and I thought you might as well have the ten thousand dollars as anyone else."

Hester whistled. "Where did a little town get so much money?" she asked in her low, husky voice.

"I thought that would get your attention," Belle said with a laugh. "Clint wrote a grant proposal to fund the project. Of course that money has to pay for the printing of the books, too, but you should receive half of it."

"Thanks for telephoning in advance; it will give me time to consider. I do need a change of pace. I've been busy with Mother's care for so long, and now I find myself at loose ends."

"Don't you have any other relatives?"

"A few cousins and an aunt on my father's side, none of whom live in Detroit."

Talking to Belle brought back pleasant memories. They had been roommates in college and had kept in touch since then. Because of Hester's busy schedule, she seldom wrote letters, though she did telephone Belle occasionally. But Belle wrote often, long narratives describing her life in Afterglow, the town where she had gone to live with her newspaper husband five years ago. She had described

Afterglow and its residents in such detail that if Hester did take the job, she would probably recognize many of the people she saw on the street.

Hester hung up the phone, feeling more at peace than she had since her mother had become ill. She heard Molly rattling pans in the kitchen, and she headed that way, a wide smile lighting her face.

Molly turned from the sink where she was preparing a salad. "It's great to see you smiling again. Must have had good news."

"Not particularly, but my friend, Belle, phoned. It always picks me up to hear from her. She wants me to come to their town to do some work."

Hester reached for a cookie, and Molly smacked her hand. "Stop that. You'll ruin your dinner, and I've got your favorite, roast beef, tonight."

Hester popped the whole cookie into her mouth and laughed at Molly's frown, wondering what she would have done without this woman over the past five years. About the time Hester's mom, Anna Lawson, had become ill, Molly's husband had died, and she had moved into the house to help Hester. She had been there ever since.

Hester inhaled the aroma of the roast beef, carrots, and potatoes as Molly set the platter on the table. It was not difficult to pray a blessing over this food.

"Thank You, God, for our food and for this kind woman who has helped me through my trouble. What would I have done without her or You during my mother's illness?" Hester prayed with tears pricking her eyelids.

Molly patted her on the back. "You're the daughter I never had, Hester. You've helped me more than I've helped you." After they had filled their plates, Molly said, "But about going to see your friend, that's a great idea. And if I can give you some more advice, why don't you sell this large house? You shouldn't live here alone. There are too many memories."

"You can always live with me," Hester said in surprise. She had supposed that Molly would continue to stay with her.

"I've been thinking of going to Florida to visit my sister. She lives in a retirement home, and she wants me to join her. At least I want to go down and check it out."

Without Molly being there, Hester wondered how she could possibly have enough courage to come home every evening to an empty house.

"I know I need to make a change. I talked to my boss today and asked him to reassign me to a job that would require some travel."

For several years Hester had been the assistant editor at a local newspaper, which kept her in the office most of the time, and, understanding her depression, the editor had agreed. But God would also understand her need for a change of pace, and she wondered if this call from Belle was the opportunity she sought.

"Do you believe in coincidences, Molly?"

"Maybe, but I believe more in faith in God and that He daily provides for us.

If it's right for you to take that job your friend suggests, you'll know it without a shadow of a doubt." Molly pointed to a framed sampler hanging above the table.

In All Thy Ways Acknowledge Him,
and He Shall Direct Thy Paths
PROVERBS 3:6

Hester had embroidered the sampler as a child, and her mother had framed it. For years she had trusted that promise as a guide for her daily living.

But at thirty years old, single and proud of it, was she too set in her ways to start a new life? Although her mental attitudes might hinder a change to another job, her physical traits would not be a detriment. She had glowing, gray eyes that took on a green hue when she became angry. She was of medium height with a supple body enhanced by a slow, graceful walk. She had worn her brown hair short for years to accommodate her busy lifestyle, and most people classed Hester as beautiful. But in her opinion the slightly long, straight nose inherited from her mother did not complement the delicate bone structure of her face.

After dinner, Hester stretched lazily, and Molly said, "Want a dish of ice cream?"

"Not just now. I'm trying to settle Mother's estate, and I stopped at the bank today and brought home a packet of documents from the safety-deposit box. If you don't need help with the dishes, I'll look through them."

"Won't take me long to put everything in the dishwasher. Do your work, but take a little time to relax. I'll be in my room if you need me."

Hester walked into the comfortable living room, cozy in its simplicity. There were deep chairs, an afghan-covered couch, an entertainment center with bookshelves holding a television set and a CD player, floor lamps conveniently located beside the comfortable chairs, and a coffee table holding several magazines, Hester's Bible, and a recently published devotional book.

Although usually not one to procrastinate, Hester had been slow to settle her mother's affairs, for once that was done, the loss would seem irrevocable. Anna Lawson had died the first week of December, and Hester had taken only her mother's will and insurance policies from the bank and had waited until after Christmas to look at these other things. The holiday had been a hard one for her, but she had struggled through it with Molly's help and by accepting the hospitality of her church friends. Since Hester was the only heir, there hadn't seemed to be any need for hurry. She put a disc in the player and turned the volume low, and the soothing piano music of Dino flowed around the room. She kicked off her shoes and spread the contents of the file folder on the coffee table.

The file contained income tax returns dating back ten years, some certificates of deposit jointly held by Hester and her mother, her parents' wedding certificate, their birth records, as well as her own. Finding nothing that needed any immediate attention, Hester laid aside all of the documents except her parents' wedding certificate. She had not seen it before, and she considered framing it to hang beside the portrait of her parents made ten years ago, before John Lawson's death.

Hester admired the colorful wedding certificate bordered with delicate garlands of roses and apple blossoms, but she gasped when she noted the date on the document. Quickly, with shaking fingers, she retrieved her birth certificate from the file. Still not certain her eyes were not deceiving her, she went into her mother's bedroom and looked at the family Bible's record. There was no doubt about it. The date on the wedding certificate was one year later than the one in the Bible. The day and month were the same, but the year in the family record was different and indicated that her parents had not been married until one month before her birth.

Hester sank weakly onto the side of her mother's bed. *Why hadn't my parents told me?* There had never been any doubt that her parents were happily married, so why had they waited so long to wed when they knew she was on the way? It was hard for Hester to accept the fact that her parents had not been perfect, but the evidence in front of her was too strong.

Hester replaced the wedding certificate in the file, and the next day during her lunch hour, she returned the documents to the bank. She no longer wanted to have the certificate framed.

Before Hester left the newspaper office for the day, her supervisor called her into his office. "I've been checking into a new line of work for you. We could possibly use you occasionally in the sports department to travel with the university's women's teams and report on their activities. At first it would be in this country, but you might eventually make it overseas."

"I'm rusty on who's who in sports now, because I haven't kept up with that information for the past few years; however, I'm sure I could pick it up quickly. When you decide, I'd like to consider it." She laughed slightly. "I had another job offer last night. I've been asked to write the history of an Appalachian town by the name of Afterglow. Ever hear of it?"

The editor shook his head.

"I wouldn't have heard of it either, except that my college friend, Belle, moved there when she married. They would give me several thousand dollars to compile the book, but that would still be a cut in my income because it would take six months or more. I'm not sure I can afford that."

"Sounds like it might be a welcome change for you. All of your friends here have been concerned about your health. Working full-time and then being on vigil in your mother's bedroom each night has drained you. The atmosphere of a small town might be good therapy for you, and you could probably send us human-interest stories from the area. We could keep you on the payroll as a freelancer and pay you for the articles you submit."

"I'm not much interested in it, though, so keep the sports job open for a few days."

❦

"Looks like the letter came from that man," Molly said when Hester came home a half hour later and entered the kitchen. "I put it on the table in the living room. Take this cup of tea and relax while I finish dinner."

Before Hester opened the letter she recalled how Belle had described their town official. *"Mayor Arthur Stepp is a short man with a barrel face and a rotund stomach, who walks as if he has bunions on both feet. . .and he probably has."*

Hester read the message thoughtfully. The mayor's letter extolled the virtues of his town. Afterglow had been founded one hundred years ago as a railroad center for the timber industry. The city council had voted to commemorate the town's origin with a six-month-long celebration scheduled to start in May and culminate with a grand-slam weekend in October. The history would need to be finished before October, therefore work on the book should be started as soon as possible.

When Molly came in to announce dinner, she said, "Any more interested now than you were before?"

"I don't think so." Hester rolled off the couch, went to the bookshelves, and took down an atlas. Turning some pages, she said, "Here it is. Looks as if Afterglow is located in a small river valley nestled among two high ranges of the eastern Allegheny Mountains."

Quickly checking the mileage, she continued, "It's about six hundred miles away and three hundred miles farther south of us, so if I do go I could avoid our Detroit winter."

"If it's in the mountains, I doubt it will be summerlike," said Molly.

For the rest of the evening, Hester pondered the situation. From her correspondence with Belle, she had deduced that nothing much ever happened in Afterglow, and no doubt the town's history would be dull. When she weighed several months of living in Afterglow with the excitement of following women's sports events, there really wasn't much choice. She hated to disappoint Belle, but tomorrow night she would write Mayor Stepp and decline his offer.

The next day, however, brought a development that not only reversed Hester's immediate plans but also set in motion a series of events that marked a complete change in her future.

When Hester arrived home, one lone envelope, a communication from the United States Postal Department, lay in her mailbox. The brief statement indicated that a bag of mail, lost for thirty years, had recently been recovered and that every effort had been made to forward the missives to the intended recipients or, lacking that, to their next of kin.

With a laugh, Hester said aloud, "I doubt anyone would have written to me that long ago." But amazed, Hester lifted a tattered envelope addressed to her mother at her childhood home in Kentucky, which was strange in itself since her mother was a child when she had moved from that town. Who would have known to send a letter there? The name of the envelope was her mother's maiden name, Anna Taylor. Another word had been written after Taylor but it had been erased, indicating the sender may have written "Lawson" and then had obliterated it.

Though her mother was dead, Hester still hesitated to open her correspondence, but she was curious. Using a letter opener, she slit the yellowed envelope and quickly scanned the contents, then read it a second time, her heartbeat accelerating with each word she read.

Anna,

    I couldn't believe that you were gone when I returned from my tour of duty in Korea. Your last letter mentioned the baby. Why did you run away? You know I would have taken care of you. Since I don't know where you are, I hope your relatives will forward the letter. You know where I live, and I beg you to contact me. I love you, but I'll not push myself on you. You must make the next move.

                                               T O By

What did this mean? Who was Toby? What baby? Hester's mind churned maddeningly, relating this letter with what she had learned just last night from her parents' wedding certificate. Did it indicate that this Toby was her father rather than John Lawson? Hester rejected the idea. John Lawson was all that anyone could have desired in a father. Of course, he was her father. And where had this letter been for thirty years?

Hester carefully examined the envelope and small sheet of paper for a clue as to the sender, but there was no return address, and the postmark on the envelope was smudged so much that she could not identify it. She made out a few letters, *Af gl w,* and then using a magnifying glass, she spelled the word, *Afterglow.* Laughter was Hester's first reaction, for it was inconceivable that she would receive two unrelated letters from this obscure town within two days. Of course, there might be hundreds of towns by that name, but after scanning the atlas for a half hour, she had not found another Afterglow. Hearing Molly entering the kitchen, Hester hastily concealed the letter. This was one thing she could not share with anyone. Surely there was some mistake!

But the coincidence was more than Hester could dismiss from her mind, and she spent a fretful night. Should she meddle in her mother's past? She might be better off not to know who had sent the letter and why. But she could not ignore the matter. She brightened a little when she thought the addressee might be another Anna Taylor rather than her mother, but she had to renounce that supposition because her mother really had lived in that Kentucky town for several years, and Anna's grandparents had made their home there until their deaths. No, the letter was to her mother, and so it concerned Hester. Could she go to Afterglow with the twofold purpose of writing the history of the town and surreptitiously searching out the mysterious Toby?

The next day Hester moved sluggishly around the office, earning her many curious glances from her fellow workers. Finally, unable to bear the indecision, she wrote a brief note to Mayor Arthur Stepp.

I'd be pleased to accept your invitation to compile a history of Afterglow.
Expect me in your town in about fifteen days.

She dropped the letter in the outgoing mail and stopped by the editor's office to tell him of her decision.

"I'll give you a year's leave of absence, if it takes that long, but still keep you on the payroll for freelance work," he assured her. "You'll probably find some great human interest stories. I understand some of those mountainous areas are fifteen to twenty years behind the times."

Once the decision was made, Hester did not fret about it, especially since Molly was enthusiastic about her plans. Molly put her bony arms around Hester. "It's for the best. I'll go to my sister's in Florida for a few months, and when you return to Detroit, I'll come to you if you need me, but I'm sure you'll be adjusted by then."

"Plan to live with me when you've had enough visiting."

"I want you to find a good man and get married, Hester, and if you do, I'll not be living here."

Hester laughed away her suggestion. She had hoped Molly would stay in the house, but she quickly found a church family who wanted to rent a place to live for six months and considered it was another reason to believe that God was guiding her decision.

When she telephoned Belle that she was coming, her friend said, "Great! You can live with us."

"I won't, although you're sweet to offer. No friendship can withstand months of live-in company. I'll roost with you for a few nights until I can find some accommodations. Is there a motel?"

"Of sorts, but you wouldn't like it."

"A hotel?" Hester asked hopefully.

"Yes, but it closed about twenty years ago. I suppose you could stay at Miss Eliza's. Her grandmother started a boardinghouse here at the turn of the century when the timber industry was strong, and Miss Eliza has carried on the family tradition. She keeps a few permanent boarders. It's not too bad."

"Oh, yes, I remember about Miss Eliza. You mentioned that she travels around town like a runaway train and that her face turns a ruddy red when she's angry."

"Your memory is too good. I hope you won't repeat any of the things I've written about our townspeople and make them angry with me. You'll be here only a few months, but this is my home."

"Trust me. I'll be discreet. But about lodging, try to find a place for me."

"Telephone the night before you'll arrive, and I'll give you directions."

"Remember I grew up in Detroit. If I can drive in our congested traffic, I should be able to find my way around Afterglow."

"Oh, you won't get lost once you arrive. It's finding the place that will pose a problem. You'd better telephone me."

Hester kept packing items into her compact car until she could not see out the rear window and knew she would have to rely on the side mirrors. Probably she was taking too much, but she would be away during the winter and summer, so that required all her clothing, and she would also have to take her computer. She bought a year's supply of paper and other office supplies, for she figured the shopping selection in Afterglow would be meager.

As she packed, Molly kept warning, "You can't put all of that in the car, Hester. Pack lightly as I've done."

Molly had packed her clothing into one suitcase and a shoulder bag, believing she would have more than enough garments to last her through the winter.

But Hester did not pay much attention. Emotionally she still could not give up her mother and the home they had shared, and she had to take some family reminders with her. Even if she had only one room in Afterglow, she wanted it to remind her of home. She wrapped several of her favorite wall hangings, but with the automobile full of necessities, she knew she would have to leave the paintings behind. She placed all of them back on the walls except two. She had to take the oil entitled, *Winter Serenity*. The rural scene had been painted by one of her professors, I. M. Thomas. A distinguishing feature of his work was that he included the figure of a bird in each of his paintings. In this work the artist had depicted a long, narrow river valley wedged between a series of mountain ranges; the tiny figure of a cardinal perched on a snow-laden spruce in the foreground.

Thomas had been an artist-in-residence one winter at Ohio State University where Hester had been a student, and she had attended two of his seminars. She recognized that she did not have any great talent, as did Thomas, but he seemed content to let her dabble. Thomas had painted *Winter Serenity* to illustrate the use of oils, and when names had been drawn for the works he had painted, Hester had won the winter landscape. Since that time she had kept it above her desk for inspiration, and she would not consider going to Afterglow without it. She took a sweater from one of her suitcases and replaced it with the painting. She tucked the sampler bearing her motto, "In all thy ways acknowledge him, and he shall direct thy paths," in beside the landscape, and her packing was finished.

Two days later, Hester saw Molly to a plane headed for Florida, and with a tingle of anticipation, she headed out of town. She had planned two days for travel to Afterglow in case she should run into slick highways, and the weather cooperated at first, but it started snowing at Pittsburgh, and she crawled for miles on Interstate 79. She stopped around dusk at a motel north of Fairmont, West Virginia, fearing to travel any longer. Accustomed to lots of snow, she had no trouble coping with the wet highway, but another concern caused tremors of fear along her spine. *Am I being stalked?*

She had first become aware of the man on Interstate 80 as she traveled across Ohio. He had smiled at her as they passed in a service area. The next time she entered a rest stop, he pulled in behind her as she started to leave. He smiled again, but this time she ignored him. His dark blue Mercedes was not hard to spot, and keeping a careful watch in the side mirrors, she noted that his car kept the same distance behind her. When she accelerated, his car sped up. When she stopped for gas in Pittsburgh, he pulled in at a pump behind her. Thoroughly angry and somewhat frightened, she drove on without filling her tank. Driving faster than she should have on the snow-covered road, she had left the man behind her, and she breathed easier when she did not see him again. She kept watch on her gas gauge and was thankful she had enough fuel to take her to a motel.

Fortunately there was a restaurant adjacent to the motel, for by the time she registered and paid for the room, the snow was several inches deep, and after bringing her bags into her room, she crossed the driveway to the restaurant. The warm food revived her spirits, and she laughed at herself for thinking the man had been following her, for he did not look like a stalker. Dressed in a dark business suit, the handsome man was of unusual height with a trim stature, and his brilliant blue eyes were both beautiful and friendly. Most women would have been pleased to have a man like that pursue them, for he was handsome enough, but she had reported too many stories about women traveling alone being assaulted.

The next morning, before she got out of bed, Hester flipped on the television, and the local forecaster announced that the snow had stopped at midnight and that road crews were busily clearing the highways. She bounced out of bed, eager to be on her way. She pulled aside the curtain and peered out the window, and her joy in the day dimmed—parked beside her loaded vehicle was the blue Mercedes that had followed her yesterday.

Chapter 1

Thoroughly frightened and without even taking time for a shower, Hester hurried into her garments and picked up her overnight bag. She opened the door and peered intently up and down the parking area. No one else seemed to be around. She pitched the door key onto the dresser, closed the door quietly, and ran to her car. She shoved some accumulated snow off the windshield and unlocked the door.

"Dear God, let this car start now." She turned the key, and the engine hummed into action as if it had spent the night in the insulated garage at Detroit instead of this windswept motel lot. She breathed easier when she pulled out onto the highway and the Mercedes had not moved. Hester drove twenty miles before breakfasting, and after she had eaten and telephoned Belle of her whereabouts, and the Mercedes and its attractive driver had not appeared, her tense nerves relaxed. No doubt she would never see the man again, but it annoyed her that she was still harassed by the memory of his sparkling blue eyes; shiny white teeth; firm, straight mouth; and magnetic persona.

As she steered her compact Ford up the curving hollow, following the twists and turns of the river, Hester appreciated the wisdom of Belle's insistence that she telephone for directions. Many unmarked roads led off from the narrow paved highway, and if she hadn't had Belle's instructions—"Don't leave the main road. Afterglow is at the head of the hollow. When you get here, you can't go any farther"—she would have gone astray more than once.

A few miles before she reached the town, the river veered to the left and her heavily loaded car slowly navigated a tortuous road up the side of a mountain. At the crest, she pulled into a lookout area for a bird's-eye view of the town of Afterglow. Although a few hemlock and spruce trees dotted the hillsides, deciduous trees, now barren of leaves, dominated the forest. Snow flurries danced in the air, but Hester left the car to peer over the precipice, jumping back in alarm when she saw the sheer drop below her. Thankfully there was a waist-high retaining wall! A sharp blast of wind swept up the hollow, so she hurried to the car and made her descent to where the river had reappeared, hugging one side of the narrow valley.

She stopped abruptly when she came to a wooden covered bridge spanning the river at a narrow spot. Although the huge timbers and beams that made up the frame looked sturdy, she wondered if it was intended for automobile traffic. She glanced up and down the river and could see no other place to cross. While she hesitated, a pickup whizzed across the structure, so Hester warily steered her car up the incline and bumped along the uneven floorboards, emerged on the other side, and crossed a rumbling, seemingly abandoned railroad track. The buildings of Afterglow spread up the valley as far she could see until a curve in the river cut off the view. Dwellings perched in neat rows partway up the mountainside.

Why, I've seen this valley before! Since she knew she hadn't, Belle's description of the valley must have been more vivid than she had imagined.

"I'll meet you at the *Courier* office," Belle had said. "It's on Main Street and easily found. You might have trouble finding our house until you grow accustomed to the narrow, steep streets."

There was only one stoplight in the town and according to Belle, after passing the light, the *Courier* was on the right-hand side of the street next to the river. Hester saw the stoplight several blocks downstream as soon as she drove out of the covered bridge, but before she came to the light, she had to maneuver around a statue in the middle of the street. Hester had a brief glimpse of the inscription: CIVIL WAR VETERAN.

Before Hester had the car parked, Belle was on the sidewalk to greet her. Hester fondly appraised her friend's slanted blue eyes, fair complexion, and tawny hair, noting with amusement that Belle was chubbier than she used to be.

Hester was soon enveloped in Belle's arms. "I was beginning to worry. You're later than I'd expected you to be."

"I'm not used to these crooked roads and then, too, I stopped a few times to gaze at the fantastic scenery. No wonder you like it here."

"Wait until you see the trees with their leaves on. It's more beautiful then. Come in and meet my family."

Tall, angular, slow-spoken Clint Noffsinger was a native of Afterglow, and he had met Belle when they both had worked in Washington, D.C. He greeted Hester with a warm handshake.

"And here's Ina," Belle said, lifting her three-year-old daughter from behind a chair where she had been peering timorously at Hester. "She's not normally so bashful, as you'll soon find out. You can see she's the spittin' image of her daddy, as the locals describe it." Belle looked fondly at her brown-haired, dark-eyed offspring.

"How was your trip?" Clint drawled. "Anything exciting happen on the way down?"

Although Hester had thought she would relish telling her friends about the encounter with the suspected stalker, she seemed reluctant to mention it. *Is it a memory I want to cherish for myself?* Strange how many times she had thought of that man today.

"I encountered about fifty miles of snow-covered roads yesterday. That wasn't exciting, but it was nerve-racking."

Belle zipped Ina into a one-piece hooded suit. "We'll go home and have dinner ready when you finish work, Clint." To Hester, she said, "The centennial commission meets tonight, and the mayor wants you to attend."

Hester moved her purse and road maps from the front seat to make room for Belle and Ina in the car. She followed Belle's directions and turned left at the next street, but Hester gasped as she looked—straight up!

"How do you ever drive off that hill when there's snow?"

"We don't; we walk."

Hester gunned the engine, and her loaded car labored up the incline. "Walking wouldn't be much better," she muttered.

"We don't have many snows down in this valley. There can be a foot of snow on the mountain, and we'll have only a smattering. Our home is the last one on this street. You can park behind the house."

"Whew!" Hester breathed deeply when she turned into the driveway and switched off the engine.

"Bring in all your things," Belle said. "I'll help as soon as I take Ina inside."

Hester shook her head. "I have everything I'll need for a couple of days in these two small bags, and I don't intend to stay here longer than that." When Belle started to protest, Hester glanced at the bungalow. "Now, Belle, be realistic. You have only four rooms, and I'm going to be here for months. I'll need working space and privacy. I'll be in and out often, and I won't stay in your house all of the time."

With a sigh, Belle agreed. "I suppose you're right, but I feel so cut off from the outside world, and I would enjoy some stimulating conversation. About the most exciting thing that's happened in the past month was when old Mr. Byrd dropped his false teeth in the soup kettle at the boardinghouse."

"I'll try to liven things up," Hester promised. "And with that comment on the boardinghouse, I don't think I want to live there."

"Oh, Miss Eliza was on the alert, and she dumped the soup. You don't have to worry about her food. She's an excellent cook."

At dinner, when they discussed a place for Hester to stay, Clint suggested, "Why not try for the furnished apartment Miss Eliza has? Her nephew lived there at one time, and she refurbished it a few years ago for a schoolteacher who moved to Afterglow. It hasn't been rented since the teacher retired and left the county. It may not be what you're used to, but you won't do much better on rental property in Afterglow."

"How many rooms?"

"Three, I think. Miss Eliza will be at the meeting. We can ask her about it," Clint said.

❧

Hester rode to the town hall with Clint, who was on the centennial commission.

She eagerly looked forward to seeing the people she would work with on this project. Clint parked along Main Street and opened the door for her to enter a building two doors north of his newspaper office.

"We're meeting in the council chamber," he explained. When they entered the room, most of the chairs at the oval table were already occupied. A rotund man standing at the head of the table sped in their direction and extended a pudgy hand toward Hester.

"I'm Mayor Arthur Stepp," he stated. "Welcome to Afterglow."

Hester considered herself of only medium height, yet she looked down on Mayor Stepp, who resembled a compact barrel. What he lacked in size, though, he made up for in action, for his body appeared to be in perpetual motion.

"Sit beside me," he said, pulling Hester along by the hand. "I'll introduce you to the commission."

As soon as Hester settled into the chair, he said, "Starting to your left is the pastor of Brown Memorial Church, Ray Stanford." When Stanford started to rise, the mayor said, "Not necessary to stand on formalities, Reverend."

The mayor talked so fast his words ran together, and she could hardly understand him, making it difficult to put names and faces together. She did note that the only other female in the room was Eliza Byrd, a woman who appeared to be in her early seventies but straight as a ramrod and with snappy, big brown eyes. Deep wrinkles encircled Miss Eliza's large mouth, and her long, thin gray hair was braided around her head.

When the mayor had finished the introductions, he said, "Miss Lawson, we appreciate that you've taken time to help us celebrate the centennial of the fabulous town of Afterglow. By writing our glorious history, you will help us honor our ancestors who settled this rugged valley and brought the benefits of civilization to kith and kin."

The mayor rambled on in this vein for another five minutes, often interspersing his words with a hearty laugh and animated gestures, causing Hester to wonder if he could talk without waving his arms.

Clint Noffsinger sat directly across from Hester, and he lowered his left eyelid slightly, suggesting to her that not all of the town's citizens shared Stepp's exalted views. But Hester was hardly prepared for Miss Eliza's interruption.

"Oh, hush, Mayor. Let's get on with the business of the evening. Miss Lawson will soon learn enough about our town."

Hester smothered a gasp at this rudeness. The mayor's face flushed, and he threw an indignant glance in the speaker's direction, but he cleared his throat and forced a laugh.

"No need to be so hasty, Miss Eliza."

"There is a need for hurry," she retorted. "With all of the highfalutin ideas you've come up with, we should have started on this project five years ago. We don't have any time to spare. Let's fill Miss Lawson in on what we want her to do so she can start."

"I'd prefer all of you to call me Hester," she said. "From Mayor Stepp's letter, I assumed that my only assignment is to research and prepare a history of the town for publication."

Mayor Stepp cleared his throat again. "And incidentals connected with it."

Ray Stanford's bass voice sounded at her side. "We've planned a drama in October to feature highlights of our heritage. Perhaps you can find time to write that as you research the history."

"I suppose I could," Hester said slowly, "although I've never written a drama."

"And to direct it, too," Clint said with a grin. "The commission wants to be sure you earn your money."

"This promises to be an interesting year," Hester replied wryly. "May I hear about the rest of your plans?"

"Miss Eliza is looking for descendants of the first settlers to bring them in for our celebration," the mayor said.

"Hester," the old woman said crisply, "this town was founded by Hezekiah Brown, who started timbering here a hundred years ago. He had enough influence to bring in the railroad, which came up the valley and over the mountain to haul his product to market. Out of his vast holdings, he gave the land for this town. It's his memory we will be honoring."

Mayor Stepp motioned to the large man at her side. "Pastor Stanford will chair a committee to emphasize the coming of the gospel to our community. Would you tell Miss Hester what you're planning?"

A massive man in his midforties, Ray Stanford resembled a lumberjack more than a preacher. His frizzy black whiskers bristled with vitality.

"The first Christian witness here was a chapel car ministry. Soon after the first train arrived, a missionary couple, Ivan and Thelma Hartwell, came into the community in a specially built car that contained their living quarters and a chapel. They pulled the car off onto a siding and stayed in the community for the better part of a year until they had organized the nucleus of our church."

"And according to my grandfather, they had a rough time of it, too," Miss Eliza said. "The wood hicks weren't pleased to have preaching in the town."

"Wood hicks?" Hester asked.

"The Appalachian word for lumberjack," Clint explained.

"Pastor Hartwell," Miss Eliza continued, "braved the saloons with a gun in one hand and a Bible in the other before he finally gathered a congregation."

"At any rate," Ray Stanford said, "we've made arrangements to have a passenger car converted into an exact replica of the one the Hartwells used, and it will remain in the town as a permanent display. It will be delivered during centennial week."

"I've wondered how the town received its unusual name," Hester said.

Bewilderment covered the faces of those around her as she looked from one to the other. Mayor Stepp stammered and cleared his throat a few times, and finally Clint said, "I guess no one has ever tried to figure that out, Hester. Maybe you can find that out for us, too."

Hester did not bat an eyelash, but by now she was convinced that she was going to earn every penny she made in Afterglow.

"And we're planning other events throughout the year," the mayor continued. "Belle Noffsinger is in charge of a big craft show in July. We're going to refurbish the covered bridge, which is almost as old as the town, and we'll reenact a bank robbery by the Benson gang."

A man across the table from Hester said, "There's still a mystery about that robbery. Lots of people at the time thought Benson stashed the gold somewhere. The law was hot on his trail, and the heavy gold was delaying him. Haven't you heard that, Miss Eliza?"

"Yes, but I think it's quite unlikely that he left the gold behind when he fled. Besides, my grandfather said that for twenty years after the robbery, there was somebody combing these mountains for the gold cache, and it was never found."

Mayor Stepp fidgeted during this exchange, and he said, "Let's not stray from the subject, please." Turning to Hester, he smiled widely. "It's going to be an exciting year. You'll be glad to be a part of it."

"Don't forget the log raft expedition in May," Clint said. "That's the way logs were transported before the railroad arrived," he explained.

"What we need now is a lot of publicity," the mayor said. "Clint, you'll have to give the centennial plans more coverage."

"I'll do what I can, but the *Courier* doesn't have a wide circulation."

"Would you like for me to run articles in my Detroit newspaper?" Hester asked.

"That would be a great idea, young lady," the mayor said. "We need all the publicity possible."

"I wonder how much leeway I'm going to have in writing this history. As a journalist I've been taught to publish the truth. How will the residents react if I uncover uncomplimentary information about the town?"

"I'm sure you'll not find anything derogatory about our citizens, but by all means, publish the truth. You have a free hand," the mayor assured her with a sweep of his arm.

"Any suggestions about where I should start?"

"There are boxes of old papers on the second floor of the *Courier*," Clint said, "left there by the former owners. I've never looked at them, but they should contain much pertinent information."

"You should check the records at the county seat, and we have several cabinets full of old church minutes," Ray Stanford offered. "You would no doubt find those helpful."

After the meeting adjourned, Clint made his way toward Miss Eliza, who had already taken her coat from the rack and was buttoning the fur collar around her neck. He motioned for Hester to join him.

"Miss Eliza, Hester wants to find a place to stay while she's here. Would your apartment be available?"

"Certainly. But it's been vacant a long time. I would need some time to have it cleaned."

"Belle will bring Hester down tomorrow morning to look at it and see if it's adequate for her needs."

As they drove home, Clint said, "The mayor gets carried away, but he means well. He's in his midfifties, and although he wasn't born here, he's become a regular chamber of commerce all by himself. He thinks Afterglow is a Garden of Eden, but we natives know plenty of flaws in our history."

"How's the mayor going to react if I do turn up some seamy stories?"

"He'll be determined that you won't publish them, that's what."

"And I'll be just as determined that I will. Perhaps I should have a written agreement with the mayor before proceeding any further."

"It's advisable."

❦

The next morning, Belle and Hester drove through town with Belle pointing out landmarks and Ina chattering from her car seat behind them.

"The old hotel is on the left, two blocks west of the *Courier*. When it was built about seventy-five years ago, the springs flowing from the mountainside supposedly produced mineral water. That didn't prove to be true, but the hotel enjoyed some success until the timber industry petered out about the time World War II started."

"What about coal mining?"

"There isn't much coal on this side of the mountains. A few mines were opened up in the county, but their supply of coal was meager. This area is in an economic slump; progress has bypassed us. Without a through road, the tourists haven't found Afterglow. Rumors have it, however, that the old Brown acreage around the town is being considered for a state park. If that happens, Afterglow's success would be assured; it would be the only town within the boundaries of the park, which should make it prosperous again. Mayor Stepp believes this centennial celebration will bring tourists to Afterglow, who will return often if the park becomes a reality."

Belle stopped her car in front of the Byrd boardinghouse, a Victorian dwelling located on the south end of town, and Miss Eliza stepped out on the porch to greet them.

"My grandfather built this house around the turn of the century," Miss Eliza explained as she ushered them through a hallway overcrowded with heavy oak furniture popular a century ago and into the large room facing the street. The living room furniture was also Victorian, but newly upholstered, so that the room was inviting and comfortable.

"He started the furniture factory," Miss Eliza added as she invited her guests to be seated.

"Oh, is there a factory?"

Eliza shook her head. "Not anymore. Ownership passed from our family many years ago, and the last owner couldn't make enough money to keep it open."

"Do you have any information on the factory that should be included in the history?"

"I have several things in the attic. And you can interview my father. He's ninety-five and still alert."

Oh, yes. . .the man with the loose false teeth.

After she contributed more information about the town's history, Miss Eliza directed them through the wide hall and out onto the back porch. She indicated a small house a few yards away.

"There it is," she said. "It was originally built by my grandfather as a stable for his horses. He was like Mayor Stepp, always thinking on a large scale. Even though he never owned more than one horse at a time, he built a stable large enough for a cavalry herd. In my youth, we used it for vegetable storage, but my nephew remodeled it into an apartment."

"I'd like to look inside."

"It's open. Help yourself."

Miss Eliza reached out her arms to take Ina; then Hester and Belle crossed the small backyard to explore the building.

"I was in this apartment a few years ago," Belle said as she opened the door.

A shivery sensation possessed Hester when she stepped into the room. Of course, the building was unheated, but it seemed that more than cold had caused the shiver. . .almost as if she were stepping back in time. *Is this centennial research getting to me?*

"There hasn't been any heat in here for years, I'm sure," Belle said, sniffing. "It will be difficult to remove the musty smell from everything."

"Except for that, it isn't so bad," Hester said as she examined the tiny kitchen with an apartment-sized stove and refrigerator, a table, two chairs, and overhead and base cabinets surrounding the two-bowl sink.

"I've considered leaving my home for smaller quarters," Hester said with a laugh, "so this should make me happy, but I won't have room to entertain a great deal."

A bed, nightstand, and a dresser crowded the bedroom, but because of its sparse furnishings—a couch, one chair, and two end tables—the living room seemed large. A garishly colored linoleum covered the floor in all the rooms.

"I'll need a desk, but otherwise, this will do quite well for temporary housing."

Surveying the sparsely furnished room, Belle said, "There's plenty of space to move in a desk."

Hester shivered and pulled her coat closer to her body. "Wonder how the place is heated?"

Belle pointed to a grill on the living room floor. "There's a gas furnace underneath this room. Only one register, but it should be enough for this small space."

"I should probably take it," Hester said, "since you think it's the best quarters available." For some reason, she was reluctant to rent this house, but she had to have a place to live.

Belle must have sensed Hester's hesitation, because she said, "There are other apartments for rent, but this one is the most convenient."

Before making her decision, Hester asked Miss Eliza about the cost of renting.

"Nothing at all, my dear. You're doing our town a favor to come here and write this history. You pay the utility bills, and we'll call it a deal. Give me a couple of days to have the place cleaned and heated, and you can move in."

With that done, Belle and Ina returned home after leaving Hester at the entrance to city hall. She entered the mayor's office at his invitation and hearty welcome.

"And what can I do for you today, Miss Hester?" he said after he ushered her to a comfortable chair in front of his tidy desk.

"Before I start working, shouldn't we have a contract citing my responsibilities as well as the obligations of the town?"

Stepp waved away the suggestion with a languid movement of his hand. "Is that necessary? A gentleman's agreement is all we usually need in Afterglow."

"But *I'm* not a gentleman, and I prefer to have a contract."

"By all means then." He hastened to please. "You write out what you think is necessary. I'll have my secretary type it, and we can both sign the agreement. It won't require much time to take care of the matter."

Hester considered it preposterous that she be asked to write her own terms, but she took the yellow pad he pushed toward her. She found it difficult to concentrate on the content while the mayor expostulated on the glory of Afterglow and its heritage, but after several erasures and additions, she produced a simple document.

This agreement is made between the centennial commission of the town of Afterglow and Hester Lawson. Hester Lawson agrees to research and compile a history of the town of Afterglow to be ready for printing within six months of this date, and also to write a centennial drama and direct its production during the month of October.

For her services, Hester Lawson will be paid approximately six thousand dollars, depending upon the cost of printing the book. If Lawson fails to meet the deadlines mentioned in this document, the centennial commission will be under no financial obligation for the unfinished work.

The commission also agrees that Miss Lawson will not be restricted in the publication of the true facts that she uncovers in her research.

Hester handed the rough copy to Mayor Stepp. "I know we hadn't discussed my rate of pay, but I understood that I was to be given the amount of the grant not used for printing. Clint says that the printing costs shouldn't exceed four thousand dollars."

The mayor scanned the agreement, smiled approval, and hustled into his secretary's office. Two copies of the document were soon duly dated and signed, and Hester returned to the Noffsingers' home with her copy.

That night, Clint looked over the agreement. "Looks legal enough to me." Then with a laugh, he cautioned, "But don't underestimate the mayor. He's been known to wiggle out of a bargain if he's displeased with the results."

Chapter 2

Hester awakened at four o'clock, her usual hour for arising in Detroit so she would be at the office in time to complete work on the early edition. Accustomed to the morning sounds of a city awakening—the delivery trucks, the garbage workers, the street sweepers—the quietness of this mountain village seemed even more thunderous than a city's clamor. After twisting and turning in bed for an hour, she heard a rooster announcing the break of day, and she decided that if it was time for him to be up, she could at least turn on the light.

The frigid room discouraged getting out of bed, so she propped two pillows behind her back and reached for a notebook on the nightstand. She studied the notes that she had made the night before, wondering if she hadn't been presumptuous in agreeing to this assignment and probably foolish to have agreed to be paid only if she completed the history on time. How could she possibly research one hundred years of Afterglow's history from an unreliable source of data, shape her findings into a manuscript suitable for a history, write a drama, and produce it in less than nine months' time? It could not be done. And how could she go about unraveling the mysterious letter addressed to her mother? It had all seemed so simple when she was in Detroit, but now she did not know in which direction to turn.

By the time she heard Clint and Belle stirring and noticed the smell of heat as the furnace warmed her room, she muttered, "I wish I'd never heard of Afterglow." But she had heard of it, and now she had to deal with the assignment she had accepted. Yet, knowing what she had to do did not make it any easier. The room seemed like a prison until Belle tapped on the door to say that Hester could take her turn in the bathroom.

After breakfast, Hester and the Noffsingers lingered over cups of coffee.

"You don't seem to be rested this morning," Belle said with concern. "Are you one of those persons who can't sleep unless you're in your own bed?"

"Usually I can sleep anywhere. But I may as well admit it: I'm terrified of what's before me, and I don't even know how to start."

"Why don't you start by taking a tour of the town?" Belle suggested. "Become acquainted with our fair city."

"That won't take long," Clint said with his one-sided grin. "Afterglow is laid out along the widest part of the river valley. You'll find most of the business district, both past and present, along the one main street, and a few of the businesses are on the side streets. The residential area is mainly spread out on the mountainside. Do you want a guide?"

"No, I got my bearings when Belle drove me around yesterday, so I'll explore on my own." But remembering her recent experience on the highway, she added, "That is, if it's safe enough."

The Noffsingers seemed not to understand until Hester said, "You know what I mean. . .what about muggers or stalkers?"

Clint and Belle laughed simultaneously, and Belle said, "Have you forgotten you're in Afterglow. . .the place where nothing happens? The last crime we had in this town was when Mayor Stepp's housekeeper took him for a burglar, hit him over the head with a skillet, and he was admitted to the hospital with a concussion. We don't even lock our doors at night."

Hester grinned wryly. "Remember I'm from the big city. How would I know?"

A wail from the bedroom indicated that Ina had awakened, and as Belle went to look after her, Hester said to Clint, "Do you know anyone in Afterglow by the name of Toby?"

Clint thought a moment. "No, I don't believe so. In the newspaper office, I come across the names of about everyone in town. Is this someone who lives here now or in the past?"

Hester kept her eyes focused on the coffee mug she held in her hands. "I don't really know. He's probably a man in his fifties. I'm not sure that he ever lived here. I wonder if there are any other towns named Afterglow?"

"I wouldn't be surprised, but I don't know of any."

Hester had considered telling Clint and Belle about the Toby letter but decided not to because it seemed to cast a shadow on her mother's character.

"Oh, well, it's of no matter anyway." She looked out the window, where the sun had finally peered over the mountain to shed a brilliant light around the Noffsinger home. "How cold is it? Do I need to bundle up?"

Belle entered with Ina in her arms and handed the child to Clint. She looked at the indoor/outdoor thermometer on the wall. "It's thirty-five degrees now, and there's a stiff breeze."

"I had the television on for the early news, and the weatherman said the temperature will reach the midfifties today," Clint added.

"Then I'll dress as I would for a brisk walk in Detroit."

After she helped Belle with the dishes, Hester put on a hooded parka over her sweats and donned heavy socks and fleece-lined boots. A pair of mittens completed her garb. Since it was ten o'clock by then, she said to Belle, "Don't expect me back for lunch. I'll find a snack downtown."

"Have fun. Dinner at six o'clock."

When Hester stepped out onto the sidewalk, a blast of cold mountain air swept over her, and she breathed deeply. But her lungs were not used to such fresh air, and she coughed lustily before she resumed her normal breathing pattern.

A downhill walk soon brought her to Main Street, where she turned left. Many buildings had empty storefronts, but she saw several restaurants, a department store, a couple of bars, some grocery stores, a pharmacy, and even a video shop, post office, and bank. She decided that Afterglow wasn't too far behind the times.

Everybody she met greeted her in some way, and she received many a hearty, "Welcome to Afterglow." Months later when Hester would ponder her sojourn in Afterglow, she would always remember this midday walk as the time when she saw small-town America at its best. Little did she know then that she was destined also to see a small town at its worst. But since she did not suspect that on her first day in Afterglow, she enjoyed her walk.

She looked with appreciation at the three-story Grand Hotel across the street from the abandoned train station. Built of red brick in the Renaissance Revival style, the hotel was by far the most pretentious building in town, and Hester thought what a pity to have it vacant but realized that the small motel she had seen down by the covered bridge could probably house Afterglow's few transients.

An elderly man passing by paused and said to her, "The hotel was built in 1915 to take care of train passengers. The ballroom on the second floor is unique, with fancy carvings, velvet draperies, and old-country murals painted by an Italian who came here to work in the woods. He wasn't any good at lumbering, but he sure had a talent with the brush. My father said the dances they used to have there were a sight to behold."

"I suppose the building would need a lot of repair now."

"Not too much, ma'am. Probably some cleaning and painting would do wonders. Good day to you," he said as he tipped his hat and went on his way.

The street ended abruptly as the valley narrowed, leaving only enough room for the railroad, long since abandoned. Hester's eyes followed the path of the ancient steel rails to a branch line that curved up the mountain about a mile down the valley before the main tracks entered a tunnel.

She turned and continued her walk on the opposite side of the street, and after she passed the city hall and the newspaper office, she wandered down a side street toward a set of low buildings on the riverbank. HARDWOOD FURNITURE FACTORY was written in faded letters over the door of one of the buildings. Hester peered through the windows, but she saw nothing, and abandoned further investigation when she stuck her face into a mass of cobwebs.

The brisk walk had warmed her, and Hester unzipped her parka and sauntered toward the statue in the middle of Main Street. She took a notebook from her pocket and copied the inscription, only part of which she had been able to read when she had entered town.

HEZEKIAH BROWN, 1835–1915
FOUNDER OF AFTERGLOW
ENTREPRENEUR, PHILANTHROPIST, CIVIL WAR VETERAN
ERECTED BY THE GRATEFUL CITIZENS OF AFTERGLOW

Nearby, the sun highlighted the spire of a buff-colored brick church facing the river. Hester walked up the six steps and pushed on the door, which opened at her touch. The sanctuary looked as if it would seat more than two hundred worshipers, which Afterglow may have had in its heyday. Stained-glass windows depicted famous episodes from the Bible, and the vaulted ceiling and the pipe organ were reminiscent of European cathedrals. Hester wondered how a small town could have financed this magnificent church until she saw the plaque in the foyer.

THIS HOUSE OF WORSHIP IS DEDICATED TO ITS BENEFACTOR,
HEZEKIAH BROWN,
WHO BEQUEATHED A HALF-MILLION DOLLARS
TO THE CONGREGATION

Hester whistled. "Let's see," she calculated, "when did Brown die?" She checked her notebook: 1915. That had been quite a large bequest in that day, so it was little wonder that Afterglow revered its founder.

She eased down onto a pew. She had missed her daily devotional period this morning, so she sat in the quiet of the sanctuary for several minutes to allow her spiritual life to catch up with the rest of her body. She focused on the window depicting Jesus calming the angry waves, and the words below the scene, "Peace, be still," helped to dispel her frustrations over the writing projects she had accepted.

Leaving the building more spiritually alert than she had been for months, Hester passed by Miss Eliza's boardinghouse, and she waved to a cane-supported elderly gentleman on the porch. Wind-wafted streams of condensation escaped from the vent pipe of the small house she had rented, and she assumed the place was being readied for her. *Maybe my stint in Afterglow won't be so bad, after all.*

When her stomach and watch reminded Hester that it was past one o'clock, she entered the first restaurant she found and sat in a booth.

Menus were not available, but a middle-aged waitress called to her from behind the counter. "Chili with corn bread is today's special, but I can fix you a hot dog or a hamburger if you'd rather."

"The chili and corn bread sounds good, and I'll take a large cola, too."

Two men sat at the counter with coffee cups before them. They looked at Hester curiously and spoke in friendly fashion. The door opened to admit a man she had seen at the centennial commission meeting, and he headed her way.

"Mind if I join you, Hester?"

Hester smiled and indicated the bench opposite her while her mind floundered. *Which one was he?*

"I've been on a tour of the town this morning to get my bearings."

"I saw you leave the church. Sorry I wasn't there to greet you."

Oh, yes, the pastor of the church, Ray Stanford.

"A beautiful building. I was amazed to find such grandeur in Afterglow until I noted the dedication plaque."

"After Brown remembered the church in his will, the congregation tore down the original log building and built the present structure."

"How long have you been the pastor?"

"Ten years. I'm a native of Afterglow. My family moved away when I was a teenager, but when I graduated from seminary, I applied for the position and was accepted. I'd missed the mountains."

The waitress hadn't even asked Ray what he wanted, but when she brought Hester's order, she set a bowl of chili, corn bread, and coffee in front on him.

When he noted Hester's questioning look, he smiled. "I'm here every day at noon, and I let Sadie choose my lunch. She knows what I like by now, anyway. I've been a widower for a couple of years, and while I can rustle up a pretty good meal, I'm usually too busy to cook. We don't have many ministers in the area, and I always have plenty to do."

"You know everyone in town, I suppose?"

"Just about. We don't have many newcomers."

"Do you know anyone by the name of Toby?"

"I don't believe so. Tommy Byrd used to live here, and I've known some Tonys and at least one Troy, but no Tobys. A friend of yours?"

"No, a friend of my mother's." His glance was speculative, but Hester changed the subject hurriedly to forestall further queries. "I'm full of questions after my morning's tour. Which house belonged to Hezekiah Brown?"

"Brown had a residence on the mountain close to his timbering industry. His heirs didn't choose to live there, so the building is in ruins now. But back to your question about a Toby. Could it be a Tubby you're looking for? That's Mayor Stepp's nickname. Of course, now that he's our eminent mayor, we try not to use that name in connection with him."

Hester lifted a hand to her burning face and sipped hurriedly on her cola. *Just my luck to have Mayor Stepp turn out to be my father.* She would have to check that signature again.

Clint Noffsinger entered the restaurant and moved toward them. Ray scooted over in the seat, and Clint sat beside him.

"Through for the day?" Ray asked.

"Yes. The presses are rolling, so I've done all I can do."

The waitress brought Clint a cup of coffee, and he smiled his thanks at her.

"Hester was wondering about Brown's residence. If you and Belle don't have plans for the rest of the afternoon, let's take her up there."

"I've walked for three hours this morning, and I doubt I could climb a mountain," Hester said.

"You won't have to walk," Ray assured her. "Both of us have four-wheelers. I use mine about as much in my work as I do the truck."

"Then that sounds like a good idea to me. I need to learn everything I can about Brown, and I feel pressured to start on this research immediately."

"I'll phone Belle and see if she can arrange for a baby-sitter." Clint moved to the telephone placed conveniently on the food counter. When he returned, he took a final swig of his coffee and said, "She can go. We'll meet you at the trail head in a half hour."

Ray stood up and helped Hester with her coat. "You can ride that far with me, if you like, Hester, so you won't have to walk up to Clint's."

They left the restaurant together and took the short walk to the parsonage adjacent to the church. The four-wheeler was parked in Ray's garage, and Hester looked at it with some misgiving while Ray put a heavy cushion behind the driver's seat and loaded the vehicle into his pickup. The thing looked like a glorified motorcycle, and she had always been afraid of motorcycles.

"We'll drive down the valley for a few miles before we take to the woods. It's illegal to drive four-wheelers on the highway, so we have to travel partway in the truck."

Her companion wore a red plaid jacket, blue jeans, a red cap, and heavy leather boots. She smiled when she remembered her first impression of him.

"You surely fit into the surroundings. I suppose this isn't very flattering, but you look more like a lumberjack than a preacher."

His dark eyes gleamed with laughter. "What's a preacher supposed to look like? Do you expect me to dress in a clerical collar and robe all the time? Come to church Sunday, and you'll see me as the stereotypical minister, but I interact with the natives better if I dress as they do. Besides, I prefer casual clothing."

"I hope you haven't adopted the tactics of the first missionary here. Didn't Miss Eliza say he invaded the saloons with a gun in one hand and a Bible in the other to gather a congregation?"

"I haven't gone that far yet, but I've been tempted."

Ray bypassed the covered bridge and traveled along a road that followed the meanderings of the river. Trees and bushes crowded both sides of the road that was hardly more than a trail.

"You will notice," he said, "that all of these trees are small. Years ago these mountains were stripped bare by the timber industry, but slowly new trees took root."

"Didn't the industry have a reforestation policy?"

"That concept was unheard of then."

After a short drive, Ray pulled into a turnout beside the road and unloaded the four-wheeler. Clint and Belle arrived in a few minutes.

"This was a good idea, Ray," Belle said. "Ina and I have gotten on one another's nerves today. It was a relief to farm her out for a few hours."

Belle straddled the back of Clint's four-wheeler when he unloaded it, and Ray indicated that Hester should ride behind him.

"We'll travel over some steep areas, so you need to hold on to me. Don't drag your feet; put your arms around my waist and keep them there. I don't want you to fall off."

Noting her look of alarm, Ray chuckled and said, "There isn't any danger if you're cautious, but I want you to hold on."

When she locked her arms around his muscular waist, he said, "Not that tight. I have to breath."

With a roar of his vehicle's engine, Clint disappeared into the forest ahead of them. Hester loosened her hold a little but kept her hands linked tightly as Ray left the clearing and steered the four-wheeler along an old logging road that wound upward through the woods over steep, rugged terrain. After Hester took one look through the barren trees and saw the river spiraling far below them, she shut her eyes and buried her face on Ray's back.

Not until the vehicle came to a sudden stop did she open her eyes. "Are we there?" she said breathlessly, looking around for some buildings. Ray helped her off the vehicle, but her legs wobbled, and she leaned against the four-wheeler.

Belle rushed to her. "Are you sick?"

"I'm sorry to be so foolish, but I haven't been in mountains before. I feel dizzy, and my ears are plugged. Your voice sounds far away."

"A perfectly normal reaction when you're unused to high altitudes. I should have though of that," Ray apologized. "We came up several hundred feet quickly. Swallow several times, and your head may clear."

"I had the same reaction when I first moved here," Belle encouraged.

Hester closed her eyes as Clint explained, "We're on a ridge now, and we won't be doing any more climbing. This is where Brown's first sawmill was located, and there are still remnants of it lying around. The house isn't far away. When you feel up to it, we'll investigate."

Perhaps the promise of no more climbing helped, because when Hester opened her eyes, she felt almost normal.

Ray and Clint led the way into the nearby forest to the site of several ramshackle log buildings.

"The wood hicks spent months in the forest, so logging companies provided accommodations for them," Clint explained. "Brown had bunkhouses and mess halls for his crews. This long building was the bunkhouse, and I imagine the smaller structure was where the men ate. The cook was usually the best-paid employee in the timber industry, because if the wood hicks didn't have good food, they would leave."

"Brown had camps all over these mountains, but this was the first site and where he had a sawmill, as I understand it," Ray added.

Stumbling over one of the many stumps protruding from the ground, Hester said, "After so many years, wouldn't you think these stumps would have deteriorated?"

"Brown's crew probably worked here no more than seventy-five years ago, and it takes longer than that for all evidence to disappear," Ray explained. "Besides, after Brown died, other companies moved in and cut the smaller trees."

"I wish I could have seen these woods when they were full of virgin timber," Clint commented. "I've seen pictures of stumps big enough for a man to lie on and take a nap."

Large timbers marked the pit where the sawmill had been situated, and the steam engine stood in the spot where it had been abandoned years ago. A rusty circular saw leaned against a tumbledown building. As they walked around the deserted site, they saw the wreckage of axes, crosscut saws, and cookware left behind by the wood hicks.

"It's rumored that this site will become a monument to the timber industry if the state park becomes a reality," Belle said.

From the sawmill they walked for about fifteen minutes to Brown's residence on a promontory overlooking the town of Afterglow. Even when it was new, the house would have been unostentatious. They stepped up onto the unstable porch and pushed aside the sagging door to enter the spacious living room. The kitchen and dining area were to the rear of this room, and three bedrooms stretched out in an L to the right of the kitchen. Dried grass, nuts, and animal dropping indicated that the dwelling had become a habitat for wildlife, but the wallpaper was still intact except for one corner of a bedroom that had been damaged by moisture from a leaky roof. The outbuildings had crumbled until only one, apparently a stable, was still standing. Hester ventured to the edge of the mountain for one quick look at the valley and scurried back to the safety of level ground.

"I don't know why that valley would appear familiar to me," she said. "Belle, you must have done a great job describing it. It's a beautiful setting for a town."

"Brown built his house here because he liked the view, or so I've heard," Clint said.

"I assume he was married. Did he have a large family?" Hester questioned.

"There's a family cemetery somewhere on this mountain, but I don't know where it is," Clint said. "Probably old Mr. Byrd knows. If you find it, that will give you some family information."

"Is Hezekiah Brown buried in that cemetery?"

"I think so," Ray told her.

"We don't have time to hunt for the graves today, but we'll help you find them later," Clint promised.

Though Ray drove slowly, Hester found the ride off the hill as terrifying as the ascent, but she had made up her mind to get over it. She had committed herself to a task in the mountains, and she had to shape up. When they returned to Afterglow, Ray drove up the hill and let her out in front of the Noffsinger house. Her ears roared, and she heard his voice from a distance. Still a bit dizzy, she held on to the truck door when she stepped from the cab.

"Thanks. Today has been a good orientation to the area."

"Sorry about the dizziness. You'll soon become acclimated to the altitude."

When Hester reached her room, the first thing she did was to unlock the case that contained the Toby letter. The unpleasant thought that Mayor Stepp might be her father had been in the back of her mind all afternoon. She scanned the signature carefully. The message had been written in pencil, and the letters were smudged. It was possible that second letter could be a *U* instead of an *O*, but if that were the case, the signature would be Tuby, not Tubby, which encouraged her considerably.

Why did the postal department have to find this letter? She moaned inwardly.

❧

The next day, after asking directions from Clint, Hester headed for the county seat twenty miles away. She wanted to begin her research with the courthouse records, and since Miss Eliza had sent word that she could move into the apartment tomorrow, today seemed like a good time to take the trip. She left immediately after breakfast.

Hester had no trouble spotting the courthouse situated on a wide lawn, and in the clerk's office she looked first among the recorded property deeds and survey plats of the towns. At noontime, she still did not have all the information she searched for, so after breaking for a sandwich and coffee, Hester reentered the courthouse to work for another two hours. Seated at the long table with more than a dozen deed books scattered around her, Hester leaned back in perplexity. Somehow the facts she sought kept eluding her, and wanting to cross the mountain to Afterglow before dark, she decided to return another day.

She stacked the books in one spot, picked up her purse, and started toward the door, which opened to admit a tall, handsome blond man whose face widened into a grin when he saw Hester.

My highway stalker!

She retreated into the room and shouted, "How dare you follow me this way!"

Surprise flitted across his face, and he plunged his hands into the pockets of his neat, navy trousers, his eyes narrowed to a frown. "Lady, believe it or not, I never expected to see you again." He moved toward her, and she glided behind the table. "Let's sit down and talk this out. It's just too much of a coincidence that we keep encountering one another. Maybe we should become acquainted."

"Are you sure you aren't following me?"

The blond-haired Apollo raised his right arm, and his eyes were laughing again. "Scout's honor."

Hester hesitated to be drawn into a conversation with him, although she could not help wondering why their paths kept crossing. She perched on the edge of a chair and favored him with a stony stare.

"Okay, I'll go first," he said. "My name is Kyle Trent. I'm an attorney, live in Harrisburg, Pennsylvania, marital status. . .unattached." He waved his arm toward her, indicating it was her turn.

"I'm Hester Lawson, journalist, live in Detroit."

He regarded her, his eyebrows raised in a questioning manner.

"Unattached, too," she admitted reluctantly.

"When I first saw you, I was returning from a business appointment in Pittsburgh. A week before that, my plans had already been made to come here and check some wills and deeds. I'm not following you; my business is perfectly legitimate. What is your reason for being here?"

Hester hesitated, not wanting him to know how long she would be in this region, but she finally said, "I'm on assignment now in the town of Afterglow."

He laughed delightedly. "Really! I have some business interest in Afterglow, too, and if you see me there, don't entertain the wrong idea. I planned this trip weeks ago."

"A likely story," she said.

"You're the most suspicious woman I've ever met. Do you consider your charms so wondrous that one fleeting look would cause me to follow you to the ends of the earth?"

Hester stood and started toward the door.

"Answer one more question before you leave. What kind of an assignment do you have in Afterglow?"

"Not that it's any of your business, but I'm doing research to compile a history of the town for its centennial celebration. I've been checking property lines today. The residents know so little about their town that I started my research with basic information. They don't even know why the town was named Afterglow."

"Oh, I can tell you that! When the founder of the town first entered the area, he stood on a high peak and looked westward. It was late in the day and the sun had already set, but the afterglow lightened the western horizon and cast its burnished hues on the valley where he eventually established a town. Hence, the name Afterglow."

"Are you making that up?"

He frowned. "Do I look like a man who would spoil a town's image and its heritage by offering erroneous facts?"

Hester looked intently at his firm chin and straight mouth. Somehow she envisioned that the expression in his unflecked blue eyes was reminiscent of the aggravating way Rhett Butler had often regarded Scarlett O'Hara. Yet her pulse vibrated with an unaccustomed emotion.

"Yes," she said deliberately.

"Then run along, Miss Suspicious. You can search out the information by yourself. See you in Afterglow."

Chapter 3

Hester braked steadily while going down the sloping hill until she reached Main Street where she drove left two blocks to the Byrd property. She was making this move reluctantly, and she could not understand why. She certainly did not want to live with Belle and Clint the better part of a year, so what was her problem? Perhaps it was because she had never lived alone, but as she negotiated the narrow driveway and parked in front of the tiny house, she felt that her hesitation had to do with the dwelling itself. She mentally chastised herself and credited her qualms as "woman's vapors," as her Kentucky grandfather used to express it.

Whatever the cause, she breathed easier when Ray Stanford came out of the Byrd house and called in his booming voice, "I'll help carry your luggage." He took two of the heavier suitcases, and since he went in the house ahead of her, she did not hesitate to enter. Ray's tall, compact body dwarfed the living room, and he measured between his head and the ceiling.

"Not more than four inches of clearance," he said with a laugh. "I was in this apartment when Tommy lived here, but I wasn't as tall then."

"It's much smaller than I'm used to, and I can think of many ways to make it more livable if I were going to live here long, but for a few months, I'll take it as it is, except I will need a desk. Is there a furniture store in town where I can buy one?"

"I doubt that's necessary. Probably Miss Eliza has a desk to lend you. She keeps some extra pieces of furniture so she can fit up rooms the way her guests wants them. Ask her before you buy one."

"Set everything in the living room, and I'll organize it later," Hester said. When they had emptied her car, the two of them crossed the twenty feet to the back porch of the Byrd house and entered the kitchen where Miss Eliza was preparing pies for baking.

"Welcome, neighbor," Miss Eliza said. "Feel free to eat with us until you're settled," she offered.

"I'm going back to Belle's for dinner tonight," Hester said, "and I'll buy a supply of groceries today, but I'd love to eat with you occasionally."

When Ray inquired about a desk, Miss Eliza said, "We have some desks in the attic. Wait until I put these pies in the oven, and we'll go look at them. Pour yourself a cup of coffee, Reverend, and get one for Hester. You're welcome to some of the nut bread in that plastic container."

Hester sat at the oilcloth-covered round table, placed two slices of nut bread on a napkin for Ray and took one for herself, while Ray brought two cups of coffee. Hester heard a cane tapping down the hallway, and a white-haired, wispy old gentleman entered the kitchen, his body bent double over the cane.

Ray stood and held a chair for him. "Mr. Byrd, this is Hester Lawson, who's doing some work for the centennial commission. Hester, meet Everett Byrd."

Hester reached out her hand, and Mr. Byrd pressed it weakly with trembling fingers.

"Larson did you say? There used to be some Larsons in Afterglow."

"No, it's Lawson," Hester said loudly, and she spelled the name for him.

Ray brought another cup of coffee for Mr. Byrd.

"I hope you'll share your recollections of the early days in Afterglow for the history," Hester said loudly.

"I was born five years after this town was founded, and I should remember a lot, although my memory ain't so good anymore."

"You remember the Hartwells, don't you?" Ray asked.

"Yeah. As a little tyke, I remember going to Sunday school in that chapel car of theirs. They had a little pump organ, and Mrs. Hartwell played it while we sang. It was a funny-looking church. . .just had two rows of seats, but it was long. We boys would sneak to the back seats and play around, and our mothers up front didn't know what we were doing." He paused, and it was obvious that his memories dwelt fondly on that period in his life.

"But my monkeyshines stopped," the old man continued, "when I found the Lord, and I started sitting up front in the 'Amen' corner. Sorta hated to see the old chapel car move away, but when we had a church building and congregation, it was time for the Hartwells to move on to another field."

Miss Eliza pushed three pies into the oven, removed her apron, and motioned toward the small set of steps ascending from the kitchen. "We'll go up to the attic now."

"Huh?" Mr. Byrd cupped his ear.

"I wasn't speaking to you, Father. We're going to the attic to look at some furniture."

Miss Eliza spoke in her normal voice, and Mr. Byrd nodded, which made Hester believe that he was not so deaf as she had thought. . .a point she must remember when she interviewed him.

Miss Eliza ascended the two flights of stairs quickly and motioned them into an attic that contained a hodgepodge of furniture, boxes, old clothing, and discarded dishes, all covered with cobwebs and dust.

"I come here only when absolutely necessary," Miss Eliza explained. "I don't know what to do with this accumulation, so I ignore it." She pointed to a handsome oak desk with a roll top. "That item belonged to my father, who gave it to my nephew. For some reason, the top won't slide anymore, so I brought it to the attic."

Hester examined the many pigeonholes above the wide, flat writing surface. The extension slides worked well, and she could see the utility of the six large drawers, as well as the card racks and the letter drops, but the roll top was stuck about six inches from the top and would not budge.

"I wouldn't have to close the desk, I suppose, and it would be useful, but will it be a problem to move downstairs?"

"We brought it up," Miss Eliza said crisply, "but by the front steps."

When they examined the other desk, a huge, flat-topped walnut piece that had once been in the furniture factory, Hester decided to use the oak desk.

"Clint and I will move it for you," Ray offered.

Miss Eliza pointed to several boxes on the walnut table. "Those are records brought from the furniture factory, Hester. You may find them useful. In fact, there's an accumulation of artifacts up here that deal with town history. Look through them whenever you want."

Hester spent the rest of the day unpacking her winter garments. Those that she would not need until spring and summer she left in the boxes and shoved them under her bed, since there wasn't any room for them in the closet. She hung the Thomas painting over the spot where she intended to place the desk, and as she backed away from the wall to be sure the painting was straight, she stared at it in amazement.

"What a coincidence!" she said aloud. No wonder she had thought the local river valley seemed familiar. She had been looking at it for years in her painting, *Winter Serenity*. Of course, there were differences, noting a boat dock in the foreground, and there was no covered bridge in the painting, but the high mountains, the narrow river valley, and the railroad disappearing into the distance were similar. Why were there so many coincidences lately?

She hung the embroidered sampler over the kitchen table and read aloud, "In all thy ways acknowledge him, and he shall direct thy paths." She was beginning to feel at home now.

Hester walked to a nearby store, bought enough groceries for a few days, and stored them in the kitchen cabinets. Then, noting that dusk was creeping over the town, she donned her coat and walked to the Noffsinger residence. She was panting when Belle opened the door to admit her.

"I'm still not used to this altitude," Hester said. "A little walk like that shouldn't make me gasp for breath."

Clint and Ina were nestled in a big chair watching cartoons, and he laughed. "You're doing the right thing, though. Keep walking, and your lungs will soon expand to take in this light air."

"That's the reason I walked, and I'll walk to the centennial meeting, too. I refuse to become a victim of fresh mountain air."

"Sit down," Belle invited. "Dinner won't be ready for a few minutes. How did your moving-in go today?"

"I'm in," Hester said, "and that's about all I can report. It will take a few days to become accustomed to the plumbing and the kitchen stove. I used an electric stove in Detroit, so I'm having trouble with gas."

"You'll soon adjust. I had the same problem when I moved to Afterglow."

"Miss Eliza has a desk I can use, and there are several boxes of records in the attic that she thinks will be helpful in writing the history."

"The Byrds are an interesting family," Belle said.

"I met Mr. Byrd today, and I keep hearing about Miss Eliza's nephew. Are there any other relatives?"

"No. The line is about to run out. Miss Eliza had only one sibling—a brother," Clint answered. "He and his wife both died several years ago, leaving one child, Tommy. Mr. Byrd and Miss Eliza raised the boy, but he's never married."

"He apparently doesn't live here. I didn't suppose a native ever left Afterglow."

Clint laughed. "A few do, and Tommy was one of them. I knew him when I was a boy, although he was probably twenty years my senior. He went into the service and then came home for another year or two—that's when he lived in the little house—but he left then to look for work. I don't know where he is now."

"Ray volunteered your help in bringing a desk from the attic to my dwelling."

"We'll do that tonight after the centennial meeting," Clint agreed.

"I'm going with you," Belle said. "The mayor wanted all of the committee chairpersons to be at the meeting and report. I have a sitter coming to stay with Ina. I haven't been out of the house all day, so I'll enjoy a walk to the town hall."

❧

Hester and the Noffsingers were the first to arrive at the council chamber, but in a short while most of the seats around the large, oval table were filled. With his usual fanfare, Mayor Stepp called the meeting to order. "We'll start with committee reports first and then take action on any items of business we have. Belle, what do you have to tell us?"

"We've advertised in the *Courier* for participants in the craft show and sale. About fifty people say they will come. Most of them are from this county, but we do have a few out-of-staters. I've made arrangements to use the first floor of the Grand Hotel. We'll need volunteers for cleaning the building, but we can arrange that later. The Fourth of July weekend seems suitable to those we've contacted."

"What about the log raft ride?"

A middle-aged man, dressed in a dark business suit stood. Hester recognized him as the city attorney, Alex Snead. "The logs will be delivered and dumped into the river by the first of May. There are still a few old-time wood hicks who remember how the logs were roped together to make rafts, and they'll give us some advice on how to maneuver our little flotilla. Logs are expensive, and we're planning to build only two rafts, which will accommodate approximately twenty-five people, so we must think of some way to choose who's going to ride. And it might be a good idea to pray for a lot of rain. If the water level is low, we can't take a raft downriver between here and the county seat without wrecking on the rapids."

"Should be enough water in May, I would imagine," Ray said.

"Hopefully," Snead said, "but there hasn't been much snow on the mountain this winter."

"I can't wait any longer to give my report," Miss Eliza said, her brown eyes snapping with excitement. "You know we've been disappointed so far in our efforts to contact any descendants of Hezekiah Brown, but just this evening, I received a telephone call from his great-grandson. He's arriving in Afterglow tomorrow and plans to stay in the area for a month or so. He has inherited the land that Brown owned in this county."

"Well, I say, Miss Eliza, that's wonderful news!" Mayor Stepp shouted, and his arms waved wildly. He pranced around the table. "I'll wager he's here to arrange for the Brown land to be converted into a state park. I tell you, folks, Afterglow is facing the dawn of a new day."

One by one, the committee chairpersons gave their glowing reports until it was Hester's turn. She knew the information she had to deliver might have the effect of an exploding bomb, but she was determined to be nonchalant in her statements as if she were not concerned.

With beaming face, the mayor turned in her direction. "And now, Miss Hester, we want to hear from you. Naturally you haven't been here long enough to accomplish much, but we would like your opinion of our fair city."

"Oh, I've been very busy. Thanks to Mr. Stanford and the Noffsingers, I've visited Hezekiah Brown's house and his mill site, and I spent several hours in the courthouse yesterday. I'm rather puzzled about something I found there, or rather that I didn't find, so perhaps you can enlighten me. Where can I find a record of Brown's transfer of this land to the town of Afterglow?"

"Why, at the courthouse, of course," Alex Snead said.

"It isn't there," Hester stated. "I found the record where Brown had bought two thousand acres of land and where he had leased several acreages. Then, in later years, there are deeds of transfer from one property owner in Afterglow to another, but nothing to show that Brown ever relinquished his claim to the land where this town is located."

"Why, that's impossible," Mayor Stepp said, and he drummed his fingers on the desktop. "Impossible."

"I don't know, Mayor. People a hundred years ago were apt to be careless in their property transfers," Snead said.

"I may have overlooked the record, but I don't think so, because I've had some experience in tracing deeds. Perhaps Mr. Snead can do some checking."

"I hope you haven't publicized this, Miss Lawson," the mayor said.

"This is the first time I've mentioned it."

The mayor swept the group with a stern glance. "And I trust the rest of you will remain equally silent. Of course, the record is there. Miss Lawson just didn't find it."

Hester judged that the mayor's formal use of her name indicated that he was unhappy with her report.

*

Later, Ray Stanford joined the Noffsingers and Hester as they walked toward Hester's house.

"You certainly opened up a can of worms, Hester," Clint said, and he laughed loudly. "Where do you think that record is, Ray?"

"Hard to tell. I don't remember that there has ever been a fire that destroyed county records. With all the moving around before the present courthouse was built, I'd just as soon think that a deed book has been lost."

"They seemed to be continuous," Hester said. "Anyway, I've tossed the ball to Attorney Snead's court. He'll have to take it from here. Obviously Mayor Stepp is displeased with me, and you'd warned me, Clint, that he would try to suppress unpleasant things."

"He might try," Ray said with a laugh, "but everyone in Afterglow will know about your report by noon tomorrow."

"You don't mean it!" Hester said.

"I do mean it," Ray said. "The phone lines are probably doing overtime right now."

Belle went home to relieve the baby-sitter, but the two men accompanied Hester to the Byrd residence. It was almost midnight before they had the bulky desk moved from the attic and situated in the small house.

Ray looked closely at the *Winter Serenity* painting. "Wonder where Miss Eliza got this picture of the valley? I didn't notice it when I carried in your luggage."

Hester laughed. "That's an I. M. Thomas original that I brought with me. I was in one of his art classes at my university. I, too, think it looks like a local scene, but I suppose not, because he just painted it freehand in a landscape workshop."

"An amazing likeness," Ray said. "I've heard of Thomas, but I hadn't seen any of his work."

After they left, Hester spent another hour washing the dirt and grime from the desk and rubbing it with a soft wax. It was a beautiful piece of furniture, and she tried to determine why the top would not slide, but her hasty inspection did not reveal the problem.

Hester still had not overcome her feeling of dissatisfaction with the apartment, but she was too tired to care, so she changed into pajamas, turned out the light, and went to bed. Afterglow's few streetlights were behind the large Byrd house, so it was dark in the room. The silence was still disturbing, but it did not bother her as much as it had last week.

Hester awakened early the next morning, and after a quick breakfast, she unpacked her computer and other writing materials and moved them into the desk. She brought a straight-backed chair from the kitchen and decided she was ready to work. It was hardly comparable to her office at the newspaper, but she had not expected this to be a luxury assignment.

When she started downtown, Miss Eliza stuck her head out the window and called, "Plan to eat dinner with us tonight at six o'clock. I want you to meet our founder's descendant."

"Thanks. I'll do that." Hester wanted to experiment with the gas stove a few more times before she tried to cook dinner. She even had trouble this morning regulating the flame to boil water for tea.

Before she arrived at the *Courier* office, Hester was stopped by three people asking about her courthouse research. Several residents passed her wordlessly but with malevolent stares, and one woman even said, "Miss, you'd be better off if you would tend to your own business. You needn't think you can put me off my property."

"Whew!" she said when she finally entered Clint's office. "I feel as if I've been through a blitz!"

"I've been talking on the phone constantly since I arrived at seven o'clock. Everybody is in a turmoil." With an amused grin, he leaned back in his chair.

"But why get so upset before Mr. Snead has checked into the matter? I'm sure there's some logical explanation. The only reason I mentioned it was to learn if anyone knew where I could find the early records."

"Oh, it will die down soon. What can I do for you today?"

"I want to start checking through those records you said were stored here."

"Would it be more convenient if I bring them up to your place? There's no heat on the second floor of this building, and you would be uncomfortable. There are six or seven cartons, and I can load them onto a dolly to bring to your house."

"That would be great."

Clint stood and said, "If you can wait a bit, I'll have someone bring them downstairs, and I'll take them as you return to your apartment."

"I would appreciate a bodyguard. If looks could kill, the ones I received on my way down here would have put me in my grave."

Clint and Hester were stopped several times on the way back to the Byrd apartment, and the story had enlarged until some of the far-fetched comments left Hester speechless. One man said, "Is it true that Mayor Stepp is trying to sell the town hall?" A woman shouted, "Nobody is going to put me off my property. I've got a deed to it." A child ran up to them and said, "I heard a big avalanche is going to bury the town."

When they arrived at the apartment, Hester silently helped Clint move boxes into her living room, but she finally said, "I wouldn't have believed it if I hadn't experienced this. Belle had written me that in a small town no one ever had a secret, and now I believe it."

"There are many advantages to living in Appalachia, and as far as I'm concerned, they outweigh the disadvantages. But there are some disadvantages. You've witnessed one of them this morning."

Hester spent the rest of the day filtering through some of the boxes, where she found a wealth of data for the history in the old newspapers and clippings dating from the early part of the century, as well as memorabilia such as political campaign signs, movie posters, high school annuals, and announcements of New Year's balls in the Grand Hotel. The ballroom was described as a fantastic place, and she wrote a memo to herself to see it soon. Hester typed notes on everything she found, delighted to have started a nucleus for the history, her excitement mounting as she worked. And as she made notes, ideas kept surfacing for the drama; these she jotted down on a yellow notepad. She envisioned a backdrop that would show the valley in a primeval setting, and an idea popped into her head that she considered both daring and brilliant.

Hester looked on the back of *Winter Serenity* where I. M. Thomas's address was listed as a post office box number in New York. Would mail still reach him there after all these years? It had been eight years since she had attended his art seminar. Impulsively, she typed a short note to Thomas, introducing herself and explaining her current project and requesting his help.

Would you think it too presumptuous of me to ask you to paint a backdrop for our performances? Your painting, Winter Serenity, *reminds me so much of this area, and it would be wonderful if you could produce something similar for the backdrop. I'm enclosing photos of the town as it is now. Please let me know if you're available to take on this project and the fee you would charge.*

Hester searched through her luggage until she found the Polaroid camera.

She would take a few pictures in the morning and send the results off to I. M. Thomas. The most he could do would be to say no. Dirty and disheveled, she realized that it was five o'clock. She had not broken for lunch, and she surely did not want to miss her dinner. She showered, washed and styled her hair, and changed into a shimmering, beige satin blouse and a pair of black slacks. By then it was almost six o' clock, so she threw a wool blazer over her shoulders and hustled up the back steps of the Byrd home.

The aroma of warm food greeted her nostrils, and she sighed appreciatively. It had been a long time since her cereal and toast this morning. A flushed and beaming Miss Eliza was carrying food from the kitchen into the dining room.

"May I help you?" Hester asked.

"Bless you, no," Miss Eliza refused. "I want you to meet Hezekiah Brown's relative. He's in the parlor with Father and Reverend Stanford. Come along."

Hester followed Miss Eliza down the hallway. She recognized Ray's booming voice and the quavering tones of Mr. Byrd. But whose was the other familiar voice? Before she could determine that, Miss Eliza motioned her into the parlor.

"Mr. Trent," Miss Eliza said, "I want you to meet our town historian, Hester Lawson. Hester, this is Kyle Trent, a direct descendant of Hezekiah Brown."

Why am I always being thrown into this man's company?

Ray and Kyle Trent had risen when the two women entered the room.

Hester opened her mouth, but no words were forthcoming, and she watched Miss Eliza's exit with a feeling bordering on panic.

Kyle, however, was not so surprised as she was, and he moved across the room and took her hand, favoring Hester with a wicked gleam from his blue eyes. "It's my pleasure to meet you, Miss Lawson."

"We hope you'll be able to help Hester unravel some of the mystery surrounding your ancestor, Mr. Trent," Ray said.

"I'll be pleased to help Miss Lawson any way that I can, but unfortunately, I know very little about Hezekiah Brown."

Hester realized he was still holding her hand, so she removed it abruptly and walked away from him. She observed a curious expression on Ray Stanford's face, and her discomfiture must have been obvious. Kyle Trent apparently intended to treat her as a stranger, so she tried to compose her features, and as pleasantly as she could, she said, "I will probably need some help, but I have done quite well in my research today using the materials that Clint has at the *Courier*. I've found many interesting facts, but it's a time-consuming job."

She turned to Ray, who was dressed in a brown suit with matching shirt and tie. No hint of the lumberjack tonight! "The desk meets my needs exactly," she told him.

"If you'll come into the dining room, we'll have dinner," Miss Eliza announced from the doorway. "My maid is feeding the boarders in the kitchen."

Miss Eliza seated Hester to her left and Kyle to her right, so that they faced one another, and Hester was so annoyed that she considered leaving. Ray sat beside Hester and to the right of Mr. Byrd, who pronounced a blessing on the food in his faltering voice.

More than once through the meal, Hester was thankful for Ray, who kept the conversation going so that she did not have to speak directly to Kyle. When she met his gaze, his expression was as bland as milk toast, but she sensed his amusement at her discomfiture in his aggravating blue eyes.

When Miss Eliza entertained, she dined in style, and the maid started with a steaming vegetable soup, followed by salad and a roast beef dinner. Dessert was apple pie à la mode. Though she had been hungry, the presence of Kyle Trent had dulled her appetite, and to Hester the deliciously prepared food was as insipid as boiled water.

They moved into the parlor for tea or coffee, and shortly afterward, Ray excused himself. "I have a visit to make," he said. "Are you going to be with us long, Mr. Trent?"

"Not long this time, but I do intend to be in and out of Afterglow quite often this year. I've rented one of Miss Eliza's rooms for several months. I wouldn't want to miss the celebration."

"We'll look forward to that," Ray said as he left.

When Miss Eliza stood to remove the tea tray, Hester said, "I'll help you." Now that Ray's stabilizing presence was gone, she wanted to escape.

"No, you keep Mr. Trent company while I organize things in the kitchen. Father isn't much of a conversationalist after he's had his dinner." She nodded toward Mr. Byrd who dozed in his chair.

"I'd be happy to have Miss Lawson's company, and I'll invite her to join me in a walk. I need some exercise after that delicious dinner."

Hester opened her mouth to refuse, but instead she said, "A walk sounds good."

"Excuse me. I'll run upstairs for a coat," Kyle said, and when he returned, Hester had put on her blazer. He opened the door for her, and they walked down the steps in silence.

"Which way?" he asked.

"We can circle the town on Main Street in a half hour. Let's go to the right first," she said shortly.

Kyle laughed, and Hester turned on him fiercely. "You're enjoying this, aren't you?"

"It does have its amusing side, you'll have to admit. You didn't do a good job of acting. I don't believe we fooled the reverend into believing we hadn't met before."

"I had no intention of fooling him, but there didn't seem to be any reason to mention our encounters. Are you really related to Hezekiah Brown?"

"There you go again! Are you just naturally suspicious of all strangers, or is it only me?"

She did not answer, but they walked a half block in silence.

"Yes, I'm Brown's descendent. I have proof of it, and I'm sure I'm going to need it."

"So that's why you knew how Afterglow received its name!"

"It's a legend that's been handed down in the family."

When they reached the statue of Brown, Hester said, "There is a memorial to your exalted relative."

"The fact that this town honored him is a surprise to me. I don't know why, but our family has never seemed to think much of the old boy. My mother told me that, when she was a child, Brown's children never mentioned his name."

"So you *don't* know much about him?"

"No, but I inherited the estate of my great-aunt, and she probably had lots of things you might use in the history. If I don't return to Harrisburg soon, I'll have my sister check through her papers."

"I suppose I was foolish to take on this task because the centennial commission keeps adding to my duties, but I'm committed to it now, and I'm going to give it my best," Hester said, wondering why she was unburdening herself to this stranger who kept cluttering up her life.

"I'm curious about how they ever found you. Didn't you say you were from Detroit?"

She explained briefly about her friendship with Belle and why she had come to Afterglow. By then they had reached the end of town, and Hester said, "We have to turn back now."

As they ambled along the deserted streets, Kyle said, "I had hoped to find a restaurant where we could stop for a soda and talk, rather than to be shivering out here on the street."

"I was up late last night, and I want to go to bed."

"Where do you live?"

"In the little building behind the boardinghouse."

"Then we'll be neighbors; I intend to stay at Miss Eliza's frequently."

Hester wondered if he intended to sell Brown's property for a state park, but she would not question him. He walked with her to the door of her apartment, and he said, "I'd come in if I had an invitation."

"But I'm not going to invite you. In the first place, I have papers spread all over the living room, and there isn't any place to sit. Besides, the people in Afterglow are gunning for me now, so I don't dare entertain a stranger after dark. I'm sure that isn't acceptable here."

"Why are they gunning for you?"

She hesitated. "I'd rather not say."

Unlocking the door, Hester said, "I suppose I should thank you for not revealing our previous meetings."

"No thanks needed. Before you go in, tell me something else. What were you looking for in those deed books at the county seat?"

She hesitated again. "I won't tell you, but I will say that's what made the citizens of Afterglow mad at me."

She slipped into her living room and closed the door.

Chapter 4

The next morning, before Hester started sorting through another box of the old papers, she wrote an article about Miss Eliza's boardinghouse to send to her newspaper in Detroit. She walked down to the riverbank and took a few pictures, enclosed them in the Thomas letter, and stopped by the post office to mail her correspondence. A few of the people she met greeted her with disgruntled nods, but for the most part, she was ignored. She encountered Mayor Stepp in the post office.

"You've certainly caused us a problem, young lady. Our phone at town hall didn't stop ringing all day yesterday."

Hester did not appreciate being treated as a child, and with a quick prayer to help her control her temper, she replied calmly, "I didn't cause any problem. I simply stated that I hadn't found a record of the land transfer in the courthouse and asked where I might locate it. The matter shouldn't have been leaked to the public until Mr. Snead checked it. Apparently the commission members discussed it because I didn't mention it to anyone. How many people did *you* tell?" she asked pointedly.

The mayor harrumphed several times. "I thought it was my duty to notify the council members of a potential problem."

"Many others must have considered it was their duty to pass the news around. I feel sure that the transfer was made, and I think the record can be found. The incident has been blown out of proportion."

"In the future, please clear any questionable information with me before you report it publicly."

"If you remember, that wasn't a part of our contract. See you later, Mayor. I have lots of research to do."

Hester had no intention of allowing the mayor to pass on everything she considered for publication, or she would never finish the research in time, but she would not argue about it this morning. She found it difficult to put up with his theatrics, and she shuddered to think of the remote possibility that this man could be her father.

When she reached her house, Kyle Trent called her name from the second floor of the Byrd dwelling. He leaned from a window that overlooked her house, which meant he could watch every move she made if he so desired. She waved to him and went on into her apartment.

Dark green blinds and lace curtains served as a window covering, so Hester pulled down the blinds in her bedroom. She had not considered that the residents next door had a bird's-eye view into her windows. At night, she should remember to pull the other blinds, too, but she needed to keep them open during daytime for extra light. The bulbs in the ceiling lights and lamps furnished inadequate lighting.

The research was slow work, but she could not complain about the amount of information she had accumulated. Numerous articles dealt with the timber industry, and not everything she learned was good. She stared in disbelief at pictures showing how the mountains were clear-cut, which in turn led to landslides. She soon discovered that Brown was unpopular with some of the residents because of his exploitation of the forest. One man in particular, Michael Ledman, had spearheaded a fight to stop Brown from leasing land.

While Hester was eating her lunch, a loud knock sounded at the door, and she laid her sandwich aside.

A masculine-looking woman carrying a briefcase stood at the door. "Miss Lawson, I'm Geraldine Ledman. I'd like to talk to you."

"Come in. May I offer you some lunch?"

"No, thank you. I've already eaten."

"Then you won't mind if I finish my sandwich." Hester pushed aside some papers to make a seat for the woman on the couch. "I'll be finished soon."

When she returned to the living room with a glass of cola that she placed on an end table, Geraldine Ledman was riffling through the papers Hester had laid to one side.

"So you're reading about the timber industry," Geraldine said.

"That and other things. Not knowing exactly what I'll need, I'm doing general reading."

"I live at the county seat," Geraldine stated, "and I have some information I want published in this history of Afterglow."

"I appreciate your interest," Hester said without committing herself to publish material she had not examined and wondering if the woman would be a help or a hindrance.

"I'm not sure you'll welcome it. My grandfather, Michael Ledman, was victimized by Hezekiah Brown, as were several other landowners in this area. He leased land from them at a minimal price, misrepresenting the facts, and then sold timber at huge profits." She motioned toward the briefcase. "I have papers showing that several of the landowners filed litigation against Brown to recover what he had stolen from them, but the issue was never resolved."

"And this is what you want in the history?"

"It is. If you'll agree to publish the material, I'll make copies of some of these documents." A shrewd look covered her face, and she added, "I can't turn these papers loose as I still believe that we have a viable case. I hear the Brown land is to be sold, and if so, we're going to block the sale until we're paid our just dues."

Wait until Mayor Stepp hears about this.

"I would appreciate having copies of the papers; I want to research every possible source before I start writing the manuscript, but I won't promise that I'll include your case. The history is limited to two hundred pages, so I can't publish everything, but it's necessary for me to follow all leads."

Ledman handed Hester a card. "My telephone number is here in case you want to contact me. But regardless, you'll be hearing from me again."

After the woman left, Hester checked the time and walked to the restaurant where Ray Stanford often ate his lunch. She peered through the window and saw him seated at one of the booths. He waved and motioned her inside. She stopped by the counter and gave an order to Sadie. "Just a piece of cherry pie and cup of coffee, please."

"How's the research going?" Ray greeted her when she joined him.

"Slow, but rewarding. It's a filthy job, too, in more ways than one. Those old papers are covered with dust and cobwebs."

"I imagined as much," he said, smiling. "Your face is dirty."

She took a tissue from her pocket and rubbed it across her face. "My hands would have been, too, but I washed them to prepare lunch. I didn't take time to check my appearance before I left; I wanted to catch you here at the restaurant."

He smiled again. "That's flattering."

"Maybe not. I'm using you for my sounding board. Do you know Geraldine Ledman?"

"I know who she is but never met the woman."

"Do you have any idea why she would come to see me?"

His fingers tried unsuccessfully to smooth his unruly beard, and his dark eyes sparkled. "Unfortunately, I have. She's made a pest of herself in Afterglow the past year or so after she found some old litigation papers that her ancestor had drawn against Hezekiah Brown. She's badgered Clint to publish her claims in the *Courier*, but he won't. There has been some publicity in the county seat newspaper, but no one has paid much attention."

"I did find some information in the old newspapers to support her claims. Should I ignore her?"

"Not as far as I'm concerned. I don't doubt that Brown did gain his wealth by unethical means, and I know we can't sugarcoat our past, no matter how much the mayor thinks so. Praise without adversity makes mighty dull reading."

"She promised to send me copies of her papers, and I'll decide what to do after I've read them. In the meantime, as I research, I'm jotting down possible scenes for the drama. Now I'm wondering if this controversy between Brown and the landowners might make a good episode for the drama. We'll need some conflict."

"Sounds good to me."

Ray and Hester left the restaurant together, and he said, "Day after tomorrow is Sunday. May I look for you at church?"

"Certainly. Is Afterglow a strict Sunday town?"

"The stores are all closed, but there aren't any blue laws nor a ban on recreation, if that's what you mean."

By nightfall, Hester had sorted through all the boxes and had separated into one large stack the items she wanted to give further attention. She stopped early enough to prepare a decent meal, and while she ate leisurely, she scanned the daily issue of the *Courier*, which had been delivered to her door, compliments of Clint. Kyle Trent's picture graced the front page, and Clint's article seemed to bear out what Kyle had told her about himself. A knock sounded at the door. *Why can't I enjoy one meal without an interruption?* Frowning, she opened the door to the smiling face of Kyle Trent. She stared at him without a greeting.

"Aren't you going to ask me in?"

"I'm eating my dinner."

"I won't take it. I've already eaten at the boardinghouse."

"Oh, come on in then," she said ungraciously. She raised the blinds and opened the curtains, which she had previously closed for the night. When Kyle looked at her curiously, she added, "I'm trying to preserve our reputations so the locals won't suspect us of clandestine activities. Come on into the kitchen. I'm not usually so inhospitable, but my lunch was interrupted, too."

She motioned him to the seat opposite her at the table. "Do you want some tea?"

"Yes, please." She reached into the cabinet for a cup and set the teapot beside him. He looked at her plate of baked pork chops, sweet potatoes, green beans, and coleslaw. "You eat well."

"I'm a busy woman. I need to be fed," she said as she resumed her seat.

"Who interrupted you at noon?"

"You wouldn't want to know. What have you been doing today?"

"Driving around, viewing my estate. I've never been here before. As a matter of fact, I didn't realize my aunt owned this land until she died and left the majority of her estate to me."

Hester pointed to the newspaper. "I see the *Courier* gave you some space. You must be the only descendant of Brown they've been able to locate."

"I don't believe he has many descendants, but as I told you, some of his relatives won't claim him."

When Hester prepared her dessert, she asked, "Would you like some frozen yogurt?"

"No, thanks. I had a huge meal at Miss Eliza's. But if you aren't too busy, perhaps you'll accompany me on another walk. That activity should be acceptable behavior, even in Afterglow. And speaking of walking, Mr. Byrd told me that there's a Brown family cemetery on the mountain. I'm going to look for it tomorrow. Want to come along?"

"I do want to visit that cemetery, but I'm not doing well in this altitude. Do you expect to walk all the way?"

"The old gentleman says you can drive partway in a car and then walk across the mountain to the Brown house and cemetery. I'm not sure that I want to rely completely on Mr. Byrd's directions, though."

"Clint Noffsinger will know. After I wash the dishes, we can walk up to his house and ask him."

To her surprise, Kyle dried the dishes. Soon Hester shrugged into a heavy coat for the walk to the Noffsingers'.

Clint had already met Kyle and was introduced to Belle. Kyle surprised Hester by picking up Ina and making an instant rapport with her. Ina hadn't even accepted Hester yet! He must have a way with children. *And women?* Hester wondered. Instinctively, her guard was up against Kyle Trent.

Answering Hester's query, Clint said, "I can tell you how to reach the logging site by taking a trail up the mountain, but I don't know where the cemetery is."

Tossing a rubber ball to the chattering Ina, Kyle said, "Mr. Byrd gave me some general directions. If we reach the house, I can probably find the cemetery."

"Drive west of town along the old railroad tracks until they disappear into a tunnel. At that point, turn left and follow an old logging road about a mile up the mountainside. It's a rough drive, so you won't want to take your car."

"I drove partway up that road today and made it all right."

Clint shrugged his shoulders. "Park your car near some dilapidated buildings, then cut across country through the forest on a small trail you'll see to the left. It's a mile and a half to the sawmill site, but it's steep climbing, and before you come to Brown's homestead, you'll think it's twice that far. If we didn't have to go to the county seat tomorrow, we could go with you. But you can borrow my four-wheeler if you like."

Hester darted a glance at Kyle. "Have you ever driven a four-wheeler?"

"No."

"Then if I go with you, we'll walk. I was terrified when I rode up that mountain with Ray Stanford, and he's an experienced driver."

"Be sure and wear serviceable shoes that have rough soles," Belle advised. "We'll lend you a backpack to carry a lunch, and be sure to take water and first-aid items," Clint said.

"We'll be gone only a few hours, won't we?" Kyle asked. "Why should we need a first-aid kit?"

"Better to be safe than sorry," Clint argued.

They watched television with the Noffsingers, staying until they heard the eleven o'clock news. Since the weather forecast was for mild weather, they agreed to take the hike the next day.

"I'll pack a lunch," Hester said when they parted at the Byrd gate. "What time?"

"Nine o'clock, okay?"

"I'll be ready."

❦

The next morning Hester held her breath as well as the sides of the seat more than once before Kyle parked the Mercedes at the end of the road. He had driven through mud holes, crept over fallen logs, and subjected the automobile to abuse on the rutted trail. Some people might call it a road, but it was nothing more than a wide path.

She trembled when she eyed the trail winding upward through the forest. "I'm not sure I can go on. When I went up with the Noffsingers and Ray Stanford by vehicle, I nearly passed out."

"The altitude change won't bother you as much when we're traveling slowly. But if you have trouble, we'll turn around and come back," Kyle said calmly.

"Doesn't anything ever excite you?"

"You should see me at my best in front of a jury. I'm excited then. I'm the best trial lawyer in our area."

"Add conceit to the list of your faults."

"It isn't conceit to tell the truth."

He fastened the backpack over his shoulders. "Here goes," he said and saluted smartly. "Forward, march!"

Hester preceded him up the trail, and it took two hours of twists and turns, panting and puffing before they finally reached the level area that Hester recognized as the Brown sawmill site.

They looked through the deserted buildings, and Hester said, "The rumor is that state officials have talked of restoring this area into a museum to the lumber industry."

"They'll have to buy it from me first, and from the looks of these buildings, I question that any of them are restorable."

They moved on to the Brown residence, and Kyle laughed when he saw it. "So this is my ancestral home. I thought Hezekiah Brown was rich."

"Perhaps the reason he was rich was because he didn't spend much on his residence. It would have been a good house for the early twentieth century, though."

Kyle leaned against a crumbling porch post and looked at the vista spreading before them. "So here's where my ancestor stood when he named the town. Pity the place didn't live up to its name. There's not much of an afterglow about it now."

After they looked over the dwelling, Hester said, "I'm hungry. Shall we eat before we look for the cemetery?"

"Suits me. Let's sit on the step. It will be warmer here in the sunshine than inside the house."

Hester spread out the picnic lunch. "I haven't bought many groceries yet, so you'll have to be satisfied with tuna salad sandwiches, apples, and cookies. In addition to the big bottle of water, I brought along two containers of fruit drink. Belle also left a sack of trail mix in the pack, so we can eat that before we start back down the mountainside."

"I found out why the citizens of Afterglow are angry with you," Kyle said as he bit into a big Grimes Golden apple.

"Oh?"

"Mr. Byrd told me. I had an idea what it was; after I saw you that day in the courthouse, I spent hours looking, and I couldn't find any indication that Brown had ever given away the townsite of Afterglow."

"It's a mystery to me, but I'm not a professional in tracing property titles. As an attorney, you should know how to look for that type of thing. What do you make of it?"

"Brown set up Afterglow as a company town, rather like the coal companies did. I don't believe he ever turned the land over to the citizens. When the timber industry declined, he just allowed them to keep their homes. And from what I make of it, I own the town of Afterglow."

Hester choked on a sip of fruit juice and stared at him. When she could speak again, she said, "That's ridiculous. What about squatter's rights?"

"Squatter's rights haven't been legal for a hundred years or so and wouldn't apply in this case. Normally I wouldn't care who owned Afterglow, but I'm trying to sell this land to the state. They're interested but don't like having a town within the confines of the park."

"There's not much you can do about it, is there?"

"Maybe not, but I'm going to suggest that the city fathers relocate the town outside the park."

Hester laughed. "You wouldn't have a chance."

"I'm not so sure. If the state wants the land badly enough, they might put pressure on the residents. For the time being, I hope you won't mention that I'm aware of the situation."

"Never fear, for I'll be blamed for telling you about the missing deed anyway. I can hear the mayor's reaction. He's heard a rumor about this state park, and he believes that will transform Afterglow into a tourist attraction."

They stored the remains of the lunch in the backpack and placed it inside the house.

"Now let's look for the cemetery. Mr. Byrd said it was due north from the back door of the house. Let's see if I can take my bearings from the sun just like a true pioneer."

Kyle's bearings indicated that they would have to climb higher to reach the cemetery.

"Not another hill," Hester protested.

"Head bothering you?"

"Not particularly, but I'm not used to this sort of terrain. In Detroit, I jog or walk every day, but climbing is hard on my muscles. The skin on the back of my legs feels stretched as tight as a bowstring, and my hip joints ache."

"I know. I felt the pull on my leg muscles while we were climbing. Why don't you stay here until I scout around? If I find the cemetery, I'll call for you."

"Since neither of us knows anything about these mountains, we should stay together, or we could easily become lost. I'll manage."

"Going back should be easy. Downhill."

"But a *steep* downhill, and Belle warned me to be careful at the steep places. Oh, for some level land again."

"Do I hear a tremor of homesickness?"

"I know I'll never become a mountaineer. Let's find that cemetery."

The trail to the cemetery was indistinct but possible to follow. To Hester's relief, the trail did not go uphill, but led around the mountainside to a small, level spot surrounded by a dilapidated rail fence. The gate was secured with a rusty wire, so Hester and Kyle stepped through a broken-down section of the rails. Hester counted twenty granite headstones and several wooden slabs marking other graves.

"Here's the old boy's stone," Kyle said. Brown's marker was unpretentious, comparing meanly to the large statue of him in Afterglow. Kyle pulled away the dead weeds so that they could read the inscriptions.

Hezekiah Brown and his wife, Elizabeth, were buried side by side, adjacent to the graves of their two infant children.

"I believe he had three children who lived to adulthood," Kyle said, "and I'll try to find that information from my aunt's papers."

"This must be Hezekiah's parents," Hester said, pointing to a double headstone of a generation earlier. "From some of the information I've read, it seems his father moved into this area so he would be away from the slave owners in Tidewater, Virginia."

"Gives me a rather strange feeling," Kyle admitted, "to be standing where my ancestors walked. I wish I knew why my family didn't think much of Hezekiah Brown."

"I may know why," Hester said, and she told him about her visit from Geraldine Ledman.

Kyle whistled. "So my ancestor was a crook! But that could be termed unethical rather than illegal. There must have been something else wrong with him."

"It's a pity this place has been neglected," Hester said as she pulled briars and undergrowth away from the plots. She took a notepad from her pocket and recorded the information from the tombstones. The graves in one section with names and dates cut into slabs of wood had no apparent connection with the Brown family nor with one another.

"No doubt these were some of Brown's workers," Kyle said. "I agree with you about the cemetery. If the state buys this property, I'll stipulate that they have to provide care for the cemetery. If not, I'll do it myself. If a man's spirit has gone to be with God, it doesn't matter much where the body is buried, but I don't like to see my ancestors' graves neglected like this."

Hester did not answer, but she was pleased to know that Kyle's spiritual priorities seemed to be in the right place.

As she plodded down the trail, tagging after Kyle Trent, Hester assessed the day's activities. Other than knowing where Hezekiah Brown was buried, she did not feel that she had accomplished much on her research. But, on a personal side, she had gained a better rapport with Kyle. He had been a great companion today.

Chapter 5

Strains of the pipe organ greeted Hester as she entered Brown Memorial Church the next morning. Her church in Detroit did not boast a pipe organ, so the town of Afterglow had one up on her there. She sat on a seat near the back, although the sanctuary was sparsely filled. She soon felt a tap on her shoulder, and Belle leaned over to whisper, "Come up front and sit with us."

Glad for their company, Hester entered another pew to sit between Belle and Clint.

"I took Ina to the nursery," Belle whispered.

As the organist built the prelude to a mighty crescendo, Kyle entered the church and sat opposite them. He smiled in her direction. Hester hated to see him sitting alone, but she could not very well leave the Noffsingers to keep him company.

This morning Ray no longer resembled a lumberjack, for he made an impressive figure in his black robe. In spite of the vaulted ceiling of the church, his massive figure dominated the room throughout the service. The choir singing was mediocre, and the congregation was sparse, but she could find no fault with Ray.

"In my research of the chapel ministry," he said, "I found a journal that Ivan Hartwell kept during his year at Afterglow. He listed his sermon texts and scriptural reference for each Sunday. Starting today and until the end of our town's celebration, I will use Brother Hartwell's ideas. Today, the text is Romans 10:13–14: 'For whosoever shall call upon the name of the Lord shall be saved. How then shall they call on him in whom they have not believed? and how shall they believe in him of whom they have not heard? and how shall they hear without a preacher?'

"This is one of the greatest missionary texts of the Bible, and one that Hartwell used to govern his actions when he first came into this area. The train that brought him to Afterglow was met by angry wood hicks, demanding that he move on. Although Hartwell was confronted with anger and violence, he persevered until he had the nucleus of a church in this community."

Ray proceeded to use the text and Hartwell's example to point out the need for a renewal of missionary activity in their town. In a final challenge to his listeners, he said, "Would God rather we had anger against our cause today, or the apathy that afflicts our friends and neighbors who have no concern for their spiritual welfare. During this year of celebration, I pray that we will not only remember the historical events of the past but once again experience the religious zeal and fervor of our forefathers."

Kyle fell into step with Hester as she started down the aisle at the end of the service. "I'm leaving this afternoon. I've been away from my office for two weeks, and I must go home to take care of the correspondence that has accumulated. I intend to be back for the council meeting ten days from now."

In a low voice, she cautioned, "You're going to stir up a hornet's nest. They'll run you out of town on a rail."

"That's probably what they should have done to my esteemed ancestor instead of erecting a monument in his honor."

Hester stood aside to wait for Belle, who was visiting with everyone as she left the church. Kyle shook hands with Ray, smiled in Hester's direction, and ran jauntily down the steps. Afterglow would seem emptier after his departure; it had been comforting to know she was not the only stranger in town.

The following week passed quickly as Hester worked out a basic format for the history book. She visited dozens of homes with her tape recorder, asking residents to share their stories of the past. She also begged for old photos until she had hundreds of them. Although she was still shunned by a few people, most of them had decided that the absence of Afterglow's deed would not cause any problem, and they had forgiven Hester's mention of it.

The most exciting event of the week was the receipt of a note from I. M. Thomas. On a small sheet of paper, he had scribbled an answer to her request.

> *Delighted to do the backdrop for drama. No charge.*
> *Will send in plenty of time for presentation.*
> *I. M. Thomas*

🦋

In spite of his advanced age or perhaps because of it, Everett Byrd provided the most information about the timber industry. Hester made arrangements to meet him one afternoon after his nap. He eyed the tape recorder with alarm.

"I don't want to talk into that contraption," he insisted.

"You don't have to talk into it. You just recount your experiences and forget the recorder is here. My memory isn't as good as yours, and I need this recording for accuracy."

"All right, young woman, what do you want to know?"

"Anything you can tell me about the timber industry in this area."

"Hezekiah Brown was the first one to start timbering here about a year before the town was started. His father had owned a little land in the county, but Brown moved away for a good many years. He said he never forgot the valley, and he came back after he made his fortune elsewhere. He was the first, but we had a lot of timbering after Brown died."

"What did you do in the industry?"

"I started working for Brown when I was just a boy. We didn't have child labor laws then. I could use an ax and a crosscut saw by the time I was twelve. I guess I did about anything that had to be done."

"Give me some examples, keeping in mind that I'm a city girl without any knowledge of lumbering."

"I can remember when there was virgin timber on these mountains. I've cut trees that measured six to eight feet through. We would have to make big notches all around the tree with an ax before we could saw it."

He stifled a yawn. Hester cleared her throat to alert him, and he continued, "Before I started cutting trees, I helped the road gang build roads so the wagons could move in to gather the cut logs. When the mountain was too steep for a wagon to travel over, we sledded the logs down."

"What kind of trees were harvested?"

"Most any kind of hardwood, but during the thirties, we cut a lot of dead chestnuts that had been killed by a fungus blight. There were thousands of those chestnuts standing around on these mountains."

Mr. Byrd started to nod, and Hester turned off the tape recorder until he had finished his nap. When he roused, she asked, "Tell me about some of the jobs you had."

"I did some swamping, but everybody had to do that. That's when the men cleared the forest of undergrowth and fallen logs to prepare the ground for skidding logs. None of us liked that, but it had to be done." He paused in his narrative and reflected while the grandfather clock in the hallway chimed the half hour.

"I was a mill-hand for a few months. As off-bearer, I took the waste wood and piled it up to use for fuel in the boiler to fire the sawmill. Once I was a ratchet man. That meant I rolled the logs down into the circular saw carriage. That was a particularly difficult job, as I had to determine how the boards were cut into widths and lengths."

"Sounds like a hard job," Hester said as she turned over the tape in her recorder.

"It was, but I didn't like working around the sawmill, so I spent most of my time with a team hauling the logs off the mountainside and down to the railroad. I guess that was my favorite job. I like horses."

"Do you believe Brown was unethical in his dealings?"

"Maybe, but it took a lot of money to finance his work. If he was, he paid it back by remembering Afterglow in his will."

"Did you ever work in the furniture factory here in town?"

"No. It took craftsmen for that work. At first they made furniture, but it proved more economical to ship the lumber out of here and have the furniture made elsewhere. Mostly they made knickknacks. It was never a profitable venture."

Hester spent several days in Miss Eliza's attic where she found numerous ledgers, invoices, and land memorabilia from the town's furniture factory. She secured a key from the real-estate agent who had the property listed for sale and took a tour of the buildings. When the centennial commission met on Tuesday night, Mayor Stepp complimented Hester on her work, and she assumed he meant to let bygones be bygones.

"As I toured the factory yesterday, I thought it would make a great tourist attraction," she reported. "I envisioned using it as a training school for those interested in cabinetmaking or in producing small wooden items for sale. Do any of the craftsmen who used to work in the factory still live around here?"

"A few, I believe," Miss Eliza said. "But it would cost a lot of money to renovate the buildings, and the factory closed in the first place because of lack of customers."

"It would have to start out on a small scale, making novelty items, as you would be appealing to a new kind of customer—the tourist. You could probably ask for a state or federal grant for expansion funds, especially if the area becomes a state park."

Even as she spoke, Hester wondered about the fate of Afterglow. Did Kyle have any possible chance of making them relocate the town? No doubt he had been working all week to shore up his defenses, determining if he had the legal clout to take over the town's land. If so, the old factory would never again operate.

When Clint smiled at her, she said, "And don't expect me to write up a grant application. If I accomplish what you've already laid out for me, it will be a miracle."

"You've opened up a new avenue of thought, Miss Hester," the mayor said, "and we'll take it under advisement."

"In the meantime, you might want to consider producing a few souvenir items for this year." She took two drawings from her briefcase. "I found these in Eliza's attic. They're sketches for a walnut vase and a curio shelf. It seems to me they would be easy to make, and I believe that tourists would purchase them."

"The only person in town who could do that is Charles Benson," Miss Eliza said briskly. "That is, if you want to involve him in this celebration."

"Why not?" Alex Snead asked. "Just because he's the descendant of Aaron Benson doesn't keep him from being a craftsman."

"Since Aaron Benson has the distinction of being the only person to rob the local bank, he should be remembered some way. By all means, contact Charles Benson if we decide to pursue this project," Clint said.

The next morning, Kyle returned and soon made his way to Hester's quarters. By now, she recognized his knock, which was a rat-a-tat rendition of "Shave and a haircut, two bits."

He entered at her invitation. "I come bearing gifts," he said. "I raided my great-aunt's files and came up with a collection of goodies on the Brown family. . .at least I hope they're goodies. I haven't read them." He placed the box he carried on the floor and perched on a chair near Hester's desk.

"What if I find something that isn't a 'goody'? May I publish it anyway?"

"Yes, as far as I'm concerned. Are you coming to the council meeting tonight to hear the fireworks?"

"Are there going to be some?"

"I wouldn't be surprised."

"I might as well come," she said. "I'll be blamed for leaking the information to you. You may have to make room for me on that rail."

"I can't think of more delightful company." He sauntered toward the door. "See you tonight. I have to check in with Miss Eliza and be sure she has enough food for me."

Hester quickly glanced through the packet of materials that Kyle had brought, noting with gratification that there was a picture of Hezekiah Brown and other members of his family. She intended to incorporate many old pictures into the history, and there definitely should be some of the Brown family. She laid aside the packet when a knock sounded at the door.

A tall, thin man stood on the low step. He removed his cap to reveal a thatch of curly brown hair. "My name's Charlie Benson, ma'am. Miss Eliza sent me around to see you."

"Come on in. Did Miss Eliza tell you what we're considering?" He nodded, and she handed him photocopies of the patterns of the vase and the curio shelf that she had made at the mayor's office.

"Could you duplicate these items if the commission decides to produce them? And could you teach others to make them?"

He whistled tonelessly while he studied the drawings. "Reckon I could, but it would take some time. If you're intendin' to have these ready to sell this summer, it's already too late to start."

"Perhaps you could have a supply ready before the big celebration in October."

"Reckon I could," he agreed.

"Will you make up a sample of these two items before the next centennial commission meeting? I'm sure the members will want to see a sample before they agree to spend any money."

After he left, Hester ate a light meal and hurried up the hill to the Noffsingers'.

"Come along to the council meeting with me tonight," she said to Clint. "I'm not at liberty to comment on it, but Kyle Trent is going to drop a bomb on Mayor Stepp. As a newspaper editor, you'll want to be present."

"I always sent the city editor to cover the council meetings because they're usually humdrum," Clint said, "but I'll take your word for it and attend. Can you find a baby-sitter, Belle?"

"No, but I'll take Ina along. She had a long nap this afternoon, so perhaps she'll behave herself. If not, I'll bring her home."

🦋

When Hester and the Noffsingers entered the council room, there was no sign of Kyle, but Geraldine Ledman sat in the front row of the spectators' chairs. When Clint looked questioningly at Hester, she whispered, "I didn't know she was going to be here." If Geraldine made public any of the papers she had brought to Hester, this was going to be a lively meeting.

The mayor had already called the session to order, and the clerk was reading the minutes of the last meeting when the door opened. Kyle slipped quietly into the room. He looked as sanctimonious as a saint, and Hester was sure he had timed his entrance for this moment. He ignored Hester, much to her relief.

When the council finished its agenda relating to repaving Main Street, the mayor turned grandly toward the spectator section. "I see we have a few visitors tonight. Do any of you ladies or gentlemen have anything to say? It isn't customary to take up any unscheduled business, but we have no rule against anyone speaking."

Kyle nodded his thanks to the mayor and moved to center stage, or at least that's the way it appeared to Hester. She believed his comment about being the best trial lawyer in the area, because from the moment he stood, he commanded everyone's attention. Dramatically his eyes roved the room, looking directly into the face of each person there. His attitude stunned the group to silence, and when the room was as quiet as a tomb, he said bluntly, "Would you have any objection to relocating the town of Afterglow?"

If it were a bomb, it did not make any noise, because no one said anything. In fact, even Hester, who had expected something of the sort, was stunned. He could have led up to the matter!

"As you know, I've inherited the land in this county that once belonged to Hezekiah Brown, and to the best of my knowledge, that includes the one hundred acres on which this town is situated. I've spent several days checking property records at the courthouse, and there is no record that Brown ever relinquished claim to this land."

The mayor and some of the council members cast angry glances at Hester.

"I've heard that Miss Lawson made a similar finding, but I learned that after I arrived in town. She didn't tell me. I found out myself."

Mayor Stepp's face had turned a dusky red and he blustered, "Are you suggesting that you own this town?"

"Just the land it sits on; any improvements are yours. I simply want the land back as it was in my ancestor's time. That's the reason I suggested relocating the town. There's a site on the other side of the mountain that would make a good place for you. The buildings could be sent downstream on barges, and the town could be reestablished in no time. Stuck up in this hollow, Afterglow will never amount to anything anyway."

"I don't believe a word of it," Mayor Stepp shouted. Turning to Alex Snead, he said, "Have you checked those deeds yet?"

Looking unhappy, Snead said, "Yes, I did, and I have to agree with Mr. Trent. There is no record of a land transfer."

"Even if there isn't," a council member said, "it's out of the question. . .ridiculous to expect us to move our homes. This town has been here for a hundred years! We're supposed to be celebrating the town's founding, not dismantling it!"

"Afterglow is dying anyway. Why not turn your celebration into a big funeral and move?" Kyle asked with a smile.

"No no no!" Mayor Stepp shouted. "Afterglow is here to stay. There has to be some mistake. We'll try this in a court of law."

"Speaking of a law court," Geraldine Ledman said as she stood, "I, myself, have a suit to present. . .against the heirs of Hezekiah Brown. And I'm pleased you're here to represent them, Mr. Trent. I have evidence," she said, patting her briefcase, "that will show how your ancestor, Hezekiah Brown, defrauded the early residents. I represent the descendants of eight landowners who were duped by Brown into leasing their land to him. He not only gave them insufficient money, but he also exploited the forests. He was to cut only the large trees, but he clearcut instead. We expect to be paid for our losses."

Kyle retained a smile on his face, but Hester could tell by the twitching nerve in his forehead that he was angry.

"If I can dish it out, I can take it," he said. "Bring on your lawsuit."

Mayor Stepp pranced back and forth in the room, wringing his hands. "Mr. Trent, Miss Ledman, you're ruining the image of this fair town." Turning to Hester, he continued, "And don't put a word of this in your history. What if the newspapers should get hold of this?"

"I do intend to publicize it. If you want tourists flocking to the town, they'll come in droves when they hear of this controversy. The public thrives on conflict; good news doesn't make interesting reading."

"I declare this council meeting adjourned," Mayor Stepp cried. Immediately those present drifted into shouting, gesticulating groups. Geraldine Ledman approached Kyle, who observed her with a cynical smile on his face.

"It's time we were getting out of here," Clint said as he shepherded his family and Hester toward the exit. They paused on the street, and he continued, "You go on home, Belle. I'm going to stop at the office and write up a news story for tomorrow's paper. Mayor Stepp's efforts to stop this will have as much effect as putting out a brushfire with a pot of tea."

"You said you would liven up things for us," Belle said to Hester, "but I don't need this much excitement. Coming home with me?"

"No. I'm going back to the apartment, write an account of this incident, then go to the county seat early in the morning and fax it to Detroit."

Hester had just written the headline SMALL TOWN'S CELEBRATION MAY TURN INTO ITS FUNERAL when she heard Kyle's knock at the door.

"Come in" she called, and when he barged into the room, she said, "I'm busy."

"And I'm elated," he said, throwing his coat across the couch. "Nothing excites me like a healthy controversy."

"If you're going to stay, open the blinds and curtains. And you'll have to be quiet until I've finished. I'm writing an account of this healthy controversy to send to Detroit."

"May I read it after you've finished?"

"Of course not. I don't need a proofreader."

"Let me ask you a question, and then I'll leave. Do you still have those papers that Ledman woman gave you?"

Hester pulled out one of the lower drawers of the desk and handed him a file labeled "Ledman Papers."

"She brought me copies of quite a few things that she wants incorporated into the history. You can take the file with you, but I want it back as soon as you've read everything."

He looked at the drawer full of neat files. "I see you're a well-organized woman. Did you bring this desk with you?"

"No, it's one that Miss Eliza had stored in the attic, but I sure like it. These big bottom drawers are just the right width for letter-sized files, and I particularly like all the pigeonholes in the upper part. I may try to buy it from her and take it home with me if I can get the top to roll down. It's stuck in this position."

Kyle peered under the lid and tugged on it. "A cabinetmaker could probably help you."

His suggestion had merit, and Hester decided she would have Charlie Benson take a look at it. Kyle picked up his coat, tucked the file under his arm, and left.

❧

The month of February turned out to be a time of bickering for the whole town. One morning Kyle discovered that all four tires on his Mercedes had been slashed. Up until that time, he had not gotten angry, but the howl he put up when he discovered the mutilation could have been heard on the other side of the mountain.

The town divided into factions; those who favored the lawsuit Geraldine Ledman proposed and those who believed the town of Afterglow should be moved. Kyle and Hester figured in every dispute, and they bore the brunt of everyone's ire. Only the Noffsingers, Byrds, and Ray remained friendly to them. On Sunday mornings, most of the disputants attended church, and Ray's sermons were designed to pour oil on the troubled waters of the town, but on Monday the citizens were arguing again.

In late February, an environmentalist group from the county seat appeared at a centennial commission meeting and demanded that the celebration be stopped. How could they honor a man who had desecrated the forests and robbed his neighbors? This added predicament unnerved the mayor to such an extent that he burst into tears in front of the commission's members.

But tempers cooled off near the first of March when a heavy snowstorm isolated Afterglow from the rest of the world. The roads were closed and telephone service was interrupted when the wet, heavy snow snapped the utility lines.

The whole area looked like a giant Christmas card, with the evergreen trees decorated with heavy tufts of snow and cardinals nestling in their branches. The citizens forgot their differences and enjoyed the only snowfall of the winter. A small knoll below the town provided a gentle downhill slope for sledders. The river froze from bank to bank, and bonfires along the riverbank each night illuminated the ice for skaters.

Kyle was gone from Afterglow during the snowfall, but Hester enjoyed the day and evening activities, coming back to the apartment cold and wet from the snow, happily alive and vibrant. After a warm shower, she would bundle up in a heavy wool robe and pore over the notes she had made during the day. The history research was going well, and she and Clint had made preliminary plans for the format and printing. True to her journalistic beliefs, she was painting Afterglow and Hezekiah Brown in their true colors, some black, some white. But one night she encountered something in the packet of papers that Kyle had brought that threw her whole perspective off balance—she had uncovered a situation where it might be best to conceal the truth.

Chapter 6

Hester scrutinized the paper carefully, trying to figure if it could be a hoax; it would be like Kyle to put in such a document just to discomfit her. But the paper was obviously old, and in Hezekiah Brown's handwriting, dated October 15, 1913, two years before Brown's death.

The idiots! Where did they get the idea that I was a war hero? When I found out what they were doing, it was too late to undo. I'd been away for six months only to return to find out they were erecting a statue in my honor. And then today, when they unveiled the plaque, I was stunned.

Let this be my witness to the world: I hated the Civil War. I enlisted first on the Confederate side because their armies controlled this area. Then when the Rebs moved out and the Federals came in, I switched sides. I watched from my safe hideout on the mountain as the Blues and the Grays in the valley spilled their blood for an ideal. While they fought, I dreamed of an empire. War hero! I didn't even care who won. All I wanted to do was get on with my life. I hate war.

Hester breathed rapidly and heat suffused her body when she read the note. She knew she had finally learned why Brown's family had not been proud of him. How could one look up to a man who showed no loyalty to his country?

What would it do to Afterglow to learn that the man they revered had not lived up to their ideal? She could not publish this. The town's pride had already suffered enough during the past few weeks, and she could not contribute added embarrassment.

When the snow melted, Kyle came back to Afterglow, and Hester sent word to the boardinghouse that she wanted to see him. He soon arrived in jubilant spirits. "At last I'm breaking through that block of ice you call a heart," he said. "You've never invited me to see you before, and you usually put me out when I do try to come in."

"Oh, be serious for once. I have something to tell you that I don't want others to hear." She took the Brown letter from a pigeonhole in the desk. "Although as a journalist it pains me to admit it, I've found something about your ancestor that I can't publish. You may want to destroy the paper. But at any rate, it's your decision now."

Kyle looked at her questioningly as he took the envelope. He scanned it, then read it more carefully and laughed.

"Don't you take anything seriously? Do you think it's funny that your ancestor was a coward?"

"I don't look at it that way. As far as I'm concerned this is the most intelligent thing I've heard that the old boy did. The Civil War was one of the most senseless incidents this country has ever experienced. If we would go to war now, do you think I'd rush off immediately, waving a flag? If he had fought in that conflict, he might have been killed, and I wouldn't even be here. Can you imagine the loss that would be to the world?"

"And to think that one reason I decided to suppress that information was to prevent you from being embarrassed!"

"I do appreciate it, and I don't think the letter should be published, mostly because Afterglow's citizens would be distressed. But it doesn't matter to me."

"Does anything?"

"You do."

She ignored his remark. "You take the letter with you. I don't want to be responsible for it. After all, you brought it to me."

He tucked the envelope into his inner coat pocket. "I won't be here long this time. Our spring court circuit starts next week, and I'll have a busy six weeks. But I wanted to check in and see how the celebration is coming along. And also to ask the mayor if he's decided to move."

"This is a laid-back town, and they don't move fast on anything. Clint and I are the only ones who are making progress. The log raft ride is supposed to be the first of May, and not one move has been made to bring in the logs or to plan the itinerary."

"Is the small-town atmosphere getting on your nerves?"

"Most of the time I accept it, but I'll be happy to return home. Many times I've rued the day I agreed to come here."

"But if you hadn't, you wouldn't have had the pleasure of meeting me."

She gave him a scornful glance, and he exited with another laugh.

Although Hester was growing weary of Afterglow and its bickering, her eventual return to Detroit did not have much appeal. She would feel the absence of her mother more keenly when she returned to the familiar surroundings, and after today's letter from Molly, she knew she would not have her friend's company, either.

Dear Hester,

I got married yesterday. That news is going to surprise you as much as it did me. I didn't suppose I would ever marry again, but I met Mario Salzabar soon after I came to my sister's.

He's from Cuba and has been living in the U.S. for about ten years. He's a retired doctor, a most handsome and distinguished gentleman. We will be living in his modest home here in Florida.

Love,
Molly

With a keen feeling of personal loss, Hester wrote Molly a congratulatory note and enclosed a check for a wedding present. *Another tie of the past severed,* she thought.

Thinking of Molly's marriage turned Hester's thoughts to Kyle. *Was he romantically interested in me, or were his comments just more of his foolishness?* If so, she could not think about it now. She also hoped he stayed away; she was beginning to feel pressured with the amount of work to be done, and she knew she could accomplish more with Kyle Trent in Harrisburg. There was one advantage to her tight schedule—she seldom gave any thought to her doubtful heritage and the elusive Toby she had hoped to find in Afterglow.

Even though Clint and Belle assured her that she was making great progress, she counted the swift passage of time by observing the progress of the awakening forest. From her living room window she looked past the Byrd house and across the river to a high mountain peak. The greening had started at the river's edge and then had gradually moved up the mountainside. By mid-April she could see some green at the very top, and by that time the trees along the river were in full leaf. When she observed a flock of robins tugging on recalcitrant worms outside her apartment, Hester knew that spring had arrived and that she had very little time to finish the history manuscript, which Clint wanted for printing by the first of August.

By now most of the citizens of Afterglow ignored Kyle's suggestion that the town be moved, had lost interest in Geraldine Ledman's lawsuit, and laughed when environmentalists talked about Brown's exploitation of the forest. The melting snow on the mountains and long periods of rain had flushed the river to its highest, and two log rafts, ready for the journey down the river, had been anchored where a boat dock had once been.

Hester refused to ride on one of the rafts, choosing rather to follow the expedition from the riverbank. She had talked to Mr. Byrd about the skill needed to manipulate one of the rafts, and she had been convinced that no one now living in Afterglow had the expertise to supervise the operation.

"Chances are they'll wreck on the rapids between here and the county seat," Mr. Byrd said. "I declined the offer to ride with the town's dignitaries. Some of the mayor's ideas for this celebration are stupid."

Smiling at his remark, Hester said, "I'll bow to the wisdom of ninety-five years, Mr. Byrd; I'll walk."

"That won't be so pleasant, either," Miss Eliza said. "You'll be going over terrain a goat couldn't cross. Besides, Father, Charles Benson is going to pole one raft. He knows how it's done."

Hester still did not choose to ride on a raft, although Charlie Benson had earned her respect. He made some beautiful replicas of the vases and curio shelves once manufactured by the old furniture factory. Several of the townspeople had met to clean out two rooms of the factory to make a place for Charlie and a few apprentices who wanted to learn the craft from him. They intended to have a good supply of souvenirs ready for the summer trade. And Hester was expecting many tourists; some of the articles she had sent to her Detroit newspaper had been picked up by Associated Press, and Afterglow's name was on the lips of people from coast to coast. She was grateful that she had some income from these articles, as she had received only a pittance of the grant money, and if it had not been for the checks for her freelance work, she would have been forced to dip into her savings for everyday expenses. Even considering the low cost of living in Afterglow, she was going in the hole on this venture, and she often wondered why God had directed her steps in this direction.

One morning in late April when she was editing an interview she had had with Sadie, the restaurant owner, about the early eating places in Afterglow, a teenager who often ran errands for Clint brought a note to Hester.

Imperative that I see you right away.

Clint

Hester turned off her computer, put on a lightweight jacket, and headed downtown, grateful for a reprieve from her desk. The weather was so beautiful that it was difficult for her to stay inside. She was in Clint's office ten minutes after she received his note. He closed the door behind her.

"I receive issues of several out-of-town newspapers, and this one from Harrisburg really gave me a jolt," he said as he handed her the newspaper and indicated an article on the inside section. The headline leaped off the paper toward her: TOWN HONORS MAN WHO SHOWED THE WHITE FEATHER.

She read the article aloud, her voice rising in volume with each word. "It isn't unusual for war heroes to be commemorated. Who hasn't heard of Andrew Jackson, William T. Sherman, Robert E. Lee? But there's only one town we know that has erected a monument in memory of someone, whom, to use a kind name, we will refer to as a conscientious objector."

There followed an unedited version of Brown's letter that Hester had given to Kyle. She felt blood rushing to her face, and her eyes blazed green when she looked at Clint. "Why did he have that published?"

"Then I take it this comes as no surprise to you."

"To see it in the paper certainly surprises me. I found that letter in a packet of papers and pictures Kyle brought me. I gave it back to him, and he agreed that it shouldn't be made public because of the impact it would have on Afterglow."

"This will put Mayor Stepp in the hospital."

"Maybe he won't see it."

"Don't count on it. This kind of news travels fast."

The telephone rang. After Clint answered, he listened silently for a few seconds, a crooked grin creasing his face.

"You're in luck," he said. "She happens to be right here."

He handed the telephone to Hester and with his lips formed the words, "Kyle Trent."

"Yes?" Hester spoke sharply into the telephone mouthpiece.

"Why don't you install a telephone at your place? I've had a hard time contacting you."

"Because I don't want to be bothered with telephone calls."

"There's something in our local paper, this morning that's going to make you unhappy." Hester held the receiver away from her ear and motioned for Clint to come closer and listen.

"I've already seen the paper here in the *Courier* office and you're right; I'm unhappy."

"And I thought I could prepare you for the blow! I'll bet nothing has ever traveled that fast in Afterglow before. Well, I didn't do it."

"You had to. You had the paper, and from the way I remember it, it was printed verbatim."

"But I didn't. I've been busy since I returned to Harrisburg, and I hadn't thought any more about my ancestor's letter. It was still in my coat pocket where I'd placed it at your apartment. I'm not the neatest housekeeper in the world, and occasionally my sister comes in and sweeps out the place. She did that last week and gathered up all of my winter suits and sent them to the cleaners for summer storage. Apparently someone at the cleaners found that note and passed it to a newspaper reporter. You won't believe me, but I am sorry."

"I do believe it. I don't think even you would be so mean as to print that deliberately."

"Thanks for your confidence," he said ironically. "Gotta run. I'll see you in a few weeks."

Hester handed the phone back to Clint, and he replaced it in the cradle. "What do we do now?"

"I'll go warn Mayor Stepp so he'll know about this before it becomes common knowledge. Then I might as well print it in the *Courier*."

"Try to assure the mayor that this is the kind of publicity needed if we're going to flood Afterglow with visitors this summer. There are hundreds of humdrum celebrations and festivals throughout this country. Nobody pays much attention when they're commonplace."

"You're probably right. Conflict commands more attention than peace."

"I'll stop by the furniture factory and tell Charlie Benson to speed up production of the souvenirs and to make a sign to advertise the factory as a tourist site. And why don't you print some 'Handmade in Afterglow' stickers to put on the souvenirs?"

Hester did not go to the next council meeting, but she heard Clint's account before reading about it in the *Courier*.

"If Afterglow isn't on the map after all of this, I'll be surprised," he said with a wide grin. "Some representatives from the American Legion Post in the county seat came to the meting and demanded that we tear down Brown's statue. The mayor really has on his sword and shield now, and he's so angry because people are picking on his town that he's gone to war. He personally evicted the men from the council chamber."

Hester wrote up an account of Brown's memo and the council meeting results after Clint went home, and the next morning she left early to take it to the county seat to fax it to Detroit. The town of Afterglow still slumbered. As she passed Brown's statue, she braked suddenly—someone had painted a vivid white feather the length of the statue! Angrily she reversed the car and headed toward the Noffsingers'. She pounded on the door until a sleepy Belle opened it.

"Hester! What's wrong?"

She pushed past Belle into the living room. "Someone has painted a white feather on Hezekiah Brown's statue! This had gone too far." Clint came yawning from the bedroom, wrapping a robe around him. "Should I telephone the mayor, Clint, and perhaps he can have the paint removed before anyone sees it?"

"I'll telephone him, but it's probably too late. It's pretty difficult to remove paint from stone. Why were you up so early?"

"Going to the county seat to fax an article to my newspaper."

"Go on. I'll notify the mayor. He's not as vulnerable as he once was. Nothing will surprise him now."

True to Hester's prediction, within a week the town's streets were crowded with curious tourists and reporters. Miss Eliza's boardinghouse and the motel were packed every night, and the owner of the Grand Hotel talked of opening up.

Belle had already rented part of the hotel for her craft show, and when the women went in to clean it for the upcoming show, they helped refurbish rooms on the second floor for rental.

"The heating system doesn't work, but I can provide electric heaters if the weather is too cold," the owner assured Hester. So in the next article to her newspaper, Hester touted the novelty of staying in the old hotel.

The furnishings are reminiscent of the early 1900s. Don't expect a plush inn for the rooms are somewhat rustic, although they do have the amenities. But the view from the windows will keep you from noticing the lack of a telephone or television. Make Afterglow a part of your vacation schedule this year.

On the day of the log raft ride, Hester, dressed in a sweatshirt, jeans, and heavy boots and with a camera slung over her back, was ready to follow the rafts downstream as far as she could. Where the river narrowed between two high peaks, she would have to climb a mountain trail, but by now she had adjusted to the altitude, and she intended to try it.

Kyle had returned from Harrisburg and without invitation had made known his intention to hike with her. When they reached the site of the old boat dock, a large group of tourists and natives were ready to follow the raft downriver, and the bank was lined with interested spectators waiting to see the departure.

Clint and Ray were the rollers on the first raft. Ray had ridden a few rafts when he was a boy, but Clint admitted that he had never been on one before. The signal was given, and the crew untied the raft and jumped aboard as the craft eased out into the current. A television cameraman rode on their raft; Mayor Stepp was intent that the camera focus on the raft bearing the town officials.

Charlie Benson supervised the second raft, and he suggested that the passengers sit down, but Mayor Stepp ignored his advice and continued to stand in full view of the camera and the spectators. When the raft was about ten feet from the bank, it tipped quickly, and before Benson could right the raft, Mayor Stepp and two councilmen tumbled into the shallow water. When the three men sputtered to a standing position, Benson helped them back onto the raft, and they sat where he indicated.

"He did that deliberately," Kyle whispered. "He's too good at the job to have made a mistake. Look at the way he crosses those logs and directs the raft out into the current."

Benson was dressed in a red flannel shirt, loose overalls, and a red cap covered his curly hair. He moved as confidently as if he were on a solid floor rather than on a log raft as he maneuvered the rough craft toward the middle of the river.

"You're probably right, and I doubt the mayor will give him any more trouble. Mayor Stepp may think he's the star of this show, but Benson is the one people will remember."

"And the preacher isn't doing too badly, either. Let's go," Kyle said. "We want to reach the rapids before they do. Should be some interesting photos from there."

They made slow progress walking along the river, as there was no trail, and their way was obstructed by fallen logs, green briars, and other vegetation. They stopped trying to find an easy route and plowed through the underbrush.

"We'll never make it," Hester complained.

"The rafts won't be going fast, either. We should make it to the rapids, but we might as well forget about following them to the county seat. Once they hit the white water, they'll travel quickly."

One of the hikers had brought a machete, so he started cutting a path for the hikers, and although their clothing was tattered, their skins bruised and briar-scratched, the cavalcade of the curious did reach the rapids before the rafts did.

"But none too soon," Kyle said, pointing upstream. "There they are."

Hester stared at the gorge below them. The mountains narrowed at this point, and as far as she could see, large boulders littered the streambed. White-capped water swirled around the rocks, and she could not see any opening large enough for the rafts to pass through.

"And you actually suggested that buildings could be moved down this river on rafts!" Hester said sarcastically.

"At that time I'd never heard of this gorge and rapids," he defended himself. "They'll have to take the buildings by truck."

"Ha!"

When the rafts approached the rapids, Benson took the lead, and while the mayor and his dignitaries sat meekly, the bank robber's descendant took them safely through the first series of rapids. The spectators cheered the wet but safe rafters. Benson poled his raft into a protected spot and took up a foghorn to transmit information to the other rafters.

"It's not so bad, Reverend. More water than it appears," he called to Ray. "Hold to the left of that jagged boulder, keep your balance, and t'won't hurt to do a little praying. When you start, you're going to come in a hurry."

Ray waved his hand indicating that he had heard the instructions. Hester felt sweat break out over her body, and she leaned heavily on the walking stick she had picked up. She forgot to breathe, glad that Belle was not here to watch. Despite the life jackets they were wearing, instant death awaited anyone who was thrown against those huge boulders.

As far as Hester could tell, Ray did exactly as Benson had done, but when he reached the first of the whitewater, a bounding wave twisted the fragile raft, and the sound of shifting logs was heard by those on shore. The cameraman was the first to topple into the water, and when the raft finally reached safety of smooth water, six of its passengers were floundering in the river.

Kyle and several other men rushed down to the water's edge to help the men to safety. With only a few bruises and cuts, they had little damage, except that the camera containing the documentary that Mayor Stepp wanted to air was lying at the bottom of the stream.

Benson and Ray agreed that the raft was damaged too much to continue the trip, so Benson and his passengers journeyed down river toward the county seat while the others tramped back toward Afterglow. By the time they returned home, a message had come from the county seat that the raft had arrived safely, but Kyle and Hester were chagrined when they realized that in all of the excitement, they had forgotten to take pictures.

A few days after the raft trip, when Hester went to the furniture factory, she congratulated Charlie on his expertise in handling the raft.

"Old game with me, ma'am. Made my living in the timber industry for a long time."

"Certainly is too bad that your skill deserted you right there at the first."

"Well, accidents happen to the best of us," he said with an amused gleam in the eye. "Better for the mayor to have a little dunking than to cause all of us to wreck on the rapids."

"Did our tourists buy many souvenirs?"

"Just about cleaned us out. We'll have to work fast before we have that craft show."

"I know you're busy, but stop by the apartment sometime and see if you can figure out why the top of my desk won't roll. I'd like to buy it from Miss Eliza if the top can be fixed."

"I'll come around after work tonight."

Later that night, Hester cleared the desk off, and Charlie spent fifteen or twenty minutes tugging gently on the roll top.

"There's some kind of paper stuck in the left slide, and that's holding it. I'll take it apart. We might jerk the papers out, but that could damage the papers or the slide. Also, the papers might be of some worth. I'll see what I can do."

Hester brought him a cup of coffee and a tray of cookies.

"At least have a snack before you start. You'll be late for your dinner."

"The old woman knows by now to cook for me when she sees me coming."

In an hour, Charlie had removed a packet of letters from the desk and had the roll top sliding up and down smoothly. The top letter was addressed to Tom Oliver Byrd, which did not surprise Hester, as Miss Eliza's nephew had used the desk. After Charlie left, Hester ate a light meal.

She was eager to take the letters to the Byrds and to offer to buy the desk. When she lifted the packet from the desk, the rubber band holding the letters snapped, and they scattered on the floor. Hester knelt to retrieve them and the first letter she picked up was addressed to Anna Taylor with a post office stamp of RETURN TO SENDER on it. In the upper left-hand corner was written, "T. O. Byrd, Afterglow."

With a *thud*, Hester settled down on the floor. Had she come to the end of her search at last?

Chapter 7

Hester's disbelief changed to shock. Surely she was dreaming! She had been in Afterglow for almost six months, and she had scanned birth, death, and property records without finding a Toby. The evidence she needed had been within her arm's reach all of the time. The Toby she sought was Tom Oliver Byrd, who sighed his name T. O. By and sometimes lazily left out the periods. Why hadn't she stumbled onto that fact?

Her fingers trembled as she sorted through the packet. A few of the letters had been written to Tom by Miss Eliza when he was in the service, but six of the envelopes were of personal interest to Hester. Two of them had been sent to her mother at an address in Kentucky, which Hester recognized as her grandmother's address. The other four were letters that Anna Taylor had written to Tom Byrd. The letters from her mother were unsealed, so she read them first, and then she opened the ones that Tom had written to her mother. In a half hour she had the answer to the dilemma that had plagued her since December.

Tom Byrd and Anna Taylor had married after a whirlwind weeklong courtship when Anna was visiting her grandmother in Kentucky and Tom had been in basic training at Fort Campbell. He was sent to Korea immediately after their wedding, and Anna had returned to her job in Detroit. Before she had gone to Kentucky, she had broken her engagement to John Lawson, but as soon as she saw John again, she realized she still loved him and that her marriage to Tom Byrd had been a mistake.

John was willing to forgive her secret marriage, and Anna wrote Tom a letter that she had started divorce proceedings. Then she realized she was pregnant. Within two months, Tom was back in the States, discharged from the service because of an injury he had received on the ship going overseas. A few months before Hester was born, the divorce was finalized, and Anna took back her maiden name. One letter contained a copy of the final divorce decree.

So Tom Byrd is my father, not John Lawson! She laughed hysterically when it dawned on her that old Mr. Byrd was her great-grandfather and Miss Eliza was her great-aunt. Then her laughter gave way to anger—anger at her mother, at John Lawson, at Tom Byrd. Anger toward her mother and John Lawson because they had not told her the truth, and anger at Tom Byrd because he had apparently given his daughter away without any desire to see her again.

Now that she knew this, was she any better off? And what was she going to do about it? After a tense, sleepless night, she knew that she would do nothing. She intended to keep the letters written by Tom Byrd and her mother, for really they belonged to her more than to anyone else, and so she locked them in her traveling case.

After she nibbled on some toast and sipped a glass of milk, she went across the yard and found Miss Eliza in the kitchen, baking her daily portion of fresh bread.

"Guess what, Miss Eliza? I found out why the top of the desk wouldn't budge. Charlie Benson worked on it last night, and he found the problem. These letters were wedged in the slide of the roll top."

Miss Eliza's hands were covered with flour, so she leaned over to peer at the letters. "Upon my word! Those are letters I wrote to Tom years ago. I'm surprised he kept them."

"Apparently your nephew was in the Korean War."

"No, the war was over by the time he was old enough to be drafted, but they shipped him out for the army of occupation. He was involved in a nasty accident on the ship going over; an engine blew up, and he was permanently injured. He was in the hospital for a few months before he came back here. That's when he lived in your little house. He wanted solitude."

No wonder I felt as if I had stepped back into time when I entered that building months ago.

"Does your nephew have a family?"

"No. He never married. He stayed with us for about a year, but he was restless for some reason. As soon as he recovered, he left and has never been back."

"So you don't know what he's done with himself?"

Eliza shook her head. "Maybe once a year I'll get a postcard from him, and he's liable to be anywhere in the world. I don't believe he has a permanent residence. He's just a vagabond."

A great guy to have for a father!

"I'll lay the letters here on the edge of the table." Although Hester's desire for the desk had dimmed somewhat because she knew it had belonged to a father who had abandoned her, she said, "I wonder if I could persuade you to sell that desk to me. It's very versatile, and I like it."

"Probably so. I'll give it some thought and decide how much I should ask for it." Miss Eliza kneaded the bread dough rhythmically. "What are your plans for the day?"

"This is the day they're going to start refurbishing the old covered bridge, and I want to copy down all of those inscriptions before they're obliterated. I tried to tell the mayor these messages add character to the bridge, but he wasn't inclined to listen."

So people in Afterglow didn't know that Tom Byrd had been married, Hester thought as she went back to her house. And they wouldn't know after she left here, either. She had been born a Lawson, and she would stay one.

On the way to the covered bridge, Hester met Ray, and she said, "If you aren't too busy, perhaps you could help me today."

"It will be a pleasure. What are you going to do?"

"Copy the inscriptions from the covered bridge before the workers destroy them."

"It's a good idea to record them, but they aren't going to be destroyed. The town council balked on the mayor last night. They told him the bridge could be repaired, but not painted inside. That's no way to preserve the history he's concerned about. Why, my own initials and my childhood love's are there! I carved them one midsummer night."

"Is that the girl you married?"

"No. I had dozens of heartthrobs after that. I met my wife when I lived away from Afterglow." A musing look crossed his face, and Hester surmised he was recalling their time together. "We had a good marriage. I still miss her."

"Have you thought of remarriage?"

"Thought of it, yes. A good wife is an asset to a minister, but I'm in no hurry. Do you want to be considered as a candidate for Wife Number Two?"

She laughed. "I wasn't hinting, but I can think of worse things. You've been a big help to me this year, but I don't have time to consider a proposal now."

They walked into the coolness of the covered bridge. "And what can I do to help you now?"

"Mostly keep me from being hit by a vehicle while I record all of this information."

Hester soon filled several sheets of yellow legal pad with notations of the type expected of teenagers such as hearts with arrows through them and bearing words like "Bob loves Susie." She found "Ray loves Bernice," and they laughed together about it.

"Ah, ha!" she cried. "Wonder if Belle has seen this? 'Clint loves Alta.'"

"There's no problem if she has. Alta moved away from Afterglow years ago, and she's happily married in California."

Hester did not mention one inscription she found: "Tom loves Anna," and underneath in small letters, hardly legible, "but she doesn't love him."

"I believe we could use a new sign," Ray said, indicating the faded words painted on a square, warped board near the entry of the structure.

AFTERGLOW BRIDGE
ERECTED IN 1915

The board hung sideways, and Hester tucked the notepad under her arm and attempted to straighten the sign. It swung slightly and slid down the side of the bridge, landing at Hester's feet. "Whoops! The nail that held it has rusted in two."

Ray waited until a car whizzed through the structure, and then he joined her. "There's a drawing behind the sign."

"Looks like a map," Hester said, peering at the blurred markings.

"You may be right. If we can get rid of all that accumulated dust, we might be able to tell what it is. I'll wet my handkerchief in the river and see if I can wash off the grime."

By the time Ray returned with the wet cloth, Hester had finished recording the other crude writings on the bridge. Ray rubbed lightly at the edge of the drawing. As the figures became plainer, he wiped more rapidly, and a smile crossed his face.

"I suppose I'm a fool to even mention it, but this does seem to be a map of some kind, and there are two initials down in the corner. Looks like 'A. B.' Do you suppose this could be a map showing where Aaron Benson stashed the gold he took from the Afterglow bank? The story has always been that he buried the treasure before he left the region."

"Yes. Mr. Byrd told me that."

Hester and Ray looked alternately at one another and then quickly away for a good two minutes. Hester's thoughts whirled.

"I suppose we're thinking the same thing. Should we nail this sign back over the map and forget what we've seen? With everything else that's happened, all we need to completely ruin the centennial celebration is to have a treasure hunt in these mountains.

"It would be great publicity for Afterglow, though," Ray said thoughtfully. "I'm for telling it."

Hester waved her arms in resignation. "You'll have to live with the consequences. I'll be leaving in a few months."

"At least let's tell Clint and get his opinion."

"Replace the sign until you've had time to confer with him. I'll stay and keep guard while you go into town."

Hester walked back and forth across the bridge, dodging from side to side to miss the occasional vehicle that crossed. She thought about the pathetic note Tom Byrd had left behind. It seemed cruel of her mother to marry him and then desert him so soon. Hester had never had any ill feeling toward her mother, and she did not like the fact that she felt this way now. If she could only see Tom Byrd, perhaps she would know why her mother had not chosen him. But on the other hand, she hoped she would never see him. It would be her luck to have him come back while she was here, but if he had already stayed away for almost thirty years, it was unlikely he would return until after the celebration in October.

In less than an hour, she heard a car coming from Afterglow at a rapid speed, and Mayor Stepp brought his Buick to a sliding halt at the end of the bridge and ran toward her.

"Don't touch it! Don't touch it! This may be important historical data."

Hester lifted her hands high. "I'm not touching anything."

Clint and Ray hustled into the bridge, and Clint and Mayor Stepp scrutinized the map.

"This must remain a secret until we can have someone interpret the map. Looks to me as if this arrow starts at the river and goes up on the western mountain about halfway, then comes down toward the river again where the route crosses to the Afterglow side."

Clint, in his quiet way, stared at the drawing a long time before he said anything, and then he cautioned, "Mayor, this may be nothing but a hoax. It could have been drawn in recent years and simulated to look old. My grandfather was always convinced that the Benson gang took the money with them. And Charlie says his ancestor left this country after that robbery and went to live in South America. That would have taken some money."

If the mayor heard Clint, he did not heed his warning. "We'll contact the university and see if they have an expert who can decipher the plan."

"The way I read it," Clint continued, "after the arrow swings around on the mountain, it crosses the river several miles below the bridge and cuts a figure eight before it points to a rock. If that indicates the money was hidden under a rock, we wouldn't have to move more than a million or so on that slope to find the cache."

"Clint, you're too conservative. What do you know about treasure maps?" Mayor Stepp said.

"Not a thing."

"Well, then, stop giving me unsolicited advice. Cover that drawing, and I'll halt repair work until we've had it analyzed. Not a word about this to anyone," the mayor warned as he hustled out of the bridge and into his car.

At least it is comforting to know that Mayor Stepp is not my father, Hester thought, the only good thing so far she could say about her discovery of the night before.

Before they nailed the board back over the drawing, Hester made an exact copy, or at least as closely as she could determine, of the map for the history book.

"I'm glad you're making a sketch of it," Ray said, "because if I were a betting man, I'd wager everybody in Afterglow will know about this before dark, and by morning the drawing will be so smudged, no one will be able to decipher it."

"I wouldn't bet you on that," Clint laughingly said. "The outcome is too sure."

"I wonder if the mayor has considered who will claim this gold if it's found."

"Good question, Hester," Ray said. "I'd assume it would go to the bank of Afterglow, or to an insurance company if the bank had been reimbursed for the loss. But that long ago, many banks might not have been insured."

"How much money was taken from the bank?" Hester questioned.

"The amount has grown with each telling through the years," Clint said, "but I think they took a bag of gold worth about twenty thousand dollars."

"No wonder the mayor is excited."

"But Kyle Trent may claim it; the chances are that the gold is buried on his land," Ray said.

🦋

Kyle had been out all day with representatives from the State Department of Natural Resources looking over the property he wanted to sell them, and Hester wondered if she should tell him about the map. But she had always heard that if you had news too good to keep, no one else would keep it quiet either, so she decided to say nothing. If the news spread, she would not be at fault. Already she wished she hadn't been curious about what was behind the dilapidated sign.

The next morning when she opened her door, Kyle called to her from the window, "Let's go look for the treasure, shall we?"

Her annoyance must have been obvious because he said, "Did you think that it could remain a secret in Afterglow?"

"No, I didn't, but the mayor did. Where did you hear it?"

"Miss Eliza told me at breakfast."

"Give me an hour, and I'll meet you at the front steps."

Hester wrote a news story about the discovery and drew another facsimile of the map, which she would fax to Detroit. She had not intended to spread the news, but the mayor apparently had already done so, because she was convinced that the leak had not come from Clint or Ray. She hurried into her car and drove out of the driveway.

When she and Kyle arrived at the bridge, people swarmed over the area. She could not even find a place to park, so she said to Kyle, "I'm going on to the county seat and send a report of this to my newspaper—that is if I can cross the bridge. I'll stop here in the middle of the road so you can get out."

"There's a policeman directing traffic. I'll ride on to town with you, if you don't mind. I want to buy a metal detector."

"Then you're really serious about hunting for the bank loot?"

"Why not? I have to do something for entertainment, and I can't meet with the Natural Resources people over a weekend, so it will help to pass the time if I'm wandering around over the mountains. Do you want to go with me?"

"No, thank you. Clint warned me of the danger of rattlesnakes on the mountain, and I need that kind of warning only once. I'll watch from the sidelines."

She maneuvered the car at a snail's pace through the crowded bridge. So many people hovered around the map that the traffic was reduced to one way in that spot.

"I'll never get close enough to look at that map," Kyle lamented.

"No need to. If you look in the file lying on the backseat, you'll find a sketch of the map. I'm faxing the original to my newspaper."

Kyle studied the map while Hester traveled several miles. "This is a pretty simple map, but I suppose a bank robber of a century ago wouldn't have been much of a cartographer. It seems to me that a person could save a lot of legwork if he would stay on the eastern side of the river and walk down the bank looking for the crossing spot. The way I read it, the route crosses the river near a clump of three spruce trees, and on the eastern bank the marker is a pile of rocks. All I need is to find that pile of rocks and go from there."

"Good luck!"

"What do you mean by that?"

"Think what floodwaters could have done to the rock pile. Also, that clump of trees would have changed somewhat since 1915. That's when the bank robbery occurred."

"Don't spoil my pleasure. This will be a fun way to spend the weekend."

While Hester used the fax machine in the post office, Kyle bought a metal detector and a shovel. When they neared Afterglow on the return trip, Hester asked, "Do you want to stop at the bridge?"

"No, I'll need to change into the rugged clothes I've been wearing the past week. And I'll snatch a bit of Miss Eliza's lunch, too."

"I'll walk to the bridge with you when you're ready to go. After all, I want to be on hand if anyone finds a fortune."

When they arrived at the bridge, Charlie Benson was leaning against the bridge, an amused expression on his face.

"Why aren't you searching?" Hester asked him. "After all, your relative was involved."

"I've heard enough about Aaron Benson to know he never left any money behind, and I also understand he had an odd sense of humor."

As Kyle and Hester walked along the riverbank, Hester pondered Charlie's amusement, and she remembered how he had dumped the mayor in the river. If this were a hoax, had Charlie perpetrated it? Hester considered him one of the most intelligent men she had encountered in Afterglow, and she knew he was cunning enough to come up with the idea. But the sign appeared as if it had not been moved for a long time, and Hester personally believed that Aaron Benson had drawn the map.

When Kyle determined he had found the correct pile of rocks and started climbing the mountain, Hester strolled back to the bridge, which was a beehive of activity. In addition to those wandering around on the hills with picks and shovels, dozens of the less active citizens lounged in the shade of trees and observed. Sadie, from the restaurant, demonstrated ingenuity, however, by peddling sandwiches and beverages from the back of her station wagon. She was doing a good business, too, for in addition to Afterglow's population, carloads of strangers crossed and recrossed the bridge.

Belle and Ina were among the spectators, and Belle signaled for Hester to join them on a blanket spread beneath a maple tree.

"Where's Clint?"

"At the *Courier* putting out a special edition. He hopes to have them here for sale in a couple of hours. He's reproduced the map and copied an account of the Benson robbery from an old newspaper. He's making a one-pager for a souvenir, but I know many people will buy it to use the map. This has been an exciting year."

Clint sent the first hundred copies of the special edition to the bridge by midafternoon, and his employee sold them without leaving the car.

Mayor Stepp, wanting to be sure he was in on the discovery, had persuaded Ray to haul him around over the mountains on the four-wheeler, but Aaron Benson's sense of humor routed the trail over rock cliffs and other places where Ray could not take the vehicle. Too hefty to do any hiking, Mayor Stepp pouted when he had to give up the chase.

By nightfall, no treasure had been found; the map had led the searchers to many false clues.

"I'm going to hold the worship service down at the bridge in the morning," Ray informed Hester as they walked back toward town at dusk.

"I had been wondering what this would do to your morning worship."

"I'd have a sparse crowd, because everyone is too excited. They want to be where the action is, so we'll gather down by the river."

"How will you pass the information to everyone?"

"You ask that after being in Afterglow for several months?" He smiled. "I'll telephone a few key parishioners and ask them to spread the word."

When she left him at the parsonage, Ray said, "I'll need to change my sermon though, so I won't have much sleep tonight."

Kyle came in soon after Hester reached her apartment, and she laughed at his appearance. He had lost his cap, and his blond hair was tangled with leaves and twigs. His clothes were torn in general, and one long scratch spread down the side of his face.

"If that map doesn't take you on a wild-goose chase," he grumbled. "One place I had to climb a tree to see the next clue."

"Look on the bright side. You've had your exercise."

"And also missed my dinner. Miss Eliza eats at six o'clock sharp, and at that time I was falling over a rock cliff. Want to come to the restaurant with me?"

"I'll prepare a sandwich for you, and I have a gelatin salad. You can wash up in the bathroom."

"Make it two sandwiches. I'm starved. . .and thirsty, too."

Kyle did not stay long after he had eaten. He said, "I'm bushed. I'm going to bed so I can be out on the mountain again tomorrow." Evidently his strenuous day had not dulled his appetite for the search.

"Ray is going to have morning worship down by the bridge."

"I'll stay for that and then start exploring again. You should come with me."

With a smile, she shook her head.

Hester and Kyle went to the bridge at ten o'clock in time for Ray's service. Ray stood behind a podium placed on a level spot near the bridge, and a large congregation had spread out on the rough ground around him. Many people had brought their picnic baskets and coolers, and a holiday feeling was in the air.

Ray's text from Matthew chapter 6 caught his hearers' attention immediately. " 'Lay not up for yourselves treasures upon earth. . . . But lay up for yourselves treasures in heaven. . . . For where your treasure is, there will your heart be also.' "

He used these words as a point of departure to indicate the futility of worshiping material possessions and to stress the importance of spiritual values. He used Jesus' parable from Matthew chapter 13: " 'Again, the kingdom of heaven is like unto treasure hid in a field; the which when a man hath found, he hideth, and for joy thereof goeth and selleth all that he hath, and buyeth that field.' "

As Ray compared the advantage of sacrificing earthly possessions for a place in God's kingdom, Hester wondered if the citizens of Afterglow held the proper appreciation for a man like Ray. They probably did not realize the treasure they had in him. Her thoughts turned to his offhand remark about Wife Number Two. Had he been serious? And how had a woman who had never considered marriage become involved with two eligible men? Perhaps that was the most noteworthy news of the summer!

By late Sunday afternoon, the trail had led the gold seekers to a knoll surrounded by a marsh, not far from the bridge. Kyle walked around the area, and his metal detector transmitted positive signals. When Mayor Stepp heard that, he plunged across the swampy area, knee-deep in the mire. But he did not go alone. Soon a dozen men were digging at the spot where Kyle had received a reading.

From their vantage point near the bridge, Belle and Hester watched in fascination. The men talked excitedly, running from one spot to another to peer over the shoulders of those who were digging in the rocky ground.

"We've found it!" a man cried excitedly.

"Swamp or no swamp, I'm going over," Hester said, and she plunged into the marshy area that tugged at her shoes. By the time she reached the knoll, she was barefoot and wet to her knees, but she pushed her way into the midst of the crowd. A rusty metal box lay in a large hole.

"Don't touch it!" Mayor Stepp shouted. He motioned to a man with a video camera. "Take a picture right where it lies, and then keep the camera going while we lift the box out and open it."

"I've had the camera going for the past two days, and I'm not about to stop now," the man retorted.

"Gently, now," Mayor Stepp admonished as three men tugged on the dirt-encrusted box. When they placed it on the ground, Mayor Stepp knelt beside it and posed for the camera. The hinges on the box had rusted, and the lid lifted easily to reveal a leather bag. The men hoisted it from the box, and with trembling fingers, Mayor Stepp untied the leather thongs. A look of consternation crossed his face when he looked inside, and one of the men peering over his shoulders groaned and muttered, "The dirty scoundrel!"

He lifted the bag and dumped the contents on the ground. Dismay spread across the face of the treasure seekers when they realized they had searched two days for a bag of pebbles. A piece of mildewed paper fluttered to the ground when the stones were dumped. Clint picked it up and read aloud, "Tough luck, Afterglow! We took the money with us. Signed, Aaron Benson."

The searchers reacted in different ways. Some of them threw down their shovels and cursed the day they had heard of Aaron Benson. Kyle laughed merrily, causing many of the sober-faced people to glare at him. Hester looked around for Charlie Benson, who stood in the background with a sardonic grin on his face. The video cameraman apparently was delighted with this turn of events; he took close-ups of the disgruntled who were too weary to even notice what he was doing.

Hester crippled around on the rough terrain to take photos of the bogus treasure. Mayor Stepp slumped on the ground, a picture of dejection.

"Look on the bright side, Mayor. It has been an entertaining weekend," Hester said.

"Why does everything we do turn out to be a joke?" he moaned.

"Not everything. The arts and crafts show will be fine."

"No, it won't. Something will happen. If nothing else, then Kyle Trent's lawsuit hanging over our heads will ruin it."

"Did I hear my name?" Kyle said, appearing beside them.

Mayor Stepp waved his arm angrily and refused to look at Kyle, who laughed and took Hester by the arm.

"Are you ready to leave? I'll help you through the mud."

"I came over by myself."

"Yes, but now you're minus a couple of shoes. Let's go."

When they passed Charlie Benson, Hester asked Kyle, "Do you think he planted that map and the rocks?"

"I'm glad you're suspicious of someone else besides me. Why not accept the incident at face value? I think Aaron Benson did it before he left here."

"But Charlie seemed so amused about it all."

"It amused me, too, but you can't accuse me of planting the evidence."

Hester was glad to reach dry land, and she gladly accepted Clint's offer of a ride back to Miss Eliza's. Her slacks were wet to the knees, and the abrasions on the bottom of her feet ached and burned. She was not in a very good humor with Aaron Benson.

Chapter 8

Belle's arts and crafts show was a success in spite of the controversy over the future of their town. The room was crowded with artisans, and a blacksmith and a cooper demonstrated their skills beneath tents set up on the sidewalk. The traffic jam was worse than during the two-day treasure hunt, and Mayor Stepp walked the streets in a state of euphoria, smiling and shaking hands as if his next election were at stake.

Hester conducted tours through the renovated furniture factory and promoted the sale of the souvenirs that Charlie and his helpers had produced. After all their worrying and planning, the centennial celebration was leveling off now into a satisfying experience.

The next week Kyle received confirmation from the Department of Natural Resources that they would buy his land for a state park, but a sale price could not be agreed upon until they knew whether the town of Afterglow was going to relocate.

Kyle pressed the mayor and council members for a decision, and when they refused to move, he instigated a suit to force them out. When he talked to Hester about it, she said resentfully, "I think you're being obstinate. It might be legal to make them move, but it certainly isn't ethical. It isn't the fault of any of these people that their ancestors didn't pay for the land. They're innocent victims. And by the way, what about Geraldine Ledman's suit against you?" she added sarcastically.

"She doesn't have a leg to stand on. There are no records to prove how much Hezekiah Brown received for the timber he sold. And as for the environmentalists who have been lambasting me, they can't do anything. I haven't cut any of their precious trees."

When she argued with Kyle that Afterglow was growing and that he should forget his claim, he said, "You prove to me that they own this land, and I'll be the first to say 'Fare thee well.' But I want things done legally. I have a lawyer's mind."

"And a scoundrel's heart."

"Maybe. Give you a few more months, and you'll join Mayor Stepp in his praise of Afterglow. A true daughter of his in spirit."

She looked at him angrily. She still had nightmares about Mayor Stepp being her father. By mid-August, Hester delivered her manuscript to Clint for printing, and then she started organizing the drama. Her first concern was a place to present it. There was no time to construct an outdoor facility, so she suggested that the hotel ballroom be converted into a temporary theater. I. M. Thomas had sent a note giving the size of the backdrop, and they had to make the stage fit that.

While she planned the drama, her mind fretted about Kyle's lawsuit. *If only there was some way to prove that Brown had donated the land to Afterglow.* She went back to the courthouse and searched for another day but without results.

When she shared her concern with Ray, he said, "I've been praying for a sane way to resolve this argument. There's still a possibility that the church minutes might make some reference to property exchanges. I haven't read all of them."

"I scanned every page when researching for the history, but I'll go through the minutes again in case I missed something."

Hester spent the next week reading through the tedious church clerk's minutes, but still she found nothing that would alleviate the tense situation between Kyle and the town of Afterglow.

"You said you had a diary of Reverend Hartwell's, the founder of this church. I don't suppose there are any clues in it."

"The diary I have deals with his year at Afterglow, and the area was a company town long after that. I'd judge that Brown turned the property over to the town about 1910."

"That's the way Mr. Byrd remembers it." Hester stared out the window of Ray's office at the shimmering sunlight on the lazy river. "If Hartwell kept one diary, perhaps he would have had others. Where did you get the one you have?"

"From a descendant of the Hartwells who lives in the county seat. It hadn't occurred to me that she could have any papers relevant to a land deal, but it wouldn't hurt to ask her."

"Do you know the woman?"

"I've talked with her on the phone several times."

"Then let's contact her to learn if she has anything else. I doubt that the Hartwells would have lost interest in the town after they left. They might have kept in touch."

"I'll telephone the woman and set up an appointment to see her."

Ray contacted Hester that night to say he had an appointment for the next day and that they should leave immediately after noon.

🦋

Iris Hambleton was a gracious sixty-year-old widow who met them at the door with a smile and a warm welcome. She led them into a small living room filled with furniture of an earlier era.

In answer to their questions, she said, "I have quite a few items that belonged to Ivan and Thelma Hartwell, and when you have the chapel car on permanent display, I will donate these things to the town of Afterglow. This huge house is too much for me, and I'm planning to move into a retirement village in Florida within a few years."

She took them on a tour of the first floor, indicating items that had belonged to the Hartwells. In the dining room, she stopped before a miniature organ, sat on the stool, and played "Amazing Grace."

"The Hartwells used this folding organ in the chapel car."

"It still has a good tone after all these years," Ray said.

She took out a few items of china from a walnut cupboard. "They used these, also." Mrs. Hambleton carefully lifted a large Bible from a drawer and handed it to Ray. "This was Ivan Hartwell's. You're welcome to use it on Centennial Sunday, if you like."

"I'd be delighted to do so," Ray said as he turned the fragile leaves of the Bible.

"A few of their possessions are stored in an upstairs closet, but I haven't looked at them for years. Would you like to see those?"

"Yes, please," Hester said.

Ray and Hester followed their hostess upstairs and into a small bedroom, and she indicated two small boxes, which Ray lifted from the shelf.

"Careful for dust," Mrs. Hambleton cautioned. "I don't keep these rooms cleaned like I once did."

Ray placed the two boxes on the dresser. "May we look through these?" he asked.

"Certainly. Draw up some chairs near the dresser so you can be comfortable."

"I'll search through one box. You check the other," Ray suggested to Hester.

Hester's box contained old store accounts that the Hartwells had kept over the years. And while historically it was interesting to learn that at one time a dozen eggs could be purchased for five cents, that butter sold for ten cents a pound, and that a yard of calico cost twenty-five cents, it did little to solve the dilemma that Afterglow faced right now.

Ray had better luck, however; he found another diary kept by Ivan Hartwell. "Aha!" he said after he scanned the pages. Then he started reading aloud.

" 'August 10, 1915. Today I returned to Afterglow to participate in an historic event. Although a dreadful controversy has rocked the little village for months, resolution of the conflict between Hezekiah Brown and his accusers proves that the gospel still has the power to repair breaches. "And you, that were sometime alienated and enemies in your mind by wicked works, yet now hath he reconciled" Colossians 1:21.

" 'The controversy was occasioned when several landowners accused Mr. Brown of unfair dealings. When they threatened to sue him to recover their losses, he rescinded his promise to turn the town of Afterglow over to its citizens. A mayor and council had already been elected to receive title to the houses and land that had comprised a company town.

" 'I counseled with Brother Brown and the others, and this morning under the sway of the Holy Spirit, I preached a powerful sermon on the text, "Therefore if thou bring thy gift to the altar, and there rememberest that thy brother hath aught against thee; leave there thy gift before the altar, and go thy way; first be reconciled to thy brother, and then come and offer thy gift" Matthew 5:23–24.

" 'When I urged a cessation of the bickering, Brother Brown and those others involved came forward, shook hands, promising to end the strife. The landowners agreed to drop their suit against Brown, and he pledged a speedy transfer of one hundred acres of valley land to the town of Afterglow.' "

Ray turned the page, but there were no more entries.

"That's what we're after," Hester said, "but is it legal enough to satisfy Kyle?"

Ray unfolded another paper he found in the back of the small journal. "If that isn't, this should be," and he handed Hester a deed to the town duly signed by Brown and witnessed, although apparently it had never been recorded.

"Is this a copy of the document, or do you think it's the original deed?"

"I'd judge it's the original, but I don't know why it would be in Hartwell's possessions."

Ray turned to Mrs. Hambleton. "Did you know this was here?"

"No, but let's check the date of grandfather's death. He had a stroke and was bedfast several months before he died. It would be in the old Bible I showed you. Bring the diary and deed downstairs, and we'll see what we can learn."

Eagerly the three of them rushed downstairs, and Iris turned quickly to the middle of the old Bible. After some calculation, Ray said, "Ivan Hartwell died three months after that deed was written. Since he's one of the witnesses, it's highly possible that he was given the document to record, but he had the stroke before he could take care of it."

"But how could people in Afterglow have received deeds to their property without this being on record?" Hester puzzled.

"I have no idea," Ray said.

Mrs. Hambleton accompanied Ray and Hester to the bank where they made copies of the church records and the deed and watched as she locked the originals in her safety deposit box.

"Shouldn't we take the deed to the courthouse?" Mrs. Hambleton asked.

"The deed is more that seventy-five years old, so I don't know that it's still valid," Ray said. "We'll have to take this up with Kyle first and then go to the mayor. I think Kyle will be reasonable."

"Yes," Hester agreed, "he wants what's coming to him, but he won't sanction anything illegal. I've found that he models his life on Christian principles."

As they drove back to Afterglow, congratulating themselves on the day's outcome, Ray said, "And of course, this shoots holes in Geraldine Ledman's suit, also, and proves why the litigation papers she has were never finalized."

"I'm glad, because I don't think it's fair for Kyle to pay for his ancestor's faults."

"Is Kyle my competitor for the winning of your hand, Hester?"

She flushed and lifted a hand to her burning face. "See how you've flustered me. Imagine anyone competing for the hand of a thirty-year-old spinster."

"I am serious, Hester. I've learned to admire you greatly this year."

"That goes both ways. But let's solve Afterglow's problems before we tackle any of our own."

🦋

When Hester and Ray returned to Afterglow, he said, "Our first move is to approach Kyle. If he's at Miss Eliza's, ask him to come to the church office after dinner."

"Why all the hush-hush?" Kyle asked when Hester sent word that she wanted him to go to Ray's office with her. "Are you trying to force me to marry you against my wishes?"

"No. It's something more important than that."

"You sure know how to hurt a guy!"

Hester's throat was dry, and she talked little on their way to the church. How would Kyle react to their discovery? She admired the man and thought more about him than was good for her peace of mind, although she sometimes suspected that he had a ruthless streak. But she did not know him as well as she thought, because when Ray explained the result of their trip to the county seat and handed him a copy of the deed and the pages from Hartwell's diary, Kyle's laughter resounded throughout the empty church.

"We haven't told anyone else about this. We thought you should know first," Ray said.

"Do you mean you've withheld this information from the mayor to cause him another sleepless night? For shame."

"Are you going to contest it?" Hester asked.

"Do you think I'm a crook? You shouldn't have such a thought when I've been working for months to make a good impression on you. Although I can't imagine how the property in this town has been bought and sold without a legal deed, it took only one mistake somewhere along the line to cause this problem." He tapped the old deed. "This is proof enough for me, but it's high time this transaction is made legal. I'll have to give it some consideration, but I should probably make a new deed."

A curious smile spread across Ray's face. "If I can convince Geraldine Ledman to drop her lawsuit, would you be adverse to having a reenactment of the settlement between Brown and the landowners in a church service? I'd use the same sermon that Hartwell did."

"Drama right down to the end, huh? I'm agreeable, but I doubt you can make much headway with Miss Ledman." He looked at Hester. "You think I have a mean streak. What about her? But she won't get a dime out of me, if I have to fight it to the Supreme Court." His blue eyes gleamed like cold steel. "It will cost me very little as I'll be my own lawyer, but she'll waste a lot in attorney fees."

So he does have a contrary streak. But, on the other hand, he is ethical and honest.

"Will this block your sale of the Brown property to the state?" Ray asked.

"It shouldn't. They've agreed to buy, but no price has been guaranteed because of the uncertainty about the town ownership of Afterglow. They may want to relocate the town, but that will be up to them."

"If we plan this church service, will that be intruding on your drama, Hester?" Ray asked.

"No. I've sketched more scenes than I can possibly use, anyway. It sounds like a good idea to me."

"The town council is meeting tonight," Ray said. "Shall we go and break the good news?"

"Wonder if Clint could take a video of our announcement? I'm sure the mayor will want this on the news," Kyle said.

"Don't worry. He'll have it aired, one way or another," Hester said.

❧

When Hester, Kyle, and Ray entered the council room, a dead silence greeted them, and hostile stares were directed in Kyle's direction.

"Mr. Trent," the mayor said at last, "we don't appreciate having you come here to badger us again. We've told you that we have no intention of moving this town and that your claims are completely erroneous."

"I couldn't agree with you more, Mayor," Kyle said.

"It's an outrage for you to even suggest that we move. We've had a glorious history for one hundred years, and we can look forward to more, especially if the surrounding land becomes a state park. You're being greedy to demand this of us. It's completely illegal."

"I couldn't agree with you more, Mayor," Kyle repeated.

"We—" The mayor stopped in midsentence. "What did you say?"

"I said, 'I couldn't agree with you more.' We come bearing good news this time." Kyle waved his arm toward Ray. "Reverend?"

Ray went to stand beside Mayor Stepp. "We have found the record of Brown's land transfer, thanks to Hester's persistence. She was determined that there had to be some record that Afterglow's title was secure."

As Ray explained the nature of their day's findings, Kyle muttered to Hester, "Well, thanks a lot!"

She nudged him to silence.

When Ray handed the mayor a copy of the deed and Hartwell's diary entry, he said, "Mr. Trent recognized the validity of these records and will not contest them."

"We no longer have a lawsuit facing us?" the mayor asked.

"That's right. There's no blot on the town's escutcheon," Kyle agreed.

The council members applauded. Mayor Stepp, unable for a few minutes to speak, took a handkerchief from his pocket and blew his nose loudly. Then he said grandly, "Then we have no more business to come before the council. We were discussing how to deal with a lawsuit. Meeting adjourned."

"We're intending to have a special service next Sunday to celebrate this turn of events. I trust you gentlemen will honor us with your presence," Ray invited.

The next day, Ray and Hester drove to the county seat again to see Geraldine Ledman. Ray was most diplomatic when he explained the situation to Geraldine, asking for her cooperation in renouncing the claims against Kyle and inviting her to participate in the church service. She heard him out, and then with a faint smile, she said, "You're most persuasive, Reverend Stanford, but your eloquence was unnecessary. Though I hate to admit it, our charges are doomed to failure anyway, because we haven't been able to find a reputable attorney to take our case. I can't speak for the others at this point, but I imagine they will drop the issue. I, for one, will attend the church service. I don't enjoy living with controversy, either."

As they left the Ledman house, Ray said, "Looks as though it will take a lot of planning to have the service ready in four days."

"I'll do what I can to help."

"I could use you to draft a dialogue between Kyle and Geraldine Ledman."

"I'll give it some thought tonight and then meet with you in the morning to draft the lines. I'm becoming adept at writing dialogue after all the trials and errors of that drama," Hester said with a laugh.

"You could assist me during Centennial Weekend, too. I'm to represent Reverend Hartwell and ride in the chapel car as it comes into Afterglow. I need someone to accompany me as Mrs. Hartwell. Will you do it?"

She darted a quick look in his direction. "Oh, Ray, I don't know! Wouldn't it be too suggestive and cause a lot of speculation? I don't think it's a good idea."

"We could announce our engagement before the celebration and end the speculation about our intentions. I want to marry you, Hester."

They traveled several miles while Hester thought of the best way to answer him. He had mentioned marriage but no hint of love.

"Ray, you've been a great friend, and I don't want to hurt you, but I believe I would hurt you more if I marry you than if I don't. I don't love you. I suppose that's the reason I haven't married before this. I've not loved a man enough to want to marry him, and I don't want a man who doesn't love me."

He threw a startled glance in her direction. "But—"

"Wait," Hester said. "You think you must marry because a minister needs a spouse. But you're still in love with your first wife. If we did marry, we're both mature enough that we would be congenial. But the marriage would be lacking something.

I believe that ultimately we would both be disappointed in the relationship."

They climbed the mountain and were headed toward Afterglow before he answered. "Perhaps you're right, but I am disappointed. I've pictured you in my life. . .and I like that image."

Hester shook her head in refusal, but tears stung her eyelids. It had not been easy to turn Ray down.

🦋

On Sunday morning, Kyle and Hester walked along with Mr. Byrd and Miss Eliza toward the church. She still had trouble remembering that these two people were her relatives. When she left Afterglow in a few months, would she put away forever the story of her heritage? Should she tell Miss Eliza? But she could not do that. If Tom Byrd had wanted to conceal his marriage from his family, it was not up to her to tell it. But what if she were to someday have a family? Would it be fair to hide her children's heritage from them?

"Why such a frown?" Kyle inquired. "This is supposed to be a day of rejoicing. If anyone should be frowning, it should be me. I'm losing a hundred acres of land in this deal."

"That shouldn't make a pauper out of you. Is the state willing to buy the rest of the land anyway?"

"Yes, and to allow Afterglow to stay where it is. The executives have decided that the town may do them more good than harm, especially with all of the publicity generated by the centennial. They're thinking of starting a new slogan. Instead of: 'Afterglow, the town where nothing happens,' they want to call it: 'Afterglow, the town where anything can happen.' "

Hester laughed. "Not a bad idea at that. Once you've sold the land then, are you going to cut all ties with the region?"

"I intend to reserve a few acres on the edge of the park."

"To live here?" Hester asked in surprise.

"No, but I've become rather fond of my ancestor this summer, and I want to keep a few acres for nostalgic reasons. I may build a vacation home on it someday."

The strains of the pipe organ greeted them as Kyle and Hester joined the Byrds in the family pew, a place she could occupy by right of birth. It gave Hester a warm feeling to know that she was a part of Afterglow's heritage.

A singer set the tone for the meeting when her solo opened with the words, "I have returned to the God of my childhood." And after Ray's sermon, not only did Geraldine Ledman and Kyle go to the altar and shake hands, but several other townspeople also presented themselves as having their differences settled.

At the conclusion of the service, dinner was served in the fellowship room. Hester had to agree with Mayor Stepp as he said over and over, "This marks a new day for Afterglow."

Chapter 9

B ut Miss Hester, what props do you need to produce the drama? Our budget is strained," Mayor Stepp protested when Hester repeated her request for extra funds.

"You can pay for them out of the price of admission."

"But we had hoped to put that in the city treasury for other expenses."

"Then you can take the cost out of my share of the grant money. I won't put my name to a mediocre production. You should have realized this drama would cost some money. Besides, with all of the tourists we've had in Afterglow, surely you've had a boost in the town's coffers."

The mayor sighed wearily. "All right. What do you need?"

"I've already received the backdrop from I. M. Thomas, and he charged nothing. I expected his fee to be in the thousands, so we've saved quite a lot of money there. We'll need a sound system, spotlights, and costumes. I've found out where those can be rented; all I need is your authorization."

The mayor grudgingly gave his consent, but because he was so tardy with it, Hester had only one week before the first rehearsal to accumulate what she needed for the drama.

🦋

As Hester surveyed the motley crowd before her, she wondered if they would ever have a drama suitable for production in six weeks. Lacking funds to hire experienced actors and actresses, Hester had to rely on townspeople for her cast.

A temporary stage had been built in one corner of the ballroom, which left capacity for two hundred rented chairs to seat the audience. Small cubicles off the ballroom, used as lounges in the hotel's heyday, made excellent dressing rooms.

Four performances were scheduled during the celebration weekend, which meant they could accommodate only eight hundred viewers, and Hester wondered if the audience might exceed that. She reached for a microphone and said, "Let me have your attention."

The roar of people's voices lowered to a hum, and Hester continued, "I've distributed copies of the script around the room, and although all of you won't have an individual copy, there are enough scripts for us to read and walk through the drama tonight. Those with speaking parts should take a copy of the script home with them and start studying their lines. As you can see, there are eight episodes in the drama."

Hester could not speak above the rustling paper as they flipped through the pages of the script, and she paused to give the people time to satisfy their curiosity about the drama. After a few minutes, she continued, "Clint will be handling the sound system to provide special effects as well as background music. And we hope our electric switches will handle the backdrop and the curtains at the proper time."

She turned to Charlie Benson, who had volunteered to handle the curtains. "Go ahead, Charlie."

From his stool behind the curtain, Charlie pulled a lever on the control system, and the heavy, rented curtains divided to show the Thomas backdrop behind the stage. An excited twitter of voices indicated the citizens' pleasure at the scene before them and Belle said, "That sure looks like our valley."

"I'm amazed at how well Mr. Thomas recreated the valley. I sent him several photos for reference; he does have a great talent."

Huge trees covered the landscape almost to the river's edge. A red-tailed hawk perched on the naked branch of a dead tree, and the valley seemed to have been painted from the bird's viewpoint. The junglelike underbrush presented a primeval appearance, but the river winding through the valley looked much as it did today. Deer and rabbits watered at the river's edge, and a lone buffalo waddled along the bank. A hint of autumn was seen in the faint coloring of foliage.

"The river forms a focal point for all of the drama, and the first scene portrays the area before European exploration. Where are our Indians?"

Six teenagers separated themselves from the audience, and Hester instructed, "You'll enter from opposite sides of the stage, close to the backdrop, to give the appearance you've come from the river. Your music teacher at school has instructed you in the dance steps you're to perform. Make this a dramatic scene, because you're worshiping the land. If Clint will start the music, we'll see how you do."

The three boys were embarrassed, but they tried not to show it, and the girls giggled, but after several false starts, they did a fair rendition of an Indian dance, as their movements followed the rhythmic beat of drums sounding from the taped accompaniment. As the low tones of cane flutes and the shrill wail of bird-bone whistles infiltrated the room, the dancers shook gourds and tortoiseshell rattles in staccato thrusts.

Two braves entered, carrying a bear on a pole across their shoulders, and two women brought baskets of acorns and dried corn and laid them on the ground. The six dancers formed a semicircle around the produce with shuffling steps. The tempo of the dance increased, and they swayed in rhythm to the music, lifting their hands toward the sky in worship.

"You'll do fine with some more practices," Hester praised them. The crowd applauded and the teenagers left the stage, exhibiting more confidence than they had at first.

"In our next episode, we see Hezekiah Brown on his first trip to the valley. Kyle Trent has agreed to play the role of his ancestor who moved to the mountains from Tidewater, Virginia, when he was a youth. Brown first entered this area as a trapper."

Kyle tiptoed onstage, hand above his eyes, peering intently from one direction to another and looking like a stereotyped explorer who expected an Indian to jump from behind every bush.

The rest of the cast tittered at his antics.

"Kyle!" Hester said crossly.

A surprised expression crossed his face. "You don't like my interpretation of the scene?"

"This isn't supposed to be a comedy."

"Let me try it again." He jumped off the stage and reentered, this time performing the scene as Hester had planned. Charlie flipped a switch, and a glow of light surrounded Kyle.

"A beautiful site!" he exclaimed. And then turning as if facing the sunset, he continued, "What a great place for a settlement. The river is large enough to provide transportation. And look at the afterglow shining on that valley. I'm going to camp here where I have a broad view of the region."

He walked around surveying the area, caressing the large trees, and set up a tent near the river. With an exaggerated bow to the audience, he exited. The girls giggled, and Hester ignored him.

"The narrator will convey the audience from Brown's arrival until the opening of hostilities of the War Between the States in this area, emphasizing how it interfered with Brown's plans.

"Episode Three centers around the battle of Afterglow. Most of you will be needed in this scene. Clint has taped the sound effects of a battle, and you'll be running back and forth, moving weapons and caring for the wounded. We won't go through this scene tonight, because the props haven't come yet. But you might give us a sample of the tape, Clint."

As the tape brought sounds of drums and bugles into the room, Hester could easily envision divisions of raw recruits moving in battle formation, drums sounding the march, flags waving, artillery rolling, heavily laden caissons plowing through the mud, with hoofbeats of a cavalry patrol moving on the flanks of the battle. Then it seemed as if a gun spoke across the narrow valley and another and another until the air above them spawned countless explosions. The whole region was filled with the roaring of weapons, the moaning of the wounded, and the neighing of injured horses.

"Do you understand what you must do?" Hester asked. "You're to pantomime what the sounds say to you. Think you can do it?"

"Sure, it said a lot to me. I was one of those groaning and screaming," a teenager said.

"Did the fight take place around the covered bridge?" Belle asked.

"No, there wasn't even a settlement here during the Civil War," Ray explained.

"I fear my knowledge of the war is skimpy," Belle persisted, "but why were they fighting if there wasn't anything here?"

"The Federals were trying to drive the Confederates east of the mountains, and they didn't want to go," Clint commented with a laugh. "Our local skirmish was an engagement between the enemies leading up to the Battle of Droop Mountain in November of 1863, which pretty much ensured Federal domination in our valley."

"Thanks for that quick history lesson," Hester said. "After the battle, the narrator will explain that Brown left the area for years, coming back as a wealthy man to start the timber industry in the late 1800s."

Hester became more encouraged as they read through their lines. Episode Four dealt with Brown's establishment of a company town and of the Irish and Italian immigrants who came to work on the railroad. Next came the Hartwells in their chapel car and the wood hicks protesting violently the advent of Christianity, but little children flocked to the Sunday school conducted by the Hartwells. Afterglow grew around the sawmill where many people could find work, but growth also brought the gamblers and the prostitutes. Scene Five closed with Brown turning the town's property over to the elected officials.

"Okay, where are our wood hicks?"

When the ten burly men came onstage, Hester explained, "You guys will have the responsibility of portraying the history of the lumber industry. Since it's a bit difficult to bring in the trains, the sawmills, the log rafts, and the like, I've planned for you men to present a day in the life of a wood hick by your conversation around the campfire. I've written a script, but please add your own comments as you go along. Some of you will be washing and mending your clothing, others will be sharpening saws and axes. This was your time of relaxation, but chores still had to be done."

The men sprawled on the platform.

"I wonder how many more of us will meet the same fate as poor old Joe. He thought he had a future, but a tree falls on him and he's gone."

"It's a poor way to make a living to my notion. I've had about all of the dirt, filth, body lice, and violence I can stand. Joe died doing an honest day's work, but Bill was killed in a street brawl last week."

"Both of them are lying up there on the mountain in unmarked graves, so I suppose it doesn't matter much which way they died."

"If you want to complain about something, what about the prices at the company store? My old woman says the groceries they have ain't fit to eat, and my paycheck is gone before she ever buys all we need."

"Great! You've gotten the idea, men," Hester interrupted. "This scene will be one of our best."

When the men left the stage amid the good-natured ribbing of their neighbors, Hester glanced at her watch. Was the time going to be right? She planned for the drama to last a bit over one hour.

"Episode Seven features the opening of the Grand Hotel with a spectacular dance in the new ballroom, and most of you will have to participate in it. That will mean a change of costumes, but we'll manage."

As the cast read the lines, Belle whispered, "I can see why you needed costumes. It's surely necessary for this scene. I can envision the women, whirling around the floor in their satin dresses with the narrow slit skirts, high-heeled shoes, and transparent stockings." A pleasant smile lit her ruddy face as she hummed softly to the tune of Beethoven's "Romance," playing softly in the background.

"The last scene," Hester explained, "will be more narrative than action. I've asked several of you to represent prominent figures in Afterglow's history in the past fifty years. We'll have a doughboy of World War I make a presentation. Mr. Snead is going to do a monologue citing the effect the Great Depression had on the town. Afterglow's participation in the Second World War will be presented by one of that war's veterans. Finally, the decline of Afterglow and our hopes for the future will be pantomimed by two of our high school students representing the Spirit of Afterglow Past and the Spirit of Afterglow Future."

🦋

After that first rehearsal, Hester felt emotionally drained, and she accepted Kyle's invitation to stop at Sadie's restaurant for a snack. Clint and Belle were invited, too, but pleading the need to put Ina to bed, they went on home.

Wearily Hester waited in the booth while Kyle placed their order for pieces of pie and cups of tea. When he joined her, she said, "I would like your opinion on the drama, and I don't want any foolishness, either."

"Yes, ma'am," he said and drew his hand across his face as if wiping away a smile. "The drama is all right, but you surely have an inadequate cast, including yours truly. I doubt you can whip us into shape by the first of October."

"We can't afford to hire professionals, so this is the best we can do. The citizens love the idea of participating in the drama. It's true they're inexperienced, but so am I. I've never written a drama before, nor have I directed one."

Sadie brought their food. As Hester sipped on the tea, she said, "I can't imagine why I ever took this assignment in Afterglow." She laughed mirthlessly. "I actually envisioned that this project could be in the class of Paul's Macedonian call. If it was, I've wondered more than once what God was doing when He sent me here."

"If you'll remember, Paul didn't have smooth sailing when he went to Macedonia, either. He was jailed and beaten and often kicked out of their towns. So you can't expect any better treatment. But I believe this was your Macedonian call so you could meet me."

Hester did not answer him, because Mayor Stepp bounded into the restaurant. "How did rehearsal go tonight, Miss Hester? Sorry I had to be absent."

"Slow, but that's to be expected on the first night. It will take much work to be ready by October."

"Care to join us for some pie, Mayor?" Kyle invited.

The mayor agreed and sat beside Kyle while they ate, commenting on the coming festivities. "It's been lots of work, but it's paying off. I had a meeting with the park officials today, and they're including Afterglow in their plans. They want to buy the Grand Hotel and set up park headquarters there. They intend to offer tours to the top of the mountain via steam-powered locomotives, and these tours will originate in Afterglow."

"Do they contemplate reclaiming the original mill site and Brown's home?" Kyle wondered.

"That's included in the long-range plans."

"Then it looks as if your faith in the future has been rewarded. I'm happy for you," Hester said.

Although she had often despaired at the mayor's pomposity, she did believe the man was sincere in his desire to make Afterglow successful. But tonight she was too tired to listen to one of his speeches, so she looked at her watch and said, "It's about time for Sadie to close, gentlemen. We should leave."

As Kyle and Hester walked toward their quarters, Kyle said, "Let's take a drive. The night's still young."

"I'm willing. I'm too keyed up to sleep, anyway."

Kyle turned on the CD player when they settled into his Mercedes, and Hester leaned her head against the seat as they drove in silence through the covered bridge and up the mountainside. Kyle parked at the turnout, and he took her hand as they walked to the overlook. A full harvest moon bathed the valley in subdued light, and the lights of Afterglow seemed dull in comparison.

Hester leaned on the stone wall at the edge of the precipice and breathed in the beauty of the night. "I'm glad I've finally gotten over my fear of heights. Now that I have, it's almost time for me to leave here."

"I understand why my ancestor liked this area. The view by night is as fantastic as at sunset. Seeing this, I'll be able to give a better interpretation of Hezekiah Brown."

"Oh, you do a great job, and you know it."

"Every attorney has to have some acting ability, I suppose. I've been doing a lot of acting this summer."

Thinking that he must have some meaning behind the words, she looked at him questioningly.

"Don't you have any idea that I'm in love with you?" he asked.

Hester's amazed look was the only answer she gave, but the sudden pounding of her heart indicated that his words were welcome.

He laughed lowly. "That's what I thought. All of these little hints and my innuendos have been wasted on you. Why else do you think I've spent week after week in Afterglow this summer, thereby driving my secretary crazy because my law business is going down the drain?"

"Why, I supposed you were here on business with the park's commission!"

"That didn't take long. No, I've stayed underfoot trying to find the right way to ask a woman who doesn't even know I exist to marry me. Will you?"

"Will I what?"

"Marry me."

Hester moved away from the wall and eased her trembling legs by sitting on a nearby concrete bench. "I sound like the heroine in a melodrama, but this is so sudden."

"Why haven't you married before, Hester? You're personable enough, and you have both beauty and brains, a hard combination to find these days. Are you in love with someone else?"

She shook her head in answer to his question. "I haven't been interested in marriage. I finished college and had just started a new job when my mother became ill and I looked after her for five years. During that time, my social life was curtailed."

"Why have you put up an invisible wall around you that says to males, 'Keep out'?"

"I don't think I have. And you're as old as I am. Why haven't you married?"

"I hadn't found Miss Right until now. Will you marry me?"

"You surely don't expect me to give you an answer now, when ten minutes ago I hadn't considered marrying anyone, especially you. I'm not sure we would be compatible anyway. It seems to me that you go out of your way to annoy me."

"That's my nature. But mostly I did that as a defense mechanism so I wouldn't be too hurt if you turned me down."

She stood up. "Most of the time I never know if you're serious or not. If I should say I'd marry you, you're apt to say it was all a joke. Let's go back to town."

Kyle pulled her roughly into his arms, and his lips stifled Hester's startled gasp. Hester had been kissed often when she was in college, but never like this, and when he released her, she sank to the bench again, her breathing difficult, her pulse racing.

Kyle looked down at her, and the moonlight revealed his face and eyes. . .eyes that gleamed with a tenderness that Hester had not seen there before.

"Does that convince you I'm not joking?"

She nodded and released his gaze. Kyle took Hester's hand, pulled her upward, and with his arm around her, steered her back to his car.

"When will you give me an answer?" he asked.

"Not until this celebration is over, and I wish you had waited until then to speak. I already have enough on my mind."

"Just forget I've said anything. We'll start over later."

"That's easier said than done."

When they parted at the steps of her apartment, Kyle said, "I forgot to tell you Miss Eliza's important news. Her nephew is coming for the celebration."

That comment wiped out the excitement of Kyle's proposal, and she was glad her face was shadowed so he could not see it.

"Which one?" Hester said harshly.

"I didn't know she had more than one, but this is Tom, the nephew who lived with her and who's been gone for years. She'll tell you all about it tomorrow."

"I can hardly wait," Hester said through lips that were so stiff she could barely open them.

Chapter 10

Hester slammed the door behind her and hurried into the bedroom. Jerking clothes off the hangers, she reached under the bed and pulled out her luggage. She would leave tonight. Mayor Stepp could find someone else to direct his drama. She had done all the hard work. She would not stay here and face Tom Byrd. Why did he have to return to Afterglow now?

Dizziness swept over Hester, and she eased down onto the bed, praying for strength to still the hammering of her heart and the trembling of her body. Wearily she pushed the luggage back under the bed and replaced her clothes on the hangers.

She could not leave. She had never run out on an assignment before, and she could not afford to work for the nine months without pay. Bitterly she thought of the contract she had forced Mayor Stepp to sign. She had received only a meager advance for her work, and if she did not stay through the centennial, she would not derive any further compensation from her hard work in Afterglow. Could it be possible that Tom Byrd would not associate her with Anna Taylor Lawson? He probably did not even know what Anna had named her, and if he did not know she was from Detroit, he might not make any connection between Hester Lawson and Anna Lawson. She looked more like her maternal grandmother than she did her mother, anyway. She would avoid the man; that's all she could do.

As for Kyle's proposal, that would have to wait. She had always thought that one would know Mr. Right the moment you saw him, that there would be magnetic vibrations from one to the other. Although he had aggravated her, she had been interested in Kyle from the first. But could it be love?

They had shared some good experiences this summer, and they had similar cultural backgrounds. But was that enough? Did love strike like a bolt of lightning, or did it sometimes develop slowly?

🦋

The next morning, Miss Eliza was on the back porch, shaking the dust mop, when Hester started downtown. Hester walked slowly toward her when Miss Eliza called, "Tom's coming home," her voice ringing with happiness. "I got a note from him yesterday. Seems he's read about the celebration in the newspapers, and he wants to be here."

So my own scrupulous coverage of the centennial in the Detroit paper may have been the cause of this visit! But Hester could not help wonder if this was the way it was supposed to be. Was this God's way of directing her path this year?

"Where was he when he wrote to you?"

"The card was postmarked Chicago. He didn't say when he would arrive or how long he would stay."

"I'm happy for you," Hester said as she continued on her way. And that was true, but she just wished Tom Oliver Byrd, alias T O By, had waited a few more months to return to Afterglow.

That night the commission met and finalized plans for the centennial weekend. A parade would start the festivities on Thursday, with the first presentation of the drama that same night. Following the drama, the centennial commission would host a reception for guests and locals. The mock bank robbery would take place on Friday, and on Saturday the chapel car would pull into its permanent home, with a worship service and dedications scheduled for Sunday.

Hester was so busy with the rehearsal every night, helping Clint distribute the histories, and working with Charlie Benson to prepare the factory for visitors that she easily pushed Kyle's proposal and Tom Byrd's arrival to the back of her mind during working hours. But they always confronted her at night when she tried to sleep, and each morning she was left listless, without any decision in dealing with either Kyle or her natural father.

One of the aspects of a future with Kyle that concerned her was the depth of his Christian commitment. She had not observed any moral or ethical flaws in his character, unless one considered his obstinacy in the conflict with the town fathers over his ownership of Afterglow, but once he was presented with legal proof, he had yielded graciously enough. And he did attend worship services, but she wanted more in a husband than just a casual churchgoer.

"Lord," she prayed, "give me a sign about this man so I won't make a mistake as my mother did."

The Noffsingers and Hester collaborated on a float for the parade by making a huge plywood facsimile of the history book and decorating it with the words A HUNDRED YEARS OF HISTORY. Clint intended to pull the exhibit with this four-wheeler, while Belle and Hester rode on the float and passed out brochures advertising the history books.

Kyle made a week's emergency trip back to Harrisburg concerning a case he was trying, and although he was missed in the rehearsal since he was the main speaking character, Hester was glad to be rid of his disturbing influence for a few days. With her thinking about both Tom Byrd and Kyle, her sleeping time was turning into nightmares. *Macedonian call, ha!* she thought more than once in the dark hours of the night when she yearned for sleep.

On the day of the parade, the weather favored them with a bright sun and wispy white clouds being wafted across the mountaintops by a gentle breeze.

Despite her worry over the drama's opening, Hester enjoyed riding the entire length of the town and back, a course planned to make the parade a little longer. It was reported that every motel and hotel room in the county seat was sold-out for the weekend and that there wasn't a room to be had in Afterglow, in spite of the fact that every household with a spare room had turned into a bed-and-breakfast. Even the mayor had laid aside his dignity and made one of the bedrooms in his spacious house available to a couple of teenagers, who in one day had raised the ire of the mayor's elderly housekeeper with their slovenly ways.

That evening, when Kyle escorted Hester to the rear entrance of the hotel, people were standing in line for two blocks, waiting to buy tickets for the drama. He squeezed her hand when he left her to go to the men's dressing room. "It's going to be great, so don't fret," he said.

Hester made last-minute checks to be sure all the participants were in place. They tested the sound system, which worked well. The drama was scheduled to begin at seven o'clock, and fifteen minutes before that, Clint started playing soft music, and the audience quieted in anticipation.

On schedule, Charlie opened the curtain, and the six Native Americans slipped onstage in their buckskin garments. Watching from the wings, Hester marveled at the skill they exhibited after six weeks of practice. The audience exploded into applause more than once during their rhythmic interpretation of the Native American music that Clint played.

In the second episode, Kyle strode onstage, dressed in the fringed buckskins of a hunter. He led two mastiffs that had given him lots of trouble during rehearsals, but Kyle had a firm grip on them, and they sat at his feet while he delivered his lines in a ringing voice.

Why, I really do love that man! Hester thought in surprise as her heart leaped in amazement. *With all the pressure on me, why did I have to realize that tonight?* But she had asked God for a sign, and she intended to wait for it.

When the curtain fell on the final scene, Hester wiped her perspiring hands on a tissue and breathed deeply. The repeated curtain calls assured her that the drama had been successful. Then Mayor Stepp took the stage, and Hester groaned to Clint, "We can't have a speech from him. It's time for the reception."

With much gesturing and clearing of his throat, Mayor Stepp said, "We want to extend a special thank-you tonight to the person who has done the most to make our centennial celebration a success. Miss Hester Lawson answered our Macedonian call for help and has kept our town from dying by bringing out the best we have to offer. Come out and take a bow, Hester."

The insufferable man, Hester thought, but with the best grace she could muster, she went onstage and received a standing ovation from the audience while the mayor awkwardly, but discreetly, pinned an orchid on her dress, sticking her shoulder in the process.

A caterer from the county seat had been commissioned to provide refreshments for the reception in the main lobby of the hotel. Hester stood in line with Mayor Stepp and the centennial commission while the costumed cast mingled with the guests. The place was so crowded that Clint echoed Hester's thoughts when he whispered, "I hope nobody shouts 'fire.' "

Gradually all the faces began to look alike, and at first Hester did not recognize the casually dressed man with white hair and whiskers and intense gray eyes approaching her with a smile on his face. After all, she had not seen him in eight years!

She gasped and said, "Why, Mr. Thomas! Can it be you? Why didn't you let me know you were here so we could have given you a public thank-you for your work on the backdrop?"

"I didn't need to be thanked, Miss Lawson; that's the reason I sneaked into town. We can talk later. I mustn't hold up the line."

He shook hands with Clint and passed on quickly.

"I want you to know," Hester said breathlessly, "that you just shook the hand of I. M. Thomas, the famous artist who contributed the backdrop for our drama."

"I thought I'd seen that guy before but hadn't heard of Thomas until you mentioned him."

"He's been on TV specials a few times. You might have seen him there."

Hester turned to smile at the next well-wisher. Her hand was numb by the time the last person in line passed her. She looked up gratefully when Kyle thrust a cup of punch into her hand.

"Come and sit down," he said as she drained the cup. "You've done your duty for the night. Belle and I have commandeered a bench so you and Clint can rest. I'll show you where it is and bring you some food."

"I'm not in the habit of having someone look out for me, but it seems rather nice. You were great in the drama tonight."

"I'm willing to take on a lifetime job of looking after you if you'll say the word," he whispered in her ear.

She smiled at him with a promise radiating from her eyes, but she could not give him an answer here. Hester eased down on the bench beside Belle and Clint, who held a chattering Ina on his lap.

"Do you suppose I'll shock anyone if I take off my shoes? I'm bushed," Hester said.

"Oh, you can do no wrong tonight," Clint said. "You're the popular one, but enjoy it while you can. You know how quickly Afterglow can change its loyalties."

Before she could unbuckle her shoe straps, Miss Eliza approached with I. M. Thomas by her side. She said, "Folks, I want you to meet the prodigal son. This is my nephew, Tommy Byrd. You probably remember him Clint, but the women wouldn't."

Hester half rose from the bench and gasped. Kyle stepped to her side, but she waved him away.

Clint shifted Ina to his left arm and rose quickly to grasp Thomas's hand. "I thought you looked familiar, but I surely didn't connect Tommy Byrd and I. M. Thomas."

"That's a pseudonym I coined when I started out as an artist. I didn't know whether my work would be successful, and I didn't want to put my real name to it," the artist said jovially, with a glance in Hester's direction.

"Oh, I get it," Clint said. "You simply used, 'I am Thomas.' Clever!"

The same way he'd turned Thomas Oliver Byrd into T O By, Hester thought bitterly. All these years when she had admired the work of I. M. Thomas, he had been Tommy Byrd. And not just Tommy Byrd, but her own father. Did he know? Had he known all along?

Hester set her plate and cup on the floor. "Excuse me," she said. Miss Eliza looked at her in surprise as she rushed away, but she did not care if she was rude. She could not tolerate this news. All these months when she had thought her natural father was a ne'er-do-well, he had been a man of fame and fortune. Thankfully this reception was not her responsibility, and someone else could lock up the place tonight.

Hester walked to the apartment, changed into a sweater, jeans, and tennis shoes, and walked the streets of Afterglow for hours, dodging anyone who looked as if they wanted to chat. She did not want to be at home when Miss Eliza and Tom Byrd returned. She could not face Kyle nor the Noffsingers. They must have been shocked at her reaction to Miss Eliza's nephew. But the most disturbing question facing her was: *Does Tom Byrd know who I am?*

It was past midnight before she went back to her apartment, and by that time the lights were out in the boardinghouse.

She dreaded having to face her friends in the morning, because she could imagine their consternation about her behavior, but as least she could put off their questions for a few hours.

As it turned out, however, the next day brought so much excitement that no one even thought to ask Hester why meeting Tommy Byrd had been a shock to her.

❧

A loud blast awakened Hester, and she stirred groggily. The little house vibrated, and she wondered momentarily if there had been an earthquake. She peered at her alarm clock and decided to get up, even though it was only six o'clock. Her body and mind were as weary as if she had not slept at all.

The mock bank robbery was not scheduled until ten o'clock, and although she did not have anything to do with the reenactment, she did not want to miss it. She put some water on the stove to heat for coffee, and she headed toward the shower.

"Hester," Kyle called, and she tied her robe and opened the door a crack. His blue eyes sparkled with excitement.

"The day has started off with a *bang!* Did you hear it?"

"Yes, what happened?"

"The bank has been robbed."

"Already? That wasn't supposed to start until ten o'clock."

"But the robbery wasn't on the schedule!"

"Do you mean the bank has actually been robbed?"

"Right. Clint telephoned me at the boardinghouse and wanted me to tell you. Let's hurry down there."

Hester dashed into the bedroom and donned sweats and a jacket in short order, and in a matter of minutes, they were jogging down the street. Kyle chuckled. "Nothing like a robbery to spice up a celebration."

Clint and Ray were in the crowd gathered around the front of the bank, which had been roped off by the police, when Kyle and Hester joined them.

"What's the story?" Hester asked, her reporter's antenna extended.

"We can't learn much," Ray said, "but apparently some robbers got into the bank and used explosives to blow open the vault. The money and the robbers were gone when the police arrived."

A siren sounded, and a police car stopped at the edge of the crowd. A deputy pushed his way through the crowd and into the bank. His voice carried to the waiting crowd. "Nobody has crossed the bridge since this explosion, so that means they're still in town."

"Or up on the mountain," Ray said, glancing around him.

"How do they know no one has crossed the bridge?" Hester asked.

"Some men have been working at the bridge's entrance most of the night to repair a rail at the crossing," Clint said. "It was damaged in yesterday's traffic."

"Of course, there's always the possibility of crossing the river by boat," Ray suggested.

A possibility the chief of police must have recognized, for he came out on the steps of the bank and called, "Folks, this is an emergency, and I'm calling for citizen volunteers. A large amount of money has been taken from the bank, and the thieves can't have been gone more than a half hour. I need men to patrol the riverbank, and I want volunteers to comb the mountains on both sides of the river."

As the men raised their hands and shouted their readiness to help, Hester noticed Charlie Benson standing to one side. Was it a smirk or a smile on his face? Hester wandered toward him.

"Aren't you going to volunteer?"

"Doubt they'd want me, ma'am. I'll probably be arrested for doing the job."

"Did you?"

"No, I didn't, but I might have if I'd thought of it. This is more sensational than a mock bank robbery."

He drifted away, and Hester joined Kyle, who had been assigned to patrol downriver. She walked with him along the river's edge. "Who do you think did it?" she asked.

"With all the strangers we've had in town, it could have been anyone," Kyle answered. "In my judgment, it was an amateur job, because professionals wouldn't have used dynamite. There are more sophisticated ways to open a bank vault now."

"And I doubt this bank kept enough money to make it interesting to big-time robbers."

"The merchants have taken in a lot of money the past few days, but you're right, no astronomical amounts."

When they reached the bridge, Hester said, "I'm going back and keep an eye on what goes on in town. Be careful."

"Is that a maternal or a wifely interest?"

She ignored his remark and turned back. If she married him, she would have to put up with his particular brand of humor, but she could think of worse characteristics in a life partner.

A roadblock had been set up at the entrance of the covered bridge, and it was not likely that any suspect could go through, but considering how easily packets of bills could be hidden in clothing, Hester thought they would need to frisk everyone. When Aaron Benson and his gang had made off with a sack of gold, it would have been more difficult to hide and to transport. Hester did not tarry at the roadblock, as the sheriff's deputy eyed her suspiciously.

When she entered the city hall to find out the fate of the planned centennial activities, Mayor Stepp told her the mock bank robbery had been canceled, and he was inconsolable. Hester tried to reason with him, "You wanted publicity. This will direct much more attention toward Afterglow than a make-believe attempt."

"But I don't like to have my plans disrupted."

Hoping to be ahead of out-of-town reporters, Hester went into the *Courier's* office. Clint was trying to use the computer while holding the phone under his chin. When he hurriedly replaced the receiver, she asked, "May I use your phone for a few minutes to call Detroit?"

"Sure. Talk on it all day as far as I'm concerned. That will keep anyone from calling me. I have to finish this article. We must start the presses in a half hour."

When she had her editor/boss on the line, Hester said, "Since you've done a series of articles on Afterglow's celebration, you won't want to miss this one, and I want you to headline the story AFTERGLOW, THE TOWN WHERE NOTHING HAPPENS."

She gave him a brief description of the robbery, as well as the parade and the drama's opening night.

"Is your work nearly finished there? When will you be returning to work?" her boss asked.

"By the middle of November, I'm sure. A few more days should finish my assignment here, but I'll need some time to readjust from Afterglow to Detroit. It's been a frustrating time."

After Hester replaced the phone, she said to Clint, "Is there anything I can do to help you? Remember, I've worked in a newspaper office."

"Yes. Edit and revise this article and do anything else around here that needs attention. I'm as bad as Mayor Stepp, so unnerved, I can't even spell correctly."

"C-o-r-r-e-c-t-l-y," she said saucily.

"Oh, cut it out. Get busy and earn your money."

She laughed at him and picked up the article he wanted her to edit. When she checked his article about the drama and reception, Hester noted his comment:

The most prominent guest at the reception was the well-known artist, I. M. Thomas, better known locally as Tommy Byrd. Afterglow welcomes home its long-lost son.

After she edited the article, Hester answered the phone and fielded questions from those who wanted information, all the while thinking of her own problems. Would the drama be showing tonight, or would the actors be on posse duty? When should she leave Afterglow to return home? Could she avoid Tom Byrd? Should she marry Kyle Trent? For the past nine months her whole life had revolved around a series of questions.

Considering the quiet life she had led in Detroit, she wondered why she had ever gotten caught up in this turmoil. Could she ever enjoy peace and quiet again? But if she married Kyle, she doubted that her life would be boring.

In the late afternoon, Belle telephoned. "They've found the robbers," she said excitedly. "The two teenagers who rented a room in Mayor Stepp's house. They were in the restaurant, and Sadie overheard enough of their conversation to make her suspicious. A policeman came in about that time, and he searched the pair, finding that they had most of the money on them. The rest was found in their luggage at Mayor Stepp's."

"But who are they?" Hester finally found an opening to ask.

"A couple of hoodlums from the county seat."

Hester quickly relayed the message to Clint before she rushed out on the street. Gunshots sounded all over the valley to recall the searchers. Dozens of irate citizens surrounded the police car when the two robbers were handcuffed and taken to the small jail in back of the mayor's office.

"The show must go on," Mayor Stepp shouted over the public address system that had been set up for the mock robbery's enactment. "Afterglow might be slowed down but never defeated. Drama tonight as scheduled."

Hester dashed back into the newspaper office to telephone this breaking conclusion to her newspaper before returning to her house. She met Kyle on the sidewalk in front of the boardinghouse. "Just look at me," he said. His clothes were covered with brown burrs, and briers had torn his jacket and made a long scratch on his chin. "And after all this misery of climbing through the jungle, I didn't even catch the robbers."

Hester laughed at him. "Quit complaining. You sound like the mayor. I'll help you pick off the burrs, but we'll have to hurry. The drama starts on schedule."

"Forget the burrs. I'm going to throw my pants and socks away. I wouldn't consider cleaning these things. But who were the robbers? I assume they've been apprehended."

"A couple of teenagers, and from all appearances, they haven't been long on the road to crime. They looked scared to death when the police handcuffed them and took them to jail."

A look of concern crossed Kyle's face, and he glanced down at his clothes.

"How long do we have before the drama begins?"

"About two hours."

"I'll have to go see those boys, but I can't go looking like this. If I hurry with a shower, I can talk with them and still be on time for the drama."

Hester laughed. "Why would you want to see them? Surely you aren't so hard up for clients that you need to solicit them in Afterglow."

He favored her with a disgusted look and headed toward the house.

"May I come with you? Perhaps I can do a feature story for Clint and for my paper."

"Be ready in a half hour."

❦

The jail consisted of two cells and a small anteroom where a bailiff stayed when anyone was housed there. It was used only as a holding area until prisoners could be taken to the county seat. Hester preceded Kyle into the bleak building. The two boys were in separate cells, each one having a metal cot, a lavatory, and a basin. Kyle pushed a chair to one corner of the room and motioned Hester toward it.

"I'll do the talking," he said, and she meekly and silently sat down.

One of the boys was stooped and lanky, with limp brown hair tied back in a ponytail, and looked to be almost eighteen. The other boy, similar in build and appearance, was a few years younger.

Kyle approached the bars. "My name is Kyle Trent," he said. "I'm a lawyer."

"Great, man," the older boy said. "It's about time they sent someone to get us out of this cage. Are you a court-appointed mouthpiece? I had one of those once, and he didn't do much."

"I didn't come here to represent you. I live out-of-state and won't be available for your defense, but I do want to help you. There are too many boys your age who are headed downhill, and I want to encourage you to stop while you can."

"Give me a break, man." The older boy did most of the talking, and he was belligerent at first, but during the next half hour, Kyle elicited enough information from them so that Hester had a good idea of what had brought the boys to this place. Her fingers flew rapidly over her notebook.

They were brothers, living with a single mother, and had no idea where their father might be. From appearances, Hester deduced that they were probably biracial. Both were school dropouts, and neither had ever held a job.

"You know, of course, that you will have to stand trial for this robbery. But I'm going to try and get some help for you. Since neither of you are eighteen years old, there may be a chance that you can receive probation. But unless you make some effort toward improvement, you'll be back in jail within a few months."

"What kind of help?" the younger boy asked.

"I'll have to explore the possibilities in this area. I know there are state programs that will put recalcitrant teenagers in schools to train them for employment, but I have in mind a camping/outdoor program that would be good for boys like you who have always lived in town."

"That camping thing sounds good to me," the older brother said. "But, man, don't those things cost money?"

"If I provide the money, are you willing to go and try to make something of your lives?"

They both nodded dumbly, looking at Kyle as if he were Santa Claus in person.

"I can't promise you anything yet, but I'll try. And another thing, this outdoor program is operated by a foundation that will introduce you to a Christian way of life. That may be the greatest need you have."

He reached inside the cells and took the boys' hands. "I must hurry away now because I have a pressing commitment, but let's take time for a word of prayer."

The two boys awkwardly bowed their heads, but Hester stared spellbound as Kyle prayed, "Lord, You see before You two of Your creation who are in need of help. During this time of trouble, will You reveal Yourself to them and give them the assurance that they need never face life's problems alone? And, God, use me as an instrument to bring healing and strength to their lives. Amen."

Still without speaking, Hester followed Kyle out to the sidewalk. As they turned toward the hotel, she stated, "This isn't the first time you've done something like this."

"I belong to a board of Christian counselors sponsored by the lawyers' bar association in our area. Most attorneys are devastated by the many youth we see going to prison. Our counselors work with first-time offenders to deter them from the path of crime. We win a few but still lose many that we want to save."

"For what my opinion is worth, I think you did a superb job with those two boys. I was impressed."

He flashed her a smile. "Thanks. It's a switch for me to receive praise from you instead of criticism."

Hester did not answer. She was too busy offering up her own prayer of thanksgiving. *I've just been given a sign.*

Chapter 11

An hour before the train was due on Saturday morning, the railroad tracks were lined with people awaiting their first glimpse of the chapel car. A platform had been built between the tracks and the river for the convenience of the dignitaries, but Mayor Stepp was far too excited to remain seated. He prowled up and down the tracks, shaking hands with everyone, saying over and over, "It's a great day for Afterglow."

A train whistle sounded nearby, and the mayor scampered off the tracks. Everyone looked for the engine, but none was to be seen. Hester, however, observed Charlie Benson slipping a wooden toy whistle into his pocket; she recognized it as one he had made for sale at the factory. He grinned slyly at Hester.

"You're always picking on the mayor," she said with mock severity.

"Someone has to keep him from making a complete fool of himself."

But soon a real whistle sounded far down the valley, heralding the approach of the steam engine, and black smoke billowed into the air as the engine rounded a bend. A shout went up from the onlookers, and Mayor Stepp hurried to his seat on the platform.

The big engine roared into town, and Hester waved away the cinders falling around her, looking in dismay at the specks of black on her beige jacket. The name, FISHERMAN'S NET, was slashed across the side of the gleaming black car that rolled smoothly behind the Shay engine. Several representatives of the railroad company, which had donated the car, rode in the chapel, as did Iris Hambleton, the descendant of Ivan Hartwell.

Ray and his sister, who had come to Afterglow to represent Mrs. Hartwell, stood on the rear platform, waving to the crowd. When the engine ground to a halt with the screeching of steel on steel and the hiss of escaping steam, ten burly wood hicks stepped close to the platform.

"Move on. Move on," one of them shouted. "We don't want no preachin' and prayin' in this town."

Ray held up his hand in a plea for silence, but the wood hicks drowned out his attempt to speak with catcalls, raucous shouting, and firing of their guns. Three policemen separated themselves from the crowd and brandished weapons to drive the hecklers away.

This bit of drama completed, Mayor Stepp officially accepted the donation of the chapel car and people lined up for tours.

Hester had her notebook handy as she entered the car, which was sixty feet in length and ten feet wide. The sanctuary was long and narrow, with wooden seats on each side of the center aisle. She recognized the portable organ standing beside the pulpit as the one they had seen at Iris Hambleton's. Counting quickly, she estimated that the seating would accommodate one hundred worshipers.

Beyond the sanctuary, a small room housed a replica of the missionary's office; a large supply of books lined the walls. The quarters for the missionary and his wife consisted only of a small kitchen and a living room/bedroom combination. Hester marveled at the dedication of those early missionaries who had sacrificed normal living conditions to take the gospel to isolated communities.

The next morning, the chapel rapidly filled for the dedicatory service, but chairs had been set up on the outside, and a microphone had been installed so that everyone could hear.

Deciduous trees on the surrounding mountains had taken on a burnished hue of brown, orange, and deep red during the past week. A smoky haze hovered over the mountain peaks, and the sun spread its warm rays around them.

Hester unbuttoned the jacket of the wool suit she had borrowed from Miss Eliza. Since everyone had been asked to wear costumes for this occasion, Kyle and Hester had raided the Byrd attic. She had been able to wear a brown traveling suit that had belonged to Miss Eliza's grandmother. Not knowing how moth-worn it was, she had hesitated sending the garment to the cleaners, but the jacket and skirt were too dusty to wear otherwise. The suit had withstood the cleaning, looking almost like new, but it was much too hot for this autumn day.

Kyle had chosen a single-breasted, grayish-brown striped cheviot suit and a stiff hat of the staple open curl style. The hat was made of fur with trimmings and had never been taken from its store wrappings. They had laughed at the price tag of $2.75. Other costumes in the crowd ranged from overalls and flannel shirts worn by the make-believe wood hicks and long full skirts and sunbonnets, to garish buckskin garments that no Indian would have ever worn.

As Hester waited for Ray to begin, she felt a touch of remorse that the celebration was nearly over. Tonight's drama would conclude the centennial observance. Afterglow had been her life for so many intense weeks that she knew she would feel bereft when it was over. Tomorrow she would start packing to leave for home before the end of the week. Detroit was going to seem dull and lonely after having had hardly a minute of privacy in this small town.

"I'm expecting my answer tomorrow," Kyle whispered as they sat side by side during the instrumental prelude.

"I know."

She still did not know what she would tell him, but right now she was more preoccupied with Tommy Byrd, who sat between Miss Eliza and his grandfather in the chapel car. So far she had been able to avoid him, and he had not made any effort to speak to her alone, so apparently he recognized her only as a former mediocre art student.

"To God Be the Glory," resounded around them as the church soloist opened the service. After responsive readings and congregational singing, Ray started his message, using the text from Exodus, " 'And this day shall be unto you for a memorial; and ye shall keep it a feast to the Lord throughout your generations.' "

During the sermon, Ray compared Afterglow's hundred years of history to the journeys of the Hebrews from Egyptian bondage, concluding his brief message with, "The years of our bondage were the times when we lived in a company town and were subjected to exploitation. During that time, Hezekiah Brown was our Pharaoh, but he also became our Moses when he deeded the town of Afterglow to our elected officials and provided a vast legacy for our church.

"We wandered in the wilderness when the timber industry played out, when our furniture factory failed, when the Grand Hotel closed. But folks, we're poised now on the banks of the Jordan and by God's grace, we're going to cross into the Promised Land. Afterglow has had a great past, but we also have a promising future."

Although Hester had practically made up her mind to accept Kyle's proposal, her thoughts took a wayward streak. Ray would certainly make a stable husband, and if she married him and stayed in Afterglow, it would be more like answering the Macedonian call she had envisioned. She sighed, and Kyle, sensitive to her mood, glanced her way.

It was not difficult to make a choice between "good" and "bad," but what was a woman to do when she had to choose between "good" and "good"? Should she follow her heart?

After the worship service, a town-wide picnic took place. The city fathers had provided a hog and a beef that had been roasting for two days in underground pits. Free beverages had also been supplied from the town's treasury, and the women of Afterglow had prepared numerous other foods that were spread on tables along Main Street.

By midafternoon, Hester and Belle left the merrymaking to make preparations for a party they had planned for the cast after the final presentation. They had reserved an empty room at the hotel, and they met there to prepare some snacks before show time.

"I am excited about Afterglow's future," Belle chatted as they spread sandwiches with meat filling. "Clint says he has reliable information that the state will buy this hotel for their headquarters."

"So Mayor Stepp said. It's such a lovely building, and I'm pleased that it won't deteriorate anymore."

"And the train excursions to Brown's camp will start next summer. I hope you'll come back to ride one of them."

"I would enjoy riding up that mountain on a train rather than Ray's four-wheeler. I'll never forget how terrified I was the first time we did that." She shuddered. "In spite of his faults, we'll have to admit that Mayor Stepp is a man with vision. I'm eager to see how he'll react to the surprise we have for him."

"Oh, he'll be excited, because he knows that Afterglow's future is secure. But what about yours, Hester? I'm not exactly blind. Is it going to be Kyle or Ray?"

"Definitely not Ray; I've told him so. I'm not cut out for small-town living. I've not given Kyle an answer, so it may not be him, either."

"We had hoped it would be Ray so we could keep you here in Afterglow, but you have our best wishes, whatever you decide."

For the final performance, the ballroom was packed. People stood around the walls, willing to pay for standing room in order to see the drama. Mayor Stepp had already asked Hester if she would return next year and direct the drama for a few weeks during the summertime, but Hester declined.

"You won't need me. You have the script, and someone else can take over."

After the final curtain call, Ray came onstage.

"To conclude our centennial observation, we want to recognize and give thanks to the person who has done the most to make this celebration a reality. Mayor Stepp, will you come forward?"

The mayor rose from his chair slowly, not with his usual vibrancy, and that uncharacteristic action convinced Hester of his surprise. When he stepped onstage, Ray continued, "Mayor Stepp, tonight we are presenting you with this plaque to recognize your belief in the future of Afterglow and for your promotion of this celebration. One hundred years ago, Hezekiah Brown gave birth to this town, but your efforts have given us a new lease on life and a hope for another century of achievement. Therefore, we award you the Hezekiah Brown Award as Afterglow's most outstanding citizen."

Ray shook the mayor's hand and gave him the plaque. The audience rose as one person and greeted the presentation with thunderous applause. Mayor Stepp clutched the plaque, and when the people quieted, Ray motioned for the mayor to speak. Tears streamed down his face, and he opened his lips several times, but no words came. With a wave to the audience, he tottered off the stage. For once, the mayor was speechless!

Hester sank wearily into a chair, but she still had the cast's party to oversee, so she could not collapse yet. She had already made up her mind that she was taking a vacation before she returned to her job. She stirred from the chair and made no effort to be entertaining, but during the two hours the party lasted, she looked forward to some rest.

Rest, though, was not to be hers for several more hours, for when she returned to her small house, Tommy Byrd was waiting on the steps. She stopped abruptly when she saw him; she was too surprised to speak but thankful she had parted from Kyle at the front of the main house.

"I'm leaving in the morning, and I thought we should have a talk before I go," he said. "You can't keep avoiding me. May I come in?"

Hester nodded and with trembling fingers, she opened the door. She took her coat and purse into the bedroom, and when she returned, Tommy was observing *Winter Serenity*.

"I always wondered why that painting resembled Afterglow."

"And now you know," he said. "But just how much else do you know?"

She went into the bedroom again to collect the letter she had received in Detroit and the pack of letters she had found in the desk. She handed those to him and motioned him toward a chair.

"That's all the information I have. You read them while I make some tea."

She took her time preparing the beverage, and when she returned with the tray, he laid the letters aside. A light rain had started, and the incessant drip on the front step set Hester's nerves atingle.

"So you know that I'm your father?"

"Yes. I learned it from that packet of letters in the old desk. But I wasn't sure you knew my identity."

"I've been a regular subscriber to your Detroit newspaper since you were born, Hester. I've kept up with you that way."

"So even when I was a student in your art class, you knew I was your daughter?"

"Yes."

"But why did you give me away?" Hester said, the pain of rejection evident in her voice.

"At the time Anna approached me about a divorce, I wasn't sure I would recover from my injury, and even if I did, I didn't know when I'd find a job. There wasn't much I could do with a baby, nor could I have paid child support at that time. It was obvious that Anna had made a mistake in marrying me. I checked out John Lawson, and he seemed an honorable man. So I had to let you go. I didn't suppose you would ever know, but I deduced that you did by the way you acted a few days ago when you saw me."

"I probably wouldn't have known if that old letter hadn't arrived. You've never married again?"

"No. I loved Anna, and there was no one to take her place."

"John Lawson was a good father, and I loved him, so no harm came to me. But I do feel hurt that I wasn't told by someone. At my age it was shattering for me to suspect that my birth was somewhat clouded."

"Except for a freak accident by the postal department, you would never have known. I probably shouldn't have said anything to you since it was obvious you didn't want to discuss it, but the truth is, Hester, I've done without my daughter for thirty years. I would never have interfered as long as your other parents lived. But now that they're gone, I'd like for us to be friends, even if we can't develop a father/daughter relationship."

"I would like that. We had a good rapport during that university class, so I suppose that was mutual blood drawing us together. And you're certainly the type of person anyone would be proud to own as a father."

"I'm proud of you, too."

"Are we going to tell the people in Afterglow?"

"They've probably had all the surprises they can take right now. Perhaps we can have Clint publish it in the newspaper a later time."

"The past six months have been frustrating, and it seems I've been in the midst of every controversy."

His smile reminded Hester of Miss Eliza. "I'm going on a photo safari to Kenya around the first of December. If you're returning to Detroit, I can contact you there when I return."

Hester brought a notepad from the desk. "I'll give you my address and telephone number. I'll look forward to hearing from you." He folded the paper and tucked it into his pocket.

"I'm intending to buy this desk and take it back to Detroit with me. Not only do I like its utility, but it has a sentimental value to me, too, since it revealed the secret of my past. I suppose it's really your desk. Do you mind?"

He shook his head, and she explained how Charlie Benson had found the letters in the top, and Tommy smiled.

"I've wondered for years what happened to those letters and feared the wrong person would find them. I suppose you were the right one to discover them."

"What's your home address? Miss Eliza didn't seem to know."

"I didn't want anyone to know. I have an apartment in Manhattan, and I'm there more than anyplace else, but I have so many appointments in and out of the country that I'm seldom at home." He handed her a card with his address and telephone number. "I won't be of much bother to you."

"I truly want to keep in touch. I've felt very alone since my mother died."

"I'm lonely, too, and I want to share your life. I'm sure we'll soon develop a filial relationship."

🦋

That night, Hester went to bed more relaxed and at peace than she had been for over a year. She looked forward to knowing Tommy Byrd. She had admired his excellent artwork for years, but now she would know him as a father. She had missed John Lawson, and she felt fortunate to have someone to take his place. She repeated slowly the words on the sampler in the kitchen, "In all thy ways acknowledge him, and he shall direct thy paths." God did have a purpose in directing her to Afterglow.

Kyle's knock came before she finished her breakfast. *Have I ever eaten a meal here that hasn't been interrupted?*

She opened the door, and he followed her into the kitchen.

"I'm packed, ready to shake the dust of Afterglow from my feet. What's your answer?" he asked.

Although he spoke in his usual jaunty fashion, Hester detected a worried look in his eyes. He obviously feared she might reject him.

"Sit down, Kyle. If you've already eaten Miss Eliza's breakfast, you aren't hungry, but pour yourself some tea."

When he sat across from her, a cup in his hand, she said, "I think it's yes."

His eyes brightened, and she lifted her hand. "But we've been thrown together under such unusual circumstances all summer that I feel we should take a few more months to make our final decision. We're dealing with a lifetime, nothing to take lightly. I'm sure I love you, but I don't know if we will be compatible."

Seriously he said, "I realize that, and I'm willing to take some more time. Why don't we start a normal courtship. . .telephone calls and visits when we have time? It isn't far from Detroit to Harrisburg on interstates, and we could visit at least once a month."

"That's what I have in mind. We've both lived alone more than most couples who marry. We're independent in many ways. It will take some adjustment."

"You don't have a family to consider, but you should meet mine. Perhaps you could come to Harrisburg for Christmas."

Deciding to wait awhile before telling him about Tommy Byrd, she said, "I don't see any reason why I can't, and this seems the best way. Hasty marriages don't always work." She had ample reason to know that from the fiasco of her parents' union.

They exchanged addresses and telephone numbers, and Kyle stood to leave. "Can't we at least seal our sort-of engagement with a kiss?"

Willingly Hester went into Kyle's arms. From force of habit, she glanced to be sure the window shades were open, but then she smiled when his lips hovered over hers. These months in Afterglow had taught her the truth of Proverbs 22:1: "A good name is rather to be chosen than great riches."

IRENE B. BRAND

Irene is a lifelone resident of West Virginia, where she lives with her husband, Rod. Irene's first inspirational romance was published in 1984, and since that time she has had thirty-one fiction books published and is under contract for three more books to be published in 2005 and 2006. She is the author of four nonfiction books and various devotional materials, and her writings have appeared in numerous historical, religious, and general magazines. Irene became a Christian at the age of eleven and continues to be actively involved in her local church. Before retiring in 1989 to devote full time to freelance writing, Irene taught for twenty-three years in secondary public schools. Many of her books have been inspired while traveling to all fifty of the United States and thirty-five foreign countries.

Still Waters

Gina Fields

This book is dedicated to: Dr. David J. Cadenhead,
Dr. Gregory V. Smith, and Dr. Everett H. Roseberry.
Thanks for allowing me to take advantage of all those office visits when I asked
and you so willing answered my research questions.
(Warning: There will probably be more in the future.)
But most of all, thanks for listening, sharing, and caring.
And a special thanks to Boyd Cantrell, for giving me the grand tour of his sawmill.

Prologue

D
r. Amy Jordan slipped into the quiet haven of her office at Mercy Pediatrics in Atlanta, Georgia. She closed the door and leaned back against it with a sigh of relief. She felt like she'd just tangled with a mama grizzly protecting her cub instead of a three-year-old boy with a one-inch laceration on his knee. It had taken three nurses plus herself to conquer the resilient tyke.

A strand of long blond hair had worked loose from her french braid and hung in her peripheral vision like a large, wet noodle. She reached up and tucked the errant lock behind her ear.

Her stomach growled, reminding her she had missed lunch and it was now time for supper. Ignoring the complaint, she pushed away from the door. She still had at least one hour of dictation to do, then rounds to make at the hospital. Plus, she was on call tonight. Who knew when she'd sit down for her next meal?

She added the file she carried to the foot-high stack on the corner of her mahogany desk then slumped down into the leathery softness of her chair. Rolling forward, she reached into her jacket pocket, but a knock on her office door stopped her short of pulling out the miniature recorder she used for dictation.

"Come in," she called.

The late-duty nurse stepped inside carrying yet another file. What was her name? Jennifer Something-or-other. Amy couldn't remember. The young woman hadn't been working at the clinic long.

"Dr. Jordan," the nurse said as she approached the desk, "I have Jessica Jones's mother on the phone. She brought Jessica in to see Dr. Cape earlier today for allergies, but she's still concerned about Jessica's cough."

Amy reached for the file. "Which line is she on?"

"One." Jennifer handed the file to Amy. "Do you need anything else before I go?"

"No, thank you." Amy smiled. "Have a good evening."

As the nurse left, Amy opened the folder and scanned Dr. Cape's notes. Jessica Jones was a perfectly healthy four-year-old except for some pollen allergies that were presently making her young life miserable.

Dr. Cape had prescribed a cough elixir and an antihistamine—exactly what Amy would have done. It appeared all she needed to do was reassure Mrs. Jones that her little girl was going to be fine.

Amy picked up the receiver and pressed the blinking button. "Mrs. Jones, this

121

is Dr. Jordan. What can I do for you this evening?"

Mrs. Jones gave Amy a brief outline of Jessica's earlier visit with Dr. Cape, ending with, "I gave her half a teaspoon of the syrup as Dr. Cape instructed, but her cough isn't getting any better."

"How long has it been since you gave her that dosage?"

"Two hours."

Amy checked Jessica's weight on the growth chart in her file. "You can go ahead and give her another half teaspoon now and see if that helps. If it doesn't, then I'm on call tonight, and I'll be happy to see her in the emergency room."

A brief silence filled with agonizing contemplation filled Amy's ear. Then the stress-weary mother sighed as though someone had unplugged a balloon of pent-up worry and frustration trapped inside her. "I suppose I should try the extra syrup and see what that does before bringing her in." She paused again, then, in a voice still laced with uncertainty, asked, "Do you really think she'll be okay?"

"I really think she'll be fine."

"Okay," Mrs. Jones said with one final sigh. "Thank you, Dr. Jordan."

Amy still sensed a perplexing reluctance on Mrs. Jones's part to break the connection and almost told her to go ahead and bring Jessica in. But on second thought she decided not to. Amy had already been approached once by the senior partners in the practice about overextending herself to her patients.

After once again stressing she'd be available throughout the night, Amy, a bit reluctant herself, hung up the phone.

A little over an hour later, after the stack of patient files had been moved from one side of her desk to the other, she switched off her recorder and slipped it back into her pocket.

Pushing away from her desk, she did a quarter-turn in her swivel chair, stood, and stretched. Massaging the back of her neck, she wandered to the wall of windows in her fifth-floor office. She peered out through the open slats of the blinds to the darkening world outside.

Skyscrapers lined Atlanta's midnight blue horizon like stacks of mismatched building blocks. Raindrops from a steady May shower shimmered in the city's awakening glow. A red, green, and blue motel sign glistened up through the mist like a neon rainbow waltzing in a waterfall.

Amy crossed her arms and leaned with one shoulder against the windowpane, a deep sense of serenity stealing over her. After what felt like a lifetime of hard work and study, she was finally a practicing pediatrician. That, in itself, would have been enough for her. But being asked six months ago to join the Mercy Pediatrics team, the largest, most successful pediatric practice in Atlanta, made obtaining her goal that much sweeter. Like an Olympic athlete going for the bronze but winning the gold instead.

And she'd done it without the influence of her father's name or money.

Amy's father, Dr. Nicholas Jordan, was one of the most sought after neuro-surgeons on the East Coast. He'd made quite a reputable name for himself—not to mention a substantial fortune—in the operating room. But Amy had never used his affluent credentials to boost her career. She wanted the satisfaction of knowing her accomplishments were her own. So she had paid her tuition with scholarships, educational loans, and part-time jobs she'd picked up whenever her schedule permitted.

An ear-piercing *beep, beep, beep* shattered her moment of reflective silence. She swept back one side of her jacket and pressed a button on the pager attached to the waistband of her slacks. The hospital number flashed across the screen. She hurried to her desk, picked up the phone, and dialed. The answering nurse immediately transferred her to the resident on duty.

"Dr. Jordan, this is Dr. Kelly," the young man said. "I've got Jessica Jones in the emergency room. Her mother said she spoke with you an hour or so ago."

"That's right." Amy wasn't surprised Mrs. Jones had decided to bring in her daughter. She opened her bottom desk drawer and reached for her purse, ready-ing herself to make the trip across the street to the hospital.

"She was brought in by ambulance a few minutes ago, and it doesn't look good."

Amy stopped short of grasping her purse. "Ambulance?"

"Yes."

"But when I spoke with Mrs. Jones earlier, Jessica was only having trouble settling down from her allergies."

"Well, her asthma is complicating things now."

Amy frowned in befuddlement. She hadn't seen anything in Jessica's file about asthma. "What did you say?"

Dr. Kelly repeated his last statement, confirming Amy hadn't heard wrong. "Her breathing is becoming more labored by the minute," he added. "She's on the verge of respiratory arrest."

Amy clamped the receiver between her ear and shoulder and shuffled through the files on her desk, pulling out Jessica's. "Treatment so far?"

While Dr. Kelly spoke, Amy searched frantically for documentation indicat-ing Jessica had asthma. The folder should have been flagged so that anyone pick-ing it up would know right away that the child had a potentially serious condition. It wasn't.

"But nothing I've tried is helping," Dr. Kelly finished.

Then, as though guided by a light beam in the darkness, her gaze fell on Jessica's birth date, and a wave of uneasiness rolled down her spine. Jessica Jones was a common name among young girls. Almost as common as John Smith.

In a voice as calm as she could manage, she asked, "How old is this child?"

"Two."

His single word confirmed what Amy most feared—she'd been given the wrong file.

Stark reality slapped her with a battering force. The room swayed. Her legs almost buckled. She grasped the edge of her desk to keep from collapsing. *Oh, dear God, what have I done?*

"Dr. Jordan?"

The panic in Dr. Kelly's voice jerked her out of her shock-induced paralysis. She swallowed the lump in her throat that was threatening to smother her. "I'm on my way."

She slammed down the phone and fled her office. She repeatedly punched the elevator button while verbally attacking the passenger cart for being too slow. She raced across the crowded city street, ignoring the blaring car horns and blatant curses angry drivers flung out their windows at her.

"Dear God, please let me reach her in time," she prayed as she sailed through the swinging emergency room door.

She sprinted down the long hospital corridor, brushing past doctors and nurses trying to sidestep her path.

But in spite of her frantic efforts and her desperate plea, Amy reached little Jessica Jones one heartbeat too late.

Chapter 1

Three months later

*T*his has been a good day.

Amy navigated her red sports convertible around another hairpin curve in the narrow road threading through southeastern Kentucky's Cumberland Gap Mountains. The earthy scent of the roadside soil and foliage awakened her senses to the untainted beauty surrounding her. Towering pines and mammoth hardwoods curtained each side of the thin highway, providing a leafy frame for the azure sky. The sun-dappled macadam carpet rolled out before her emitted a sense of tranquillity.

She reached over and popped a cassette into the car's tape player. One of her favorite easy listening tunes floated through the air.

Yes, this has been a good day, she told herself once more. *Better than yesterday. Better than the day before.*

A fading green sign attached to a rusting metal pole read CEDAR CREEK, 5 MILES. Amy smiled. What would Robert and Linda think when she showed up on their doorstep unannounced?

The doctor-and-nurse couple had moved from Atlanta to Cedar Creek two years ago to open a much-needed medical clinic in Linda's economically repressed hometown. Since that time, they'd extended many invitations to Amy, but it seemed like she was always too busy, too pressed for time to fit in a visit to her two best friends from college.

But not anymore. Now, at the ripe old age of thirty, she was a lady of leisure with nothing but time on her hands. She held onto her smile even as she felt the joyless lump rise in her throat.

Think positive thoughts, she reminded herself. Isn't that what her therapist had instructed her to do?

As she rounded the next curve, the car's engine sputtered. A ripple of panic flitted through her. "Oh no. Don't quit on me now." As she uttered the words, the motor coughed twice more. She barely managed to pull the two right tires off the narrow road before the engine died completely.

Releasing an annoyed sigh, she scanned the instrument panel, trying to recall if any warning lights had come on. She knew virtually nothing about automobiles, except that they were made to be driven.

When her gaze fell on the fuel gauge, she stared at the gas hand resting below the *E* for a disparaging moment, and then her eyes slid shut. She shook her head. "Stupid, Amy. That's what you are. Stupid, stupid, stupid!" She'd passed scads of service stations on the expressway before taking the Cedar Creek exit. Why hadn't she thought to stop for gas before entering such a sparsely populated area?

She shifted into PARK and switched off the ignition to the dead motor. Then she dug her thin cellular phone and address book out of her purse and looked up Robert and Linda's telephone number. Flipping open the phone, she started to punch in the number but paused with her forefinger a mere inch above the first digit. The words NO SERVICE blinked at her from the digital display screen. Her dampening spirits plunged like a lead weight to the pit of her stomach. The area was apparently too mountainous to make a connection.

Slapping the phone shut, she crammed it and the address book back into her purse. She'd have to walk the rest of the way. Not a pleasant thought considering the heat and humidity of the late August afternoon.

She raised and secured the top of the car and locked the doors. Then, slinging her thin purse strap over her shoulder, she set out for Cedar Creek.

Around yet another sharp curve, she met with the remains of a tree that had been cut out of the road. A dense scattering of brown leaves still dangled on its gnarly branches. She sidestepped a large rock and lumbered over several limbs. When she was halfway across the last bough between her and the main trunk, a high-pitched *buzz* rose and reverberated through the air.

She froze, a chill of apprehension coursing her spine. Glancing down, she found the source of the sound and fought to keep her legs from buckling. Next to the tree trunk, less than three feet from her unprotected ankle, lay a large, coiled rattlesnake. The serpent's tail beat the air so fast it merely blurred. Its forked tongue darted in and out of its triangular head like scarlet streaks of lightning.

Amy stood stock-still, even though blood raced through her veins at record breaking speed. She knew if she moved she risked a bite. On the other hand, how long would it take the snake to lose interest in her and slither away? She decided she didn't have the nerve to find out.

Keeping her gaze fixed on the snake's black eyes, she withdrew her foot degree by degree. As her sole floated over the height of the branch, the rattler hissed.

Without further thought, Amy turned and fled, scaling the scattered logs as fast as her legs would carry her. Just when she thought she'd escaped to safety, the toe of her tennis shoe snagged a limb.

Ground and rock flew up to meet her. A piercing pain shot through her head. Then nothing.

❧

Hal Cooper shifted his logging truck into third gear. The vehicle hesitated, groaned under its cumbersome burden, then continued plugging along at its own leisurely speed.

Hal hunched his shoulders and tilted back his head in an effort to ease the tension building in his neck. He'd hauled timber since he was sixteen. Half his life. He'd traveled every single roadway carved into these mountains, and few he found intimidating—including this one. But on this particular day, pulling his bulging load over this desolate route was proving to be a ruthless test of patience.

The sun bowing toward a craggy mountaintop reminded him what a long day it had been. His right-hand man had called in sick that morning. He'd spent his lunch hour delivering his newest truck to the mechanic—for the second time in two weeks. And that afternoon, another truck had suffered a broken chain and a flat tire.

He shifted gears again as he approached a sharp curve. Thank goodness tomorrow was Saturday. He'd reserved the entire day for his five-year-old daughter and fishing.

When he rounded the embankment, his grip tightened on the steering wheel. "What the—?"

He swerved, barely missing a red convertible sitting half in, half out of the road. Once he cleared the automobile, he glanced in the mirror attached to the passenger door. A disgruntled frown marred his forehead. Only an imbecile would leave their car parked in such a dangerous place.

Around the next bend, he found that "imbecile" in the form of a woman lying beside the road in a crumpled heap.

Adrenaline kicked in, sending a spasm of alarm through his chest and moisture to his palms. He pulled his truck and trailer off the road as far as possible, set the emergency brake, and switched on the hazard lights. Jumping out of the truck, he reached under the seat for the first-aid kit.

A short sprint took him to her. She lay on her side, her head close to a large rock. Thick, dark blond hair, secured by a green scarf at the nape of her neck, fanned out over the ground behind her. Long, slender arms and legs extended in all different directions from the green T-shirt and white shorts she wore. A thin leather purse strap looped the crook of one elbow.

Kneeling, he checked her pulse and breathing and found both strong and steady. He inhaled deeply then exhaled slowly. This was a first for him. As a volunteer firefighter, he'd had emergency training and, a few times, rescued people and animals from burning buildings. But he'd never run upon anyone unconscious in the middle of nowhere.

Pursing his lips, he looked up at his truck and contemplated his next move. He had a cellular phone, but little good that would do in a no service area. He glanced up and down the road, but with little hope. Who knew when someone would come along on this scarcely traveled route?

His gaze slid back to the unconscious woman. He'd have to move her, regardless of the risks.

Fighting the stubborn sense of trepidation stealing over him, he closed his eyes. "Dear Lord, please guide my hands. Let me not make one move that will cause this lady further injury."

Opening his eyes, he set aside the first-aid kit and slipped the purse strap from around her elbow. Gently he straightened her arms and legs, checking for broken bones. Fortunately, he found no evidence of any.

Holding his breath, he turned her onto her back. When her head bobbled from one side to the other, his chest contracted. An inch-long wound gaped open on the right side of her forehead next to her hairline. A droplet of blood oozed from the cut and trickled across her temple, spreading a crimson stain into her honey gold hair. Gooseflesh raced down Hal's arms despite the warmth of the late summer day.

He wiped his wet palms on the thighs of his jeans before reaching for the latch on the emergency kit. After cleaning his hands with an antiseptic towelette, he withdrew a thick gauze wrap and a roll of white tape. With shaky hands, he cleansed her wound with antiseptic and applied a tight bandage. Then he sat back on his heels and allowed his gaze to linger a brief moment on the woman's striking features.

She was young, probably in her late twenties. She wore little, if any, makeup, but she needed none. Her tanned complexion was naturally smooth and unblemished. A small, straight nose and full pink lips graced her delicate oval face. Thick, tawny lashes curled against slightly sun-kissed cheeks. Clearly, God had been generous when He passed her way handing out physical assets.

Setting his mind back to the task at hand, he pulled a packet of smelling salts from the white box. He squeezed the tube, plastic crackled, and ammonia permeated the air. Then, leaning forward, he eased his free hand beneath her head. "Okay, Sleeping Beauty. Here we go."

❦

A sharp, burning sensation seared Amy's nose and throat. She coughed, and an excruciating explosion ripped through her head. Wincing, she stilled herself against the pain.

"Ma'am, can you hear me?"

The softly spoken words penetrated her subconscious, pulling her up out of the black void she had fallen into. Slowly she opened her eyes to a fuzzy world. As she blinked away the fog, a ruggedly handsome face materialized above her. A pair of piercing brown eyes peered down at her from beneath a brow creased with an unreadable frown.

Who in the world was this man? Someone she should know? His chocolate-colored hair was barely long enough to part and comb over to one side, and a dark five o'clock shadow shaded his dimpled chin and wedge-shaped jaw. His lips were drawn into a thin line.

To her dismay, she found nothing familiar in his aristocratic features.

The faint scent of sawdust mixed with the pungent odor of antiseptic wandered into her muddled senses, and she realized the stranger pillowed the back of her head in his hand.

Fear quickened her pulse. She curled her hands into tight fists. Grit imbedded underneath her fingernails. "Wh–who are you?"

He smiled, and his grimacing features softened. "Hal Cooper," he said in a velvet-edged voice. "I found you alongside the road a few minutes ago, out cold. Apparently you fell and hit your head on a rock."

Her gaze traveled downward, over wide shoulders and a broad chest. When she read the words "COOPER LUMBER MILL, CEDAR CREEK, KY" stitched on the pocket of his light blue shirt, where she was and what had happened came back to her like a whirlwind. She noticed an open first-aid kit on the ground beside him, and her fear dwindled. Considering the kit, he probably was telling the truth. She relaxed her fists.

"What about you?" he asked. "Do you have a name?"

She swallowed and tried to wet her lips. Her throat and mouth were so dry. "Amy Jordan," she finally managed to croak.

"Can you tell me what happened, Amy?"

She let her eyelids slide shut against the pain behind them. "I was on my way to Cedar Creek to visit friends when my car ran out of gas. I started walking but ran into a snake. I tripped trying to get away."

"A snake?"

She nodded once.

"Did it bite you?"

She heard the rise of panic in his voice and opened her eyes, meeting his concerned expression. "No," she assured him. "Just scared me half to death."

"Do you know what kind it was?"

"A rattlesnake."

"Where was it?"

She pointed toward the cut-up tree. "Over there, next to those logs. . .on this side of the trunk."

"I'm going to go see if he's still there." Hal gently replaced the hand holding her head with her purse. For some reason, the small gesture for the benefit of her comfort touched her.

With her head elevated by her handbag, Amy could watch his progress. He carefully prodded and parted each branch in front of him, then made each step with cautious hesitation. So sleek and graceful was each movement, he could have been a mountain lion sneaking up on unsuspecting prey.

After a thorough search along the logs, he returned and knelt back down beside her. "He's gone. You probably scared him as much as he did you."

"I hope so."

One corner of his mouth twitched in amusement.

"He hissed at me!" Amy added offensively.

He pursed his lips, Amy suspected, to keep from laughing out loud. And Amy silently berated herself for sounding so petty, as though she thought the snake had invaded her territory, not the other way around.

She raised her head and started to sit up but immediately found her shoulders pinned to the ground by his hands.

"Whoa! Wait a minute," he said. "Where do you think you're going?"

She eased her head back down. "I was hoping you would take me somewhere to get some gas so I could get my car out of the road."

"Not so fast. You have a head injury."

"Head injury?" she repeated in a small voice, hoping she'd heard wrong.

He nodded. "You cut your forehead when you fell. But it doesn't look too serious, and you're plenty coherent." He gave a nonchalant shrug. "A few stitches and I'm sure you'll be fine."

His seemingly unconcerned gesture and calm tone gave her a tenuous sense of relief. She raised her hand to her forehead and her fingers came in contact with a thick gauze bandage.

"That's my menial work," Hal explained, tossing the roll of tape into the white box at his side. "Dr. Sanders will do a much better job."

She blinked. "Dr. Sanders?" she repeated. "Do you know Robert?"

Hal closed the first-aid kit. "Yep." Without giving her a chance to respond, he leaned forward, slipped one arm under her shoulders, and the other under her knees.

"What are you doing?" she wanted to know.

"Carrying you to my truck so I can get you to the clinic."

"There's no need. I can walk." At five-ten and one hundred thirty-five pounds, she considered herself no small burden for any man. But this one lifted her off the ground and into the cradle of his strong arms, it seemed, with little effort.

"My purse," she reminded him as her arm circled his muscular shoulders.

"I'll come back and get it."

He carried her to a large white logging truck with a long skeleton bed weighed down with a massive load of timber. He set her on her feet and supported her with one arm around her back while he opened the passenger door. He then held onto her waist while she climbed up into the cab.

Amy settled herself on the worn leather seat and found a spot for her feet on the gritty floor among several large wrenches and an empty soft-drink bottle.

When he closed the door, the resounding *clang* shot into each ear and clashed head-on in the center of her aching head. She winced.

While Hal retrieved her purse and his emergency kit, she examined her surroundings with a touch of curiosity. She'd never seen the inside of a logging truck before. Beyond the items absolutely necessary to operate the vehicle, the cab possessed an AM/FM radio with a missing knob and an air conditioner/heater. A cellular phone and two orange grease rags lay beside her in the seat, and a trace of diesel fuel hung in the air.

Amy's gaze settled on a wallet-sized picture of a little girl taped to the paint-chipped dash. An abundance of dark curly hair framed dimpling cheeks and sparkling blue eyes. The child looked to be about four years old. Who was she? Amy wondered. Hal Cooper's daughter?

The photo reminded Amy that most of her friends were married and had children of their own. Robert and Linda were expecting their first in November. In the past, Amy hadn't had much room in her life for romance, much less commitment. She couldn't even recall the last time she'd had a date.

Hal opened the door, set her purse in the middle of the seat, and scooted the first-aid kit beneath it. "How's your head?" he asked, climbing into the cab.

"A little better." The pain had diminished to a dull throb.

"Good." He pressed in the clutch with his left foot and reached for the key. "I'll try to take it easy, but sometimes this old truck has a mind of her own. She may jerk us around a bit."

Amy nodded, a little amused that he spoke of the vehicle as though it were an obstinate female.

He cranked the engine and released the emergency brake. Amy prepared herself for a jolt. Good thing she did, too, because the truck bolted a couple of times before settling down and offering them a smooth ride.

Once they were well under way, Amy motioned toward the picture taped to the dash. "Is that your daughter?"

Hal glanced at the photo, a lazy half grin tipping one corner of his mouth. "Yeah. Her name's Krista. She just turned five but thinks she's fifteen."

Amy could almost see his chest swell with pride, and a wistful longing settled deep inside her. Swallowing, she said, "She's beautiful. You and your wife must be very proud."

His smile waned. "Krista's mother died four years ago."

Amy immediately regretted her remark. "I'm sorry. I didn't mean to pry."

"You didn't." He shifted gears. "Say you know Robert?"

A quick change in subject, she noticed. Of course, he didn't want to be reminded of what was probably the most painful time in his life. How many times over the past three months had she detoured around an unpleasant topic?

"Yes," she replied. "Since high school. I met his wife, Linda, at Emory while she was studying to be a nurse there. Of course, that was before she and Robert married."

"So you, Robert, and Linda all went to the same college, right?"

"That's right. In fact, they're the friends I was going to see when I ran out of gas." A brief silence passed while he adjusted the air conditioner, then Amy added, "You apparently know Robert and Linda pretty well if you know where they attended college."

An easy smile tugged at his lips. "I've known Linda all my life. We're first cousins."

Amy looked at him a thoughtful moment, taking in the information.

He arched his brows. "Surprised?"

"A little, I guess. Although I suppose I shouldn't be. I remember Linda saying once she was related to half the people in Cedar Creek."

"She is." He shrugged. "We both are." He pressed a red button anchored to a small metal pole in the center of the floorboard. The truck seemed to gain a second wind, picking up speed as it started up a sharp incline. "Are you a nurse, too?"

An ache that had become as familiar as Amy's mirrored reflection rose in her chest. "No," she rasped past the tightness in her throat.

She knew propriety demanded some sort of explanation follow her blunt answer, so she cleared her throat and said, "I used to work in a doctor's office, but that was a long time ago."

A lifetime ago, she added to herself. At least, that's what the last few months had felt like.

Fearing her feelings would show on her face, she turned her head and stared out the dusty window, hoping Hal would ask no further questions about her former vocation.

After several long seconds, Hal replied, "I see."

Amy closed her eyes against the bitter sting of unshed tears. *No, Mr. Cooper, you don't see.* And she wanted to keep it that way. That part of her life was history. Best leave it where it belonged—in the past.

She drew in a ragged breath. This wasn't turning out to be such a good day after all.

Chapter 2

During the remainder of the trip, Amy made no effort to resuscitate her conversation with Hal. Fortunately, neither did he.

Had it been another place, another time, she might enjoy an amicable talk with the handsome lumberjack. But not right now. She was too close to losing control.

Her chin quivered. She bit her lower her lip to stop it. Just that morning she had resolved to put Jessica's death behind her and move forward. Yet Hal's one innocent question, "Are you a nurse, too?" had reminded her of what she once had and all that was lost in the space of a single heartbeat. Would she ever be able to put her life back into order? Would she ever find a way to escape the pain, the disappointment, the guilt that constantly nipped at her heels no matter how hard she tried to outrun it?

She struggled to focus on the present, the here and now. But after a few rebellious seconds, the mental scale holding her fragile thoughts in balance tipped to the negative side, and her mind traveled back to that dreadful night and the debilitating days that followed.

The morning after Jessica's death, Amy had gone to the senior partner at Mercy and explained what happened. Standing in front of his desk, her heart lodged in her throat, she'd asked him, "How am I going to tell Jessica's parents about this?"

"You're not," came his blunt reply.

"But—"

"But nothing, Amy. If you tell that little girl's parents what happened, we could very well find ourselves saddled with a wrongful death suit. Now, I don't want that, and I know you don't."

Of course she didn't. But she also thought Jessica's parents had a right to know why their daughter had died.

"Look, Amy," Dr. Dayton continued, "we're doctors, but we're also human. Mistakes happen. Take my advice and put last night behind you. Don't think about it; don't discuss it with another soul."

Amy stood there in bewilderment. How could Dr. Dayton, her mentor, Mercy Pediatrics' lead doctor, treat a child's death with such indifference, especially one that should never have happened? "What about Jennifer? Shouldn't I tell her to be more thorough in obtaining patient information before pulling a file?"

"I'll talk with Jennifer."

Numbly Amy nodded and turned to go. What other choice did she have? He was her senior partner. He'd hired her. He could just as easily fire her and see that she never worked in another reputable clinic again.

"Amy?" Dr. Dayton's gravelly voice stopped her as she reached for the door. When she looked back, he added, "This conversation never happened." The underlying warning in his words rang clear. *Talk, and you're history.*

That evening, Amy noticed, Jennifer was gone.

In the days that followed, Amy tried to follow Dr. Dayton's advice and carry on with her practice as she had before. But more often than not, she found herself second-guessing every diagnosis, every decision she made. She spent evenings pacing her office floor, reviewing files of the patients she'd examined that day, worrying she'd missed something important, something vital to one's health. She arrived at work each morning fearing she'd hear another child had died because of a careless mistake she had made.

Her colleagues had tried to encourage her, tell her it was normal for a doctor to question their abilities after losing a patient, especially their first. They'd tried to assure her that, eventually, things would get better.

But things didn't get better. They only got worse until, one day, after examining another asthmatic patient, Amy collapsed. When she woke, she was in the hospital, suffering from exhaustion and a nervous breakdown.

In two weeks her therapist deemed her strong enough to return home, but she'd never found the strength, or the courage, to return to her practice.

That one small oversight had cost her everything she had ever dreamed of— and a little girl her life. When comparing the two, Amy knew she had paid a much smaller price.

"Well, here we are."

The lumberjack's smooth voice mercifully interrupted Amy's dismal thoughts. She took a deep, calming breath and forced her mind back to the present.

Hal turned off the road and into a parking lot just beyond a sign that read CEDAR CREEK MEDICAL CENTER. A solitary vehicle, a tan sport utility Amy recognized as Robert's, sat in front of a one-story brick building.

"Good," Hal said. "It looks like Robert is still here."

The clinic was smaller than Amy had imagined, but, she suspected, plenty big enough to serve the citizens of Cedar Creek. If memory served her correctly, they hadn't run upon a single traffic light in the small town they had just passed through.

Hal eased his truck to a stop, taking up one entire side of the parking lot. "Wait. I'll come around and give you a hand." After switching off the engine, he set the emergency brake.

While he got out of the truck and circled in front of the cab, Amy opened the door and twisted around so her legs dangled over the side of the seat. When she glanced down, her world tilted. She steadied herself by bracing a palm on each side of the door frame.

Hal stepped into her line of vision and looked up at her. "Are you okay? You look a little pale."

"I'm fine. I just didn't realize the ground was so far away."

His lips curved in understanding. "Put your hands on my shoulders, and we'll get you down."

She did as he instructed, and as he reached for her waist, she stretched one foot toward the step. When the sole of her tennis shoe touched the rubber-coated surface, her foot kept right on going. Before she could regain her balance, she slid off the seat and slammed into Hal's hard body. His arms closed around her in an instant.

Amy's mouth dropped open, but she couldn't think of a thing to say. The manly smell of salt and sweat and sun-baked skin seeped into her senses like water to a thirsty sponge. She felt the rise and fall of his chest with each breath he took. She noticed his brown eyes had little gold flecks in them.

"Are you all right?"

His question jerked her out of her stupefied state, and she snapped her mouth shut. Sliding her hands off his shoulders, she pushed away, but the feel of his sinewy chest lingered on her fingertips.

Warmth crept up her neck and over her face. She glanced down, brushing her hands down her shirt and shorts in a pretense of straightening them. "I'm sorry," she muttered. "I slipped."

"That's okay. How does your head feel?"

In the wake of the jolt, the throbbing had increased. She felt like someone was using her forehead for a dartboard but didn't want to complain. Lifting her eyes to his, she forced a smile. "Fine."

"Let's get you inside." He bent to pick her up.

She placed a hand on his shoulder, stopping him. "Mr. Cooper, I can walk."

Straightening, he pinned her with a dubious look and, after a second's hesitation, said, "Are you sure?"

She nodded.

"Okay," he said, but his tone held a trace of uncertainty.

They started across the parking lot, but three steps into the trek, the clinic teeter-tottered. Amy stopped, reaching for her forehead.

In one smooth motion, Hal stooped and swept her up in his arms. She didn't argue, just slipped her arm around his neck, closed her eyes, and rested her head against his shoulder. Above the pain, she was aware of firm stomach muscles rippling across her hip with each step he took.

She heard a door open and raised her head to find Robert stepping outside the clinic.

"Hal?" he said, his voice elevated by surprise. Then he yanked off his wire-framed glasses. "Amy?"

"In the flesh." She tipped her head toward a raw scrape on her knee. "What there is left of it."

Still holding the door open, Robert stepped to the side. "What happened?"

"She met up with a snake out on Bear Slide Hollow," Hal explained, breezing past Robert and into the clinic without breaking his stride. "She fell and hit her head on a rock trying to get away. I think she'll need a few stitches."

"Take her into room four. There's an X-ray machine in there."

Hal carried her into the room and eased her down on the examining table, taking care when he pulled his arms from beneath her.

"Got a pillow?" he asked as Robert entered.

"The cabinet beneath the bed," the doctor answered.

Hal bent, opened and closed a door, then came up with a pillow clothed in a startlingly white pillow case. Leave it to Robert to always consider his patients' comfort.

Gently Hal slid his hand beneath her head and raised it enough to slip the pillow underneath.

She met his gaze, and he smiled. "How's that?" he asked.

"Good. Thanks."

Robert put on his glasses and washed his hands. Then, stepping up to the table, he reached for the bandage on her forehead. "Now let's see how much damage you've done."

Amy flinched twice when the tape tugged at her hair.

"Is there anything I can do to help?" Hal asked, as though sensitive to her discomfort.

"Yep," Robert answered, examining the laceration. "First, I'm going to take a couple of X rays to make sure she's not cracked anything important, then I'll need you to hold her head while I numb her. She hates shots."

Amy glowered at Robert, who, in turn, ignored her. Her fear of needles was not something she cared to have advertised, even if it was true. She could give a shot without batting an eye. But when on the receiving end, she had to lie down to keep from passing out.

Hal pointed his thumb over his shoulder. "Do I have time to make a couple of calls?"

"Sure." Robert tossed the bandage into the trash. "You can use the phone in my office."

Two X rays revealed Amy had gotten by with only a minor concussion, nothing to be overly concerned about. When Hal returned, Robert was filling a syringe. The lumberjack stopped at the sink to wash his hands, and when he finished, Robert said, "Okay, Hal, you come around here and hold her head."

He pumped a couple drops of medication into the air.

A sick knot twisted in Amy's stomach. She closed her eyes and balled her fists in anticipation of the injection. She heard shuffling, then two callused palms, slightly damp from their recent washing, framed her face. In a few seconds, a biting sting shot across her forehead and temple.

After the pain subsided, Hal withdrew his hands. She felt the heat emitting from his body move from the top of her head to her side. Then his strong, work-roughened fingers captured her fist and wormed their way inside until his hand circled hers.

Amy didn't open her eyes, just allowed the methodical stroke of his thumb across the back of her hand to work its magic on her taut nerves. By the time Robert pulled the first stitch, the queasiness in her stomach was gone.

Twenty minutes and six stitches later, Amy, after taking a few trial steps down the hallway, walked out of the clinic on her own, despite the disapproval of the two men with her. She and Robert waited next to his car while Hal retrieved her purse from his truck.

She reached for the handbag when he held it out to her. "Thank you so much, Mr. Cooper. For everything."

"Hal, please. And you're quite welcome."

"Could I pay you for your time and trouble?"

He hooked his thumbs in his back pockets. "Oh no. I didn't do anything anybody else wouldn't have done. I'm just glad I came along when I did."

"Me, too." She slipped her purse strap over her shoulder. "Well, I guess I've taken up enough of your time." Turning to Robert, she said, "I need you to take me to a station for some gas so I can get my car out of the road."

"Oh yeah," Hal injected, drawing her attention back to him. "I almost forgot. I called the local mechanic here. He has a tow truck and is going to deliver your car to Linda and Robert's house a little later on this evening."

Amy brushed a windblown strand of hair away from her face. "That was thoughtful of you."

He shrugged off the compliment. "It was sitting in a dangerous place. I was afraid someone would hit it or get hurt."

"Let me get the name of the mechanic so I can get a check to him before I leave tomorrow." She slipped her purse off her arm and slid her thumb beneath the front flap.

"Oh no. It's already taken care of."

Pausing, Amy looked up. "I can't let you do that."

Again, he shrugged. "The guy owed me a favor."

"But you should save the favor for yourself. Not waste it on a stranger."

He started walking away backward. "Take care of your head, Ms. Jordan."

"Amy," she corrected.

"Amy. It was nice meeting you." His gaze shifted to Robert. "See you at church Sunday. Tell Linda I said 'hey.' " With that, Hal turned and sauntered to his truck.

Amy watched as he circled the cab, climbed inside, and fired the engine. She thought of the caring way he'd held her head and then her hand while Robert sewed her up, and a sad thought slipped into her mind. Tomorrow she'd be leaving Cedar Creek. She'd probably never see the disarming lumberjack again.

She released a disheartened sigh. It was probably for the best. He struck her as someone she'd like to have as a friend, but her life was too messed up right now to involve anyone else in it. This way, she'd be left with a pleasant memory of his coming to her rescue. Hopefully he would, too.

She pivoted to face Robert, who now leaned back against the passenger door of his vehicle with his arms and legs crossed. "Are you ready to go?" she asked.

Grinning as though he'd been reading her thoughts, he said, "I'm waiting on you." He pushed away from the car and opened the door for her. She slid inside.

When Robert took his place behind the steering wheel, he turned on the ignition, and a warm but welcome blast of air rushed into the car's steamy interior. Then, instead of shifting into reverse and backing out of the parking space as Amy expected, he sat back in his seat, clasped his hands in his lap, and stared straight ahead like a man with a heavy thought on his mind.

Amy leaned forward and peered at him. "Is something wrong?"

He shifted his gaze to her. "Amy, what were you doing out on Bear Slide Hollow?"

"I was on my way to see you and Linda, but I ran out of gas. You know the rest of the story."

His dark brows rose, arching above the rim of his glasses. "*You* ran out of gas?"

"That's right," Amy answered, although she understood his surprise. She was notorious for keeping her fuel tank above the one-quarter mark for those times when she got stuck in Atlanta traffic. She lifted her shoulders in a helpless gesture. "How was I supposed to know there aren't any gas stations out on Bear Slide Hollow, or whatever the name of that road is?"

He didn't respond immediately, just continued looking at her like she was a puzzle with a piece that didn't fit. "Linda didn't tell me you were coming," he finally said.

"Linda didn't know."

"What do you mean, 'Linda didn't know'?"

"I mean, I didn't call and tell her I was coming. I just got up this morning and decided to come."

"Just like that?"

"Just like that," she confirmed.

"On the spur-of-the-moment, you got up this morning and decided to come and see me and Linda."

"Yes. What's so unbelievable about that?"

"Amy, you've never done anything spur-of-the-moment in your life."

"There's a first time for everything." She hoped her attempt at putting lightness into her voice sounded more convincing to him than it did to her.

Apparently it didn't, because he narrowed his eyes and studied her. His perceptive gaze told her he saw right through her cheerful charade.

Slowly he shook his head. "No, Amy. Something's wrong. Something's happened since you got out of the hospital."

The oppressive weight bore down on Amy's chest. Yes, something had happened. She'd walked away from her career, her life.

Robert knew about Jessica's death. He and Linda had been the first persons she'd called that night. He also knew about the nervous breakdown. But he didn't know of her decision to quit practicing medicine.

Perhaps subconsciously that's why she had come to Cedar Creek, to tell her two closest friends in the world that she had left her practice. After all, she'd told her father, her partners at Mercy Pediatrics, and a couple of close acquaintances in Atlanta. There was no one else left to tell—at least no one that mattered—except Robert and Linda.

"Well," Robert jabbed at her non-response. "Are you going to tell me what's wrong?"

Amy drew in a deep breath and gave Robert what she hoped was a convincing smile. "Sure. I'll tell you. But let's wait until we get to your house, so I can talk to you and Linda together."

"Okay," Robert said and shifted the car into reverse.

Amy turned and stared absently out the window. How would Robert and Linda react when she told them she'd had to turn away from everything she knew and loved? Shocked? Bewildered? Disappointed—like she had seen in the face of her father?

Thankfully, Robert had agreed to wait so she could talk to him and Linda at the same time. That way, she'd have to retell the unpleasant story only once more.

She tucked her right lower lip between her teeth. Then maybe she could figure out what to do with the rest of her life.

❧

"We want you to come and work with us."

At Linda's comment, Amy paused, a piece of jam-covered toast halfway to her mouth. She glanced across the breakfast table at her petite, dark-haired friend. Last night, Linda and Robert had taken the news of Amy's leaving the medical field better than Amy had expected. At first, they had been surprised and, like everyone else, tried to convince her to "give it a little more time." When they finally realized she was adamant in her decision, they hadn't looked at her with disappointment, but with a sad, relenting expression of acceptance.

Or so she thought.

Now here they were asking her to come and work with them. Amy's gaze shifted from wife to husband, then back to wife. "You mean at the clinic?" she asked, to make sure she had heard correctly.

Robert swept his plate aside and folded his forearms on the table. "Amy, Linda and I have been talking about hiring an office manager. When Hal brought you into the clinic last night, I was still there because I was trying to catch up on paperwork. Linda usually helps, but her doctor has ordered her to slow down. It's getting really hard for me to run the office now, and it'll be impossible when she takes maternity leave. Plus, I'd like to be able to spend my evenings with her and the baby instead of tied down at the clinic filling out orders for medical supplies."

Amy returned her toast to her plate and pushed it away. "Robert, I don't think I need to work in a clinic, much less be around patients, right now."

"You won't be around patients. Our receptionist makes appointments and answers the phone, and we've just hired another nurse. You'll have your own office, away from the waiting area. You'll be in charge of things like supply orders, payroll, and accounting. Basically you'll see that the office is run smoothly and handle minor problems without the other employees having to come to me."

Amy leaned back in her chair, crossing her arms. "You can't be serious. I don't know anything about acquisitions and payroll."

Robert settled back and crossed his arms, matching Amy's position. "You're a quick study and have a lot of common sense. You'll do fine. Besides, if all goes well, Linda will have time to train you before the baby comes."

Amy glanced from Robert's staid expression to Linda's hopeful one. She couldn't believe it. They were serious.

With the fingertips on one hand, she rubbed her forehead in contemplation, wincing when she came in contact with the bandage on her head. Then she clasped her hands in her lap. "Look, guys, I don't know about this. I mean, I'm a city girl. I like the feel of concrete beneath my feet. I'm used to living next door to every modern convenience known to man. I don't know if I would be happy living here."

"Are you happy where you are now, Amy?"

The question came from Robert and pierced Amy's soul like a flaming arrow. She met his perceptive gaze. Did he mean geographic location or the pitiful state of limbo her life was in? It really didn't matter; the answer to both questions was no.

Amy swallowed, fighting the onslaught of moisture pooling in her eyes and making Robert look like an oblique, crystallized blur.

"I'm sorry, Amy," he added, his voice full of remorse. "I didn't say that to hurt you. But I know you. We both do and only want what's best for you. You'll never be happy living an aimless life. You know that." A fuzzy grin spread across his tear-clouded face. "And, at the risk of sounding a little selfish, we really could use your help right now."

Linda reached across the table and placed a warm hand over Amy's. "Come on, Amy. It would mean so much to me and Robert, having you here."

Amy blinked away the tears she had somehow managed to hold at bay and studied the two people who were more like a family to her than her own. They had always been there for her, put up with her on holidays when her father had been too busy to even call, encouraged her through medical school whenever she felt like giving up. After her breakdown, they had flown down and stayed with her those first few days she was in the hospital, when she felt like she was broken into a million pieces and her world would never be sane again.

And now they needed her. Maybe not as much as she needed them, she acknowledged begrudgingly. But they did need her. How could she refuse their request?

"You can stay with us," Linda offered in a small, earnest voice.

Amy raised her hands in surrender. "Oh, all right. I'll help out. At least until after Linda has the baby and gets back into the swing of things. Then," she shrugged, "if I don't like it, I suppose I can always quit."

A relieved smile stretched across Robert's face. "Great."

"I won't live with you guys, though. I want to find a place of my own." Amy reached for her plate, pulling it back in front of her. "There's only one condition to this deal. I don't want anyone here to know that I am. . .*was* a doctor." She hesitated for a thoughtful second. "Or who my father is." Nicholas Jordan had been in so many medical journals, he was practically a household name in the field of medicine. Who could say he wasn't known to someone in the Cumberland Gap region? For all she knew, he could have performed surgery on someone in the area.

"You mean you don't want anyone to know you're filthy rich," Linda said, training shrewd eyes on Amy.

Yes, Amy was wealthy, thanks to an early inheritance from her father. And more than once she'd wondered if her so-called friends—Robert and Linda excluded—were loyal to her, or her money. "Right," she said with conviction. "I want to be known as plain old Amy, Miss Average, for a change."

"Pardon, me, sweetie, but that's two."

Amy arched chiding brows. "Promise, or I'm outta here."

"I promise," Robert said. "Besides, that might not be such a bad idea. The locals in this area tend to shy away from prosperity."

Good. She'd convinced Robert. But he understood her. They came from similar molds. His own father had accomplished fortune and fame as a stockbroker. Now to convince Linda, who, bless her heart, wasn't all that good at keeping secrets.

Amy fixed her gaze on Linda, and an understanding smile tipped the nurse's lips. "I promise," she said, then propped her elbow on the table and her chin in her hand. "Now, about finding you a place to live. I know someone who just might have a rental house available."

"Who?" Amy picked up her toast and started to take a bite.

"My aunt Ellen, Hal's mother."

At the mention of the lumberjack's name, a small tremor ran down Amy's arm to her fingertips, and a dollop of strawberry jam dribbled down her chin.

Chapter 3

One week later, Amy sat cross-legged in the center of her new living room floor, surrounded by a semicircle of four cardboard boxes. Three of these cartons held symbols of her future—new clothes to suit her new lifestyle and a few treasured books and compact discs. The other held remnants of her past—her physician's bag and medical degrees. Everything else she had donated to charity when she canceled the lease on her apartment.

She'd considered hanging on to the Atlanta condo in case things didn't work out in Cedar Creek but, on second thought, decided not to. That part of her life was over. Why leave excuses to go back?

She glanced around the cozy room. Ruffled eyelet curtains added a crispness to the pale yellow walls, and a red brick fireplace offered a touch of nostalgia. Everything about the small rental house was quaint and charming, much more homey and unpretentious than anything she'd ever lived in before. To her surprise and delight, she liked it.

According to Linda, after Hal's wife died in a tragic plane crash, his mother had moved in with him in order to take care of his daughter during his long, unpredictable work hours. Ellen Cooper, Linda had said, firmly believed a child's life needed structure and solidity. A sense of belonging. She had willingly given up her home of thirty-something years in order to help Hal provide that for his daughter.

Amy agreed with the older woman's way of thinking and thought it wonderful a family would pull together in the face of a crisis for the sake of a child.

A telephone rang, startling Amy out of her reflective daydream. Hand pressed against her chest, she whipped around and stared at the phone on the end table, where the sound had come from. She didn't know service had been connected. She'd arrived only an hour ago and hadn't had a chance to go by the telephone office. Since it was Saturday, she figured they'd be closed anyway.

Another jangle reverberated the air. Amy twisted and stretched her hand toward the receiver, interrupting the third ring. "Hello."

"Amy! I see you made it."

"Linda. I should have known that was you. Do you have any idea who had this telephone connected?"

"Robert did that a couple of days ago. You need to drop by the telephone office one day next week and sign the order."

"You mean they hooked it up without my signature?" Amy asked in disbelief. In Atlanta, a signature was required for everything.

"One of the benefits of living in a small town, dear."

"If you say so," was the only response Amy could think of. Using her free hand for leverage, she scrambled up off of the floor and onto a green and yellow floral-patterned sofa. Turning sideways, she stretched out her legs, crossing them at the ankles, and leaned back against the settee arm. How long had it been since she'd allowed herself to relax in such a way? She couldn't remember.

"Robert and I are asking a few friends over for supper tonight," Linda said. "Wanna come?"

"Sure. My cupboards are still bare. I haven't had a chance to check out the food markets yet."

"Market," Linda corrected. "There's only one grocery store here."

Amy looked heavenward and shook her head. Did this town have more than one of anything? "Does this market have a deli?"

"No."

Amy funneled her fingers through her hair. "Good. I guess that means I don't have to bring anything."

"Nothing except yourself. We'll eat around six."

"I'll be there."

❧

When Hal pulled into Robert and Linda's driveway that evening, he immediately smelled a rat—a matchmaking rat in the form of his meddling first cousin. Linda had phoned him at work that afternoon and invited him to supper, explaining she and Robert were having a few friends over to meet their new employee. But the only other vehicle in sight, besides Robert's SUV and Linda's compact sedan, was a little red convertible with a Georgia tag, which meant the only guest present besides him *was* their new employee.

He got out of his ten-year-old white pickup and ambled to the door. Eight days ago, when he'd driven away from the clinic, he thought he'd never see the green-eyed beauty again. Then, the next afternoon, his mother told him she'd rented her house to Robert and Linda's new office manager. "You'll never guess who it is," his mother had said.

"Who?" he'd asked.

"Amy Jordan. You remember, the young woman you found unconscious out on Bear Slide Hollow."

Yes, Hal remembered. Unusual circumstances of their first meeting aside, Amy Jordan was not a woman a man could easily forget—even if he wanted to.

And Hal wanted to.

She was too beautiful, too perfect on the outside to not have some serious flaws inside.

Just like Adrienne.

The thought flitted through Hal's mind unbidden. He just as quickly pushed it away. The last thing he wanted to think about right now was his deceased wife and their stormy four-year marriage.

The front door opened before he had a chance to knock. "Come in," his ever-buoyant cousin said.

He stepped inside and followed Linda to the kitchen, where she'd apparently been cutting vegetables for a salad. He glanced around the room. "Where is everybody?"

Linda, seven months pregnant, waddled to the sink and picked up a tomato. "Robert's gone to the store for more milk—we're having homemade ice cream for dessert—and Krista's keeping Amy busy in the backyard."

Since it was Hal's mother's weekend to sit with her sick aunt in Lexington, Linda had volunteered to keep Krista that afternoon so he could get in a few hours' work at the sawmill.

Hooking his fingers in the back pockets of his jeans, Hal traipsed to the bay window overlooking the backyard and there she was—the woman who had crossed his mind at least once every waking hour over the past eight days. She knelt with her shoulder angled toward him, one arm draped loosely around his daughter's back. With her free hand she pointed toward a yellow butterfly on a wilting fuchsia crepe myrtle blossom.

She wore her tawny mane in a french braid that hung down between her shoulder blades. With each small movement she made, rays from the setting sun bounced off her crowning glory like a radiant halo. She tilted her head, giving Hal a shadowed view of her profile. But he didn't have to see her face to remember every delicate feature, each minor detail, right down to the tiny brown mole next to her left eye.

Amy was the kind of woman who stood out in a crowd. Hal knew; he'd seen it all before. She'd walk into a room and men would turn their heads in awe, women in envy. One coquettish smile from her could set a man's heart to racing. One sensuous touch could sear a man's soul and take possession of his God-given free will.

He noticed Krista studying Amy's hair and saying something. Amy looked at Krista, smiled, and said something back. Krista nodded and wrapped her arms around the woman's neck. Amy closed her eyes and returned the hug.

The scene kindled a spark of anger inside Hal. Of course, if Amy was in on Linda's matchmaking scheme, she'd try to gain his good graces by using his daughter.

Out of the corner of his eye, Hal saw Linda step up beside him.

"What do you think of our new office manager?" she asked.

Given his most recent ruminations, he chose not to answer her question.

Instead, he looked down at her and asked a question of his own. "What happened to everyone else that was supposed to come?"

Linda crossed her arms over her extended middle. "Well, as you know, your mom's sitting with Aunt Lucille. My mom and dad had already committed to the senior supper at church. Bill, Judy, Jeff, and Debbie all had other plans. And Kip and Nancy weren't home when I called."

"Sounds convenient." He heard the hard edge in his voice but couldn't help it. He didn't appreciate being taken for a fool.

Linda studied him for a moment with a blank expression, like she was searching for the meaning behind his comment. Then a quizzical frown wrinkled her forehead. "What's that supposed to mean?"

"Linda, I know a setup when I see one."

Her mouth dropped open in offense. "Is that what you think this is?"

"Kind of obvious, isn't it? I mean, out of all the people you were supposed to invite, the only two who showed were me and Amy."

Linda drew her lips into a thin line, and her eyes flashed with fury. Perching her fists on her hips, she did a quarter-turn and faced him squarely. "Hal Cooper, I'll have you know I did ask the others to come. Or, at least, I tried. If I were going to try and set you and Amy up, I might be a little sneaky about it, but I wouldn't tell a flat-out lie."

Guilt pricked Hal's conscience. What Linda said was true. She had been guilty of trying to fix him up on blind dates before, but she'd never been dishonest about it. And she wouldn't be now.

His shoulders drooped. Suddenly he felt tired and weary and wanted the evening to be over so he could go home. "I didn't mean to accuse you of lying. It's just that, the whole thing looks so. . .suspicious."

"Hal, all I wanted to do is introduce Amy to a few of our friends, let her get to know them. It just happened you're the only one who could make it."

"Okay. Point taken." He stepped around her and strode toward the door. "I think I'll go see my daughter."

"Hal."

He stopped with his hand on the knob and looked at her.

"Is something bothering you?" she asked.

"No. Why?"

"You're. . .I don't know. Not acting like yourself tonight."

"Nothing's bothering me, Linda. I guess I'm just a little tired. It's been a long day." He started to open the door.

"Hal."

He gave her a *What now?* look.

"I know you're tired, but would you please try to make Amy feel welcome? Life hasn't been so good to her lately, and she could use a good friend right now."

Hal wondered what Linda meant but didn't ask. He didn't want to feel sorry for Amy Jordan. He didn't want to feel anything for her. "Of course, I'll make her feel welcome. What do I look like? A monster?" With that he pulled open the door.

"A grouch," he heard her say before he closed it.

"Daddy!" Krista yelled when she saw him.

He lumbered down the deck steps and kneeled on one knee just in time to catch her. "Hey, buttercup. How's my girl?"

"Doin' good, Daddy." She circled his neck with her arms and squeezed. Just as quickly, she pushed away, planting an enthusiastic kiss on his cheek. With her tiny hands resting on his shoulders, she looked at him through huge blue eyes alight with youthful exuberance. "Daddy, Amy said she would fix my hair like hers tonight."

Hal tugged on one of his daughter's dark curly pigtails. "You mean 'Miss Jordan,' don't you?"

"I told her she could use my first name," Amy said from where she'd stopped a few feet away. "It doesn't bother me, if it doesn't bother you."

He slanted her a glance, then focused his attention back on his daughter. "Well, it was very nice of Miss Amy to offer to fix your hair like hers, but it'll have to wait until after supper. I think Aunt Linda's about got everything ready, and you need to wash up." Even though Robert and Linda were actually Krista's second cousins, the child had always referred to them as Uncle Robert and Aunt Linda.

Her cherubic cheeks dimpled. "Okay." She skipped away like a dandelion dancing in the wind, her pigtails bouncing along behind her.

As Hal stood, Amy took a couple of steps forward. He noticed the stitches were gone from her forehead, and her wound appeared to be healing well.

"It's nice to see you again, Hal," she said, extending her right hand. "I didn't get a chance to thank you for having my car filled up before you had it delivered here last week."

Her hand was soft and smooth, but her grip firm and confident, like she'd made the move a thousand times over. She was, Hal gathered, comfortable greeting people.

"I hope you'll allow me to reimburse you for the expense," she added, releasing his hand.

Hal expected to find something beguiling in her smile, something intentionally provocative in her stance. But all he saw was open friendliness coupled with a touch of decorum—and class. Hal recognized class when he saw it. And Amy Jordan had it.

"No, Miss Jordan," he said. "I'll not allow you to reimburse me. I was just glad I could help. How's your head?"

She blinked, her smile faltering at the formal use of her name. "Fine. Much better than a week ago. Thanks."

He tucked his thumbs in his back pockets. "Did you find everything okay at the rental house?"

"Yes, I did." She stuffed her fisted hands in the front pockets of her jeans. "The house is charming. I think I'm going to enjoy living there."

"I'm glad to hear that. If you need anything or any problems come up, just let me or Mom know."

"I will." She trapped the right side of her lower lip between her teeth and studied him a silent moment, her expression turning serious. Then, releasing her lip, she said, "Hal, have you noticed the bruises on Krista's arms?"

The unexpected question caught him off guard. His brow dipped. "Of course, I have," he said, biting back a sharp retort. "She's my daughter."

A frown Hal read as concern creased her smooth forehead. "Do you have any idea how she got them?"

"Probably playing. She's a very active little girl."

A timid smile tipped her lips, but her countenance remained solemn. "I see."

Hal narrowed his eyes. He wasn't sure he liked where her line of questioning was headed. "Why do you ask?"

"Because the bruises don't look normal. Not like those a child would receive as a result of everyday play."

He cocked his head to one side. "Just what are you trying to say?"

"That maybe Krista's bruises should be checked out by a doctor to determine exactly what caused them."

"How do you know they haven't been checked out by a doctor?" came Hal's quick response, then he clamped his mouth shut. The welfare of his daughter was none of Amy's business.

His rational mind told him to turn and walk away before he lost his temper, but his already wound up emotions got the best of him. His breathing became labored. He unhooked his thumbs from his back pockets and curled his hands into fists at his sides to keep from pointing a finger in her face. "Let me tell you something, Miss Jordan. When Krista's not with me, she's with my mother or, on a rare occasion, Linda. And none of us are child abusers."

Amy didn't flinch. "I didn't imply that you were."

His eyebrows shot up. "Didn't you?"

Her expression remained steady, unreadable. "No, Hal, I didn't. I merely suggested you have her checked out by a doctor."

He stared at her a dumbfounded moment. "What are you? Some kind of child care expert who thinks she can look at a bruise and tell what made it?"

She closed her eyes and ran her fingertips across her forehead, like she was counting to ten. Then, opening her eyes, she tucked her hand back into her jeans' pocket and released a long, slow sigh. "No, Mr. Cooper. I'm no expert."

"Then I think you should keep your opinions concerning my daughter to yourself." With that, he turned and stormed to the house.

When he stepped inside, Linda took one look at him and said, "I take it that didn't go well."

"That, my dear cousin, is an understatement." He scanned the room and found no sign of his daughter. Turning toward the bathroom, he yelled, "Krista, let's go!"

❧

"Hal did bring Krista into the clinic about a month ago," Robert told Amy after she explained what had transpired between her and Hal earlier. "He expressed concern over some bruises on her back. I did a full workup on her, and everything checked out fine."

Amy, Linda, and Robert had been sitting at the couple's dinner table for ten minutes, but Amy hadn't touched her food.

"Did you do a complete CBC?"

"Yes."

Amy didn't know what was driving her to question Robert. She knew he was an excellent physician. "Platelet count, red blood count, and white blood count were all normal?"

"Lymphocytes. Everything. I even sent her to a specialist in Lexington. He didn't find anything either. He concluded Krista had to be receiving the bruises during her playtime. She is pretty much a tomboy."

Amy pursed her lips. She'd already figured out Linda and Robert adored Hal and his family. She didn't want to ask her next question, but her conscience wouldn't let her keep it to herself. "Hal. . .or his mother. . .would never. . ."

"No," came Linda's quick answer. "In fact, when it comes to discipline, Hal could use a little firmer hand. And his mother? A child has never been blessed with a better grandmother."

Amy felt all her old insecurities closing in on her, feelings she thought she'd left behind in Atlanta. She ducked her head and fiddled with her napkin.

"Why don't I have Hal bring Krista into the clinic and you do a workup on her?"

Robert's question brought Amy's head up. "You know I can't do that."

"Why not? You still have a license."

"I can't practice medicine anymore, and tonight was a perfect example why. I second-guess and question everything. I'm suspicious of the most innocent circumstances. Besides, Hal thinks I accused him of child abuse, and, in a way, maybe I did. I'm the last person on earth he'd want examining his daughter."

Robert studied her for a pensive moment. "But I get the feeling your instincts are telling you something's been missed."

"My instincts can no longer be trusted, Robert." She pushed away from the table. "I'm sorry, but I'm not really hungry right now." She lumbered to the front door, retrieving her purse from a nearby hall tree.

"Wait a minute," Linda said. "Where are you going?"

She stopped and looked back. Robert and Linda were both standing, a befuddled expression on their faces.

"I'm going to apologize to Hal," Amy said. "And then I have a feeling I may be looking for another place to live."

Chapter 4

Hal lived just two curves—one-quarter mile—away from Amy. The rugged Cumberland Gap Mountains, silhouetted by the setting sun, provided a picturesque background for his two-story brick house with its wraparound porch.

Amy parked in front of the two-car garage and, upon stepping out of her car, was greeted by a friendly golden Labrador retriever. Stooping, she rubbed the dog behind his ears, noting the identification tag on his collar read H. COOPER, then listed an address and telephone number.

"Hi there, fella. Is your owner home?" Since the garage doors were closed, Amy had no way of knowing if Hal's vehicle was inside.

The canine, apparently pleased with her attention, jutted his nose forward. Amy saw what was coming and jerked back her head, barely dodging the dog's tongue. "Oh no, you don't," she said with a laugh. "You're a handsome guy, but no kissing on the first date." Giving the dog one last tousle on his head, she added, "I'd like to hang around and play a game of fetch with you, but right now I really need to talk to your master."

She stood, tucking her hands into the pockets of her green sports jacket. Strolling up the curving walkway leading to the front porch, she wondered what kind of reception she'd receive. At this point, she didn't know what to expect from the handsome lumberjack. Thinking back to eight days ago, it was hard to believe he was the same gentle-natured man who'd so tenderly held her hand while Robert sewed up her head.

Her mind sprang forward to today and the first few minutes of their meeting in Robert and Linda's backyard. Even before she'd approached him about his daughter's bruises, Amy sensed a guarded wariness about him. The moment he first referred to her as "Miss Jordan," she'd gotten the feeling he was drawing a boundary line between them and daring her to cross it.

She climbed the two wide brick steps leading up to the porch. Maybe her first impression of him had been wrong. Maybe he wasn't someone she would want as a friend after all.

A touch of irony tipped her lips when she stepped onto the "Welcome" mat. Just how *welcome* would she be?

"No time like the present to find out," she muttered. Taking a deep breath of courage, she rang the bell. Slipping her hand back into her jacket pocket, she straightened her spine and prepared herself for whatever.

She waited only a few seconds before the overhead porch light came on and the doorknob rattled. Then Hal's voice, outlined with a rough edge, spilled out of the yawning opening.

"Okay, Linda, if you came to tell me what a jerk I acted like tonight, I already—" He stopped short when he saw it was not his cousin, but Amy on the other side of his threshold.

Hand still grasping the doorknob, he stood transfixed in the luminous glow of the porch light, his face frozen in an unguarded expression of surprise. He'd untucked his blue-and-red plaid shirt from the waist of his blue jeans, and his short brown hair appeared at bit unruly, like he'd recently run his fingers through it.

For an instant, Amy sensed she was catching a glimpse of the real Hal Cooper, the one who'd picked her up off the side of the road last week and driven her to the doctor. The one who'd held her head while Robert gave her the shot. The Hal who'd stayed beside her, holding her hand, while Robert pulled the stitches. The same man considerate enough to have gas put in her car before having the vehicle delivered to her friends' house.

Amy opened her mouth to greet him, but the words got stuck in her throat along with her breath. The sudden manly awareness of him scattered her common sensibilities in a dozen different directions. Her purpose for being there temporarily deserted her.

Then he blinked, and whatever had cast the entrancing spell over her dissipated like a warm vapor in a cold wind. His guard came back up as quickly as his surprise had fallen over him when he first opened the door and found her standing on his front porch.

As though summoned by the chilly atmosphere, a cool breeze stirred, brushing Amy's flushed face. She reached up and tucked the wayward strand of hair that was always working loose from her french braid behind her ear.

"Hello, Hal," she said, breaking the expanding silence between them.

He braced his free hand on the door frame as though barring her from entering. "Miss Jordan." He nodded curtly.

"I was wondering if I could speak with you a minute."

At first he didn't respond, merely studied her with an indefinable expression.

Amy was beginning to think he was going to refuse her request and ask her to leave, when he finally stepped back and motioned for her to come inside.

As she walked past him, the essence of soap and man, a pleasant scent undisguised by cologne or aftershave, wrapped around her senses.

She padded through the foyer to the living room where a hunter green leather sofa with a matching recliner flanking each side faced a rock fireplace. She stopped in the center of an Oriental rug spread over the hardwood floor and scanned the room. "You have a lovely home."

"Thank you, Miss Jordan. But I'm sure you didn't—"

She pivoted to face him. "You're right. I didn't come here to talk about your house, or your daughter. I came to apologize."

He studied her with a look of skepticism, like he was checking and rechecking her words to see if he could find a hidden motive or an unscrupulous meaning behind them.

Swallowing, she continued. "When I questioned you about Krista's bruises, I stepped over a line I had no right to cross. It won't happen again." *Maybe*, a stubborn sector of her conscience whispered.

In spite of Robert's logical explanation for Krista's bruising, Amy could not quell the gut feeling telling her something was still amiss where Krista was concerned. In the past, Amy had depended on that internal instinct whenever she was dealing with an out-of-the-ordinary case. The only time she had chosen to ignore it, a little girl had lost her life. An alarming thought spurred Amy's conscience. Was she making that same mistake again?

Hal shifted his weight, tucking his thumbs into his back pockets. The movement jerked Amy out of her musings, and she reminded herself—for about the tenth time that evening—she was no longer practicing medicine. Even if she were, Krista would not be her patient but Robert's. Amy knew the little girl was in capable hands.

"You've apparently talked to Robert," Hal said.

"Yes. But that still doesn't excuse the way I approached you this evening."

Hal brushed a hand down over his face, then hooked that same hand around the back of his neck. The action seemed to wipe away his cryptic edginess, leaving behind a very weary man.

Shoulders drooping, he said, "I think I owe you an apology, too, Miss Jordan. I was in a foul mood when I got to Linda's this evening, and I'm afraid I took my frustrations out on you. I'm sorry. I shouldn't have lost my temper."

Amy was lost for an immediate response. He was like the wind during the changing of seasons: warm one minute, cool the next. And right now he was once again showing her the side of him she wanted to know a little better, learn more about.

Suddenly she felt a magnetic pull toward him and an overwhelming urge to step forward, reach up and lay a comforting hand on his wedge-shaped jaw, feel the roughness of his five o'clock shadow. But prudence prevailed, and she quelled her overactive emotions, which seemed to be struggling to go in a direction that contradicted Amy's usual levelheadedness.

Hal Cooper was an avenue Amy couldn't afford to explore right now. She was in Cedar Creek to start a new life, not make friends who might ask questions about her old one.

Reminding herself she'd done what she came to do and it was now time to go, she said, "Thank you for understanding. I suppose I've taken up enough of your time."

A door to Amy's right swung open, and Krista walked into the room with a jaunty bounce in her step. When she saw Amy, she stopped short, her mouth forming an *O*, and her sparkling blue eyes stretched wide in surprise. "Miss Amy, did you come to fix my hair?"

Amy's mouth dropped open. She'd forgotten all about the promise she had made to the child. What in the world should she do? Sure, Hal had seemed to mellow out after her apology. But in light of their confrontation that afternoon, would he want Amy spending more time with his daughter?

Amy bent down, hands on knees, to tell the little girl that tonight might not be such a good time.

"Of course, she did," Hal said before the words formed on her lips.

Surprised, Amy glanced up. "You don't mind?"

"Number one rule of parenting, Miss Jordan. Never break a promise to a child."

Well, he really hadn't answered her question, but at the moment Amy didn't care if he minded or not. She was simply grateful she wasn't going to have to go back on her word to Krista.

Amy turned her attention back to the child. "Why don't you show me where you keep your brush and comb, and we'll get started."

Stepping toward the door Krista had just come through, Hal mumbled something about cleaning up the kitchen.

A beaming Krista curled her hand around two of Amy's fingers and led her into a bedroom decorated for a little princess. A white canopy bed with a fluffy floral spread was complemented by a matching dresser with a vanity mirror, a chest of drawers, and desk. White Priscilla curtains added a touch of warmth to the pale pink walls.

But one area contrasted sharply with the rest of the room. Trucks, cars, brightly colored building blocks, balls and bats, all scratched and showing signs of frequent use, lined the shelves along one wall. Amy did notice three dolls perched high on the top shelf, looking abandoned. One of them hadn't even been taken out of her box.

Robert obviously hadn't been stretching the truth when he said Krista was a tomboy.

Amy noticed a framed picture of a woman sitting on Krista's nightstand. Curiously drawn to the photo, Amy picked it up and studied it. The woman, with dark curly hair and brilliant blue eyes, leaned against a tree, posing confidently for the camera. A seductive curve tipped the corners of her red painted lips. She was, Amy acknowledged, a rare beauty, possessing the kind of face one expected to find on the cover of a first-class fashion magazine.

"That's my mama," Krista said, answering the question roaming Amy's mind. "She died when I was little."

Amy smiled down at the little girl who looked so much like the woman in the photograph. "I know, and I'm very sorry." She returned the picture to the nightstand and scooped up the brush and comb from the dresser. She didn't want to dampen the child's high spirits by reminding her of her deceased parent. Amy knew from experience the heartache of growing up without a mother. Her own had died when Amy was only three.

She sat down on the bed, positioning Krista between her knees, and unwound the band from the child's ponytails. She was grateful Hal hadn't followed them. His absence allowed her to enjoy this time with his daughter without feeling under pressure from his judgmental parental eye. Amy was usually comfortable around people, new acquaintances included. But Hal Cooper's mere presence unnerved her in a way she couldn't define.

"Do you have any pets?" Amy asked as she pulled the brush through Krista's thick curls.

"Yes. I have a dog. His name is Rufkin."

"Is he that beautiful golden Lab I met outside a while ago?"

"Uh-huh." Krista nodded. "And I have a guinea pig named Scooter."

"That must be that orange and white hairy thing over there in the cage in the corner?"

"Uh-huh." Krista bobbed her head up and down again, and Amy grinned, not bothering to remind the child she needed to be still while having her hair fixed.

"We can play with him when you get finished, if you want," Krista added.

"We'll see." Amy had never petted a guinea pig before, but the furry little creature darting around the cage, stopping occasionally to twitch his nose, appeared harmless enough. At least he didn't have a long tail like a mouse. Amy shuddered. She hated mice.

While she finished Krista's french braid, the child kept up an incessant chain of chatter. Amy was wrapping a band around the bottom of Krista's hair when Hal poked his head and one shoulder through the open doorway. "How's it going? You girls through primping yet?"

"Going great," Amy said. "We're just finishing up." She slipped the final loop around Krista's hair.

Krista abandoned Amy, running to her dad. In one smooth motion, he stepped through the door, bent, and lifted his child to his hip.

Amy stood back, watching the interaction between father and daughter.

"Am I pretty, Daddy?" Krista asked, turning her head and touching her braid.

The corners of Hal's eyes crinkled. "Yes, you sure are, buttercup."

"Am I pretty as Miss Amy?"

Amy's heart tripped, although she couldn't fathom why. She knew how unpredictable kids could be. And she knew adults could be put on the spot in trying to answer a child's innocent yet awkward questions. She'd learned during her short career to take in stride any unorthodox thing that came "out of the mouths of babes." But for some reason, she held her breath in anticipation of Hal's answer.

After only a second's hesitation, he said, "You're as pretty as the prettiest angel in heaven."

His wife, Amy immediately concluded. That's whom Hal was referring to. Though Amy knew little about the Bible, she had, over her years of sporadic church attendance, gleaned enough knowledge to know angels weren't human and humans weren't angels. But she could also see why Hal thought of his deceased wife as one. She was certainly lovely enough.

Figuring now was a good time to make her exit, Amy stepped forward. "I really should be going."

Hal looked back at his daughter. "Why don't you run and hop in the bathtub, and I'll walk Miss Amy to the door."

"Can Miss Amy give me a bath?"

"Now, Krista, how long have you been giving yourself a bath?"

Krista ducked her head. "Since I been four."

"We wouldn't want Miss Amy to think you're not a big girl, now, would we?"

Krista shook her head.

"Why don't you go thank her for fixing your hair, then go do as I asked. But leave the bathroom door cracked so I can hear you."

Hal set down his daughter. Artfully pouting, the child traipsed over to Amy.

Amy kneeled down, putting herself on the child's level. "You think I could get a hug?"

Krista reached up and wrapped her arms around Amy's neck. Amy returned the embrace, closing her eyes and relishing the feel of a child against her breast. These last few minutes with Krista had reminded Amy of how much she missed the time she'd spent with children while practicing medicine.

While Krista padded off to the bathroom, Hal followed Amy outside. Amy noticed he left the door open, apparently so he could listen for his daughter.

Stopping and looking up at him, Amy said, "Thank you."

He tucked his fingertips in his front pockets. "For what?"

"For allowing me to keep my word to your daughter. She's a lovely child. I enjoyed the time I spent with her."

"Thank you. I think she enjoyed herself, too."

"You're blessed to have her."

"Yes, I am."

An awkward silence passed between them, as though they were both unsure of what to say next.

Hal recovered first. "I'd walk you to your car, but. . ." He pointed a thumb over his shoulder.

Amy held up a palm. "Oh no. I understand. You need to get back to your daughter."

Reaching for the doorknob, Hal nodded. "Good night, Miss Jordan."

"Good night." She started to walk away, but when she heard the door *click* shut behind her, she looked back and, like an obstinate child wanting to get in the last word, added, "Hal."

Amy didn't go home but returned to Robert's and Linda's for two reasons. Number one, she found the idea of facing four unpacked boxes so late in the evening depressing. Number two, her appetite had returned, and her cupboards were still bare.

After eating her fill at her friends' table, she followed Linda to the living room where Robert sat back in a recliner with his face buried in a newspaper.

Adjusting a pillow along her side, Linda curled up on one end of the sofa. Amy slumped down on the other end, stretching out her legs and crossing them at the ankles. Lacing her hands over her stomach, she lay her head back, closed her eyes, and waited for the question she knew was coming. As expected, she didn't have to wait long.

"How did it go at Hal's?"

The inquiry, of course, came from the overly curious Linda, but Amy suspected Robert was indiscreetly directing an interested ear her way.

"I think your cousin hates me," Amy answered.

"Hate?" Linda's voice rose in surprise. "That's an awful strong word to use when referring to someone you know so little about."

Amy detected a note of defensiveness in her friend's voice but wasn't surprised given Linda's fondness of Hal. Amy rolled her head to the side, opened her eyes, and met Linda's chiding expression. "Okay. 'Dislikes me' then."

The expectant mom crossed her arms. "Look, Amy, I know Hal lost his temper with you this afternoon, but that was because he's so defensive when it comes to Krista. He's not usually like that. I mean, he does have a temper when he's pushed too far, but he's not one to hold a grudge or hate someone because they ask a few questions about his daughter."

Amy shook her head. "I don't think it has anything to do with our discussion over Krista. In fact, he apologized for losing his temper with me."

"What, then, makes you think he dislikes you so much?"

Using her hands for leverage, Amy pushed herself up out of her slumping position. Folding one leg in front of her, she angled her body so she faced Linda. "For one thing, he insists on calling me"—she drew quotations marks in the air— " 'Miss Jordan.' For another. . ." Amy paused here, trying to find the right words to describe the resistance she sensed whenever she was around Hal. Finally figuring there was no clear way to explain something she didn't understand herself, she forged ahead. "For another, he seems to put up his guard around me, like he's wearing this iron shield of suspicion. It's as though he feels threatened by me in some way." She shrugged. "Only I can't fathom why."

Linda chewed on her thumbnail, studying Amy with intensity, then narrowed her eyes as though she were on the verge of figuring out some complicated math equation. "I think I know why."

Amy gave a helpless palms-up gesture. "Then, please, tell me what great trespass I've committed to warrant his standoffish attitude."

"You remind him of his wife."

Amy's eyebrows rose. "His wife?"

Linda nodded.

Amy scratched her forehead in confusion. "Ah, Linda, you're not making any sense. I saw a picture of Hal's deceased wife when I was at his house awhile ago. I look nothing like her."

Linda adjusted her pillow. "No, you don't. She had dark curly hair, blue eyes, and probably stood at least a head shorter than you. But you do have one thing in common with her."

"What's that?"

"Beauty."

"Ha!" Amy's response rang with satirical disbelief. In her opinion, she was too tall and gangly. Maybe she had one or two good features to her benefit, but *never* had she thought herself beautiful. She certainly wouldn't put herself in the same class as a woman as lovely as Hal's deceased wife. "Linda, I think your pregnancy is doing weird things to your brain."

Tucking in one corner of her mouth, Linda shook her head. "Never mind. You don't get it. You never will."

An annoyed "Uh" left Amy's lips. "Linda, I do wish you'd stop talking in circles and explain what any of this has to do with Hal's attitude toward me."

"Adrienne, like you, was an extremely beautiful woman. She literally glittered when she walked into a room. Only, she knew it and took advantage of it."

Amy worried her right lower lip with her teeth. Was her friend saying what she thought? That the "angel" she saw in the picture at Hal's wasn't really an angel at all? "You mean, she used people?"

"Yes, she used people, including Hal." Pain surfaced in Linda's eyes just before she averted her gaze downward. "Especially Hal."

Amy waited, wondering if Linda would explain what she meant by Adrienne using Hal. But she didn't, and Amy, although curious, didn't ask.

Amy wasn't quite sure what to make of this new revelation. Perhaps Hal hadn't been referring to his wife when he told Krista she was "as pretty as the prettiest angel in heaven." Guilt pricked Amy's conscience when she found a small degree of solace in that thought.

But she still couldn't see how she reminded Hal of his deceased wife, unless. . .

An alarming thought pierced her mind. She had grown up in a world where almost everybody used everybody else to get what they wanted. She had tried hard not to let herself fall into that self-serving mold, but maybe she hadn't tried hard enough. Her brow creased with concern. "Linda, I don't use people. . .do I?"

Linda rolled her eyes. "Of course you don't. That's exactly what I'm trying to say. All you have in common with Adrienne is your good looks, and, right now, that's all Hal can see."

Amy sent her friend a dubious look. "You mean, you think Hal somehow finds me attractive, and that turns him off?"

"Yep. My guess is he's trying to push you away because he's afraid of making the same mistake with you he made with Adrienne." She gave a nonchalant shrug. "But give him time. He'll eventually figure what really lies beneath your surface." An impish gleam lit up her dark brown eyes. "And when he does, it'll be interesting to see what happens between you two."

Amy recognized that look. Where her love life—or rather her lack of a love life—was concerned, her friend sometimes couldn't resist playing Cupid. "Don't go there, Linda. I didn't come to Cedar Creek looking for romance."

The warning didn't seem to faze Linda. Amy could already see the matchmaking wheels spinning in the brunette's head.

Amy made a pretense of examining her fingernails and, more for her own benefit than Linda's, added, "Besides, I get the feeling your cousin is a very complicated man. And the last thing I need in my life right now is another complication."

Chapter 5

H al eased his pickup to a stop in the driveway of Amy's new home and got out of the vehicle. He'd come to the rental house out of obligation, not desire. Most weeks, Sunday was his only day off, and he didn't want to miss an opportunity to spend a few quality hours with his daughter. But at church that morning, Linda had told him Amy was having trouble with the plumbing at the rental house. Since his mother was still out of town, he felt duty-bound to see if there was anything he could do to help out.

He climbed the steps and rang the doorbell. In a few seconds, a window curtain fluttered then the door flew open.

Amy met him with a look of mild surprise. "Hal?" The inflection in her voice reflected the unasked question *What are you doing here?*

"Good afternoon, Miss Jordan." He tipped his head politely. "I saw Linda at church this morning, and she mentioned you were having trouble with the water."

Her shoulders drooped a bit. "I wish she hadn't told you that. I was going to wait until tomorrow before I called your mother. I didn't want to bother her. . .or you. . .on a Sunday."

"It's no bother." In the same breath, he asked, "What seems to be the problem?" He wanted to stay on track. The sooner he finished here, the sooner he could get back to Krista, who had conned him into letting her stay with Robert and Linda while he saw to his mother's new tenant.

"Well, the hot water runs, but it doesn't get hot. And I just now tried the range top and found it doesn't work, either." She gave a helpless palms-up gesture. "Am I doing something wrong?"

"Have you tried lighting the pilot lights?"

She blinked. "Pilot lights?" Sweeping a stray lock of honey-colored hair behind her ear, she added, "Excuse my ignorance, but I have no idea what a 'pilot light' is."

"Propane gas supplies the energy for the hot water, stove, and heat," he explained. "But to get those things to work, you'll need to light their pilot lights."

She looked at him like he'd just handed her an unassembled bicycle with no instructions on how to put it together.

He held on to his stoic expression despite the amusement threading through him. This girl was city through and through, just like Robert had been when he first moved to Cedar Creek. But from Day One, Robert had put forth a dogged

160

effort to fit in with the people of Cedar Creek. He'd determinedly learned their ways, accepted their lifestyle, and extended the first friendly hand.

It had taken some time, but eventually Robert's persistence paid off, and the usually reserved folks of the Cumberland Gap highland town had embraced the doctor as one of their own.

But what about this newcomer? Would she rise to the challenge like Robert had? Or would she find the old-fashioned and conventional world of Cedar Creek too inconvenient for her and run back to the city, like Adrienne had?

"Would it take you long to show me how to do that?"

Amy's question penetrated Hal's errant thoughts, which had strayed from amused to grim in a matter of seconds. He shook his head. "No. Not at all."

She stepped to the side and motioned him in, closing the door behind him. "Where do we begin?"

"How about the kitchen stove?"

She led him through the living room, where four cardboard boxes sat scattered about the floor, then continued on through the door leading to a modest dining room and on to the tiny kitchen located at the back of the house.

When she stopped in the center of the room, Hal walked past her to the pantry. "Mother always leaves a supply of matches in here on the top shelf." He opened the folding doors then froze, taken aback by the unexpected barrenness of the cupboard. He stared a blank moment at the empty shelves then reached up for the matches. He withdrew a small cardboard box then closed the doors on the pantry—and on the disturbing wave of concern that had washed over him upon first viewing the stark shelves.

Amy was an adult. A grown woman who, he was sure, could manage to find something to eat if she was hungry.

He turned away from the pantry and faced her. She stood next to the stove, her hands tucked in the back pockets of her jeans. When their eyes met, a timid smile touched her lips—and Hal thought he felt something thump him in the chest.

An uncanny sense of déjà vu swept over Hal, sending a wave of uneasiness up his spine. Why did she suddenly have such an arresting effect on him? There was absolutely nothing special in the way she wore her hair—pulled back in a pony-tail with that one stray lock trapped behind her ear. Neither was there anything deliberately provocative in what she wore—a simple white sleeveless blouse tucked into a pair of loose-fitting jeans.

Yet something twisted inside Hal. Something vague and abstract, yet all too familiar.

Reining in his emotions, he walked over to the stove and turned a knob. He would not let her innocent facade or her seemingly helpless state get to him.

He lit a match, then touched it to the mouth of a tiny valve leading from one burner, explaining his actions as he went. A steady blue flame appeared.

Watching and listening intently, Amy leaned over his arm. Not close enough to touch him, but close enough that he felt the heat emanating from her body. And close enough that her pleasant, balmy scent slipped unbidden past the shaky control he held over his senses. He had to concentrate to remain focused on the task before him.

He turned the knob farther, and a sapphire and orange circle of fire danced to life around the stove burner. "You see," he said, turning the control back and forth, making the blaze bigger then smaller. "You can adjust the flame, depending on how fast your food needs to cook."

"Neat," she said in awe. "Now I can cook over an open fire anytime I want, regardless of the weather."

A sting nipped at Hal's fingertips, and he remembered he was still holding the lighted match. He quickly blew it out.

He turned off the burner then strolled to the sink, where he turned on the faucet and held the blackened matchstick under running water. "Where's your trash can?" he asked, turning off the spigot.

"I haven't bought one yet. I went to the market this morning to buy a few supplies and some groceries." She shrugged. "I didn't realize it was closed on Sunday."

So that explained her empty pantry. Hal laid the matchstick in the sink, reminding himself once again that Amy's plight wasn't his problem. He was only there to light the pilot lights. "I'll show you how to light the water heater now. It's in the basement."

Hal led the way downstairs but at the bottom remembered he'd left the box of matches on the kitchen counter. "Wait right here," he told her, turning back, "I forgot the matches."

He trotted back up the stairs and was reaching for the matchbox when a piercing scream rent the air. Panic ripped through his chest. "Amy?" He abandoned the matches and ran for the stairs.

She met him at the top, flying into his arms and wrapping her own around his neck. He teetered back a couple of steps, struggling to maintain his balance. "Amy, what's wrong?"

She jumped and squirmed and latched onto him like a python squeezing the life out of its victim. "Get it, Hal! Get it! Get it!" she screamed in his ear. "Don't let it come up here!"

"Amy, what are you talking about?" He tried to loosen the grip she had on his neck, but she merely tightened her hold. Burying her face in the crook of his neck, she mumbled something unintelligible.

Hal somehow managed to slip one arm beneath her gyrating knees and lift her twisting body up into the cradle of his arms. The second her feet left the floor, she stopped squirming. But she didn't loosen her ironclad grip on him, and she kept her face hidden against his neck.

He lumbered to the living room and lowered her to the sofa. When he tried once more to pull her arms from around his neck, she only squeezed harder. Hal had no choice but to ease down and sit on the edge of the sofa next to her.

"Amy, sweetheart," he said, cajoling her with the same firm but gentle voice he sometimes used on Krista, "you're choking me. You're going to have to let go."

Her arms relaxed a bit, but she still didn't release him. So he let his hands rest on her waist and waited. Soon her labored breathing steadied, and her arms slackened a little more.

"There you go." He slid his palms up her sides to her upper arms. Finally she allowed him, albeit reluctantly, to draw back enough so he could see her face. She released his neck, letting her hands fall to her lap.

The look of fear in her green eyes hit him full force. His chest contracted. The errant lock of hair had worked free from her ear and now curled along her jawline. Reaching up, he tucked the wayward strand back behind her ear. Then he cupped the side of her face with his palm and brushed her cheek with his thumb. "Now, tell me what happened."

"I saw a m—mouse."

Hal's caressing thumb went still. "A mouse?" He couldn't believe it. All this excitement over a harmless little rodent?

She nodded. "Yes. Oh, Hal." She shook her hands like she'd stuck her fingers in something slimy. "It was big and hairy and had a long tail. And its eyes. . ." Tears pooled on her lower lids. "Oh, Hal, it looked at me."

Hal wrapped his arms around her and pulled her close, trapping her fluttering hands between them. He rocked her back and forth, holding her head against his shoulder, trying to console her. But at the same time, he fought hard not to laugh. He'd seen the reaction of people who were afraid of mice before— he'd danced around one or two himself. But never had he witnessed such a desperate response as Amy's. It almost made him pity the mouse, which was probably huddled in some dark hole right now still trying to recover from Amy's earth-shattering scream.

"It's okay now," he said when he finally regained control of his mirth. "The mouse is downstairs. You're up here."

"Will it stay down there? I mean, can it get up here?" Her voice sounded so small. So. . .*defenseless.*

Hal became acutely aware of her long lashes fanning his neck every time she blinked. A peculiar flutter rose in the pit of his stomach. His remaining mirth fled.

Slowly he stopped rocking as an intense stillness settled over the room. The kind of heart-stopping, motionless silence that preceded a first kiss.

Amy drew in a shaky breath and released it with a shudder. The warm air slipped inside his collar and whispered against his chest, tugging at a forbidden place there, a door he'd long ago locked and vowed to never reopen again. Gooseflesh pricked the back of his neck.

He closed his eyes, battling temptation. He wanted to kiss her. Tip her chin and taste the sweetness of her lips. Quench the thirst parching the back of his throat.

But he wouldn't. Not this time. He'd fallen for a beautiful woman once, but never again. He was eight years older and a hundred years wiser now. Clinging to his last thread of resistance, he captured her upper arms and backed away.

Amy gazed up at him with misty green eyes full of an emotion he did not want to define. Unshed teardrops glistened on her tawny lashes. He resisted the urge to reach out and wipe the moisture away.

"Tell you what I'll do," he said. "I'll go to my house and get some mousetraps and put them out. I'll set two on the top step. There's not a mouse alive that can resist a baited trap."

Her eyes searched his with skepticism. "Are you sure?"

Hal smiled. "I'm sure." Although he really wasn't. But going after the traps would at least get him out of her presence long enough for him to cool off.

"Okay," she finally replied, her voice still weak and trembling. She leaned back, pulling her knees to her chest and wrapping her arms around them.

Hal rose. "I'll be back in a few minutes."

Amy nodded, but her gaze roamed the floor like she expected a beady-eyed rodent to dash across the room at any given second.

Hal made his way outside and to his pickup, drawing in a deep, settling breath of pine-laced mountain air. Thank God, he'd made his escape.

As he reached for the truck's door handle, he heard the front door of the house open and close. Looking up, he found Amy dashing down the porch steps, slipping her narrow purse strap over her shoulder.

"Wait up," she said. "I'm coming with you."

🦋

Hal set the second baited trap in the corner of the top basement step. "There you go." Standing, he glanced over at Amy, who stood with her back hugging the opposite wall. "Do you want me to show you how to light the pilot light on the water heater now?"

Her gaze darted past him to the darkened stairway tunnel; then she looked back at him like he was daft. "You mean, go back down there?"

"Never mind," he said, wondering why he'd even bothered asking the question. "I'll do it." He held up a paper bag containing four more traps and some cheese. "I'll set these out while I'm down there."

"Okay," she readily agreed.

Flipping on the light, Hal loped down the stairs. Before he reached the bottom, he heard the door at the top close. Shaking his head, he couldn't help grinning.

When he came back up, he found Amy pacing the living room floor, her arms folded across her midsection. She stopped and faced him as he entered.

"You should have hot water in a couple of hours," he told her.

"Did you set the other traps?"

A smile tugged at his mouth. Apparently hot water had slipped down a notch on her list of priorities. "Yes." He tucked his thumbs into the back pocket of his jeans. "Try not to get too close to them, though. They're quite easily sprung and painful if you get a finger caught in one," he added, although he felt quite certain he didn't need to worry about her getting close enough to one to trip it.

"What do I do if I catch a mouse?"

"Dispose of the body," he said, just to see her reaction.

"What!"

Guilt pricked his conscience at the sight of her wide-eyed terror. "Call me, and I'll take care of it."

Her entire body relaxed.

Raising her right hand, she ran her fingertips across her forehead, focusing on some unknown spot below his chin. "It must seem silly, me being so afraid of a mouse. But I can't help it." She dropped her hand and met his gaze. "Some people are afraid of heights, some closed-in spaces. My phobia is mice."

"Don't worry about it. I understand." Hal was afraid of horses—almost as much as Amy was of mice. But he decided he'd keep that bit of information to himself.

He glanced at the boxes scattered about the room. "I see you haven't finished unpacking."

"Finished? I haven't even started yet."

Frowning, he looked back at her. "Is this all you have?" The words slipped out ahead of his thoughts. He realized too late the question was a personal one.

Dropping her gaze back to the unknown spot below his chin, she shifted her weight from one foot to the other, and Hal sensed his thoughtless inquiry made her uncomfortable.

"Well, sure," she said. "My apartment in Atlanta was furnished." Once more lifting her eyes to his, she smiled, but it seemed forced. "You don't know how grateful I am that this house is, too."

Hal studied the woman in front of him, Linda's words from the evening before coming back to him. *"Would you please try to make Amy feel welcome? Life hasn't been so good to her lately, and she could use a good friend right now."*

What had Linda meant? Hal could only guess.

Amy Jordan possessed class and sophistication, grace and beauty. That much he knew. But what else did she own?

Her personal belongings were contained in four cardboard boxes sitting in the middle of the living room floor of a rented house. Her food pantry was empty, and she drove a fourteen-year-old car. Granted, that car was a convertible and in mint condition, but it was an older car just the same. Perhaps a remnant from better days?

Like a wave cresting in the ocean, a desire to pull her into his arms, tell her everything would be all right, that he'd be her friend and take care of her swept over Hal.

But his common sensibilities rose to do battle with his tumultuous emotions and won. He'd be a fool to think allowing himself to become personally involved with Amy would stop at friendship. She was too alluring, too tempting. Too beautiful.

All he felt for her was physical attraction and pity. He didn't know her well enough for the churning in his stomach, the pounding of his heart, and the sweat on his palms to be anything else. And he knew too well where surface attraction and sympathy for a seemingly defenseless woman could lead if he wasn't careful.

He decided he'd done his duty to his mother's tenant. He'd seen she had a stove top to cook on, hot water, and set some mousetraps. He'd worry about lighting the furnace later, when the weather, and he, had cooled off a bit.

"Well, I guess I should go pick up Krista. Robert and Linda are watching her for me and are probably ready to pull their hair out by now."

Amy followed him to the door, which he opened without hesitation. When he stepped outside, her soft-spoken "Hal?" stopped him. He turned around to face her.

She leaned in the doorway. "Thank you for lighting the pilot lights and setting out the mousetraps. I apologize for disrupting your Sunday afternoon."

He gave her a curt nod. "No problem. Have a good afternoon, Amy."

She smiled, her eyes sparkling like a kid's on Christmas. "I see you remembered my name."

Hal hadn't meant to call her by her first name earlier. It'd just slipped out when she screamed, and when she was hanging onto him for dear life—when his guard was down. Now he feared going back to the more formal 'Miss Jordan' would sound a little ridiculous, making his efforts to keep her at arm's length too obvious. "If you prefer, I can—"

"Please, no!" She grimaced, holding up a protesting hand. "I hate being called 'Miss Jordan.' It makes me feel too old." She hunched one shoulder. "Besides, we're neighbors. I'm your mother's tenant. There's no reason we can't be on a first-name basis, is there?"

"No," he had to begrudgingly agree. "I suppose there isn't."

"Good." She pushed away from the door frame and reached for the doorknob. "I'll see you later."

He started to walk away, but a rumbling sound stopped him in his tracks. He glanced at Amy's midsection, where the noise had come from.

She folded her hands over her stomach. "Excuse me. All that excitement awhile ago has kicked up my appetite."

He met her gaze. An embarrassed blush was rising in her cheeks.

"Amy, how long has it been since you've eaten?"

She frowned thoughtfully, like she was trying to remember. "Last night. I went back to Robert and Linda's after I left your house."

That did it. Knowing she was hungry coupled with her having no food in the house ripped away the defenses he was barely managing to hold intact.

He captured her wrist, pulling her across the threshold and closing the door behind her.

"What are you doing?" she wanted to know.

"Taking you to get something to eat." He led her to the steps.

She resisted. "Like this?"

He stopped and looked at her. "What do you mean, 'like this?' "

"I'm a mess. I need a bath."

She was a mess all right. The prettiest mess he'd ever laid eyes on. "You won't have any hot water for at least another hour and a half," he reminded her.

Her gaze darted to the front door, then back to him, like she was torn between making herself presentable and satisfying her hunger.

As though rallying for her attention, her stomach growled again. She released a relenting sigh. "At least let me get my purse."

Why women insisted on carrying around extra baggage had always been a mystery to Hal. But he knew better than to argue with a woman over her handbag.

He released her wrist. "Okay. I'll wait right here."

When she disappeared into the house, he drew in a deep, replenishing breath. He could do this. He could take her to his house, fix her a meal, fill a bag with enough food for a couple of days, and bring her back here without allowing himself to fall under her spell.

But first, he'd go pick up Krista. Having his daughter around to provide a buffer between him and Cinderella Jordan would definitely help.

And it did.

While Hal cooked Amy a man-sized hamburger and a generous serving of french fried potatoes, Krista kept Amy occupied in the living room building a log cabin—with the same set of wooden logs he'd played with as a child. Then, during the meal, his daughter sat at the table and chatted with Amy while he packed two bags with food from his own pantry.

Two hours later, still unscathed by the fierce attraction he felt for her while in her presence, he delivered her back to the rental house.

Or so he'd thought.

But later that evening, as he sat in his easy chair, his Bible open to a still-unread passage of scripture, images of the green-eyed beauty pushed everything else from his mind.

He thought of the way her hair, a honey-hued mixture of white, gold, and brown strands, caught the light when she tilted her head a certain way. The way her eyes, as bright and green as new leaves in spring, captured and held his gaze at an unexpected moment. The way she smelled, like a dew-kissed field of clover, when he held her close that afternoon. The feel of her warm breath against his neck. . .

Those memories of her, he feared, would linger deep in his conscious for a very long time.

But he had other memories. Shattered fragments from his life with Adrienne he gathered up now to remind him where his attraction to Amy could lead if he wasn't careful.

"I'm doing good, ain't I, Daddy?"

Krista's young voice penetrated Hal's reflective reverie. He shifted his gaze from the obscure spot he'd been staring at on the opposite wall to his daughter. She sat cross-legged in the middle of the living room floor, finishing the miniature log cabin she and Amy had started earlier that afternoon. He didn't bother correcting her grammar. In Cedar Creek, "ain't" was an accepted part of the everyday vocabulary.

Krista peered up at him, her blue eyes wide in anticipation of his answer. Her dark curls were once again secured in a neat french braid, compliments of Amy.

Odd, he thought, Krista had never really cared how she wore her hair before. Of course, he probably couldn't have done anything about it if she had. He still found getting her pigtails straight a challenge.

"Yes, buttercup," he said in answer to her question. "You are doing good."

"Wanna help me finish?"

"Sure."

He rose, sauntered over to his daughter, and lowered himself to the floor. He had more important things to focus on than his attraction to Amy Jordan. The most important of all was sitting right here in front of him.

He picked up a log and showed Krista how to start building the roof. He'd done his neighborly duty this afternoon by lighting the pilot lights, setting the mousetraps, and seeing that Amy had food through tomorrow. But given his reaction to the newcomer, he'd be wise to avoid any close encounters with her in the future.

In the past, he had always looked after the minor repairs to his mother's rental house. But while Amy lived there, he'd simply hire someone to take care of whatever problems arose.

Yep, he thought with determination as he placed another log on top of the cabin. The safest path he could take was the one leading away from Amy Jordan.

Chapter 6

"Well, here it is." Robert said as he pushed open the door of Amy's new office.

Amy stepped forward, scanning the modest room. A computer sat on a simple oak desk, a built-in supply cabinet lined the wall on one side of the room, and a long credenza stood beneath a single window along the back wall. A hand-carved coatrack was nestled in one corner, a tall ficus tree in another.

Simple and unobtrusive, Amy thought. Exactly what she needed. A place where she could fade into the woodwork. No excessive demands. . . No parents wanting her to wave a magic wand and instantly make their child well. . . No eminent expectations. . . Just a steady nine-to-five job she could leave at the office at the end of the day.

"I know it's not what you're used to," Robert added, stepping up next to her.

"It's perfect, Robert."

"I figured that's what you would say. You never did care much for glitz and glitter. It was always the people. That's what made you such a good doctor."

Amy felt Robert's gaze on her but refused to look at him—and she chose to ignore his last comment. She didn't want any reminders of what had been. Walking down the hallway a short while ago had been hard enough. Each examination room she passed brought back a bittersweet memory.

Shaking off the melancholy spirit threatening to dampen her enthusiasm for her new job, she strolled to the desk and brushed her fingertips across the smooth desktop, then thumbed through the stack of invoices resting in a letter tray. She opened a top desk drawer and found an assortment of gem clips, ink pens, and notepads all neatly organized inside.

Overcome with gratitude, Amy shook her head. Robert and Linda had done everything possible to make Amy's transition to this new world an easy one. They would have probably had her pantry stocked with food had she not insisted she was going to take care of buying groceries the day she arrived in town. But after her distressing tryst with Hal that first evening, the last thing on her mind had been grocery shopping.

A smile touched Amy's lips as she thought of the time she spent with Hal yesterday. He had been cool and aloof when he'd first come to check on her hot water problems, but before long his gentle nature had shown through. He was, Amy suspected, a generous and caring man. A softy at heart.

He was also the most virile man Amy had ever met in her life. Whenever she was in his presence, everything and everyone else just seemed to fade into the background.

Then there was his daughter. The little girl had managed to worm her way into Amy's heart the first time Amy had laid eyes on the child.

A dreamy sigh left Amy's lips as she sank down in her chair. Hal and Krista Cooper. Now *there* was a pair a woman could easily fall in love with—if that woman were in a position to fall in love.

"What's that smile about?"

Robert's voice shattered Amy's daydream, jerking her back into the real world. She looked up to find him standing in front of her desk, his arms folded across his chest, grinning at her like he knew her innermost thoughts and found them amusing.

"I, um, was just thinking how fortunate I am to have you and Linda as friends. You've made this move so easy for me."

As though summoned by the mention of her name, the spunky, expectant mom poked her head inside the open door. "Robert, Ann Peters is on the phone. She said the cream you prescribed for Casey doesn't seem to be helping his rash."

"Okay," Robert said, turning toward the door. "I'll talk to her."

When the couple disappeared around the doorway, Amy breathed a sigh of relief. Somehow she had to stop thinking so much about Hal. He had been on her mind almost constantly since Saturday night.

Rolling up to her desk, Amy reached for the invoices in the letter tray and went to work. Although Linda or Robert hadn't had a chance to show Amy anything about how to operate her new terminal, she plunged right in, completely undaunted by her lack of computer skills. After all, how hard could posting a few accounts payable be?

By midmorning, she'd found out. The computer kept telling her she was performing an illegal operation. About the sixth time the ornery machine told her she was breaking the law, she wanted to toss the thing out the window. She thought an illegal operation was something performed by a shady doctor, not a novice office manager trying to work her way through a stubborn software program.

She left work at the end of that day with a new respect for the office staff she had, in the past, taken for granted. By the end of the week, she was beginning to fear she had made a mistake in trying to tackle her new position.

But she gave herself a dozen pep talks over the weekend, then approached week number two with a new determination. By the end of her tenth day at work, things had settled down to a dull roar. But Amy's initial enthusiasm for her new job was fading fast.

Even though she was feeling more comfortable and confident with the position, the daily tasks didn't offer her the excitement and challenge practicing medicine had. But, she reminded herself often, it did fill her days. And to occupy the long, lonely evening hours, she took up a new hobby—house painting.

"You lied, Joe."

Paint roller in hand, Amy stood in the center of the extra bedroom of her new home, studying the wall she had, with her landlady's permission, started painting. A drop cloth covered the carpeted floor. A paint can, paintbrush, and a half-full paint tray sat at her feet.

Joe, a nice, friendly man at the hardware store, had helped her choose the supplies she needed for the project. When she had checked out, he'd smiled, winked, and told her, "You'll do fine, ma'am. They ain't nothin' to paintin' a bedroom."

Well, she begged to differ with Winking Joe. She had more paint on her T-shirt and jeans—which she'd worn only twice before—than she had on the wall.

With a disparaging shake of her head, she bent down to moisten her roller, but a smile of deliverance touched her lips when the phone rang. Leaving the roller in the paint tray, she abandoned her task and raced to the living room, answering on the third ring. "Hello."

"Hey, Amy. This is Robert."

"Hi, Robert. What's going on?"

"I'm at the clinic."

Amy frowned. It was Saturday evening. What was Robert doing at the clinic—unless he had an emergency?

"What's wrong?" As the question left her lips, a picture of Robert's pregnant wife flitted through Amy's mind. When Amy had spoken with Linda earlier that day, the expectant mom hadn't been feeling well. Amy's pulse accelerated. "Is Linda okay?"

"Linda's fine. But. . .Amy. . ."

Something in the way Robert said her name sent a chill of apprehension down her spine. After a long, tense pause, he added, "I need your opinion on something."

Amy's grip on the phone tightened at the same time a lump of dread rose in her throat. "What?"

"A patient's blood work."

Bingo! Amy had feared Robert would eventually try to involve her with his patients, try to convince her to return to practicing medicine. Her only surprise was that he'd waited two weeks to make his first move.

"Robert, you know just as much about analyzing blood counts as I do." She heard a defensive ring in her voice but couldn't help it. Robert needed to realize her decision to quit practicing had been final.

"Not in this case, Amy. This is a child. And quite frankly, I have no idea what I'm dealing with here."

Amy found that hard to believe. Robert graduated medical school in the top 3 percent of his class. He certainly wasn't lacking knowledge when it came to analyzing blood samples.

Mentally she put up a shield of resistance. Robert had always had a knack for talking her into doing things she didn't want to do. But not this time. She would stand her ground. Her emotional survival depended on it. "Call a specialist if you have a question," she suggested.

"I could, but. . ."

Robert paused again, and Amy tapped an agitated foot while she examined the white paint freckles on her hand. She would not let Robert's persuasive plea get to her. *She would not.*

"Amy, it's Krista."

Amy's petulant world stopped spinning so abruptly the room tilted. The specks on her hand blurred and the *tap, tap, tap* of her foot fell silent. "Krista?" she repeated in a small voice.

"Yes."

A picture of the little girl flooded Amy's mind. Her sparkling blue eyes, her cherubic smile—the ugly bruises on her arms. Amy's eyelids slid shut. Krista really was sick after all.

"Amy? Are you still there?"

"Yes." Opening her eyes, she swallowed. "Robert, I don't know if I can—"

"Please, Amy. Krista looks like someone has beaten her black and blue. Both she and Hal are really scared right now, and to be honest with you, so am I."

Amy raked a lock of hair away from her face and squeezed her eyes shut. For the love of Pete, what should she do?

"Amy?"

Robert's voice sounded urgent and small, like a lost little boy wandering the aisles of a huge department store in search of a parent.

She swallowed hard, fighting the fingers of fear closing around her throat. "Okay. I'll be there in a few minutes."

"Thanks." Amy heard relief in Robert's sigh.

She hung up the phone and retrieved her purse from the bedroom. As she climbed into her car, the thought crossed her mind that she was about to see Hal. She was even less presentable now than she had been the last time she'd seen him—when he showed up on her doorstep two weeks ago to tackle her hot water problems. But there was no time for vanity now. A child was sick and needed her.

She started to whisper a prayer but stopped herself short of uttering the first word. The last time she'd asked God for help, a little girl had died. Either He had chosen to ignore her plea, or He didn't exist at all. She cranked her car, shifted into reverse, and backed out of the driveway. Either way, she didn't see much point in wasting her breath on prayer now.

Krista sat on Hal's lap, her head resting against his chest, his arms wrapped loosely around her. Although he wanted to hold her tighter, he was afraid to. It seemed everywhere he touched her, she'd bruise right before their very eyes.

"Daddy, I want to go home now."

Her small, scared voice echoed exactly what Hal felt. He raised a hand and ran his palm down her dark curls. "I know, sweetheart. Uncle Robert will be back in a minute; then maybe we can go home."

Hal checked his watch then glanced at the door. What was taking Robert so long, anyway? When he'd pricked Krista's finger and drawn blood, he'd said he'd have the results in less than five minutes. That had been twenty minutes ago.

Hal's fear increased with each passing second. Something was terribly wrong. He knew it. Why else would Robert be gone so long?

A few minutes later, Hal could stand it no longer. But at the same time he decided to go in search of Robert, the door opened, and the doctor walked into the room. Hal searched his friend's face. Robert was smiling, but the two undeniable lines of strain creasing his forehead didn't go unnoticed by Hal.

"Well?" Hal asked, both anxious and afraid to hear what Robert was about to say.

Although moving at his normal pace, Robert seemed to take an eternity to pull his stool from beneath a built-in desk and sit down. Then he took the time to take off his glasses, fold them, and tuck them into his shirt pocket. For the first time in the two years he'd known the doctor, Hal wanted to choke the man.

Folding his arms over his chest, Robert finally spoke. "Hal, Krista's platelet count is low."

Hal swallowed, but the fist of fear refused to dislodge from his throat. Somehow, he managed to speak around it. "What, exactly, does that mean?"

"To be perfectly honest with you, I don't know."

"You don't know?" Hal's voice rose in uncontrollable ire on the last word.

"No. But I've called in another doctor. A pediatrician who may be able to shed some light on what might be going on with Krista."

Hal took a moment to rein in his frenzied emotions. "Okay. When will he be here?"

"*She* is already here, and with your permission, I'd like her to come in, do an examination on Krista, then speak with you about Krista's blood workup."

Hal was totally baffled. Where had Robert found a pediatrician in Cedar Creek this fast, at this time of night? But those questions would have to be answered later. All Hal wanted right now was for someone to tell him his daughter was going to be all right. He nodded his consent. "Sure. Send her in."

Robert rose and opened the door, peeking around the corner and motioning for the mystery doctor to enter. Amy Jordan, the enchantress who had haunted

Hal's dreams the past two weeks, appeared and stepped into the room.

Shock sent his caustic nerves reeling. He looked from one solemn face to the other then his brow dipped in befuddlement. "Robert, what's going on here?"

"Hal, Amy is a licensed pediatrician," Robert explained. "She practiced in Atlanta before coming to Cedar Creek."

A pediatrician, my eye, thought Hal. *If Amy Jordan was a doctor, what was she doing working as an office manager?* Instinctively his arms tightened around his daughter, and he turned away slightly.

"Hal, Amy is a good doctor," Robert added, apparently noticing Hal's protective gesture. "In fact, she's the best pediatrician I know."

Hal didn't know what to do. He knew he could trust Robert, but what did he know about Amy? Not much, he quickly concluded.

As though reading his thoughts, Amy raised a hand and ran her fingertips across her forehead. "Look, Robert, I don't want to do anything that makes Hal uncomfortable. I'll call the specialist in Lexington and see how soon he can see Krista." With that, Amy turned and strode out of the room.

Hal leveled Robert with a dark scowl. "Robert, what's going on here?" he demanded for the second time.

The doctor looked at the door thoughtfully, as though he could still see the woman who had just walked through it. "Hal, you've just met the real Amy Jordan." Then he looked back at Hal. "I think she can help Krista, if you're willing to let her."

🦋

Amy was seated at her desk, about to dial the phone when Robert walked into her office. "Amy, wait." He closed the door and stepped closer. "Hal's changed his mind."

Amy returned the receiver to its cradle. "Robert, I don't think this is such a good idea."

"Hal was just surprised to learn you're a doctor. That's all."

"Duh." Amy leaned back in her chair and gave an *I wonder why?* palms-up gesture. Then she leaned forward on her folded forearms. "I'm *not* a doctor anymore," she reminded her friend. "All I agreed to do was come in and give you my opinion on Krista's blood work." Shaking her head in disbelief, she added, "I don't know why I let you talk me into examining her."

"Because you care."

Amy dropped her gaze to her desktop to escape Robert's knowing expression. She did care, she begrudgingly admitted to herself. More than she wanted to.

Robert released a despondent sigh, and Amy looked up to find him rubbing his closed eyes with his thumb and forefinger. He looked tired. And worried. And Amy knew he had reason to be.

"Amy," he said, dropping his hand, "I'm dealing with a monster here I've never run across before."

"I'm not one hundred percent sure I have, either, Robert," Amy answered, repeating what she'd told him in the lab room earlier while studying Krista's blood sample through a microscope. "Further testing needs to be done by a pediatric hematologist. Krista is going to have to see a specialist anyway."

"I know. But the closest one is in Lexington, which is two hours away, and that's if we can get Krista in to see him tonight. Can you imagine how long the next few hours are going to feel to Hal if he doesn't have a clue as to what's going on with his daughter? Couldn't you at least go in there and give him something to hang on to until he gets Krista to Lexington?" Robert braced his hands on Amy's desk. He searched her face a moment with intense brown eyes, as though trying to find a part of her that was missing. "Then it'll be out of your hands," he finally added, "and you can walk away. . .if you want to."

That's exactly what Amy wanted to do—what she intended to do. She leaned forward on her elbows, closing her eyes and circling her temples with her fingertips. Tears pushed at the backs of her eyelids, but she refused to let them escape. In spite of the heaviness bearing down on her chest and the tightness in her throat, she voiced her biggest fear. "What if I'm wrong, Robert? What if Krista is sicker than I suspect?"

"Then at least you'll know you tried."

Amy squeezed her eyes shut tighter. She didn't want to do this. She didn't want to walk back into that examination room and face her old demons. But the mental picture of Krista sitting on her daddy's lap, looking all bruised and battered, and Hal, looking like he'd lay down his own life for a tiny thread of hope, became larger than her own fear. And somewhere deep inside her, she found a remnant of strength and knew she could make it through the examination. Somehow, some way, she'd make it. Then she'd go home, break down, and start putting the past behind her all over again.

Opening her eyes, Amy met Robert's hopeful expression. "Okay, Robert," she said. "I will tell Hal what I suspect. But I'm only doing this as a friend. Not as a doctor."

His entire body slumped with relief. "Thank you."

Walking down the hallway alongside Robert, Amy drew in a deep breath of courage. Why was she doing this? *How* could she be doing this? What was propelling her forward? One short month ago, thoughts of walking into an examination room again as a doctor sent her emotions spiraling out of control, like a penny in a wishing well. And each time she found herself, like that copper coin, at rock bottom.

The answer almost knocked Amy's wobbling legs out from under her. Hal and Krista. She was doing this for a charming lumberjack and his sparkling-eyed little girl. The realization touched on something inside Amy she never knew existed, a door that had never before been opened. She wasn't sure what it was, or that she even wanted to open that door and explore what was beyond it. She just knew her legs quit shaking and her steps grew faster—and stronger.

Then a voice Amy had never heard before rose from somewhere deep within and told her that for the sake of Hal and Krista Cooper, she could do just about anything.

Chapter 7

When Amy and Robert reentered the examination room, Hal gave Amy a quick head-to-toe perusal. He still had a hard time believing she was a doctor. She certainly didn't look like his perception of the high-class pediatrician Robert had described a few minutes ago. Her hair was pulled back in a ponytail—except for that one wayward lock that insisted on curling along the soft curve of her right jaw. She'd twisted the ponytail and fastened it at the crown of her head with a gold barrette, leaving the ends of her long golden strands fanning her head like a peacock's tail in full spread. She wore a green T-shirt, light denim jeans, and pale blue canvas shoes, all of which appeared relatively new, but they were speckled and smeared with something that looked like white paint.

But in spite of her less than professional appearance, Robert had assured Hal she was a *good* doctor. No, not just a good doctor—the best pediatrician he knew. And given the current dilemma Hal faced, he had little choice but to entrust his daughter to the care of this woman he knew so little about.

May as well start off on a good note, he thought. "Look, about the way I reacted awhile ago, I—"

"It's okay," she said with a wave of her hand, cutting off his weak attempt at an apology. "I understand."

Hal nodded, relieved she didn't appear offended.

Without looking at Robert, Amy held out her hand. At the same time, he unhooked his stethoscope from around his neck and handed it to her, as though he'd read her mind as her thoughts unfolded. Hal was surprised when a spark of jealousy shot through him.

Hooking the earpieces of the stethoscope around her neck, Amy strolled across the room, knelt beside Hal, and laid her hand on Krista's back. The child responded by burying her face in the front of her daddy's shirt.

Dread rose in Hal's stomach. Krista hated coming to the doctor, and he had a feeling she was about to show one unsuspecting pediatrician just how stubborn she could be.

"Krista, honey," Amy coaxed, "have you ever listened to your heartbeat?"

Krista turned her head and peered at Amy, who held up the cupped end of the instrument. After a few thoughtful seconds, Krista shook her head.

"Would you like to?"

To Hal's amazement, Krista nodded, pushed away from his chest, and reached for Amy. Reluctantly he released his daughter to the doctor, who gently carried the child to the examination table and set her down.

Amy fit the earpieces of the stethoscope into Krista's ears then held the cupped end to Krista's small chest. After waiting a few seconds, Amy asked, "Do you hear that?"

Krista nodded.

"That's your heart."

A brilliant smile accompanied by an expression of awe spread across Krista's face.

Amy waited another moment, then said, "May I listen now?"

Krista's head bobbed up and down.

While Amy fastened the earpieces into her own ears, Krista asked, "Are you a real doctor, Miss Amy?"

Amy paused, looking at Krista as though the question had caught her off guard, then smiled. "Tonight I am." She lifted the instrument to Krista's chest.

"Just for tonight?" Krista wanted to know.

With the forefinger of her free hand, Amy touched Krista's nose. "Just for you."

In a matter of seconds, the examination was well under way. Hal stood close by watching in amazement as Amy teased and cajoled his young daughter, who only a few short minutes ago had been just as scared as he, into full cooperation. Before long, Krista was so entranced by Amy, Hal had a feeling the child had forgotten all about his and Robert's presence.

Mentally, Hal shook his head, thinking back to two weeks ago, when he'd witnessed Amy's panicked reaction to a mouse. Could this really be the same woman he thought so helpless and vulnerable?

Upon finishing the examination, Amy helped Krista slip her shirt back on. "Do you like to draw?"

"Uh-huh."

"Good." Amy lifted Krista off the table, but instead of handing her back to Hal, passed her to Robert. "Let's see," Amy said, looking around. "You'll need some paper." She snapped her fingers, like she'd just received a bright idea, then circled around to the head of the examination table and slipped the large roll of white paper off the end. She held the paper out to Robert, whose mouth dropped open in surprise. "Relax," Amy told him, "I'll order an extra roll next week."

Robert snapped his mouth shut and gave a consenting one-shouldered shrug. "Whatever you say, Doc."

"Now for some pens." Amy rummaged around in a drawer until she found a red and a green felt pen, then she plucked Hal's pen from his shirt pocket, and Robert's from behind his ear and held them all out to Krista. "Here's red, green, blue, and black. I want you to go with Uncle Robert to my office and draw me a pretty picture for my wall."

Face brightening, Krista reached for the pens. "Will you really put it up?"

"Of course. You can help me pick out a frame, and we'll hang it together."

"Promise?"

"Promise."

Krista left a happy camper, and Hal found his own spirits a little lighter at seeing his daughter's jovial mood. But when Amy turned and faced him with a serious expression, he sensed the worst was yet to come, and his brief moment of ease dissipated like steam in a cold wind.

She motioned for him to sit. Then she rolled the doctor's stool directly in front of him and eased down onto its bright yellow cushion. Crossing her long legs, she grasped the sides of the seat and leaned forward slightly. "Do you know anything about platelets, Hal?"

"Just that they have something to do with clotting the blood."

"That's exactly what they do. A normal platelet count is between one hundred forty thousand and four hundred thousand." There was a short pause, then, "Krista's is fifteen thousand."

Hal's eyebrows shot up and his head jutted forward. "Fifteen thousand!" He did some quick calculating in his head. "That's only about ten percent of what she should have."

Amy nodded. "That's why she's bruising so easily right now. She doesn't have enough platelets in her bloodstream to clot her blood properly, so she's bleeding underneath the skin."

Hal wanted to scream—to stand up and ram his hand through the wall. Why was this happening to his daughter? Struggling to keep a cap on his tumultuous emotions, he swallowed the fist of fear threatening to choke him. "Can you tell me what's wrong with my little girl?"

"I think so." She shifted, uncrossing then recrossing her legs in the opposite direction. "Has Krista had a viral infection over the past few days? Something you wouldn't normally bring her to the doctor for, like an upset stomach or a cold?"

"Well, yeah. She had an upset stomach and ran a low-grade fever a couple of days ago." Guilt stabbed at Hal's conscience. Should he have brought Krista in sooner? "She was better the next day, though, so I figured she just had a twenty-four hour bug."

Amy smiled as though that bit of information pleased her. "I'm sure she did."

"Does Krista having a stomach virus have something to do with her low platelet count?"

"I think it has everything to do with it."

He shook his head. "I don't understand."

"I think Krista has a rare blood disorder known as idiopathic thrombo-cytopenia purpura."

He pulled a face. "Idiowhat?"

"I know." Amy rolled her eyes as though the long, complicated name frustrated her as much as it did him. "Let's just call it ITP for short." She shrugged. "Besides, by the time you learn to say it, I'm counting on Krista being better."

Hal saw a ray of hope and grabbed it. "You mean there's a cure?"

"No, there's no cure—"

His shoulders drooped.

Amy held up a protesting hand. "Now wait a minute. Hear me out."

Hal nodded.

"With ITP, when a child gets a virus, for some reason yet unknown to the vast array of researchers in the medical field," she made a wide sweep with her arm, "her antibodies attack her platelets, destroying them faster than her bone marrow can reproduce them. Now, while there is no cure, there is treatment."

"There is?" He leaned forward slightly.

"Yes. In fact, there are several; the most recent drug is given through an IV over a twenty-minute period."

"Can you do that here?"

"I'm afraid not, at least not in the beginning. Krista needs to be under the care of a pediatric hematologist, and the closest one is in Lexington. Also, just to be on the safe side, the doctor there will probably want to do a bone marrow test to make sure nothing else is going on with Krista. And since this is her first known bout with low platelets, I suspect he'll want her to stay in the hospital for a few days, at least until her platelet count returns to a safe level."

"So, what you're saying is, this can happen over and over again, right?"

"It's possible. For a little while, anyway. But remember what I told you. I'm counting on Krista being better by the time you learn to say the"—she drew quotation marks in the air— " 'ITP' word." She dropped a warm hand to his knee. "Hal, I know the cloud hanging over your head right now looks pretty dark, but I assure you, there are some silver linings, and I want you to keep those in mind." With her free hand, she ticked off the silver linings. "Number one, this is not a terminal illness; number two, it's not communicable—she can't pass it on to anyone else; and number three, 90 percent of the children with ITP completely recover within one year."

He considered what she said and had to agree things could be a lot worse. At least his daughter had a 90 percent chance of recovering. "What about the ten percent that doesn't recover?"

The optimism in her eyes faded a bit. "If Krista happens to be among the ten percent that doesn't recover, then you deal with it. While she will have bouts with low platelets, and during those times you'll see the inside of a doctor's office so much you'll be tempted to take her and run the other way, remember there is treatment. But the majority of the time her platelet count will most likely be normal, and with a few precautions, she should be able to lead a full, productive life."

He nodded. "I'll try to remember that. In the meantime, I'll pray for her healing."

Amy dropped her gaze and pulled her hand away from his knee. "I'm going to go make the call to Lexington," she said. "My feelings are they'll want you to take her in tonight. I'll have Robert bring her in so you can prepare her."

"Okay. Thanks."

He thought she was going to get up then, but instead, she reached over and slipped her long, slender fingers around his hand resting on his thigh. Squeezing his hand, she said, "I really think Krista is going to be fine, Hal."

Their eyes met, and Hal felt the warmth of her gaze slip past his defenses. He curled his fingers around hers, drawing strength from her touch, and studied the sincerity in her expression. For the first time since meeting her three weeks ago, he allowed himself to catch a glimpse of the gentle, caring person emerging from behind her exquisite beauty, and, he had to admit, he was beginning to like what he saw.

🦋

Amy breezed back into the room after making the call. "All set. They'll be waiting for you as soon as you can get her there."

Hal stood beside the examination table, where Krista sat finishing her picture. "Great," he said, reaching for his daughter. "I'll leave from here." He propped Krista on his hip.

Amy's heart twisted. The poor man appeared ready to do whatever he could as fast as he could to help his daughter.

"Do you have anyone to go with you?" Robert asked.

Hal shook his head. "No. Mom left early this morning. It's her weekend to sit with Aunt Lucille. I'll call from the car and let her know what's going on. She'll probably want to get one of her sisters to swap out so she can come to the hospital. Krista and I will be fine until she gets there, though."

"It's a two-hour drive to Lexington, Hal, and Krista may need your attention during the drive," Robert reasoned. "Let me make a quick call to Linda, and I'll ride up with you." Turning to Amy, he said, "You don't mind staying close by in case Linda needs you for anything, do you?"

"Of course not."

"Thanks. I'll be right back." He headed for the door.

"Wait," Amy said, stopping him. When he turned back, she said, "I know Linda wasn't feeling well this morning, and I'm sure you don't want to leave her. Why don't I go with Hal and Krista?"

"You don't mind?"

She shook her head. "No. Not at all."

Robert shifted his gaze to Hal. "Is that okay with you?"

Amy's stomach knotted then. What was she doing? She had vowed to remain uninvolved, to walk away after the examination. Glancing at Hal, she held her breath. Maybe he'd say he had someone else who could ride with him, then she'd be off the hook.

"Sure," he answered to her dismay. Turning to her, he added, "In fact, I'd appreciate it. . .very much."

Amy forced a smile. So much for walking away.

Chapter 8

As Amy expected, the pediatric hematologist at Lexington diagnosed Krista with ITP and recommended she be treated just as Amy had described to Hal. Once in the bloodstream, the medication would attract the attention of the antibodies that were attacking her platelets and give the blood-clotting cells a chance to rebuild to a normal level.

Amy had witnessed countless children being hooked up to IVs and each time had managed to remain emotionally detached. But not this time. Hearing Krista cry when the nurse injected her tiny hand almost broke Amy's heart.

Fortunately, Krista's pain was short-lived, and now, two hours later, Amy stood just inside the door of Krista's hospital room watching Hal while he watched his sleeping daughter. His mother, Ellen, stood on the opposite side of the bed.

This wasn't the first time Amy had witnessed a family pulling together in a crisis, but it was the closest she'd ever come to being a part of that experience. After her own mother died, it had been the nanny who'd bandaged her boo-boos, driven her to the doctor when she was sick, sat beside her hospital bed when she was eight and had to have her tonsils removed. Her father had been there before the surgery, but he hadn't been there when she had awakened in the recovery room. He had merely telephoned from time to time, whenever his surgery schedule allowed.

Whenever there wasn't a crisis in Amy's life, he usually didn't check in at all.

A nurse coming in to check Krista's vital signs interrupted Amy's somber ruminations. Amy shook off the melancholy spirit threatening to overshadow her. But she couldn't shake off the fatigue and weariness invading her body—that all-too-familiar feeling that had been her constant companion the weeks immediately following her breakdown.

Suddenly her surroundings closed in on her. Visions of another hospital, another room, another little girl rose up to haunt her. A smothering weight bore down upon her chest.

She needed to get out. Out of this room, out of this building, out into the night air where she could look up at the sky and see the stars and remind herself that another world existed. A world that didn't include hospital rounds, late nights at the office, an endless list of patients. . .dying children. A world where she now belonged. Somehow she had to find her place in it.

She retrieved her purse from the chair where she had dropped it earlier and eased the thin strap over her shoulder. Just before slipping out the door she glanced back at the people, the family, she was leaving behind. Her gaze lingered on Hal. He leaned over and lightly brushed his daughter's forehead with his lips.

A lump caught in Amy's throat. It was the most beautiful sight that she had ever seen.

Gazing down at his daughter, Hal shook his head in awe. "It's amazing how she can sleep so well after all that excitement awhile ago." The child lay in peaceful slumber, as though the trauma she had experienced two hours before had been two years earlier and long forgotten.

Ellen Cooper reached over and swept a curl away from her granddaughter's cheek. "Children are resilient that way."

"Yeah. That's what Amy said on the way up here," Hal replied without looking up.

A half smile tugged at the corner of his mouth as he recalled that moment. They had been en route to the hospital, and Amy was behind the steering wheel of his SUV, leaving him available to Krista should she need him. After Krista had fallen asleep in the backseat, he'd told Amy he was worried about how Krista would handle the tests and treatments when she got to the hospital. Amy had reached over, squeezed his hand, and said, "It'll be rough at first, but once treatment is over, she'll settle down pretty fast. Children are resilient that way. They usually handle things a lot better than grown-ups do."

Pulling his thoughts back to the present, Hal, not for the first time, silently thanked God for Amy's presence. She had a way of knowing what to say to calm his fears whenever they started getting the best of him. It was as though she had some sort of internal sensor his nervous system activated whenever he was on the verge of panic.

"Speaking of Amy, where did she go?"

Hal glanced up at his mother, who was looking past him with a befuddled frown creasing her forehead. He turned toward the door, where Amy had been standing a few short minutes ago, only to find her gone. He slid his gaze to the chair where she had earlier dropped her purse and discovered it missing, also.

He left his daughter's bedside and ambled to the door, looking both ways when he stepped out into the hallway. Midnight had come and gone over an hour ago. The dimly lit corridor was empty except for two nurses busy with paperwork at the nurses' station. Hal traipsed down the hallway and checked with the nurses. One had seen Amy leaving, but neither knew where she had gone.

Puzzled, Hal turned and walked away. Where could she have gone, and why hadn't she told him or his mother she was leaving?

Stepping back into the room, he said, "I think I'll walk around a bit, see if I can find her."

"Oh, Hal, give the poor girl a few minutes to herself." The slim, agile grandmother left her granddaughter's bedside and plopped down in a nearby chair. "She's probably just gone to freshen up a bit, scrape off some paint she didn't have a chance to get rid of before coming up here. I'm sure she'll be back in a minute." Brushing a strand of short silver-streaked hair away from her face, she laid her head back and closed her eyes.

Hal stood there, considering his mother's theory, and figured it was more logical than anything he could come up with.

Ellen cracked open one eye and patted the seat beside her. "Why don't you come over here and rest while Krista's sleeping? You never know when she may wake up and need you."

Hal lumbered to the chair and sat down but found his gaze slipping to the door every few seconds.

Less than two minutes later, his mother, without opening her eyes, said, "Don't worry about Amy, Hal. She's a big girl. She can take care of herself."

Hal didn't know how to respond. After thirty-two years, his mother's perceptiveness still sometimes amazed him.

He settled down in the chair. He knew his mother was right. Amy was a big girl; she could take care of herself.

Still, something about not knowing where she was made him uneasy, raised his protective instincts. Knowing she had the keys to his car in her purse didn't help any, either. But surely she wouldn't leave the hospital alone in the middle of the night. . .would she? That last thought subtly reminded Hal of how little he knew about Amy Jordan.

He stretched out his legs, crossed them at the ankles, and clasped his hands over his abdomen. One hour. He'd wait one hour; then he'd go look for her. After another vigilant glance at the door, he laid back his head and closed his eyes.

Four imperceptible hours later, he opened them.

He sat up, massaging the kinks out of the back of his neck. Blinking the sleep from his eyes, he checked his watch. 5:30 a.m. Man, he hadn't meant to fall asleep, much less check out for four hours.

He looked up at the hospital bed and found his daughter still resting peacefully, then glanced over at the only chair in the room that had been unoccupied when he drifted off, expecting to find Amy curled up there. But the chair was empty. A quick glance around the room told him she had either returned and left again, or she hadn't come back at all. Something akin to panic rose in his chest.

His mother stirred, rubbing her eyes as she sat up. "Krista apparently rested well. How about you two?"

"Amy's not back yet," Hal said, carefully guarding the tone in his voice against his rising anxiety. He did not want to alarm his mother. "I'm going to look for her," he added, standing. "If Krista wakes up, tell her I'll be right back."

Eyes widening with concern, Ellen nodded, and Hal strode from the room in search of Amy.

His search ended a few minutes later when he found her in the pediatric waiting area, sound asleep.

Smiling, he stepped into the room. She made quite a fetching picture lying there curled up on the sofa, one flattened hand serving as her pillow, her purse held securely against her chest. The light from the lamp on the end table above her head reflected off her hair like sunshine on a field of ripened wheat.

Then Hal's steps slowed. She looked different than when he'd last seen her. Instead of a twisted ponytail, she now wore her hair in her characteristic neat french braid. She'd also replaced her paint-spattered T-shirt, jeans, and tennis shoes with a pale yellow blouse, a full-length light green skirt with a pale yellow floral pattern, and brown sandals. His smile faded, and his brow dipped in a disconcerting frown. Where had she gotten the change of clothes? He searched his brain for an answer and soon came up with the only possible one. She *had* left the hospital. . .in the middle of the night. . .*alone*.

He clenched his teeth, a swift surge of anger shooting through him. Didn't she know what kind of crazy perverts roamed the city streets at night?

🦋

Something awakened Amy. Not a sound or a touch, but a sense she was not alone. She opened her eyes to find Hal standing in the middle of the room, gazing down at her with the oddest expression on his face. His scowl reminded her of the time she had fallen running away from the snake out on Bear Slide Hollow and knocked herself out. She had awakened then to find him frowning down at her pretty much the same way he was now.

Amy's stomach fluttered. Hal Cooper, with his full day's growth of beard shadowing his wedge-shaped jaw and cleft chin, and his finger-combed short hair, was not a bad dream to wake up to.

Sitting up, she sent him a sleepy smile. "Good morning." She shielded a yawn behind one hand. "What time is it?"

"Five thirty," he answered without looking at his watch, then he strode over and sat down beside her. Leaning forward, he propped his elbows on his knees and let his hands dangle between them. Instead of looking at her, he stared straight ahead in pensive silence, like he had a heavy thought on his mind.

"Is Krista okay?" Amy asked, hoping his somber mood didn't mean otherwise. Everything had appeared fine when Amy returned to the hospital a little over an hour ago. She'd peeked in the room and found him, his mother, and his daughter all sound asleep.

"She's fine," he answered to Amy's relief. "Still sleeping."

"That's good. How about you and your mom? Did you get much sleep?"

"A little."

Amy chewed her right lower lip, considering the firm set of his bearded jaw and his clipped answers to her questions. "Is something wrong, Hal?" she finally asked.

He turned his stoic expression on her. "Amy, where have you been?"

"Oh." She looked down at her new outfit, only then remembering her middle-of-the-night shopping spree. Raising her head, she met him with a pleased smile. "Shopping."

His eyebrows inched upward. "Shopping," he repeated in an *Are you serious?* tone.

"Yes." Amy bent forward, reached way back beneath the sofa, and came up with a large plastic shopping bag. "I found a variety store that was open all night and bought us all a change of clothes." She reached into the bag. "I hope everything fits. I had to guess at the sizes."

"Amy, what on earth were you thinking?"

She detected a note of ire in his voice and stopped short of pulling out a pair of jeans. Looking up, she found his expression belligerent. She frowned in befuddlement. "I was thinking if we all wore the same clothes the entire time Krista's in the hospital, we wouldn't find much pleasure in each other's company," she told him.

"Don't you realize how dangerous it is for a woman to be out roaming the city streets at night alone?"

His condescending tone sparked her indignation. It had been a long time since anyone had reprimanded her for anything she did—*a very long time*. She leveled him with a *Just who do you think you are?* glare and said, "I suppose it's a lot less dangerous for a man to be out roaming the city streets at night."

"That's not the point."

"Oh?" She lifted a cynical brow. "Then what is the point?"

Clearly frustrated, he ran a hand down his face.

"Are you upset because I drove your car?" she asked, then before he could answer added, "Because, if you are, I can assure you I brought it back without a scratch and with a full tank of gas."

His brown eyes turned two shades darker. He clenched his teeth. "You mean you stopped at a service station?"

She refused to flinch under his mounting wrath. "Yes."

"And got out of the car?"

"Yes."

"And pumped gas."

"Yes."

He shook his head, looking at her like she'd just lost her last marble.

She gave him a palms-up gesture. "I don't understand what you're so upset about."

"I'm upset because. . ." He hesitated, his mouth hanging open as though whatever he meant to say had gotten lodged in his throat. After a brief paralytic moment, his features softened and his shoulders drooped. In a much gentler, much softer voice, he said, "I was worried about you."

In his now tender eyes, she saw how much that admission had cost him, like he'd let go of some sacred part of himself.

Her anger fled and any further argument died on her tongue. For years she had traveled the streets of Atlanta at all hours of the night, going to and from school, work, and the hospital, and no one had ever worried about her safety before. A warm glow settled deep within her chest.

"It's probably because I'm from such a small town," Hal injected, like he'd jumped back on his treadmill of thought after temporarily slipping off. "You know how it is." He gave a nonchalant shrug. "We're pretty snoopy people, us mountain folk. We know every time our neighbors go out their back door, we watch each others' houses during vacations, we always tell someone when we're leaving. . . ." His voice trailed off like he'd just run out of bumbling excuses.

Amy grinned.

"What?"

"Stop apologizing, Hal, before you convince me you really didn't mean it."

Aiming a thumb toward the bag, he said, "What'd you get me?"

A quick change of direction, she noticed. Pulling out a pair of jeans, she said, "Jeans, relaxed fit. Hope you can wear thirty-three thirty-threes."

One corner of his mouth tipped. "That's exactly what I wear."

"Good."

She also showed him the plaid cotton shirt she'd bought him, pink overalls for Krista, and khaki slacks and a peach blouse for his mother. She left the toiletries and bare essentials in the bottom of the bag. She didn't have the nerve to ask him what size underwear he wore.

"I don't have enough cash on me to reimburse you for the clothes right now," he said while she stuffed the clothes back into the bag, "but I'll pay you back when we get home."

"That's okay. You don't have to."

"Of course, I do," he said, sounding a little offended.

Men and their pride, she thought. "Whatever," she said, figuring arguing with him was pointless.

He nodded, apparently satisfied with her answer.

Amy slipped her hand through the hand-holes at the top of the bag. "Let's go see if Krista's awake."

He reached over and took the bag from her—another gentlemanly gesture she wasn't accustomed to. "Okay, but. . ."

She cocked a brow. "But?"

He playfully bumped her shoulder with his. "Next time you get the urge to run off in the middle of the night, let me know, and I'll go with you."

Amy's moonstruck heart wanted to believe he was talking about forever, but her rational mind told her he was only referring to their stay at the hospital. Reminding herself that now was not the time in her life to engage in foolish romantic notions, she sent him a mock salute. "Aye, aye, sir."

He rewarded her with a heart-stopping grin. "Come on," he said, pulling her up as he stood. "Let's go see my daughter."

He dropped her hand before they took the first step. Amy tried to convince herself the letdown feeling spearing her heart wasn't disappointment.

As they walked down the hallway, Amy couldn't help breathing an inward sigh of relief that he hadn't asked her the big question: Why had she left her practice?

While she realized she had gotten through one conversation without having to answer the question, she also knew that eventually he would ask. And when he did, she'd have to tell him. After all, she'd examined Krista. As her father, he had a right to know.

Then he'd probably never let her touch his daughter again.

❦

"Amy?"

Hal and Amy stopped and turned to see who had called her name. A tall, sandy-haired man with a stethoscope draped around his neck stood in the middle of the dimly lit hospital corridor, a look of utter disbelief on his face.

"Brandon?" Amy said, her voice ringing with surprise.

"Well, I'll be," the man responded. He stepped forward, his arms wide open. "It *is* you."

Amy left Hal's side and floated, it seemed, into the man's embrace.

The hug was. . .friendly. Too friendly for Hal's liking.

An unpleasant memory flashed through Hal's mind. He mentally pushed it away, reminding himself this was a different woman, different circumstances. He had no claim on Amy, no right to feel such intense jealously at seeing her in another man's arms.

When Amy and the man she'd called "Brandon" released each other, the stranger kept her close by holding on to her upper arms. "Girl," he said. "I was afraid I'd seen the last of you when I left Atlanta."

"I hate to disappoint you," Amy told him, "but here I am."

"The last thing you could ever do by showing up unexpectedly is disappoint me."

Hal noticed the way the man looked at Amy, like he couldn't get enough of the sight of her. And Amy smiled up at him like she'd found a long-lost treasure.

I should leave, Hal thought. Slip away so Amy and her old acquaintance could reminisce. Better that than what he *wanted* to do—step forward and physically remove the other man's hands from her arms.

"Are you on staff here?" Brandon asked, hope evident in his question.

Amy's expression changed. Both the sparkle in her eyes and the smile on her lips faded. "No," she said, the delight in her voice gone. "I'm here with friends." She stepped back, breaking contact, and turned to Hal, bidding him forward.

As Hal approached them, he read the name tag attached to the man's shirt pocket. DR. BRANDON L. COPELAND. MIDLAND PEDIATRICS. So he was a pediatrician. Was he merely an old colleague of Amy's? Or more? Hal tried to ignore the unsettling wave of disquietude the thought brought to his stomach.

Amy slipped her hand into the crook of Hal's arm and introduced him to the doctor. The two men shook hands.

"Hal's daughter is here; she's being treated for ITP," Amy explained.

"Oh, man, I am so sorry," Brandon told Hal. "How is she doing?"

"She had a good night. We won't know if her platelets have gone up, though, until after blood counts are done later this morning."

"I hope she does well."

"Thank you."

Turning his attention back to Amy, the doctor said, "I ran into Dr. Cape at a convention a couple of weeks ago. He told me you'd left Mercy."

Hal felt Amy's hold on his arm tighten. "Yes. I did."

"Where are you practicing now?"

Her gaze dropped to the doctor's neck or his tie or some point well below his face. "Actually, I'm not practicing anywhere."

Brandon's jaw dropped in an incredulous gape. "What?"

Amy said nothing.

Now would be the proper time to leave, Hal thought. But Amy's hold on his arm kept him glued to the spot. It was as though she clung to him for support.

"Amy," Brandon said, inching forward, his expression full of concern. "What happened?"

"It's a long story, Brandon. I really don't have time to get into it right now. We need to get back and check on Krista."

"Sure. Maybe we can all get together for lunch while you're here."

Brandon glanced at Hal, and Hal nodded his approval. But Amy said a more negative, "We'll see."

The doctor studied Amy another bewildered moment, his face etched with a dozen unasked questions, then he turned back to Hal. "I'll keep your daughter in my prayers."

Hal nodded. "Thank you, Doctor. I appreciate that."

Brandon reached over and squeezed Amy's hand, giving her one more worried look, then turned and walked away.

With a forlorn expression, Amy watched the doctor retreat. What was she thinking? What was she feeling?

"Life hasn't been so good to her lately." For about the hundredth time over the past two weeks, Hal recalled Linda's words about Amy.

What happened, Amy? he wanted to ask. *What made you leave such a successful career and come to work as a clinical office manager in a town where people still, at times, barter to pay their medical bills?*

She'd traded so much for so little. Why?

The question would have to remain unanswered for now. If she didn't want to talk about it with an old friend like Brandon, then she wouldn't want to talk about it to Hal, whom she'd known hardly a month. And as much as he wanted to, he had no right to ask.

In silence, Amy turned and continued toward Krista's room. Hal followed suit, wishing he could do or say something to wipe the sad look off her face.

If he only knew what put it there.

❧

Later that afternoon, Amy began to wonder if she should remain at the hospital for Krista's entire stay. It wasn't like she didn't have a way home; both Hal's and his mother's vehicles were at the hospital. There was nothing to prevent her from taking one of them and going back to Cedar Creek.

What would Hal and Ellen want her to do? If they wanted her to go, would they say so? Or would they, out of politeness and propriety, put up with her unwanted presence?

Amy chose a moment when she and Hal were in the vending room getting soft drinks to find out.

She leaned with one shoulder against one cola machine while he fed coins into another. "You know, Hal, if you want me to, I can take your mother's car and go home."

He stopped short of pushing the selection button and looked at her like he didn't quite know how to respond to her statement.

"Or I can stay," she added, hunching the shoulder not leaning against the machine. "It's up to you."

"What do you want to do?" he asked, his finger still poised over the button.

"Whatever I need to do. I mean, I don't want to get in the way. On the other hand, if there's anything I can do here to help out, I don't mind staying."

He pressed the button. The machine groaned, then spat out the can. Leaning forward, he retrieved the drink, the entire time remaining quiet and pensive. Was he stalling, trying to figure out how to tell her to go home without sounding like he really wanted her to?

Straightening, he finally said, "What about the clinic? Can Robert do without you there for a few days?"

"Yes. I'm sure he'll understand, and I'll have plenty of time to catch up when I get back."

"Then stay." He paused long enough to pop the top on the can. "Krista may need you."

Krista may need me, but what about you, Hal?

The instant the question popped into Amy's head, she mentally shoved it away. She wasn't sure she would want to know the answer.

Chapter 9

On Wednesday morning, after three days with a steadily climbing platelet count, Krista was released from the hospital. But paperwork, at-home instructions, and a delay in the arrival of the required departure wheelchair prevented the Coopers and Amy from leaving Lexington before early afternoon.

Upon arriving back in Cedar Creek, the first stop was the Cooper house where Krista, tired from the busy morning and the long ride home, fell promptly asleep. Hal tucked Krista into her bed, then, with his mother there to watch over his daughter, he drove Amy home.

Somewhere between his house and hers, a melancholy spirit fell over Amy. While she was thrilled at Krista's speedy recovery, she was also saddened her time with the Cooper family was coming to an end.

For the past three days, Hal, Ellen, and Krista had treated Amy like a veritable member of their family. They'd included her in their decisions, their worries, and their concern and shared with her their laughter. No doubt Amy would miss their companionship.

She cast a sidelong glance at Hal. She'd miss being with him most of all. A comfortable camaraderie had developed between her and the handsome lumberjack during Krista's hospital stay. What would happen to their budding friendship now that they were returning to their separate lives?

As Hal turned into her driveway, imminent loneliness welled up inside Amy. In a few short minutes, she'd be right back where she'd always been. Alone.

Hal eased his SUV to a stop and switched off the engine. "Well, here we are."

" 'There's no place like home,' " Amy quipped, forcing counterfeit cheerfulness into her voice. "Thanks for the ride, Hal." Without hesitation, she reached for the door handle. *No point in putting off the inevitable.*

"Wait a minute. I'll get that." Hal was out the driver's seat and circling the front of the vehicle before she could protest.

Ever the gentleman, he held on to her hand while she stepped out of the four-by-four. His touch spawned a giddy flutter in the pit of her stomach. That same peculiar sensation had visited her often over the past three days—every time Hal was close enough for her to inhale his pleasant outdoor scent or feel the heat emanating from his body. Like he was now.

He dropped her hand, and, side by side, they ambled up the walkway. The sun cast long, dreary shadows across the yard. A slight nip in the air and nearby shade trees touched by gold and brown hinted that fall was just around the corner.

Autumn, Amy thought as she climbed the front porch steps, *a time of year when the earth's bounty dies, wasting away like sand filtering through a bottomless hourglass.*

Digging in her purse for her key, she thought of spring, hoping to dispel the somber mood she'd slipped into. Her efforts did little good. No matter how many images of March flowers and daylilies she summoned to mind, at that particular moment, the season of rebirth and new beginnings seemed too far away, a place in time she simply couldn't reach.

Hal took the key from her, unlocked, and opened the door. As he passed the key back to her, she turned to face him. "Maybe I'll see you and Krista in a couple of days, when you bring her to the clinic to have her platelets rechecked." She cringed inwardly. She'd failed miserably at trying to keep the *wishful thinking* tone out of her voice.

He hooked his thumbs in his hip pockets. "I wanted to talk to you about that."

"Oh?"

He nodded once but said nothing.

After a few bewildered seconds, Amy figured out he was waiting for her to ask him in. "Would you like something to drink? Coffee or tea?" she asked.

"Coffee sounds good."

Stepping across the threshold, she tipped her head sideways, silently welcoming him inside.

🦋

"Can I do anything to help?" Hal asked, following Amy into the living room.

"No. Just make yourself comfortable, and I'll be back in a few minutes." With that, she disappeared through the door leading into the kitchen.

Hal sank down onto the sofa, taking in his surroundings as he did so. Nothing much had changed since the last time he'd been there. The cardboard boxes were gone. A decorative white ceramic jar and a half-burned green candle in a brass holder had been added to the mantel. A green and white afghan was neatly draped over a rocking chair sitting next to the fireplace. But he didn't find a single family photo, memento, or anything that appeared to have any sentimental value. Nothing that would give him a glimpse into her past, except the white Bible with gold lettering lying on the coffee table.

He leaned forward and read the inscription on the bottom right corner of the book. "Amelia Nicole Jordan." The name beheld a classical, yet mysterious presence. Much like the woman herself.

Reaching over, he picked up the Bible, testing the feel of it between his hands. He loved God's Word. It and its author had seen him through the most trying times of his life.

He opened the book and found a note written to Amy in a bold, familiar handwriting inside the front cover.

To Amy on her sixteenth birthday.
Welcome to the family of God.

Your friend forever,
Robert

A thread of envy wove through Hal. Robert knew Amy so well, knew things about her he himself was only beginning to catch a glimpse of. Her likes and dislikes. Her pet peeves and common idiosyncrasies. . . Had Robert's relationship with her ever gone beyond friendship?

Hal shook off the unsettling thought. Even if it had, it was in the past. Robert was now happily married to Linda, and they were expecting their first child. And Linda seemed just as devoted to Amy's friendship as Robert.

Hal read Robert's note to Amy again. It appeared Amy had become a Christian shortly before her sixteenth birthday. Something akin to hope sprang up inside Hal. If she shared his faith, then maybe. . .

Before the entire thought could evolve, Hal pushed it away. It took more than one hand to count the reasons a relationship between him and Amy wouldn't work. She was everything he wasn't—elegant, cultured, highly educated. She was a doctor. She'd probably been to school twice as long as his twelve years. Then there was the money—the evil root that had destroyed his marriage.

During Krista's hospital stay, Hal had learned Amy was not only a doctor but also a doctor's daughter. Physicians from cities like Atlanta made big bucks compared to a sawmill operator from the Cumberland Gap Mountains. Amy had most likely grown up surrounded by wealth and luxury. Although, glancing around her sparsely decorated living room, one would never guess her affluent background. If she had money, why did she choose to live so simply?

Hal shook his head, mentally putting a halt to the confusing questions crowding his mind. If he wasn't careful, he'd start inventing reasons why a relationship between him and Amy might work.

He closed the Bible and set it back on the coffee table, reminding himself why he was there—to see if Amy would agree to be his daughter's pediatrician. Not explore ideas of starting a romantic relationship with her.

Hal had just leaned back on the sofa when Amy reentered the living room carrying a mug in one hand and a large foam cup in the other.

"Straight up, no cream or sugar," she said, handing him the mug. "Sorry about the caffeine, though. All I have is decaf."

He smiled. She'd learned he liked his coffee strong and black and loaded with caffeine during their stay at the hospital. "Decaf's fine. Thanks."

Amy sat down in the recliner flanking his side of the sofa, kicked off her sandals, and curled her legs beneath her. Holding up her foam cup, she said, "I couldn't find any cups when Linda and I went to the flea market last week.

Thank goodness, Frank sells these in his grocery store."

"I don't mind drinking out of the foam cup," he told her.

She grinned. "I'd trade, but I've already poisoned mine with cream and sugar."

"In that case, I guess the mug will have to do." He raised his drink in a mock salute, then took his first sip of coffee. The thick ceramic container he drank from, he knew, was a free giveaway for opening a new account at the local bank. He'd received one just like it last week when he'd opened a savings account for Krista.

He watched over the rim as Amy gingerly drank from the large gaudy cup that looked totally out of place in the circle of her slim, delicate hands. She was a woman meant to hold fine china.

What happened, Amy? Why are you here? Why did you leave Atlanta?

The questions remained unanswered. Since her encounter with Dr. Copeland Sunday morning, she hadn't mentioned her practice, and she deftly dodged questions about her past. Sometimes Hal wondered if she'd evolved from thin air, a figment of his imagination too good to be true.

After her second dainty sip, she lowered the cup to her lap. "What was it you wanted to know about Krista's appointment on Friday?"

Raking aside his plaguing thoughts, he balanced his mug on one thigh. "I was hoping I could convince you to see Krista through her illness. At least until we know she's completely recovered from the ITP."

Some indefinable emotion flickered in her eyes. "In what way?" she asked, her voice underlined with caution.

"She needs a pediatrician."

"She already has a good doctor."

Sensing resistance, Hal shifted in his seat. This was going to be harder than he thought. But his daughter needed a pediatrician, and Amy was the top candidate, so he plowed ahead. "You're right. Robert is a good doctor. One of the best, as far as I'm concerned. But the hematologist in Lexington said Krista needs to be under pediatric care between her visits to his office, and Robert's not a pediatrician. He said himself he has no experience with ITP."

Amy lowered her lashes, focusing on the milky liquid in her cup. Her rebellious lock of hair slipped free from her french braid and curled along her jaw. "I can't do what you're asking, Hal," she softly said. "I no longer practice medicine."

Why? The question circled his mind like horses on a runaway carousel. Should he press for an answer?

He wasn't sure if it was his growing need to know more about her or a selfish desire to satisfy his own curiosity, or both. But something urged him forward. He slid to the edge of the sofa, setting his mug on the timeworn coffee table. Bracing his elbows on his knees and clasping his hands between them, he willed her to look at him. When she did, he chose his words carefully.

"Amy, you diagnosed Krista's blood disorder when Robert couldn't. I've watched you interact with my daughter for more than three days. You're obviously a very gifted doctor."

"So why did I quit?" she said, supplying the question he so desperately wanted answered.

He nodded.

A sad smile touched her lips. "I've been wondering when we would get around to this conversation."

"I don't mean to pry. If you don't want to talk about it, I understand."

She shook her head. "You're not prying, Hal. You need to know."

"I do?"

"Yes, you do. You're Krista's father, and since I examined her, you need to know why I no longer practice medicine. Then you'll understand why I can't take over as her doctor."

His interest acutely piqued, he settled back in his seat.

She lowered her gaze to her cup once more, tracing the rim with one fingertip. "It happened almost four months ago. I had just finished with my last patient and was about to start some paperwork when a nurse brought me a file. . . ."

Hal listened intently while Amy told him about a little girl named Jessica Jones, the critical error that led to the child's mistaken identity, and the little girl's untimely death. While she spoke, her voice remained steady, almost a monotone, like she was intentionally keeping her emotions detached from her words.

After she finished, Hal sat in silence, considering what she'd said. Was she telling him she'd left her practice because she lost a patient? For some reason, Hal didn't think so.

Doctors lost patients. That was an unfortunate fact of life that went with their vocational territory. Robert had lost a young woman to leukemia last year. Hal remembered the haunted look the doctor had worn for several days after that. But Robert didn't give up. On the contrary, he got up each morning and went to the clinic more determined than ever to serve the patients that remained.

What had been the difference for Amy?

Now that he thought about it, she didn't seem like the type, either, who would walk away from a career she obviously loved and had spent years preparing for because of a patient's death—tragic as that death was. Hal had spent enough time with her over the past three days to know she was levelheaded, strong, and intelligent—too smart not to have considered the repercussions of losing a patient before ever entering into the field of pediatrics.

A sixth sense told him something was still missing, a small kernel of understanding he hadn't grasped.

Driven by his need to know more, he leaned forward again, planting his elbows on his knees. "What happened after Jessica died, Amy?"

Her head came up. "I went back to work." Then, as though she couldn't bear facing him, she glanced away, but not before he caught a reflection of shame in her eyes. "I know that sounds hypocritical, Hal, being in the profession of saving lives when you're responsible for the loss of one."

So that was it. She blamed herself for Jessica's death. He could only imagine the torture she'd put herself through over the past few months.

"It didn't last, though," she went on, her voice still lacking luster. "A month later I had a nervous breakdown and spent two weeks in a mental hospital." One shoulder lifted in a seemingly nonchalant gesture. "I just never could go back after that."

The pain in her voice cut at Hal's soul like a sharpened razor. He found himself wishing he'd known her then, so he could have been there for her.

Finally she looked back at him. "I'm sorry I didn't tell you about this before I examined Krista. You had a right to know, but there wasn't enough time. And I didn't want to put more stress on you than you were already dealing with."

"It's okay, Amy. You have nothing to apologize for."

One cynical brow inched up her forehead. "Oh? Are you saying if you had known about Jessica's death before I examined Krista, you wouldn't have hesitated before handing your daughter over to me?"

He thought for a moment. "I don't know."

"Well, at least you're honest," she said dryly.

Hal slid forward another inch or two. "Amy, I can't tell you what I would have done that night. I didn't even know you were a doctor before then. But now I do, and these past three days with you have shown me not only what a good physician you are but also what kind of person you are"—he touched his fingertips to his chest—"right here." He shook his head. "I know you'd never do anything to hurt a child."

"But I did—"

"No, Amy, you didn't," he countered, his voice rising with conviction. "You were given the wrong file."

Her green eyes sparked with anger. "I was the doctor in charge that night, Hal. Jessica was my responsibility."

Hal noticed the firm set of her jaw and the stubborn glint in her eyes, and his respect for her doubled. Most people in her situation would have pointed the finger of blame elsewhere and gone along on their merry way, leaving the accused party, guilty or not, to suffer the consequences. But not Amy. She was determined to bear the responsibility for Jessica's death—alone.

Hal released a slow, labored sigh. He felt helpless. He wanted to do something to wipe the sadness from her face, erase the guilt and shame from her tortured conscience. But he didn't know how.

Help me, Lord. Show me what to do to make her see that only You hold the keys to life.

TELL HER I'M IN CONTROL, came the still, small voice that so often directed Hal in times of confusion.

He rose, taking her cup from her and setting it on the coffee table. Then he knelt in front of her and gathered her hands in his. "Amy, I don't know why Jessica died that night. But I do know you're not responsible."

She shook her head, rejecting his attempt to comfort her, and looked away.

Reaching up, Hal curled a finger beneath her chin and urged her to face him. "Listen to me, Amy. Suppose everything went exactly as it should have that night. Suppose the nurse had brought you the right file, and after talking to the little girl's mother you told her to bring Jessica in, and you did everything that doctors do for children having an asthma attack. How do you know Jessica would not have died anyway?"

"How do you know she would have?"

"Because God was in control of Jessica's destiny that night, Amy. Not you."

Amy flinched as though the finger still curled beneath her chin had shocked her.

Hal dropped his hand to the chair arm. "You do believe in God, don't you?"

She opened her mouth to respond, but no immediate words came.

Sensing a denial on the tip of her tongue, Hal held his breath in dreaded anticipation.

But the denial never came. Instead an expression of anguish followed by dazed bewilderment crossed her delicate features, and her gaze darted to the coffee table.

Hal knew she was looking at her Bible. Remembering what, he did not know. He wished he could read her mind, know the thoughts she was thinking, the memories she was recalling.

But he couldn't. All he could do was wait and pray that when her answer came, it would be what he wanted, what he needed to hear.

Finally she shifted her eyes back to his. "Yes, Hal," she softly said, "I do believe in God."

Her humble confession sent Hal's heart soaring. He released a relieved breath. "But—"

That one tiny word clipped a wing. "But?" he repeated, urging her on.

"I have to be honest with you, I'm having a difficult time with my faith right now."

"I understand," Hal told her honestly. He remembered a time in his life when he'd lost faith in both himself and God.

Tears pooled in her eyes. "I prayed that night, Hal," she said, her voice sounding as lost and forlorn as an orphaned child. "I asked God to let me reach Jessica in time, but He didn't. I got there just as the heart monitor went flat, and I couldn't revive her."

A visible tremor skipped across her body. She pursed her lips, obviously battling for self-control. "I'll never forget the look on that mother's face, her screams, the way she begged for God to have mercy."

Amy squeezed her eyes shut. Twin tears trailed down her cheeks. "Why, Hal? If God was in control that night, why wasn't He there for me? For Jessica? Why did an innocent child have to die because of my carelessness?"

Her tears ripped away the last of Hal's resistance. He slid his arms around her trembling body. She slipped her arms around his shoulders, grasping the back of his shirt in her fists. Then, burying her face in the crook of his shoulder, she released a heartrending sob.

Hal slid one hand up her spine and cupped the back of her head with his palm. Gently he rocked her back and forth. Closing his eyes, he silently prayed.

Help her, Lord. Please take her pain away.

Little by little, her trembling ceased, and her crying subsided. Hal gradually stopped rocking, and a calming stillness settled around them. After awhile, she inhaled deeply then exhaled, releasing a shuddery sigh. Her feathery breath whispered against Hal's neck, cooling the moisture put there by her tears. Gooseflesh pricked the back of his neck, and his arms tightened around her.

Conflicting emotions rose to do battle within him. His common sensibilities told him he should let her go, but his heart and soul told him he wanted to stay there and hold her this way forever.

Too soon, it seemed, she released the back of his shirt and withdrew from his embrace. Reluctantly he let his hands fall heavily to the chair arms.

She wiped her face with the backs of her hands, then gingerly reached over and straightened his collar. With a small smile she said, "Sorry I got your shirt wet."

"That's okay." He reached up and brushed a wispy strand of hair away from her flushed cheek. "You can borrow my shoulder anytime you need to."

Her hand stilled, and so did his. Their gazes fused, and, like a thrown power switch, a jolt of electricity surged between them. A breathless moment passed, then her gaze dropped to his mouth. She raised her hand from his collar and brushed feather-soft fingertips across his lips.

Desire, fierce and strong, shot through Hal. He wanted to pull her back into his arms again, breathe in her sweet scent, kiss her long, slender neck, feel her pulse beating beneath his lips. . . But a thin thread of rationality that had somehow remained intact warned him if he did, he'd cross a line neither of them was ready to cross.

Her raw vulnerability gave him the strength to stand and step back, putting much-needed space between them.

Her eyes, wide and luminous, followed him as he rose, tugging at his emotions like a lighthouse beckoning a ship on a dark, stormy night. To be on the safe side, he stuffed his hands into his pockets.

He knew he should leave, but he couldn't with their conversation unfinished. There was more he needed to say to her about God's enduring love and mercy.

But with her sitting there looking up at him that way, he didn't trust his own will-power. He needed more air and space than the small living room provided.

"Would you walk with me outside?" he asked, not at all surprised by the huskiness in his own voice.

She nodded.

Hal waited while she slipped on her sandals, then followed her to the front door, wiping tiny beads of perspiration from his brow. He hadn't felt this much like a flesh-and-blood man in a long time. A very long time.

When he stepped outside, he pulled the door closed behind them, firmly. The coolness hovering beneath the shade of the front porch brought blessed relief to his heated face. He drew in a deep, calming breath of the crisp air.

With her back to him, Amy stared thoughtfully at the mountains banking the meadow beyond her yard, then, crossing her arms, turned to him. "Hal, about my taking over as Krista's doctor—"

He pressed a finger to her lips. "Don't answer right now. Wait until you've had time to think about it."

She blinked in surprise. "You mean you still want me to be your daughter's doctor?"

He nodded. "Yeah. Whenever you're ready."

He found the feel of her soft, pliant lips beneath his fingertip a bit too distracting and dropped his hand. Hooking his thumbs into his back pockets, he took a few seconds to weigh out his next words. He'd never considered himself much of a verbal witness for Christ before. Eloquent speeches and well-honed grammar skills were not among his strong suits. But for some reason, this door had been opened to him, and he felt it was God's will he finish walking through it.

"Amy," Hal said at last, "you asked awhile ago why God left you the night Jessica died."

Amy's gaze dropped to his chest, and Hal's confidence slipped a bit. The last thing he wanted to do was offend her, make her feel he was trying to preach a sermon.

TRUST ME, HAL, the still, small voice reminded.

"I don't know why things happened like they did that night," Hal plunged forward. "But I do know that God didn't leave you. . .or Jessica."

She didn't speak, didn't raise her eyes.

"Think about it," Hal continued. "Do you honestly think God would allow an innocent child to die because of someone else's mistake?"

Her gaze darted back to his. Something he said had apparently captured her attention.

"Of course He wouldn't," Hal said in answer to his own question. "He's not that kind of God." In a softer, gentler voice, he added, "He loves you, Amy. He only wants what's best for you."

She tucked her right lower lip between her teeth and shifted her weight from one leg to the other. "I hear what you're saying, Hal. It's just that. . ." She glanced away, her ponderous thoughts hanging heavy between them.

Hal searched his mind for something else to say, something that would erase the doubt and confusion etched on her lovely face. But no more words of divine wisdom came. So he just waited.

Finally she looked back. Uncrossing her arms, she inched forward and laid a palm against his chest. Of its own volition, his hand rose to cover hers.

"Thank you, Hal," she said, "for listening and for your words of encouragement. You've given me a lot to think about." She searched his face for a fleeting few seconds, then added, "I mean that."

And somehow, Hal knew she did. Smiling, he squeezed her hand and was rewarded with a soft smile in return.

It was now time to go. He had said all God wanted him to say. He had no other excuse to prolong his stay. Stepping back, he broke the contact between them. "I guess I'd better run."

"Yes," she said, recrossing her arms. "You'll want to be there when Krista wakes up."

Hal paused, taking in Amy's lovely features. She was like a beaming light at the end of a long, dark tunnel. The closer he got to her, the brighter she shined.

"Amy," he felt compelled to add, "anytime you need to talk, just let me know. I may not have many of the answers you're looking for, but I can always listen."

"I'll keep that in mind."

With a "See you later," he turned and headed for his SUV. Before sliding behind the steering wheel, he looked back toward the front porch, intending to send Amy one final wave good-bye. But to his disappointment, she'd already slipped inside and closed the door.

Chapter 10

A s soon as Hal turned and walked away, Amy slipped inside and closed the door, berating herself for falling apart in front of him. She hated losing self-control. It was an arduous reminder of how volatile and unpredictable her emotions had become, how far removed she was from the confident, self-assured doctor she'd been just a few short months ago.

Odd, she thought as she wandered back to the living room. She'd known when she'd chosen a career in pediatrics it would be a long, slow climb to the top. But she'd never once stopped to consider what a fast, hard fall it could be to the bottom. Or how difficult it would be to get up when she got there.

She slumped down on the sofa, mentally and physically drained. Not surprising, considering extreme exhaustion always followed an emotional visit to her not so distant past.

How did people like Hal do it? Maintain their unwavering faith in God even in the face of a crisis, like the one he'd recently experienced with Krista.

Amy propped her elbows on her knees and her chin on her fists, thinking back on the last three days she'd spent with Hal. Every evening, without fail, he'd read from the Gideon Bible placed in Krista's hospital room. More than once he'd visited the hospital chapel to pray. He'd even told another couple, practical strangers, that he'd pray for their daughter's speedy recovery from pneumonia.

Yet not once had she heard him say anything or react in any way to indicate he blamed God for his daughter's rare blood disorder—a malady she may have to deal with for a long time.

Obviously he was a man of devout faith, a man who depended on divine authority rather than his own, a man at peace with himself. . .and with God.

A thread of envy wove through her. "How do you do it, Hal?" she muttered. "What's your secret?"

When he'd asked her if she believed in God, she'd almost said, "Not anymore." But then she'd stopped and thought about the acrimony and bitterness she'd lived with for the past three and a half months and decided yes, she did still believe in God. How could she not believe in someone she was so angry with?

But Hal's relationship with God, she suspected, went beyond belief.

She ran her fingertips across her forehead, trying to dissuade the dull throb building there. A mental picture of Hal sitting in the corner of Krista's hospital room reading the Gideon Bible floated through her mind. Her eyes shifted to her own Bible lying on the coffee table. Robert had given her the testament on her sixteenth birthday, shortly after she'd made a commitment to follow Christ. She'd felt so close to God then, so cherished and loved. But somewhere between then and now, all that had changed, and, in all honesty, it had started long before Jessica's death.

Leaning forward, she picked up the white leather-bound book. How long had it been since she'd used God's Word for something other than a table decoration? Weeks? Months? Guilt pierced her conscience. No, it hadn't been weeks or even months since her daily devotions ended. But years. She truthfully didn't know how long. She'd lost track. Her life had become so busy. . . .

The shock of realization hit her full force and shame washed over her. Yes, her life had been busy. Too busy to include God.

Tears blurred her vision as the reason for all her pain, confusion, and loneliness became startlingly clear. God had not left her; she had left Him.

She hugged the Bible to her chest, and a life-changing warmth spread through her, like the book sprouted wings and hugged her back. She may not know what she was going to do with her life and where she was headed, but she did know, wherever that was, she didn't want to go there without God.

Closing her eyes, she bowed her head, and for the first time since Jessica's death, and only the second time since she could remember, Amy prayed.

🍂

The ax fell full force against the wood, splitting the fire log into two even halves and launching them in opposite directions. Hal bent, picking up the piece of timber that had landed nearest him, then stood it upright on the large round stump he used for a chopping block.

The damp night air and the sweat seeping from his pores merged on the surface of his skin, wrapping his bare upper body in cool, dank clamminess.

Glowing from the back corners of his house, flood lamps cast long, eerie shadows across the yard. And beyond the beaming lights, in the stillness of the forest, crickets sang a rhythmic, peaceful song.

Peace, Hal thought with another deliberate swing of the ax. That's what he'd come out here seeking. But with each smack of the blade and each ear-shattering separation of wood, he only became more confused.

Seemed like fate was determined to make Dr. Amelia Nicole Jordan an imminent part of his life. And feelings beyond his control had already granted her a continuous place in his thoughts, a constant presence in his dreams.

He liked her. Not just how she looked, but how she walked, how she talked, how she laughed. How she touched a place inside him no one had ever touched before—not even Adrienne.

And that realization, staring him square in the face, scared him to death.

Falling in love may feel great. But falling out could cut a man's soul so deep that only the healing power of God could close the wounds. And nothing could take away the scars, those ugly, deeply embedded reminders of what can happen when you give too much of yourself to someone.

"Hal Cooper, put your shirt back on before you catch your death of cold."

Glancing over his shoulder, he found his mother, wrapped in a terry robe, her feet tucked into untied hiking boots, standing several yards behind him. In each hand she balanced a heavy ceramic mug.

"Hi, Mom." He leaned the ax against the chopping block and reached for the shirt he'd tossed over the back of a nearby lawn chair. Slipping first one arm and then the other through the sleeves, he grinned at her, silently telling her he didn't take her scolding seriously but would do as she ordered simply to appease her because he loved her.

She waited until he'd buttoned the last button then passed a mug to him. The hearty scent of strong black coffee rose to tempt his senses.

Ellen studied the diminishing woodpile then shifted her gaze to two waist-high rows of split fire logs Hal had neatly stacked on the opposite side of the chopping block. "Goodness," she said, "I don't think we've ever been so well prepared for winter."

Yes, Hal could argue, they had. Once. That week almost five years ago when he'd finally agreed to give Adrienne a divorce. The same week she'd died alongside her newest lover in a single-engine plane crash.

"Do you want to go inside?" he asked his mother. "It's kind of chilly out here."

She looked up, where a half moon and a brilliant canopy of stars illuminated the midnight blue sky. "No. It's such a beautiful night. Let's sit out here a few minutes."

She eased down into the lawn chair. Hal settled on the chopping block.

After taking one generous sip of coffee, he leaned forward, elbows on knees, cupping the warm mug in his hands. "I hope my wood chopping didn't wake you."

"You woke me, Hal, but it wasn't your wood chopping."

Hal quirked his brows in question.

"You're my son," she answered his silent query. "I always know when something's troubling you."

Hal wasn't surprised. He and his mother were close. She knew him better than anyone else. And he knew there was no point in dancing around the issue. She'd probably already figured out what was bothering him.

He focused on the steam rising from his mug. "It's Amy."

"Oh?"

"I like her."

"What's not to like? She's beautiful, generous, intelligent. . ."

He met her gaze. "I like her. . .a lot."

His mother's eyes filled with understanding. "I see." Several pensive seconds ticked by. "Any idea how she feels about you?"

Hal nodded. "I think there's something there."

"But you're afraid."

Again he nodded.

Ellen leaned forward, elbows on knees. "Hal, Amy is very different from Adrienne."

"I know, Mom." *Now,* he added to himself. "Even so, I've got a lot to consider before entering into a relationship. . .with anybody."

"Such as."

"Well, Krista for one." He shook his head. "I don't want her to get hurt. And that's exactly what will happen if Amy steps into our lives and then, for some reason, walks out."

"Like Adrienne did."

A distant but all-too-clear memory rose up to taunt Hal. Krista had been six months old the last time Adrienne had walked out. Too young to understand that her mother didn't want her. But Krista was older now. What would it do to her should she fall in love with Amy then lose her?

"Hal," his mother said, "I don't want Krista to get hurt either. And if I felt that were going to happen, I'd be the first to state my opinion."

Hal stared into the darkness beyond the yard, where crickets continued to chirp and an owl released a lonely sounding *hoot-hoot.* For a heartbeat, he wished he could erase twenty or so years. Go back to a time when his life was much simpler, when deciding what was best for him was someone else's responsibility. Finally he said, "How can I know for sure, Mom?"

"You can't. Life holds no guarantees."

"It's not worth the risks, then."

"Are you sure about that?"

Yes, he was sure. . .he thought. But for some reason, he couldn't voice that conviction to his mother. He felt her touch his knee and looked back at her.

"Sometimes, son, when you feel God leading you in a new direction, you have to step out in faith and trust Him to take care of your loved ones."

A silent understanding passed between them. How many times had she, during his tumultuous marriage, stepped out in faith, trusting God to take care of Hal and his family? Only she and God knew.

Patting his knee, Ellen stood and drew back her shoulders as though shaking off the dismal mood. "I'm going back to bed, and I suggest you do the same. It's just a few hours until sunrise." With that, she turned and headed back to the house, leaving Hal with his thoughts.

The wind whispered by, slipped inside the porous material of his shirt, and fingered a chill across his skin. Trust God, his mother had said. Hal thought he could do that. But what about Amy? Could she learn to trust God again?

Hal would not consider a future with anyone who didn't share his faith. He'd made that mistake once, and it'd cost him—dearly. So for now, it seemed, all he could be to Amy was a friend.

Standing, he dumped his cold coffee on the ground and set the mug next to the chair. Reaching in the woodpile, he grabbed a log and stood it upright on the chopping block. Then, wrapping first one hand and then the other around the ax handle, he continued splitting wood.

Chapter 11

Later that morning, Hal slid into a booth at Grace's Café across from Amy. She'd phoned him as he was headed out the door for work and asked him if he could meet her for breakfast. She said she had something she wanted to tell him.

Hal suspected her invitation had something to do with their conversation the night before. He'd told her to call anytime she needed someone to talk to, and he'd meant it. Still, hearing her voice when he'd picked up the receiver that morning surprised him. He hadn't expected to hear from her so soon.

"Thanks for coming, Hal," she said, folding the newspaper she'd been reading and laying it on the seat beside her.

"No problem."

She asked about Krista and his mother, and he told her they were both doing fine, but Krista was a little disappointed she couldn't return to school this week. She loved kindergarten.

The waitress came and took their order, and as she walked away, Amy leaned forward on her forearms. "I asked you to come this morning, Hal, because I wanted to thank you."

He arched his brows. "Thank me?"

"Yes. . .for what you said last night. After you left, it didn't take long for me to realize that you were right. God hadn't left me. He'd been there all along, waiting for me to return to Him."

Hal leaned forward, matching Amy's position. Could this mean what he thought? "Go on," he urged.

"I'd let so many things come between me and God. School, my studies, my practice. . ."

The waitress brought their coffee, but Hal hardly noticed.

"When I first began praying last night," Amy continued. "I thought it'd take awhile for me to get through to God. You know, gain His forgiveness. But it didn't. I asked, and right there He was, waiting to answer." The corners of her mouth turned up softly, and Hal noticed for the first time since he'd met her, her smile reached her eyes. "God's given me a second chance to live my life for Him. I intend to do it right this time. Not fail Him like I did before."

She reached over and covered his hand with her own. "I just wanted to share that with you, Hal, and let you know what you said last night made a difference."

He turned over his hand and wove his fingers with hers. "I'm glad you did, Amy. You have no idea what that means to me." *No idea*, he added to himself.

They sat there holding hands, talking about her newfound faith, until their food arrived. While they ate, their conversation wandered to more general topics: the weather, their work, the upcoming Harvest Festival.

About halfway through the meal, which neither of them seemed particularly interested in, Amy glanced at her watch and gasped. "Oh, dear! I'm going to be late for work."

She reached for the check, but Hal beat her to it, stuffing the slip of paper into his shirt pocket.

"I don't have time to argue with you, Hal Cooper," she scolded good-naturedly. "But the next one's on me."

Outside, he walked her to her car and opened the door for her. Before slipping behind the steering wheel, she turned to him with another radiant smile. "Thanks again, Hal. You're a good friend."

Hal drove to work a little in awe of what Amy had told him. She'd made peace with God, which meant she was now equally yoked with Hal in faith.

The main obstacle standing between him and Amy had just fallen away.

Hal felt like he'd just been given the green light, a "go-ahead" signal from God to take his and Amy's relationship one step further. And that's exactly what he intended to do.

He rolled down his window and folded his arm over the door. Talk about an answered prayer. God had been a few steps ahead of Hal on this one.

🦋

"Come in," Amy called in response to the knock on her office door Friday afternoon.

The door swung open and a curly-haired bundle of energy sprinted toward her. "Miss Amy!"

"Krista!"

The sight of the child sent a bolt of joy through Amy. She rolled away from her desk and swiveled sideways just in time to scoop the resilient tyke up onto her lap. Inconspicuously, she examined the child's arms. The bruises had faded to a pale greenish purple, and she saw no new discoloration. A good sign.

Krista gave Amy an enthusiastic hug, which Amy returned. Then, in one quick motion, Krista planted her small hands on Amy's shoulders and pushed back, looking up at Amy with blue eyes stretched wide with excitement. "Me an' Daddy's got a surprise for you."

"For me?"

"Uh-huh." Krista's head bobbed up and down.

Amy looked toward the open doorway, where Hal leaned with one shoulder against the frame, his thumbs hooked in his back pockets, looking like a heavenly dream. He dazzled her with a broad smile that dimpled both cheeks. For about the space of four heartbeats, Amy forgot to breathe.

"Tell me, Doc," he said. "Why do women have such a hard time keeping secrets?" There was a teasing note in his voice, a lightheartedness she'd never noticed before.

She tried to think of a quick-witted comeback, but his presence had scattered her senses. "I don't know," she finally managed to mumble then wanted to kick herself for sounding like a bumbling idiot.

"Show her the 'prise, Daddy," an impatient Krista urged.

He shoved away from the door frame and reached behind the exterior wall, withdrawing a large framed. . .something. Amy couldn't tell what, with him holding it down by his side.

Stepping forward, he lifted and turned the frame so that Amy could see, and her mouth dropped open in surprise. Inside the smoothly finished oak casing was the completed picture Amy had asked Krista to draw for the office wall.

Amy reached out and ran her fingertips across the polished wood then over the non-glare glass protecting the picture. "It's beautiful."

"I helped Daddy make it for you," Krista said.

Amy lifted her gaze to Hal's. "You guys made this?"

He gave a modest shrug.

A warm glow coiled in Amy's chest, and unbidden tears stung her eyes. She'd received her share of gifts in the past. Expensive trinkets and frivolous commodities bought without thought or sentiment. But no one had ever taken the time or gone to the trouble to make something for her with their own hands.

"Do you like it, Miss Amy?" Krista wanted to know.

Amy blinked the moisture away. "I love it. It's the best present I've ever received," she said, and meant it.

Krista beamed, and Amy felt a maternal tug on her heartstrings. Why did this pair have such an enchanting effect on her?

"Can we hang it up now?" Krista asked.

"Sure," Amy said. "Let me go see if I can find a hammer and some nails in the supply closet."

"I've already got it covered." From his back pocket, Hal withdrew a child-sized hammer and a small plastic bag of picture hangers.

"Well, aren't you Mr. Resourceful," Amy said without thought.

He wiggled his brows. "I try to be."

Amy blinked in surprise. Was he flirting with her? Or had she imagined it? She swallowed nervously and wet her lips. "Okay. Let's get started." Setting Krista on her feet, Amy stood on legs that felt a bit like jelly.

Ten minutes later, they all stood back and admired the new addition to Amy's office. In the picture, three stick people and a stick creature of some sort stood side by side between a house with a chimney and a tree.

Amy lifted Krista to her hip. "Tell me about the people in the picture."

Pointing, Krista said, "That's Daddy, and that's me, and that's you."

"Me?"

"Uh-huh."

But Amy thought it was. . . "Where's your grandmother?"

"She's in the house, cookin' chicken for the picnic."

"Oh," Amy replied, not allowing herself to contemplate why she herself was included in the picture. She pointed to the stick creature. "Who's this?"

"That's Rufkin."

Of course, Amy should have remembered the dog.

The door cracked open, and Linda poked her head inside. "Want to get a treat from the treasure chest, Krista?" Every child who visited the clinic was rewarded with a trip to Dr. Robert's treasure chest of toys and treats.

"Yes!" Krista said, squirming for release.

Amy set Krista on her feet, and in a split instant the child was gone.

After the door closed behind Krista and Linda, Amy turned to Hal. "How did the checkup go?"

"Great. Krista's platelet count is up to one hundred fifty-three thousand."

"That's the best news I've heard all day."

"Me, too." Hal leaned back against the wall, apparently in no hurry to leave. "I asked Robert if I could take her on a picnic tomorrow."

"What did he say?"

"To ask you."

Mentally Amy planned a slow session of torture for Robert. He knew very well that Krista could return to normal activity with a platelet count of one hundred fifty-three thousand. He'd asked Amy's advice on the child's limitations that very morning.

Amy didn't mind sharing her knowledge of ITP with Robert, but she had asked him to keep her involvement in Krista's case behind the scenes. Lot of good that request had done.

Feeling she'd been given little choice but to answer Hal's question, Amy leaned back against the desk. "A picnic sounds fine, Hal. As you know, Krista's platelet count has returned to normal. However, you do need to keep her out of trees and off bicycles for a while, away from anything where there's a risk of head injury. At least until you're sure the ITP isn't going to reoccur."

Hal looked perplexed. "That's not going to be easy."

Amy's lips tipped. "I know." Krista's liveliness could drain the stamina of a world-class athlete.

"What about you, Doc?" Hal asked. "Want to come along?"

The invitation caught Amy off guard. "You want me to come?"

"Sure," he responded, as though asking her to a picnic was an everyday occurrence. "That is, if you'd like to."

If she'd like to. Of course, she would. But *should* she? Every minute she spent with Hal, she lost another little piece of her heart.

She glanced at a generous but neatly stacked pile of paperwork on her desk. "I really should work tomorrow." Inwardly she cringed at how lame her excuse sounded, like she'd intentionally left the door wide open in hopes that he'd ask again. Why hadn't she simply told him she *was* going to work tomorrow, as she'd intended to do before she opened her mouth?

"Aw, come on, Doc," Hal said. "Surely after spending three days cooped up with us in the hospital this week, you could use a break, too."

The guileless plea in his voice and the boyishly charming expression on his face beat down Amy's feeble resistance and steered her thoughts in another direction. What could one little picnic hurt? A friendly family outing to celebrate Krista's quick recovery.

"Well, what do you say?" Hal cajoled. "Is it a date?"

Her heart took off in a giddy sprint across her breastbone. "Sure. What time should I be ready?"

His grin broadened, and Amy allowed herself to believe he was thoroughly pleased she'd accepted his invitation.

"How does ten sound? That way, we can get in a little fishing before we eat."

"Sounds great," Amy said, even though she had never been fishing in her life. He'd probably have to show her which end of the pole to hold.

He pushed away from the wall and tucked his fingers into his jeans' pockets. "Well, I guess I'd better go find Krista. Linda probably needs rescuing by now."

"Okay."

"Well, I'll see you tomorrow, Doc." He headed for the door.

"Hal," she said as he reached for the doorknob.

He looked back at her.

"I wish you wouldn't call me 'Doc.' "

He winked at her. "Anything you say, Doc." With that, he opened the door and slipped through it.

Amy looked heavenward and shook her head.

Then she stood staring at the space he'd just vacated. Something had definitely changed in him. Before, he'd always been intensely serious, cautiously guarded where she was concerned with what Amy thought of as a *you-can-get-close-but-not-too-close* mentality. But today, that shield had dropped, and she couldn't help wondering why.

Shaking her head, she circled her desk and sat down. He was obviously thrilled Krista had gotten such a good report. That was all. What caring father wouldn't be elated to hear his daughter could return to normal activities when she'd been in the hospital a few short days ago?

Amy pulled up patient accounts on her computer, then glared absently at the screen, unable to dispel the sanguine thoughts swirling through her mind. Hal had teased and joked with her. *Flirted* with her. She was sure of it. And Hal Cooper was not a man who made amorous advances lightly. Amy knew, because he'd had at least a dozen opportunities to do so while Krista was in the hospital. Practically every pediatric nurse that had visited the child's room, both young and aged, had taken their turn at trying to impress him with coquettish looks, impudent giggles, and seductively swaying hips.

But, like a granite statue, Hal had remained unimpressed. Either that or he'd done a very good job at covering up his interests.

Now here he was cracking carefree jokes and winking at her—harmless gestures had they come from someone other than the usually serious and brooding lumberjack. Plus, he'd asked her to go with him on a picnic, then referred to the outing as a date. Amy worried her right lower lip with her teeth. Good report on Krista aside, something had changed.

The screen saver popped on, throwing a multitude of shooting stars in Amy's direction. She swiveled away from the computer and propped her elbows on her desk, plopping her chin in one hand. A despondent sigh slipped past her lips. "What's going on here, Lord?"

She didn't receive an answer, but she really wasn't listening for one. She had her own ideas about what was happening between her and Hal. Something wonderful and exciting. . .

And. . .

Possibly impossible, she reminded herself, jerking her thoughts out of the castle in the air they'd drifted into. A disgruntled frown creased her forehead. She had no business engaging in romantic fantasies about Hal until she figured out what she was going to do with the rest of her life.

She turned back to the computer, striking a key that banished the shooting stars from the screen. In all fairness, she should tell Hal just how uncertain her future was before their ill-timed attraction for each other evolved into something more.

She glanced at the door. He was probably still at the clinic. She could go find him and tell him she'd changed her mind about the picnic, decided not to go, nip a possible romance in the bud before it got off the ground floor.

Or she could wait and see how the outing went, just in case she was reading more into his sudden effervescence than what was really there.

Amy drummed her fingers on her desk. Keep the date or cancel. What should she do? She weighed the decision in the balances a few more deliberating seconds, then turned to her computer and went back to work.

Chapter 12

W hoa, Doc!"

Hal captured Amy's wrist, thwarting her attempt to throw her line back out into the gently flowing waters of Cedar Creek, the watercourse for which the town Cedar Creek was named.

Amy looked behind her to see if her line was tangled in the drooping branches. When she saw her hook dangling idly at the end of her rod, she looked at Hal and frowned. "What's wrong?"

"I'm hungry," he said, "and before I untangle one more hook from one more tree, I need to eat."

Her frown turned into a scowl. "If I remember correctly, this was your idea."

"I know. But now I have a better idea." He started peeling her fingers from around the rod. "It's called *lunch*."

Reluctantly and with a small degree of disappointment, she released the pole. She never realized fishing could be such fun.

Of course, it probably hadn't been much of a treat for Hal. He'd moved her to three different locations along the creek bank. Still, about every other cast, she somehow managed to get her line tangled in some obtrusive form of plant life. So he'd spent the better part of the morning untangling rather than fishing.

Poor man. No wonder he looked so frazzled.

He laid aside Amy's rod and turned to Krista, who stood a couple of yards away, ankle-deep in water, her own child-sized pole clutched in her hands. Intently she watched her line, waiting for the slightest nip or tug that would indicate she'd snagged a fish.

It dawned on Amy that Krista hadn't once needed her father's assistance. "Do you suppose I'll ever get the hang of it?"

She hadn't realized she'd voiced her thoughts until Hal glanced back at her. "Sure, you will. It just takes a little time and practice." His response was polite enough, but considering his finger-combed hair and haggard expression, he was probably thinking, *Lots of time. Lots of practice.*

He turned his attention back to his daughter. "Time for lunch, buttercup."

Krista, her face framed with corkscrew curls that had escaped her pigtails, looked up at her father with moping eyes. "But I want to fish some more."

"I know, and you can. After we eat." Hal's words, while gentle, brooked no argument.

Lower lip protruding in an artful pout, Krista reeled in her line.

The day had turned out to be the perfect one for a picnic. The wind was calm and the air full of sights and sounds of nature: whistling songbirds, barking squirrels, the *swish-gurgle* of the crystalline stream.

Amy spread a wedding-ring quilt in the shade of an ancient oak while Hal hauled the picnic basket from the car. "Can I help?" she asked, reaching for the lid when Hal set the basket down.

He brushed away her hand. "Nope. You're our guest. That means we serve you."

Feeling a bit useless, she sat back while Hal and Krista started pulling out food and arranging it on the quilt. The father-daughter pair uncovered fried chicken, potato salad, green beans, corn-on-the-cob, and rolls. And if that wasn't enough, an apple pie—fresh baked from the looks and smell of it—and a frosty pitcher of tea.

"Wow!" Amy said, her mouth watering. "Did you cook all this?"

"I wish I could take the credit," Hal said. "But I had Sal down at Grace's Café whip up the potato salad and apple pie."

Amy narrowed her eyes suspiciously. "Your mom didn't have a hand in this? Not even the chicken?"

"Unfortunately, no. She's tied up at a church yard sale today. So I'm afraid you're stuck with my cooking."

"Well, you shouldn't have gone to so much trouble."

He stopped short of handing a stack of napkins to Krista and captured Amy's gaze with his own. "I wanted to," he said softly.

Amy's breath caught in her throat. She tried to glance down or look away, but she couldn't escape the hypnotic pull of his intense chestnut eyes. The birds still sang, the squirrels still barked, and the brook still gurgled. But for one breathless moment it seemed time stood still.

"Dad-*dy*, hand me the napkins."

Krista's impetuous voice broke the enchanting spell. Amy finally managed to drop her gaze, and Hal went back to arranging food fit for a southern governor's dining table.

Hardly ten minutes into the meal, Krista set her plate aside and wiped her mouth with a napkin. "Can I go fish some more, Daddy?"

"You've hardly touched your food," he pointed out.

Krista folded her arms over her stomach and filtered a laborious sigh, like she'd just finished her third helping of a Thanksgiving feast. "But I'm full."

"Okay," Hal relented. "You can go on and fish some more, but stay on the shore until Amy and I get back down there."

Wise move on Hal's part, Amy thought. It caused more grief than glory to force a child to eat when he or she wasn't hungry or interested.

The child's doleful expression blossomed into a brilliant smile. With the buoyancy of a prima ballerina, she jumped up and skipped down to the stream, her curly pigtails bouncing along behind her.

Concern creased Hal's brow as he watched his daughter flutter away. "You know, I worry sometimes about her not eating enough."

Hal's anxiety spawned a sense of servitude in Amy, nudged her to do what she was trained to do, what once came so naturally for her. She reached over and laid a hand on his knee. His skin, exposed by the denim shorts he wore, felt warm beneath her palm.

When he looked at her, she gave him a reassuring smile. "Krista's fine, Hal. She'll eat when she's hungry."

Hal shook his head. "You sound like Robert."

"Well, Robert's right. She's healthy and happy. As long as she doesn't lose weight, she'll be fine. She is a little petite, but I suspect that's hereditary."

"Yes. Her mother was small. Five-two."

"There you go, then. I hate to have to break this to you, but you've got one perfectly normal child."

He grinned sheepishly. "I still worry about her, though." He hunched one shoulder. "I can't help it."

She patted his knee. "Spoken like a true father."

Turning her attention back to the food, she dug into a bowl for a piece of chicken, settling for a leg. She was about to sink her teeth into the first bite when she felt him watching her. Slanting him a glance, she found him grinning, his brown eyes dancing with laughter.

She closed her mouth and waved the drumstick at him in a mock threat. "Don't you dare say one word about my appetite, Hal Cooper. I've never tried it, but I think I could pack a pretty powerful wallop with this chicken leg if provoked."

Hal held up a hand in surrender. "Hey, you'll not hear me mention that that's your second piece of chicken, or that you've already finished off two helpings of potato salad."

She narrowed her eyes. "Bet I can still beat you down to the river."

One dark brow rose in amusement. "You think so?"

"I *know* so."

"Okay. On three."

Amy set her plate down. So did Hal. While they scrambled up off the ground, their gazes remained locked, each gauging the other's movements.

"One," Amy said slowly, taking the initiative in starting the count. Then, without warning, she took off running, tossing a quick "two-three" back over her shoulder.

"Hey!" Hal called after her. "That's cheating!"

Halfway to the river, she glanced back and found him close on her heels. She squealed and picked up speed. But just as she reached the water, his arm snaked around her waist. In one fluid motion, he bent and came up with her cradled in his arms. She hooked her arms around his neck.

"You cheated," Hal repeated. "And for that, you're gonna pay."

Krista, who'd abandoned her fishing pole, danced around them, clapping her hands. "Do it, Daddy! Do it!"

Amy looked from the rakish lumberjack, to the child, then back to the lumberjack, who suddenly reminded her of a wolf, a magnificent creature of the wild that had just captured some unsuspecting prey.

"Do what?" she asked, her voice small and totally void of the brazen confidence she'd possessed less than two minutes ago when she'd first issued the challenge.

"When you don't play fair, you get dunked."

Her confidence returned. "Oh yeah, right." She was fully clothed in shorts, shirt, and shoes. So was he. He wasn't going to dunk her.

He stepped into the water.

Then again, he might.

Her momentary cocky self-assuredness fled like a scared rabbit. Unlooping her arms from his neck, she braced her palms on his shoulders. "Come on, Hal. You don't want to get wet."

He merely curled his arms tighter around her. "Says who?"

"Does my opinion count?"

"Huh-uh." He stepped farther out into the water.

Amy continued to struggle, but pushing against Hal's chest was like trying to move Stone Mountain. "Come on, Hal. I have on new shoes."

"I'll buy you another pair."

"Can't. They're one-of-a-kind. Tailor-made."

His cocky grin tipped sideways. "Yeah, right. They're canvas. Very rare."

Amy looked down. Hal was thigh-deep and sinking with each step. He was going to do it. He was really going to dunk her. And that water was ice-bucket cold. In an act of desperation, she flung her arms around his neck and buried her face against him. "Okay, lumberjack. I go down, you go down."

"Have it your way, Doc." With that, he plunged beneath the frigid water.

The chill shocked her. Struggling not to gasp—which could result in her swallowing one of the scaly creatures swimming below the creek's surface—she tightened her hold on Hal.

He released her legs and slipped his arms around her waist. Then, with her body clasped tightly against his, he brought her back up.

They stood a moment holding on to each other, trying to catch their breath. Then, drawing back, Amy raked the hair away from her face and scowled at Hal, who looked tremendously pleased with himself.

"Are you happy now?" she asked, trying to sound disgruntled. Not an easy thing to do with laughter bubbling up from her chest, threatening escape.

The merriment in his eyes faded. His gaze dropped to her lips, then rose again to her eyes. "Yeah, Doc," he answered, his voice husky. "I'd say I'm pretty happy right now."

Amy's frozen body thawed in a heartbeat. She became acutely aware of his warm breath caressing her face, the rise and fall of his chest with every breath he took, his hand pressing against the small of her back.

Kiss me, she thought. *Kiss me and watch me disintegrate into a million brilliant pieces.*

"Dunk me, now, Daddy. It's my turn."

Krista's voice, although coming from the nearby shore, sounded faint and far away.

"We need to talk," Hal said.

"I know," Amy whispered.

"Tonight?" His brows rose in question. "I'll ask Mom to watch Krista."

Amy nodded.

Hal released her and turned his attention toward his daughter. "Okay, buttercup, you ready to get wet?"

Krista jumped up and down, squealing with delight.

"Wait," Amy said before Hal took his second step toward the creek bank. "You forgot something."

Hal glanced over at Amy as she stepped up beside him. "What?"

"Just this." She looped an arm across his chest, kicked his feet out from under him, and pushed him under. She was halfway to the cove when he popped up, giving her a wicked *I'll get you back* look.

She shot him an impish grin and headed for the quilt. She couldn't wait to see how he intended to "get her back."

After packing the food away and setting aside the picnic basket, she pulled the quilt around her shoulders, then sat, watching father and daughter. Amid the child's squeals of laughter and shrieks of delight, Hal would dip underwater with her, then he'd allow her to dunk him.

What a relationship, Amy thought. Would Krista, as she grew, come to realize how blessed she was to have a father like Hal? Not an action, thought, or decision was made without consideration of his daughter.

The scene opened up a bittersweet trail leading back to her own childhood. She remembered being Krista's age, the nights she fell asleep holding the book her father never got home in time to read, the dance recitals he missed, the birthday parties he never made on time. . .or forgot altogether.

Amy shook her head, forcing her thoughts back to the present, chiding herself for venturing down memory lane. When she'd rededicated her life to Christ, she'd promised herself to let go of the past and stay focused on the future—whatever that future may be.

Something pricked Amy's awareness. A sound, faint yet urgent, muffled by the gurgle of the stream and Hal and Krista's laughter. Frowning, Amy tipped her head, straining to hear.

"Help! Somebody! Please, help! Anybody! Please!"

Gooseflesh raced down Amy's arms. Someone was in trouble, and if she wasn't mistaken, the voice belonged to a child. Adrenaline kicking in, she threw off the blanket and jumped up. "Hal!"

The frolicking stopped as both father and daughter looked at Amy.

"Someone's in trouble downstream. I'm going to see what's going on."

"Wait," Hal said. "I'll go with you."

But Amy was already sprinting toward the desperate young voice. She knew when help was needed, milliseconds mattered—could even make the difference between life and death.

She tackled a dense area of growth, slapping branches out of her way, plowing through the low-growing foliage clawing at her ankles. "Hang on! I'm coming. Hang on!"

When she finally broke through to a small clearing, the sight before her threatened to stop her in her tracks, but pure gut instinct and inborn ineptness propelled her forward.

A boy around the age of ten kneeled on the creek bank. In front of him, on the rocky ground, lay another boy, perhaps a couple of years younger. He was pale and lifeless, with a pool of blood forming at the top of his head.

Amy fell to her knees on the opposite side of the injured child. "What happened?" she asked the older boy while she took a quick glance at the scarlet soil above the younger child's blond hair to gain a vague idea of how much blood had been lost.

"He—he's my br—brother," the older child managed to croak past his sobs. "I think he's dead."

While the boy explained, Amy checked his brother's breathing and found none. She tilted back his head, covered his mouth with her own, and blew.

His chest rose and fell.

She checked for a pulse. Faint but steady. "What's your name?" she asked the older child while watching, praying the younger child's chest would rise and fall on its own. It didn't. She gave another breath.

"Joey," the boy answered.

When Amy raised up to gauge the rise and fall of the child's chest, Hal was there, kneeling beside her. "Heaven help, Joey," he said. "What happened to Timmy?"

Timmy, Amy repeated to herself. Good. She had his name.

She watched Timmy's thin chest, silently willing an unprovoked rise and fall of the child's rib cage.

"H–he dove off the rocks," Joey explained. "I dared him, but I didn't think he'd really do it." A heartrending sob tore from his throat. "I killed him, Hal. I think I killed my brother!"

"You didn't kill your brother, Joey," Amy heard Hal tell the child. "You probably saved his life by getting him out of the water."

Amy hoped, prayed Joey had gotten his brother out in time. She gave another breath. Timmy's chest rose and fell, then, again, nothing. *Help me, Lord. If it be Your will, help me save this child.* "Come on, Timmy," she muttered, willing the child to fight for his life. "Breathe for me, baby. Breathe." She bent to supply him with another breath but stopped when he drew in a deep breath on his own.

"He's breathing," she said, more for the benefit of his brother than anyone else. Timmy's eyes fluttered open, and Amy felt the sharp sting of tears. She batted the moisture away. At the moment, she didn't have the time or luxury to cry.

"Hold his legs, Hal." She placed a firm hand on each of the child's shoulders. "We've got to keep him as still and calm as possible until I can check him out."

As anticipated, fear leapt into Timmy's blue eyes, and he started to struggle against them.

"Listen to me, sparky," she said in a firm but controlled voice. "You're hurt, but you're going to be fine." Still the child struggled. "Your brother is here with you, and so are your friends Hal and Krista."

"That's right, buddy," Hal said. "I'm right here. We're going to take care of you."

The struggle ebbed a bit.

Joey reached over and placed a hand on Timmy's shoulder. "Me, too, Timmy. I'm here."

At the sound of his brother's voice, the struggling ceased.

"An' me, too, Timmy," came another small voice. "I'm here, too."

Amy glanced sideways and, for the first time since running upon the injured child, noticed Krista. She kneeled at Timmy's feet, patting his ankle. Amy would smile about the precious scene later, when she knew Timmy was out of danger.

She turned her attention back to the patient.

A scowl creased his forehead. "Who are you?" he asked bluntly.

"My name is Amy. I'm a doctor." She watched his eyes, his breathing, and his head, which was still oozing blood. She held her hand out to Hal. "Give me your shirt."

He did as she requested, and she placed the shirt against the two-inch laceration on top of his head. "Does your head hurt?"

"Yes."

"Well, it should. You took quite a lick when you dove into the creek, sparky."

She glanced at Joey. "Could you please hold this cloth against your brother's head while I check out a few things?"

Nodding, Joey wiped his wet face with the back of his forearm, then reached for the shirt.

"Not too tightly," Amy instructed. "Just enough to stop the blood flow."

Palms resting on her thighs, Amy leaned over Timmy, looking deep into his eyes. "Okay, sparky, I need to ask you a few questions."

"My name ain't Sparky."

Amy quirked a brow. "Oh? It's not?" She emphatically rolled her eyes. "Right. Hal called you Buddy. That must be it."

"No. It's Timmy. T-I-M-M-Y."

"Are you sure about that?"

"I'm sure."

Thank God, Amy thought. He was coherent. "Nice to meet you, Timmy, although I would have preferred we got to know each other under different circumstances. I need to check you out before we move you. First I'm going to check your eyes. Okay?"

" 'Kay."

She bent so that she was practically nose to nose with the child, cupping her hand over one of his eyes, then pulling it quickly away, checking for proper dilation and contraction of the pupils. A darkened room and an ophthalmoscope would have been much better, but she had to do the best she could with what was available. Satisfied his eyes were both functioning properly, she proceeded to check for feeling in his arms and legs. He had equal strength in his hands when she asked him to squeeze her fingers, and he indicated he felt her brush her fingertips across his palms, his legs, and the bottoms of his feet. She found nothing in the examination indicating he shouldn't be moved. Yet something didn't feel right. Something in the pit of her stomach told her to proceed with extreme caution.

Sitting back on her heels, she muttered half to Hal, half to herself, "Everything checks out all right."

"Good. I'll carry him to the car." He leaned forward and started to pick up Timmy, and Amy almost let him. But just before Hal slipped him arms beneath the child's knees and shoulders, she placed a hand on his forearm, stopping him. He met her gaze.

"I don't think we should move him," she said.

Hal studied her face a few seconds. They both knew they could get Timmy to the clinic faster than the EMTs could get to that area on the creek and transport the boy. But Amy couldn't quell the sixth sense warning her not to move him.

"Okay," Hal agreed, sitting back on his heels.

"There's a cell phone in my purse," she told him. "I need you to call the ambulance service. You'll need to hit the SEND button twice after dialing the number."

Hal nodded and started to rise. Before he could, Amy remembered Cedar Creek had only one ambulance and grabbed his arm again. "Hal, if the EMTs are tied up, find a flat board big and strong enough to support Timmy, and a thick towel so I can brace his neck. Then call Robert and tell him to meet us at the clinic ASAP. Krista and Joey can stay here with me."

"Got it, Doc." With that, he leaned over, planted a quick kiss on her mouth, then jumped up and trotted away.

The warmth of his lips lingered on hers, even after he disappeared from sight. But she had little time to consider what the intimate gesture meant or where it would lead.

Because right now, she had a patient to see to.

Chapter 13

Forty-five minutes later, Hal, Joey, and Krista sat waiting in the clinic's reception area while Amy and Robert treated and assessed Timmy's injuries.

After five minutes of solemn silence, Joey asked in a small voice, "Hal, is Timmy going to die?"

Hal looked over at the boy, whose eyes swam with worry. The child's knuckle-white hands were clasped in his lap, and his bare feet dangled a couple of inches above the clinic's white-tiled floor. A colorful beach towel Hal had retrieved from his SUV was about to slip from the boy's shoulders.

"No, Joey, Timmy's not going to die," Hal said, adjusting the towel. "But he may have some serious injuries."

Joey's chin quivered. "I didn't mean for him to get hurt. I just dared him because he's such a wimp most the time. I didn't think he'd really do it."

Aw, man, thought Hal. He wished Joey's mother would hurry up and get there. Hal's parenting skills were limited to his five-year-old tomboy. What did one say to an adolescent boy consumed with guilt over his younger brother's injuries? Both kids knew better than to sneak down to the creek alone and without their mother's permission. Hal didn't want to excuse their disobedience, but at the same time he didn't want to make Joey feel worse.

Hal leaned forward, elbows on knees, rubbing his palms together as he gathered his thoughts. "You know, Joey, when we do something we know is wrong, we might get by with it once, maybe even twice. But eventually disobedience will result in unpleasant consequences, like it did today. You and Timmy disobeyed your mom, and the result was an accident that hurt Timmy."

A tear slipped from the inner corner of Joey's eye. He ducked his head. "I'm sorry, Hal. I didn't mean for it to happen."

"I don't want you to feel the fault's all yours, Joey. You and Timmy both knew better than to slip down to the creek alone. Besides, if you let Timmy know you think this is all your fault, he'll have you waiting on him hand and foot the rest of your life. Now, you don't want that, do you?"

Joey looked back up at Hal, the corner of his mouth twitching in a teary smile. "No."

The boy's weepy grin lifted Hal's spirits a bit. "Let this be a lesson to you," he said. "Never go down to the creek again without your mom's permission, and never *ever* go swimming without adult supervision. Got that?"

Joey nodded.

Hal gave Joey a playful elbow-to-shoulder shove. "I'm proud of you. If you hadn't pulled Timmy out of the water, he would have drowned for sure."

Joey's spine straightened a bit. Sniffing, he wiped his nose with the back of his hand, then lifted one shoulder in a seemingly nonchalant shrug. "Just did what I had to do."

Hal detected a note of pride in the boy's voice and couldn't help smiling. "Well, you did good," he said, giving Joey's shoulder another playful shove.

The front door swished open and a petite woman with short brown hair and a multitude of freckles sailed into the waiting room. "Joey, Hal, where's Timmy?"

Hal stood and gently captured Maggie Brown's upper arms. "Timmy's with the doctors," he told her. "He had a cut on his head that needed stitches, and they were going to check him out for other possible injuries."

She looked up at Hal through dark brown eyes rounded with a mixture of fear and worry. "Is he going to be okay?"

"I think so," was all Hal could tell her. Giving her arms a gentle squeeze, he added, "He's in good hands, Maggie. He's got the best with him right now."

"You're right. Robert is the best."

In her concern for her child, she'd apparently missed the information contained in Hal's words when he'd told her Timmy was in with the *doctors*. Hal was about to explain that Robert had some very reliable help when the door leading to the examination area opened and Amy stepped through it.

She paused, her eyes quickly scanning the four people in the waiting room, then her gaze settled on Maggie. "You must be Timmy's mom."

Hal dropped his hands from Maggie's arms as she turned to face Amy. "Yes, I am," Maggie said. "Are you the nurse?"

Amy didn't seem at all offended. She simply stepped forward and offered her right hand to Maggie. "My name is Amy Jordan." Then, with only the slightest hesitation, she added, "I'm a doctor. A pediatrician."

Maggie took Amy's proffered hand. "I see." Her face registered a fleeting flicker of surprise; then her son's welfare apparently took precedence over all else. "How's Timmy?" she asked, dropping Amy's hand.

"His prognosis is good, Mrs. Brown."

"Oh, thank God!" Tears sprang into the mother's eyes, and a trembling hand fluttered to her chest. "When can I see him?"

"I think right now is as good a time as any." Amy captured Maggie's elbow and guided her toward the door. "I think Timmy's pretty anxious to see you, too. Then Robert and I will need to talk to you about treatment."

Joey jumped up from where he'd been quietly sitting. "Can I come, too?"

Amy looked back and offered the boy one of her heart-stopping smiles.

"I think little heroes are allowed." She motioned with her head. "Come on." Then she shifted her gaze to Hal. "I'll be back in a minute."

With nothing else left to do, Hal sat back down beside Krista, but his thoughts remained on Amy. How would today's events affect her? Just a few short days ago, she'd told him she blamed herself for a patient's death and could no longer practice medicine. But today she hadn't been given a choice. Out there on that creek bank, she'd been forced to give a child the medical attention he needed.

On the outside, Hal had seen a doctor in complete control, confident of her every move, administering treatment with a strong and steady hand.

But what about on the inside? When the dust from Timmy's accident settled and Amy had time to think about what had taken place, how would she deal with it? Would she retreat into that shell she had helplessly fallen into after Jessica's death?

Hal refused to believe she would. She was a lot stronger than she gave herself credit for. Plus now, she had God to lean on. . .and Hal. He'd be there for her no matter what. He loved her that much. . .and more.

Fifteen minutes later, Amy strolled back into the waiting room alone.

Hal rose and opened his arms to her. She gracefully stepped into them as though their union was the most natural thing in the world. He wrapped her securely in his embrace in hopes of comforting her but wondered if he wasn't more on the receiving end. She slipped her arms around his waist and rested her head on his shoulder, then she took a deep breath and exhaled slowly. Her chest rose and fell softly against his.

Hal sighed in contentment. Having her in his arms felt so right, like they were both exactly where they were supposed to be, were born to be.

He drew back so he could see her face. That gorgeous face with the emerald eyes and the full, soft lips. How much more could his poor heart take before he sated himself with a kiss? Not something like that mindless and impulsive peck he'd given her at the creek before he dashed off to find help for Timmy, but a real kiss. He wanted to taste her, savor her, pour his heart and soul into hers, show her how much he cherished her.

But right now, standing in a waiting room while his daughter watched them with curious little eyes, was not the time or place.

Tonight, he decided. Tonight he'd tell her how he felt about her, then kiss her until they were both breathless and weak in the knees. Hopefully his heart would hold out until then.

He tucked her stubborn lock of hair behind her ear. "How's Timmy?"

"It took twelve stitches to sew up that hard head of his. I don't think he's going to like his haircut."

"I'd say right now he's just happy to be alive."

Amy worried her right lower lip, her expression turning serious. "We're transporting him to Lexington."

Surprised, Hal stepped back, but kept his hands on her upper arms. "Why?"

"He has a hairline fracture in his fifth cervical vertebra." Amy demonstrated by lifting a finger to a spot low on the back of her neck. "Right here."

"How serious is that?"

"It could have been very serious, but like I said, it's hairline, and fortunately the bone stayed intact. As far as Robert and I can tell, there's no nerve damage. That's why he still has feelings in all extremities.

"We both agreed he needs to see a specialist and probably spend a few days in the hospital, but I think he'll be fine once he heals." Her lips tipped. "To be honest, his head will probably give him more grief than his cracked vertebra. That's why he needs to be somewhere the doctors can watch him and keep him still for a while."

Hal ran his hands up and down her arms. "What about you? How are you doing?"

Her smile faded a bit, and her face took on a thoughtful expression. Her penetrating gaze captured his then slipped beneath the surface to touch that place inside him that now belonged to her.

"I'm fine," she finally said. "Really fine," she repeated with unequivocal conviction.

Hal studied her expression and in it saw a serene glow. Yes, he thought with relief, she really was fine.

He felt a tug at the bottom of his shorts and glanced down to find Krista looking up at him with somber eyes. "Daddy, will you hold me now?"

Amy pulled away from him, apparently sensing what he did—that his daughter was feeling left out, perhaps a little jealous of the new woman stepping into her father's life. A spur of panic jabbed at Hal's chest. He hoped this wasn't going to be a problem, because no matter how much he loved Amy, his daughter's happiness had to come first.

He bent and scooped up Krista, hoisting her to his hip and embracing her in an enthusiastic hug. "There's always room in my arms for you, buttercup."

Krista laid her head on her father's shoulder and peered stoically at Amy for a few seconds. Amy smiled warmly at the child but kept her distance, as though she dared not tread on forbidden territory. Hal felt the bitter hands of disappointment close around his throat. *Dear Lord, please let Krista learn to love Amy as much as I do.*

A few more pensive seconds passed, then Krista extended her hand toward Amy, curling a forefinger to summon the doctor forward. Cautiously Amy stepped up to Hal and his daughter. Raising her head, Krista curled one arm around Hal's neck and the other arm around Amy's. "I love you, Miss Amy," she said, then brushed a butterfly kiss across Amy's cheek.

Hal's knees almost buckled with relief, but he still somehow found the strength to wrap his arms around his young daughter and the woman of his dreams.

"I love you, too, Krista," Amy said, and returned a kiss to his daughter's cheek.

Oh, this is good, Hal thought. *No, not just good. Wonderful.* He had all his hopes, dreams, and happiness right here in the circle of his arms, and he knew of only one thing that could make it better.

Amy was the first to pull back. Looking down at her bloodied and muddied shirt, she said, "You know, I could really use a shower."

"So could I," Hal agreed. After handing over his shirt to stop Timmy's bleeding, he'd found a clean one in the back of his Blazer and slipped it on. But the day's events had still left him with his own share of sweat, mud, and blood. "Come on. I'll take you home so you can change, and I'll go home and do the same. Then I'll be back at your place around seven. We've got a lot to talk about."

Hal set Krista on her feet, and she immediately slipped one small hand into Hal's and the other into Amy's, establishing her place between her father and the doctor.

With a heavy heart, Amy walked outside with Hal and Krista. Hal was right, she agreed to herself. They did have a lot to talk about. Only she didn't think he was going to be pleased with what she had to tell him.

🍂

Later that evening, Amy lit the two candles she had set on her dining room table. Between the candles stood a vase of roses she'd dashed out to the florist to get. She had offered to cook—something she rarely did, but she made a pretty good beef stroganoff, and fortunately she'd had the ingredients on hand.

She wanted tonight to be special, a night to remember. She wanted to sit across from Hal and look at him through the candlelight and engrave every detail of his handsome face onto the pages of her memory. She wanted to capture the essence of his generous heart and tuck it away inside the center of her being so she could carry a part of him with her wherever she went. And she would go. It was inevitable.

A pressing ache rose in her throat. Fate had dealt her a bittersweet blow today. Sweet because Timmy's accident had forced her to accept one solid, unchangeable truth—she was a doctor. Practicing medicine was not just something she did for a living. It was her vocation, her calling. She had known it the second she put her mouth to Timmy's and offered him her breath in hopes of giving him back his life. She had known, at that moment, whatever the outcome, she would have done her best.

Like she had with little Jessica Jones that fatal night four months ago.

Amy filtered a sigh and wandered to the bay window, where she looked out at a brilliantly orange sun bowing to kiss a mountaintop in the western sky. She realized now Hal had been right about the events surrounding Jessica's death. Any doctor could have been given that file that night, and he or she would have probably done exactly what Amy did. The lot just happened to fall on her. Now Amy realized God had a reason for that. Had she not been the doctor on call that night, she'd still be in Atlanta, working ruthless hours, trying to climb the ladder of success ahead of the next guy, putting everything else in her life before God.

And while Amy knew she must go back to practicing medicine, she also realized she couldn't do it without God. He was the calm in the midst of her storm, the strength in her weakness.

"And he said unto me, My grace is sufficient for thee: for my strength is made perfect in weakness."

She'd read the verse just yesterday and remembered pausing to ponder the words, and now she stood in awe of their meaning. In her weakness, she'd found the source of her strength. That was one sweet comfort she could take with her as she stepped back into the world of medicine.

The bitter was that her return to practicing medicine meant she would have to leave the man and child she had fallen in love with. Cedar Creek already had one doctor—an excellent one. Amy didn't think the sleepy little town was quite big enough for two. Even if she went into practice in one of the nearby larger towns, she knew firsthand the sacrifices forced upon a doctor's family. She'd never ask that of Hal and Krista.

She shifted her weight and leaned a shoulder against the window frame. Tonight she would be with Hal. Perhaps, if fate would allow, she'd hold him in her arms once more.

And then. . .

Tears blurred the sun's orange blaze. Then she would break his heart. That thought hurt worse than the breaking of her own.

The doorbell rang. Amy blinked away the moisture and checked the table one last time to make sure everything was in place. Then, pulling back her shoulders and drawing in a deep breath, she went to answer the door.

🦋

When Amy opened the door, she took Hal's breath away. She was beyond beautiful. She wore a sleeveless teal dress, belted at her tiny waist, with a full skirt that whispered around her ankles. A rosy blush touched her cheeks, and her lips shimmered with pink gloss. And for the first time since he'd met her, her hair was down. Those glorious tresses hung in soft curves around her shoulders and shone like a golden halo under the foyer light. His hands itched to touch it, test its silkiness between his fingertips.

Later, he reminded himself. He wanted to woo her in little by little, show her he knew how to treat her just like the lady she was.

"Come in," she said with a radiant smile.

As he stepped over the threshold, the hearty scent of stewed beef greeted him, but her own elegant scent slipped past the cuisine's aroma and coiled around his senses, drawing him into a heady dream with her at center stage. He stuffed his hands into his pockets to keep from reaching for her.

She led him into the dining room, where he found the table draped in white linen and bathed in candlelight, with a crystal vase of six red roses for a center-piece. He released a silent sigh of contentment. Tonight was going to be perfect. Just perfect.

During the meal they engaged in small talk, and thirty minutes later, Hal pushed away an empty plate and folded his arms on the table. "That was delicious."

"Thank you," she said quietly. Come to think of it, she had been quieter than usual since his arrival. He had done most of the talking. She'd pushed her plate away several minutes ago, having eaten very little, and Hal noticed her eyes looked tired. Perhaps it was the excitement of the day catching up with her.

"Are you okay?" he asked.

"Yes." She sat up a little straighter and sent him a smile that seemed forced. "I was, um. . .just thinking about Timmy."

"Have you heard from him since we left the clinic?"

"I called the hospital in Lexington about an hour ago. He had arrived and they were headed to X-ray with him."

"Tell me something, Amy. When you were examining Timmy at the creek, did you find anything to indicate his neck might be broken?"

Leaning on her forearms, she clasped her hands. "No, I didn't."

"Then how did you know not to move him?"

She focused on a candle for a moment, the reflection of the flame dancing in her eyes, then looked back at him. "It's hard to explain, really. There are times when I'm examining a patient that I get this feeling"—she pressed a fist against her diaphragm—"right here. It's like a sixth sense telling me what I should or should not do."

"Gut instinct?" Hal guessed.

One corner of her mouth tipped. "Yes. Gut instinct. I know that sounds crazy, but—"

"No, it doesn't. I get the same feeling sometimes when I'm talking to God. It's like He nudges me in the right direction whenever I'm in doubt or confused about something."

She cast her eyes downward. "I know what you mean. I've been experiencing a little of that lately myself."

He reached over with one hand and laced his fingers through hers, willing her to look back up at him. When she did, he said, "You say that like it's a bad thing."

With her free hand, she brushed a lock of silky hair over her shoulder. "I didn't mean to. I'm just. . ." She paused, worried her right lower lip, then smiled. "I'm glad you came tonight, Hal. It means a lot to me."

"Me, too." He squeezed her hand. "Why don't we move this conversation to the living room?"

She merely nodded.

He circled the table and held her chair while she rose, then followed her into the living room. Her steps slowed and stopped in the center of the room, and she just stood there with her pencil-straight back to him for a long moment. What was she thinking? Surely she sensed things were about to change between them. Destiny had been leading them this way from the moment they met.

Finally she turned and looked at him, and his world spun out of control. Every enamored emotion he had held at bay since the moment he first found her unconscious on the side of the road rushed forward and crashed head-on in the center of his chest. His heart pounded with such fury, he thought it would burst right through his rib cage and fall at her feet.

Now. It had to be now.

"I love you, Amy." His racing heart slowed a bit, like the release of those four small words was just what it needed to calm its erratic beat.

He held his breath while he waited for her reaction.

For what seemed like an eternity, she stood statue still, her expression stoic, her body rigid. Then tears rose in her eyes, and she began to tremble.

A dark hand of foreboding reached inside Hal and pulled the plug on his rising tide of happiness. Somehow he knew the moisture pooling on her lower lids was not tears of joy.

"I love you, too, Hal." Her soft voice was brimming with pain.

Hal stepped forward, raised his hands, and slid his palms up and down her upper arms. Her heart was breaking. He could see it in her face, in the tear that escaped from the corner of her eye. "Tell me what's wrong, Amy."

Wetting her lips, she swallowed. "I'm leaving Cedar Creek."

His hands stopped moving and he just stared at her, wondering if he had heard correctly. "Leaving?" he finally managed to ask.

"Yes."

No!

The silent scream ripped through his veins. This was not happening, Hal told himself. He was merely having a bad dream. He'd fallen asleep in his easy chair at home and would soon wake up, rush to Amy's house, find her table dressed in white linen and candlelight, sweep her into his arms, and tell her he loved her. And that would be that. Fifty years from now, they'd be sitting on their front porch swing holding hands while watching their great-grandchildren play in the yard.

But the burning ache rising in his chest told him he wasn't having a dream. He was wide awake and being catapulted into a living nightmare.

She raised a palm to his cheek. "I'm sorry, Hal."

Sorry? She tells me she loves me but she's leaving in almost the same breath, and all she can say is "I'm sorry"? He grasped her hand and pulled it down to his chest. "May I ask why you're leaving?" His voice rang bitter with frustration, but he couldn't help it. Her leaving had not been in his plans.

"I'm going back into practice."

Somewhere amid the disillusionment and confusion dousing his hopes and dreams, a spark of jubilation ignited. He framed her face with desperate hands. "Amy, that's great. No one could be happier for you than me, because no one could love you more than I do. You're a wonderful doctor and have a lot to offer others. But why can't you practice in Cedar Creek?"

"Oh, Hal. I wish that were possible. But Cedar Creek already has a doctor. I don't think the town can support two. Besides, if I opened a practice here, it would be like going into competition with Robert, and I could never do that to him. He's been too good of a friend to me."

"You know he wouldn't look at it that way."

"You're right, he probably wouldn't. But I'd have to live with myself."

Hal searched for another argument but couldn't find one. His mind had gone numb, his legs felt like they'd been chopped off at the knees. He slid his hands to her shoulders. "When?" he wanted to know.

"I promised Robert and Linda I'd stay until after the baby was born. Two months, three at the most."

"What do we do 'til then?"

"Nothing."

"Nothing?" He shook his head in indignant disbelief. "Tell me how I'm supposed to live this close to you, in the same town with you, feeling the way I do about you and do nothing about it."

Her eyes brimmed with sad acceptance. "Hal, we have to think of Krista."

Ice water splashed in his face couldn't have jolted his senses more. She was right. He couldn't bring her into his daughter's life knowing their time together would be limited. In the end, it'd break his little girl's heart.

Hal dropped his hands and stepped back. He felt cold and empty, which was probably good. Because when the numbness wore off and the pain set in, he didn't know how he would bear it.

He raked a hapless hand through his hair, trying to collect his wits enough to figure out what he should do next. "Well, I guess that's it, then," he finally managed to say. "I should be going."

He took one last look at Amy, standing in the middle of the living room, her arms crossed, her eyes now dry but her face still streaked with tears. Oh, how his arms ached to hold her, his hands longed to touch her. But it wasn't meant to be. She'd been no more than a beautiful dream after all.

He drew in a deep, painful breath of resignation. She'd done the right thing in ending it now, before his daughter got hurt. A small part of him had to be grateful to Amy for that.

He crammed his hands into his pockets. "I. . .uh. . .guess I'll see you around."

"Yes," she whispered, like a single breath of air was all she had left.

A suffocating sensation pressed on his chest, overwhelming him. He had to get out now, while he still had the strength. "I'll see myself out." With that, he turned and walked to the front door on unsteady legs, then he wandered to his car like an aimless drunk, putting one wobbly foot in front of the other until he reached his destination then wondered how in the world how he'd gotten there.

He opened the car door but stopped short of getting in and gritted his teeth. *How dare she.* His grip on the door handle tightened to knuckle-white. Anger coiled inside him like a boxer's fist, pushing upward until he saw red. *How dare she tell me she loves me then dash my hopes like they were thin bubbles floating on the air! If she is so bent on leaving, fine. But by Ned, I'll give her something to remember me by.*

He slammed the car door and marched back up the sidewalk. Without bothering to knock, he opened the door and sailed through it.

"Amy!"

In an instant she stepped from the living room, her already tear-dampened eyes wide with question. "Did you forget something?"

"Yeah." He strolled forward, pulled her into his arms, and covered her mouth with his with all the finesse of a hungry lion.

At first, she was too shocked to do anything and just stood there, her eyes wide and her body rigid. Undaunted, he deepened the kiss, unleashing all his anger and frustration on her soft, pliant lips.

When he felt her arms circle his neck and her body go soft against his, a moan of release escaped his throat. He slid his hand up her spine and buried his hand in her hair, curling his fingers around its silky softness.

The kiss turned tender, seeking, like two desert dwellers drinking from a well about to go dry, greedily savoring every pure, sweet drop. They may not have each other, but at least they'd have this. This kiss, this memory.

When Hal's lungs were about to explode, he pulled back and studied her face, her eyes, her mouth, so he could lock every detail of her away in his dreams. Because he knew with certainty no woman would ever fill them the way Amy did.

She looked at him through misty eyes full of question and bewilderment. "Hal, I—"

He pressed a finger to her lips. "Gut instinct," he said, then turned and walked away.

Chapter 14

A my?" The receptionist's voice filtered through Amy's telephone intercom. With her gaze fixed on her computer screen, Amy absentmindedly reached over with one hand and pressed a button, leaving the other hand on the keyboard. "Yes."

"You have a call on line two."

"Thank you." Amy pulled her gaze away from the screen long enough to pick up the receiver, target the blinking button, and punch it, then, sandwiching the receiver between her ear and shoulder, she turned her attention back to the monitor. "Amy Jordan. May I help you?"

"Hello, sweetheart."

Amy straightened her spine, barely catching the handset before it slipped from her shoulder. "Dad?"

"How are you doing?"

"Fine," she said a bit too quickly. Actually she was shocked. Since she'd rededicated her life to Christ, she'd phoned her father twice. The first conversation had been a bit stilted, like two strangers sharing a bus seat and searching for something to say to break the monotony of their journey. The second had been a little easier, more like old friends trying to catch up after a long separation. But this was the first time since she'd moved to Cedar Creek that he'd called her. There had to be a reason.

"Is everything okay, Dad?"

"Yes," came his quick reply. "Everything's fine. I was just. . ." He cleared his throat. "I was just thinking about you."

And I've been praying for you, she wanted to say but didn't. She didn't want to push. If they were ever to have a congenial father-daughter relationship, it would have to be in God's time. All Amy had felt led to do so far was reach out to her father. And pray.

Amy swiveled away from her computer and propped an elbow on her desk. "I've been thinking about you a lot lately, too, Dad."

"Yes, ah, well. . ."

Amusement tipped Amy's lips. Engaging in personal conversation made Nicholas Jordan as comfortable as a novice public speaker delivering his first speech. But her father was trying, and with time, he'd get better at it. She was sure.

"I'm taking a couple of days off week after next," he continued. "I thought

233

I'd fly up your way. You know. . ."

Amy could almost see him shrugging one shoulder, almost hear him jangle the keys in his pocket. Character traits she somehow remembered even though they'd spent so little time together.

"Spend some time with you," he finished.

Amy smiled her first heartfelt smile in three weeks. That's how long it'd been since Hal had walked into her house, kissed her senseless, then walked back out the door. . .out of her life.

Thoughts of Hal brought a lump to her throat. Swallowing the knot, she said, "That would be nice, Dad."

They talked on a few more minutes, then Amy hung up the phone with an imminent sense of peace. She and her father were finally connecting, communicating after a lifetime of alienation. It made her wonder what would have happened if she had reached out to him sooner.

She released a despondent sigh. At least something was going right in her life. She stood and wandered to the window. For almost three weeks now, in a desperate attempt to stay close to Hal and Krista, Amy had searched—and prayed—for a nearby town that needed a pediatrician. Maybe a small community within reasonable commuting distance where she could put in a satisfying day's work and still have time for Hal and Krista. . .

A place like Cedar Creek.

But every inquiry she'd made, she'd met with a dead end.

Resting her forehead against the cool windowpane, she looked out at the rugged Cumberland Gap Mountains, christened by a kaleidoscope of fall color: golds, oranges, and reds. And at the foot of those mountains the tiny town of Cedar Creek lay like a precious jewel cradled in her majesty's lap.

A reminiscent smile touched Amy's lips. Just a few short weeks ago this charming little community with its friendly but wary population and its solitary grocery store had felt like a strange and foreign country to her. Now it held a special and permanent place inside her, just like Hal and Krista.

Her smile faded as a dull ache rose in her chest. Hal and Krista. How would she ever live without them?

Her chin quivered. She pursed her lips. *Accept it, Amy,* she told herself. *It just wasn't meant to be.*

A shuddery sigh left her chest. Deep down, she knew she would be all right. God was big enough and strong enough to fill the gaping wound in her heart. And somehow, someway, she and Hal would both move on. Someday they'd be able to look back on the short time they'd had together as a fond and cherished memory.

Amy had told herself that countless times over the past three weeks. And she'd pretty much made up her mind that was how things must be. She would leave Cedar Creek. It was God's will.

Now all she had to do was convince her heart.

Much later that day, Amy was reorganizing a file cabinet when a knock sounded on her office door. "Come in," she called in response.

The door opened, and Robert stepped inside, frowning when he saw her. "You don't look so good."

She closed the file drawer a little harder than intended. "You and Linda are the only two people in the world who could get away with telling me that."

He strolled to her desk, pulled out one of the guest chairs, and sat down. "We're worried about you. You look like you haven't slept or eaten in days."

She hadn't. Not much, anyway. And her weariness and loneliness were apparently beginning to show.

Drawing back her shoulders, she ambled to her desk. "I'm fine, Robert." She pulled out her chair and sank down. "I'm just a little tired. That's all."

"Then why are you still here? The office closed over an hour ago."

Just trying to stay busy, she thought. *Trying to keep my mind occupied and my brain busy so I can get through another day without Hal's presence in my life.*

Oh, she had seen him a few times, around town and at church. But the encounters had been awkward, like two bad actors in an amateur play forgetting their lines and bungling through a lousy ad-lib. And the meetings always managed to leave her missing him more than if she hadn't seen him at all.

How was she going to survive living in this town two more months, looking for him around every corner, seeing him from time to time but never able to reach out and touch him or satisfy her need to hold him?

"Amy?"

She blinked, snapping back to the here and now. "Yes?"

"Didn't you hear me?"

Yes, she'd heard him. But what had he said? She searched her short-term memory and came up empty. "I'm sorry, Robert. My mind strayed. What was it you said?"

"I said if you're tired, why are you still here? The office closed an hour ago."

"Oh." She hesitated, searching her mind for an excuse. She couldn't tell him the real reason she was spending so much time at work. "I'm just trying to catch up," she finally said.

"By cleaning out a file cabinet you organized less than two months ago? I don't think so."

She hunched one shoulder. "Has to be done sometime."

A brief silence fell between them, and an instinctive knot twisted in Amy's stomach. Somehow she knew where Robert was headed with the conversation, and she didn't want to go there.

But before she could change his direction, he said, "I saw Hal yesterday."

A smothery feeling rose in her chest. Dropping her gaze, she thumbed a stack of outgoing mail. "That's nice," she muttered as nonchalantly as she could manage, hoping she sounded more convincing to Robert than she did to herself. "How are he, his mom, and Krista doing?"

"I imagine Krista and Ellen are doing fine, but Hal looks as miserable as you."

Her busy hands stilled. She raised her lashes, meeting his smug expression with an irritated scowl. "Just what makes you think you know so much about Hal and me?"

A knowing grin curved his lips. "I may be a busy man, Amy, but I've got eyes." With a forefinger, he tapped the rim of his glasses. "Twenty-twenty with these babies. And I think I know my two best friends pretty well. You two were headed down lovers' lane just a few weeks ago. Now, whenever you meet, it's like two porcupines passing each other in a drainpipe."

She didn't argue. What was the point? Robert pretty much had her pegged.

Leaning on her forearms, she clasped her hands tightly. "I really don't want to talk about Hal," she said past the catch in her throat. "We do need to talk about my job here, though." Robert had been so busy at the clinic lately that she hadn't had a chance to talk to him about her plans to leave after Linda had the baby. But since he was here now, sitting at her desk and obviously in a talking mood, she figured she'd better seize the opportunity so he could be working on her replacement.

He settled back, crossing an ankle over the opposite knee. "You're right," he surprised her by saying. "We do need to talk about your job."

"Is something wrong?" She wouldn't be surprised if he said yes. After all, she hadn't been on top of things lately.

"Yes," he said, echoing her thoughts.

With her fingertips, she kneaded her closed eyes, gritty from loss of sleep and tears. "I'm sorry, Robert. I guess I'm just not cut out to be an office manager."

"Boy, I'll say," came his quick reply.

That did it. She was tired and irritable, and his impudent response rubbed her the wrong way. Opening her eyes, she dropped her hands to the desktop with a *thud* and leveled him with a glower. "First you tell me I look horrible, then that I'm doing a poor job. I'm beginning to wonder if I want to keep you as a friend."

He shook his head. "You misunderstand me, Amy. You're doing a wonderful job. But you don't belong in here behind a desk. You belong out there"—he pointed a thumb over his shoulder—"with your patients."

Propping her chin in her hand, she released a weary sigh. "I know."

Surprise jerked his head back a couple of inches. "You do?"

Her lips tipped. "Yes, I do." She went on to tell him how her experience with Timmy and her newfound faith in God had given her the courage to return to practicing medicine. By the time she finished, he was all smiles.

Sitting back, he pushed his glasses up the bridge of his nose. "Good. Now you can come into practice with me."

This time, it was she who yanked her head back in surprise. "You can't be serious."

"On the contrary, Dr. Jordan. I am *very* serious."

As she studied his zealous expression, suspicion crept in. "Has Hal been talking to you?"

Robert's brow dipped in confusion. "About what?"

"About my going into practice with you."

"Why would he?"

"To keep me in Cedar Creek."

"Oh." Robert nodded in understanding then shook his head in denial. "No. Hal hasn't said anything to me about you."

She glanced away in order to mask her disappointment. "Good. Because I don't need any favors. I can always go back to Atlanta to practice." Looking back at him, she added, "The senior partners at Mercy told me I had a place there if I ever decided to go back."

He raked his fingers through his thick brown hair. An unruly lock fell across his forehead. "At the risk of sounding selfish, I'm not offering you a partnership so much as a favor to you as I am a favor to myself."

She scrutinized him a moment, wondering about the truth in his statement. She knew he *would* offer her a partnership as a favor to her, just as he knew she would *never* accept a handout. But the earnestness in his eyes and the sincerity on his face told her he was being honest with her, and a thin thread of hope wove through her.

Still, she had to be sure. "Robert, you always manage to see all the patients. How would I be doing you a favor by taking half of that away from you?"

Settling back in his seat, he laced his hands over his flat stomach. "Amy, one of the reasons I came to Cedar Creek is because I didn't want to get caught in the same trap our fathers did. Working night and day and having nothing left over to give my family. But lately that's exactly what I've been doing. I knew when I came here it would take awhile to earn the community's trust, but it looks like I finally have. More and more patients are coming to the clinic rather than driving to a neighboring town to see a doctor like they once had to do, and I'm having to work like crazy to see them all.

"Right now it's"—he checked his watch—"six o'clock. This is the first time in weeks I've finished up before seven. Not to mention the three emergency calls I received in the middle of the night this week. And no offense to you, but I'd much rather be home right now, cuddling with my pregnant wife, than sitting here trying to persuade you to go into practice with me. But I know this discussion is necessary. The sooner I can convince you how much you're needed here, the better for the both of us."

Amy sat in shocked silence. Was she dreaming? Or was this a splendid reality? A prayer answered?

Her mind spun with confusion. She pressed her fingers to her temples. "Robert, I don't know what to say."

"Say yes." When she didn't immediately, he once again leaned forward, folding his arms on his desk. "Think about it, Amy. I'm a family practitioner; you're a pediatrician. I'll see the adults; you'll see the children. The balance would be perfect. This town is small enough and the patients few enough that we could both put in a satisfying day's work and still have time to spend with our families."

His features softened. "Amy, I want to have time to hold my daughter when she gets here, rock her to sleep, even change a diaper or two. I want to go to bed at night and hold my wife when I'm not so tired I'm asleep before my head hits the pillow.

"And you, Amy. I know you. If you go back to Mercy, you'll end up meeting everyone else's needs but your own. If you stay here, you can pour yourself into your work and still have time to watch Krista grow. You can be there for Hal when he's put in a hard day at work, and vice versa."

In her mind Amy repeated Robert's list of reasons for her to accept his offer.

Pour herself into her work.

Watch Krista grow.

Be there for Hal.

Everything she wanted. Exactly what she'd prayed for.

The shadows lifted from her heart, and the confusion vanished from her mind. No wonder she hadn't been able to find a nearby town to practice in. God already had a place picked out for her, right here in Cedar Creek.

Robert leaned back. "If you want to take a few days to think about my offer, then, of course, I understand."

A few days? She didn't even need a few minutes. "I have only one question for you," she said.

"What's that?"

"When do I start?"

A huge grin split Robert's face. "How about Monday? We'll shuffle the paperwork between us until we find another office manager."

"Great." She grabbed her purse from her bottom desk drawer, jumped up, and flitted around her desk like a hummingbird. Bending down, she planted a sisterly kiss on Robert's cheek. "Lock up for me, will you?" With that, she headed for the door.

"Hey, where are you going in such a hurry?"

Without breaking her stride, she glanced back. "To see Hal, of course."

When Amy knocked on the door, Ellen Cooper opened it. "Oh, Amy, dear, I am so glad to see you." She captured Amy's upper arm and pulled her inside. "Our woodshed is overflowing."

"Pardon?" Amy said, not having the vaguest idea what the older woman was talking about.

Ellen fanned a hand through the air. "Never mind. Hal's out back. Follow me." She led Amy through the foyer and living room, stopping at the french doors leading out onto the patio.

Beyond the door's clear panes, Amy saw him. Ax in hand, he stood next to a woodpile at the far edge of the backyard, his sinewy, sweat-dampened back glistening in the setting sun. Drawn by the mesmerizing spell he always cast over her, Amy inched forward until her breath painted a small foggy circle on the glass.

With his free hand, he withdrew a log from the woodpile and set it end-up on a large stump; then he raised the ax over his head and brought it down with whiplash force. The log split, the two halves launching in opposite directions. He bent, picking up the half nearest him, and stood it upright on the stump.

"Well," Ellen said from where she stood beside Amy, "I'll let you take it from here." Then, shaking her head, the older woman walked away muttering, "That boy never could keep his shirt on."

Amy opened the door and slipped outside but didn't leave the patio; she just stood watching the finest specimen of a man she'd ever laid eyes on. And he loved her.

For a split instant, her mind spun to her old life and what she was leaving behind. She'd experienced the glitter and glamour of city life, rubbed shoulders with some of the world's most renowned doctors, known the privileges wealth could buy. But all that paled when compared to what lay ahead of her—the love of an honorable man and faith in a God who would never forsake her.

A window of revelation opened up to her and words from the popular Twenty-third Psalm poured from her memory.

"He leadeth me beside the still waters. He restoreth my soul."

Her entire being overflowed with peace, filling her joy cup to the brim. Truly when God led her to a sleepy little town called Cedar Creek, He had led her to still waters—and restored her soul.

Hal started to raise the ax once more, then, as though sensing her presence, twisted his upper body around. Their gazes locked, and at least a dozen giddy butterflies took flight in Amy's stomach. She felt like she was about to step into the happy ending of a fairy tale.

Without taking his eyes off her, he laid aside the ax and reached for a shirt draped across the back of a nearby lawn chair.

Simultaneously they started toward each other, he fastening buttons, and she so light on her feet, she barely felt the ground beneath her. They stopped with less than a foot separating them and stood looking at each other for a moment in silence.

Dark circles ringed his eyes, and his face appeared thinner. Had he lost weight? Regret pressed down upon her. Whatever made her think she could leave him? "Hi," he finally said.

"Hi."

His gaze roamed her face. "You look good."

Liar, she thought. "Thank you," she said aloud. "You don't."

Shaking his head, he released a halfhearted chuckle. "You never cease to amaze me, Doc." Then his spiritless joviality faded. "I was going to call you tonight."

She arched her brows. "You were?"

"Yeah." He nodded. "I wanted to come over and talk to you."

"Oh? What about?"

He slipped his fingers into his jeans' pockets. "I've been thinking. About us." He glanced away for a few seconds, as though considering his next words, then looked back to her. "You know, if you practiced somewhere like Lexington, we could move halfway between here and there. At the most, each of us would only have an hour's commute."

So he'd come up with a plan for them to be together. She almost laughed out loud with delight. He wasn't any more willing to let her go than she was willing to lose him. Feeling a bit impish, she crossed her arms. "You think that would work?"

"I think we could make it work. Don't you?"

She cocked her head to one side. "What if I don't want to practice in Lexington?"

His shoulders drooped. "Then Krista and I will go with you wherever you want to go."

Tears burned the back of her throat. "You'd do that for me?"

He raised his hand to her upper arms and rubbed up and down. "Amy, I'd do anything for you. I don't particularly want to leave Cedar Creek. But I'd do it before losing you."

Amy would have never thought it possible, but at that moment, her love for him grew. Heart overflowing, she lifted her hands to his face, reveling in the prickly feel of his day-old beard beneath her palms. The windows of heaven seemed to open and flood her soul with liquid sunshine. She loved this man. Oh, how she loved him.

"What if I were to tell you I've been doing some thinking of my own," she said, "and I've come up with a way we can be together without leaving Cedar Creek?"

The rise and fall of his chest intensified. "I'd be interested in hearing it."

She let her hands fall to his chest, just to feel his rapid heartbeat keeping time with her own. "What if I were to tell you Robert's offered me a partnership in his practice, and I accepted?"

The pulsing beneath her fingertips quickened even more. "You did?" he asked, sounding like a kid afraid of getting his hopes up.

"Of course, silly. Why should we live halfway between here and anywhere else when we don't have to?"

She felt his arms circle her waist and saw hope rise in his eyes. "Tell me this is real, Doc. Tell me I'm not dreaming."

A coy smile tipped her lips as she slid her arms around his neck. "Why don't I just show you?" She pulled him close and kissed him, telling him with her heart what she knew he wanted to hear. When she drew back, she said, "Well, what do you think? Dream or reality?"

He pulled her back into the circle of his arms, tipping his head toward hers. "I don't know," he said with a rakish grin. "I haven't made my mind up yet."

Chapter 15

Five months later

Outside the Cooper home, a frigid March wind sliced through the crisp evening air. But inside, all was warm and cozy.

An inviting fire popped and crackled in the fireplace. In a rocking chair flanking the hearth, Ellen sat, reading glasses perched on the end of her nose. Her agile hands skillfully worked her knitting needles, building stitches on what would soon be a new afghan for Krista's bed.

On the sofa, between Hal and Amy, Krista sat with her rosy cheek resting against Amy's upper arm, listening while Amy read the story of Hannah and Samuel. Amy paused a moment and glanced over at her husband. He sat with his legs stretched out and crossed at the ankles, his hands clasped over his abdomen, his head laid back on the top of the sofa. His chest rose and fell with the steady rhythm of slumber.

Poor guy. He'd had such a hard day at work. She felt an overwhelming need to reach over and brush the backs of her fingers across his jaw.

"Tell me what happens next, Mama."

Krista's voice penetrated Amy's thoughts, and she continued with the story.

The four months Amy had been married to Hal had been the best of her life. The immense pleasure she found in simple things—the feel of Krista's hand in hers, a quiet evening spent with her new family, hearing Hal say "I love you" every day—never ceased to amaze her.

Only one thing could make her life more complete, and she'd see what Hal had to say about it later on tonight.

"So," she continued, finishing the story, "God gave Hannah a son, and Hannah named the child Samuel."

She looked down at Krista, who stared at the book, her lips pursed, one corner of her mouth tucked in. Amy knew that expression well. It meant her daughter was doing some heavy thinking.

After half a minute of thoughtful silence, Krista glanced up at Amy. "Do you think if I pray for a baby brother, God will give me one?"

Before Amy could respond, Hal snapped to attention, opening his eyes and sitting up straight. "Okay, buttercup," he said. "Time for you to go to bed."

Amy grinned. Her husband hadn't been sleeping after all.

Later, while Amy sat at the dresser in her and Hal's bedroom, brushing her hair, he came in, closing and locking the door behind him. A giddy flutter of anticipation fluttered in her chest.

He stepped up behind her, and with his gentle, work-roughened hands, started kneading her shoulders. "So, my beautiful wife, I finally have you all to myself."

Laying aside the brush, Amy rested the back of her head against his abdomen, meeting his reflected gaze in the mirror. "I love you, Hal."

A lazy half smile touched his lips. "I love you, too, Dr. Cooper."

Sweeping aside her hair, he leaned down and pressed a whisper-soft kiss just below her ear. Gooseflesh raced over her body, but she resisted the desire to turn into the embrace she knew awaited her. She had something to tell her husband, and if she didn't do so now, she'd never get to it tonight.

"Hal?"

"Mmm?" he responding, still raining kisses on her neck.

"Do you think Krista will be disappointed if God gives her a baby sister instead of a baby brother?"

He mumbled something that sounded like, "Don't know."

Amy's shoulders drooped. She rolled her eyes. "Honey, you're not listening to me."

He raised his head, looking at her mirrored reflection with a confused and somewhat impatient frown marring his forehead. "Do we have to talk about this now?"

"Better now than when he or she gets here. . .don't you think?"

Amy watched while Hal's disgruntled expression changed to one of wonder. "Exactly what are you saying, sweetheart?"

"That come November, Krista should get her wish. That is, if it's a boy."

Hal blinked. "You mean. . . ?"

Amy nodded.

He kneeled, turning her around to face him. Mixed emotions played across his face—awe, amazement, unquestionable love. He laid his palm on her flat stomach. She covered his hand with her own.

"Wow," he whispered, as though he could already feel the baby kicking.

"Yes," she whispered back. "Wow."

Hal closed the distance between him and his wife, a tear of joy in his eye and a prayer of thanksgiving in his heart.

GINA FIELDS

Gina is a lifelong native of northeast Georgia. She is married to Terry, and they have two very active young sons. When Gina is not writing, singing, or playing piano, among a hundred homemaking activities, she enjoys volunteering for Special Olympics.

Come Home to My Heart

JoAnn A. Grote

To the members of the Forsyth Fellowship of Christian Writers,
who believed in my writing before I sold a single manuscript:
Margaret Dyson, Martha Green, Debbie Barr Stewart, Allene Robinson,
and the late Catherine Jackson.
Thank you for your prayers, advice, encouragement, and love.

Prologue

Ellie Carter reached one red-mittened hand out and slowly lowered the door on the mailbox. The cold metal screeched in protest. The December wind spiraled through the Blue Ridge Mountain village's short, winding main street, tugging at the brown hair that escaped Ellie's stocking hat. She didn't notice.

Her mittened fingers squeezed more tightly about the square envelope. If she mailed it, it would change her life and her son Corey's life.

She pulled the envelope back and released the door. It closed with a *bang*.

Ellie stared at it unseeing. She trembled all over. She'd spent months building the courage to mail this letter. If she turned away now, would she ever regain the strength to send it?

She grasped the door, opened it, and dropped in the envelope. It disappeared silently into the black hole. Her chest felt as though it would split open in fear. *Have I just destroyed my son's life?*

Chapter 1

I *have a son.* The thought filled Travis Carter's mind and heart to the exclusion of everyone and everything else.

The sanctuary was fragrant with the scent of pine and burning candles. Organ, trombones, clarinets, and trumpets burst forth in a joyous rendition celebrating the gift of God's Son. The music filled the Los Angeles church with glorious expectation while parishioners waited for the Christmas Eve service to begin.

Travis wasn't thinking of God's Son. His mind was filled with the stunning knowledge that he had a son of his own. He slipped his hand beneath his finely tailored gray suit coat to rest over the monogrammed pocket on his white shirt. He could feel the picture through the cloth. He'd placed the picture there so it would be close to his heart during the service. He wished he could pull it out and stare at it, drink in the image of the laughing two-year-old.

Not that he needed to see the photo to remember what the boy—his son, Corey Travis Carter—looked like: a mass of curly blond hair, blue eyes, pointed chin, a face filled with every two-year-old's joy in discovering something new every day about this experience called life.

The news about Corey had come in an innocent-looking envelope that arrived with the usual handful of Christmas cards in the mail. His heart had stopped beating for a moment when he saw his estranged wife's name, Ellie, in the return address. His hands shook as he opened the envelope. Inside was a simple Christmas card, a picture, and a short, to-the-point note from Ellie saying her conscience wouldn't allow her to keep the knowledge of their son from him any longer.

How long had he stood, not moving, staring at that picture? Disbelief, shock, anger, and finally joy had swept over and through him, leaving him feeling as weak as if he'd swum a mile through heavy surf. When he'd finally roused himself, he'd barely had time to make it to the Christmas Eve service.

As Christmas music swelled about him, questions raced through his mind. Why hadn't Ellie told him about Corey before? She must have been pregnant when they separated three years earlier. His heart burned at the realization that she may have known she was pregnant when she left. Why had she decided *now* to tell him about Corey? Did she need financial help? She hadn't said anything in the note about child support.

Ellie hadn't said anything about arranging for him to meet the child either.

Had she thought he wouldn't want to meet his own son? Of course he wanted to meet him, get to know him. Would Ellie consider bringing Corey to Los Angeles? Not likely, given how eagerly she'd fled back to the North Carolina mountains when they separated.

Pain ribboned through him as he recalled the days leading up to the separation. He'd been in his first year at the prestigious Los Angeles law firm of Longfellow, Drew, and Prentice, where he still worked, and nervous at attending the company's first Christmas party at the senior partner's home. . . .

Travis paused, one hand tight about Ellie's arm, and stared at the brilliantly lit, huge house in front of them. He took a ragged breath. Anticipation was edging out the anger that filled him from the argument he and Ellie had had earlier. "This is it. See you don't do anything to embarrass me."

"I'm sure you can accomplish that without any help from me." She jerked her arm, but he kept his hold on it and started up the walk. He stared straight ahead and could tell she was doing the same.

Travis plastered on a smile when they entered, though it was only a servant who greeted them at the door. Moments later they stood at the edge of the largest living room Travis had ever seen. He counted six overstuffed white sofas and love seats, mixed with antique chairs which looked too uncomfortable for a man to sit upon, arranged in three groupings for easy conversing. Original oil paintings graced the walls. A fire danced and crackled merrily in the fireplace. A Christmas tree which reached the vaulted two-story ceiling glistened with crystal ornaments and perfumed the air with pine scent. A wall of windows, also reaching from floor to ceiling, looked out upon a stone-walled patio. In front of the windows a string quartet played baroque music. Men in tuxedos and women in gowns and jewels mixed laughter and voices with the music.

He heard the sharp intake of Ellie's breath. She touched the fingers of one hand to the base of her throat. "It's beautiful."

It was beautiful. A fierce desire filled him. This home was a symbol of Edward Longfellow's extraordinary success as a lawyer. Travis could see the tall man's head of thick white hair above a group of guests ten feet away. Longfellow glanced in their direction, smiled in recognition, and started toward them.

Travis leaned toward Ellie and said in a low voice from which he couldn't disguise his eagerness, "One day we'll have a place like this."

"Glad you could make it." Edward Longfellow shook Travis's hand then turned to Ellie. "Good to see you again, Ellie."

It was so like the man to remember Ellie's name, Travis thought, though he'd met her only once before. The partner made it a point to know everything and everyone important to the people important to him. Travis knew he was important to Longfellow, though only because as a member of his firm—even a lowly first-year lawyer—clients and potential clients saw him as a representative of the older man's company.

Travis was glad to see Ellie greeting Longfellow graciously. No hint of the anger between husband and wife remained in her face or in the set of her shoulders.

Mrs. Longfellow, with carefully styled blond hair Travis suspected was as white as her husband's underneath, slipped up beside them. After greeting them warmly, she stood back and looked Ellie up and down. "My dear, what a lovely gown."

Ellie flushed and darted Travis a short look of triumph. "Thank you."

His anger surged back. He tried to swallow it. It was the dress over which they'd argued earlier. It was long, flowed easily along her slender body. She called the color ice blue. Her dark hair and dark coloring looked good with it, but she'd made it herself. Not that it wasn't beautiful. She was good with a sewing machine, but he'd told her he expected her to wear an expensive gown like the rest of the women would be wearing tonight. She'd refused.

Fury filled his chest to the point of pain. He was sure Mrs. Longfellow was only being kind. Likely tomorrow all the women at the party would be talking about his wife's homemade gown. Not that Ellie had told the woman it was homemade, but a sophisticated woman like Mrs. Longfellow would be sure to know just by looking at it.

He was relieved when Mrs. Longfellow drew Ellie away to introduce her to some other women. He was too angry to be civil to his wife at the moment. He wouldn't want to lose his temper in front of the senior partner.

Travis moved from one group to another, laughing and joking with fellow employees and avoiding Ellie whenever possible. It grew easier to carry on conversation as the night went on and people drank more and more from the partner's generous bar. Travis limited his own drinks to ginger ale or orange juice, and he knew Ellie did the same.

At some point he hooked up with Michelle, another first-year lawyer with the firm. They worked together often. She was smart as a whip and easygoing, fun to work with.

There was only friendship between them, but when Travis looked up and caught Ellie jealously watching Michelle, he decided to show his law associate a little more attention than usual.

It didn't hurt that in addition to being intelligent and funny Michelle was single and had a great figure and long honey-blond hair. She was six inches shorter than he, even in her heels. Between the guests and the music from the string quartet, she had to lean close and lift her head to make him hear her. He was well aware it only made them look more intimate. He smiled to himself, smugly aware of the effect it would have on Ellie. *Serves her right*, he thought, *refusing to dress properly for a party she knows is important to my success at the firm.*

"I'm going to get another drink," Michelle said. "Be back in a minute."

Standing beside the Christmas tree, momentarily alone, Travis stared over the group at Ellie on the other side of the room. She was smiling, but when her gaze met his it grew cold. He knew his own was icy in return.

"Hey, buddy." Don Alexander stepped up beside him, his cheeks only slightly flushed from the effects of liquor. Travis knew Don was always careful of the way he appeared to others. Getting drunk at the boss's party was no way to make an impression and get ahead. Now Don's gaze followed where Travis's had been a moment before. "Not many men watch their own wives at a party. Must say, your wife is something to look at. A real beauty."

Travis grunted what he intended to be taken as agreement. Ellie was a looker all right, with high cheekbones, large brown eyes beneath perfectly shaped dark brows, her face framed with shiny brown hair. If only she hadn't worn that awful gown.

Don cleared his throat and rubbed his hand over his mouth. "You and Michelle are pretty chummy tonight."

He sounded embarrassed, and Travis thought he well should be embarrassed. "We're good friends. You know that."

Don wouldn't meet Travis's gaze. "I'm only going to remind you of this once. I've told you before I think Michelle's interest in you goes beyond friendship or work."

Travis snorted with laughter. "And I said you're wrong."

Don took a deep breath and hiked at his trousers with one hand. "That's what you said all right. See someone over there I need to talk to." He walked away without looking back.

The evening wasn't as much fun after Don's comments. Travis and Ellie left as soon as Travis felt they could do so without appearing overly eager.

The ride home was chilly for a winter night in California, at least in the car. Ellie sat with her arms tight across her chest and stared out at the road, her jaw tight. It was fine with Travis that she hadn't anything to say to him. *What could she say?* he thought. He was the one who'd been wronged. She knew how important it was to his career that they put forth the right image, and she'd purposely worn that. . .that *thing*.

Back in their apartment—the apartment they couldn't quite afford but which had an impressive-sounding address—they continued their non-verbal argument in the manner familiar to most couples. Both pointedly refused to look at each other or speak, both kept their backs to each other whenever possible, both closed doors with a little more effort than necessary.

Rather than relieving his anger, his refusal to address the issue made the anger build inside Travis. By the time they entered the bedroom, he felt like a red-hot boiler about to burst.

Ellie seated herself on the bench before her vanity and glared into the mirror as she removed the diamond-stud earrings which had been his wedding present to her.

Travis slipped off his jacket and threw it on the bed. "Are you happy now that you wore your stupid dress to the party?"

Ellie silently continued removing her jewelry.

"You can apologize any time for embarrassing me in front of my coworkers and partners," Travis blurted out, hands on his hips.

Ellie's eyebrows lifted. Her gaze met his in the mirror, her brown eyes glittering with a mixture of shock, anger, and pain. "*I* can apologize? If anyone deserves an apology it is me. As for embarrassing you, you managed that all by yourself, trotting around with that woman on your arm all night."

"She wasn't on my arm. Anyway, you could have been beside me. You chose not to be." He looked over her head into the mirror and began loosening his tie.

"You made it obvious you didn't want my company."

His fingers stopped on his tie, but only for a moment. He wasn't about to let her transfer her guilt to himself. "You specifically chose to wear something you knew would embarrass me."

"Did it ever occur to you that as a woman I might know better than you what is appropriate for me to wear?"

He refused to look at her, refused to admit to himself the guilt the pain in her voice shoved toward him.

She swung around on the vanity bench and stood to face him. "I suppose Michelle's off-the-rack dress made it appropriate for you to be seen with her instead of me. Don't you think the colleagues and partners whose good opinion you are always seeking might wonder why you spent the evening with a woman other than your wife?"

"They all know Michelle and I are only coworkers."

"Two of your associates warned me tonight that Michelle is interested in you romantically."

"There's no reasoning with you." Travis grabbed his coat from the bed and headed toward the door.

"Where are you going?"

"I have no idea."

Once in the car Travis drove around aimlessly, his frustration level growing. His intention in spending time with Michelle tonight had been to anger Ellie, not to embarrass himself. Ellie's take on the evening was wrong, he assured himself.

Don's comments about Michelle wriggled into his consciousness. Maybe Ellie was right.

"No!" He slammed an open fist against the steering wheel. He went through all the reasons he was right and Ellie and Don were wrong. When he was done, discomfort still wormed about inside him.

"For a lawyer, I'm a miserable failure at convincing arguments tonight."

It seemed fate when he discovered himself on the street where Michelle lived. He'd dropped her off after work one day when her car was in for repairs. Now he parked in front of the apartment building. If she was home from the party, she most likely hadn't gone to bed yet.

He was right. She was still up. Her voice registered surprise when he announced himself over the security system. Her face registered welcome when he arrived at her door.

She invited him to sit down on the sofa, then she went into the kitchen to get some sodas. Travis slipped off his overcoat and jacket, tossing them over a chair. Relaxing into the overstuffed cream-colored sofa, he undid his cuff links, set them on a side table, and rolled up his sleeves.

Unease slipped through his chest. Maybe this wasn't such a bright idea, he thought. He shook his head quickly. There was nothing wrong with his being here. He'd tell Michelle about Ellie and Don's accusations, she'd reaffirm how ridiculous the accusations were, and he'd go home with a clean conscience.

"What's up?" Michelle handed him a soda and settled herself on the sofa facing him, her legs drawn up beneath the skirt of her red party dress.

Her easy manner reassured him. He set the soda on the table and leaned back into the cushions, running both hands through his short sand-colored hair. "Ellie and I had a fight tonight. Not a fight exactly, more like an argument. I had to get away for a while."

Michelle's brows met in concern over large blue eyes. "Do you want to talk about it?"

The sympathy in her manner and soft voice was soothing after the tension between him and Ellie. "Yes." He didn't get any further for a moment. "I don't know where to start."

"Someone once suggested beginning at the beginning."

He gave a short, polite chuckle.

Michelle ran a pink-tipped index finger around the top of her can. Her gaze followed her finger. "Did it begin before the party or afterward?"

"Before. Mostly before."

She set her can down on the glass coffee table. "Then it didn't have anything to do with me."

Her blunt suggestion caught him off guard. He felt like he'd had all the breath knocked out of him. It was a minute before he could respond. "Why would you think it was about you?"

"I noticed you two didn't spend much time together this evening." She looked down. "And we did." She glanced up suddenly. Her gaze caught his.

He wanted to pull his gaze away but wouldn't let himself. It would be too much like admitting he had done something wrong. He forced a smile and shrugged one shoulder. "I knew you wouldn't take it the wrong way."

She tilted her head, her eyes filled with questions.

"I mean, we work together every day."

"What did you and Ellie argue about?"

Travis hesitated. He'd all but denied Ellie had a problem with him spending so much time with Michelle, yet that was the very thing about which he wanted reassurance. In spite of his confidence in stopping here, he wasn't prepared to be as forthright as Michelle and didn't like the added discomfort of feeling the need to slip sideways into the topic.

"It doesn't matter what it was about. I wanted to get back at her, so I spent more time with you than I probably should have."

"I assume your ploy worked."

"I'll say it did. She's furious. She insists I embarrassed myself and her and you by spending so much time with you that the partners and our colleagues will get the wrong idea."

"The wrong idea would be what?"

He recognized that tone. It sounded a lot like Ellie when he'd put his foot in his mouth. Why did women always want you to put things in black and white? "You know exactly what I mean. Do you think anyone from work would get the impression from the party that we're more than friends and coworkers?" *Anyone besides Don,* he added silently.

"Let's see. First you drop your wife like a hot potato as soon as you arrive. Next you latch onto me for the rest of the evening." She counted the items off on her pink-tipped fingers. "Then you arrive on my doorstep at midnight." She leaned closer. Her shoulder touched his. She looked directly into his eyes. "I don't know about everyone else, but I'm getting the impression you want to be more than friends and coworkers."

Travis's mouth went dry. His mind went blank.

Michelle slipped a hand around his neck. "I don't mind."

He grabbed her shoulder, stopping her before her lips could meet his. "Wait a minute." He stood, holding his hands up, palms toward her. "This isn't what I want."

"Then why are you here?"

He shoved a hand through his hair. "Obviously this was a really dumb move. I'm sorry. Your friendship means a lot to me. I thought you understood."

Michelle crossed her arms. "Do you treat all your friends as weapons against your wife?"

"I'm sorry." He picked up his coat and jacket and backed toward the door.

In the car he leaned his forehead against the steering wheel. "What was I thinking?" In astonishment, he realized he was shaking. Until Michelle made that move on the sofa, he hadn't let himself believe he'd been playing a dangerous game, that he'd been unfair to Michelle as well as to Ellie. He'd come so close to cheating on his wife, something he deplored in others.

He was still shaking when he arrived back at his and Ellie's apartment and lay down on the sofa to sleep.

The next morning, Sunday, Travis slept late and woke up stiff. He and Ellie went through the entire day without speaking. It was too humiliating to admit to Ellie that she was right about Michelle's intentions.

He was glad when Monday morning arrived and he could escape to the office. Delving into preparation for a court case gave his mind welcome relief from his personal problems. He was only assisting a senior partner, but it was an interesting case involving a major movie star's claim against a movie production company for withheld pay.

It was almost eleven when he glanced up from his desk and saw Ellie coming down the hall toward his office with a bounce in her step and a smile on her face. Relief washed away tension he hadn't realized had tightened his shoulders. She'd forgiven him. He could tell by the happy-shy smile on her lips and in her eyes. He was tired of guilt and anger and ready for a reconciliation.

Ellie was almost at his door when Michelle slipped into his office. Travis glanced at her with impatience and opened his mouth to ask her to leave. He never got the words out.

Michelle held a fist toward him. "Here are your cuff links. You left them in my apartment after the party Saturday night."

He barely noticed her triumphant glance before she turned and left the room. His attention was on Ellie, on the stunned look of betrayal in her eyes.

"Is it true?" Ellie asked in a quiet, controlled voice. "Did you go to Michelle's when you left the house Saturday night?"

Travis wished he could deny it honestly. He took a deep breath. "It isn't the way it looks. I went there, yes, but—"

Ellie turned on her heel and started down the hall, her back stiff.

"Ellie!" He hurried after her, all too aware of the other lawyers and clients in the office. Catching up to her, he matched his steps to hers, keeping his voice low, but not managing to keep the desperation from it. "I can explain everything. I promise. I can't leave right now. Longfellow and I are meeting with an important client, but I'll explain everything when I get home tonight."

She left the building without looking at him or saying a word.

Even work couldn't keep his mind from his problems with Ellie the rest of the day. Longfellow kept him late discussing the case. It was almost eight when he finally arrived at the apartment.

Ellie wasn't there. He sensed it as soon as he walked in, but he didn't begin worrying until he opened the bedroom closet door. He stood grasping the handle, staring in disbelief. All her clothes were gone. All of them, that is, except the ice blue gown.

He found a note from her on the kitchen table, short and to the point. She was returning to her hometown in the North Carolina mountains.

In the first anger and pain of her leaving, he didn't go after her. *Good riddance, if that's all the trust she has in me,* he thought. He tore the note in half and flung the pieces to the floor. "She'll be back. I give her a week."

Days slipped into weeks, then months. At first his pride wouldn't let him go after her. Later he reasoned that if she loved him she would return without his asking. There was no point in going after her if she didn't love him, didn't want to be together, was there?

And the months slipped into years.

🦋

There was a shuffling of feet and pages as the congregation stood for a hymn. Hastily, Travis rose, jerked back to present reality. The Christmas hymn was a familiar one; he didn't need the hymnal, but his throat was too tight from painful memories for the words to get through.

Try as he might to focus on the sermon, his thoughts drifted away to Ellie and Corey in North Carolina. *How could You have let this happen, God?* he raged silently. *How could You have kept me from knowing my son for two whole years? Corey and I will never be able to regain that time. It's lost forever.*

He squeezed his eyes shut. It wasn't God's fault he'd acted like a fool and lost his wife's trust.

It didn't make him feel any better to realize the separation from his son was his own fault.

When he opened his eyes again, his gaze rested on the nativity scene at the front of the church. The pastor's voice barely dented his conscious mind. The baby doll in the manger had captured his attention. He'd never held his son when he was new to this world. The thought gripped his heart and squeezed painfully. Tears pooled in his eyes, blurring the manger and the precious gift it symbolically sheltered.

Had it felt like that to God? Travis sat up straighter, still staring at the manger. Had it felt like that to God, sending His Son to earth? Travis had always heard Christ was thirty-three when He was crucified. The two years Travis had been separated from Corey seemed forever, and Travis had only discovered Corey's existence. How could God have sent His Son to earth, knowing they would be separated for thirty-three years?

Of course, it was a different kind of separation. After all, Jesus was both Son of Man and Son of God. Still, even knowing They would have the rest of eternity together and that thirty-three years is a short time out of eternity, how could the

Father have borne the thought of the separation? *I'm sorry, Lord,* Travis whispered in his mind. It had never before occurred to him to feel sorry for God.

The realization he might never be part of Corey's life dragged Travis's spirits down again. Spending the rest of his life without Ellie wasn't going to be easy either. He didn't speak of it to others, but he still missed her.

Why had she never sent a separation agreement or divorce papers? Had she been afraid he'd find out about Corey and demand custody?

Travis had never filed for divorce either. Even before he became a Christian, he'd believed marriage was for keeps. Now he felt guilty every time he read a Bible passage dealing with divorce.

He'd tried to assuage his conscience with the fact that he and Ellie weren't legally divorced. It hadn't worked. He'd wondered whether God wanted him and Ellie to reunite and argued with God against it. It was Ellie who left. He couldn't force her to spend her life with him.

He and Ellie never attended church after their wedding day. He wouldn't want his son brought up not knowing God loved him and would always be there beside him, helping him stand through the tough times that come to everyone. God wouldn't want that either, would He?

Was it only silly pride that had kept him from trying to win Ellie back? That and the fear of failing, he realized, the risk that she could break his heart all over again. He doubted she'd come back just because he asked her to do so. She thought he was a liar, a cheater. Despair spiraled through him. She didn't trust him, and he hadn't the slightest idea how to go about winning back her trust.

Couldn't the Lord change that? He drew himself up a little straighter in the pew, hope filling his heart. If it was the Lord's will that they be back together, couldn't the Lord show him, dense as he could be about relationships, how to win back her trust?

What if she's found someone else?

He pushed away the voice that whispered in his mind.

The thought of God's separation from Christ returned. Thirty-three years. Travis was only twenty-nine. What if he had to live another twenty-nine years, or thirty-three, or longer without Ellie and Corey?

The congregation rose for the final hymn. As the organ began the introduction to "Joy to the World," Travis lifted a silent prayer. *Please, Lord, restore Ellie to Yourself and me to my family. In the name of the Son You love, amen.*

Chapter 2

In the back room of her boutique, Ellie Carter carefully stuck in the last pin, connecting the finely crafted lace collar to the high neck of the peach linen jacket on the dress form. It was only two weeks after the new year. The boutique was in the middle of its after-Christmas sale, but she'd already completed most of her spring designs.

Ellie darted a glance into the main shop through the workroom door. Brass bells were situated above the boutique door to announce shoppers' arrivals, but she was concerned the bells' music might be drowned out by the *bang, bang, bang* of the carpenter's hammer as he worked on new display shelves.

She lifted the ivory lace gently with one finger. "It's the perfect touch, Anna. My designs wouldn't be the same without your exquisite lacework."

A rose color as gentle as Anna's spirit spread over the woman's wrinkled, soft face. Her faded-blue eyes glowed with pleasure. "I love creating lace. I'd have nowhere to use it if it weren't for you. I'm glad your customers like my lace and your designs."

Ellie fingered the soft linen material and gazed at the simple but sophisticated design. People did seem to appreciate her unique pieces. She hadn't been certain her idea of a boutique made up primarily of her own designs could be successful. She'd been told by a number of owners of more traditional shops that such a shop wasn't possible unless it was in an area which catered to the wealthy, such as Rodeo Drive. This small mountain town was definitely no Rodeo Drive. Still, even though the shop was only three years old, she managed to earn enough to pay the expenses. Barely.

"Travis would never believe it." Instantly she wished she could catch back the words, though they were true.

"He wouldn't believe people like unique things?"

Ellie unnecessarily straightened the jacket sleeve. "He wouldn't believe I've made a success of this boutique, selling my own designs."

"Whyever not?"

"He's the practical type. Logical. He's a lawyer, remember?"

Anna nodded. "He believes more in statistics than in the power of dreams and inborn ability."

"Yes, that's it exactly." Kinship spread sweet warmth through Ellie. She should have known Anna would understand.

Anna was Ellie's idea of a perfect grandmother, though they weren't related. She was short and petite with sagging jowls, sagging upper arm skin, and sagging just-about-everything-else except her spirit. Though she worked about her house and yard, she didn't bother trying to keep her body looking twenty-five years younger than its seventy-nine years. She claimed she liked being her age, that each age has its own beauty and excitement, and she couldn't wait to see what the rest of her years held.

Ellie's thoughts drifted back to Travis and the letter she'd mailed three weeks earlier. Why hadn't she heard from him? Turning the form with the peach suit around, she let out a deep sigh.

"What's wrong, dear?" Anna's voice was filled with kind concern.

Ellie hesitated a moment. Anna was always a trusted and wise confidante. In a rush Ellie spilled out the story of the letter. "I thought I'd have heard from him by now, but I haven't."

Anna made a sympathetic sound.

"I don't know whether to be relieved or hurt." Ellie realized she was twisting the peach jacket sleeve in both hands. She dropped it, disgusted with herself. "Is it possible he doesn't even care that he has a son?"

She glanced at Corey, who was sleeping on his back with arms flung out at his sides in complete abandonment in the playpen in the middle of the workroom. Surely if Travis saw Corey he would never be able to leave him.

That thought wasn't comforting.

"Travis may not have received your letter yet. Perhaps he was out of town over the holidays."

"Maybe." Ellie thought a moment. "Some of Travis's law partners used to spend the Christmas and New Year holidays at Aspen."

"Even if he's received the letter, it must be quite a shock to suddenly find oneself a father. You said you weren't sure whether you should have sent the letter," Anna reminded Ellie gently. "Will you be relieved if you don't hear from Travis?"

"I don't know." Ellie plopped inelegantly onto a scruffy bentwood chair, situated where she could keep an eye on the shop. "I argued with the Lord for months over whether to tell Travis about Corey. Every negative thought plagued me. What if Travis wants custody and is granted it? It would be like tearing out my heart to lose Corey."

Anna lowered herself to the oak stool beside Ellie. "I know, dear. No use pretending it might not come to that, but I'm sure at the worst the judge would only award Travis partial custody."

"Maybe." Ellie wasn't convinced. She'd heard of too many decisions by judges in child custody cases that made no sense to her at all.

"Would you trust Travis to raise Corey?"

Ellie's gaze moved again to her son. She felt her face soften. He looked so much like his father with the blond hair and blue eyes. "I don't know. When I met Travis in college, I thought he was the most wonderful man in the world. He wanted to fight for people who need justice."

"He sounds like a good man."

"Mmm. We married right after graduation. Then he entered law school. He did brilliantly, and his instructors predicted a great future for him." She shook her head. "He interned with a major law firm. Soon he was more in love with the idea of becoming a big-bucks lawyer than with the ideals of justice."

Anna shook her head, making a "*tch, tch, tch*" sound.

"The scariest thing," Ellie continued, "is that Travis doesn't believe in God. I hate to think of Corey being raised by someone who doesn't love Christ."

Ellie hadn't believed in God either when she left Travis. Out on her own for the first time in her life with a baby on the way, she discovered she needed a firm foundation on which to build her and her baby's lives. She'd sought help in church and eventually came to believe in Christ. Now He was like a close friend. *I would never have made it without Him.*

Anna sat quietly, apparently turning over in her mind everything Ellie had said. The banging of the carpenter's hammer continued while Ellie waited. When Anna spoke, her tone was sincere. "You decided it was right to tell him of Corey in spite of those fears?"

"Yes. I couldn't erase the conviction that Travis has a right to know his own son. Believe me, I tried for years to erase it. I kept hoping for a sign from God, assurance that everything would work out in a way I could easily accept."

"You didn't get an answer like that."

"No." Ellie could tell from Anna's tone that she'd learned through her long life such easy answers are rare. "The only answer I received was that God loves Corey and wants the best for him more than I do." She turned to Anna. "I've learned to trust the Lord in so many ways in my life during the last three years. Trusting Him with Corey is more difficult than anything I've ever had to do."

One of Anna's soft, wrinkled hands patted Ellie's. Anna's smile was filled with a joy and peace that made her eyes sparkle. "It's a great blessing to our Father when we trust Him with the things we love the most."

Ellie darted Anna a look of surprise. "I never thought of anything we do as blessing Him." Her gaze swiveled back to sleeping Corey. He looked so innocent, so. . .vulnerable. A sudden lump of pain filled her throat. "What do parents do who believe God will protect their children, and yet awful things happen to their sons and daughters? How do they ever reconcile that with a loving Father God? How would I?"

"That is the hardest test of our faith, when painful things happen to our children." Anna's voice had dropped to such a soft level that Ellie instinctively leaned forward to hear her better. "We're tempted to forget at such times that the children don't really belong to us at all. They belong to God, the same as we do. I believe each child has his own mission on this earth, a mission that doesn't always coincide with what we with our limited sight believe is right for that child." She was silent a moment. "It's the only way I've been able to keep my faith through some things."

The last sentence hung in the air with an emotional force Ellie seldom felt. Her chest tightened in compassion. Anna had lost a grandchild to leukemia. A difficult way to learn the lesson she'd just shared. It was a lesson Ellie had no wish to learn from experience.

The carpenter stopped in the workroom doorway. "You want to see what I've done so far?" He jerked his head back over his shoulder toward the shop.

"Sure, Chuck." Ellie stood up.

Corey let out a tentative cry, a typical I'm-awake-is-anyone-going-to-pick-me-up cry. Ellie laughed. "I guess the quiet after your hammering woke him." She gave Chuck a teasing grin.

Anna shooed Ellie away with a wave of her hand. "I'll take care of Corey. You go check out Chuck's work. Have to keep an eye on that young man, you know." Anna chuckled at her own joke.

Chuck looked down from his six feet to Ellie's five-foot-five and grinned. "Does she mean me or Corey?"

Ellie laughed. "Both of you, probably."

Chuck stopped beside the shelves on which he'd been pounding for what seemed like hours to Ellie. "What do you think? Do they blend with your cabinets all right?"

"They're perfect." They were. Chuck had gone to a lot of trouble to match the new shelves to the antique cabinet she had bought last month. He'd stained the wood to match as closely as possible, aging it in some way mysterious to Ellie. Unable to locate molding to match, he'd carved it himself. Ellie ran a hand lightly over the side of the cabinet. "You put so much of yourself into your work. No wonder everything you make is wonderful."

His already straight shoulders straightened slightly more in pride and pleasure. "Wouldn't go to all this trouble for just anyone."

"Yes, you would. You're an artist with wood."

His posture relaxed a little. His gaze traveled over the cabinet. "It feels that way sometimes."

Ellie breathed a soft sigh of relief. She'd successfully turned his comments to his work. Perhaps she was misjudging him. Perhaps he hadn't meant that he had gone to all the trouble with the cabinet because she was more than a friend or client. All too often, however, his normal friendliness had taken on more intimate tones. Nothing out-and-out romantic, but too close for comfort.

She opened the doors of the antique cabinet she was using to display sweaters which had been knit by a local woman and trimmed in Anna's crocheted lace. "Could you check the hinge on this door, Chuck? It's loose, just a smidgen."

"Best time to catch it." He moved close behind her, reaching both arms to check the top hinge.

Ellie slipped from between him and the cabinet door and watched him work. He was so different from Travis. About the same height, but built slighter. Not skinny. The muscles in his forearms reminded her of taut rubber bands. His hair was straight and dark brown beneath one of the baseball hats he always wore. Travis's hair was curly and blond, and he wouldn't be caught dead in a baseball hat. Just the thought of him in one made her smile.

Chuck turned to reach for a screwdriver from his small red tool chest and caught the smile. "What's the joke?"

"Nothing."

He brushed unnecessarily at the front of his long-sleeved gray T-shirt. "Did I get something on me?"

"No. I was just thinking of a funny memory."

"I can always use a laugh."

"It's the kind of thing that doesn't translate well."

Chuck shrugged, turned back to the cabinet, and began removing screws in the lower hinge. "You and Corey have plans for dinner?"

She didn't answer immediately. Often during the last three years, she'd shared meals with him without giving it a second thought. His calm wisdom had always been available when she needed a friend. But now. . .

"I won tickets for two free meals at the Black Bear Café's New Year's drawing. Thought maybe you'd help me use them."

It sounded innocent enough. "Thanks. It will be nice for both Corey and me to get out for a little while."

Maybe she was building a mountain out of the proverbial molehill. Maybe he wasn't showing undue interest in her. Maybe she was tired of being alone and wanted to believe a man was romantically interested in her. She caught back a groan. A romantic interest was a complication and temptation she didn't need in her life.

The brass bells tinkled, announcing a customer. Ellie swung about, her usual welcoming smile in place.

It froze. All of her froze.

"Travis."

Chapter 3

Ellie's thoughts tumbled about like sticks in rapids. She'd thought he would write or call, not travel across the country without letting her know he was coming.

"Hello, Ellie."

"Hi." The word sounded as breathless as she felt.

Hands in the pockets of his gray wool jacket, he glanced about the shop. "Nice place."

Her fears rushed back full force. *Why is he here? Does he think by arriving unexpectedly he can gain an advantage? He's a lawyer. He must know all kinds of legal tricks to help him gain custody of Corey.*

Chuck moved close behind Ellie. "You here on business, mister?"

Ellie could hear the threat in his calm, even voice. She was grateful for his support, even though she didn't need his protection. "This is my hus. . .this is Travis. Travis Carter, Chuck Beckett."

The men exchanged curt nods. Neither one offered his hand. Ellie felt Chuck tense. "It's all right," she reassured him.

Chuck took a step, slapping the screwdriver lightly against an open palm. "I'll be in the back room if you need me."

She nodded. Neither she nor Travis spoke until Chuck reached the workroom.

"He acts like I'm a serial killer." Travis's voice was low in an obvious attempt to keep from being overheard. It carried a rumble of anger. "What have you been telling people about me?"

She began straightening the sweaters inside the cabinet, not wanting to face him. "I don't spread my personal life around as though it's everyone's business."

A moment of silence. "I'm sorry. I guess I jumped to a conclusion. I didn't mean for us to start out this way. It's just. . .a little uncomfortable."

How could it not be uncomfortable? Ellie stared unseeing at her hands resting on a rose sweater. She took a deep breath and turned to face him. "You must have received my card."

He nodded once, briskly. "And the picture."

Silence again. It strained Ellie's muscles, as if she were trying to bring a wild bronco at the end of a rope under control. Travis's unspoken accusations hurled themselves through her brain: *Why didn't you tell me earlier that I had a son? How could you leave me knowing you were carrying our child?*

"I want to meet him, Ellie." Determination underlined the simple, quiet words.

"Of course." She wondered that her voice didn't tremble the way her heart was trembling. She'd known when she mailed the card that if he chose to see Corey she wouldn't fight it. Still, the reality frightened her.

Travis let out a sigh of relief, and she realized he had actually thought she might say no. *Why, he's afraid, too!* The knowledge calmed her somewhat.

"Tonight?" he asked.

"I. . .I have dinner plans."

"When, then? I'd like to meet him as soon as possible."

Ellie ran the palms of her hands down the sides of her skirt then caught her fingers together in front of her to end their betrayal of her nervousness. She should tell him Corey was in the back room. They could meet now. But she wasn't ready yet. Tonight or tomorrow was too soon, even though she'd set the meeting in motion by letting him know of Corey's existence.

It was too late to turn back. She'd cancel her plans with Chuck. "Tonight, after dinner, if that suits you."

"That's fine." Travis's shoulders dropped a couple inches.

"It will have to be early. I usually put Corey to bed about eight. Could you be at my place about seven?"

"I'll be there. Are you still staying with your folks?"

"They spend winters in Florida now that they're retired. I have a place of my own." She gave him directions. As soon as they were out of her mouth, she regretted her decision. Perhaps it would have been wiser to meet him on neutral ground, not to let him know where she lived. She dismissed the thought. It was a small town. If he wanted to know her address, he could find it out with little trouble.

"I'll see you at seven." The brass bells tinkled merrily above his stiff back when he walked out.

She shivered. The chill winter air his leaving let in bit at her body as his arrival had bitten at her spirit.

❧

Travis went quickly up the wooden front steps of the old two-story frame house. It was a modest place, but so were most homes in the small mountain village. A porch, its floor slightly slanting from age, crossed the front of the building. Lace curtains at the large windows discreetly and daintily allowed a sense of privacy. The front door, which he guessed was original to the house, had a large oval etched window.

Travis frowned. A door like that wasn't safe. Anyone could break in without half trying. He pushed away the thought, reminding himself this wasn't Los Angeles.

He became aware of the tension in his shoulders. He took a moment to breathe deeply, then roll his head to loosen the muscles in his neck. He snorted in disgust. He hadn't been this tense since his first appearance as a lawyer before the bar.

He admired the workmanship of the beautiful window while he knocked. He could see through the lace-covered window that it wasn't Ellie who was answering. The door was opened by a slender blond woman about his own age, wearing tight jeans and a cropped red top.

"I'm sorry. I thought Ellie Carter lived here." He took a step backward, his glance darting to the tarnished brass numbers beside the door.

"She does. You must be Travis."

At his nod, the woman opened the door wider. "Come in. I'm Jessica. My son, Brent, and I share the house with Ellie and Corey." She reached out a hand, and an armful of silver bracelets jangled.

Travis shook her hand.

Jessica pointed to the large stuffed gray horse with a white mane and tail tucked under one of Travis's arms. "Good choice."

His cheeks heated. "Thanks." He'd wanted to buy the whole toy store for Corey. A stuffed animal seemed like a mundane first gift for his son, but in the toy store he'd faced the sobering fact that he didn't know what toys Corey had or what kind he liked.

He'd barely entered the house when a wailing call came from the second floor. "Mo–o–o–m!"

Travis's heart lurched at the toddler's voice. Was that his son?

Jessica groaned and rolled her eyes, then grinned. "That's my son."

Travis's chest deflated.

"Make yourself comfortable in the living room. Ellie will be down in a minute." She hurried up the open staircase that bordered the hall, climbing over a gate at the top. Travis recognized it as a child safety device.

Jessica was a surprise. Travis was relieved to find Ellie wasn't sharing the house with a man. If she was seeing someone, she must not have made a commitment to him yet.

Travis walked slowly into what was obviously the living room. The room opened directly onto the hall by an open wall. Tall, brightly polished wooden columns stood on each side of the opening.

The room was high ceilinged with thick dark woodwork in the tradition of the early 1900s. The furniture looked like it came from the same period. The navy blue overstuffed sofa and chairs were worn until the cushions were almost bare, yet they looked comfortable and welcoming. Dark wooden tables with intricate carvings were similarly worn.

The difference between this shabby room and the smart apartment he and Ellie had shared in Los Angeles made him shiver.

He set the horse behind one of the chairs where Corey wouldn't see it as soon as he entered the room.

Making his way toward the old-fashioned piano with a display of pictures covering the top, he stumbled. "What. . . ?" A yellow and black plastic dump truck rolled slowly across the faded, rose-covered beige rug, propelled by the energy of his errant foot.

A glance about showed it wasn't the only toy. Other plastic trucks and autos in bright reds, blues, and yellows were scattered about the floor. A Nerf ball so orange he wondered if it glowed in the dark rested beneath the piano bench. A pale brown teddy bear with a well-loved look reclined upside down on the sofa. Was the bear Corey's or Brent's? Would Corey prefer it to the horse?

Unexpected joy curled through Travis. Some of these were his son's toys. Travis crouched down, balancing himself on the fronts of his shoes, and pushed the dump truck around one of the piano bench legs before winding up the box on the back of the truck. The hours he'd spent playing with a dump truck just like this when he was a boy came back in a rush.

"Don't drive too fast. You wouldn't want to get a speeding ticket."

At Ellie's voice, Travis jerked his head up so fast he fell back on his bum. Ellie's smirk turned into a laugh.

Travis's neck and face heated, and he grinned sheepishly. "Just remembering when I was a kid." He got to his feet. "Where's Corey?"

"Jessica will bring him down in a minute. She thought we might want to say hello first." Ellie swung her weight from one foot to the other, her long brown skirt swinging gracefully. Her eyes seemed to look everywhere except at him.

We're like two cats trying to decide whether to be friends or attack each other, Travis thought.

"Can I take your coat?"

He handed it to her, noticing the wedding band on her left hand. Surprise danced through him at the encouraging sign. Why had she removed the solitaire diamond engagement ring and left the wedding ring?

He glanced about the room. There were no mementos from their life together. No wedding picture on the wall. Why should he have thought there would be? Their wedding photo still hung on the wall of the California apartment, right where she'd hung it the day they moved in. She'd left the wedding album, too, he remembered, trying to ignore the pang that shot through him.

When she returned from the hall closet, Travis searched his mind for something neutral to say, anything but what he wanted to say, anything but the questions that had built up inside him since he'd received her card on Christmas Eve. "How old is Brent?"

"Three and a half, a year older than Corey. They're best buddies."

"That's good. That he has a friend near his own age, I mean."

"Yes." Ellie's gaze again searched the room.

The sound of footsteps and boyish voices came from the stairway. Ellie turned toward it. "Here they come." Travis thought from her face that she looked relieved, but her shoulders appeared tense, riding a bit higher than normal beneath her burgundy-colored sweater.

Then he noticed his own shoulders were tense, and he realized he was watching Ellie to avoid looking at Corey. He hadn't expected this wonderful moment to be ribboned through with fear. Maybe fear wasn't the right word, but he knew his life would never be the same once he looked on the face of his son.

Travis turned his head slowly. There was one boy on either side of Jessica, one brunet and one blond, each clutching one of her hands. They leaped bravely down one step after another as though descending the stairway were an exciting adventure. Travis recognized Corey immediately. The blond curls and laughing blue eyes were the same as those in the picture Travis had carried with him since the day it arrived at his apartment.

He rubbed a hand over his mouth, trembling with the effort to stay where he was and not rush across the room and wrap the boy in his arms. To do so would only frighten Corey.

Ellie held out a hand to him. "Come and meet your. . .our friend, Travis."

Travis glanced at her face. It was noticeably paler than a minute earlier. It hadn't occurred to him that she wouldn't introduce him to Corey as his father. Of course, it was only sensible that she didn't push it on the child right away. Still, he hadn't been prepared for how much it would hurt to be introduced as anything less than Corey's father, how much it would hurt not to be able to acknowledge their relationship. He wished he and Ellie had discussed this before Corey came downstairs. How many other things should they have resolved before he met Corey?

The boy hurried to Ellie, smiling. Even that simple act cut through Travis's heart. Would his son ever come to him in that trusting manner?

Corey leaned against Ellie's leg. Curiosity filled his face as he looked Travis over. He held up a hand, fingers splayed. "Hi."

"Hi, Corey." Travis mirrored the boy's gesture, then stuffed his hands into the pockets of his khakis. He smiled at Corey, meeting the boy's curious gaze, waiting patiently while Corey studied him.

"You've met Jessica," Ellie said. "This is her son, Brent."

Travis tore his gaze from his son to glance at the other woman and boy. Travis lifted his palm again. "Hi, Brent. Nice to meet you."

"Hi." The word was muffled as Brent burrowed his head into his mother's thigh, while trying to keep one eye on Travis.

Jessica smoothed Brent's long brown hair with one hand. "We're going out to eat," she explained to Travis, pulling on a jacket. "We won't be late."

Jessica hesitated at the door, looking at Ellie uncertainly. Travis had the uncomfortable feeling Jessica was afraid to leave Ellie and Corey alone with him.

He was glad when the front door shut behind them. He studied Ellie's face. Surely she wasn't afraid of him. Her wide brown eyes and broad face did seem tense, though. Likely she felt as uncomfortable and uncertain as he did about this evening.

Corey hurried across the room with his wide-legged two-and-a-half-year-old's gait. His eyes sparkled when he picked up the dump truck. He held it up for Travis to see. A grin dotted with baby teeth spread across his face. "Mine."

Travis dropped to one knee. "That's a great truck."

"Look." Corey squatted down and turned the handle that lifted the dump truck.

"Wow. That's pretty terrific."

Corey grunted agreement and concentrated on winding the dump truck back down. "See?"

"I sure do."

Corey searched the floor with his gaze then pounced on a tiny stuffed dog. He dropped it into the truck. "Look," he demanded again. Once more he twisted up the back of the truck then opened the back and let the dog slip out. His mission a success, he dropped back his head and beamed up at Travis, awaiting praise.

"Good job. Do you haul things besides dogs in your dump truck?"

Corey nodded and looked for another load.

Travis was amazed at the joy that filled him watching his son perform these simple acts. How was it possible he hadn't known Corey existed, even without being told? Travis couldn't take his gaze from the boy, couldn't bear a moment in Corey's presence without watching him.

It was obvious Corey enjoyed having such a rapt audience. He pulled toy after toy from the wooden box with the hinged top beneath a window, showing each toy to Travis, who dutifully exclaimed over it and asked how it worked. As each toy was discarded for the next, Ellie tried replacing it in the box. Sometimes she actually managed to put a toy away without Corey catching sight of her and issuing a loud and demanding "No!"

Ellie ignored the command the sixth time and put a plastic tool bench back in the box.

Corey rushed over to recover it, his face red with fury. "No!"

"We put our toys away when we're done, remember?" Ellie reminded gently.

Corey didn't answer. He retrieved the tool bench, sat down on it, and went back to showing off his large red fire engine.

Travis roared with laughter.

Ellie's hands landed on her hips. "Don't encourage him."

"He wants to show me his toys. What's the harm in that?"

"He wants to have his own way, you mean. I don't need anyone encouraging him to disobey me."

"You're right. I'm sorry." Travis couldn't help smiling. He and Ellie sounded like any two parents.

Travis thought it all too soon when Ellie announced Corey's bedtime. Corey thought it was too soon, too. He sat among his toys, refusing to look at her, and repeated his favorite word. "No."

Ellie wasn't about to be deterred. She picked up the worn teddy bear from the couch. "Here's Teddy. Say good night to Travis, and we'll take Teddy upstairs to bed."

Corey shook his head until his curls bounced. His bottom lip stuck out in a pout, and he concentrated harder on the toy in his hands.

Travis gave it a try. "If you go to bed with your mother, I'll give you a present."

Corey's head lifted. His eyes brightened.

"Travis." Ellie's one word was a protest.

Travis took the stuffed horse from behind the chair, knelt down, and held it out. "Here you go, partner."

Corey's face lit up. "A pony!" He couldn't get to it fast enough. The rest of his toys were instantly forgotten. He held it tightly, brushing the mane and tail with one hand.

"What do you say to Travis?" Ellie reminded.

"Thank you." Corey was too busy studying the horse's face to look up.

Corey's obvious pleasure was nothing compared to Travis's joy that his gift was so well received. "What will you name the pony?"

"Pony," was the instant and decisive answer.

"Very appropriate." Travis exchanged an amused glance with Ellie.

Ellie held out a hand to Corey. "Say good night to Travis."

Corey ignored her, devoting his attention to the horse.

"Pony hasn't seen your bedroom yet. Don't you want to show it to him?" she suggested.

Corey appeared to consider this. "Okay." He struggled to his feet, the large horse hindering his progress. " 'Night T'avis."

" 'Night, so—Corey."

"Do you want to give Travis a hug?"

Travis could have hugged Ellie for suggesting it, even though he detected a strain in her voice.

Corey shook his head and leaned against Ellie's leg, eyeing Travis warily.

His lack of trust lacerated Travis's heart, but he forced a smile. "That's all right, partner. No one should hug anyone they don't want to hug. I'll be glad to be your friend anyway."

"I'm sorry," Ellie mouthed.

"Any chance I could help put him to bed?"

"No." She blurted the word. "It will only take longer to settle him down if you do." The excuse sounded lame to Travis, but he hadn't any choice but to accept her decision. He watched the two until they reached the top of the stairs and were lost to his sight.

A minute later Jessica and Brent returned. After a few brief words they also went upstairs. Travis could hear the women talking.

Travis picked up the toys scattered about the floor and put them back in the toy box. He plopped down on the sofa and poked an index finger into the worn teddy bear's stomach, fiercely glad his son had chosen the pony over this old favorite.

I love that boy, he thought. He'd loved him from the first time he read about him in Ellie's note on Christmas Eve. His own son, the only person on earth who was literally a part of him. Travis had heard a father's love could be like that, instant and complete, but he hadn't believed it. He'd seen too many cases in his law practice where blood ties apparently meant nothing.

"I only want the best for you, Corey." Travis rested his head against the sofa, reliving the time spent with Corey, watching his eyes shine with fun and excitement, listening to his wonderful little-boy laugh, sharing the joy of him with Ellie. If he and Ellie got back together, they could spend every evening like that, like a real family.

The vision caught at his heart, both in hope and in pain at the fear it might never happen. *God is in control,* he reminded himself. *He will work everything together for good.*

He tried not to dwell on the fact that the separation was his own fault, the result of his own foolish actions. Flirting with Michelle had been the most unwise choice of his life. He shifted uneasily. Would one of the consequences of his flirting be a lifetime separated from Ellie and their son?

When Ellie returned he immediately sat up straight. He caught her amused look, realized he was hugging the teddy bear to his chest, and hastily tossed it back onto the couch.

She walked across the room slowly with her hands caught behind her back. "Your horse was a big success."

"I'm glad."

Ellie sat on the edge of the cushion on the other end of the sofa. "We have some things to discuss."

Travis agreed. He was aware of the boundaries between himself and Ellie, boundaries he wasn't willing to test or cross over. He could sense Ellie's defenses were up. He began with a simple question. "When is Corey's birthday?"

It was his unspoken questions he most wanted to ask. Was she afraid he might try to take Corey away from her? What would she think if she knew he'd been entertaining the thought of the three of them together as a family? If that didn't happen, he couldn't promise he wouldn't try to gain custody if he decided it was in Corey's best interest. The connection he'd seen between Ellie and Corey tonight looked healthy. Travis wished everything could be resolved immediately, but he knew it would take time for him and Ellie to know what they each wanted and what each of them could give in the situation.

"Corey seems happy. You must be a good mother."

She slipped her hands about one knee, looking instantly more relaxed. "Thank you."

"Do you need financial help?"

Ellie bristled visibly. "My boutique hasn't made me wealthy, but I manage to support Corey and myself."

Travis felt like he was interviewing a hostile client, trying to lessen Ellie's tension with conciliatory and non-threatening comments and actions. "I'm sure you do, but it's my responsibility as much as yours to support Corey. How about if I give you a check each month?" He suggested an amount.

Ellie hesitated. "Shouldn't that be determined by the courts or something?"

He started sweating. He hoped things would never come to a divorce or custody hearing. "I'll give you whatever amount you think is fair. The courts can change it later if they wish." He might advise against this if he were his client.

She agreed to his offered amount. "I'll put it in a savings account for him." She glanced down at her hands. "I. . .I owe you an apology. I should have told you about Corey earlier. You have every right to be angry with me."

"I was at first. Now all I want is for us both to put away blame and anger and get on with our lives. I only want to know my son, to be part of his life."

Ellie's gaze met his. "How do we do that?" she asked quietly.

He shrugged. "I guess we figure it out as we go."

The silence between them grew long, and the longer it grew the thicker with tension the air became.

He swallowed hard, his heart speeding up as he considered the question burning his tongue. "Did you know you were pregnant with Corey when. . ." He searched for a phrase that wouldn't sound accusatory. "When you came back here to your hometown?"

Ellie's face became masklike. Her arms folded over her chest, her hands clutched her upper arms. "I found out the morning I left. I went directly to your office from the doctor's office to share the news with you." Her voice was as emotionless as her face.

Travis stared at her in shock, remembering the joy on her face when she came to his office that morning. He'd thought she'd merely forgiven him. Pain charged through Travis's chest like a lightning bolt. If he hadn't acted the fool with Michelle, he wouldn't have been separated from Ellie and Corey all this time, wouldn't be sitting here now afraid he might be separated from them for the rest of his life. If only he could make her understand. "About Michelle—"

"I don't want to hear it." Her angry words cut through his attempt.

"But it wasn't what you think."

"I said I don't want to hear it." Ellie shot to her feet, her brown eyes flashing. "It's in the past."

"All right." He rose to face her. *If we can't discuss it, how can there be forgiveness and healing for us, and without healing, how can it ever be in the past?* he wondered.

Ellie crossed her arms tightly over her chest. She rocked slightly back and forth. "What do you plan to do now?"

About Corey. The unspoken words shouted in the air between them.

Suddenly Travis knew exactly what he was going to do. "I don't want Corey to grow up not knowing his father, not knowing me. I'm moving here as soon as possible."

Chapter 4

Ellie and Jessica left Corey and Brent playing in the church nursery and walked together into the sanctuary, greeting friends on their way to the pew where they always sat with Anna.

Ellie glanced about with a puzzled frown as they took their seats. "I wonder where Anna is? She's usually here by now."

"I hope she isn't ill." Jessica paged through the hymnal locating the first song. "We know last night's snowstorm didn't keep her away." Anna lived two houses from the stone church, so even inclement weather never kept her away in spite of her seventy-nine years.

"Let's stop and check on her on the way home."

Jessica nodded agreement. Then her face brightened. "Here she is."

Ellie turned toward the aisle. Her smile froze. Anna was coming toward them on Travis's arm, looking positively delighted with the attention the two of them were drawing from the curious congregation.

Anna's eyes sparkled as she and Travis stopped beside the pew. Ellie wouldn't have said Travis's eyes sparkled, but he looked pleased at her surprise.

"There isn't room for both of us in your pew," Anna whispered loudly. "We'll just sit in this one." She indicated the pew in front of them.

"What is he doing here?" Ellie mouthed to Jessica.

Jessica shrugged and sent her a look of pity then stood with the rest of the congregation as the opening strains of the first hymn swelled through the church. Ellie belatedly followed.

She tried to keep her mind on the service. It wasn't easy with her estranged husband seated directly in front of her. What was he doing at the service? She hadn't seen him in a church since their marriage ceremony. In college they'd had many long discussions about what they believed, or rather did not believe, about God. Travis always said he didn't know and didn't care whether there was a God. "If there is," he had said more than once, "He can mind His business, and I'll mind mine, and we'll get along just fine."

Perhaps Anna had invited him, Ellie speculated, and he'd thought it rude to refuse. He was living in Anna's home, after all, renting her upstairs apartment. He'd moved in two days ago, just over a month after he announced in Ellie's living room his intention to move to town.

Ellie could hardly believe Travis had given up his position with the prestigious law firm to live in this small mountain village to be closer to Corey. She knew he was planning to practice law here but didn't know any details about his business plans.

Likely he'll soon tire of our village, she thought. He probably hadn't quit the Los Angeles law firm, merely taken a leave of absence and sublet the apartment. Maybe he was only here to win over Corey and determine the best way to gain custody.

That's not fair. Perhaps it wasn't, but this small-town, church-going lawyer certainly wasn't the man she'd left three years ago. So who was the real Travis Carter now?

She wished he wasn't sitting right in front of her. In spite of distrusting his motives, an old familiar longing stirred in her. The shape of his head and shoulders, the way he moved, his hair: All brought back memories of the time she'd loved him completely, memories of laughter, of struggling together, of loving together, intimate memories she'd been trying to forget for three years.

Memories from when she'd been innocent and naive, when she'd trusted him with every inch of her heart and being.

The harshness of broken trust mixed with desire for the time before disillusionment had changed her life forever. She hated the painful way the conflicting emotions twisted inside her.

Had she been wrong to tell Travis about Corey? she wondered for what seemed the thousandth time. *Lord, I need Your guidance now more than ever.*

During the last three years, she'd relied on the Lord's guidance constantly. Everything had been new and frightening: being a first-time mother and the only support for herself and Corey, finding a place to live, beginning her own business. Everywhere she'd turned stood unfamiliar challenges to face. Struggling to learn to hear the Lord's voice, she'd come across Colossians 3:15 in her Amplified Bible. "And let the peace (soul harmony which comes) from Christ rule (act as umpire continually) in your hearts [deciding and settling with finality all questions that arise in your minds]."

Now, when she needed guidance desperately, she kept concentrating on her fears and couldn't feel peace. She'd dealt with fears before, but this time she couldn't seem to get past them.

When the service was over, Travis turned around with that broad smile Ellie loved and distrusted at the same time. "Hi. Where's Corey?"

"In the nursery."

"Do you attend here often?"

"Every Sunday." Ellie could hear Jessica and Anna chatting beside them. "I'm surprised to see you here."

"I could say the same."

Ellie placed the hymnal in its holder on the back of the pew. "I've changed. I'm not the person you knew."

"Me either."

"Really?"

He ignored her sarcastic tone. "I'm glad you're raising Corey in the church."

His statement shocked her so that she couldn't think of a reply. She was glad when Anna turned to them with an invitation. "I've a roast in the oven. Won't you and Corey join Travis and me for dinner? Jessica has already agreed to come."

Ellie hesitated. All she wanted was to take Corey home and get away from Travis's disturbing presence, but Anna loved to have company, and she was such a dear. "Of course. It's lovely of you to ask us."

Anna beamed. "I love doing for folks. I'm so glad Travis moved into my apartment. It's nice having company for meals again. The last tenants kept to themselves."

"You're cooking for Travis?" Ellie directed the question to Anna but her disapproving gaze fixed on Travis.

He spread his hands in a how-could-I-say-no-to-the-sweet-lady gesture, but his smile told her he was pleased with the arrangement. "Anna is a great cook."

His charm obviously worked on Anna, who couldn't have looked more pleased. Ellie remembered how well his easy charm had worked on her during most of their relationship. She determined to steel herself against it in the future, for her own sake and for Corey's.

Anna introduced Travis to Pastor Evanson at the church door. "He just moved here."

Pastor Evanson invited him to join the men's weekly prayer breakfast.

"I'd like that. Where and when?"

"The Black Bear Café, Wednesday mornings at six thirty."

"I'll be there."

Ellie eyed Travis with suspicion. Travis at a prayer breakfast? She couldn't imagine it. What was behind this apparent change of heart? Did he think becoming involved in the church was a good way to meet potential clients?

Ellie had to agree with Travis on Anna's baking talents as they finished up her coconut cake dessert a couple hours later. The meal had been more pleasant than Ellie expected. Travis kept them all entertained with stories of a lawyer's life in L.A., which could easily have been the basis for a television program titled *Funniest Courtroom Videos*.

Corey and Brent had tired of the dinner table. They were arguing over a stuffed dog on wheels in the living room. Ellie kept an eye on them, hoping the argument would stay mild, while Anna served coffee in delicate porcelain cups.

"Isn't it difficult to start a law practice from scratch with no clients?" Anna asked Travis when she sat down.

Ellie was glad Anna had asked the question. She'd wondered the same but hadn't wanted to show an interest in Travis's life by asking.

He took his gaze from the boys reluctantly to answer Anna. It seemed Travis hadn't stopped watching Corey since they arrived. Ellie hated to admit it, but Travis's apparent fascination with their son was so touching it made her chest glow with warmth. She was sure he'd rather be on the floor playing with the boys now than drinking coffee from fragile cups with three women. She took a sip, repressing a giggle.

Travis rested his elbows on the table. "It is hard starting from scratch. With that in mind, I spoke with a large regional firm in Charlotte. I'd met one of the partners on a ski trip last winter. I suggested opening a branch office here, with me as the firm's representative. He and his partners agreed to give it a try. That way I don't carry all the financial risk myself, and the firm's name, which is well known in the Carolinas, will draw some clients."

"Where will you work?" Ellie asked.

"I've arranged to rent the downstairs of the vacant Brandywine building for an office. It needs remodeling to meet our needs, of course. I've talked with your friend Chuck, Ellie. He's agreed to start working on it next week."

"That's wonderful." Anna smiled at him over the rim of her cup.

Ellie didn't think it was at all wonderful. Wonderful would be if Travis had stayed in L.A. and been content to send Corey birthday and Christmas presents.

Her conscience tweaked. She did want Corey to have a regular father, one who would be there for him through good times and hard times and growing times, but was Travis capable of being a responsible father?

Corey threw himself against her thigh. She barely managed to keep her coffee from sloshing over the rim onto Anna's antique lace tablecloth. "Whoa! Careful, Corey."

He looked up at her eagerly. "Want to go outside."

"We have to help Anna with dishes first."

Corey's face fell.

"Please," Brent cajoled Jessica.

Travis shoved his chair back. "I'll take them outside while you clean up if you'd like." He sounded as eager as the boys.

While Travis went upstairs to change from his suit, Ellie found the boys' snowsuits, and she and Jessica dressed Corey and Brent for the outdoors. By the time the two were ready, they could barely walk for all the protective clothing.

Travis laughed. "They look like they're ready to walk on the moon."

Ellie couldn't help grinning. "Remember what it felt like to try to play in a snowsuit?"

"Do I. I had a red one, with a matching red hat that looked like an old cloth football helmet with a bill, and waterproof red mittens that were so slippery snowballs slid right off them."

"And the mittens were so stiff you couldn't pick up anything with them."

"And the muffler Mom tied around my face was so long it got caught beneath the sled runners."

It was fun sharing similar childhood memories, even though they hadn't known each other until college.

"Remember the snowball war we had our sophomore year in college?" Travis asked.

Ellie groaned. "You and me against your entire fraternity. How could I forget?"

"We didn't do so badly, considering."

"We came out of it alive, which is about the best one could say for that battle."

"Outside." Corey tried unsuccessfully to tug at Ellie's skirt with his mittened hands.

Ellie and Travis chuckled, their gazes meeting. An exciting thrill danced through her, like sparks on a sparkler, at the pleasure of sharing the moment.

Travis held out his gloved hands to the boys. "Come on, partners. Let's brave the elements."

"Okay, pa'dner," Corey agreed happily.

Ellie was sure the boys didn't understand Travis's words, but they knew he meant they were going outside together. Each lifted a hand trustingly and eagerly to Travis's, and the three went out the back door together.

When Ellie turned back to help Jessica and Anna with the dishes, she found Anna watching her with concern etched on her wrinkled face. "Are you sure you don't mind Travis living here, dear?"

"Of course not. I told you that when you asked me last week."

"I know, but with the trouble between the two of you. . ." The words trailed off. "You mean the world to me, Ellie. I won't have him here if it hurts you."

Ellie squeezed Anna's hands. "Thank you for caring, but it's fine. Travis needed a place to stay, and you had rooms to rent. He may not make a very good husband, but there's no reason he shouldn't make a good tenant." Travis's living arrangements were a bit uncomfortable for Ellie, but she wouldn't admit it to Anna. The older woman needed the money from the rent.

Ellie released Anna's hands and picked up a dish towel. "I hope Travis isn't making too much work for you."

"Not at all. I like him."

Ellie didn't respond. She wasn't sure she wanted her friends to like her estranged husband too much.

"I think he'll be a help to have around. He shoveled the walks and driveway for me after last night's storm." Anna plunged her hands into the dishwater.

Ellie wandered to the back door, looking out the window at Travis and the boys while wiping the platter in her hand.

Jessica retrieved the platter. "It's dry. It's going to shine like a waxed car if you don't stop polishing it."

"They're building a snowman."

Jessica and Anna peered out, both grinning as the boys together attempted to roll a lopsided ball. The ball wasn't very large before its mass was too great for their combined muscles. Travis leaned over and helped them complete the snowman's stomach.

Reluctantly, Ellie and Jessica went back to help Anna.

Ellie kept returning to the door to check on the snowman's progress while helping with the dishes.

Finally Jessica threw up her hands in disgust. "This is the fifteenth time you've checked on them. You're wearing a rut in Anna's linoleum. Why don't you go outside and join them?"

"Yes, go ahead," Anna urged. "Jessica and I can finish up here."

Ellie refused. She forced herself to stand by the cupboard with Jessica and Anna.

They were almost done with the dishes when the back door opened. All three women turned around at the rush of cold air.

Corey stood panting in his blue and red snowsuit, his cheeks and nose bright red from the winter chill. "We need a cawwot, muvver."

Ellie stared at him. "A carrot?"

Corey frowned. Ellie sensed his impatience with her. "For his nose. We're makin' a snowman."

"Can we see it?" Jessica asked while Anna opened the refrigerator to procure a carrot.

"No. We're not done." He grabbed the carrot between his mittened hands and left, his snowsuit *sh-sh-sh-ing* as he walked.

Ellie turned to the other women. "I must design some decent boys' snowsuits for next winter's children's line, something practical that a child can move in easily."

"That should be easy," Jessica encouraged dryly. "That's why no one's figured it out before this."

"Just because it's difficult doesn't mean it's impossible."

Only a couple minutes passed before the door opened again. This time all three males stood there. Ellie noticed Travis's cheeks and nose were as red as the boys', and his eyes as filled with fun.

"C'mon and see our snowman," Brent demanded.

"C'mon." Corey waved an arm, urging the women outside.

"C'mon." Travis imitated Corey's gesture.

Ellie, Jessica, and Anna hurried to put on their boots and coats while the boys waited impatiently. When they all finally went outside, the women admired the boys' handiwork loudly and profusely. The boys looked like they'd burst with pride, but no more so than Travis.

"His name's Snowy," Corey informed them.

"Where did you get the eyes?" Ellie asked.

"Over there." Corey pointed to the gravel driveway.

"They aren't really eyes. They're stones," Brent explained gravely.

"I like the hat." Jessica was struggling to keep her mouth straight.

"It's T'avis's," Corey told her.

Red berries from a nearby dogwood tree made up a crooked smile. Twigs worked for the skinny arms. Likely the world had seen more original snowmen, but none that were so dear in Ellie's eyes as this one created by her son, his father, and her son's friend. She blinked back sudden tears. "Good job, guys. Your snowman has everything but a belly button."

Corey's mouth formed a large *O*. He turned to Travis. "What makes a belly button?"

Travis looked at a loss for a moment. "How about another stone?"

"Okay!" The boys stumbled through the snow, looking like penguins as they hurried toward the driveway, the only place in the snow-covered landscape where they could hope to find a stone. When they reached their goal, they plopped down on their knees to search.

Jessica and Anna decided to take a walk in the crisp air, leaving Ellie and Travis to watch the boys. Ellie was suddenly uncomfortable.

"The scenery here is beautiful," Travis said quietly. "The mountains look like they go on forever."

The village was built on a low mountain. The Blue Ridge Mountains of North Carolina and the Smoky Mountains of Georgia could be seen in the distance, row after row of snow- and pine-covered peaks. Ellie never grew tired of their beauty. "They seem to change every day," she told him. "Sometimes every hour as the sunlight and shadows change, or a storm moves in, or the fog settles or rises."

"It'll be fun to live in a place where it snows. In California, I had to go to the mountains to ski and snowboard. Now that I'm in the mountains, I can just go out the back door." He grinned at his own joke.

"Some people do ski or snowshoe to work when there's enough snow," she admitted, "but most people commute the way people in the rest of America do, by foot or car."

"Here's the belly button." Corey held up a round stone.

"Looks good," Travis approved. "Better put it on Snowy."

Corey shoved the stone into the round, white belly. Brent gave the stone an extra push.

Ellie and Travis shared a chuckle.

Satisfied they'd completed the snowman to the best of their ability, the boys looked for other entertainment. Spotting the sled on which Ellie and Jessica had pulled the boys to church and then to Anna's that morning, Brent let out a whoop and headed toward it. Corey followed, stumbling and falling flat on his face in the snow, then pushing himself up and starting out again.

"Looks like he's a veteran at that," Travis commented.

"At what?"

"Falling and starting over."

"All kids are accustomed to that. It's when they're older that the courage to try again is bred out of them."

"I guess you're right."

She felt his gaze on her but kept her own on the boys. At Brent's urging, Corey had climbed on the wooden sled. He sat with his legs straight forward and his hands clutching the sled's sides, his face shining with eagerness for the ride ahead. Brent leaned into the rope with all his weight, the intensity of his effort showing in the way his face screwed into lines. The sled jerked forward half a foot, then another. The boys were as happy as if they were moving a hundred miles an hour.

I wish I had their courage, Ellie thought. It exhausted her to consider the effort she and Travis would need to put into working out a lifetime of sharing the parental responsibilities and joys of raising Corey.

"It was good to see you in church this morning, Ellie."

Travis's jump to the topic of church surprised her. It took her a moment to change her line of thought. "I've been going for years."

"Why? Did you think it was a good idea to raise Corey with a faith in God?"

"Of course, but I started attending for myself before Corey was born. I wasn't doing such a good job of figuring life out by myself. I knew I needed to find help. I found what I needed when I decided to trust God."

Travis's smile was broad. "Me, too. Amazing what a difference believing in Him makes, isn't it?"

Surprise shot her eyebrows up. "Are you saying that you believe in God?"

He nodded. "Yep. Best thing that ever happened to me."

His new faith was a wonderful thing—if it was real, Ellie thought. "What happened to your conviction that 'God can mind His business, and I'll mind mine, and we'll get along just fine?'"

"Same thing that happened to you, I guess. I found out I wasn't getting along fine without Him at all."

Ellie wished she could believe him. Was his declaration of faith a way of convincing her, and maybe others, that he'd make a good father for Corey? Rather than take him at his word, she'd wait and watch. If his faith was real, his actions would show it over time.

The boys were getting nearer—Brent still bending into the rope for all he was worth and Corey urging him on between giggles and lurches of the sled.

Travis shook his head at the scene. "I like to think I'm in pretty good shape, what with the skiing and jogging I do, but if I worked at anything as hard as Brent is working now, I'd wake up so stiff the next day I couldn't get out of bed."

"Brent's muscles won't even remember this tomorrow."

"I'm beginning to feel old."

Travis didn't look old to Ellie. He looked a lot better than she would have liked. He was altogether too attractive for a man she didn't trust.

"I wish I'd brought my camera." Ellie would have liked to have pictures not only of the boys, but more importantly of Corey with his father making this first snowman.

"Do you have pictures of Corey when he was younger?" Travis asked quietly.

Ellie laughed. "What kind of mother would I be if I didn't?"

Travis didn't smile. "May I see them sometime?"

Ellie's smile died. She'd been thoughtless not to realize he would want to see them. She should have offered to show them to him before this. "Of course."

"Tonight?"

She hesitated. She was already worn out emotionally from being so near him today. Maybe she needed a break before they spent more time together.

"Please, Ellie."

Why not? It wasn't as if he was inviting her out for an intimate evening. He'd be looking at pictures. How long could it take? "All right."

The boys finally reached them. Brent dropped the rope. He was panting so hard the pale blue snowsuit rose and fell over his chest. His face showed his complete satisfaction with his Olympian effort.

Travis patted him on the back. "Good job. You're mighty strong."

Brent beamed.

"More," Corey urged.

"How about if I pull both of you?" Travis picked up the rope. "Jump on, Brent."

Brent hastened to join Corey. The boys giggled in their anticipation.

Ellie watched Travis pulling the boys around the yard. Their calls urging Travis to "go faster, faster" were clear in the cold air. She was surprised they hadn't urged him to take them down one of the many steep hills in town. It probably wouldn't be long before they did. Or before Travis thought of it himself.

Could it be any more dangerous than the emotional mountains she and Corey were traveling by allowing Travis back in their lives? Shivering, Ellie wrapped her soft black muffler closer about her neck.

Chapter 5

orey and Brent were already in their pajamas when Travis arrived at seven that evening. "The boys are in the kitchen," Ellie explained. "Jessica is making hot chocolate."

"Hot chocolate?"

The hope in his eyes and voice showed clearly he'd like some hot chocolate, too. Ellie groaned inwardly. She didn't want to do anything to encourage him to stay longer than necessary. She was already regretting she'd agreed to meet with him. Oh well, if he drank the hot chocolate while they looked at the albums, the drink shouldn't extend his visit. "I'll ask Jessica to make you a cup."

He grinned and pulled off his coat. "Thanks."

The swinging door between the kitchen and hall banged open. Corey barreled toward them in footed yellow fuzzy pajamas. "Hi, pa'dner." He threw his arms around one of Travis's legs.

"Hi, partner." Travis lifted Corey into his arms.

Ellie's heart lurched. The two were taking to each other altogether too quickly for her comfort. The thought sharpened her tone. "Jessica is waiting for you in the kitchen, Corey."

"Okay. Want hot choc'late, pa'dner?"

"Sure do."

"C'mon." Corey wiggled.

Travis got Corey's body language message and set him down.

"The albums are on the living room coffee table. You can drink your hot chocolate while you look at the pictures."

"No." Corey grabbed one of Travis's hands with both his own. "Dwink with me."

Ellie wasn't about to give in this time. "Travis can't stay long." She felt Travis's gaze on her, and her face grew hot. She reached for Corey's hand. "You can say good night to Travis after you're done with your snack."

"No." Corey ignored her hand and tugged on Travis's. "C'mon."

Travis gently removed Corey's hold. "Mom's the boss."

Corey's lower lip trembled.

Travis squatted down. "I promise I won't leave until you've come in to say good night. Is it a deal?"

"Okay." Corey made it clear it wasn't a satisfactory deal.

Jessica appeared in the dining room. "Hey, Corey, we almost forgot your favorite mugs. Are you going to help me get them down?"

"Yes." He hurried into the dining room. Travis followed.

Feeling defeated, Ellie trailed along.

Jessica opened the china closet and lifted Corey so he could reach a porcelain mug shaped like an elephant. The elephant's trunk made the mug's handle.

He held it toward Travis. "Look."

"Wow. Great mug."

Jessica pulled out another mug. "This one's Brent's." A giraffe's long neck made up the handle of Brent's mug.

Ellie closed the china closet doors. "Would you bring Travis and me some hot chocolate, too? No special mugs required."

Travis chuckled.

Corey decided someone must have said something funny. He threw back his head and laughed, watching for the adults' reaction. He wasn't disappointed.

When the laughs died down, Travis nodded at an old print hanging on the wall. It was of a log cabin on a snow- and pine-covered mountainside. "That looks like a romantic place."

Jessica grimaced. "Not to me. My husband and I have a cabin that looks a lot like that. Former owners made moonshine in it."

Travis burst into laughter. "You're putting me on."

"Nope, but I promise your hot chocolate will be nothing but chocolate and milk." She carried Corey and the mugs into the kitchen.

At this rate it was going to be a long evening, Ellie thought. "Ready to look at the pictures?" She led the way back to the living room.

Travis swung a hand over the three albums on the coffee table. "Which is first?"

She handed him an album with a white satin cover trimmed in baby blue. "This one." She sat beside him on the worn blue sofa while he opened the book as though it contained a fragile treasure.

She heard his sharp intake of breath as he looked at the first page. The pictures were of Corey and herself in the hospital right after Corey was born. She felt suddenly vulnerable. She shrank away from him, sinking into the back of the sofa.

Travis ran one large, blunt, trembling index finger over a picture of a naked, wrinkled, screaming Corey, then over another of Corey wrapped in a blanket of palest blue and lying on her chest. "I should have been there for you, for both of you."

Her heart contracted at the words which had been spoken in a cracked whisper. Her gaze darted to his face. Were those tears causing his eyes to glisten?

He turned his head so their gazes met.

They are tears. It was as though they trickled into her heart.

283

Guilt flooded after them. He was right. He should have been there, holding newborn Corey. She'd deprived him of that experience and could never give it back.

Did Travis's arms ache for that loss? Was that the pain she saw in his eyes now? Her own arms ached to hold Travis and make the pain go away.

Ellie broke their eye contact, looking down at her lap.

I'm sorry. She pressed her lips hard together against the words. She was sorry, but if she said the words, he might misunderstand. He might think she was apologizing for leaving him, for no longer trusting him. She wasn't sorry for those things. It wasn't safe for her or Corey to trust him. She didn't want to give him any emotional ammunition to use against her. So she swallowed the words and tried to swallow her guilt, too.

From the corner of her eye, she watched him turn the page. She gave her attention back to the album. Family pictures covered this page. Her family. Her mother holding Corey. Her father holding Corey. Her younger brother, Alan, holding Corey. Herself holding Corey and grinning from ear to ear. Only her family, her friends, not Travis's.

The guilt increased.

Jessica came in and set two steaming mugs on the coffee table, grinned at Ellie and Travis, and returned to the kitchen. Her entrance lessened Ellie's tension a trifle. She reached for the mug, glad to have something else to concentrate on.

Travis paged through the record of Corey's first few months of life: first day home, baby gifts, his first Easter, his first bath at home, his first bottle, his first time in a swing, his first time sitting up by himself, his first Christmas, in a stroller, in a playpen, crawling, his first steps—or maybe his second. Then there was Corey playing with his toes, playing with his toys, studying his belly button, laughing, crying, at the service dedicating him to God, and lots of pictures of Corey doing nothing but sleeping. Ellie gave brief explanations when necessary or in response to Travis's questions.

They'd just started on the second album when Corey hurried into the room.

He flung himself against Travis's knees. "You still here."

Travis ruffled Corey's golden curls. "Of course. Told you I would be."

If only his promises were that trustworthy, Ellie thought bitterly.

Corey struggled to climb up on the sofa. Travis lifted him effortlessly. The boy plopped down beside Travis, snuggling close to his father. Noting the pictures, Corey squealed in delight. "That's me!"

Travis frowned. "Are you sure? The boy in the pictures doesn't look old enough to be you."

"Uh-huh, is too." Corey's head bobbed up and down. "I was little."

"Really?"

"Uh-huh. I was one. See?" Corey shoved a pudgy finger over a picture of himself in a white short-sleeved top and white shorts seated beside a birthday cake with a single blue candle in the middle of it. "That's my bi'thday cake."

"Did you have a party?"

"Uh-huh."

"Who was at your party?"

Corey turned the page and pointed to people in the pictures as he rolled off, "Mommy an' Gwamma an' Gwampa an' Jessie an' Bwent."

Ellie watched the exchange silently, joy at the interaction between father and son braiding with regret and trepidation to form a confusing, bittersweet sensation.

"How old are you now?"

Corey held up two fingers.

Jessica and Brent came into the room holding hands. "Brent's going to bed now. We came in to say good night."

Ellie hugged Brent when he came over to her. "Good night. Sweet dreams. I love you."

"Love you." Brent looked at Travis, hesitating as if not certain how personal to be with him. Ellie knew he liked Travis, but he obviously wasn't as taken with the man as Corey was.

Travis gave him a grin. "I had fun building the snowman with you today. Maybe you'll let me play with you again sometime."

Brent nodded. A moment later he lifted his arms. Travis leaned forward and gave him a tight, quick, one-armed hug. "Good night."

" 'Night. Comin', Corey?"

Corey shook his head. "I'm showin' Twavis my pictures."

Ellie groaned inwardly. Usually Corey was good about going to bed when he was asked to. She hated the battles when he didn't want to go, but she refused to let him win those battles. "It's your bedtime, Corey."

He shook his head harder and stared at the photo album, refusing to meet her gaze as though that refusal strengthened his position.

Jessica held out a hand. "Why don't you come upstairs with Brent and me? I'll read you a story after you're tucked in."

Corey repeated his silent battle.

Ellie sighed. Before she could say anything, Travis caught her gaze. The appeal in his eyes for more time with his son was unmistakable. She caved in to guilt. "You can stay up for a few more minutes."

"Thanks." Travis smiled.

At first Corey eagerly told Travis about each succeeding picture, but it wasn't long before Corey was yawning. Travis slipped an arm around the boy, and he slumped against his father as he grew more tired.

Ellie could tell Travis was treasuring this time, the feel of his son resting against him in the manner all boys should be able to rest trustingly in their fathers' arms. But could Corey trust Travis? She'd discovered in a painful way that she could not. She didn't want that to happen to her son.

Soon Corey's explanations petered out. His head bobbed then rested against Travis's chest.

Travis and Ellie exchanged amused glances as Corey struggled to stay awake, his eyes closing and opening repeatedly. Finally the battle was over. His eyes stayed closed, long lashes resting against round cheeks like pencil-thin shadows of trees against snow in moonlight.

"Should I carry him upstairs for you?" Travis whispered.

She started to say no but then realized that putting his son to bed was another experience Travis hadn't had before, and she nodded.

They went up the stairs together. Ellie led the way to the bedroom the boys shared. A night-light kept them from tripping over a few scattered toys as they crossed the room to Corey's crib.

Corey stirred slightly when Travis laid the boy down. Ellie took from the crib rail the teddy bear quilt her mother had made and placed it over Corey. She touched his cheek lightly, saying a silent prayer that the Lord would keep him safe throughout the night, the prayer she said every night.

At that moment she felt Travis's hand on her shoulder. Her heart jumped and began racing.

She couldn't move. The moment was too sweet, too much the ideal family scene as she'd pictured it when she was younger and naive, with parents gazing together adoringly at their sleeping child. A moment too precious not to savor in spite of the legacy of broken trust.

Travis's touch felt familiar even after three years. She'd always loved the gentleness in the way his large hands touched her. It had been hard after she left him to make herself refuse to remember his touch, refuse to remember what it felt like to be in his arms. Now memories flooded back, sending waves of longing through her.

He squeezed her shoulder and smiled tenderly at her.

She stepped back quickly before her body and emotions could betray her further and led the way from the room. Ellie tried to slow her breathing as she walked down the stairs, but it was difficult with Travis right behind her.

She walked directly to the tree rack, removed his jacket, and held it out to him. She forced herself to look him squarely in the eyes and smile, refusing to allow him to see how she was quaking inside from her desire to allow all the walls she'd built to fall down and let herself know the joy of his arms once more.

He didn't put the coat on. He crushed it between his hands, his gaze boring into hers. "Thank you."

Sincerity rumbled through the quiet words, weakening the foundation of the distance Ellie was trying to keep.

Travis cupped her cheek gently in one hand, sending tremors through her.

"Thank you for tonight, Ellie, for the pictures, for the time with Corey. Thank you for raising our son with such love." The last words were a whisper.

Travis's jacket dropped to the floor. One arm slid about Ellie's waist, pulling her slowly against him. The familiar scent of his Langenfeld cologne enveloped her.

Ellie knew she was going to be in trouble if she didn't stop him, but she couldn't make herself say no. The palms of her hands trembled against his chest. Some traitorous part of her wanted to feel his kiss again, to live in the dream of desire satisfied in loving and trusting this man.

Travis's hand on her cheek tenderly urged her face toward his. His lips touched hers, lightly, testing, warm. Then again, and she leaned into his kiss, welcoming it, remembering it.

It felt so good it was frightening.

She pulled her head back, breaking off the kiss, and closed her eyes. "No."

His forehead touched hers. His heart banged beneath her palms. "Okay." The word was barely more than a ragged breath.

Ellie lifted her hands from his chest and stepped back.

He released her instantly. Regret and relief washed through her as the warmth of his body was removed.

She tried to regain a semblance of control. "You can have the negatives if you want."

"Negatives?"

"Of the pictures of Corey."

"Oh, right, negatives."

"Do you want them?"

"I was just thinking."

"What?"

"I wouldn't need my own copies of Corey's pictures if we lived together as a family again."

Ellie stared at him in disbelief. The blood pounded in her ears so loud she was sure she'd misheard him.

"What do you say, Ellie? We're still married. All we'd have to do is move in together."

Chapter 6

Y ou can't be serious." Ellie widened the gap between them.

Travis mentally kicked himself. He'd jumped in too fast. He should have known better. He did know better. Only everything had felt so good tonight, so right, with Ellie and Corey. His longing for them had outrun his judgment.

Now that he'd jumped in with both feet, he might as well continue. He took a deep breath and plunged both hands through his hair.

"I am serious. I want to be with my son. And I've missed you like crazy."

"We can't just. . .just move in together again after all this time."

"How long do we have to wait to make it proper?"

"Maybe a lifetime. I'm not sure we should get back together."

Travis was terrified to ask the next question, which was the very reason he knew he must. "If that's the way you feel, why haven't you filed for divorce?"

"I. . .I don't know."

"I hoped it was because you still love me." How could admitting his need for his wife's love feel as terrifying as jumping out of a plane without a parachute?

Ellie rubbed her arms and refused to meet his gaze.

Travis swallowed hard. "Maybe it was because you were afraid if I found out about Corey I'd try to take him away from you."

Her head swung up.

The fright in her eyes made Travis sick to his stomach. "That's it, isn't it?"

"You can't take him away." The words were raspy with fear. "I'm a good mother. There's no reason the courts would let you take him away from me."

He laid a hand on her upper arm in an attempt to calm her.

She jerked away.

"Sorry." Travis held up his hands, palms out. "I'd never take Corey away from you unless I thought it was necessary for Corey's well-being."

Ellie's eyes flashed.

Travis's heart sank. Another bad error. He rushed on, hoping to divert her defensive anger. "I haven't any reason to believe you aren't a wonderful mother. That's what I'd expect you to be, a wonderful mother."

A little tension left her face, and he allowed himself a small sigh of relief. "We're both Christians now, Ellie. We're still married. I believe it's God's will families stay together. Don't you?"

"I can't trust you. How can I live with you when I can't trust you?"

"I tried to explain about Michelle before, but you wouldn't let me."

"I know what I saw, and I know what I heard. I trust my eyes and ears more than I trust your explanations. I'd be a fool not to."

"But—"

"I've no one to blame but myself for falling in love with a man who treated me the way you did, but I don't want Corey to be hurt by you, too."

Shock exploded inside Travis. "You can't think I'd hurt my own son."

"I want Corey to have a father he can trust, whose values don't include humiliating him in front of others, belittling his dreams and abilities, breaking promises, and betraying him." Ellie's eyes snapped with anger. Her hands formed into fists. "That's why I didn't tell you about Corey earlier. Every day since I mailed that letter I've worried that it was a horrible mistake. I can't keep you from seeing him, but I don't have to let you live with us and pretend we're a happy family. If I did, and you broke your trust again, the betrayal would be that much worse for Corey."

Travis felt like he'd been kicked in the stomach. "You think I can't be trusted? What about a mother who abandons the man she's promised to live with forever, who leaves without even saying good-bye? What about a mother who won't even try to work things out when there's a problem?"

"I did try, before you spent the night with that Michelle woman."

"Ellie, Travis, keep it down!"

Travis looked up in surprise to see Jessica leaning over the stairway banister in flannel pajamas. In a flash he realized he and Ellie had raised their voices to the point of yelling. He closed his eyes and rubbed his hands down over his face. "Did we wake the boys?"

"I didn't take time to find out. You woke me." Jessica's troubled gaze moved from Travis to Ellie. "You okay?"

Ellie nodded.

"Are you sure?" Jessica gave Travis a look that made him feel as if she was considering making a domestic violence report.

"I'm sure," Ellie said. "Sorry, Jess."

Travis dug his hands into the pockets of his khakis. "I'm sorry, too."

"Call me if you need me," Jessica ordered Ellie.

When Jess was back upstairs, Travis walked into the living room where their voices wouldn't carry upstairs as easily. Ellie followed. "I am sorry. I shouldn't have yelled," he admitted. "I think Jess is afraid I'll raise more than my voice."

"Her estranged husband has a mean temper. Dan beat her. That's why she left the marriage. She was afraid he'd start hitting Brent, too."

Travis gave a low whistle. "No wonder she's worried about me."

Ellie brushed her thick brown hair behind her ears. With a catch in his chest, he realized she looked suddenly tired.

"Did you mean what you said? I never thought of it as abandoning you when I left. I was only protecting myself from being hurt by you further. I never saw it from your point of view."

"I guess both of us could have acted wiser." He felt miserable—about tonight, about what had happened between them three years ago, about the years they'd lost in between. Could they ever repair it all? "I still love you, Ellie. I've never stopped loving you."

"I want to believe you, but I don't dare let myself trust you. I'm so afraid you'll hurt me again, and more afraid you'll hurt Corey." Her eyes looked haunted. "Besides, I don't think love treats people the way we treated each other."

He hated the pain in her eyes. He wanted to hold her and make all the pain he'd caused her go away. The knowledge that his comfort was the last thing she'd accept right now intensified his own pain.

"Would you please leave?" She brushed her bangs back in a weary gesture. "I'm tired, and I don't want to argue anymore."

He couldn't stay if she wanted him to leave. He picked up his coat from the floor. At the door he turned, studying her face. He wanted desperately to tell her again that he loved her. "Thanks again for tonight. It meant a lot to me."

He reflected on the evening while he walked the few blocks back to Anna's house, the crisp winter night quickening his steps as they squeaked on the snowy sidewalk. He'd made a huge blunder, suggesting he and Ellie get back together. He'd been moving way too fast.

He groaned, remembering the way it felt to hold her again, the feel of her hair soft against his cheek, the gentle floral scent she wore, her lips soft beneath his, hesitating before they yielded to his invitation, then drawing back. It was going to be harder slowing down again now that he'd held her.

How was he ever going to get past the pain he'd inflicted on her? "Lord, show me how to convince her she can trust my love."

What had she said right before he left? "I don't think love treats people the way we treated each other."

I'll just have to prove my love for her a day at a time, a step at a time. Baby steps.

❧

Ellie found it difficult concentrating on work at the boutique the next morning. The memory of the kiss she and Travis had shared kept getting in the way. If only it hadn't felt so good. Ellie groaned.

Jessica looked up from the sketch she was showing Ellie for a necklace of dogwood blossoms in silver. "What's the matter?"

"Nothing. This sketch looks great. Could you make a bracelet to match?"

"Sure. It's Travis, isn't it?"

"What's Travis?"

Jessica's bracelets jangled as she propped her fists on her narrow, jean-covered hips. "The groan. Your absentminded attitude this morning. You're thinking about the argument you had with Travis."

"Not really." Ellie's lips lifted in a slow smile.

Jessica's eyes narrowed. "I don't think I like that twinkle in your eyes. What exactly happened last night? The part I didn't hear when you were yelling at each other, that is."

"I think Travis proposed to me."

"He can't propose to you. You're already married."

"It sounded a lot like a proposal. He wants us to live together again."

"That's indecent."

"It isn't indecent. Like you said, we're already married."

"Ellie, get a grip. This is the man who cheated on you. You aren't going to let him hurt you that way again, are you?"

"No." Ellie examined the wonderful blue and green fabric on her worktable. "I dreamed that he and I were back together. When I woke up I could almost feel his arms around me. My first thought was how in the beginning of our marriage we would fall asleep with his arm around my shoulders and my cheek against his chest. Sometimes I miss that, you know?"

"I do know." A wistfulness slipped into Jessica's tone, like fog softening the edges of jagged mountain bluffs. "Sometimes I wonder if I'll ever experience that with anyone again." She picked up Ellie's open shears, clapped them shut, and slammed them down on the worktable. "But I never make the mistake of thinking I can have true intimacy with Dan or with any other man who beats women. And you can't have it with a man you can't trust, either."

"I guess. . .it feels nice to be wanted again."

"Ellie—"

"Don't worry. I told Travis we can't live together, that I don't trust him not to hurt me and Corey."

"Good. We all hurt others without trying to. It's when people do it on purpose it's a problem. When a man cheats on his wife, he's hurting her on purpose."

"I know." Ellie wished Jess would stop repeating that Travis had cheated on her. She hated those words and the emotions they evoked.

A question she'd pushed away repeatedly popped into her mind. Why hadn't Travis filed for divorce so he could marry Michelle? Maybe he didn't think he needed to, since he'd been seeing her while he was married to Ellie anyway.

"You have to protect yourself and Corey. Especially Corey. You're the adult. If you want to let yourself in for a life filled with pain, no one can stop you." Jessica threw her arms up in a gesture of disgust, her bracelets saucily adding their tinkling music. "Corey hasn't a choice in the matter. You're the only one who can limit the pain he's exposed to."

Ellie sighed and dropped her head into her hands. "I know you're right."

"If all you're looking for is a man to make you feel wanted, what about Chuck? Lately I've had the impression all he's waiting for is for you to give him an indication you're a teeny bit interested in him."

"Chuck is nice, but I'm married to Travis."

"Maybe you shouldn't be."

"Maybe." Ellie had gone back and forth on this issue for three years. She had friends who knew a lot more about the Bible than she did who believed God never allowed divorce, and others who believed He allowed it in certain circumstances. She respected what others believed for themselves. She certainly felt Jessica had been wise to leave Dan to protect herself and Brent. For herself Ellie only knew she'd promised to love and stay married to Travis for the rest of their lives. Even knowing he'd been unfaithful, she wasn't quite ready to sever her ties with him completely. She knew people who would consider her emotionally unhealthy because of that, but that's where she stood.

The tinkle of brass bells and the laughter of young women announced new customers. Ellie glanced into the shop. She didn't recognize the women. They were probably visitors at the nearby ski resort, as so many of her customers were this time of year.

"I'll wait on them," Jessica offered. "I know you want to get this outfit cut out." She entered the shop with her usual quick pace and greeted the women warmly.

Ellie turned gratefully to her work. She'd asked Anna to watch Corey and Brent today so she and Jessica could work on some one-of-a-kind spring pieces. She hadn't put many spring pieces out in her shop yet, but she was well aware major department stores had already cleared out much of their winter merchandise and were filling the space with spring outfits. Most of her designs were ready to be hung out.

This gorgeous silk material was for a summer ankle-length shift and shawl. The color was a rich blending of blue and green, with a jewel-like depth to it. The material was so soft it felt like she remembered the water of a lake feeling against her skin on a calm summer day.

Ellie had a moment of regret. It would be fun to make the gown for herself. She'd designed the dress for Jewell Landry, a wealthy local woman, one of Ellie's most loyal customers and one of her best advertisements. Every time Mrs. Landry wore one of Ellie's outfits, women came into the shop asking for similar outfits. Since Mrs. Landry insisted everything she purchased be one of a kind, Ellie never had exactly the same thing available, yet she seldom sent these women away empty handed after they'd seen her stock.

Humming to herself, Ellie pinned her hand-cut tissue paper pattern to the material. She was glad Anna had agreed to watch the boys at home today. There were too many dangerous things in the workroom, she thought, picking up her expensive shears.

Jessica bounced into the workroom, brushing the palms of her hands back and forth, obviously pleased with herself. "They bought one of those wonderful cardigans with the mountain design, and a blue tweed suit, and a pale blue silk blouse with one of Anna's lace collars."

"That is a good sale." Those were among Ellie's most expensive winter pieces.

"Here we go again," Jessica said as the brass bells gave the message of a new arrival. "Here's hoping they're in as much of a buying mood as the last customers."

She swung about and stopped. "It's Dan."

"Oh no, Jess."

"Some customers came in right behind him."

"I'll wait on them. Why don't you ask Dan to come back here to talk? Just be careful."

"He won't hurt me in a public place." Jessica went to meet him.

Ellie wasn't so sure. She started toward the door to the shop, turned around, and stuck her scissors into her skirt's deep pocket, then hurried to greet her customers.

"Hi, Dan." She gave him what she hoped appeared a welcoming smile when they passed each other. He'd think up enough reasons to act obnoxious without her encouraging him by being unfriendly.

The customers were a middle-aged woman and her teenage daughter, again taking a break from the ski slopes. They chatted pleasantly with Ellie in between exclaiming over her sweater collection.

Ellie's stomach tightened in dread anticipation when she first heard the angry rumble of Dan's deep voice, too loud for normal conversation. She sent up a silent prayer for God to protect Jessica and give her wisdom in her words so that she would not anger Dan unnecessarily. Not that the man needed a reason to act angrily.

The customers darted curious glances toward the workroom, and Ellie's stomach cinched tighter.

Dan's voice suddenly became almost inaudible. The women's attention went back to the soft sweaters before them. Ellie stole a glance toward the back of the shop. The swinging door separating the shop and workroom had been closed. Ellie didn't know whether she felt relieved or not. She was glad Dan was no longer disturbing her customers, but the closed door made Jessica more vulnerable to Dan's anger.

The daughter decided on a pale peach sweater with a heart-shaped pocket and matching silver heart-shaped buttons designed by Jessica. The sweater had been one of Ellie's most popular with teenage girls that season. Ellie was ringing up the sale when Mrs. Landry entered the shop.

When Ellie handed her customer her package, she looked relieved to hurry out of the shop with her daughter.

Ellie put on her most professional smile. "Hello, Mrs. Landry."

"I just stopped by to see how my new gown is coming."

"I started cutting it out this morning. It's in the workroom."

Dan's voice rose again. Ellie's heart plummeted. Mrs. Landry was the last person Ellie wanted to have hear his tirade in her store.

Her customer frowned. "What is going on back there?"

Ellie spread her hands, searching her mind for an answer that wouldn't reveal things Jessica preferred remain private. Chuck walked in just in time to give her a reason not to answer.

Dan's voice had risen so loud that Mrs. Landry looked uneasy. There'd been a couple *thuds* and *thunks* Ellie hadn't liked the sound of, either.

Ellie hurried across the room to Chuck. His smiling greeting quickly turned to a frown as he became aware of Dan's bellowing.

"Dan?" he asked before Ellie had a chance to say anything.

"Yes."

He started toward the back room. She stopped him with a hand on his arm. "Please," she urged in a low voice, "will you get the sheriff?"

He looked toward the back room uncertainly.

"Please, Chuck. Hurry."

He pressed his lips together and left, angry determination in every stride.

Ellie breathed a sigh of relief. The sheriff's office was on the next block. Help should arrive any minute.

She started toward the back room. Mrs. Landry clutched Ellie's arm with a well-manicured hand. "Be careful."

Ellie opened the swinging door slowly, not knowing whether Jessica or Dan was behind it. Entering the room, her gaze immediately searched out Jessica. She was on the opposite side of the room, the large worktable between her and Dan. Ellie felt as though she could collapse in relief when she saw her friend apparently hadn't been hit.

Dan's face was red with unrepressed fury. He glared at Ellie and barked, "This is a private discussion."

"Not that you'd notice." Ellie pushed the door back and locked it open. She hated to expose Jessica to Mrs. Landry's curiosity, but she didn't dare leave her friend alone with Dan any longer.

Mrs. Landry stayed back by the counter, stretching her neck to see. Dan didn't notice her.

Ellie leaned back against the door. One sweeping glance told her what had caused the noises she'd heard earlier. Her dress form was on the floor, as were the beautiful material with which she'd been working and numerous supplies.

Dan grabbed the edge of the door. "Get out of here." His voice was jagged-edged with anger.

The brass bells jangled.

"More customers," Ellie announced, not leaving her post. Maybe he'd be too embarrassed to continue acting out his anger if he knew people could see who was making all the noise.

Dan glanced into the shop. His mouth tightened. He jammed his hands into the pockets of his brown suit coat.

Ellie followed his glance. Travis was coming toward her, a bounce in his step and a smile on his face. "Hi, Ellie. I was hoping we could have lunch together."

He gave Dan a short curious look, started to greet Jessica, and stopped short, taking in the mess in one sweeping glance. "What happened in here?"

No one answered.

Travis looked at Ellie with raised eyebrows.

She bit her bottom lip. If she said anything, it might set Dan off again.

His eyes narrowed as he looked at Dan. "I don't think we've met. I'm Travis Carter, Ellie's husband." He didn't offer his hand.

"Dan Robbins, Jessica's husband." Dan's chin jutted out belligerently.

"Soon to be ex," Jessica reminded him.

Travis's eyes widened a sliver, and Ellie knew the information was registering, that he was remembering what she'd said about Dan being an abusive husband. "Are you okay, Jess?"

Jessica nodded and knelt down to gather up the blue and green silk.

"Jess and I were having a private conversation. If you two will leave, we'll finish it." Dan jerked at the door behind Ellie, causing Ellie to stumble forward.

Travis caught her. She felt the strength in his arm as he drew her against him. "Don't do that again." Travis's words were a quiet threat.

The two men glared at each other. Dan was the first to look away. "If you'll just leave us alone a couple more minutes. . ."

"I don't think we'll be doing that." Travis's voice was still quiet and even. "Ellie and Jess obviously have work to do in here."

The front door crashed open. Chuck rushed in, a sheriff in an official brown jacket right behind him with one hand on his holster.

Thank You, Lord. Ellie's stomach muscles slackened the tautness that had started when Dan entered the shop.

Chuck stopped just outside the back-room door. Mrs. Landry moved quickly to stand behind him, peeking over his shoulder into the room.

Ellie watched Sheriff Eric Strand take in Jessica's condition and the condition of the room in a moment.

"Jess, Dan, Ellie, Travis." Sheriff Strand greeted them with cautious friendliness.

Ellie was surprised he knew Travis, then realized of course a law officer would be familiar with even the newest of the town's lawyers.

"Any trouble here?" The sheriff's eyes questioned each of them in turn.

Dan's chin jutted out again. "No trouble." He caught sight of Mrs. Landry and Chuck, and Ellie saw him struggle to gain some composure.

"Jess?" The sheriff singled her out.

Jess shook her head. She still had the worktable between herself and her estranged husband. Her arms were crossed tightly over her chest, as though she were hugging herself to feel safe. Ellie's heart went out to her.

Sheriff Strand looked pointedly at the items Dan had knocked onto the floor. "Things are kind of a mess here, Ellie. Anything damaged?"

"I don't think so." The material for Mrs. Landry's dress probably needed cleaning, but it didn't seem worth mentioning. The sheriff was probably talking about the kind of damage for which Dan could be charged, and Ellie doubted the material qualified.

Chasing off Ellie's customers with his angry, loud voice likely wasn't a chargeable offense, either. Jessica's soon-to-be-ex-husband probably couldn't be charged for anything he'd done today, unless it was disturbing the peace.

"It's almost noon, Dan. How about if we have lunch together? It's on me." Sheriff Strand laid a hand on Dan's arm.

Dan shook it off under the guise of straightening his suit coat. "Thanks, I have other plans for lunch." He stalked out of the room and out of the shop without looking back.

Ellie drew a shaky breath. "Thanks, Eric."

"Anytime." The sheriff looked from Ellie to Jess. "Either of you decide there's something you think Dan should be charged with, let me know." He lowered his chin, raised thick eyebrows, and stared pointedly at Jess. "I mean it. Don't you let him get away with anything he shouldn't. A man with a temper like Dan's is dangerous."

"I know." Misery looked out of Jess's eyes.

Ellie's heart wanted to burst at the sight of it.

The sheriff left, looking dissatisfied with the results of his call. He offered his arm to Mrs. Landry. "Why don't we let the ladies get things organized again, Mrs. Landry? Then they'll be able to devote all their time to you."

Ellie was glad to see her wealthy customer leave with Sheriff Strand, though Mrs. Landry looked back over her shoulder until they reached the outside door.

Throughout the sheriff's questioning, Chuck had stood just outside the workroom door. Now he asked quietly, "You sure you're okay, Ellie?"

"I'm fine." It was only then she realized she was still standing in the safe circle of Travis's arm. Blood raced to her face. She stepped away from Travis. She could feel his gaze on her as his arm fell away, but she refused to meet it.

Curiosity and something which looked suspiciously like pain filled Chuck's eyes as they studied hers. Angry with herself for feeling compromised for being in her husband's arms in what had been a dangerous situation, she put more warmth than necessary into her appreciation. "Thanks for getting Eric for us, Chuck."

She moved quickly around the table to where Jessica was picking things up from the floor. Ellie's heart contracted at the way her friend was trembling. "It's okay. I'll pick it up later."

Jess shook her head hard. "It's my fault. I'll clean it up."

"It isn't your fault."

"If it weren't for me, Dan wouldn't have been here."

"He's responsible for his actions, not you. You know that. Why don't you go get some lunch, or go home and lie down for a while?" Ellie slipped an arm around Jess's shoulder and gave her a loving squeeze.

"I'm sorry he got so loud." Tears filled Jessica's green eyes. "Did the customers say anything?"

"No." Not for the world would Ellie admit the customers' horrified looks or that Dan's angry voice had frightened customers away. "What was he so upset about this time?"

"Same old, same old." Jess's voice cracked, betraying her in her attempt at lightness.

"He wants to get back together with you," Ellie clarified.

"He's using Brent as a threat if I don't agree."

"What do you mean by 'threat'?" Travis asked sharply.

Jessica's slim shoulders lifted her white cotton sweater in a shrug. "The usual, I guess. He says if I don't agree to get back together with him, he will sue for full custody of Brent."

"What makes him think he could win?" The lawyer in Travis was in full force now.

"He's a professional with a good income. He can afford to give Brent anything he needs. I, on the other hand, couldn't make ends meet on my income from my jewelry and working here if Ellie and I didn't live together and share expenses."

"You give Brent a good and love-filled home," Travis assured her. "No judge would give Dan full custody based on what you just told me." His brows drew together. "From what Ellie told me, I thought. . .didn't you ever have Dan charged for hitting you?"

Her face flushed. "No."

"It sounded like Sheriff Strand knew about. . .the situation."

"It's no secret Dan has a bad temper and a loud, vile mouth. Some people suspect him of hitting me, but I've only admitted it to Ellie, Anna, and Chuck. I needed someone to know in case. . .in case something happened to me and I couldn't be there to protect Brent."

"Why didn't you report Dan?" Travis persisted.

Jessica straightened some of the supplies she'd picked up from the floor. "He said if I reported him he'd hurt Brent."

"You could have had a restraining order issued against Dan."

"Do you honestly think that would keep Brent safe from Dan?" Jessica's eyes flashed with disdain.

Travis looked like he wanted to argue for the system but couldn't. "No."

"People who haven't been in relationships with people like Dan don't understand," Jessica asserted. "They think the solution is so easy. Just walk away. Just report him. Well, it isn't so easy to walk away knowing there isn't any way the law can protect you and your children from a man who wants to harm you."

A customer entered the shop, and Ellie reluctantly left her friend with Travis, closing the door to the workshop. Chuck was still in the shop, too, she discovered. He appeared to be examining his workmanship on the display shelves he'd put in a couple of months ago.

The customer wanted to browse, so Ellie made herself busy straightening displays where she would be readily available if the customer had questions. No questions were asked. The customer soon left without making a purchase.

The door hadn't closed behind her before Chuck was at Ellie's side at the sales counter. "What exactly happened here?"

Ellie gave him a brief explanation. "I was afraid Dan would hurt Jess. She says he'd never do that in public. She's probably right. He'd know his reputation would be finished in this town if he was convicted of beating his wife."

Chuck snorted. Ellie suspected he was biting back a few choice words about Dan. Jessica had discussed the situation with Ellie and Chuck many times. Neither of them had been able to change Jessica's mind about the manner in which she dealt with Dan. They just tried to never leave their friend or Brent alone with Dan and listened when Jessica needed to talk to someone.

Chuck stuffed his hands into his pockets. "About when I came in," he started. "The second time, I mean."

"Yes?" Ellie encouraged when he stopped.

"I thought you and your husband weren't back together."

"We're not." A hint of reserve stiffened her spine.

"It kind of looked like you are."

"He only had his arm around me because—" She caught herself. She didn't owe Chuck or anyone else an explanation. "We're not back together." She stared back at him boldly. What did she have to hide?

"I stopped to ask if you wanted to go to lunch."

"I don't think I can today, not after what happened. Jess will probably need to get away for a while. Anna is watching the boys, so I can't ask her to come down."

"Another time."

"Sure."

There was an awkward silence.

Ellie tried to get past it. She didn't want anything to destroy their friendship. "Thanks again for coming to the rescue with Sheriff Strand."

He nodded. "I'll see if there's anything I can do to help in the back."

"Thanks." Ellie genuinely liked and respected him, but it was growing more evident all the time that he no longer wanted to keep their relationship on a platonic level. She certainly wasn't ready to move on to anything else. She doubted her beliefs would ever allow her to, regardless of what happened between her and Travis.

The relief she'd felt when Travis came into the shop, the security she'd known with his arm around her, washed over her. She'd known she and Jessica could rely on him.

Rely on him. The thought stopped her hands on the sales slips she was riffling through. Relying on him sounded awfully similar to trusting him. Of course, this situation was nothing like Travis choosing to be with another woman. Faithfulness in one way didn't ensure faithfulness in another.

Still, she discovered she was profoundly grateful she never had to fear Travis would physically harm her or Corey. No question that adultery was a betrayal, but what could possibly be worse than worrying that your child might be harmed by his father?

Travis came out of the workroom and stopped beside her. His face still looked tense. "Are you all right?"

"Yes."

"I hadn't realized Jess's husband was the Dan I knew through work. Even though our law firm had wealthy clients who were abusers, I always picture violent men as biker types, not professionals."

"It would be nice if we could tell by looking at someone whether they'd hit us or rob us." *Or have extramarital affairs,* she thought. She changed the topic. "I'm glad you came by when you did, though."

"I am, too. I expect it wasn't a coincidence. Our heavenly Father probably had something to do with the timing."

Ellie grinned. "I expect He did."

"And here I thought I was only coming by to ask you out to lunch."

"I can't leave the shop."

"Is Corey with Anna today?"

"Yes, and Brent, too." Ellie laughed. "Anna has a lot of energy for a woman her age, but she'll probably be 'tuckered,' as she says, by the time Jess and I pick up the boys."

Travis's blue eyes grew darker, and his jaw tensed. She wondered what she'd said to disturb him then decided she'd imagined the reactions, for his next words gave no hint of anger.

"Maybe I'll stop home for lunch and give Anna a break. I like having lunch with our son, anyway."

A pleasant tingle ran through Ellie as it always did when he referred to Corey as "our" son. "One of Anna's homemade meals doesn't have anything to do with your plans, I'm sure," she teased.

"Her cooking is quite an incentive," he admitted lightly, "but not quite on par with Corey's company. See you later."

Ellie's fingers rested lightly against the wooden counter while she watched him leave, watched as he passed the shop's windows on his way to Anna's, noting the swing of his strong shoulders, remembering the safety she'd felt with his arm taut around her in the workroom.

And the familiarity she'd known in his arms last night. The memory of the kiss they'd shared warmed her with its sweetness. It had awakened the longing for the intimacies they'd shared in the early, happy days of their marriage.

She sighed deeply. She shouldn't have allowed the kiss. Any physical intimacy between them would only complicate matters.

But it had felt so good.

"Hi."

Jessica's arrival at Ellie's side jolted her from her reverie. "Hi, yourself. You doing okay?"

"Yeah. A little shaky still, but that will pass. I, uh, was talking to Travis. . ."

"Yes?"

"Maybe I misjudged him. A little. Maybe."

Ellie frowned. "What do you mean?"

"Maybe every guy who raises his voice in an argument isn't going to raise his fists, too."

"I really don't think Travis would ever strike me or Corey," Ellie said gently.

"Maybe not. It's hard to trust any man not to act violently, though. When Dan and I first started dating, he treated me like a princess. I never expected I'd one day be a. . .a battered wife." She wrinkled her nose. "It's still hard to use that term about myself."

"It's in the past. You were a battered wife. Now you're a wiser, stronger woman."

"Thanks." Jessica gave Ellie a quick hug. "Travis offered to represent me for free. He wants me to tell him everything I can remember that Dan's done, in the way of hurting me and such."

"Sounds like a good idea."

"Yeah. He seems like an okay guy. Except. . .except I guess you still can't trust him not to. . .you know."

Her words trickled through Ellie's veins like poison, killing her heart's tender new shoots of hope. "Yes. I know."

Chapter 7

As soon as Travis was out of sight of the shop, he set off in a jog. His heart was already beating as hard as though he'd run ten miles. He had to get to Corey and Brent. Dan's anger likely escalated when his ego was bruised, knowing so many people saw him out of control. What if he decided to take it out on Brent? Only fragile Anna would stand between the three-year-old and the furious man.

The slick soles on Travis's wing tips slipped on a patch of ice, sending him crashing to the sidewalk. He picked himself up and took off again. He wished he'd worn his sneakers or sure-soled boots to work today.

He wished he'd taken the car to work instead of walking the few blocks between his office and Anna's.

He wished he hadn't worn his long camel-hair coat over his suit today; it caught the wind and slowed his speed.

He wished fear wasn't tying his stomach into knots and building that hard ball at the base of his throat that made it hard to breathe as he ran.

He wished his law experience hadn't left him with too many vivid memories of what out-of-control dads could do to their own kids.

Prayers he couldn't express in words wafted heavenward while his feet flew over the snow-edged sidewalks.

He raced up the wooden steps, across the porch, flung open the front door, and rushed into the house. The design of the home was almost identical to Ellie's, and he could see from the front hall through the living room into the dining room—where three pairs of eyes stared at him in surprise.

Travis halted, his hand still on the open door's brass knob. His lungs all but collapsed from relief. Brent was fine. Corey and Anna were fine. Obviously Dan hadn't been here. *Thank You, Lord.*

He wanted to pull both boys into his arms, hug them hard, and never let them go, never allow them into a place where they could be harmed.

"Travis?" Anna's voice was a mixture of concern and amusement.

He was suddenly aware of how strange his bursting into the house that way must appear. He raised a hand, feeling sheepish. "Hi. Okay if I join you for lunch?"

Anna pushed back her chair. "Of course. We're having tomato soup and grilled cheese sandwiches. It will take only a couple minutes to heat some for you."

"Thanks." Travis closed the door, looking for the lock as he did so. There was only a keyhole in the original ornate brass door handle plate—a keyhole Travis suspected hadn't seen a key since the house was built.

He started for the kitchen, surprised to find himself panting. He made time to jog each day. Normally the run from the boutique to Anna's house would cause his breath or heart rate to rise only slightly. Amazing the effect fear had on the body.

Anna was already at the stove. He moved quickly across her cheerful blue and white kitchen to check out the back door. Only a simple hook lock. He fastened it.

Anna stared at him with a puzzled expression, a spatula in one hand. Her gaze slipped to his feet, where a small muddy puddle was forming, then back to his face. "You're acting strangely."

He grimaced. "Sorry, forgot to take off my shoes." He slid them off.

"Is something the matter?"

He could have kicked himself for being so transparent. He hadn't meant to frighten her, but maybe it was safer if she were a bit frightened. He glanced into the dining room. The boys were laughing and chatting.

Travis moved close to her so that the boys wouldn't overhear and told her about Dan's outburst and Travis's worry for the boys.

"I've been concerned for Jessica ever since she told me about Dan's abuse." Anna's eyes were troubled beneath a furrowed brow. "But it never occurred to me Dan might show up here."

"Does he know you watch Brent sometimes?"

She shrugged. "I suppose so."

"Do you have keys for your doors?"

"No. I've never seen the keys, though my late husband's parents built this house."

"Would you mind having locks put on?"

"No, not under the circumstances."

Travis didn't want to leave her alone with the boys even for the time it would take to run to the local hardware store and pick up some locks. "If it's all right with you, I'd like to call Chuck and ask him to bring some locks up. Maybe he can put them on right away."

She swung a hand toward the wall beside the dining room door. "There's the phone."

Hand on the phone, he turned to her. "You're handling this pretty well. I thought you'd be more upset."

"You mean because I'm an old lady?"

He grinned in surprise at her description of herself. He'd never have had the nerve or lack of tact to call her that to her face. "A sweet little lady," he qualified.

"Sweet little old ladies don't grow to be sweet little old ladies without living through a lot of troubled times. That's why there's nothing tougher than a sweet little old lady." She winked at him.

He laughed and lifted the receiver. He reached Chuck on his cell phone and the carpenter readily agreed to come.

Next Travis called his temporary secretary and let her know he would be late getting back to the office. *Good thing I don't have any appointments this afternoon,* he thought, entering the dining room.

The boys greeted him with an enthusiasm that made his heart expand with gratitude for the gift of having them in his life. He'd met his son a little over a month ago and been in town only a few days, and already he could barely remember what his life had been like before Corey.

He reached over and rubbed Corey's blond curls. "Hi, partner." Then he did the same with Brent's straight, thick brown hair.

Both boys giggled.

Travis loved the funny little-boy sound and the tiny-toothed grins that went along with it. Joy spiraled through him. "So what have you two been doing all day?"

"We went shoppin' with Anna," Brent announced.

Corey nodded, speaking around his grilled cheese sandwich. "For groc'ies."

"I'll bet she was glad you two helped her out with that chore."

Both boys nodded. "She didn't let us take the sled, though," Brent said.

"Too bad." Travis imagined it would be hard for Anna to pull both boys and carry the groceries at the same time, and the boys could hardly pull each other the few blocks to the store and back.

"We made cookies." Corey's wide-eyed grin showed he thought Travis should be especially impressed with this feat.

"Can I have one?"

Corey nodded.

"Have to clean your plate first," Brent qualified.

Travis swallowed a laugh. "It's a deal." He dipped his spoon into his soup.

"Here." Corey grabbed a handful of oyster crackers from the blue and cream pottery bowl in the middle of the table and dropped them into Travis's soup.

"Thanks." Travis rubbed a hand across his mouth, hiding another laugh. The boys each had so many of the small crackers in their bowls that he could barely see the soup.

"Look. You can do this." Corey pushed a cracker down into his soup with the bottom of his spoon.

Brent did the same thing.

In a moment it turned into a contest as to which boy could push the most crackers down the fastest.

Travis's heart seemed to reach outside himself and hug both the boys. They were like brothers. Living together, they must feel like brothers. If anything happened to Brent, it would break Corey's heart.

And his own, Travis realized. Amazing how quickly a boy could take root in a man's heart.

Bang!

Travis leaped to his feet as the front door crashed open. His heart lodged in his throat. Had Dan found them?

He was dimly aware of Anna's gasp.

The boys' heads swiveled toward the door.

It wasn't Dan standing at the door.

"Ellie!" Travis dashed to her. Grabbed her arms. Looked her over, searching for any sign of harm. "Are you all right?"

She nodded, barely paying him any attention. Her gaze looked over his shoulder.

Travis knew she was reassuring herself the boys were safe. "They're fine," he told her in a quiet voice that wouldn't carry to the boys.

She braced herself against his chest then, gulping huge breaths of air. Corey was calling to her eagerly, but she spoke first to Travis. "I was so worried. It suddenly occurred to me that Dan might have come here when he left the shop. I got here as fast as I could."

Her unbuttoned coat and windblown hair were evidence of that fact. "I had the same idea. Better say hi to Corey."

Ellie hugged the boys and listened with rapt attention as they repeated their tale of their morning adventures. After a couple of minutes they were willing to share her with Travis and Anna again.

"Won't you join us for lunch?" Anna asked when the three adults entered the kitchen where they could talk privately. "There's plenty of soup, and it won't take a minute to make another sandwich."

"Thank you, but I must get back to the shop."

Travis was instantly alert. "Is Jess there alone?"

She shook her head. "One of the women who knits my sweaters came by. I asked her to help Jessica out until I get back. I didn't say where I was going. I was afraid she'd insist on heading here herself, and if Dan was here, that might have only made things worse."

"You're probably right," Travis agreed.

"As long as I know you are all right, Ellie," Anna said, "I'll return to the dining room. I don't like to leave the boys alone too long."

Travis told Ellie he'd contacted Chuck to put locks on Anna's doors. "Do you and Jess have good locks on the doors at your house?"

"Yes, that was the first thing we did when we moved in. A lot of people in Blackberry don't lock their homes, but we didn't want Dan to stroll in unannounced."

"I don't remember the doors being locked when I've been there."

"I guess we don't always remember. We've become a bit too secure after all these months."

"It's time you start remembering."

Ellie eyes widened at the sharpness in his tone.

He winced. "Sorry, it's just that I don't want anything to happen to any of you."

"You're right, we should be more careful. When a person's as volatile as Dan, you never know when something might set him off. From now on we'll lock the doors as soon as we enter the house, as well as whenever we leave."

"Good girl."

"That sounds like I'm a dog."

Travis laughed. "You are definitely not a dog." He wished he dared tell her how beautiful she was to him. "Be careful."

She wrinkled her brow and tilted her head to one side. "How long are you planning to stay here? Don't you have to be at your office?"

"I told my secretary I won't be back for a while. I won't leave until Chuck arrives."

"Thank you." Ellie's voice was so thick with gratitude that it felt like a hug.

After Ellie left, Travis found the old-fashioned dining room in the midst of transformation. Anna and the boys were spreading quilts over the dining room table. The colorful bedding hung to the floor and was weighted down on the tabletop with large books. "What's going on?"

"Makin' a fo't," Corey informed him.

"A fort?"

"Uh-huh." Corey dropped to his hands and knees, lifted a quilt, and crawled beneath the table. A moment later he stuck his head out, the quilt draping it like a heavy peasant shawl. "See?"

Brent immediately followed suit.

Travis and Anna left the boys to their play and went into the living room. Anna sat down in a tapestry-covered rocking chair from the turn of the century and picked up some handwork.

"What's that?" Travis asked, more to make conversation than from true curiosity.

"A raffia purse. Ellie asked me to crochet some for the shop. She thinks they'll be popular with the customers this summer."

Hands in his pockets, he watched her nimble fingers. "Ellie's doing pretty well with that store, isn't she?"

"Wonderfully. She has a true gift. She knows how to take the picture of an outfit or accessory in her mind and turn it into the real thing. Not everyone can do that. She's a shrewd businesswoman, too."

Travis didn't like the shame that crawled through him when he remembered the way he'd belittled Ellie's talents in the past.

He examined an old oil painting hanging above a camel-back sofa.

"My ancestors, Samuel and Jane Goodson. That was painted in the early 1700s."

"Wow! You're fortunate to have it." He moved on to another picture, this time a large sepia photograph in a wide tortoiseshell frame.

"My grandparents, Andrew and Sophia Goodson," Anna offered.

On the long, narrow table beneath Andrew and Sophia's likenesses were a number of smaller, more modern pictures. Anna described each. There were pictures of her parents on their wedding day, and of Anna and her husband, George, on theirs, and pictures of Anna and George's children.

Travis learned that George had died five years earlier, suddenly, of a stroke. All their children were grown and moved away.

It should be like this with Ellie and me, Travis thought. Part of a long line of families blending together through time, pictures scattered about their home of their parents and grandparents and their children and, one day, their grandchildren.

Goose bumps ran up his arms. Grandchildren. Corey's children. Hard to imagine the little boy with the golden curls and chubby cheeks as a man, a father.

It was new to Travis, this sense of his place in the order of life, in its continuity. He liked it. There was a stabilizing feeling to it.

Or there would be, if he and Ellie and Corey were together as a family.

Baby steps, he reminded himself.

He glanced at his watch, wondering what was keeping Chuck. Restless, he wandered back over to Anna and sank onto a huge, round, leather ottoman.

"You're thinking about Ellie, aren't you?" Anna's question was asked in her low, gentle voice, her gaze on her flying fingers and the tan raffia. "You're wondering whether you'll ever be together again."

Travis rested his elbows on his knees and his chin on his folded hands. "Am I that easy to read?"

Anna only smiled.

"How long were you and George married?"

"Fifty-five years."

"Were you happy?"

"Very. He was more than a man to whom I was legally bound. We loved each other. We were best friends."

It was a gift, Travis realized, to find that kind of love and have all those years to share it. "I suppose Ellie has told you about us, why she left, I mean."

Anna nodded. "She's confided in me, yes."

"Did you and George ever have any problems like that to get past?"

"Problems, yes. Some that seemed mighty large at the time. None that were like yours, no."

He dropped his hands between his knees. "I didn't do it, you know," he said quietly. "Cheat on her, that is. I know it sounds like I did, but I didn't."

Anna didn't respond.

"You don't believe me?"

"I think I do, but it doesn't matter what I believe, does it?"

Travis pushed his hands through his hair and sighed. "I've gone over the months before our breakup a thousand times in my mind, trying to figure out how we reached the place where we were so far apart we could hurt each other as deeply as we did."

"What were the places you stopped listening to each other? George and I found those were the places we needed most to hear each other, the places we needed to grow together, toward each other and forward together." She shrugged her fragile shoulders beneath her soft pink sweater. "Maybe it's not the same for you and Ellie."

Maybe, maybe not. He'd have to think about it.

"One thing I'm sure is true for everyone," Anna continued. "I believe that everything that happens to us is another opportunity to learn to love more like Christ."

"Do you have any advice for me, any wisdom of the ages on how to regain Ellie's trust?"

Anna's hands stilled. She looked directly into Travis's eyes. "How much do you love Ellie and Corey?"

He spread his hands. "More than anything. I've given up my law practice and friends in Los Angeles and moved across the country to be close to them. I've told Ellie I want us to live together like a normal family. I'm giving Ellie money for Corey and setting more aside for his future."

"That's a good start."

"A good start?" Frustration washed through him. What more could a man do than he had already done?

"Is your greatest desire to be together with Ellie and Corey at any cost? Or is it for their lives to be filled with happiness, with God's best for them?"

"Aren't they the same thing? Ellie and I are married. The Bible tells us God doesn't care much for divorce. Doesn't that mean His best is for us to be together as a family?"

Anna went back to her crocheting. "Very likely His perfect will includes the three of you living together as a family and acting in pure love toward each other."

Travis shook his head. One corner of his mouth lifted in a wry grin. "Why does that sound straightforward but feel like a puzzle?"

Anna only smiled her mysterious, gentle, wise smile.

A strong knock at the door jerked Travis out of his reflective mood and back into the role of protector. "That must be Chuck."

He approved of the dead-bolt locks Chuck brought. "Do you have time to install them now?"

"I'll make the time," Chuck replied grimly.

"Have you been in Ellie's house? Do you happen to know what kind of locks she has?"

"Dead bolts. I installed them."

Was that challenge he saw in Chuck's eyes before the carpenter turned away?

Travis wondered about the look as he walked back to the office. He'd noticed the way Chuck had looked at him and Ellie at the shop earlier, too, when Travis had his arm around Ellie, a look of surprise mingled with distaste. Travis hadn't thought much about it at the time. His attention had been on Dan and Jessica.

Uneasiness vined through his chest. Was Chuck interested in Ellie? Were they perhaps seeing each other? She'd told him she wasn't seeing anyone, but Chuck seemed to be around quite a bit. Was he hoping to be next in line in case Ellie filed for divorce?

Travis tried to push the ugly thought away. He couldn't do anything about other men in Ellie's life. He could only concentrate on loving Ellie himself, in whatever ways she'd let him.

Anna's questions skated through his mind. *"How much do you love Ellie and Corey?" "Is your greatest desire to be together with Ellie and Corey at any cost? Or is it for their lives to be filled with happiness, with God's best for them?"*

He wanted to spend his life with Ellie and Corey so deeply the ache for that life seemed part of his bones, but he couldn't make that happen.

"I don't have to wait until we're living together to love them," he spoke fiercely into the mountain winds. He knew suddenly and in a deep sense that his love wasn't to be given only in the hope of winning these two precious souls into his home and his arms.

The realization terrified him so much he stopped in his tracks. He started forward again slowly, exploring the new and troubling thought. Amazed, he found that along with the fright he felt freedom; freedom to be vulnerable and love Ellie and Corey completely.

Show me how to love them, Lord, he begged. *Show me how to love them the way You love them, how to be a blessing to them whether or not we ever live together as a family.*

Chapter 8

Ellie stopped on the sidewalk in front of Travis's office, hugged the package wrapped in mauve and blue marbled paper to her chest, and took a deep breath. She'd never been to his office. For some reason she couldn't understand, visiting him in his new professional home seemed an acknowledgment that he was here in Blackberry and her life for good.

Still, today was his open house. The remodeling was completed, and Travis was ready to show off his office to the community. She thought it only right that her gift be part of his office.

"Quit stalling," she admonished herself. Straightening her shoulders and lifting her chin, she reached for the door of the old brick building with the new interior. The skirt of her gently shaped pale peach corduroy dress brushed against her calves as she slipped inside.

Ellie entered directly into a large reception area. It looked very contemporary with stained wood timbers bordering white walls and the high white ceiling. She recognized the work of local artists in the wooden tables and lamps, in the pottery decorating the bookcases, and in the Native American pictures by her favorite Cherokee artist on the walls. The earthen colors in the artwork were perfect for the room.

Plants and bouquets were on the tables, bookcases, and floor. Ellie guessed most were gifts from local businesses congratulating Travis on joining their business community.

A middle-aged woman with a professional manner and gray hair cut in a short, contemporary style looked up with a smile from the one desk in the room. "May I help you?"

"I'd like to see Travis, please. Mr. Carter, that is, if he's free." Ellie was surprised she didn't recognize the woman. She knew almost everyone in Blackberry. The nameplate on the desk said MRS. SUSAN NORTHRUP.

"I'll ask whether he has time to speak with you. Who should I tell him is here?"

"Ellie."

Mrs. Northrup hesitated. "Ellie. . . ?"

Ellie flushed. Obviously the receptionist didn't know she was Travis's wife. Ellie wasn't inclined to inform her. "He'll know who I am."

Mrs. Northrup pressed a button on the phone. "Mr. Carter, a young woman named Ellie would like to speak with you if you have a moment."

Ellie started at Travis's voice over the speakerphone. "I'll take the call."

"She is in the office, Mr. Carter."

A moment later the door behind the desk was flung open, and Travis strode out to greet Ellie with a huge smile. "This is a pleasant surprise."

"I hope I'm not taking you away from anything urgent."

"Not at all. I haven't any court dates today, and I asked Mrs. Northrup not to schedule any appointments for me in case any last-minute things came up with the remodeling. I needn't have worried. Chuck and the men he hired to help him finished up two days ago."

"It looks great."

"I'll give you a tour." He took her elbow. The simple action sent shivers down Ellie's spine. "First, let me introduce you to my secretary. Mrs. Northrup, this is Ellie Carter. Ellie, Susan Northrup."

Mrs. Northrup's eyes widened slightly at Ellie's last name, but she gave no other indication of her curiosity. The women smiled and nodded at each other as Travis continued. "Any time Ellie calls or stops by, you are to let me know immediately."

"Yes, Mr. Carter."

Ellie indicated the walls and bookshelves with a wave of her palm, freeing herself from Travis's hold at the same time. "I like what you've done in this room. You chose your artwork well."

"I followed your lead, using local artisans as much as possible as you do with the boutique. I think it's important people in a community support each other's business in art as well as the professions and retail stores. Besides," he said, flashing a smile, "I genuinely admire the work of the artists represented here."

His appreciation of the talent of the people among whom she'd been raised warmed Ellie's heart, and she returned his smile. "I do, too."

He led her down a hallway off one side of the reception area. Even here his dedication to local artists continued, with photographs of mountain scenes by an award-winning photographer lining the walls, and a runner on the floor by a local weaver.

The last room he showed her was his office. Ellie stood in the middle of the room, her package still clutched to her chest, and looked around. The room was almost as large as the reception area and decorated in the same manner. A frieze of Native American design topped the wall behind Travis's immense desk.

Everywhere she looked, Ellie saw dollar signs. She knew how much it had cost her to make the simple renovations necessary for the boutique, how much money was tied up in her inventory, and how much she had outstanding in business loans. "The company must think the opportunity for growth is large in this area to invest so much in your office."

"Lots of wealthy men and women retire to this area of the mountains and still need legal advice, even though they've left their business worlds behind them. There's lots of investment going on in these hills, too. The firm is hoping its reputation in the Piedmont will bring clients familiar with the name through our doors. They want the office here to represent the firm's successful image."

"I'm sure it will do that." Obviously he still liked the money and prestige of a large firm. He wasn't the village type.

"Have you and Jessica had any trouble with Dan lately?"

"No. Jessica is on pins and needles every other weekend when Brent goes to stay with Dan. She's afraid one of these times Brent is going to come home with bruises, if not broken bones."

"It's a valid fear." Travis's comment was grim. "She told me he hasn't made any threats since the incident at the boutique, but I wasn't sure she was being honest with me."

"She hasn't told me about any more threats. I expect the old ones are still good."

Travis grimaced.

"Thank you for offering her free legal advice. I know she's talked with you about the situation with Dan."

"There's not much I can do to help her at this point. Are you two remembering to keep your house locked?"

"Yes." Now it was Ellie's turn to grimace. "We're beginning to feel like prisoners."

A wooden carving on the edge of his desk of a Cherokee man, woman, and child caught her attention. The woman was looking over her shoulder, sadness in every line of her face. Ellie reached out and ran a finger lightly over the wooden cheek. She felt as though she wanted to wipe away a tear the artist hadn't put there but whose presence could still be felt. "I haven't seen this artist's work before. It's magnificent."

"I bought it from the artist at his shop near Cherokee. He told me it's of a family just starting out on the Trail of Tears." He cleared his throat and shrugged his shoulders, looking a little embarrassed. "I haven't had it long. Still chokes me up to look at it."

Ellie could understand that. She liked him all the more for allowing himself to feel the emotion of this family's story, of the Cherokees' story.

"Makes me think we have life pretty easy." Travis was looking at the carving. "The thought of being forced to start out on a journey like that into the unknown with Corey—" He shivered. "It's terrifying."

"Yes." More terrifying than when she'd first told Travis about Corey and wondered whether he'd try to take the boy away from her. She was convinced now that he wouldn't do that, but she was still not ready to trust him to stay faithful to their marriage vows.

"Sit down." Travis waved her toward the pair of leather wing chairs facing his desk.

"I can't stay."

"I've been so busy showing off the office that I didn't think to ask why you stopped. Is it a legal matter?"

"No." She held out the package. "I thought you might like this for your desk."

His face lit up like a kid's at Christmas. He tore the paper away. Emotions chased across his face like clouds across a sky: disbelief, gratitude, joy.

"I thought you should have a picture of your son for your office." It was a framed eight-by-twelve print of the wallet-sized photo she'd sent him months earlier. "It's the most recent professional shot I have of him. He's changed quite a bit since it was taken, but—"

"It's perfect." His husky assurance stopped her excuses. "It's perfect. Thank you."

Ellie took a couple of steps backward toward the door, glad Travis's desk was between them. The way he was looking at her, his heart in his eyes, made her ache to be in his arms. She moistened her suddenly dry lips with the tip of her tongue. "I'd better be getting back to the boutique."

"You're welcome to stay for the open house, or come back for it. It starts in an hour." He set the picture in a prominent place on his desk, ran his hand caressingly across the top of the cherry frame, and started toward her.

"I don't know if I can get away from the shop again today." Too many townspeople knew she and Travis were married. She didn't want people to think they were more of a family than they were in fact. If she were here during an important event like his open house, people might think they'd reconciled. Maybe Travis would take it as a sign she wanted to reconcile. She wasn't ready for that yet.

What made her tack *yet* on the end of that thought? Dismay twisted her stomach into knots. Was it possible her heart wanted to let him back into a real marriage, under one roof and in one bed? Or was it hormones speaking and not her heart?

Travis had been altogether too appealing since moving here. In spite of the hours involved in getting his office and business up and going, he made sure he saw Corey every day. He'd been faithful to his promise to provide a weekly check to help with Corey's financial support. He hadn't pressured her anymore to get together. She was beginning to feel almost relaxed around him, at least most of the time. It was plain he enjoyed the time he spent with her and Corey. But she didn't dare let herself trust him.

In the reception area she saw a long table had been set up along one wall. Mrs. Northrup was straightening a white tablecloth.

Anna came from the hallway with a tray of chicken salad on bite-size buns. Her wrinkled face broke into a sunny smile when she recognized Ellie. "Are you here to help with the open house, too?"

"No." Ellie shook her head vehemently.

Anna set the tray down. "I'm so excited that Travis asked me to help serve the refreshments and greet guests. He insisted on buying me a new dress. I bought it at your shop, of course. Jessica helped me pick it out. What do you think?" She spread her arms wide and turned about like a little girl.

The dress was a total departure from Anna's usual traditional lace-trimmed pastels. It was a sunlit chestnut brown with a crinkle skirt of fluid rayon challis and matching blouse with a small Native American design in black on the collar and placket. A matching embroidered vest added an elegant touch. A braided leather belt with a round silver buckle completed the ensemble. Ellie recognized Jessica's handiwork in the rectangular silver earrings and pin with a jack-in-the-pulpit design.

"You look spectacular," Ellie told Anna sincerely, squeezing the older woman's hands.

"I feel brand new," Anna confided in a loud whisper.

"I hope you're the same old Anna underneath," Ellie teased, "but the new style looks good on you."

"I'm glad you think so, since you designed it."

Travis followed her out of the building. "Ellie, I was wondering if we could go to church together this Sunday, you and me and Corey."

Like a family. Ellie shivered. "I. . .I don't think so, no. I hope your open house goes well." She turned on her heel and hurried off before he could press her further.

Conflicting emotions tumbled through her heart and conflicting thoughts through her mind as she headed toward the boutique. She wished the spring breeze could blow away the fog of confusion concerning her feelings for Travis. Should she trust him or shouldn't she? The chant went on day after day. It was fatiguing her.

She greeted townspeople along her way with absentminded smiles. How many of them would be attending Travis's open house? The town had taken him to its heart in the short time he'd been here. He'd accepted the church's request to join the board. He met with other businessmen over lunch and dinner in the local restaurants. He attended the weekly prayer breakfasts. Even Mr. Hobson, the elderly gentleman who had been the village's primary lawyer all his professional life, had told her Travis was an asset to the community. Everyone but Ellie seemed smitten with Travis.

Maybe not everyone. She suspected Dan didn't care for Travis one bit.

"I wish I could trust him completely," she whispered into the spring air. She was tired of worrying whether she had been right to let him back into Corey's life, tired of worrying whether Travis might hurt her again, tired of trying to deny her enjoyment of his company, tired of fighting her desire to be in his arms again.

I wish it could be one way or the other, she told the Lord silently. *I wish he was out of our lives completely or in our lives completely. Trying to balance between friendship and intimacy is like walking along the top of a picket fence.*

Ellie shivered and hugged her arms. *How long before I lose my balance and fall off?*

That evening Ellie and Jess had sloppy joes and potato chips for supper. It was one of the boys' favorite meals. Jess always liked to make sure Brent's time was pleasant right before Dan picked the boy up for a weekend.

Ellie watched the boys giggling as they ate, finding typical little-boy humor in the way the meat and sauce were dripping from the sandwiches, dribbling from chins, and tumbling down the fronts of their T-shirts. She and Jessica had given up trying to convince the boys to wear bibs on sloppy joe nights. Corey and Brent insisted they were too old for bibs. Their mothers gave in, and instead of bibs, allowed the boys to wear their oldest T-shirts.

Ellie knew Jessica had a clean shirt ready to put on Brent as soon as he was done eating. Neither of the women liked the boys running around in clothes covered with food, but the sight made Dan livid.

Jessica glanced at the clock, grimaced, and shifted her weight.

Ellie checked the time. Almost seven. Dan would be here any minute. Her stomach tightened in the familiar response to Dan's imminent arrival. She set down her own sandwich. She couldn't eat it now.

But when she answered the door a few minutes later, with the sound of Jessica's voice hurrying Brent to finish eating in the background, it wasn't Dan who entered but Travis.

She looked at him in surprise. "I wasn't expecting you. Did we agree you'd see Corey tonight? If so, I forgot."

"No. Jess stopped at the open house. She was upset about Dan picking Brent up for the weekend." He shrugged. "I thought if I was here when Dan arrived, things might go smoother."

"I'm not sure it will make any difference. Dan is never actually violent when he picks up Brent. It's the boys who get upset, not wanting Brent to leave. And Jessica gets upset worrying what might happen to Brent while he's with Dan."

Travis raised his eyebrows in question marks. "So this was a dumb idea?"

"It was a kind gesture, and maybe your presence will make Jessica feel better." She waved a hand toward the kitchen. "The boys are eating. You can go in and say hello if you'd like."

"Dinner smells good." He raised his face as if sniffing the air. "I came directly from the office. All I've eaten today are the cookies and minuscule sandwiches Anna and Mrs. Northrup provided for the open house."

Ellie laughed. "If that's a hint that your man-size stomach is growling, you're welcome to have a sloppy joe with the boys."

"Thanks." He headed down the hall, sliding his coat off as he went.

Ellie leaned against the kitchen wall with her arms crossed over her coppery chenille sweater and watched Travis and the boys.

As usual, Corey and Brent were delighted to see Travis. He'd barely sat down when he commented on the blobs of sloppy joe that decorated the boys' shirts. "Don't you think you need bibs?"

They shook their heads vigorously.

Travis looked down at his white shirt. "Think I need one. Do you have one that will fit me?"

The boys burst into giggles.

Ellie smiled. She could never help smiling when the boys giggled in the full-fledged manner that jiggled their entire little bodies and shined from their eyes.

"No," Corey managed to force out in between the giggles.

"No?" Travis looked crestfallen.

Corey shook his head, his giggles diminishing.

"Guess I'll need to use this then." Travis stuck a napkin in his collar.

It set the boys into stitches again.

Warmth filled Ellie's chest. It took so little to bring joy to the boys. All they wanted was a few minutes of uncritical, undivided attention.

The doorbell's ring brought Ellie out of her reverie. As she hurried to answer it, the bell rang again and again, pushing away the comfortable, warm moment. She pressed her lips together in irritation and yanked open the door.

Dan entered without an invitation. Annoyance filled his eyes. His hands were plunged into the pockets of the lined trench coat he always wore. He didn't bother with a friendly preamble. "Where's Brent?"

"He's just finishing supper." Jessica spoke from the kitchen doorway.

Dan's mouth tightened. "Why isn't he done? You knew I'd be here at seven."

Ellie could see Jessica working to control her temper and knew she was afraid if she said what she felt, Dan would take his anger at her out on Brent later.

"Sorry," Jessica apologized, "he's almost done."

"Get him out here. I want to get going."

Ellie wondered what he could possibly have planned for the evening that would be ruined if he waited for Brent to finish eating, but she didn't ask.

"Let him finish his sandwich," Jessica asked reasonably.

Dan flashed her an impatient look. "If you won't get him, I will." He started for the kitchen.

He stopped abruptly inside the kitchen door.

Behind him Ellie saw the satisfaction in Jessica's face at Dan's surprise and knew she was glad Travis was there. A gloating sense of satisfaction filled Ellie, too.

Travis looked up calmly. "Hello, Dan. Going to join us?"

Dan hesitated, obviously put off by Travis's unexpected presence and friendly gesture.

The boys had stopped eating and were watching Dan warily.

Dan strode toward Brent. "Get your coat on."

"The boy hasn't finished his dinner." Travis's quiet but firm tone made the simple words a threat.

His hand on Brent's shoulder, Dan threw an uneasy glance at Travis.

Without standing up, Travis drew out a chair. Its legs squeaked across the linoleum. "Why don't you sit down and join us?"

Dan ignored the chair. "Hurry up and finish eating."

Brent obediently took another bite.

Ellie could have cried at the boy's forlorn face.

"Thanks for stopping by the open house today, Dan." Travis's voice and face revealed nothing of what he might be feeling. "And for the plant you sent."

Dan grunted something that might have been "You're welcome" and finally dropped into the chair. "Nice office."

Ellie could hear the envy in Dan's voice. His office, though nice, didn't begin to compare to Travis's, but Dan didn't have a large regional firm behind him like Travis did. She was surprised Dan had sent a plant to the open house, let alone shown up. He probably only did so because he thought it was expected by the rest of the business community. The open house was a good place to network.

After only two bites, Brent set his sandwich down. "I don't want any more."

"Are you sure, honey?" Jessica leaned over him. "You haven't eaten much. Maybe you'd like to take it along with you."

"No!" Dan exploded. "He's not going to eat in my car."

Ellie grinned at the vision of tomato sauce spotting the interior of his Mercedes.

Jessica evidently had no such cheering vision. "Do you have anything to feed Brent if he's hungry later?" she asked Dan.

"Of course I do." Belligerency drenched his words.

Ellie wondered, as she was sure Jessica did, whether Brent would have the courage if he was hungry to ask Dan for food.

Dan scowled. "Don't you have a clean shirt for him, Jessie? He's a mess. I don't know why you don't make him wear a bib since he's not grown up enough to eat like a man."

Brent's mouth turned down at the corners, and he climbed off his chair.

Corey stared wide-eyed at Dan.

Ellie was glad her son apparently knew instinctively that this was a man who could not be trusted.

Travis deliberately wiped his mouth with the napkin still stuck in his collar. He winked at Brent and grinned. "Next time we have sloppy joes, you and Corey can wear a man-sized napkin like mine."

Brent rewarded Travis with a smile, though it wasn't a wholehearted one.

Jessica took Brent's hand. "Come on, honey, let's change your shirt."

"Hurry it up." Dan scraped back his chair. "I haven't got all night."

While Jessica was changing Brent, Ellie wrapped a couple of chocolate chip cookies in a napkin.

She collected Brent's jacket and gloves, surreptitiously sticking the cookies into a jacket pocket before handing it to Jessica.

Travis, who was standing with Corey in his arms in the kitchen doorway, winked at Ellie.

She allowed herself a small smile back, one that wouldn't catch Dan's attention.

Corey's arm was about Travis's neck. Ellie hated the resignation in Corey's wide-eyed gaze. He always hated to see his friend head off for the weekend.

Jessica pulled a billed blue corduroy hat over Brent's forehead and gave him a big hug. "I love you, Brent."

Brent clung to her.

Ellie blinked back tears as Jessica gently but firmly removed her arms. Tears shone in Jessica's eyes, too.

"You'll make sure Brent is dressed warmly if you take him outside, won't you?" Jessica asked Dan as she stood up.

"Of course. Think I'm some kind of moron?" Dan lifted Brent's red and blue duffle bag.

Ellie knelt down and surrounded Brent with her arms. "I love you, sweetheart."

" 'Bye, partner," Travis said.

Brent waved forlornly at Travis and Corey.

Dan reached for Brent's hand.

Brent extended his reluctantly. "Can Corey come?" His gaze sought his friend.

"No." Dan tugged at Brent's hand.

The boy followed along with his father for a couple of steps. At the door he looked back over his shoulder. "I don' wanna go, Momma!" His face crumpled into tears.

"Don't be a baby." Dan scooped the boy into his arms and headed out the door before Jessica had a chance to reply.

Jessica sank to the bottom step of the hall stairs and dropped her face into her hands. Her shoulders shook with quiet sobs.

Corey stared at her and hugged Travis's neck.

Travis's face was a study in controlled fury.

Ellie darted out the door. She reached Dan and Brent at the open back car door. Brent was climbing into his car seat.

In the front seat was Sissy Barr, a young woman Ellie recognized as having graduated from high school only two years ago. This, then, was the reason Dan was in even more of a hurry than usual. The girl wiggled her fingers at Ellie in a wave.

Dan looked at Ellie in surprise. "Did I forget something?"

"No. I did. I forgot to tell you that I'm not afraid of you like Jessica is. You better watch Brent very carefully and hope he doesn't fall down or run into anything. If he comes back with so much as a penny-sized bruise, I'll tell the sheriff what you've done to Jessica in the past."

Dan's eyes were black with rage. "I've never laid a hand on Jessie."

She ignored his protest. "I promise you I'm not going to let you get away with hurting this boy. He's a treasure."

Dan leaned into the car and fastened Brent's car-seat belt, then slammed the car door. Glaring at her, he climbed into the front seat, turned on the ignition, and closed the door.

Ellie smiled and waved at Brent as the car started to back out of the driveway.

Turning back to the house, she saw Travis, Corey, and Jessica standing in the doorway. Ellie caught back a groan and smiled as she walked toward them, shivering in the early spring evening.

"What did you say to him?" Jessica asked, closing the door behind Ellie.

Ellie shrugged. "Just wanted to say another good-bye to Brent."

Jessica eyed her suspiciously but didn't push it.

Ellie gave her a hug. "You doing okay?"

Jessica nodded, but her face was still flushed and her eyes red from the tears she'd shed. "Why don't I do the dishes while you guys visit?"

"I can help," Ellie offered.

"No. I. . .I'd like to spend a few minutes alone. Might as well spend them doing something worthwhile." Jessica stopped just outside the kitchen door and turned to Travis with a small smile. "Thanks for coming."

"Sure."

Travis, Corey, and Ellie wandered into the living room. Corey wiggled to be let down, and Travis obliged. The boy went to the TV stand, picked up a video tape, and brought it to Ellie. Ellie rolled her eyes.

"What is it?" Travis took the tape from her and scowled down at it. "Teletubbies?"

Ellie nodded. "A Teletubbies movie. It's his favorite video. We've seen it so many times I've lost count."

"Put it in," Corey demanded, pointing to the TV.

Ellie nodded in response to Travis's questioning look. "We might as well. Maybe it will take his mind off his little friend for a while."

Travis stuck the tape into the recorder. Corey picked up the gray horse which had been Travis's first gift. The boy hugged it to him as he sat down in front of the television.

Travis picked up a small book with a red leather cover from the end table beside the sofa. "*In His Steps*. I've heard of this. Are you reading it?"

"Yes. Rereading it actually."

Travis riffled the pages and set it back down.

Ellie sat on the sofa, dropping her head against the back. "I feel like I've been through a war."

Travis dropped down beside her. He leaned close, speaking low, glancing at Corey. "Is it always this way when Dan picks up Brent?"

"Oh, no. Sometimes it's worse. I think it did help that you were here. Brent hates spending weekends with Dan. Knowing it sets Dan off."

"Something should be done to prevent it then."

"You're the lawyer. You know how hard it is to keep a father from his children. Besides, the separation agreement says Brent will spend every other weekend with Dan."

"If I didn't know the law, I don't think I would have allowed Dan to take Brent out of here tonight. It was all I could do not to grab that boy and hold on for dear life."

Ellie's chest flooded with admiration. Regardless of anything else she might feel for this man, she loved the way he loved Corey and Brent.

A muscle jumped in Travis's cheek. "I wanted to wallop the guy."

"I know the feeling." She sighed and brushed back her hair. "So much for walking in Christ's footsteps."

"Wanting to protect the boy has to be a Christ-inspired desire. Knowing how to go about it in a Christ-centered way, that's the difficult part."

"Yes." She studied his face thoughtfully. It was only a few inches away, as they were still trying to prevent Corey from overhearing their conversation.

Travis slid down a bit so he could rest his head against the back of the sofa, too. His shoulder pressed against Ellie's. The hint of intimacy in the simple touch filled her stomach with butterflies. Was it playing with fire, sitting with him like this, with Corey in the same room watching television, acting like a family?

"I don't get it." Travis's gaze was on Corey. "Dan doesn't seem to even like Brent."

"I know." She told him about the girl in Dan's car. "I wonder how much attention Brent will receive from Dan tonight with Sissy around."

"Why does Dan want to spend every other weekend with the boy when he doesn't like having him around?"

"To hurt Jessica."

Travis turned his head to face her. "He hates her that much?"

"He says he loves her, but love doesn't act that way."

"Love doesn't. Wounds do."

Ellie studied Travis's eyes, thinking about his words. She wasn't sure she agreed with him. There was only acting from love and not acting from love, wasn't there?

Was there ever an excuse to choose to not act from love?

Her conscience made her squirm inside. Had she acted in love when she left Travis? Hadn't her actions resulted from her wounds? She'd defended her actions ever since by saying she'd been protecting herself from being hurt again. Her excuses had since grown to protecting Corey, too.

She'd think about it later. Maybe. Right now it was more comfortable to talk about Dan and Jessica. "I think it hurt Dan's ego when Jessica left, not his heart. Now he's trying to pay her back."

"He's doing it all too well."

"Yes," she whispered, remembering the pain in her friend's eyes and in Brent's, "but it's his own fault she left. If he hadn't hit her, she'd have stayed with him."

Pain shot through Travis's eyes. "I know."

Was Travis thinking that it was his own fault that she had left him, too? Ellie wondered. Travis thought it all right for Jessica to leave a man for causing her physical harm. What did he think about Ellie leaving him because he'd caused her emotional harm?

She wasn't about to ask. Her thoughts went around in the familiar circle. She wasn't sure how she felt about it herself. All she knew was that she didn't want Corey to experience the betrayal she'd felt, and she didn't want to experience it again, either.

Travis's hand enveloped hers. She shifted her glance from his eyes to their joined hands. His thumb played lightly over the back of her hand, sending delightful shivers down her spine and wonderful memories echoing through her mind.

"I'm sorry, Ellie."

Her gaze darted back to his eyes, but now he was watching their hands.

"I'm sorry I hurt you so much." His husky whisper cracked on the words.

She wanted to say it was all right. She wanted to tell him she believed him. She wanted to tell him she still loved him. She wanted to tell him how much she missed being in his arms. She wanted to tell him she was sorry she'd hurt him, too. She wanted to tell him how glad she was they saw each other every day, and she knew he was all right. She wanted to tell him how much she loved seeing him and Corey together.

She wanted to never doubt him again, for her sake and for Corey's. But she did doubt him. A piece of her couldn't let go of the fear he'd betray her again.

Still, she left her hand in his, remembering the beauty of his touch when her trust in him had been complete. Her shoulder continued to rest comfortably against his. Their heads remained so close together she could feel his breath.

"Let Co'ey up."

Ellie and Travis started at Corey's demand.

Corey shoved his stuffed horse into their hands. "Up."

Chuckling, Travis settled the boy on his lap. Corey wasn't content. He tried wiggling in between Travis and Ellie. They got the message and moved to allow him room.

Travis slipped an arm over Corey's shoulders, and Corey leaned back, content written wide on his face. "Look." He pointed toward the television where the Teletubbies were running about.

Ellie smiled as Travis made some appropriate noises of appreciation.

Travis pointed out different Teletubbies. He looked delighted when Corey was able to name each one.

"Think your mom will let us have some of those chocolate chip cookies that are out in the kitchen?" Travis asked Corey.

Corey nodded. "Mom, can we have cookies?"

"I'll bring you some. Do you want a glass of milk, too, Corey?"

Corey nodded. "Uh-huh."

Ellie smiled mischievously at Travis. "How about you, milk or coffee?"

He met her mischievous smile with one of his own. "Do I have any other choices? Besides beverages, I mean."

His meaning wasn't lost on her. The old phrase "coffee, tea, or me" jumped into her mind, sending heat racing to her cheeks and her feet heading for the kitchen.

At the entry to the hallway she glanced back at the two men in her life and smiled. Already Corey had Travis's undivided attention again.

Reluctantly she left her view of them for the kitchen. The sight of them together always made her feel downright mushy. Would the three of them ever be together like this as a family in every sense of the word?

Chapter 9

Ellie hummed as she went about her work Monday. Sunny, warm spring weather was bringing tourists from the Piedmont into the mountains and into her store. Her spring line was selling well.

The cash register provided background music for the brass bells above the door, until Ellie decided to keep the door open. The air carried in fragrances of spring blossoms and grasses, a pleasant change from the potpourris which scented the shop in the winter months.

"There should be spring tunes blaring from loudspeakers today the way Christmas carols do in December," she told Anna with a laugh.

"Easter hymns would be nice."

A thirtyish woman with a red pageboy stepped into the shop about noon. Ellie eyed the woman with curiosity. She was dressed in a lovely designer suit, not typical tourist attire. Ellie wondered if the woman was a new professional in town.

She was examining a pale blue linen suit when Ellie approached her. Expensive perfume overpowered the spring scents. "May I help you find something?"

The woman's face brightened. "You must be Ellie Carter."

"Yes." She always felt uncomfortable when people she didn't know recognized her.

"I recognized you from Travis's description." The woman held out a hand. "I'm Angie Adams."

Ellie met Angie's hand with her own, though dread and caution were winding through Ellie's breast. How well did Travis and Angie Adams know each other? She wanted to ask how they'd met but chose not to. Ellie wasn't about to let this woman she'd just met know it mattered to her one iota what women Travis knew. "Do you live in Blackberry?"

"Oh, my, no." Angie gave a dismissing little wave with a finely manicured hand. Ellie noticed there were no wedding or engagement rings on it. "I'm from the law firm's Charlotte office. I'll be helping Travis out on a case."

"I see." Ellie's dread lifted somewhat but not totally. "I hope you'll like our village."

"It's charming." Angie leaned toward Ellie in a confidential manner that made Ellie want to back away. "Travis offered to take me to lunch today, the way people in the firm always do when someone from one of the other offices is working with them. I turned him down because he told me about your shop. I knew

I had to visit it first thing."

"How kind of you," Ellie murmured.

"He raved about your talent as a designer. Positively raved." Angie flipped her hand in the annoying waving motion again.

"He did?" Surprise and pleasure surged through Ellie like a dancing mountain creek.

"Raved," Angie assured her, widening her green eyes and leaning even closer to emphasize her point.

"How nice." Ellie tried not to beam on the outside the way she was on the inside. It might be springtime, but she felt like a Christmas tree in full dress and brilliantly lit.

She wondered whether Travis had told Angie that he was married to Ellie, and, if so, whether he'd told Angie he was separated. She wasn't about to offer the information herself.

When Angie left the shop forty-five minutes later, she was carrying the blue linen suit and was assuring Ellie that Travis had been right about her designs and promising she would return another day. "We simply must do lunch while I'm in town."

Ellie waited until Angie had passed the shop windows, then looked at Anna. The older woman's blue eyes were dancing. A moment later both women burst into laughter.

"Can you imagine that woman in court?" Ellie asked when she could breathe again. "She looks the perfect professional, but her mannerisms. . ." Ellie couldn't find the words. "Judges probably rule in her favor just to get her to stop talking."

"Or to get her perfume out of their courtrooms."

They broke into giggles again.

Ellie dabbed at the corner of her eye to catch a laughter tear. "I suppose that was catty of us. She was nice enough. She didn't have to buy that suit or even stop at the shop or tell me Travis had complimented my designs."

"Or gush over the lace collar I made for the suit she bought." Anna lifted her white blouse's Peter Pan collar and pretended to preen.

"I was a little afraid. . .a lot afraid. . .when she told me she was working with Travis." It was hard to admit, even to Anna, in whom Ellie had confided so much.

Anna patted her hand. "That's only natural, dear."

"Do you know Travis's receptionist, Susan Northrup? I didn't recognize her when I met her at his office the other day, and I thought I knew everyone in town."

Anna brightened. "Oh yes, I know her. Her oldest sister is a friend of mine. Susan and her husband live in Blowing Rock."

"Why did he hire someone who lives over thirty miles away? I would think he could have found a receptionist and secretary who lived closer."

"A couple of young women applied. He wanted someone more mature. He was afraid if he put that in the ad or told the employment agency that he'd be accused of reverse age discrimination." Anna chuckled, her soft rosy cheeks wrinkling pleasantly.

Ellie smiled with her. "Did he think that someone older would be more experienced?"

"Not necessarily." Anna hesitated, fingering her collar. "He thought you would be more comfortable if his secretary were older."

"Me?"

"Yes. He didn't want to give you any reason to be. . .suspicious. . .that there might be something improper going on between him and his employee."

Ellie stared at her, amazed Travis had given a moment's thought to his wife's reaction to whom he hired.

"He says he wasn't unfaithful to you with that woman in Los Angeles," Anna said quietly. "You do know that, don't you?"

"I know." Ellie's lips were suddenly stiff. She knew he'd said that he wasn't unfaithful, but she also knew what she'd seen and heard.

She was spared expanding on her thoughts to Anna by Chuck's arrival.

He greeted them cheerfully, leaned his elbows on the counter, shoved up the bill of his ever-present baseball hat, and grinned at Ellie. "Have you had lunch yet? I'd be glad to treat at the Black Bear."

"Thanks, but I can't make it today. Anna will be heading home any minute. Jessica has been watching the boys this morning while she worked on some jewelry sketches. Anna's going to take over for her for the afternoon, and Jessica's coming down here to help me out."

Ellie was glad Chuck left without appearing too downhearted.

A few minutes after Anna left, Chuck returned with a brown paper bag which emitted the tempting aroma of a Black Bear hamburger and french fries. "Since you won't go to the food, I'm bringing the food to you. You go without lunch all too often."

"Thanks. I didn't realize I was hungry until you walked in with this."

"I brought something for both of us, so you don't have to eat alone."

"We'd better go to the back room." She didn't want customers to see her chomping away on a burger or have the odors she found so tempting to her taste buds assailing her customers in the shop. She didn't want to encourage Chuck, either. Of course, he hadn't crossed the line of friendship yet, but she didn't want him to think she was encouraging him to do so, either. She knew how easy it was for men and women to misinterpret each other's actions.

They ate standing beside the worktable where she could see into the shop. Unfortunately for her cash register but fortunately for her digestion, no customers entered the shop while she and Chuck ate.

Conversation between them was easy at first, as it had always been. From the beginning they'd found it easy to be together, sharing many interests and a common sense of humor. They were almost done eating when he told her he'd been to Travis's open house.

"He has a nice office, doesn't he?" she said.

"Yeah."

His almost surly tone alerted her to a shift in his mood. For a couple of minutes neither of them spoke. She searched her mind for a non-controversial topic and finally told him about Dan picking up Brent at the beginning of the weekend. She even told him about her challenge to Dan in the driveway.

"I assume he returned Brent in good health."

"Yes, in physically good health, at least. The way Dan treats the boy has to be taking its toll emotionally."

"I saw Dan Friday night about nine. He was at a movie with Sissy Barr."

"They took Brent to a movie?"

Chuck shook his head. "I didn't see Brent there."

Anger rose in her as quickly as a creek overflowing its banks in a flash flood. Dan had cruelly rushed Brent away from his mother and Corey to leave him with a sitter while he, a married man, went out on a date.

"Didn't Brent tell you?" Chuck asked.

"He's too young to tell us. He might tell us he'd played with the baby-sitter, but. . ." Dawning realization cut short her thought.

"But what?"

"He didn't mention a baby-sitter. Maybe. . ." She didn't like what she was thinking. It made her stomach feel like she'd just had a glass of sour milk. "Maybe there wasn't a baby-sitter."

"Even Dan's not enough of a creep to leave a youngster Brent's size alone." Chuck's eyebrows met above troubled eyes. "Is he?"

Ellie didn't answer. She didn't know the answer.

"Thinkin' of that little guy maybe left alone. . ." Chuck removed his baseball hat and wiped his forehead with his forearm. "Makes my skin crawl."

Neither of them spoke for a couple of minutes, each examining the horrible thought in the privacy of their own minds.

There was nothing to be gained by it, not at the moment. "I'll ask Jessica about the baby-sitter tonight," Ellie told him. "Maybe Brent said something to Jessica."

"I hope so."

Ellie searched for a more pleasant topic.

"Does Corey miss Brent when he's with Dan?" Chuck asked.

"Yes. We watched a Teletubbies movie with him after Brent left, hoping to divert his attention for a while." She laughed and told Chuck about Travis's funny ways with Corey while they watched the movie.

Chuck didn't find them amusing. "Travis spent the evening at your house?"

"He's Corey's father," she reminded him gently. "They need to spend time together."

"Have you told Corey yet that Travis is his father?"

"No."

"Aren't you afraid Travis will tell him before you do?"

She went numb at his question. The possibility hadn't occurred to her. She and Travis had never discussed when and if they would reveal Travis and Corey's relationship to the boy, though she had no intention of telling that to Chuck. "I don't think Travis will do that. Even if he did, I'm not certain Corey is old enough to understand."

"Are you sure?"

She didn't answer. Ellie met his gaze evenly as he studied her eyes.

"Am I prying, Ellie?"

"You've been a good friend to me ever since I moved back to Blackberry, but this part of my life. . .my family, my marriage. . ."

Chuck's jaw tightened. "Have you decided to go back to Travis?"

"No. That is, I don't know. I'm praying about it."

"Don't do it, Ellie."

"Don't pray about it?" she asked, purposely misunderstanding, trying to lighten the emotions between them.

His eyes flashed, but his voice only registered frustration. "Don't go back to Travis. You can't trust him." He crumpled up his sandwich wrapping and tossed it onto the worktable. "Once you've let him back into your life and he feels secure, he will hurt you again. Leopards don't change their spots."

"Oh, please." Ellie rolled her eyes. "That's not very original."

"Most sayings that last do so because they have a lot of truth in them."

She knew he was right. It was what she feared most, that leopards didn't change their spots, that Travis hadn't changed his unfaithful ways, either. After all, he'd moved to Blackberry because he'd discovered he had a son. He'd known she'd moved to Blackberry when she left Los Angeles. He'd known how to reach her through her parents if he'd wished. He hadn't. Now that he was here, now that he knew Corey, Travis had told her he'd missed her and wanted to be back together, but was it truly because he loved her or only because he wanted to live with their son?

Ellie shivered, hating the way the cruel thoughts wormed into her heart and mind and clouded the sunshine of the spring day.

Chapter 10

S ay yes, Ellie," Travis begged, keeping his tone light with an effort. "It's going to be a beautiful April afternoon. We should take advantage of it. The forecast is for a snowstorm to move in tonight."

The mountains in springtime couldn't be any more beautiful than Ellie, he thought. She was lovely today as always, wearing a simple light blue shift with a blue sweater over her shoulders. Sunshine poured through the stained-glass windows, delicately lighting her chestnut hair.

People passed them in the aisle, making their way to the church doors now that the service was over. Many smiled or raised a hand in hello. Travis returned their greetings, liking the way it felt to be part of this church family.

Jessica laid a hand on Ellie's arm. "Go ahead. It will be good for you. You've been working like a slave laborer the last few weeks."

"I hate to leave you with the boys."

"We can take them with us," Travis offered immediately. He and Ellie hadn't spent any time alone since he moved to Blackberry, but if the only way he could get her out on a picnic was with the boys, that was fine with him. "They're always good company."

"I will watch the boys," Jessica informed them in a tone that invited no argument. "Brent spent last weekend with Dan. I'm not giving up my Sunday with my boy. Speaking of the boys, I'll head down to the nursery and round them up." She leaned close to Ellie and said in a stage whisper, "Go. Get out of town. Corey will be fine with me and Brent."

Travis tried again. "Anna promised to send a picnic basket with us. If that doesn't tempt you, nothing will."

Ellie spread her arms and laughed. "All right, I give in. What else can I do with all of you conspiring against me?"

An hour later with the picnic basket in the back of Travis's red Jeep and Ellie and Travis in the front seats, they were headed down the Blue Ridge Parkway. Both had changed from their Sunday finery into jeans, sweatshirts, and short leather boots which would be good for walking mountain trails.

Ellie stretched. "I feel as if I've been kidnapped."

"I promise to return you safely with no ransom demand."

His words brought a lazy laugh from Ellie, but he knew the promise would be harder to keep than she realized. Not that he had any fantasies of a money ransom. Daily trying to love her and Corey the way Anna suggested was difficult; loving them without asking to be loved and trusted in return. That was the ransom that was so hard not to demand: love and trust and a life together under one roof.

He wanted them to be living together and loving each other in a family setting so badly there were times he could hardly bear it. He wanted Ellie the way every man wants the woman he loves. He didn't dare press it.

Baby steps, he reminded himself.

Right now he tried to content himself with sharing one of the most beautiful places in the world with his wife and cheered himself with the reminder that she was still his wife, that in spite of everything, she hadn't divorced him.

They oohed and aahed over the views of mountains and valleys as they traveled along. There appeared to be only a few areas of private land along the parkway. Most of the road traveled through natural settings.

"I've been over this drive many times, but I never grow tired of it," Ellie said. "I'm glad you talked me into coming up here today."

His heart ballooned with joy. "I'd take credit for the views if I could. As it is, I'm grateful for the people who set this land apart for a national treasure so many years ago. If they hadn't, it would likely be covered with condominiums, private resorts, and billboards announcing tourist sites."

He pulled to the side and parked where they had a view of a private hillside covered with trees that were a froth of pink blossoms. He rolled down his window and welcomed in their fragrance. "Apple trees?"

"Peach trees. Unfortunately, if the weather forecast is correct, those blossoms will be covered with snow by tomorrow. I hope the farmer doesn't lose his entire crop."

He stared at the rosy pink beauty, and a little sadness crept over him. "Nature can be cruel."

"Yes." A minute later she amended her response. "Sometimes what seems cruel isn't, or at least it has beautiful benefits. I remember when I was a teenager, a bad windstorm toppled hundreds of trees on the mountain behind my parents' home. I felt as devastated as the mountain looked. The next spring, dogwoods and rhododendrons blossomed where the tall trees had stood. The blossoming trees had been there before, of course, but the older trees had shadowed them. Now the smaller trees could reach wide for the sun. I remind myself of that when life is hard." She bit her bottom lip, looking embarrassed. "I guess that sounds hokey."

He shook his head. "No, not a bit."

He hoped that would happen for them; that the storm of separation would pass and leave their life more beautiful. He popped his palms lightly against the steering wheel and took a deep breath, breaking the sentimental spell. "Ready for lunch?"

Travis took the picnic basket and red-and-black plaid blanket from the back of the Jeep. Together he and Ellie spread the blanket on the ground.

"When did you buy the Jeep?" Ellie asked as he opened the picnic basket.

"Last week. I decided sports cars weren't made for mountain living, at least not if you plan to drive them all year."

"You traded your car? You loved that car."

Travis shrugged. "I decided a four-wheel-drive vehicle made more sense."

"Don't tell me you, the citified lawyer, are becoming a red—true mountain man." Her teasing tone kept the statement from sounding like an insult.

He chuckled. "What was that you almost called me? A redneck?"

She tossed her head in a delightfully flirtatious manner, her chestnut hair catching the sunlight. "I grew up in these parts of the woods, mister. We don't like menfolk hereabouts called such names. Our men are good old boys."

He threw back his head and laughed at her husky voice until his ribs hurt.

"Did you really trade your car in," Ellie asked when his laugh mellowed to a chuckle, "or do you have both the car and Jeep now?"

"I traded it in. I'll probably be trading the Jeep soon."

"Why? Doesn't it run well?"

"When I showed Jess my new wheels, she said that fathers own vans."

It was like a curtain dropped over Ellie's face. It caused a shadow on his own good spirits.

Ellie busied herself with removing things from the wicker picnic hamper. "This is a lovely old basket."

"Anna said she and George took it on picnics. It hasn't been used since he died."

Ellie sat back on her heels and gazed at the basket. "That's rather bittersweet, isn't it? The basket must have brought back happy memories for her when she brought it out for us to use."

She continued unloading it: Red-and-white checked cloth napkins and colorful plastic plates and forks were followed by ham and cheese sandwiches on Anna's homemade sourdough buns, homemade watermelon pickles, potato chips that were definitely not homemade, and Anna's chocolate-cherry cake. "Nothing to drink?"

Travis retrieved sodas from the small cooler in the Jeep. When he returned, Ellie was holding a paperback copy of *In His Steps*. "I found this in the basket. Are you reading it?"

"Yes. I've known for a while it's considered one of the classics of Christian literature, but I never made the time to read it before. When I discovered you were reading it, I decided to read it, too." He opened a can of soda and handed it to her. His gaze caught hers and held it. "I wanted to know what thoughts and stories fill your mind, what ideas you find fascinating."

She studied his eyes for what seemed a short lifetime. He didn't know what she was looking for. He allowed her to look her fill. He had nothing to hide.

He heard her swallow. "I think," she whispered, "that's the nicest thing you ever said to me."

Her words touched him deeply, making him feel strangely and unexpectedly humble. He hadn't known she would respond that way, hadn't known this would strike such a chord in her heart. He hadn't chosen to read the book to impress her.

He cleared his throat of an obstruction that seemed to have suddenly grown there. "It would be great if everyone lived by the motto in this book, wouldn't it— 'What would Jesus do?' "

"Yes." Her smile was radiant. "Yes, it would."

Travis remembered Christmas Eve in the Los Angeles church when he'd prayed for Ellie to believe. Now they shared their belief. Peace enwrapped him. Whatever happened between himself and Ellie, at least their son was being raised by a wonderful woman who would teach Corey the joy of believing.

They were beginning their chocolate cake when Ellie came back to the subject of asking "What would Jesus do?" Her eyes looked troubled. "I love designing clothes and running the boutique, but sometimes I wonder whether Jesus would think it too materialistic a way for me to make a living."

Her statement would have shocked him in the days before she left Los Angeles. Now it seemed to him a natural thing for a person to wonder. "From where I stand, it looks like you are doing work for which He's gifted you, work that brings enjoyment to others. And in doing so, you give others an opportunity to earn a living and practice their own talents and skills. None of that sounds like a bad thing. I guess it boils down to your attitude."

"Mmm. I guess." She gazed off at the peach tree–covered mountainside.

He allowed her to reflect in silence, or in nature's idea of silence. A light breeze stirred the redbud maples and fragrant pine trees. Small birds hopped about on the grass nearby, scratching in last autumn's crunchy leaves and chirping messages to one another. Were they hoping he and Ellie would leave some crumbs?

Ellie swallowed her last bite of cake. "There was a time you didn't think very highly of my designing." She studied her plate, scraping up the crumbs with her fork.

He chose his words carefully. He knew his attitude in the past had hurt her. "I wasn't too wise back then about a lot of things. I expect I still have a lot to learn, but some of the lessons are behind me. When I joined the Los Angeles firm, I thought in order to be successful we had to be carbon copies of the firm's other lawyers and their wives. I was wrong to want you to give up who you are. I'm sorry."

She studied his eyes as she had before, as though trying to probe into his soul. After a minute, she nodded. Moving to her knees, she started cleaning up their things and repacking the basket.

That's all? he thought. He tried to keep his frustration from showing. She'd acted like he'd given her the world's greatest jewel when he told her he wanted to know what ideas she found interesting, but when he admitted he'd been wrong about her life's work, she said nothing. He'd never understand women. But he wasn't going to quit trying to understand this one.

"Do you ever wonder about your own work, your law practice?" she asked.

"You mean, do I ever ask myself in my work, 'What would Jesus do?' " She nodded.

"Sure. Maybe not in so many words, but yes."

"You don't find it compromising to practice law?"

"I try to practice Christ's love by serving my clients the best I can."

"Through legal actions?" Her voice was drenched with doubt.

"I help people whose legal rights are challenged. Don't you believe it's possible that can be a loving act?"

"Maybe, but there's so much conflict and pain in court battles. Doesn't the Bible tell us that we should go to court only as a last resort, that we should try to work things out first?"

"Yes, but there are legal acts that are necessary and don't hurt people, like making out wills or examining documents to determine the legal status of a situation. What about people like Jess, who want to protect their children from violent fathers? You'd want her and Brent to have legal protection from Dan if it becomes necessary, wouldn't you?"

"Of course." Ellie shuddered visibly. "That reminds me. Chuck told me he saw Dan and Sissy together at a movie last Friday night."

Chills crawled up Travis's spine when she related her suspicion that Dan had left Brent home alone. Travis wouldn't be a bit surprised if Dan had done such a low-down thing. "Did you ask Brent whether he had a baby-sitter?"

"I never think of it at the right time. If Dan did leave Brent alone, would a judge take his custody rights away?"

"Depends on the judge and the proof."

Ellie's shoulders slumped. "I guess a judge wouldn't take the word of a three-year-old boy."

"We could try to verify it, assuming he was left alone, that is."

"How?"

"First things first. We'll ask Brent if he had a baby-sitter last weekend."

"And if he says no?"

"We confront Dan."

"He'll lie."

"Most likely. So we'll ask him to give us the sitter's name and address."

"What if he refuses?"

"Then I'll threaten to talk to the local children's services."

"I'll ask Brent about the sitter when we get home. He might not remember or might mix up that night with another time. I don't think he'd lie about it, but he is only three, and kids don't have a great sense of time at that age."

"We'll hope he remembers the name of a sitter and what a great time they had together."

"Yes. I worry and pray a lot about Jessica and Brent. I'm glad you're here to share this with."

Travis knew it was a huge admission for her to concede that she was leaning on him in any manner at all. "Then I'm glad I'm here, too."

Ellie took a deep breath and stood, lifting the blanket to shake it out. "There's a great waterfall near here. Want to see it before we head back?"

"Sure." Did he want to spend more time alone with her? Did birds fly? He felt like he was walking on air as they went back to the Jeep.

"Pull over here," Ellie said a few miles farther down the parkway.

Travis obediently pulled into the paved parking area of a well-marked lookout, one of many the parkway builders had provided so people could safely enjoy spectacular views of valleys and distant mountain ranges.

He looked out over the valley before them. It went on for miles and miles. "I don't see any waterfalls."

"You have to walk to the falls, silly. It will be good for you. Wear off that wonderful chocolate-cherry cake of Anna's." She pointed toward a wooded area to one side of the lookout parking lot. "The path to the waterfall is over there."

Travis climbed out of the Jeep after her. "Are you sure there's a path there? Maybe this isn't the right place." He saw nothing but trees and underbrush.

"The path's here." She headed toward the trees with a confident stride.

He followed, doubting.

Ellie tossed a triumphant look over her shoulder when they reached the trees. There was a path, two or three feet wide. She started down it.

Travis followed. Happiness for the simple time they were spending together bubbled up out of him. He hummed as they went along.

Ellie turned, stopping to stare at him with amusement written large across her face.

"What's so funny?"

"You're humming a Barney song."

Heat raced over his neck and face. Embarrassed laughter strangled his words. "How the mighty are fallen. A couple of months ago I was a big-city lawyer attending symphonies and opening-night movies and eating at spectacular restaurants among the rich and famous. Now I spend my evenings with a little boy whenever possible, watching Barney movies and dining at McDonald's—and loving it."

"I like this man better than the Los Angeles man."

Ellie's quiet words tied his heart and tongue into a tangle. She stood a few feet ahead of him, framed by rhododendron bushes and tall pines, watching him with her lips lifted in a small, sweet smile. She'd never looked so attractive to him. He wanted to haul her into his arms and kiss her eyes, her neck, her lips—for starters.

Baby steps. He could barely hear the words through the roaring in his ears. Trying to break the spell, he did a little shuffle, his boots scuffing in the dirt path. "I do a pretty mean Barney dance, too."

Her laugh rang out. "I don't think directors will be breaking down your door to sign you to remake any Fred Astaire films." She pivoted and started off again. "We're getting closer to the falls. Can you hear them?"

He chuckled as he followed after her. And he'd thought the roaring he'd heard was his blood racing in his ears. Maybe some of it had been, but not all.

The path had been meandering down the hill. Now it steepened. He could see a wooden footbridge with a peeled log railing crossing the river that came into view. Their footsteps quickened on the steep, twisting incline, and in a moment they were at the picturesque bridge.

They stopped in the middle, hands on the log that was worn smooth, and peered into the clear, shallow water gurgling beneath them over pebbles of gold, gray, and brown. The peaceful, cheerful sound fit his mood perfectly.

The gravel path continued on the other side of the bridge, continuing along the river. The waterfall's roar grew louder as they followed the path. Soon the path began a gradual descent, then a steeper descent, until the trail alternated between the gravel pathway and wooden stairs.

Eventually the trail led to a landing with a picturesque two-foot-high rock wall which offered limited protection to hikers. The falls were only beginning at this point. The water was shallow across the large flat stones.

Travis leaned over the wall to peer down the gorge. The river continued its sloping way toward the bottom. "Looks like it would make a great slide."

"Until you reached the drop-off a few hundred feet farther along."

Travis laughed at her dry tone.

She pointed to a wooden sign nearby. He read that people were to stay behind the rock wall, that the river's stones were slippery and people had fallen to their deaths on these falls. The news sobered him but took away none of his fascination with the river's beauty.

"There's another viewing point farther down the mountain." Ellie started off.

He reflected on the deceptive river as he and Ellie continued along the meandering path. It looked like a fun and beautiful place to play, but it was a death trap to those who didn't pay attention to nature's laws. *Like many places in life,* he thought, *when we don't listen to God's hints and continue on in situations where He has put up signs and rock walls telling us the places are unsafe. The situations look fun or beautiful, and we ignore the warnings, to our peril.*

He shared his comparison with Ellie.

She smiled and nodded her agreement. "One of the things I love about living in the mountains are nature's lessons. God teaches us so many things about life through nature, if we'll only open our eyes and ears to learn the lessons."

Travis recalled her earlier comments about the storm opening up the forest's ceiling to sunlight for the forest's shorter plants. He noticed the rhododendrons along the path where man had opened an area of mountain forest to sunlight. He looked at the mighty tree trunks fallen in the nearby forest floor and the occasional trunk which had fallen across the path with new eyes.

When they reached the next viewing point, he exclaimed in delight. Above them the river ceased its lazy meandering down the mountain. It dropped in a thick white veil, spraying Travis and Ellie as it passed, and continuing to plummet toward the bottom of the mountain.

"This is certainly worth the climb." He couldn't see the bottom of the falls. He wondered how far they fell. "You were right about the drop."

A shiver ran through him. How frightening to be playing in the river and find yourself at the top of this huge drop with no chance of preventing yourself from falling along with the water.

"It's one of my favorite waterfalls." Ellie sat down on the rock ledge and watched the tumbling waters. "Jessica and I have brought Corey and Brent here a number of times."

"Do they like it?"

"They're fascinated by it. I don't think they understand what they're seeing yet."

Travis liked what he was seeing: Ellie seated in this natural setting with the magnificent waterfall for a background. He pulled a camera from the pocket of his lightweight tan jacket. He'd bought the camera to begin his own photo collection of Corey. He wouldn't mind a few pictures of Corey's mother mingled in with those of Corey.

He caught her gazing at the falls. She turned her head immediately after he took the shot.

"Oh no, not a picture." Her hands flew to her hair in an unnecessary attempt to straighten it.

"Your hair is fine. This will be a terrific shot. I'll make a copy for you if you'd like."

She wrinkled her nose. "No thanks. I see this face enough."

I wish I did, he thought, *like first thing every morning and last thing every night, for starters.* "It's a beautiful face."

Ellie flushed and changed the subject. "Why did you decide to move to Blackberry? I know you wanted to be part of Corey's life, but you could have done that without moving. You could have asked for shared custody."

"I didn't want to do that to my. . .our son." Travis sat down on the cold rocks beside her. "Taking him away from the only parent he knows for half the year," he shrugged, "what kind of love is that? He'd be terrified and lonely without you. He's too young to understand what shared custody means." Memories of other families with children of varying ages whose parents' divorces had been handled by his Los Angeles firm ran through his head. "Sometimes I think shared custody terrifies children of all ages."

"And their parents."

"Yes."

"You could have asked me to move back to Los Angeles with him."

"I had no right to ask you to move across the country for my convenience. You'd established a successful business here."

"There was a time when that would not have stopped you."

A hardness had crept into her tone. He chose his words cautiously. "There was a time when we had agreed to move together through life as one. Somewhere along the line, we started moving in different directions instead of taking the same path."

Sadness rolled across her face like a wave. She straightened her back and shoulders as though trying to throw off unhappy memories. "Moving to Blackberry was a major career decision. Don't you miss working for the Los Angeles firm? The famous clients, law cases that are unusual or involve lots of money, that are high profile, that take lots of research and new ways of interpreting the law?"

"I miss all of that. On the other hand, there's more variety in my everyday work here. I accepted a case last week that promises to be very interesting. A group of individuals concerned for the area's environmental integrity wants to limit a planned development."

"You must worry that, even if you return to Los Angeles eventually, you'll never be able to pick up where you left off in your career."

"I'd be lying if I said the thought hadn't occurred to me, and more than once or twice, but I know beyond doubt it was the right choice. More than anything else, I want to know Corey, to be there for him in every way I can."

Ellie stared at her hands in silence for a few moments then stood.

"Ellie." Travis caught one of her hands and drew her gently toward him until she stood between his knees. He took her other hand also and played his thumbs along the smooth skin on the backs of her hands.

He was surprised she'd allowed herself to be drawn so close to him, that she allowed him to hold her hands, that she allowed him this simple caress. He was almost afraid to speak for fear he would break the sweetness of the moment.

"What?"

Her breathless question forced him to speak. "I'd like to tell you about that night."

"What night?"

He knew by her defensive tone that she knew exactly what night he meant.

"The night of the Christmas party in Los Angeles." The night that changed his life. Or had that night only been the culmination of a series of small choices he'd made in the days and months and years leading up to it, choices to put his own happiness above Ellie's, to put himself before his wife and before God?

Ellie took a step back. An emotionless shield seemed to drop over her eyes. He felt the pull of her hands, but she didn't tug them away. With immense gratitude for that tiny gift, he squeezed them tighter.

He waited for permission to speak before plunging into the place that had brought them both such pain. He wanted desperately for her to understand what had happened that night, but he wouldn't push her to open the wounded place in her heart so he could absolve himself.

He wondered if she could hear his heart beating over the rush of the waterfall behind them.

"All right."

Travis could hardly believe she'd agreed to his request. He realized he hadn't expected it. He'd imagined this discussion many times, but now he couldn't think how to start. He sent up a silent prayer asking God to give him the right words, that he might not cause Ellie to shut the door she'd just cracked open between them.

He stumbled into the beginning. "When I left our apartment that night, I was furious. I drove around, telling myself all the reasons I was right to be angry and you were wrong to be angry." He shrugged and lifted one corner of his lips in an embarrassed grin. "The usual human reaction, I guess. Anyway, I found myself near Michelle's apartment and decided to stop. I thought she'd laugh at the idea that she and I were more than friends, and then I'd really be vindicated. Only she didn't laugh."

He continued with the story, telling Ellie what had happened in the apartment, how he happened to leave his cuff links behind, the whole sordid mess.

When he was done, he waited for her to say something. She didn't. The stiffness he'd felt in her at the beginning hadn't loosened an iota.

"Do you believe me, Ellie?"

"I don't know."

His heart sank. He'd begun with such hope. After all this time of refusing to listen, she'd allowed him to tell his story. She hadn't pulled away during the telling of it, and with each sentence he'd felt the excitement of hope rising within his chest. Now it fell and smashed, and he felt empty inside, not knowing what he could do to prove the truth of his story.

"I want to believe you."

Her unexpected admission sent the hope leaping up within him again. *Thank You, Lord.* "You do?"

"I want to, but I don't dare. Part of me is still terrified of trusting you."

Travis's throat thickened with tears he couldn't shed. "I'm sorry I hurt you."

"I know that you've made an incredible sacrifice moving to Blackberry to be near Corey. You've been wonderful with him. And I'm so grateful for the way you've helped Jessica out. I wish those things made the distrust go away. Maybe they should. I don't know. I only know there's part of me that throws up flares and caution signs and says, 'Don't trust him. Don't let him in your heart again.' I don't dare not listen. Not yet. Maybe later."

Later wasn't as good as now, but it was a lot better than an outright rejection. "Maybe never."

His heart plunged again. He stared at her hands, trying to accept what she was saying. Finally he nodded. "Thank you for listening anyway." He took a deep breath and looked up at her with a smile. "You're in charge of this expedition. We'll take it a day at a time. Baby steps."

"Baby steps."

The term brought a smile to her lips and the sparkle back to her eyes.

It loosened the tightness in his chest. If she could smile with him like that, surely there was hope.

He stood quickly, dropping a quick kiss on her lips before she could step back. "To seal the bargain," he defended himself lightly. He gave her hands a squeeze before letting them go.

To his surprise she didn't move. A wistful longing looked out from her brown eyes. Her lips, which had been so warm and soft beneath his brief touch, were open slightly.

"I wish I could trust you," she whispered. "Sometimes I miss you. I miss us."

"I do, too." His heart hammered. Where was she taking them?

Ellie lifted both hands and laid them against his cheeks. He barely breathed, drinking in the wonder of her soft caress. Rising on her tiptoes, she touched her lips to his, gently, in a kiss that lingered longer than his quick peck. He returned it, slowly, not forcing it into something more passionate.

Ellie groaned softly against his lips and leaned against him, her arms slipping around his neck.

Travis's arms held her close. He buried his face in her neck, loving the feel of her skin, the familiar scent of her light floral cologne, the silkiness of her hair against his cheek.

She gasped slightly as he kissed her on the side of her neck, the place that he'd always delighted in knowing she loved to be kissed. He held her tighter, rejoicing that she was in his arms again, that she was there of her own choice.

He wasn't sure how many minutes passed before she withdrew slowly from his arms. Too few minutes to satisfy him, more than he knew he'd had a right to hope for.

With a shaky smile, Ellie turned to start up the path. Travis took her hand,

and she allowed him to hold it. He watched her from the corner of his eye whenever he dared take his gaze from the path, loving the slightly mussed hair and flushed cheeks that were a visible reminder of the intimate minutes they'd spent.

Maybe never.

The words whispered through his thoughts, reminding him that kisses aren't guarantees.

Chapter 11

Ellie's thoughts tumbled through her mind and her emotions through her body as the water tumbled over the rocks in the river they left behind as they climbed up to Travis's Jeep. Her cheeks were still warm from the time she and Travis had spent in each other's arms.

She kept her gaze out the windows while they drove back to Blackberry, not willing to look into his face and possibly see his desire for her there.

Had she been a fool, kissing him that way? Undoubtedly. But it felt so good.

In the years between her departure from Los Angeles and Travis's arrival in Blackberry, she'd kept the door slammed and locked on their intimate memories. Once she'd let him through that door when he'd kissed her in her hallway weeks earlier, she'd been allowing herself to remember the early days of their romance and marriage, how special and beautiful his kisses and touch had been to her.

You'll be sorry for those kisses later, she admonished herself.

Her emotions weren't ready to go along with logic and reality. They were still wrapped up in Travis's kisses.

Ellie was out of the Jeep almost before it stopped in her driveway. "Thanks for a wonderful afternoon."

"Wait, Ellie."

She waved over her shoulder, grinning a broad, friendly grin, and pretending she hadn't heard his plea.

She could as well have waited. He was beside her with a few long strides. "Mind if I say hello to Corey?"

Ellie's ego deflated instantly. "Of course."

Their kisses so occupied her mind that she'd forgotten he would want to see their son.

She groaned silently. Had she created a hopeless emotional pool of quicksand when she kissed Travis? For Corey's sake if not her own, she mustn't allow her physical attraction to Travis to muddle her decisions.

At the front door she laid a hand on Travis's chest. "Wait. There's something I must say."

He waited while she struggled for the right words.

She took a deep breath, then blurted, "About the kiss—"

"Kisses." His smile teased her.

"Yes, well, about them." She linked her fingers, twisting them back and forth

339

while she fumbled. "I don't want you to think I meant. . .that I didn't mean. . ."

"I know." He cupped the side of her neck with one hand and lifted her chin with a thumb. "Your kisses didn't mean you trust me."

She nodded, part of her glad he understood, part of her miserable.

"I hope," he continued, "they meant you're trying to forgive me and believe in me again."

"Yes." That was exactly what they'd meant, though she hadn't understood it herself until he put it into words.

"You're in charge. If I start moving too fast, say so and I'll slow down. I promise." His hand at her neck drew her only close enough for him to drop a kiss on her forehead. "Let's go see our son."

The house was very still when they entered. Ellie called out, but no one answered. "They're probably in the backyard."

But they weren't.

"That's strange." Uneasiness spread tentacles in Ellie's chest.

"It's five o'clock. Maybe Jess took the boys out to eat."

"Probably. Or to Anna's."

"Or to the park. They love the playground there."

Ellie reminded herself there was no reason for her to experience the uneasiness that wasn't quite fear. The tentacles only grew and gripped harder.

"Maybe Jess left a note," Travis suggested.

Ellie ran back inside, allowing the screen door to slam behind her, and hurried to the kitchen table, willing a note to be there.

There wasn't one.

"This is where we leave notes for each other," she told Travis when he reached her. "There's nothing here."

His arms went around her shoulders from behind. He gave her a comforting squeeze. "Don't make up any awful scenarios in your mind. Maybe Jess took the boys on a picnic. Remember how they were clamoring to join us on ours?"

"Jessica and I share a car. It's parked in the drive."

"So maybe they went for a walk."

"You're right. I'm being silly. Any minute they'll walk in the door, and I'll feel like a fool for worrying."

She didn't even dare voice her fear that one of the boys had been hurt and Jessica had taken him to the clinic or to the hospital in a neighboring town. Travis would think she was hysterical. Besides, Jessica would have left a note in such a case.

"Maybe they're in the garage. Jessica uses it for her studio." Ellie hurried toward the back door. "Jessica usually doesn't allow the boys in there. She thinks it's too dangerous with her tools and paints and all."

Jessica and the boys weren't in the studio either.

"They're fine," Travis insisted. "You're going to make yourself sick worrying this way. Why don't you come back to Anna's with me? Visiting with her will keep your mind off fictional problems. You can leave a note asking Jess to call when she gets back."

It was the sensible thing to do, of course. Yet when they were back in the Jeep, Ellie asked Travis to drive past the park and check the store before going to Anna's. Ellie was glad when Travis did as she asked without ridiculing her fears further, but they didn't see Jessica and the boys.

They weren't at Anna's either, nor had Anna heard from them since church that morning.

Ellie consciously pushed away her fears. She complimented Anna on the picnic lunch and listened to Anna's stories about her own and George's experiences with the picnic hamper. Travis and Ellie told Anna of their afternoon—leaving out the kisses.

Through it all, Ellie never stopped straining to hear the phone's ring announcing the call from Jessica. The call never came.

In the middle of one of Anna's stories about her and George's experiences as young parents when their first child was Corey's age, a picture flashed in Ellie's mind: an ornate oval brass door handle plate.

Ellie went cold from head to foot. She turned to Travis. "The doors weren't locked."

His eyebrows scrunched together. "What?"

"The doors at my house. They weren't locked. We always lock them now when we go out, because of Dan's threats."

She saw by the way his eyes widened slightly that he realized the implications, but his voice and manner were reassuring.

"There weren't any signs of struggle in the house. How about in Jess's studio?"

"No, everything looked normal there, too."

"Then most likely Jess forgot to lock the doors." Travis grinned. "A person can forget anything while trying to keep up with Corey and Brent."

That was true. Ellie's alarm calmed somewhat but didn't go away. Anna picked up her story, and Ellie pretended to turn her attention back to it.

Before long Travis stood and stretched. "Think I'll run down to the grocery store and pick up some soda. I'm about out."

The waiting was harder after he left. At least he wouldn't be gone long, Ellie thought, turning her attention to a new lace design Anna was showing her.

❧

Travis stood inside Sheriff Strand's door and finished telling the little bit there was to tell about Jessica and the boys. "I know there isn't any reason to believe there's been any. . .foul play, but I thought. . .just in case something's wrong here, I wanted you to know."

The sheriff's round face looked grim. "I'm glad you came to me. There's no big-city police department here, just me. I know almost everyone in this town. I don't have to be told Ellie knows Jessica's habits. If Ellie says it's unusual for Jessica to take the boys somewhere without leaving a note, then it's unusual. I don't like it that the house is unlocked, not with what I've seen of Dan's temper over the years."

"His house was dark when I drove past, but I didn't stop to see if he was there."

"I'll check it out. But first I'll try Doc Swenson and then the nearest hospital."

Travis paced the small entryway while Sheriff Strand made his calls. *Corey's fine. They're all fine. There's nothing to worry about. This is only a precaution.* He repeated the phrases again and again. They did nothing to stop the fear that rose like bile in his stomach.

"Doc hasn't seen them, and there's no record of any of them checking in at the hospital." The sheriff grabbed his official brown leather jacket from the closet.

"If you're heading to Dan's, I want to come along."

Strand hesitated with his hand on the doorknob. "I should order you home, but I won't. Follow in your own vehicle if you want. See that you stay in it. I don't want any fool John Wayne–type stunts. If Dan's home, I'll talk to him alone. Got it?"

"Got it."

Travis was glad to be doing something, even something as mundane as following Strand to Dan's house. Sitting around waiting for Jess and the boys was making him crazy. He knew Ellie felt the same. Part of him wanted to be with her, comforting and reassuring her, but if there was any chance Jess and the boys needed help getting back home, he wanted to make sure they had every possibility of receiving that help.

He hadn't anticipated how difficult it would be to stay in the car once they were at Dan's. He watched as Sheriff Strand knocked at the front door of the darkened house, then watched him walk around to the back. Travis gripped the wheel so tight his hands hurt.

The sheriff peered into windows as he made his way back to the cars. Travis realized he could barely make out the man's form. The sun was setting. Travis had never minded that the mountains made the sun appear to set earlier than in flatlands. Now the evening darkness was like an enemy.

Sheriff Strand stopped beside Travis's window. "Nothing there. Can't go inside without a warrant, as you know, and I don't have a legitimate reason to request one yet. Dan's Mercedes is in the garage, but his new pickup is gone. Let's drive by his office."

Dan wasn't at his office.

Travis remembered Dan's girlfriend, Sissy, and mentioned her to the sheriff. "I know where she lives."

Sissy was home, but she hadn't seen Dan.

They headed back to Ellie's, hoping Jessica had turned up and that the men were on a wild goose chase.

The house was as still as Travis and Ellie had left it hours before.

Travis flipped on the lights and checked the kitchen table. No note.

The sheriff hiked at his pants. "Did Ellie check to see if anything was missing? Kids' clothes, toys, Jess's clothes, a suitcase, that sort of thing?"

"No. You don't think Jess kidnapped the kids, do you?"

"One thing I've learned in law enforcement. Usually it's people the victims know who hurt them, the very people they're most apt to trust."

Travis's stomach turned over at the word *victims*. It brought his worst fears too close to home. He knew from his law practice that what Sheriff Strand said about victims knowing the people who harm them was true. "So now, assuming something is amiss here, we have at least two suspects, Dan and Jess."

"Why don't you get Ellie back here to check on what's missing? Before you leave, do you know where Ellie keeps pictures? A clear picture of Jessica and the boys might be a good thing to have to show around. While you're picking up Ellie, I'll start asking neighbors if they saw anything suspicious around here this afternoon."

Travis could have kicked himself for not thinking of speaking to the neighbors earlier, but he'd believed at first that Ellie was making a mountain out of a molehill, being a typical worrywart mom.

Travis didn't have to dig out the albums. Pictures of Ellie and Jess and the boys were displayed all over the house. He selected one with Jess and the boys kneeling in front of the Christmas tree, grins on all their faces, Jess's arms about the boys. It was a good likeness of each of them.

When he arrived at Anna's, Ellie's first words were, "That was a long trip for soda pop." She looked pointedly at his empty arms. "Didn't the station have any?"

Travis had forgotten there weren't any stores open on Sundays in Blackberry, only the superstation on the edge of town. Ellie must have suspected all along he'd left about the boys.

He sat down on the sofa near Ellie's chair, not bothering to remove his coat. In a few sentences and in as emotionless a tone as he could manage, he told Ellie and Anna what he'd been doing. "Sheriff Strand wants you to go home and check to see if anything's missing."

Ellie's face went white.

Travis thought she might scream or faint or react like women in movies and books so often do when faced with a frightening situation. Then he realized she'd already been facing the possibility that the boys were in danger. He was the one who hadn't believed it right away.

She stood. "All right. Let's go."

Anna stood, too, laying a wrinkled hand on Ellie's arm. "I'll go with you." She hurried to the hall closet to retrieve her and Ellie's coats.

Travis put his arms around Ellie. Her arms gripped his waist like a vise but only for a moment. Then she pulled away, her face set as if in stone.

His heart ached for her pain and for his own.

Corey's fine, he assured himself for the umpteenth time. *All this is precautionary.*

By the time they reached Ellie's place, sleet started falling, nasty little pellets that drove the doubts in Travis's mind into full-fledged fears that twisted his gut. He'd forgotten the snowstorm that was predicted to move in.

The sheriff wasn't at the house. Ellie made a quick pass through the downstairs. "Nothing missing down here but the spring jackets Jess and the boys would have worn."

They were coming down from her upstairs search when Sheriff Strand returned.

"Anything missing?"

Ellie described the outfits she thought the three were wearing.

"Sure about that?" Sheriff Strand had a pencil poised over a small notebook.

"I'm sure about the boys' outfits. I'm pretty sure about Jessica's."

Strand's pencil scratched across the pad. "Anything else missing?"

"The gray stuffed pony Travis gave Corey. That's not unusual. Corey carries it everywhere."

Travis's heart expanded. If Corey was in trouble, Travis hoped the pony made him feel braver, safer, loved.

The smell of fresh coffee wafted into the hallway and brought a small smile to Travis's lips. Anna was already at work in the kitchen.

There was a knock at the door, and Ellie opened it. "Mike. What are you doing here?"

"Sheriff asked me to stop over."

Travis recognized the man but had never met him. He ran a local shop that performed a number of services businesses and individuals in a small town needed. He provided one location for people to copy things, fax things, use a computer, make posters, and use various shipping services.

Mike gave the sheriff a friendly smile. "What do you need?"

Sheriff Strand handed him the picture of Jess and the boys.

Ellie gasped in recognition, one hand flying to cover her mouth.

Travis slipped an arm around her shoulders.

Strand darted them a glance before answering Mike. "Can you make up some copies of these, quicklike? Maybe some blowups, too."

Mike shrugged. "Sure. What's the problem?"

"Not sure there is any yet," Strand answered. "Just taking some precautions." He explained the situation succinctly.

"I'll get them back here as soon as I can." Mike sent a pitying glance over

Strand's broad shoulder to Ellie. "Sorry, Ellie. Hope this is just a false alarm."

Sheriff Strand spoke over his shoulder as he walked out with Mike. "I'm going to make some calls from my car. I want your line kept clear, Ellie, in case Jessica tries to call you."

The sleet had turned to snow, and the dusk to dark. Travis could hear the *shhing* of the snowflakes, could see them thick in the light from the old-fashioned street lamp before he closed the door behind the two men. Usually he loved the beauty and winter-wonderland sense such a snow brought. Tonight it chilled his bones.

Travis wondered whether the sheriff was putting out a bulletin on Jessica and the boys. It was early in the game for that, but Travis hoped the lawman was doing it anyway.

When the sheriff returned, he and Travis and Ellie moved into the living room. Travis sat beside Ellie on the sofa and reached for her hand. "Did you have any success with the neighbors, Sheriff?"

"No one saw anything or anyone unusual."

"Dan?"

"No one saw him either."

Travis's shoulders dropped. He hadn't realized how much he'd hoped one of the neighbors had seen something that would explain everything or that Jessica had told one of them where she and the kids were going.

Strand lowered himself to the edge of an overstuffed, worn maroon chair. "I have some questions for you two. Travis gave me a rundown on the situation, but I want to hear everything again from the beginning, from both of you."

The questions were simple and straightforward. When had they last seen Jessica and the boys, where exactly had Travis and Ellie spent the afternoon, had anyone else been with them, when had they noticed Jessica and the boys missing, was there a vehicle Jessica might be driving?

Travis and Ellie answered everything honestly. Travis knew Sheriff Strand needed the information. Travis had no qualms in answering the questions fully and completely and knew Ellie felt the same. Yet memories of newscasts with other parents of missing children flashed before him, parents who begged convincingly for their children's safe return, only to be exposed later as their children's killers. And he knew that in Sheriff Strand's mind, he and Ellie had been added to the list of suspects.

It was a strange feeling, but as a lawyer, Travis knew the sheriff was acting wisely in considering them suspects. Secure in their innocence, the knowledge wasn't disturbing.

The questioning was interrupted by the arrival of two deputies. While Sheriff Strand was talking with them in the hall, Anna brought in a tray with mugs of coffee, cream, sugar, and doughnuts.

Anna set the tray on the coffee table. "I found these doughnuts in the cookie jar."

"Thanks, but I'm not hungry right now." Ellie gave Anna a slight smile.

"Maybe not, but have a doughnut anyway. They're calming."

Travis wondered whether that was true. If it were, wouldn't the caffeine in the coffee counteract the doughnuts?

Anna must have anticipated the question. "Decaffeinated. I made a pot of each." She winked at them. "I'd like Sheriff Strand to stay awake until Jessica and the boys arrive home."

Travis couldn't help grinning at her attempt to lighten their emotions for a moment. Tension made the air in the room feel thicker than the snowflake-filled air outside.

Anna sat down beside Ellie on the edge of the sofa cushion and patted Ellie's hand. "I made a quick call to Pastor Evanson. He and his wife will make calls to start a prayer chain. I didn't want to make any more calls. I thought you'd want to keep the line clear."

Ellie clutched Anna's hand with both her own. "Thank you."

"Thanks." Travis's voice was husky. He'd learned to rely on his own prayers and those of friends in the last year or so but never had the prayers meant so much. Travis believed in the power of prayer, but before tonight he hadn't understood what an expression of love it was to pray for another.

As the evening wore on, concerns for the safety of the missing people increased. The storm grew in intensity. Wind picked up, driving the snow into a whirling, biting enemy. The wind whistled around the corners of the house, rattling the storm windows and making it impossible to forget the storm's ferocity.

Ellie stared out the front window, hugging her arms over the sweatshirt she was still wearing. "They were only wearing spring jackets. I hope they are someplace warm."

Travis slipped his arms around her from the back and drew her against his chest, resting his cheek on her hair, wishing he could absorb all her fear and pain into himself.

Beside them, Sheriff Strand said, "Wherever they are, they're likely holed up. From the highway patrol's reports, it sounds as if the roads will soon be impassable if they aren't already."

Travis felt a shiver run through Ellie and hugged her tighter, knowing that like him, she was imagining Corey freezing in the winter storm. "Jess is with the boys," he reminded her. "She'd lay down her life to protect them, you know that. She'll take care of them."

Ellie nodded and patted his hand.

He hoped she wasn't thinking what he was thinking: that there were limits to Jess's ability to protect the boys. He believed what he'd said, that she'd give her life for the boys. He only hoped Jess didn't have to do just that.

As evening grew into night, people began stopping by. Neighbors came with sympathy and food. Pastor Evanson came to pray with Ellie and Travis and stayed on to support them. He reassured them that all the members of their church family his wife had called had readily agreed to partake in the prayer chain.

Mike returned with the enlarged copies of the Christmas picture and a sample of a poster with the three faces smiling large at the viewers.

"Great," Sheriff Strand approved. "Make up some more of these posters. Charge them to my office."

"I'll get right on them." Mike yanked on his gloves. "There'll be no charge."

Travis gripped his hand. "Thanks." He could barely get the word past the lump in his throat.

Mike gave a sharp nod, then hugged Ellie. "Keep your chin up, kid." A minute later he headed back into the storm.

"I'm going back to the office." Sheriff Strand was pulling on his jacket. "I want to get these pictures distributed and put the news out over the wire. Other law enforcement agencies or other emergency groups trying to reach us will try my office first."

Travis knew it was the wisest move, but he wished the sheriff wasn't leaving. It made Travis feel left out of the information loop.

"Deputy Rogers will stay here." The sheriff nodded toward a tall young man with curly red hair cut so short it looked crispy. "He'll have a shortwave radio and a handheld radio to keep in touch with my office in case the phone lines go down."

Travis's stomach tightened. He hadn't even thought of that possibility.

"I'd better get candles and flashlights together, just in case." Ellie started toward the dining room.

Anna followed. "We'd best make extra coffee, too. Mrs. Schneider from next door brought over an urn. The coffee will stay warm quite awhile in there."

Travis wandered into the dining room after Ellie. The old print of the cabin beneath tall pines on a snow-covered mountain caught his attention. He remembered telling Jessica he thought it looked like a romantic spot, a place of rustic beauty and serenity. Now it only spoke to him of a cold, dangerous land.

Ellie was looking through drawers, pulling out candles of various sizes and colors. Travis wished he had something to do, anything at all to take his mind off Corey. Something besides praying, that was. The same prayer had been running through his mind for hours, *Keep them safe, Lord. Please, keep them safe.*

It was almost midnight when Travis heard footsteps crossing the porch in running *thumps*. Even with the snow cover and all the people coming and going, these were distinctive in their rush and the loudness that spoke of the person's urgency. The door crashed open before Travis could reach it.

Chapter 12

Ellie heard the door crash, followed by Travis's shocked, "Dan!"

She ran through the living room to the front door. "Dan, what are you doing here? I thought. . ." She snapped back the incriminating words on the tip of her tongue, the belief that he was with Jessica and the boys, that he was responsible for their disappearance.

The wind howled through the door, whisking in snow. Travis shut it out.

Dan wasn't wearing his usual long khaki coat. Instead he was dressed in jeans, a flannel shirt, and a lightweight jacket, all of which were covered in snow. His hiking boots dripped melting snow onto the hallway runner. His eyes were wide, and his chest lifted and fell with his panting. "Have you heard anything about the boys yet?"

Ellie shook her head. "Not yet."

Travis stepped beside her, arms crossed over his chest. "How did you hear about them, Dan? Stopped by your place to tell you about them, but you weren't there. Figured you were out of town."

"I was. Tax season just ended. Needed a break. I got back in town about ten minutes ago. Barely got out of my truck before one of my neighbors rushed over and told me the boys and Jessie are missing."

Deputy Rogers stood behind Dan. He'd moved so quietly that Ellie hadn't heard him coming. "When was the last time you saw them, Dan?"

"Me?" Dan shrugged. "This afternoon."

"When? Where?" Rogers's questions were asked in a friendly, eager tone. "We need all the information we can get."

Ellie wondered whether the officer trusted Dan as much as he appeared to.

"I stopped over early, not long after noon. Jessie said Ellie had just left with Travis for a picnic in the mountains. So I invited Jessie and the boys to drive over to Blowing Rock for lunch."

"Why Blowing Rock?"

"The boys like the fast-food restaurants, and we don't have any of the chain restaurants here."

"That's true, the boys love those places," Ellie confirmed.

"What did you do after lunch?" The officer was writing Dan's information down in his trusty notebook.

"Came back here and dropped them off. Then I took off for a drive in the mountains. Nowhere special. I just wanted to get away. Like I said, tax season is finally over. Haven't had too many minutes to call my own the last few months."

What minutes he'd had, he'd spent with Sissy rather than his son, Ellie thought.

She wandered away, not wanting to be near Dan. He made her skin crawl, treating Jessica and Brent the way he did and then acting the concerned husband and father.

Her conscience nipped. Even though he wasn't the epitome of the perfect father, she shouldn't assume he didn't care whether Brent was safe.

Back in the dining room, she opened the door of the built-in china cabinet and reached for a pair of pottery candlesticks. She gasped when large hands settled on her shoulders. She relaxed when she realized they belonged to Travis. He kneaded her shoulder and neck muscles. "Mmm. That feels good."

"Your muscles are so tied up in knots, you could qualify for a human pretzel." She let him work at the knots.

"What do you think about Dan's alibi?" he asked.

Alibi? she wondered. "It's not like Jessica to go to lunch with Dan, with or without the boys."

"That's what I thought, but I expect he's too smart to lie about it. He must know all our stories will be checked out."

"They'll have a hard time verifying ours." She laid her hands over his, which were still on her shoulders. "I'm so afraid. I was sure Jessica and the boys were with Dan. There was no proof, but I was so sure. Now. . .they could be anywhere, with anyone."

"Wherever they are, God is there, too."

She wished that comforted her more. She supposed it should make the fear go away, but awful things happened to lots of people even though God was there with them. What would she do if something awful happened to Corey? How would she go on?

Anger at her lack of control of the situation rose inside her until she wanted to scream and scream and scream. She knew that wouldn't help. The anger kept churning inside her instead.

"It looks like Dan's decided to stay." Travis nodded toward the living room.

Dan, minus his jacket and wet hiking boots, was pacing the floor, rubbing his hands together, looking for all the world like a worried, loving father.

Deputy Rogers came back into the dining room with a hot mug of coffee and a sugar cookie, which Ellie recognized as a contribution from one of the neighbors.

"Shouldn't someone let Eric. . .I mean, Sheriff Strand, know Dan's here?" Ellie asked.

"I called him." Rogers spoke around a bite of cookie. "He'll probably stop by after awhile to talk to Dan."

The dining room table looked like a command post with the deputy's radio, notebooks, and maps. Rogers opened one of the maps and studied it, leaning over the table to do so.

Ellie wondered whether he was looking for anything special or just trying to keep from being bored while they waited. She wished she could think of something to do to keep her mind off Corey and all sorts of horrible possibilities. *Keep him safe, Lord. Keep them all safe.* The refrain never stopped running through her mind.

It was past midnight. Neighbors' visits had dribbled off and finally stopped. Pastor Evanson was still there; sometimes talking quietly with one person or another, sometimes sitting by himself and, Ellie was sure, praying. Faithful Anna was still there, too, offering coffee and food to people without pushing it on them, offering comforting pats and hugs, neither giving false hope nor voicing despair.

The night went on forever.

Or so it seemed to Ellie. Logic told her dawn would come eventually. Honesty told her dawn would banish darkness but not the fear that was burning inside her.

She tried to avoid looking at the pictures of the boys and at their toys strewn around the house. She was afraid she'd break down and start crying if she paid those things too much mind, and if she let herself start crying, she might never be able to stop.

When dawn came, there was no blush on the horizon. The only announcement of its arrival was a lightening of the outside world. The storm still swirled around the house and through the village streets and valley and over the surrounding mountains. The winds still howled, and the snow still fell.

"We must have had eighteen inches of snow so far." Dan blew on his clasped hands as though he were outside in the fierce cold.

Beside him, Ellie stared at his hands. "What happened to your thumb?" It was purple beneath the nail.

Surprise registered on his face. He looked at his hand as if it was a foreign object, then stuffed it into his back pocket. "Slammed it in my truck door."

Ellie winced. "Nothing more painful than that."

"That's for sure."

Ellie looked out the window at the white blanket covering the ground, walks, and street.

Dan shook his head. "No one's going to be able to get through that to help the kids and Jessie."

"Don't say that." Ellie clenched her fists. She was so angry at him she could spit, but all he'd done was say aloud what she'd been thinking, what she didn't want to believe.

Travis looked like he'd like to slug Dan. "Ellie's right. We must keep believing Jess and the boys are okay, that we'll find a way to find them, or they'll find their way back to us."

"There are ways to get around out there." Rogers appeared with his ever-present coffee mug. "Snowmobiles, snowshoes, skis, four-wheel drives. Sheriff contacted me a few minutes ago. He's been making some calls, arranging search parties."

Hope shot through Ellie, dashing away her fatigue. She grabbed the deputy's arm. "Are they really planning to go out in this storm? I hadn't dared hope—"

"They'll head out as soon as the winds die down enough that we don't have to worry about losing anyone else on the mountains."

Ellie's spirits were dampened but not drowned. Surely the winds would calm before too long. The storm had already been raging for more than twelve hours. *You control the winds, Lord. You calmed the sea in the Bible. You can calm the wind now. Please. Please.*

There wasn't any question in anyone's mind that something was terribly wrong. Everyone knew Jessica would have found a way to get news to Ellie about her and the boys' whereabouts if at all possible. Jessica would never have let Ellie worry overnight and through a major storm.

Unless she wants to disappear with the kids herself. Ellie tried to push away the thought, but it persisted. Finally she broached the possibility to Travis in a corner of the living room where they couldn't be overheard.

Travis shook his head. "Why would Jess do that?"

"To get Brent away from Dan."

"She wouldn't be so cruel as to take Corey, too, keeping his location a secret from you. If the plan had been to keep Brent from Dan, Jess would have left Corey with Anna or Pastor Evanson or one of the neighbors."

Ellie sighed and pushed her hair back off her forehead. "You're right. I hate that I would even entertain the possibility that Jessica would steal the boys away."

"You can be sure that Sheriff Strand has considered the possibility."

The whine of a snowmobile screamed up the street and stopped in front of the house. Ellie darted a curious glance at Travis and moved to the window. She couldn't make out who the rider was who made his way through knee-high snow to the front porch. The person was wearing a helmet and dressed head to toe in a thick black and purple snowmobile suit.

Once inside with his helmet off, Ellie was touched to see it was Chuck who had made his way through the early morning storm. He pulled off his thick gloves and touched her face with a cold hand. "You doing okay?"

"I'm holding up." She pressed his hand with her own warm one for a moment in an expression of thanks.

"I had to come over and check for myself before heading to the sheriff's office."

"You're going out to look for Corey?"

"Yes."

Gratitude filled her like a physical thing. Tears smarted her eyes. She beat them back. "Are they planning to start out soon?"

He hesitated slightly. "As soon as possible."

She knew he meant when the winds died down, as Deputy Rogers had said. "I'd like to be in the search party."

Ellie whirled around at Travis's announcement. He hadn't made it to her but to Rogers.

Rogers shrugged. "No one can keep you from joining it if you want."

"Me, too."

Dan's declaration surprised Ellie even more than Travis's.

Rogers raised his red eyebrows. "You both understand the party will work in teams or groups. We don't want to lose anyone out there."

Both men nodded.

"Neither of you needs to do this," Rogers assured. "We have plenty of volunteers, experienced and otherwise. The ski rescue team from the resort will be helping out. Sheriff's even arranged for a helicopter once the weather allows."

Neither man backed out.

"I'd better head home and change," Travis said.

"I have an extra snowmobile suit if you need one," Chuck offered.

"Thanks, but I think my ski outfit will do. Can I talk to you for a minute?" Travis held out a hand to Ellie.

Curious, she took it and walked with him to the dining room where they could speak privately.

He placed his hands on her shoulders and looked into her eyes. "I won't go if you want me to stay."

"Thank you." Her tight throat made the words a whisper. "I appreciate your offer, but I'll be all right. Anna is still here, though she's finally napping, and Pastor Evanson and Deputy Rogers. Now that morning's here, I'm sure friends will be stopping again. Do what you feel you must."

"You're sure?"

"Yes. I understand that you want to be out there looking for Corey. Part of me wants to do that, too. But I want to be here for Corey if. . .when he comes home. Maybe you should get some sleep before you go out, though." Reddish gray circles beneath blue eyes showed he hadn't slept all night.

"I couldn't sleep now." He pulled her into his embrace with his arms around her shoulders. His stubble caught at her hair, but she didn't mind. "I'm praying for Corey and the others all the time," he said. "I'll be praying for you, too."

She smiled a bittersweet smile into his shoulder before lifting her chin enough to say, "I'll be praying for you, too. Be careful out there."

Ellie darted a quick glance at herself in the mirror over the dining room bureau. She had circles beneath her eyes as deep and dark as Travis's. Her hair was a dirty mess. With a start, she remembered she hadn't brushed it since she and Travis had shared kisses on the mountain trail beside the waterfall.

She ran a hand over her hair when they started back to join the others, then shrugged. It was only hair. What did it matter what it looked like at a time like this?

"I'll have to call Mom and Dad." She dreaded it. "The news will all but kill them, but they need to know."

Travis agreed. "It would be worse if the news services got hold of the story and your folks heard about Corey first in a newscast."

"Dan's left already," Chuck informed them. "If you want, I'll run you over to your place on my snowmobile, Travis."

The men left minutes later. Ellie stood alone at the window, watching the whining machine carry them away into the snow. She shivered.

Chapter 13

Eight hours later Travis shivered as he slid off another snowmobile in front of the sheriff's office. He'd never been so cold in his life, in spite of all the time he'd spent skiing in the Rockies. It wasn't that he wasn't dressed for the weather. The sheriff had handed out hand warmers in the form of dry heat. They looked like small bandages. Travis had them stuffed into his mittens and boots. They'd helped, but they couldn't keep the cold out forever.

Maybe because the chill he felt wasn't all from the weather.

Every minute his fears for Corey, Brent, and Jess grew. The fears were like a rain forest out of control, smothering the life from his heart.

Ellie must feel the same. I should be with her, he thought.

The man walking beside him slapped him on the back. "Maybe we'll have some good news inside."

Travis forced a smile through cracked lips. "Maybe."

Sheriff Strand didn't have good news. He shook his head and sighed, staring at the floor, before lifting bloodshot eyes to meet Travis's gaze. "It's dark. We've had to call in all the searchers. We can't have people running around in the mountains at night."

Travis nodded, numbness enveloping him. His mind understood the logic, but his heart cried out against it.

"We're fortunate the wind died down this morning and let us get out today at all."

Travis nodded again. He looked around the room. It was filled with searchers who were watching him with pity in their eyes or avoiding his gaze so he wouldn't see their pity. He recognized many of the men and women, but not all. Some attended the church. Some ran local businesses. Some worked in local shops. The owner of the Black Bear restaurant was there, and so was the waitress who served him coffee and pancakes every morning. The owner of the local dry cleaner where Travis had his suits cleaned was there. The editor of the small Blackberry newspaper was there—to help, not to get a story. Then there was the mechanic from the shop where he'd had the Jeep serviced, the man who ran the garbage truck, the woman who ran the small local greenhouse and serviced the plants at his office, the photographer whose work hung in the hallway at the law office, and one of the church deacons. And Chuck.

Travis tried to swallow the lump in his throat. He'd never felt so much love directed toward him in his entire life. "Thanks. Thanks to all of you for coming out. You can't know how much this means to Ellie and me."

They started filing out, heading for home. Each one shook his hand or laid a hand on his arm or said a word of sympathy or encouragement as they passed. Almost all of them said they'd be back at dawn.

"I know when people are missing in Los Angeles there's a lot of angels on earth out looking for them," Travis told Sheriff Strand, "but mostly those human angels are people who search for missing people as part of their job. These people. . ." He was at a loss for words.

"Every one of them knows it could be them or someone they love lost on a mountain next time."

"We don't even know Jess and the boys are out there. They could be anywhere. They could have caught a plane in Charlotte and be in the West Indies, for all we know."

"Yep, but we don't believe that, do we?"

Travis studied the sheriff's face, not certain what the law officer thought. "No, at least I don't. I think they're out in these mountains, but I don't have a tangible reason for believing that."

"There's still people out searching, but I've called all the teams in. Dan's with one of them. They should be here shortly." Strand's shoulders heaved. "Sorry we haven't discovered any sign of your son."

He's taking it as if it's a personal defeat, Travis thought. "Something keeps tugging at my mind, as though the Lord's trying to remind me of something, but it's just out of reach."

"I know the feeling. Frustrating."

"It sure is."

🦋

After a hot shower and change of clothes at his apartment, Travis headed back to Ellie's house. His mind felt as fuzzy as an open pussy willow. The lack of sleep combined with the emotional turbulence inside him was taking its toll.

A snowplow had been out during the day, and his Jeep made the short journey to Ellie's house easily, though the roads were anything but clear by Los Angeles standards.

Ellie's house was lit from top to bottom. A number of vehicles lined the street and filled her driveway. Someone had shoveled the walk.

Travis grimaced. Chuck's snowmobile was parked on the front lawn. He must have come directly from the sheriff's office.

Warmth and the smell of stew met him when he entered. People filled the living and dining rooms, sitting or standing in small groups and speaking in low tones. Travis knew they were there to support Ellie, and he was glad for that, but the atmosphere was that of a funeral.

Ellie was in the dining room, her back to him, talking with Deputy Rogers and Chuck. Travis slipped off his boots, threw his jacket over the banister, and started toward Ellie.

An attractive middle-aged woman with heavily highlighted hair and a perfectly made-up face reached out a hand with rose-tinted nails and a huge diamond ring and laid it on his arm as he passed the overstuffed chair where she sat. He recognized her immediately. Mrs. Landry, wife of one of the wealthiest men in the area. Their mountain home was only one of three of their residences. He'd met her first at the boutique the day Dan was there. He'd met her since with her husband when they'd come in about a legal entanglement with a real-estate purchase they planned to make.

"Good evening, Mrs. Landry."

She stood up. "My dear boy, I am so sorry about your little boy. I had to come over to tell Ellie my thoughts and prayers are with her and Corey. And you, too, of course."

"That's very kind."

"Ellie designs many of my clothes, you know."

He hadn't known, and though he knew it was a compliment to Ellie's talents, he didn't particularly care at the moment.

"That's how I know your son. He is the dearest boy."

Travis's impatience died an abrupt death. "Thank you. We think so."

"He and Jessica's little boy are such a cute twosome." She shook her head, making a *tsk-tsk-tsk-ing* sound Travis thought people made only in books. "So hard to believe all three of them are missing. I spoke with Jessica's husband, Dan, only yesterday."

"Yesterday? I thought he was out of town most of the day."

"I wouldn't know about that. I spoke to him in the morning. He's been preparing our tax returns—that is, my husband's and my personal tax return and my husband's business return—for the last few years. We picked our returns up yesterday morning. I'm afraid we had to tell him he will no longer be our accountant." She laid a bejeweled hand on his arm again and leaned closer.

Travis instinctively reacted by leaning closer to her.

"It's his temper, you know." Her loud whisper wouldn't have required such close proximity. "We've no complaint with his professional abilities, but I don't trust a man with a temper like his. He created quite a scene at Ellie's boutique one day."

"Yes, I was there."

"So you were. I'd forgotten. Well, I told my husband about it, and he began asking about town, discreetly of course, concerning Dan's temper. My husband heard enough to convince him he no longer wants this man involved in any way with his business returns. He doesn't trust angry men. He says an angry man thinks with his emotions and not with his head."

Travis silently agreed. "Not a good plan for an accountant."

His dry humor appeared lost on Mrs. Landry, who only murmured a stammered, "N–no," and creased her perfectly made-up brow in a puzzled frown.

Travis politely excused himself and started toward Ellie once more. This time he was interrupted by Anna.

"Did you just arrive? You must be exhausted. There's hot stew in the kitchen. Are you hungry?"

Travis laughed and gave the woman a hug. "Yes, I just arrived. Yes, I'm exhausted. Yes, I'm hungry. The stew smells great. Did you make it?"

"One of the neighbors brought it in. I did make biscuits to have with it, though."

"I'll be in the kitchen for a bowl of stew and one of your biscuits after I say hello to Ellie." He glanced at her curiously. "Isn't that the same pants and top you were wearing when I left this morning?"

Her wrinkled cheeks flushed a pretty pink. "I didn't want to leave Ellie to go home and change."

"Have either of you slept at all?"

"I took a couple naps. Ellie laid down once or twice, but I don't think she slept. She took a shower a couple hours ago and said that refreshed her a bit. I think she's running on adrenaline, fear, and hope." She studied his face a moment. "Looks like you're doing the same."

"I think you're right. See you in the kitchen in a couple minutes."

He poked Ellie lightly on the shoulder with an index finger when he walked up behind her. She looked over her shoulder with only mild interest. When she recognized him her face lit up, lighting up his heart.

"You're back. Chuck said you were, but then. . ."

"I stopped for a shower and change of clothes. Wish I brought good news."

Her face fell into weary lines. "Deputy Rogers told me none of the search parties found any signs of Corey or the others."

Travis pushed her hair behind her ear with one hand. He could feel its dampness. She hadn't taken the time to dry or style it after the shower.

He wished they were alone. He wanted to pull her into his arms and pray with her for their son. He wanted to tell her he loved her and he loved their son and what a terrible failure he felt as a father that he couldn't protect Corey from whatever it was that was happening to him. But he was afraid to do that would frighten her more. "How are you holding up?"

She nodded, closed her eyes a moment, and opened them again. "Fine."

It was a lie, of course. She wasn't doing fine. Neither was he. Admitting it in words might mean they would both break down. They couldn't afford to do that. What if Corey needed them and they weren't emotionally ready to help him?

"You should get some sleep. Anna and I will wake you if there's any news."

She hesitated, then nodded. "All right. I'll try. But you promise you'll wake me, no matter what the news?"

Even if it's the worst possible news. The words hung in the air between them.

He kissed her forehead, aching for her pain and fear, and for his own, and for their helplessness. "I promise."

"You need sleep, too."

"I'll lie down when you wake up. Right now I'm going to get something to eat."

As Travis headed for the kitchen, his gaze caught sight of the old print of a cabin on a snow-covered, wooded mountain hillside. It was a picture that kept recurring to him when he was out looking for Corey.

The picture had been interspersed with pictures of Corey and Brent: Brent pulling Corey on the sled, the boys helping him make the snowman, Corey dancing to a Barney song, Corey pushing his way in between Travis and Ellie on the sofa, the boys drowning oyster crackers in bowls of tomato soup, their joy filling their faces and giggles filling the air.

He hoped they had something warm and nourishing to eat tonight. He hoped they were out of the cold, maybe in a place like that log cabin in the print. He hoped they were playing and giggling together. He hoped they hadn't been caught out in the storm. He hoped. . .

Change the picture, he demanded of his mind.

The one that replaced it wasn't a keeper: Chuck placing his hand against Ellie's cheek that morning, and Ellie covering the man's hand with her own. Travis wondered as he had so many times what Chuck meant to Ellie. He was pretty sure Chuck was sweet on her.

Travis remembered Ellie's kisses, the feel of her in his arms. Had it only been yesterday they'd embraced at the waterfall, that they'd laughed together running along the mountain path?

He hoped Ellie would decide to stay with him instead of choosing a life with Chuck or someone else, but whatever she decided, what he wanted most was her happiness. At least Travis was glad she was alive—she wasn't missing, maybe stranded on a mountain after a major snowstorm.

The thoughts had come full circle back to what he'd been trying to avoid, the thoughts that fatigued him to his very bones. *Keep Corey safe, Lord. Keep them all safe.*

Travis stopped, his hand on the swinging kitchen door.

A log cabin. That's what had been teasing at his fuzzy mind all day. The mountain cabin Dan and Jessica owned.

Would Jessica have taken the kids there? It was a long shot, but just maybe. . . .

His pulse raced. He turned and started running through the dining room. "Ellie!"

His shout stopped conversation. Everyone turned to watch him.

Ellie was in the living room, stopped by sympathetic friends before she could reach the stairway. She stared at him openmouthed. "Corey? Is there news?"

He grabbed her hand. "No, sweetheart, no news. I just thought of something." He tugged her along with him toward the door, not bothering to apologize to their guests. "Get your coat. We're going to the sheriff's office."

She didn't protest or ask any more questions. She pushed her feet into her boots and stuffed her arms into a red parka.

"What's going on?" Chuck stood with arms spread and a bewildered look on his tired face.

"Tell you later." Travis reached for Ellie's hand, and they hurried out the door together.

The group Dan had searched with had just returned when Travis and Ellie arrived at the sheriff's office.

"Didn't find anything," the leader was telling Strand. He jerked a thumb at Dan and grinned. "Almost had to break off the search to go looking for this guy. He took a wrong turn in the woods."

Dan shrugged. "I would have realized my mistake before long."

Travis wondered. He'd seen for himself today how easy it would be to get lost in the thickly forested mountains.

Dan wiped a hand over wind-ruddied cheeks. "I was almost falling asleep out there."

Strand grunted. "Better go home and get some sleep."

"That's my plan. See you in the morning." The leader headed out. The rest of the search team followed. Dan was the last to head for the door.

"Wait a minute." Travis stopped Dan with a hand on his shoulder but spoke to the sheriff. "I finally figured out what's been nagging at me all day." He told them about the print of the log cabin.

Sheriff Strand rubbed a hand over his stubbly jaw and looked at Travis as if he'd lost his mind. "You're here about a painting?"

"Not exactly. The picture triggered a memory, a memory of a mountain cabin Jess and Dan own."

Travis felt Dan's shoulder tense beneath his palm. "Where'd you hear about that?"

"Jess told me. A lawyer remembers things like shared assets when he's helping a woman with a divorce case." Was it his imagination, or had Dan's eyes grown suddenly darker? The law firm he was with was big on watching body language. Sudden enlargement of pupils could denote fear or lying. Dan hadn't said anything that could be construed as a lie, had he? So what was he afraid of?

Strand beckoned Travis with a crook of his index finger. Travis followed him to a corner on the opposite side of the room from the sheriff's desk. "What's going on here, Carter? We don't have any reason to suspect Dan of foul play. His story of eating lunch with Jessica and the boys at the fast-food joint in Blowing Rock checked out. We had a copy of the photo you gave us and one of Dan sent over the wire and one of the workers at the restaurant remembered them. Right now you're as much a suspect as he is."

"I know all that." Travis was almost trembling from the energy racing through him. "I know the cabin is a long shot. We don't have any reason to believe Jess took the boys there. Maybe it's a coincidence that the picture of the cabin kept flashing in my mind all day while I was out searching. I can't explain it, but I have this urgent feeling that we should check that cabin out."

Sheriff Strand rubbed his jaw again. Travis could almost see Strand's tired mind going over the possibilities, weighing the chances of finding the three at a cabin against going home to a good night's sleep.

"Come on. The worst that can happen is that we eliminate one more possibility."

Strand heaved a huge sigh. "All right."

Back on the other side of the room, Travis fought his impatience and waited for Strand to ask Dan the questions.

"About this cabin of yours, exactly where is it?"

Dan spread his arms and looked bewildered. "It's pretty remote. I can't imagine Jessie would go up there. She never liked the place. It's not some fancy vacation cabin. I use it mainly for hunting, let some of my cross-country skiing friends use it. Like I said, Jessie never liked the place."

"He's right." The look on Ellie's face told Travis she thought this was a wild goose chase.

"I still say we check it out." Travis held his breath, waiting for Strand to agree or nix the idea.

Dan's eyes sparked. "It's a waste of time, I tell ya."

"Don't you want to check out every possible lead in finding your son?" Travis made his voice as smooth as pudding.

"This isn't a lead. It's a fantasy. The best way I can help my son is to get a good night's sleep so I'll be fresh to go out with the search party again come dawn."

Strand walked over to a detailed map of the county that covered most of one wall of the office. "Where exactly did you say that cabin is located? Can you show me on this map?"

Dan made his way to the map wall, his boots clomping loudly on the linoleum-covered floor, his glance shooting daggers at Travis.

He studied the map for a minute, then jabbed an index finger at it. "There. That's where it is."

Strand shook his head. "You weren't kidding when you said it's a remote area. Is there even a road to that cabin of yours?"

"Only an old logging road. Not much more than a trail."

Strand stared at the map, considering.

If this idea about the cabin came from You, Lord, Travis prayed, *convince him to check it out.*

The sheriff turned and gave a stiff little nod. "All right, we'll see what's there."

"Yes." Travis lifted both fists in a triumphant gesture.

Immediately Sheriff Strand changed into a human efficiency machine. He ticked off what they'd need: a couple of four-wheel drives with trailers to carry snowmobiles, blankets, first-aid equipment, energy bars, and coffee. "We'll contact the Highway Department and see if they can send up a plow if we decide we need one. And ask the hospital to have an ambulance standing by. I'll give Doc Abrams a call and see if he feels like making a house call. Ellie, you said Jessica and the boys were wearing spring clothes. Why don't you run home and get some warm things, just in case we have a break? Be back here in fifteen minutes."

Travis and Ellie made the trip in seventeen minutes. Sheriff Strand was ready to go when they arrived. A deputy Travis hadn't seen before was there, as was Doc Abrams. Travis nodded at them. "Thanks for coming."

"Yes, thank you." Ellie's smile made her face brighter than Travis had seen it since they'd discovered the boys were missing. Whether Jess and the boys were at the cabin or not, selecting warm clothes for them was good for Ellie's spirits. Travis knew it made her feel she was contributing something important to their rescue.

Dan, still scowling, was pacing the office.

"We want to go along." Travis wasn't about to take no for an answer. If nothing else, he'd follow in his Jeep uninvited. Strand would have to jail him to stop him.

"All right, but no back talk and no arguments."

"Done."

"You coming, too?" Strand slid into his jacket as he waited for Dan's answer.

"Yeah." He shuffled along behind the others toward the door.

Travis and Ellie were already outside when Travis heard Dan's wail.

"I can't. I can't do this. I can't do it."

Travis spun around, shock spiraling through him.

Ellie spoke sharply. "Get hold of yourself. If Brent is there, he might need you."

In the light from the office, Travis watched Dan's face crumple. Dan dropped his face into his hands. A keen split the night. He rocked back on his heels. "What have I done? Oh, what have I done?"

Chapter 14

Ellie stared at Dan, fear twisting through her, rooting her to the snow-covered ground. What was he talking about? Why was he making that high crying noise?

She dashed forward. Grabbed his hands. Pulled them from his face. "What are you talking about? Did you take Corey? Tell us." She shook his arms. "Tell us."

Travis's hands closed about her arms and pulled her back.

"Tell us."

Dan ignored her screaming demand and sunk to his knees on the ground just outside the door, rocking back and forth, continuing his keen.

Travis yanked him up by one arm. Dan hung from Travis's grip like a rag doll. "Where are the boys?"

"At the cabin. They're at the cabin."

Ellie could barely believe the words that jerked out between Dan's sobs.

"Are they all right? Have you hurt them?" Travis's voice sounded ragged, as if he'd torn the questions from his heart.

Ellie strained to hear the answer.

"They. . .were. . .okay. . .when I. . .last. . .saw them."

Ellie dropped to the ground.

"Ellie." Travis was beside her instantly, his arms cradling her.

"I'm okay. I'm just so relieved." She giggled, feeling a bit hysterical. "My knees turned to mush."

Travis helped her up.

Sheriff Strand and his deputy had taken over when Travis dropped hold of Dan. They carried him inside and dropped him into a vinyl chair by Strand's desk. The others followed, Travis and Ellie last. Ellie's legs were still wobbly.

Someone brought Dan a cup of coffee.

Doc Abrams had other ideas. Ellie saw him pull a bottle and a syringe from his bag. Was he planning to sedate Dan?

Evidently the sheriff thought the same thing. He held out a palm in a stop gesture. "Hold it. We need some more information here." His sharp tone held a note of something that sounded all too like anxiety to Ellie. "When did you leave them at the cabin, Dan?"

"Last night."

Ellie gasped, clasping her hands to her mouth. She'd been so relieved to hear

362

Corey was all right when Dan last saw him that she hadn't thought how much time might have passed. Travis put his arms around her. She leaned into him, glad for his strength.

Sheriff Strand's face was grim while he pulled the information he needed from Dan. Dan continued his rocking motion throughout the questioning.

"Does Jessica have transportation?"

Dan shook his head.

"Why did she and the boys agree to go there with you?"

"I made them."

"How?"

"I had a gun."

Ellie groaned. She hid her face against Travis's shoulder to keep from crying out at the picture Dan created in her mind. Poor Corey. Poor Brent. They must have been so terrified.

"We don't have time for anything but the most important questions right now." Travis's words rasped above her ear. "Did you leave them food, Dan? Water? Firewood? Matches?"

Ellie felt the blood leave her face as all the possibilities were spoken.

"No food. But they'd just eaten. We went to the restaurant in Blowing Rock, remember?"

For lunch, Ellie recalled. That had been at least thirty hours ago. The boys would be hungry. They'd be crying.

A worse thought tightened her stomach. "Did you tell them you were coming back? What if they started walking and got caught in the storm?"

"They couldn't leave." Dan was rocking again, staring at the floor. "The windows were boarded shut. Before I left, I nailed the door shut, too." He glanced up, searching the faces of the men standing about the room.

Ellie followed his gaze. Disgust and horror filled each face.

"I didn't plan it." Justification filled Dan's yelled words. "It was a spur-of-the-moment thing. I'd lost my most important client that morning, Landry. It was Jessie's fault. Landry's wife heard us fighting at the dress shop and decided I was unstable." He snorted. "I can tell you I handled Landry's tax returns quite competently for an unstable person. It's Jessie who's unstable. I was angry, and I went over to Jessie's. The hunting rifle was in the truck and. . .and the plan just popped into my mind, and I went with it."

"Let's go get the kids and Jess." Travis's tone said clearly that he had no more time for Dan.

Strand slapped a handcuff on one of Dan's wrists.

Dan cringed at the sight.

Strand cuffed the other hand. "You're coming with us. We don't want to miss that cabin. We want to find it on the first try."

Ellie and Travis followed the sheriff in Travis's Jeep. Every once in a while, Travis reached over and squeezed her hand. Most of the time he kept his attention on the road. They didn't say much to each other. A couple of times they prayed together. The rest of the time, prayers for Corey and Brent and Jessica's safety ran through Ellie's mind. She was sure they flashed through Travis's also.

The trip was a blur in Ellie's memory later. Travel was slow along the icy roads. The plow the sheriff had requested met them near the logging trail. Sheriff Strand, his deputy, and the doctor rode snowmobiles down the trail to the cabin. Ellie and Travis were left to follow the plow. Not even in the Jeep could Travis follow an unplowed logging trail through the woods at night after all the snow the storm had dropped.

When Ellie finally arrived at the cabin, the door had been removed. The boys and Jessica were wearing the clothes she'd sent ahead with the deputy. All three of them were seated on a hard bunk built into the wall, gulping down doughnuts.

"Corey." Ellie rushed to the bunk, feeling she couldn't get there fast enough. She wrapped her arms around him, burying her face in his neck. Tears ran down her cheeks.

"Oof." One of Corey's little palms pushed at her.

She loosened her hold only enough to see why he wanted out of her embrace. The half-eaten doughnut reminded her. With a laugh that was half sob, she released him.

She decided she couldn't stand it. Settling down on the bunk, she leaned back against the wall and hauled Corey onto her lap. He rested his back against her chest and kept eating. Satisfaction, contentment, and gratitude she hadn't known since the night he was born seeped through every cell of her body.

Ellie reached out a hand and ruffled Brent's hair. "Hi, Brent."

He looked back at her with unsmiling eyes.

Her heart clenched. Brent and Corey had a lot of memories to undo. First thing tomorrow, she'd make an appointment for them with a counselor.

She met Jessica's gaze over Corey's head. For the first time she noticed her friend's black eye. Had she received it trying to protect herself and the boys from Dan? "Are you okay?"

Jessica nodded, touching a finger lightly to her bruise. "I was never so glad to have someone break down my door."

Ellie smiled gently. "Thank you for taking care of Corey."

"Anytime. Did you and Travis have a nice picnic?"

Ellie heard Jessica's message loud and clear. They'd talk about the ordeal later out of the boys' hearing. Ellie smiled across the room at Travis. "I thought the picnic went well."

"Me, too." Travis's smile didn't quite reach his eyes. The expression in them was hungry as he watched Ellie and Corey.

Ellie's smile widened. "Why don't you come over and say hello?"

Travis crossed the small space in three slow steps, his gaze never leaving their son. He squatted beside the bunk. "Hi, partner."

Corey lifted a palm. "Hi, pa'dner."

"Hi, partner," Brent chimed in.

Travis grinned. "You two ready to go home?"

"Yes." Corey reached his arms toward Travis.

Travis hesitated. He glanced at Ellie.

Ellie nodded. Pure joy flooded her when Corey's arms hugged Travis's neck and Travis's eyes filled with tears.

Travis was almost at the door before Corey cried out, "Pony. Need Pony."

Ellie retrieved the gray horse from the bunk. Corey clutched it with a sigh of relief.

Ellie waited by the door for Jessica and Brent. The three of them walked out into the moonlit forest together.

❧

Ellie slept late the next morning, but as soon as her eyes opened she was wide awake. She stretched her arms toward the ceiling, unable to contain her joy. "Thank You, Lord."

She slipped out of bed and hurried into the boys' room. Both were still sleeping. She stood beside Corey's bed for a long time, absurdly happy just watching him breathe.

If Travis hadn't remembered the cabin, Corey wouldn't be here now. She recalled the love and relief in Travis's eyes while he'd watched Corey at the cabin, the way Corey had reached for him, clung to him.

She'd clung to him, too, emotionally. What would she have done if he hadn't been with her through the ordeal? It seemed hard to believe she'd ever wondered whether she could trust him with Corey's love. She'd asked the Lord so many times whether Travis was trustworthy, or whether she was a fool to trust him with her and Corey's hearts. In every way, Travis had acted lovingly and faithfully and trustworthily. After the last couple of days, she couldn't imagine asking him to continue as a father who didn't share their lives in every way.

Her growling stomach reminded her she'd hardly eaten anything since she'd discovered Corey missing. Reluctantly she left Corey's bedside. She pulled on a sunny yellow sweater that matched her mood and comfortable jeans for a stay-at-home morning. She wouldn't bother to open the shop today.

She was breaking eggs for an omelette when Chuck arrived.

"I heard the good news. I had to stop and tell you how happy I am for you."

"Thanks. And thank you for helping to search for them and for being here for me. You're a good friend."

He pulled his brown and blue corduroy baseball hat from his head and twirled it between his fingers. "Yeah, well. Guess you figured out I was hoping to be more than a friend one day."

Ellie wished he hadn't raised the subject. She hated coming right out and telling him again there was no place for him in her life as anything beyond a friend. "You're a good man. You'll make someone a—"

"Good husband one day," he finished with her.

They laughed together.

"About that husband of yours. . ."

"Yes?"

"I'm still not convinced that leopards change their spots. I don't know if you can trust him to be faithful to you. But I know he'd give his life to keep you and Corey safe, and that's not a small thing. If what you're looking for in a husband is a good father for Corey, you couldn't do better than the one he's already got."

"Thanks." Ellie knew how much it cost him to admit that. On impulse, she threw her arms around him. "Thanks for everything. You're the best."

He gave her a squeeze.

"Guess I came in at the wrong time."

Ellie started at Travis's unexpected voice. He was standing in the doorway. Chuck's arms fell away.

Ellie brushed a lock of hair behind her ear. "Travis. I wasn't expecting you."

"That's obvious. Don't let me interrupt." He turned on his heel. The door swung gaily in his wake.

Ellie turned pleading eyes on Chuck.

"Don't just stand there. Go after him."

It took a moment for his words to register. Then she grinned and gave him a silly little salute. "Aye, aye, sir."

He returned the salute and stepped out the back door as she rushed into the hallway.

She reached Travis on the front porch and grabbed his arm. "Don't go. Please. We have to talk."

He didn't look as if he wanted to talk, but he allowed her to lead him back into the house and into the living room. They faced each other in the middle of the room.

"Travis, I—"

"You don't have to apologize."

"But I—"

"Let me finish. This isn't easy to say."

She pressed her lips together to keep back the words of love she wanted to shout.

He took a deep breath. "These last couple days not knowing whether Corey was alive or dead taught me a lot. I learned what Anna tried to tell me."

"About what?"

"She asked me how much I loved you and Corey, whether I loved you enough to want what was best for you even if that meant I didn't share your lives. I've tried to love you that way. After this weekend I think I finally understand what she meant, understand it in my heart, not only my head. I want us to live together under one roof as a family in every sense of the word. But more than that I want you to both be healthy and safe and happy. I never want to go through another sixty seconds of the kind of fear I felt this weekend. I don't know how to make you trust me as a husband and father. I can only leave you in God's hands. I know you'll try to follow God's leading in your life. Whatever your decision is about us, I'll respect it, even if you choose to marry Chuck."

She shook her head, smiling softly. "I have no romantic interest in Chuck."

Travis jerked his gaze to the ceiling and snorted. "Right. I saw the evidence for myself. You were in his arms not five minutes ago."

"Well, yes, but—"

"I heard you tell him. . .you told him he's the best."

She heard the pain in his voice. "It wasn't the way you think." A memory popped into her mind, a memory of herself saying, "I heard you; I saw you." She pressed her fingertips to her lips to suppress a laugh.

"What's so funny?"

"You're the lawyer. Evidence isn't always what it seems, is it?"

"Not always, but when there's an eyewitness—"

"Like I was an eyewitness to Michelle returning your cuff links and saying you'd left them in her apartment?"

He swung an arm toward the kitchen. "It's not the same thing. I saw. . .I heard. . ." His arm fell. He stared at her. "Wow. So that's what it was like for you." He wiped a hand over his face. "No wonder you left. No wonder you find it so hard to trust me. When I saw you and Chuck. . .it hurt so much I thought I couldn't bear it. And then when I thought you were lying to me about caring for him. . ."

Ellie's throat constricted painfully. "Yes, that's what it was like."

His hands enveloped hers. "I promise what I told you about that night at Michelle's is true. She was never more than a friend to me. I've never been unfaithful to you."

She looked down at their joined hands. All the fears she'd nursed so attentively the last three years filled her mind and twisted her stomach. What if he was lying? What if she opened her heart to him completely and he betrayed her? But there was no way to guarantee another person's love and faithfulness. Only God's love came with a guarantee. Trusting anyone was a choice, a calculated risk. Travis's actions the last few months seemed those of a faithful, loving man, she reminded her fears. How long and in how many ways did she expect him to prove himself before she gave him her trust?

She made her choice. She took a deep, shaky breath and looked into his eyes. "I believe you. What I told you about Chuck is true, too. He's only a friend. Believe me?"

He nodded. He lifted a hand to cup her cheek, caressing her face gently with his thumb. "It must have taken so much trust in God and so much Christ-like love for me for you to tell me about Corey. You had so little reason to trust me then. You still believed I'd been unfaithful. You didn't even know I'd come to believe in God."

"Corey is your son. You had a right to know him."

"I'm sorry about the whole Michelle incident."

"Don't." Ellie pressed her fingers to his lips. "Don't speak about it again. It's behind us. I shouldn't have run out on you that way. I should have given you a chance to explain. I wanted to protect myself from any more emotional pain more than I wanted to stay faithful to the 'us' that is you and me. I guess there's more than one way to be unfaithful in a marriage. By not giving you a chance to explain, I was unfaithful to you. I'm sorry."

He kissed the fingers that were still at his lips, sending tingles along her nerves. "Like you said, it's behind us. I believe God meant for us to stay together as a family instead of separate the way we did, but God never wastes any experience. He's used our time apart to bring each of us to faith in Him and to teach us more about love."

"Yes." There was no doubt left in her heart as to what she wanted with this man, but she trembled inside at the risk. Living together as husband and wife would make her so vulnerable again. Was that life's next lesson, staying vulnerable to those she loved?

She took a shaky breath. "If you don't mind, I'd like us to learn the rest of God's lessons together, as husband and wife and as Corey's parents. That is, if you still want us to be a family."

The joy in his eyes told her everything she needed to know, but he answered anyway. "If I still want us to be a family?"

He caught her in his arms, lifting her from her feet and swinging her around in a circle. When he stopped, his kisses started. Gently he touched his lips to her temple, her eyebrow, her eyelid, her cheek, making a trail to her lips.

"Any doubts left about whether I still want us to be a family?"

She smiled against his lips.

He led her to the sofa and pulled her back into his arms on the comfy cushions. "Let's talk about our plans."

"What do we need to talk about?"

"Where we'll live, for starters."

"Don't you want to live here?"

"It's a great house, but do we plan to keep living with Jess and Brent?"

"I hadn't thought about it. I guess getting back together isn't going to be as simple as I thought."

Travis chuckled. "I think we'll be able to work it out if we keep our heads together."

For the next few minutes they sat quietly, content to hold each other and bask in the joy of rediscovered love.

Ellie stirred slightly. "Next Sunday is Easter."

"Mmm. So it is. We have a lot to be thankful for this Easter."

"Will you go to church with me and Corey?"

"We've never gone to church together, except for our wedding. What a great way to begin our new life together."

"There's something we need to do first."

"What's that?"

"Introduce Corey to his father."

He didn't respond.

Ellie pulled her head from his shoulder to look at him. Tears glistened in his eyes.

"You sure Corey will want me as his father?"

She pictured the way Corey had reached for him at the cabin. A slow grin spread across her face. "I'm sure."

❦

With the inconsistency of spring weather in the Carolina mountains, Easter was sunny and warm. The little snow that had survived the week since the storm ran in cheerful rivulets down the village's hillside sidewalks and streets. Birds sang their songs and searched for food in the grass sticking through the last of the snow.

Inside the stone church, the sun's rays fell warmly through the stained-glass windows. Music rejoicing in God's gift of His Son swelled, filling the sanctuary to the rafters.

Travis looked down at Corey. The boy sat between Travis and Ellie in a sharp little blue suit Ellie had designed for him. His pointed chin rested on the gray pony he clutched to his chest.

Travis felt as if his heart would explode from ecstasy. At Christmas he hadn't known if he'd ever have a chance to meet Corey. *Thank You, Father, that I won't be spending Corey's first thirty-three years apart from him. Thank You for sending Your own Son, Jesus, to show us the way of love.*

Ellie's gaze met Travis's above Corey's golden curls. She smiled, and Travis felt wrapped in her love.

Together the three of them waited patiently after the service in the line to shake Pastor Evanson's hand, with Corey in Travis's arms. They visited with friends and neighbors, acknowledging the many who expressed their thanksgiving that

Corey, Brent, and Jessica were safe.

Sunshine warmed them as they stepped through the large wooden doors onto the church's front steps. Ellie grasped the pastor's outstretched hand. "Thank you for all the prayer support you gave us last week."

"Yes, thank you." Travis grasped the man's hand warmly.

Corey stuck out one little hand.

Pastor Evanson shook it with a laugh.

Corey pointed at Ellie. "That's Mom." He shoved an index finger against Travis's white shirt. "This is my dad. We're a fambly."

"So you are." The pastor grinned.

Ellie gave Travis a flirtatious grin that made his heart jump. "So we are."

Travis held Corey securely with one arm. He slid the other around Ellie's waist and smiled down at her as they started down the stone steps. "Amen."

(Photo by Carol Owens of Winston-Salem, North Carolina.)

JOANN A. GROTE

JoAnn lived in North Carolina for many years and loves the Blue Ridge Mountains. Most of JoAnn's stories are set in Minnesota, where she was raised and presently lives. An award-winning author, she has had over thirty-five books published, including several novels published with Barbour Publishing in the **Heartsong Presents** line as well as in the American Adventure and Sisters in Time series for kids.

Eagles for Anna

Catherine Runyon

Chapter 1

The rending screech, like fingernails on a blackboard, brought Anna fully awake. She sat straight up in the confining motor home bed, tired and aching after a restless first night in the Smokies. Hoping the noise she had just heard was only a part of her dreams, she shivered and wrapped the insulated blanket around her shoulders against the early June morning chill and listened, half afraid, the confusion of sleep just beyond her senses.

Perhaps the noise was only within her own skull. The trip from New York, driving the unfamiliar vehicle, had been exhausting. She had begun developing a headache long before she crossed the Tennessee state line. Then, instead of being able to drive to Granny's old homesite as she had planned, she had driven for hours looking at one place after another, recognizing none and wracking her brain for memories of the trips she had made with her parents so many years ago. Finally, with the gas gauge fluttering on empty, she had given up, pulled the small motor home off the road, and fallen into bed disappointed, lost, and confused.

Above the pounding of blood in her temples, Anna heard a noise something like soft knocking. *Of course,* Anna thought, *I've parked on someone's property, and they've come to investigate.*

❦

She called, "Who's there?" but no voice answered.

Whump! Whump! came the sound at the side door. Then Anna heard the awful screech again. Shivers moved in waves across her body.

"What are you doing?" she cried, then jerked back the curtains on the window near her bed, not caring if someone saw her smeared makeup and tousled hair.

A black bear grinned back at her through the window.

Anna gasped and whipped the curtains together. She jumped into the middle of the bed and pulled the covers close. What could she do? Could the bear get in? Quietly she peered out the window again. The bear was walking around sniffling, pawing at the side of the vehicle, and occasionally rising up on hind feet to give it a good cuff.

Anna felt the vibrations from the blows. Climbing out of bed, she went from window to window, watching the bear. Apparently it was not angry, only curious. The bear walked around, nose to the ground, and finally found the apple core that Anna had tossed out the window last night just before dropping into bed.

Great! Now it thinks this is a traveling restaurant. It will probably be here all day! She sighed, a sudden image of Barry Carlson coming to her mind. If he were here, he would be laughing at her, she thought. Sometimes she wondered what kept her attached to this man who managed her career. He was seldom available when Anna wanted his companionship, but he expected her to be ready at a moment's notice to accompany him to a party or show. Though he was witty and fun, he sometimes seemed quite insensitive about things that Anna felt were important, such as this trip to Tennessee. He certainly was good-looking and was always fashionably dressed with his jet black hair elegantly styled. His dark mustache was so thin and perfect it could have been penciled on. He carried an aura of excitement about him, was always in a hurry, and always laughing.

Anna could still hear Barry making fun of her decision to come to Tennessee. "Anna, dear, don't you know that after you get south of D.C. you drop off the edge? And in a camper at that!"

"It isn't a camper, Barry. I've rented a motor home. It has a bathroom and everything."

He had waved away her explanations and flashed the brilliant smile that was probably his greatest asset.

"Tell me the truth. You've been out digging for accounts behind my back, haven't you? You've been hired to do a spread for *National Geographic*. . .no, they don't use models. I know! It's *Farm Journal* or something like that, isn't it?"

Anna could not help but laugh with him, though she wished he could try to understand the feelings that had brought about her decision to come south. Anna knew she should have said yes immediately when Barry offered her a partnership in his modeling agency a few weeks ago. It was the chance of a lifetime in some ways, but Anna had doubts.

Anna had confidence in her own ability to manage a business and to work with other models as a manager, but she was unsure just what her relationship with Barry should be. He had said he wanted her to share his business and his life but had said nothing about marriage. He said, "I love you," as casually as he said, "Good morning," and Anna wondered if he understood how much she wanted the deep, passionate commitment for life that she had witnessed in her parents' marriage. If he understood, did he care?

As a child Anna had visited the Smokey Mountains with her parents. She remembered a loving great-grandmother, standing in a farmhouse doorway waiting for Anna to come in, a woman out of tune with her times but completely at peace with herself. Anna had experienced a deep sense of wonder while standing on the high ridge near the house, gazing out at wave after wave of blue green hills. The memory of that feeling had helped seal her decision to return to the mountains.

Anna peered out the window again. The bear was still nosing about. With a burst of determined energy, Anna pulled on the red plaid shirt and khaki pants she had worn the night before, rolled her sleeves up past the elbows, and headed for the door. As soon as she opened it, the bear trotted toward her.

"Scram!" Anna yelled as loudly as she could. "Get away from here! You don't scare me, understand?"

The bear continued toward her. It knew as well as Anna did that her threats were empty.

Anna scurried backward, closing the door just as the bear reached it. Again she heard the awful screeching of the claws on the metal.

"You're ruining the paint!" she screamed. "This thing is rented, you know! I have to take care of it." Anna rubbed her tired eyes with the back of her hand, taking off some of yesterday's makeup. With a deep sigh she got into the driver's seat. If the bear wouldn't leave her, maybe she could leave it.

Anna had been hoping to get directions from a passing motorist before she started out on the road again, but it was full daylight now, and there had been no sign of a car. Now she was going to get out of here as fast as she could and just hope she found a gas station before the tank went completely dry.

With one bare foot on the accelerator, Anna turned the key. The engine started, then died.

"Come on, come on," she begged. "If there's enough gas to start this thing, there must be a little bit left to get me out of here." She turned the key again. The engine came briefly to life, then died. Anna leaned her head against the steering wheel, drew a long, deep breath, and exhaled slowly, trying to relax. She forced down the rising panic that accompanied the knowledge that she was no longer in control.

Maybe this is a sign, she thought. The letter from her lawyer, urging her to revisit the property where Granny Huddlestone's home had been located in order to determine whether she wanted to sell it, had seemed like a message from the God she had so recently discovered.

"The Tennessee property that once belonged to your mother's grandmother is included in your parents' estate," the letter had said, and the laywer had mentioned a copy of a deed that had been in her parents' safe deposit box. She had not seen nor thought of the old place for years. "If you wish to sell the property, I will arrange for the sale through local Realtors. However, in your own best interest, I urge you to visit the site if at all possible to help determine its true value."

The timing was perfect, taking her away from her work to a serene place just when she needed to think over her relationship with Barry, but maybe she had been fooled by her own emotions. She had certainly been fooled by her memory and had behaved like a fool when she took off without first obtaining a copy of the deed with its indications of location and property boundaries.

On impulse, she decided to pray. "God, I think You brought me here, but things are not what I expected. Help me."

The motor home began to sway a bit. The bear had stopped clawing at the door and was pushing against it with its full weight. The small vehicle began to rock, and Anna's throat once again tightened in fear. Was the bear strong enough, heavy enough to overturn the motor home? Anna began to look for some sort of safety in case that happened. Just as she started to crouch beneath the dash in front of the passenger seat, she thought she heard a car approaching.

🐾

Peter McCulley had plenty of time. He had been up since five o'clock and didn't have to be at work until eight. *The nice thing about tourists,* he thought, *is they usually like to sleep late.* That gave Peter time to enjoy the best part of the day before having to give himself to meeting their needs at the Sugarlands Visitors' Center. He had already been fishing and had taken a drive up on the ridge to catch the last reflections of the sunrise on the dew. He began whistling "Wildwood Flower," feeling good, knowing he could make it through one more exasperating day at the park information center now that he had some good memories to carry him along, and now that he decided that after fulfilling the one-week notice he was giving today, he would never have to go back to work there again.

Peter had no idea where he would go or what he would do. He only knew that the thought of leaving Gatlinburg was the most satisfying idea he had had in years. It did not matter where he went. Even if he moved only as far away as Sevierville, he would not have to make excuses for not coming to Sunday dinner with his mother. He would not have to pass the little strip mall where his photography studio had been four years ago. He would not have to feel guilty about hating his own brother if Darron did not honk and wave on his way home from work each day.

He knew he was leaving nothing in search of nothing, but he had made the decision, and it seemed right. The only question he had now was why he had not made this decision sooner. There was nothing here for him. He should have left long ago.

The sight of a bear, scratching its back against the door of a motor home, caught Peter by surprise as he came around a bend in the road. He hit the brakes and his pickup slid around on the loose gravel then came to a stop. Seeing the New York license plates, Peter shook his head and sighed. When would people learn that they could not use the entire state of Tennessee as their personal backyard?

He honked the horn to get the bear's attention, but nothing happened. For some reason, this bear was particularly taken with the motor home. Peter took his mess kit from behind the seat of the truck. He got out slowly and began to beat on the skillet with a wrench.

"Hey!" he shouted. "Git! Beat it!" Slowly he advanced toward the bear, pounding the pan, carefully judging the distance between himself and the bear, and between himself and the truck. The bear sat down on its haunches, scratched behind one ear, and gave a tremendous yawn. Peter scooped up some small rocks and threw them one by one at the bear's feet.

"Go! Scat!" he shouted.

Finally the bear reared halfheartedly, shook its head, and got up. Lazily it ambled off toward the woods. Peter watched until it was well out of sight, then walked toward the motor home. He wondered why anyone would be parked here so far from the main road.

Just as he was about to knock, the door flew open in his face and a woman stepped out, almost knocking him over.

"Thank you, thank you!" she cried. "I was trapped in there. I was so afraid the van was going to tip over. I. . .was just. . .afraid." Anna closed her eyes and breathed deeply, welcoming the flood of relief though it threatened to make her knees buckle.

"You weren't in any real danger," Peter said. "That ol' mamma bear would have left soon to take care of her cubs, but she just came to see what you all were having for breakfast. You never know. Maybe it was better than what she was having herself."

Anna covered her eyes with one hand and Peter saw, with some alarm, what looked like a wide bruise across the back.

"I feel like a complete fool," she said, "and most of all, I can't believe I was so frightened. I should have known that bear wasn't a real threat." She felt her face growing hot. All the poise and sophistication that she had cultivated over the years vanished. "I'm a first-class dunce, and you put yourself in danger to help me. If you had been hurt, it would have been my fault."

The sarcastic speech that Peter had prepared moments ago faded from his mind as he watched the woman in front of him. She was nearly as tall as he was, very slim, but without the fragile look that he disliked in some women. Peter was forced to admit to himself that when he went to the door, he had been expecting the kind of gushy gratitude he usually received when he helped people out of the stupid situations they got themselves into. Now he hardly knew what to say.

"What are you doing here anyway?" he said at last. "This road's hardly wide enough for your vehicle. Where are you headed?"

Anna, her strength returning, smiled ruefully. "I was asking those very questions of myself just as you came along. I was looking for a place. . .my great-grandmother's farm. . .that I thought was right around here, but I couldn't find it last night. Or maybe it's gone. That's a possibility. To be honest, I don't know where I am. . .or where I'm going."

"Got a map?" Peter asked.

Anna nodded and went inside the motor home, glad to be away from the eyes of the man who had rescued her. She could not remember a time when she had felt so awful. She picked up the map of Tennessee that lay spread out on the dash where she had left it last night. As she turned to go back outside, she caught a glimpse of Peter through the window. He had an air of patient suffering about him that made Anna feel more ashamed of her own thoughtlessness and lack of preparation for this trip. She had never run out of gas before in her life. To Anna, it symbolized a total lack of responsibility and organization.

Suddenly it seemed important to her that this man should not think badly of her. She glanced in the rearview mirror, grabbed a tissue from the dispenser on the sun visor, and rubbed out the worst of the makeup smudges, then quickly combed her hair and fluffed it with her fingers. She went back outside to greet this welcome stranger with her best professional smile.

"Let me start over, please," she said, extending her hand. "I'm Anna Giles. I live in Manhattan."

"Peter McCulley, from over near Pittman Center," he said. Anna liked the way he spoke.

"Are you hurt?" Peter asked. Instead of releasing the hand she had offered, he turned it slightly, looking at the smear across the back.

The small gesture touched Anna, and for a moment she wondered what to do. It was such a little thing, but so close, so personal and caring. It made her realize how alone she had been since she had left New York.

"It's just makeup," she said, laughing slightly. "It will wash off. I must really be a mess."

"No, ma'am, you're sure not," Peter said, glad that she seemed more at ease. "You look just fine." He made an effort to control his voice because she certainly did look fine to him. Her hair was expertly cut and hung in a plain, natural style. The color reminded him of good honey held up to the sun. She had very large eyes, blue gray with dark-rimmed pupils, with a quality like deep, clear water, set above sculpted cheekbones. Peter allowed himself the pleasure of glancing down the length of her legs and was startled to see bare feet with pink polished toenails.

"Let's see that map now," he said to keep himself from staring. He took the map and refolded it so the Gatlinburg area was clearly visible.

"I came in this way last night," Anna said, pointing to a red line on the map, "and turned off. . .here I think. . .south of Sevierville somewhere, but I got turned around. There are so many little roads that aren't on the map, and they all seem to go in circles."

"Well, the place we're standing on isn't marked on this map. You'd need a pretty detailed county map to find this road. You sure did drift, though." He drew a tiny circle on the map with a ballpoint pen. "Here's the approximate location. Now, where do you want to go?"

Anna chuckled ruefully. "If I only knew! I'm afraid I can't tell you. You see, I came down here to find my great-grandmother's place, but I can't give you an address. I just thought that once I got here, I'd be able to find it. Pretty stupid, right?"

Peter paused, his quick reply checked by a note of sadness in Anna's voice. "Maybe not, if it's important to you." He wondered at the odd expression that came over Anna's face. "Does your granny have a phone? Maybe she could give you directions."

"Oh, Granny isn't here anymore. She's been dead for years. My parents are gone, too." She didn't tell Peter that it had been only two months since her parents had died in a plane crash and that their deaths were the reason the Huddlestone property now belonged to her. The memory was still painful.

"I haven't been to Granny's place in twenty years. When I was little my parents would bring me to visit, but, of course, I only have mental pictures of the trips, not road numbers, in mind. I'm not sure whether my mind has gone bad or whether the landscape has changed. The memories are so vivid that I was just sure I could drive right there."

Peter smiled. He knew the power of memory both for good and for ill. "Did you ever know of a name she called her place? Where did you send letters to her? Was it Gatlinburg or some other place, like Coon Creek or Pine Bluff?"

"Yes, it was something Hollow, someone's name. Marshall Hollow? Does that sound familiar?"

"How about Martin? Martin's Hollow?"

"Yes! Is that on the map?"

"Not on this one. A lot of those little places are just wide spots in the road. Only the people who live there know where they are."

"But you know where Martin's Hollow is, don't you? If I could just get in the general area, I know I could find Granny's place. It's so clear in my mind!" Anna put her hands together, her fingers touching her chin, and gazed at the tops of the pines. "There were trees that we don't have up north. Granny called them cucumber trees, and I learned in school that they are a kind of magnolia that has a long, cylindrical seed. There were tall pines, but not the same color as these, and they were a deeper green and not as bushy looking. The road went practically to the door of the farmhouse, which was low and near a creek. The rest of the land rolled away behind the house, rising and rising." Her voice was soft now. "It was the happiest place I've ever known."

Peter listened quietly, amazed at the freedom Anna felt to express her feelings, her fears, her joy. She was looking for more than the land. She was looking for something, some part of her that had remained there since childhood, something that was lost to her as an adult. He felt a quiet stirring deep inside, an idea he had pushed away for a long time, but today, now, for just a fleeting moment, he remembered its presence, and it was because of Anna. It was the hint of a possibility that he might still share the beautiful things of life with someone who could appreciate them.

"Look here, Miss Anna. I've got to get on over to Sugarlands. I want to help you find your granny's place, though. Why don't you follow me over there and we'll do some asking in the right places."

"But I can't let you do that!" she protested. "You must have work to do and—"

Peter cut her off with a gesture of his large hands. "You got my curiosity up now. Besides, how could I keep on telling folks about Tennessee hospitality if I let you wander around with no help?"

Anna shrugged and rolled her eyes. "What can I say? I'd be a liar if I said the help wouldn't be appreciated. Oh! I forgot! This thing is out of gas," she said. "That's why I couldn't pull out and get away from the bear. I can walk to a gas station and get some gas if you need to get to work."

"I guess you could, if you really like walking. It is fourteen miles, though. . . one way." Peter laughed at the look of despair that came over Anna's face. He remembered the humble gratitude when he had not berated her for having no travel plans and the softening of her sophisticated smile when he had remarked on what he thought was a bruise on her hand. *She can't hide anything! Everything she feels is written all over her face.*

"Just hold on a minute," he said. He went to his truck and got a three-gallon can from the back. Anna unlocked her gas cap, and Peter poured in the gas, then helped Anna get the vehicle started, pouring gas into the carburetor until the engine continued to run.

"Now follow me," Peter said. "There's just barely enough gas in that thing to get you to the station, so don't get lost on me, hear?"

Anna nodded silently, got back into the motor home, and put the vehicle in gear. As she followed him along the winding road, she wondered if God ever sent angels in pickup trucks.

Chapter 2

When Anna came out of the ladies' room at the gas station, she saw Peter hanging up the receiver of the pay phone. She had changed into fresh clothing, brushed her hair, and properly cleansed her face, restoring the natural dewiness of her skin. A dash of eye shadow, mascara, and some light plum lipstick would be all the makeup she would use for the day. As she put her bag back into the motor home, now refueled, Anna knew that Peter was watching her.

She did not mind. She was used to the admiring glances of men and accepted the silent compliment that this one offered. In fact, his dark brown, slightly wavy hair and his tan, angular face worked together to make Anna take a second look. He had none of the polish of the men in her life in New York and certainly did not have the pretty good looks of the men with whom she modeled. His clothes were useful, purchased for durability instead of to emphasize the strengths of his build. Anna could not help but notice, though, that the simple uniform with its poor cut and careless fit could not hide the deep chest; the thick, strong arms; and the solid figure of the man who wore it.

As Anna approached Peter, he waved a finger up and down, indicating the denim jacket, cotton turtleneck, and pleated duck pants, all in shades of blue and purple.

"L.L. Bean?" he asked.

Anna drew back slightly in surprise. "How did you know?"

"I just know," he said, a mischievous look on his face.

Anna was just a bit defensive. "Why not? I figured if I was going to rough it, I might as well rough it in style. Besides, I love nice clothes."

Peter lounged against the phone booth, his arms crossed. He winked broadly, pulling down one corner of his mouth. "We'll keep your tenderfoot status a secret, but if you want people to think you're a native, don't wear new boots. It's a dead giveaway."

Anna laughed at his teasing and good humor. "Mr. McCulley, I can't thank you enough for all you've done. Now I've made you late for work. Please let me at least pay you for your time lost on the job."

He shook his head. "No need for that, Miss Giles. I called and told my boss I won't be in. He can find somebody else to empty the trash cans today." He dropped his eyes, suddenly self-conscious. He would prefer that Anna thought of him as a hero than the glorified janitor he really was. . .or had been until five minutes ago. Angered by his manager's patronizing refusal when Peter had asked for the morning off, he decided to skip the week's notice.

"Find yourself another boy," Peter had said. "I quit."

"Well, you won't be hard to replace," he had heard as he replaced the receiver.

"Anyway," Peter continued, "you caught my interest. Your granny's place, I mean. Well, you, too, but. . .I was kind of hoping you'd let me tag along and see that old farm. There aren't too many of them left."

"Are you interested in old houses?" she asked.

"Yeah, and young women." Peter was rewarded with another laugh from Anna, and it seemed to him like a Christmas gift. Even if it had meant being fired, at this moment he felt it was worth it.

"Did you get any breakfast before that bear came to call?" Peter asked.

"No, and I'm starved. The last time I poked food into this mouth I was in Kentucky. It seems like a long time ago, and like forever since I left New York."

"Tell you what," Peter said. "Let's park that monster here at Albert's place. You can ride with me. I'll find you a real Tennessee breakfast, and we'll figure out which direction to take looking for your granny's place. I can get us a county map at the ranger station at Greenbrier. . .if the rangers aren't all out feeding the bears."

"I can see it's going to be awhile before I. . .live this down." Anna giggled. "I said I was sorry. Don't tell me you're the kind who carries a grudge."

Without time to wonder at what was happening, Anna found herself getting into Peter's truck while he expertly backed the motor home into a space between two buildings. The smell of sheepskin seat covers, wood smoke, old metal, earth, and general manliness assailed her senses, which were sharpened by hunger. The smells seemed odd to her at first, far removed from her experiences in a scrubbed city environment, but quickly they were accepted as right. The sight of Peter, approaching the truck and holding her pink enameled key holder between his thumb and forefinger, made her think, *There's a real man, a good man who doesn't depend on the company of a woman to make him feel adequate.*

As they drove toward the ranger station, Anna told Peter more of what she remembered of the surroundings in the area of Granny's house.

"The thing I remember most vividly is a log church," Anna said. "Granny didn't go there to worship. She said the church was from the old days and there were no services held there, but you could see it from the road coming to her place. There was just a faint track leading off to it, not even noticeable enough to be called a trail."

"Was there a Grandpa Huddlestone?"

"Not in my experience, I'm afraid. He died when my mother was just a girl, shortly after her own mother died. Granny never remarried. Her life was very simple. The house is just an unpainted old frame place, all gray boards inside and out. She didn't have electricity or inside plumbing. I remember when she finally had electric lights put in because she was afraid of fire with the kerosene lamps, but she kept her wood-burning stove and carried in water from the pump. Isn't that odd? That was in the early seventies. I guess she didn't live much differently than her own grandmother did."

"Was it because of her religion?"

Anna hesitated. "No, my granny was very religious, but not in the way that inhibits the enjoyment of living. My father used to encourage her to get some comforts, like a gas furnace or an electric range, but she was just. . ." Anna spread her hands wide, her mind searching for the proper word.

"Satisfied?" Peter suggested.

"Exactly! She never seemed to feel she was underprivileged in any way. She didn't feel she was missing or lacking anything. She said she was happy and as long as she could take care of herself, why change what worked well? She would say, 'If it ain't broke, don't fix it.' I used to love going there, the strangeness of it all, the feelings, my granny. . . ."

Her voice trailed off, and Peter did not question her further, leaving her alone with her memories. He wished his own thoughts were as pleasant.

He was glad the break with his job had been made, glad it was clean and final, but wished he had been more in control. *Control!* That was the magic word, the quality Peter was seeking, the one that always seemed to elude him, even as it had this morning.

Peter and Anna were both silent when they finally pulled up to the ranger station, got out, and in a few minutes returned with a map.

"Now we'll get something to eat and have a look at this map and make some plans," Peter said. "I know a little place—"

That phrase grabbed Anna's attention. It was so typical of Barry's conversation. "I know a little place where we can have some privacy," he would say, or "He's got a little place up in the Catskills that has to be seen to be believed," or "There's a little place just on the edge of the district where they've got an old Italian woman who cuts without a pattern but faster than a stamper."

By now, midmorning, Barry would be in the thick of his business day.

"If I don't make a thousand by noon, the day's a waste," he sometimes said. Always trying to find the inside track, the inside tip, was Barry's approach to life. He never actually cheated, of course, but he was not above using people in subtle ways. He was so good at it they did not mind, if they ever actually knew. Anna knew Barry would certainly never lose a morning helping some poor lost tourist whom he had discovered alone in the park while jogging.

As Peter and Anna waited for breakfast to arrive, they studied the map. No Martin's Hollow appeared amid the dozens of locations noted in tiny letters between the winding roads.

"How can that be?" Anna asked. "I know we used to write letters to her at Martin's Hollow."

"Probably there was a post office at the general store and gas station. In the last twenty years, a lot of those little places have closed up and consolidated with the bigger stations. When the store closes, there's no more indication on the map. You said your granny was religious. Did she go to church anywhere?"

"Yes, when we visited we used to take her to church. There was a little town, just a few buildings, with a white church." Anna frowned at the map again, saying the names of the towns out loud.

"This one! This is it. McMahan."

"Now we're getting somewhere," Peter said with obvious satisfaction. After the waitress placed plates of sausage and eggs, biscuits and gravy, and potatoes in front of them, he said, "McMahan's not all that far. We'll truck on over there after we eat and find that church. Could be someone still remembers your great-grandma and can tell us how to get to the place. In fact, that might be the postal station now, too." He scooped gravy onto his eggs, buttered a biscuit, and began to eat, his five o'clock breakfast now only a dim memory.

Anna stared at the food. "How many people were you expecting? This would feed a basketball team."

Oh, no, not another dieter! "Try a biscuit," he coaxed. "They're not the same as homemade, but they're real good."

She shook her head and sighed. "I wish I could. They look terrific." She sipped her orange juice and cut a small piece of egg, which she chewed slowly.

"What's the matter? Scared you'll get fat?"

"Not scared, just disciplined. Fat models don't make much money."

Peter did little to conceal the sudden look of surprise and distress that came over his face. "A model! You don't look like a model."

"Oh? What do the other models you know look like? Two heads, or what?"

"Well. . .it's not that. . .I mean, I don't know any other models, but—"

"No one? Surely you base your opinion on wide research, Mr. McCulley. If I don't look like a model, what does a model look like?" She stared at him unmercifully, enjoying his embarrassment and wondering how he would get himself out of this.

"I mean. . .you said 'model' and I just thought. . .well, you know, those funny dresses and piled-up hairdos, and the women all bent into unhuman shapes and their hollow cheeks and all. You're not that kind of model, are you?"

"What if I am?" Anna replied coldly. "High-fashion modeling is a very demanding profession. There are very few women who have the talent to make it in that area."

"Well, you'll have to skip more than biscuits to get cheeks like a corpse," Peter grumbled.

"Oh yeah? Well, how's this?" Anna sucked in her cheeks and moved her lips like a fish.

Peter looked at her and his face brightened. He snapped his fingers. "Now I know where I've seen your face. I thought it looked familiar! You're on the cover of some magazine I just saw."

Anna was immediately pleased. "Which one did you see?"

"*Field and Stream*," he said.

Laughter burst from Anna like summer rain. "Just wait until I get hold of Barry!" she said, shaking her head. "Just see if I ever let him handle another account for me! *Field and Stream*. He'll love that."

"Barry?" Peter asked, relieved that he had managed to get his foot out of his mouth.

Anna looked at her plate and took another bite of her egg. She shrugged. "He's my agent, sort of." For some reason she did not feel like saying more. She looked longingly at the basket of still-warm biscuits. "I think I will eat one of these," she said. "I've got plenty of time to get back in shape." She spread a tiny dab of butter and some honey on half of a roll and munched happily. "I really do like good food," she confessed.

"Well, if you don't eat biscuits, you'll starve to death here," Peter said. "Now, how about some gravy to go with it?" He held up the small bowl of milk gravy flavored with spicy browned sausage and smiled appealingly.

Anna took a spoonful, tasted it, and sighed. "That is so good! It's been years since I've had gravy." The taste of the plain, delicious food, so far removed from her urban lifestyle, merged with the memories she had dredged up earlier. Nostalgia came in a wave. The smell of the sausage and biscuits put her back in her granny's kitchen, warming her feet at the wood-burning stove, hearing Granny hum, her small, thin body moving efficiently about the sparsely furnished room.

"Funny, isn't it," she said softly, "how you seldom appreciate the good things in your life until after they're gone. . .maybe forever."

"Don't be sad, Anna," Peter soothed. "It could be worse. You know they say, 'Better late than never.' It would really be a shame if you didn't understand how valuable your memories are or how important she was to you. Some people never do."

"Yes, that's true. I was only twelve when she died, and I hadn't seen her for a couple of years then. It's hard for a child that age to get a picture of things that last." She shook her head slowly. "I'm still wondering if I've done the right thing by coming here. Sometimes the reality is less than the hope."

"But you are here, and we'll find—"

"Mornin', Peter," came a soft male voice behind them. "Mornin', Miss—"

"Hey, Darron." Peter stiffened and did not look around. Anna sensed the tension immediately. Peter nodded in the other man's direction. "My brother, Darron

McCulley. This is Anna Giles. She's visiting from New York City."

Darron's face showed childlike delight. "New York? No kiddin'? That's a good ways off. Come to see the park?"

Anna smiled. "No, not really, but I can see why so many people do. It's certainly beautiful here."

Darron pulled out a chair and sat down.

"Help yourself, Darron," Peter offered. "Anna won't eat her share, so you might as well finish it."

"Dorothy, bring me a plate, will you?" Darron called to the waitress. "I'm glad I stopped," he said to Peter. "I saw your truck outside. I'm just on my way up to Sevierville to pick up some parts for the shop, but I can count this for coffee break."

He proceeded to fill the plate the waitress brought him and, with obvious enjoyment, ate the cold biscuits and gravy. "Actually this might be lunch, too. Alysia wasn't feelin' too hot this mornin' and didn't pack me a lunch. That's my wife," he said to Anna.

"Nothing serious, I hope."

Darron beamed. "She's pregnant, if you call that serious. I'm havin' lots of fun babyin' her. She cries a lot and runs me off, tells me I'm bein' silly and can't love a fat old woman like her, but I know she's teasin'." He dug a thick wallet out of his back pocket. "We got two kids already. Here. Here's Alysia with Wilford and Emily, taken a year back. This one's Alysia and me just after we got married. Peter took the pic—"

"Miss Giles is here looking for some family property," Peter interrupted. "You know anybody around McMahan who might know Martin's Hollow?"

Darron continued to eat in silence for a moment. "Can't think of a livin' soul, Pete. There was Hobe Gillman, but he's passed away."

"Well, we're going to drive over there and ask around town." Peter stood up and held Anna's chair, hurrying her a bit.

Anna handed the wallet back to Darron. "You have a lovely family, Darron. I can tell you're proud of them all." As Darron stood up and offered a firm handshake, she added, "I'm glad I got to meet you. I hope your wife doesn't feel ill for the whole pregnancy."

"Oh, she won't. Say, where are you staying?"

"I don't know yet," Anna shrugged. "I guess that depends on what I find in my travels today."

"Listen, you get set somewhere, you call me." He grabbed a paper napkin from the black metal dispenser and began to write on it. "Here's my number. We live up toward Cosby, and you just have Peter bring you over and have supper with us. Tomorrow, next day, be fine." He pushed the paper in Anna's direction.

"Why. . .thank you." Anna glanced at Peter, who seemed irritated and anxious to leave. "I'll try to let you know what happens," she said.

She waved as she left the restaurant, and Darron called, "Y'all come."

"That's what I call a proud papa," Anna said as she climbed into the truck. "Is Darron's wife as cheerful and pleasant as he is?"

Peter shrugged and concentrated on getting the door closed firmly.

"So! You're an uncle," Anna tried again as Peter got behind the wheel. Still he said nothing, and Anna decided it was best not to pursue the issue. She could not understand how anyone could be at odds with someone as delightful as Darron McCulley, but strange things happened between brothers sometimes. Besides, Peter McCulley's personal life certainly was none of her business. She had totally forgotten that Peter was really a stranger. A day like this could never happen in New York, at least not to a New Yorker like Barry. She had heard of the magic of the South, the friendliness and easygoing attitude. Perhaps it was true. Still she could not help but wonder at the sullenness that had overcome Peter since meeting Darron.

🦅

When Anna and Peter finally reached the town of McMahan, the small white church where Granny had been a member was not hard to find. The maddening slowness of the mountain roads had begun to irritate Anna, who was still in tune with the pace of New York. It was nearly two o'clock, and they were just on the verge of getting real information. First, they had gotten the name of the pastor from the sign on the church. They had driven to the pastor's home only to find that he was a young man who had been at the church for only two years and knew nothing about Granny Huddlestone. He sent Anna and Peter to find Deacon Parker. Deacon Parker had no telephone, so they drove to his farm, but he and his wife were both gone.

Peter was driving Anna crazy. He was silent in the truck, but when he got out to ask a question, he first had to chat about crops and weather before getting to the point. Didn't anyone in this part of the world hurry?

After leaving the Parker farm, they headed back toward McMahan to find the post office. Anna chafed as Peter made another of his leisurely inquiries as to the location.

"Well, what did you find out?" she demanded as he came back.

Peter turned the truck around in the middle of the street. "It's this way."

This time, when Peter pulled up in front of a small grocery store, Anna got out and went ahead of him. There was a desk in one corner with a red, white, and blue sign and the familiar white eagle. Anna walked briskly to the desk, but no one was there. She rang the small bell. A girl who appeared to be about eighteen years old came from the office. "What can I do for ya?" she drawled.

"I'm trying to locate an old address," Anna began. "The name is Huddlestone and the previous address was Martin's Hollow."

The girl looked confused. "I don't know anybody by that name," she said. "You could try mailin' a letter and see if it gets forwarded, or you can have it returned with an address correction. That's what we do when we get bad checks here at the store."

"The woman is dead," Anna said.

"Then how come y'all want to write her a letter?"

Peter stepped in. "Howdy. This the post office?"

"Of course it's the post office, can't you see?" Anna snapped.

"No, sir," the girl said emphatically. "This here's just a contract station. We sell stamps and stuff. We don't handle any mail."

"Do you live here?" Peter asked.

The girl nodded.

"Have you ever heard of Martin's Hollow?"

She shook her head.

"Peter, my granny lived in this county for sixty-three years! Why doesn't anyone know anything about her? How can someone just disappear without a trace?"

"She was your granny," Peter said quietly, the accusing tone all too obvious.

Anna had to look away. Part of her frustration was a sense of guilt at having lost such an important part of her life. Her pride injured and her energy sapped, Anna sighed, "What now? Should we look for a main post office somewhere?"

Peter shook his head. "I doubt we'll get any help that way. We could go on up to the county seat and check the tax rolls and so on."

Anna did not answer but wearily headed for the door. The day was ruined. She was looking forward to getting back to Albert's, pulling that motor home out onto hard, blacktop road, and finding the nearest stretch that would get her out of Tennessee. After a day of being shackled to a stubborn man in a bad mood, she felt that an evening of Barry's caustic humor would be great by comparison.

She glanced sideways at the man walking beside her through the parking lot, and suddeny she was ashamed. No doubt he was as tired and disappointed as she was, even if not for the same reasons.

"Peter, you've done so much for me. Why don't you take me back to Albert's? I'll look up the tax rolls by myself. If I don't find anything, it will be a waste of time for only one of us."

"Time is something I've got plenty of," Peter said flatly. "We are going to find this place, if it still exists. We will! I'm not going to quit. Even if you head for the city, I'm going to keep looking."

"But why? It doesn't mean anything to you."

"Do you want me to leave you alone? Is that it? Well, if you think I want to share in the work but not in the success, you're wrong."

"No, of course not, but it seems so hopeless—"

He gripped her shoulders with a fierceness that startled her. His face made her afraid, not for her own safety, but at the thought of what such intensity might accomplish if misdirected.

"Maybe you get only one chance, Anna," he said, his grip firm but not painful. "You came here looking for something. I don't know exactly why, but I'm mixed up in it now, too, and I'm not sorry. It isn't just the house and all your warm, fuzzy memories about your old granny, and it isn't just the challenge of finding something as big as an elephant that still can't be seen. It's you. . .something about you."

Anna stared at him, her lips parted, hardly breathing. What was he trying to say?

He let her go and stepped back, his face softening a bit. "If you really don't want me along, I understand. I know I'm not always great company. I apologize."

"Oh, Peter, why are we arguing?" said Anna, feeling weak with the tension of the moment added to the fatigue and frustration of the day. "I certainly didn't mean to imply that you weren't wanted."

He said no more, and Anna tried to sort out the tangle of emotions that crowded the hot cab of the pickup. Unbidden, the thought came to her that perhaps Peter was seeking an intimacy that she had not offered. That almost brought a smile. Anna Giles had achieved notoriety in her social circle for her creative ways to say no.

Anna didn't ask for anyone's understanding or need anyone's approval. For her, it was all or nothing, and so far it had been nothing. She knew what she wanted and no one—not even Barry—had offered it to her. She wasn't about to settle for anything short of her own expectations when it came to commitment to a man. For Anna, that meant marriage to a full-time husband, a home, and children, in that order.

Anna's friends would have been amazed to know that Anna had never accepted anything more from Barry than a few living-room kisses. Not that he hadn't offered more! In fact, lately it seemed that every date ended in an argument over what he and she wanted from a relationship. Perhaps that was why Barry had offered her the partnership with its implications of marriage. Maybe he was ready to settle down now, in business and in personal relationships. If so, was he the man she wanted?

Anna glanced toward Peter again. What exactly would he be expecting later this evening? Suddenly her thoughts were violently wrenched away as they came to the top of a ridge. She sat up straight and grabbed the dashboard.

"Stop!" she demanded. "Stop! There's the old log church."

Chapter 3

This is the same church! It's exactly as I remember it, but it's in the wrong place," Anna said. She and Peter walked around the ancient building, peering through the tiny windows at the rough benches inside. A wooden lectern with a yellowed, ragged Bible on it stood at the front of the room. The door had been sealed, and a thick bronze plate anchored to a boulder outside the church gave the history of the building. Anna sat on the boulder and read the information.

"It's been moved. The county historical society brought the building here to preserve it when the highway went through eight years ago. It used to be on County Road 406, south of McMahan." Anna stared at the plaque as though it had fallen from space. "What does that mean? Did they call that trail a county road? If they had to move this building, what's happened to Granny's place?" The doubts came rushing in, and Anna no longer had the strength to hold them off. Tears began to come, and she shoved both hands hard against her mouth to keep from sobbing aloud.

Peter approached tentatively. He had no encouragement to offer. He remembered hearing Darron remark on the extensive improvements in the area some years back, but it had meant nothing to Peter then. No doubt if they did find the Huddlestone home, the area would be drastically changed. Should he give in, tell Anna to forget it rather than be disappointed any further? He placed a gentle hand on her shoulder, not knowing what else to do.

"I'm just as out of place as this church," Anna managed to say. "I don't belong here. I'm just chasing some kind of foolish dream, and I've wasted your time and mine, too. I'm going to find a telephone and call my lawyer and tell him to sell. What would I do with the place even if I found it? I don't know anything about property values."

Peter sat beside Anna on the rock, his arm falling naturally across her shoulders. "Do you really want to leave without knowing for sure?"

Anna breathed deeply. "Ever since last night when I couldn't find Granny's, I've had this fear that the house would be gone. I think that's why I didn't do more calling before I came all the way down here. I was afraid to find out the truth. . . that I am really all alone now, without anything left of my family."

"Your momma and daddy didn't leave you anything to remember them by?"

"Last fall they sold their house in Maryland, but it was just a house. We lived in so many places that no single house ever seemed like home. We were happy together, and my parents had a beautiful marriage, but we didn't have. . .oh, you know, a place. I never thought about it much, but they were going to retire. Daddy was in the army, and he was going to get out, and they were going to build their dream house in the mountains. They had sold the Maryland house, and they were on their way to look at a piece of property when they died."

Peter held her close beside him, knowing the sorrow was still so new to her. At last he said, "You know your granny's place will never make up for them being gone, don't you?"

Anna nodded, then leaned against him and sobbed openly, feeling the warmth of tears flood the fabric of his shirt. He said nothing, letting her cry until she was ready to stop.

He took a blue paisley bandanna from his pocket and offered it to her. "Come on," he said gently and led her to the truck. He helped her inside, hating to be separated from her even by inches, but knowing she would not want him near when she recovered her resolve, and he believed she would do that very soon. He got behind the wheel and waited until her breathing was once again regular and quiet.

"Anna, it's after five o'clock. It's a good hour to the area where this church came from. I think you ought to get some supper, then some sleep, and start again in the morning. There's probably still a lot of time on the road ahead of you. You'll feel more like it tomorrow."

Anna nodded wearily. "Take me back to Albert's."

They got hamburgers at a drive-through restaurant and talked about nothing on the way back to the garage. The stillness of evening had begun to set in when Anna found the owner, gave him ten dollars for using the space for the day, and chatted with him for a moment.

"Albert says he'd rather not have the motor home here tomorrow because of the liability," she told Peter. "I don't blame him. I know about insurance and all that. Besides, I wasn't looking forward to sleeping here with cars coming and going all evening. Maybe I should just look for a motel. I really hate motels, but it's probably for only one night, after all."

That was exactly what Peter was afraid of. He was ashamed to admit, even to himself, that he was just a bit satisfied that they had not found Anna's property today. A feeling that could only be called panic rose within him when he envisioned her in the motor home, heading north and out of his life forever. For a brief moment he thought of manipulating the situation, hiding evidence that might be discovered, in order to prolong her stay, but, of course, that was absurd.

The knowledge that Anna was once more in control made him realize she would not need him forever and, in fact, was already separating herself from him. He did not want to share her with other people at a campsite or at a motel, people who would have no idea of what she was going through and what the bond was that the two of them shared. His big question was whether Anna herself felt the unity that he was experiencing.

"If you want to stay in the motor home and aren't afraid to stay by yourself, I can take you to a place I think you might like," he said, trying to keep his voice steady.

"It isn't in a park, is it?" she said. "I think I might like a motel better than a trailer park."

Peter laughed. "No, it's not a park. Why don't you just follow me? If you don't like it, you can leave the motor home behind, and I'll take you to a motel. . .I mean, I'll show you where you can get a room." He spun around and jumped in his truck as Anna smiled, remembering her thoughts of the afternoon.

Once again Anna was following Peter's truck. As the sun began to cast longer shadows, she barely recognized the scenery along the road they had traveled this morning. It seemed so long ago! The sight of the taillights ahead of her were both comforting and upsetting. She followed Peter off the good gravel road onto a narrow dusty one where she wondered if there would be room for a passing car. The motor home was difficult to handle. What if she had to slow down and she lost sight of Peter? No, of course he would be watching for her. As they wound upward into the hills and then down into the hollows, the darkness deepened abruptly and she turned on her headlights.

It was the awkward time of day when headlights made no difference. Anna tried not to think about the steep dropoff on one side of the road and the sharp rock wall on the other side that had a tendency to shed loose boulders from time to time. The way she was driving reminded her of the way she had played as a child, twisting the wheel back and forth, back and forth, working the brake feverishly in an exaggerated manner. But this was for real.

At last Peter turned from the small road onto an even smaller one and slowed his truck even more as he went along a steep decline. Now thick clumps of laurel threatened to swallow the road that was little more than a path. Just as Anna wondered how much farther they could go, Peter pulled ahead into an open area and stopped.

He got out of his truck and walked back to the motor home and got into the passenger seat. "You all right?"

Anna nodded. She mustered a false good humor and said, too brightly, "Some drive! Well! Is this the place? I don't see anybody else camping."

"Come have a look," Peter said.

When they got out of the vehicle, Anna was immediately cheered by the effect of the sunset above the distant mountains, the soft light reflected on the late spring colors of the surrounding woods. The shadow of an early full moon hung in the east, waiting its turn. The chill of evening had settled the breeze, and the air was perfectly still and crisp as she followed Peter along a footpath of bare rock toward a rushing creek that glistened in the fading light. As they came closer, she could hear its frantic mutterings as it whizzed along through the shallow bed, following its destined course toward the big river.

"Like it?"

"Peter, this is like something out of a coffee table picture book! It's hard to believe that such a place actually exists." She looked around at the variety of trees, the shapes of chinquapin bushes and honeysuckle vines, and breathed in the rich aroma of blossomed air. The steadfastness of the rocks and trees, the purposeful journey of the stream, settled her senses and reminded her once again of her own mission. She was happy. Somehow, she knew things would work out.

"Yes, Peter, this is exactly right. I remember now. It was this sense of peace that I was really hoping I'd find once I got away from the city and back into the mountains that my parents and Granny loved so much. It is here, after all."

Peter touched her shoulder. "Do you have enough water for the night?"

"Yes."

"Are you afraid to stay alone?"

The question that had nagged at Anna's mind earlier returned. Was it payoff time? What exactly did he want her to say? More disturbingly, Anna found herself wondering what she wanted to say. Today she had seen a melancholy, brooding Peter and a teasing, fun-loving Peter and an understanding, thoughtful Peter. All of them were good-looking and evidenced a definite appreciation for women. What if he wanted to stay? Could she say no?

Peter, suddenly aware of her silence, slapped his forehead. "I did it again, didn't I? I meant that I would sleep in the truck if you didn't feel like camping out here in the wilderness all alone. If you want to be alone, I'll go home. What's your choice? I'm here if you need me."

Yes, as usual, it was her comfort, her well-being that he had in mind. *I should have known he isn't the type to use people in any way.* "I'll be fine, Peter," she said. "Please get a good night's sleep and don't worry about me. If there aren't any people around, I guess I don't have anything to be afraid of, do I?"

She pulled his bandanna from her jacket pocket, then turned and met him face-to-face. The light of the rising moon fell on one side of his face, and Anna felt for a moment that it was the face in a painting, one of the old Dutch masters where the faces were full of wonder and curiosity, shining through a dark world. She handed the still-damp fabric to him. "Sorry about all that crying."

He took the kerchief and held it. "I'll come back first thing in the morning, and we'll know soon enough if what you're looking for still exists."

For a moment, they simply stood together under the trees, the darkness falling rapidly around them.

Anna murmured, "This land belongs to someone. You're sure it's all right if I stay here? I should make arrangements with the owner, shouldn't I?"

"It's mine," Peter said and deliberately folded the bandanna so that she would not see in his face the feelings that came with those two small words. He began walking toward the truck and she walked with him.

As he reached for the door handle, he stopped and turned to her. "Anna, I hope. . .hope. . ." What could he say? He had no right to tell her that whatever it was she was looking for, he wanted her to find it here and that he wanted to be the one who showed her the way. He looked at her trusting, open face, and for one horrible moment he visualized himself coming back in the morning and finding her gone without a trace, back to New York and out of his life as though she had never been stranded on that road this morning.

She's a stranger, a city girl who'll run back to Barry Whoever-He-Is as soon as she disposes of her inheritance, or finds out it's nothing but an improved public roadway, he told himself. But more than anything he could remember in a long time, Peter did not want that to happen.

"I hope you get a good rest," he said, despising his lack of skill in the language department.

"Thank you again, Peter. I never imagined anything like this."

"I'll be out early. I'll cook. You get some rest."

Anna wanted to ask another question to hold him there for a few minutes, but he was gone, bumping over the rough trail. The sound of the engine faded, and she knew she was more alone than she had ever been in her life and yet not alone at all.

Chapter 4

The persistent knocking at the door of the motor home penetrated Anna's sleep, and for a moment, she thought of the bear. Then she remembered. Peter had said he would be there.

"Peter?" she called. "Is that you?"

"Were you expecting somebody else? Come on out, or I'll eat everything myself."

Anna snuggled deeper into the blankets, savoring their warmth in contrast to the cold, crisp air inside the motor home. She had left one window open and slept deeply. She felt rested. The problems of yesterday did not seem so insurmountable this morning. Peter had been right.

Still reluctant to leave the warmth that surrounded her, Anna dragged the blankets along as she crawled to the end of the bed. She reached into the small bureau built into the motor home and took out a pair of jeans and a heavy cowl-necked sweater. She dressed quickly, brushed her hair, and fastened it at the back of her head, then stepped outside into the morning. The smell of ham and wood smoke went straight to her stomach, and Anna was suddenly ravenous.

She saw Peter near the stream and jogged toward him. "I hope you have tons of food," she said. "I'm so hungry I could die."

"What about your diet?" He broke an egg into the skillet and put the shells back into the carton.

"What good is being thin if you're dead?" she asked, sitting down on an outcropping of rock beside him.

Without makeup, Peter noticed, Anna's face lost some of its definiteness. She looked softer, more vulnerable. Her hair was bundled into a granny knot and small tendrils escaped around her neck and ears. A little air of sleepiness remained about her as she huddled close to the fire and hummed to herself. She held her hands out to the warmth, and Peter saw that her nails were of a moderate length and bore no polish. His image of the big-city fashion plate was fading. He began to feel that Anna was something else entirely. Suddenly he felt a need to concentrate on his cooking.

"Why are you doing that?" Anna nodded at the skillet as Peter moved it in and out of the small flames.

"Regulates the heat," he said, "so the eggs don't burn."

"You must cook this way a lot. You don't waste any movements."

"A fair bit. Not as much as I'd like to. Having a job tends to interfere with living sometimes." But now there was no job. Maybe he could live again.

Anna smiled. "I get the impression that you aren't exactly fond of your job."

Peter shrugged. He scooped the eggs onto tin plates, served thick slices of ham from a plate that had been resting on the rocks near the fire, and then poured coffee from a battered and blackened percolator. Anna took the plate then watched as Peter scraped away hot coals and pulled out a small dutch oven. He lifted the lid, and Anna saw that it was filled with golden brown biscuits. The heat and aroma rose to her face, and she knew that she would rather be here than in the most exclusive supper club in New York.

"Peter, I almost hate to eat this. You've worked so hard. You must have started breakfast hours ago!"

He sliced a chunk of butter from a stick, slipped it inside one of the biscuits, and handed it to her. "Believe me, I can't think of a better way to spend a morning. Don't feel too sorry for me. I didn't butcher the hog and cure the ham and feed the chickens and gather the eggs the way our grannies did."

"I used to feed the chickens when I came to Granny Huddlestone's," Anna remembered. "I was so afraid of them! I used to stand just at the edge of the yard and throw handfuls of feed overhand like a baseball. Granny coaxed me and encouraged me until I got over the fear. She would say, 'People are like chickens. There's banty roosters, all noise and feathers and no meat. There's old hens that are always in a stew. There's little biddies that don't know enough to stay home in their nests.' She called me her little chick, said I belonged right next to her under her wing."

"I like the way you talk about her. You're a good talker."

Anna grimaced. "That's a very nice way of putting it. My friends tell me my mouth needs a new transmission because it won't stay in neutral."

"Nice friends you got. Want another biscuit?" He handed her another without waiting for her to answer. "How did you get into the modeling business? Were you discovered, or what?"

"My high school home and family living teacher encouraged me to try it," Anna said. "I went to a big consolidated high school in eastern Virginia."

"What? I thought you were a Yankee."

"Oh no. I didn't go to New York until. . .oh, a little over six years ago. I went to one of those charm school places when I was a senior and learned how to walk straight and keep my nose in the air, you know. I started working in Richmond, then I went to Baltimore for a few years before trying the big time. Believe me, the girls that come to New York straight from Iowa or Tennessee. . . they seldom have a chance."

"Where were you born?"

"I was born in Tennessee, and my family lived here for two years after I was born. My father was in the army. We moved around a lot, four years here, two years there. New York is as much my home as any other place I've ever been. What about you? Is Tennessee home to you?"

"Sure. Born and bred in the briar patch, you might say. I only left Seviere County to go to college in Memphis, and I stayed there for two years."

"Tell me about your work, Peter. You must like helping people all day. You certainly saved my life yesterday."

"Well, it was my gain," he said, beginning to stamp out the fire without answering her question. Anna watched him as he quickly disposed of the garbage and cleaned the utensils without leaving any sign of human presence. From the bank of the stream where he cleaned the skillets using only sand and the cold water, he called, "As soon as you're ready, we'll drive over to the county seat. They can look up the location of your granny's property. We might as well get scientific about this thing."

As Anna and Peter drove toward the county offices, she once again broached the subject of work. "I'm really afraid you're giving me too much time, Peter. I'd hate to have you lose your job because of this."

"It's all right," he said. "I'm taking some time off. Stop worrying."

The tone of his voice told Anna the subject was off-limits, but her curiosity burned on. He was so full of secrets and so full of surprises! She wondered if, when the time came to leave, she would still be trying to figure him out.

She also wondered if her questions would be answered. Would she know if the new faith she had adopted as her own just weeks ago would really change her life, as her friend Brianna had promised?

Brianna had taken Anna to a luncheon where a businesswoman had shared with the listeners how she had asked God to forgive her sins and make her life His own. Anna had heard such stories before but had assumed such experiences came to one in a supernatural, mystical way, not through logical decisions like the ones the speaker asked the audience to make. Still, when Brianna explained to Anna that without the forgiveness of God through the death of Jesus there could be no communion with the creator, Anna decided to pursue the idea. After reading the Bible and talking more with Brianna, she decided to make the personal connection to the God she had always assumed was rather disinterested in individuals.

The opportunity to get away from her work and her surroundings had so far given her little insight into the effects of that decision, but Brianna was right about one thing. Anna knew there was a divine presence in her life now, guiding her, helping her, though she could not guess in advance where it might lead.

As she listened to Peter talk about fishing, she knew he had come to her for some reason known at this time only to God. Maybe it was simply to help her find the property or to solve some problem connected with it. Maybe it was to be a friend at a time when she especially needed one. She didn't know.

The county clerk sent them to the assessor's office, who first did a flurry of computer work, then rummaged in a large file drawer and pulled out a yellowed document.

"There's good news and bad news," said the man. "I'd say from the records I've got here, the Huddlestone house is still standing, though the road right-of-way has been changed considerably. The bad news is, the taxes haven't been paid in nearly two years. Actually, that property's due for sale in about. . ." He glanced at a large calendar on the wall. "Let's see, the auction is in four days."

"But my attorney didn't say anything about taxes," Anna protested. "He has the deed. The property belonged to my parents."

"I can look up the correspondence for you, if you like," the clerk said. "All I know right now is that this parcel is on the list for auction unless we get full cash payment."

"Well, I'm not going to pay it until I see the place," Anna said, trying to control her emotions. "Can you tell us how to get there?"

The assessor showed Peter the location of the property, and he and Anna quicky got back into the truck.

"Two years," Anna said. "How could that have happened? Tax notices must have been mailed to the wrong address after my parents moved the last time. Two years' worth of taxes!"

"If you need money, Anna, I've got some put away. I can help."

She stared at him. "Peter, you are a wonder. I've known you for only a day and a half, and you're behaving like family. That's the most generous offer I've ever heard."

He reddened a bit. "Oh, well, you didn't hear the terms of the contract yet. I demand you name your firstborn child after my grandfather."

"Is it worse than Rumpelstiltskin?"

"Jonadab Subulocious McCulley," he said.

"What if it's a girl?"

"She'll really hate her name," he said.

As Peter slowed the truck, Anna at first thought they were in the wrong place, but then she saw the house, standing as always near the ancient pines. The house had not moved, but the road had changed so much that she was at first disoriented. She had thought she would jump from the truck and run to the old place the minute she saw it, but now she hesitated.

"Come with me, Peter."

He walked quietly beside her as they walked down the hill and stepped up onto the porch. On the kitchen door was the tax notice. Anna took it down and tried the door. It was open, as always. Granny had no locks.

Anna pushed open the door and smelled the rush of air with its odor of vacant rooms, spiderwebs, earth, and insects. Carefully she stepped inside and surveyed the room she had not seen for so many years.

"I would give anything to see my granny one more time," she whispered.

Peter said nothing for a time then asked, "Did your mamma and daddy ever come back here after she died?"

"They came for the funeral, of course. They took some of the things that were left in the house. But I have a feeling they never quite got around to making any decisions about the place. See? So many things have just been left here. How can it be that vandals haven't destroyed the whole place? There are some dishes still in the cupboard. Here's a can of corn still in the pantry."

"It doesn't make sense," Peter said. "Seems like a perfect place for a high school beer bust or worse. For some reason, the place escaped damage. It must be well-built. The weather doesn't seem to have done much damage."

Roused from her reverie, Anna began looking through the rooms, one by one. As she did, the memories of her early years came to life. The house was no longer a sad place but the piece of her own history she had hoped it would be.

"Peter, I'm going to keep this place. I might even fix it up and keep it for a vacation home or something like that. Do you think it needs much work?"

"I'm not much of a builder," he said, "but Darron's pretty good at it. He could tell you what would have to be done to put it in shape. Of course, you'll want plumbing, maybe a bigger electrical service, but it doesn't appear there's much structural work."

"I never thought to ask how much the taxes were. Let's go back and find out. Then I'm going to rent a car for a couple days. . .that is, if you don't mind if I leave the motor home on your land."

"Wouldn't have it any other way," he said, delighting in her enthusiasm and purposefulness. This was the Anna he had seen yesterday morning, set on a purpose, knowing her mind, yet not afraid to admit she needed help.

🦋

Anna and Peter reached the assessor's office about fifteen minutes before closing then were sent to the treasurer who obviously didn't appreciate their visit.

"You owe three hundred twenty-two dollars and sixty-eight cents," she said abruptly, staring at Anna.

"No, I want to know the total amount," Anna said firmly.

"That is the total amount," said the treasurer. "That's the taxes for two years, plus interest and penalites."

Anna paused, not wanting to be rude, but said once more, "That's all? Are you sure?"

The treasurer wearily laid the tax bill before Anna for her approval, and suddenly Anna laughed out loud. "Three hundred and twenty-two dollars? For two years?"

The treasurer was surly. "Well, I'm sorry, but we built a new school a few months back. The money mostly goes to the schools, you know, and there is a house on the place. If you have a problem with the charges, you could ask for a hearing."

"Can you take an out-of-state check?" Anna asked.

"I'd rather not," said the treasurer.

"I'll be in tomorrow with the cash," she said. "Thank you."

Once outside Anna wrapped her arms around Peter and hugged him tightly. "I thought it would be thousands!" she gasped between peals of laughter. "It's a gift! An outright gift!"

"Real-estate values are different here, I guess," Peter said, laughing with her.

"I guess I don't need the loan," Anna said. "Thanks anyway."

"Too bad," said Peter. "Jonadab would have been proud."

"Peter, come and celebrate with me, please. I need to go to Gatlinburg and arrange for a transfer of some money from New York. I can also rent a car there. Then I'd like you to come out to the motor home and have supper with me later. Would you? I haven't been able to do anything for you, and you've been wonderful. Say you will."

"I wouldn't miss it," he said. "Are you cooking?"

"Well, I'll serve something," she said. "I don't promise to cook, but it will be something edible, trust me."

❦

When Peter opened the door for Anna at the bank in Gatlinburg, he said, "I'll see you about seven. Are you sure you can find your way back now?"

Anna patted her handbag. "I've got my map, and as long as I don't wait until after dark, I'll be fine." She waved as he drove off, then she went into the bank.

After getting a rental car, Anna visited a grocery store and then did some shopping. She found a dark mauve jumpsuit in a quasi-military style that she decided she would wear for the evening. She rationalized her own motives for the purchase, telling herself she was not really dressing to please Peter, just making a wardrobe investment.

When paying for her clothing, Anna noticed in her handbag the napkin on which Darron had written his phone number. She remembered what Peter had said about Darron's talents in the building trades, and she decided to call him before she left town.

"Is this Darron?" she asked the person on the phone. "This is Anna Giles. Do you remember me? We met at the restaurant."

"I wouldn't forget you, Anna," Darron answered. "Are you all ready to come and have supper with us? I'm fixin' spaghetti."

"I'm afraid I can't tonight, Darron. You're awfully free with your hospitality, aren't you?"

"You know what they say. Love isn't love 'til you give it away. Just remember you're always welcome. Is there something else you need?"

"Well, I found my granny's house, the one Peter and I were looking for in Martin's Hollow."

"You did? For sure?" He lowered the receiver, and Anna heard him call, "Alysia, Peter and that gal I told you about found that old house." To Anna he said, "Is there anything left of it?"

"It seems to be pretty sturdy, but Peter said he wasn't qualified to give any kind of estimate on repairs. He said you were good at building. Would you be willing to look at the place and tell me if you think it's worth fixing up? I don't want it to completely go to ruin. It's already been vacant for several years."

"I'll be glad to look at the place. Can you tell me where it is?"

Anna hesitated. "You know, I'm afraid I can't. I have the map we got at the clerk's office, but I couldn't tell you how to get there. For one thing, I don't know where you are. I could bring the map to you, though. I've rented a car, and I'm doing some shopping in Gatlinburg."

She told Darron where she was, and he gave her directions to his home in a neighboring small town. Anna was surprised to find the home was in a crowded and not-too-pleasant area. The duplex where Darron stood waiting on the porch was in need of paint, and the small patch of grass was rimmed with bare dirt. Anna would have thought she was being welcomed into a palace; however, by Darron's warm, enthusiastic reception.

"I'm sure glad I was home a little early today, otherwise I would have missed your call. Come on in and meet my wife."

Alysia was short with dark eyes and hair and a cupid's bow mouth. Her hair was windblown and curly, and she wore a huge T-shirt over walking shorts. Though more shy than Darron, she welcomed Anna with a handshake and a smile.

"You'll know the place when you see it," Anna said after showing Darron the map. "For one thing, there are those huge pine trees below the house." She took a hundred dollars out of her bag and handed it to Darron. "This is just for your gas and time," she said. "If you need more to pay for estimates from contractors or anything like that, let me know."

Darron stared at the money. "I didn't think about getting paid."

"But. . .I couldn't ask you. . .this kind of work is expensive, Darron," Anna stammered. "I wouldn't feel right asking you to use your time and your own vehicle and not pay you."

"Well, if it makes you feel better, I won't say I don't need the money," he said, but he was obviously uncomfortable. He excused himself and left Anna with Alysia.

"Oh, I hope I haven't offended him," Anna said.

"You can't offend Darron," said Alysia. "It just never would have occurred to him to ask for payment, and he wishes he could afford to give it back, that's all. He won't think badly of you for it."

"Alysia, I've never met people like you and Darron. I don't know anyone who would invite me to their home on a moment's notice like this. They might meet me somewhere, but this is wonderful."

"Don't give us too much credit," said Alysia, laughing. "It's the way we were raised. We don't know any other way. Anna, I hope you stay a bit. I really like talking to you. I'm going to tag along with Darron to the house, too, if you don't mind."

"I don't mind at all. I think I'd better go now, though. I know you'll want to be feeding your family soon, and I've invited Peter to the motor home for supper. He's been such a big help."

A shadow of sadness passed across Alysia's face, and a small smile that was not a happy one lingered. "Peter has so much to give," she said. "I hope you and he can be friends." Suddenly she thought of something. "Anna, would you like to come to church with Darron and me? It's a little place, but we're happy there. We'd love to have you come."

Her invitation prompted Anna to share her own recent spiritual decision. She was pleased to see that Alysia understood perfectly what had happened.

"Darron and I both love and follow the Lord Jesus," she said. "Now I just know you and I are going to be friends even if you don't get to stay in Tennessee."

"Oh, I couldn't stay," Anna said. "I have my work, you know, but I am beginning to think I might be staying longer than the week I had originally planned. We'll see what happens."

Chapter 5

After she got things ready for a light meal, Anna still had time for a relaxing beauty treatment and the production of a more sophisticated hairdo. Her feeble attempts to convince herself that Peter would not be expecting her to dress up were lost in her natural love of elegance. When she opened the door to Peter's knock, she was surprised to see that she was not the only one who had dressed for the occasion.

"Peter! You look very nice," she said. He was freshly shaved, and Anna caught a hint of spicy cologne as he brushed past her. He wore cotton slacks that broke precisely over casual but well-polished loafers. His plaid sport shirt, though it bore no designer label, was crisp and bright and, Anna noted approvingly, tailored nicely.

Briefly Anna wondered if she had misled Peter. Had he dressed out of courtesy, or was he trying to please her? Then she mentally slapped herself. Of course he would shower and shave for dinner. He was not a slob. And what if he were trying to make an impression? He had already done that, but the new image he presented to her this evening made him seem less like a wise uncle but more like an available man.

Serving the fondue supper that she had prepared, Anna said, "Sorry, no biscuits."

"I don't mind a bit," he said. "I can go without biscuits when the cook wears such a nice uniform."

"Oh, thank you," she smiled. "I saw this in Gatlinburg, and it called my name. It's my favorite color. Let me guess yours. I'll bet it's blue."

He nodded. "What was your clue?"

She shrugged. "Most people like red or blue, and you don't seem to be the red type. Anyway, I think you're a bit romantic. I'll bet you even keep souvenirs."

He reddened at the thought of the small cedar box in his bedroom that held treasures from past years. Why could he not read her the way she read him? The only thing he had learned to predict about this woman was her definitely female effect upon him. He thought of the vulnerability she had shown last night. She had made no move to conceal it, nor had she used it as a ploy to gain his sympathy and attention. She simply had a need, and he had been present to assist her.

Anna was saying, "Peter, are we friends?"

He smiled. "If I have anything to say about it, we are."

"I want to ask you something. . .tell you something, I guess. A few weeks ago something happened to me. I went to a luncheon with a friend of mine and heard a woman talk about how she had given her life completely to God. She said she realized she was separated from Him because of her sins. She asked God to forgive her and make her acceptable to Him. Have you ever heard anything like that?"

Peter nodded. "Sure, lots of times. It's what they call the gospel message."

"Yes, she used that word, gospel. She said it meant 'good news,' and the news was we could have peace with God and a personal relationship with Him. I prayed that God would take away my sin, too, Peter. I believe, though it's all new and strange to me, that I'm changed somehow. It isn't that I was some kind of lowlife before and now I'm an angel. I just know God is at work in my life. I can say now that I know Him. Does that make any sense?"

Peter nodded. "Around here people would say you got converted or maybe saved or just got religion. It depends on if you're Baptist or Methodist."

"This is important to me, Peter. It's one of the main reasons I came here, maybe the whole reason. Do you think it's weird?"

Peter could hardly believe she could lay before him perhaps the most personal decision any person could make. Didn't she fear his laughter and rejection? Could she be so sure of herself that his opinion would not change her mind? He understood that she was not seeking his approval but only asking whether her experience paralleled anything in his own life.

"It isn't weird, Anna. If it's real to you, that's all that matters."

"I want to know if it is real or just an emotional reaction," she said. "That's why I decided to get away from work and the city and my friends and just think about this for a while. It's easy to get separated from the really important things when you are so busy and the lights are so bright." A picture of Barry flitted through her mind. He would be telling her that her ears were deaf from hearing things like horns and sirens and that there was something basically unwholesome in silence. He would not even try to understand the quiet stirrings in her soul.

Peter searched Anna's face. "It doesn't much matter where you are, Anna. You can still lose touch with what's real."

"What's real, Peter?" Anna asked softly. "What's important to you?"

He shrugged slightly. "A few things. . .land, family. Maybe only those two things."

"Speaking of family, I met Darron's wife today. She's the most friendly, relaxed person. They invited me right in."

"You went to Darron's place?"

"Yes, he's going to look at Granny's house and help me get some idea of whether it's worth investing money in repairs. Alysia seems to think highly of you."

"I don't appreciate people talking about me behind my back," Peter snapped.

Anna stiffened. "No one was talking about you behind your back. What a thing to say!"

"Neither one of them will be happy until they. . .just leave them alone, all right? They can't do anything for you."

"Maybe they can. They can be my friends, which, by the way, I choose without your permission." Anna felt her own temper rising and was unhappy with herself for sniping at Peter.

"Well, I won't stand for you all taking me apart. Darron knows better. I've told him to let the past rest, but he won't."

"Peter, I have no idea what you're talking about. Darron wasn't even in the room when Alysia said—"

"So now it's Alysia," he shouted. "I should have known she couldn't live with it forever. She just had to tell somebody. Did she tell you the whole story or just her side? Did she tell you everything?" He was standing now, leaning over Anna in an almost threatening manner. "Did she tell you we had been engaged?"

"You? You and Alysia?"

Peter sat down again, obviously struggling for control. "What's the use? Everybody in this town who knows me knows what happened. Eventually you would have known, too. You might as well hear it from the source."

"Peter, Alysia didn't say anything about it." Suddenly the animosity she had seen between Darron and Peter made sense. Certainly Peter would resent the younger brother who had stolen his sweetheart, but that had happened years ago! Anna looked at the man before her, knowing at once that he was capable of such intense feeling and that he was also paying a price for his emotions.

"It doesn't matter," he said, calmer now. "It was a long time ago. Anyway, they won't have to be reminded of me much longer. I'm going to be leaving Tennessee."

Anna was stunned. "Peter, you love this place. It's as much a part of you as your own nose. You couldn't leave Tennessee."

He shook his head slowly. "You don't know anything about me, Anna. You think I've got some exotic, glamorous job. Did you know I am actually unemployed? The job I left was sweeping out bathrooms and cleaning windows. I assume I've already been replaced."

Anna did not know what to say. It must have happened recently, because Darron didn't seem to know his brother was no longer working. She remembered the phone call at Albert's garage. Could it have happened then?

"Oh, Peter, I knew you were going to get in trouble for taking time off to help me!"

"Anna, I was on my way to work yesterday with one thought on my mind. I was going to get free. I had my plan all figured out. I was going to give my notice yesterday, then serve my time, and get away from here. Quitting over the phone just moved the timetable up a bit, I guess. I should have left years ago. There's nothing for me here."

"But you might find someone else, Peter. Don't throw away everything you love because one relationship didn't work out. It's true I don't know you very well, but the sound of your voice when you talk about Tennessee is like love. And your land! I know it's important to you. Give yourself time."

"My mind's made up, Anna, but thanks for listening. Don't worry, I know this is the best way. I need to make a new start, and Darron and Alysia sure don't need me hanging around town, bumping into them on every corner. It's best for everybody."

"What will you do?" she asked.

Peter smiled. "I'll find something. Meanwhile, though, I would like to help you with your granny's house. You'll need someone to run you around the county, and Darron's a working man with three and a half mouths to feed."

"I'd love to have your company, Peter, and your help."

He stood up to leave, and Anna found herself feeling unsettled, wishing he would stay and somehow talk through the hurt she knew he must be enduring. But she had no control over him. Maybe, as Alysia had said, they could learn to be friends.

🦋

The next day, Saturday, Anna decided that she would not see Peter for a few days. She wanted to settle her own feelings, and she knew he would be uncomfortable with her after having shared such a rare confidence. She met Darron at the Huddlestone home for an initial review of the property, and she was pleased to see that he had brought not only his wife but also both of their children.

"Well, what do you think of the old place?" she asked Darron after a brief tour through the house.

"They sure don't build them like this anymore," he said. "I suppose by today's standards this wasn't a luxurious home. But look at the wood. Look at the way the doors and windows are set. It's as strong as iron."

Anna was as proud as if he had directed the compliment to her personally, for in an odd way, since she had found the place and decided to keep it, it was her home.

"Would you like to help me fix it up?" she asked.

Darron squinted up at the tin roof. "What are you going to do with the place once it's fit to live in?" he asked.

Anna shrugged. "I don't know. I might rent it or just keep it as a vacation home. Who knows? I might come back here someday when I'm too old to be a model anymore."

The words had a hollow ring in Anna's own ears. Even if she decided to stop modeling, there was the agency and Barry's offer waiting for her. Anyway, she was not exactly at the end of her career, though she had noticed many of the new models seemed like children to her. The truth was that she simply couldn't bear to see the old place empty and bare, remembering the home that it had once been. She wanted to give it life again.

Darron kicked at a loose board on the front porch. "How far do you want to go with this? Do you want to make it into a new house or just put it back the way it was?"

Anna hesitated, trying to focus the picture in her mind. "I just want it to be a home again," she said. "No one today would want to live here without plumbing and electricity, of course, but I wouldn't want to change everything. The place is sturdy, as you said. If the roof is sound, don't change it. If the windows keep out the cold, don't change them."

Darron nodded. "I always did want to do this kind of work, but I never figured I'd get the chance. I'm handy enough with a hammer, and I can find good people to do the plumbing and wiring, if you trust me. I can only give you Saturdays and evenings, though. I have to keep my job."

"Of course you do," Anna said. "Would you try to get some cost estimates for me pretty soon? If I could get some idea of how big the project is, in say a week or ten days, before I go back to New York, then I could make some plans. Pay yourself whatever is fair, Darron. I'm not rich, but I can just about do what I want right now, since there's only myself to think about, and this is important to me."

Over Alysia's picnic lunch, while the children climbed trees and raced in and out of the laurel thickets, Anna, Darron, and his wife worked out details. Anna would open a bank account for the project, and Darron was to draw a weekly salary from the account, pay all contractors, and get the necessary permits.

"Anna, why don't you and I come out this evening and clean the place up?" Alysia said. "It can be just us women, and we'll tie our hair up in rags and do some good old spring cleaning."

"Whoa, now!" Darron cautioned. "The place is just going to get dirty again once the electricians get started."

"Oh, I know," Alysia said, "but we could do the windows and get rid of the cobwebs."

"I'd like that," Anna said. "I don't mind doing some of the work twice if I can see good results right away. There's nothing like a little success to keep hope alive."

Darron took the children home with him, and Anna and Alysia headed toward the library to see if there were any historical records about the house or family.

"I can't get over how different Peter is from Darron," Anna commented. "Darron seems to be the most. . .well, I hardly know what to say without making it sound derogatory."

"Average? Normal?" Alysia prompted. "That's what he is, Anna, just the kindest, most self-sacrificing man in the world, and I love him to death. They aren't so different, though, really. See, they're like two Confederate soldiers who believed in the cause and were willing to die for it. One went off to the battle, that's Peter, and one stayed on the farm to grow food for the troops, that's Darron. Trouble with Peter is he keeps thinking that because he can't win the war and plant the corn, too, there's something wrong with him."

Alysia, who had gone to the same high school with Peter and Darron, told Anna that their father had died when the boys were in junior high school. The man had charged his sons to be faithful, to take care of their mother and sister, and to honor the family name.

"Peter thought that meant becoming rich and famous," said Alysia. "He had so much talent and potential, but he practically killed himself trying to be absolutely the best at everything. He was class valedictorian and football captain, held down an almost full-time job, and hated it all. Darron practically worships the ground Peter walks on, but his heart's just about broken because Peter won't ever forgive him for marrying me."

"Peter told me you two had been engaged," Anna said.

"He did? He never talks about it anymore. I thought his head would fly off the night I broke our engagement, but the day Darron told Peter he was going to marry me was worse. Peter never said a word. He packed up and headed for the woods and didn't come back for a week. Peter's special, all right, and real fine, but he's just not the man for me. I knew that years ago. I wanted a man like Darron who would just love me to pieces and be as dependable as the sunrise and not think about everything so much."

While Anna turned the car into the library parking lot, she was thinking of Alysia's words. She had had glimpses of the fiery Peter, and unlike Alysia, the image was exciting to her. If only she could find a man whose strength and determination would be directed toward the same goals as her own, she knew she would snatch him up in a minute.

🦋

Later that evening the two tore into the upstairs bedroom where Granny Huddlestone had given birth to Anna's grandmother, who had died before Anna was born, and where the old woman had quietly died in her sleep at the age of ninety-seven. In the room was a bed so large and heavy, her parents must have decided to leave it when going through her things after her death.

Anna dusted and polished the bed while Alysia washed the inside of the windows and swept down cobwebs. They cleaned the floor, and the smell of wet wood rose to Anna's nostrils.

"Oh, wouldn't this be pretty with some good hard wax rubbed into it?" Alysia said, touching the boards. "You weren't thinking about a carpet, were you?" she asked.

Anna shrugged. "To be honest, I haven't thought about much of anything. Sometimes I feel like I'm just riding a wave where this house is concerned. It seems to be pulling me along toward something. . .I don't know what."

"God is in charge of your life now," Alysia reminded her, "because you gave Him permission to take over. You might find a lot of your ideas will change." She picked up an oversized trash bag she had brought with her, and which Anna had assumed contained cleaning rags, though she wondered why Alysia would bring so many. Alysia removed the twist tie and withdrew a quilt made of blue and white cotton in a double wedding ring pattern. She spread it on the bare bed springs, and the room came alive.

"Alysia! It's beautiful. Where did you get it?"

"Made it. I make about one a year, and I've had lots of time to work since I got pregnant and haven't felt so good. Anyway, that's as good an excuse as any to waste time on foolishness." Though Anna's obvious pleasure embarrassed her slightly, she could not hide the pride in her work. "Anyway, you keep that," Alysia said, patting Anna's arm. "The place isn't a home without a quilt."

Impulsively Anna hugged her new friend. "Thank you, Alysia. I feel that all of you—Darron, Peter, and you—have given me so much, and I don't have anything to give back."

"No matter. We don't keep accounts on friends, and you musn't either. Come on, let's go home. I need to get things ready for church tomorrow. Would you like to come with us?"

"I would love to. I haven't been to church very much. I just started going with my friend in New York before I came here."

"Well, our church is little and plain, but we like the people. Darron likes it because it's country people, and he doesn't have to wear a tie."

Anna pulled into the driveway at Alysia's home. "I'll come and meet you in the morning," she said, "and we can ride together if you like."

Alysia waved from the porch, and Anna backed out, somewhat reluctant to return to the motor home but knowing it was only because of the closeness she had enjoyed today with Alysia.

❦

As Anna lay in the dark, the moon shining through the window, she wondered what God had planned for her. Alysia had said that her plans—her very life—might change. Did that mean she and Barry would become partners? Had God directed her to this new friend to help her make that decision? As she thought of Barry, however, she remembered the analogy Alysia had used to describe Peter and Darron. Barry, she knew, was neither the soldier nor the farmer. He was more like a Rhett Butler, turning every situation to his advantage, regardless of the cost in terms of relationships. Oh, he would never be cruel or even dishonest, but he would manage to avoid any association with the cause itself.

When she finally drifted off to sleep, it was Peter who stalked her dreams.

It was also Peter who, on Sunday morning, walked into the church and sat down in front of Anna, his hair freshly cut and his white shirt emphasizing his deepening tan. As Anna listened to him sing, she was more confused than ever. It had never occurred to her that Peter attended church anywhere. Darron and Alysia did not seem surprised, so it apparently was a normal occurrence.

When the fiery message, followed by a long altar call, was over, Peter turned and met Anna eye to eye but did not smile. He nodded curtly at her, then at Darron and Alysia, and left the church.

"Did you know he's going to move away?" Anna asked Darron.

Darron's lips tightened, and he seemed to droop like a flower in the sun. "I suppose he will someday. I just don't know what else to do."

"Darron, does Peter have convictions about following Christ the way you and Alysia do?"

"You'd have to ask Peter. It's been so long since we said more than hello and good-bye, I hardly know him anymore. In fact, he's told you things I thought he'd never tell anyone. You just might be good medicine for him."

Chapter 6

While Anna was trying to cut the tallest weeds in the yard with a grass whip that she had bought, Peter drove up. Anna saw him take ladders and a toolbox from the back of his truck and come toward the house. "Am I too late?" he called.

"I think we can still find something for you to do," she said, glad to see him but embarrassed to admit it, even to herself.

"I was surprised to see you in church yesterday," she said.

"I was surprised to see you, too, so I guess we're even," he answered. He set up a ladder to reach the top windows and began pulling away the old sealer and replacing it with soft, pliable glazing. "Are you going to try to make the old place energy efficient?"

"I told Darron I didn't want to change things too much. As long as the doors and windows keep out the weather, I would be happy to keep them."

Just then Peter glanced through the window and caught sight of the quilt on the bed. "Alysia gave you that, didn't she?"

"Yes. It's perfect for the room, and she does lovely work."

"I can't argue with that. She's a good wife to Darron, always has been."

Anna waited, saying nothing, but Peter did not continue, and so she returned to cutting weeds. After half an hour, she slumped on the porch, her nails broken and small blisters forming between her thumbs and forefingers.

Peter came down the ladder and sat beside her. "I suppose you don't do a lot of physical labor."

Anna smiled. "Well, whirling and twirling in front of a camera can be tiring, but I admit it's nothing like whacking weeds."

"Got to be done, though. Fact is, the copperheads have probably already nested around here somewhere. They love old deserted places where there's an old porch to get under and weeds to hide in."

Anna glared at him. "I don't scare easily, mister, and I'm not afraid of snakes." A sudden movement at her feet, however, caused her to gasp and jump up on the porch. When she saw the small twig in Peter's hand, she pummeled him soundly on the shoulders while he laughed and covered his head with his arms.

"You're just plain mean," she said, knowing that if she had not boasted, he would not have been tempted.

"True, true. I ought to be staked out on an anthill and have honey dripped on

413

my nose. I'm serious about the snakes, though. Be careful working around here. They love any old quiet spot like this away from the road."

"I've been thinking I might bring the motor home over here," Anna said. It would save miles on the rental car, but I hate to leave the hollow. It's so beautiful and peaceful there." Suddenly she remembered her discovery. "Peter, come and see what I found! I had forgotten all about this." She hurried to the back of the house and farther down the hill to a place where a rock ledge protruded from the ground. A thin trickle of water came from below it and traveled downward on a path devoid of soil.

"I'll bet this was your granny's water supply," he said.

Anna nodded. "I used to bring the dipper from the house and come here to get drinks because the water was so cold. There was a pool then. I think there's a creek down there where the springwater runs." She stooped down and let the cold water run on her hands, relieving the burning of the irritated flesh. When she stood up, she said, "I hate to say it, but I think I'm done for the day."

"Would you like to go exploring?" Peter asked. "I'd like to show you some more of the mountains before you head for the flatland. Let's go on a hike over on my land."

"That sounds great. I usually do a lot of walking and running, but since I left New York, my life is all turned around. I could use some good exercise."

Peter followed her car to the motor home where she put on jogging shoes, and together they started out along the road, which was little more than a two track. Gradually the track became a path, and within twenty minutes they were hiking up a steep grade on which a thin layer of soil hosted mosses, short spring vegetation, and an occasional white pine.

Anna was exhilarated by the exercise, especially when combined with the beauty of the landscape. She and Peter spoke only occasionally, when he pointed out a tiny flower or spectacular view. All the while she sensed they were moving up and up.

She took great deep breaths of the morning air, glad that she had resisted the temptation to begin smoking in order to stay thin. At this moment, however, her modeling career seemed faraway and almost unimportant. For the first time she realized with wonder and amazement that everything before her was the product of the creative mind of God, the God whom she could now say was her friend.

"You should be here in the fall," Peter said. "The hardwoods turn, and it looks like the mountains are on fire. The air is different, and the earth gives off an aroma. You can hardly walk by here without stepping on a squirrel." A few minutes later he said, "You really ought to be here in the winter when the tree cover is gone and you can see the way the land swells and rolls. Even when there's only light snow, the bareness and wildness of it all is like a sweet sadness. There's nothing like the mountains in winter."

For a change, Anna just listened. The unfamiliar terrain was demanding, and she needed to concentrate on her footing, but hearing him talk in such a relaxed way was refreshing. When he started to say, "You should be here in the middle of the summer. . . ," she couldn't help but laugh.

"Why don't you just say it's always beautiful here?"

Peter offered the crinkling grin that Anna had not seen since their first morning together. "I do love this place," he admitted.

"How can you think of leaving, Peter? You'd be so unhappy. You know you'd be longing for this sight with every change of the seasons."

"Well, we don't always get to have what we want. Anyway, this will be here if I want to come back."

They were approaching a summit where a tall pine pointed straight to the sun. When they got there, Peter leaned against it and said, "This is the middle of my property. I bought my first two acres when I was still in high school, and I've kept on adding to it every time something came available. It's one of the few things I've done right in my life."

Anna surveyed the timbered hills before her, over two hundred acres according to Peter. "Do you plan to build anything on it?"

"Under the right conditions I would put in a few homes, but it won't happen soon. There aren't any roads, and there aren't any plans for them, either. Besides, I don't have any investment capital. For now, I just like the idea that it's here."

Anna sat down, feeling the effects of the exercise and the thinning air.

"Have we come too far?" Peter asked. "I can carry you piggyback if you're too tired." He sat down beside her, his back against the tree.

"I just need a few minutes to catch my breath. I get a lot of exercise, but it's all on cement."

"You're strong. You weren't even winded when we got here, and it's a pretty rough climb."

"I have to stay in good shape. These last few days have been a lazy time for me."

"I figured all you had to do was stand around and look pretty. Tell me about your job."

Hearing her life's work referred to as a job rankled Anna, but she did not comment on it. "Modeling is very diversified. Most people are familiar with the real stars who get the big name-brand television commercial accounts, but there's a lot more to the industry than that. Usually those girls start working at fourteen or fifteen, some as young as twelve, and in five years they disappear. When their faces aren't new anymore, they're out of the business. I didn't begin that way. I went to a modeling school and started out small and worked into a good, steady career."

"But what do you do all day long?"

Anna hesitated then burst out laughing. "I stand around and look pretty! I have my picture taken all day long. Sometimes I do department store fashion shows or some other kind of live product demonstration. I work through an agency, and Barry Carlson is my agent. He's responsible for making sure that I have enough work to keep bread on the table. He screens the offers, and I make the final selection, now that I don't have to take just any job I can get."

"Do you just model clothes?"

"I've done makeup ads and posed with dishes and pots and pans. Like I said, any time you see a picture of someone in a magazine or on a billboard or a package, it's a paid model like me. I get lots of work because I'm versatile and I'm not temperamental."

"And you left it all to wander in the woods and think philosophical thoughts."

"Barry has asked me to go into partnership with him," she said. "I don't know if that's what I want. Then, on top of that, I'm seeing a whole new facet of life. . . a spiritual dimension. . .that I still don't understand. When my lawyer wrote to me about Granny's property, it seemed like a good time to take a vacation and sort out the pieces of my life."

"You didn't mention any man being one of those pieces."

"Well, there's Barry."

"But do you love him?"

"I don't know. Maybe I could."

Peter offered a small, derisive laugh. "If you have to get away from somebody to decide if you love him or not, it can't be too great. You're too smart and too determined to settle for less than exactly what you want, Anna. I don't know another woman in the world who would do what you've done. Don't sell yourself short. I don't know Barry, but if it were me—" He stopped talking abruptly and pulled a candy bar from his pocket and began to eat.

Anna stared at him. "What?"

He shrugged. "I guess I'm not the one to give advice about love." He stood up and pointed to the east. "We better head back. Looks like a shower's coming up on us."

As Anna stood up, she noticed something in the sky. "What is that bird, Peter? It looks like it's coming right toward us."

He moved behind her, looking over her shoulder. "It is. Watch a minute."

Larger and larger the bird loomed in their vision, the filtered sun glinting on waxy feathers and giving the creature the stark contrasts of renaissance art. Anna's heart beat faster, and she stood absolutely still as the bird, a golden eagle, pounded the air in its steady course. When she thought it would surely smash into them, it veered upward, spiraling into the sky until it was lost from her view.

"There's a nest just on that next ridge," Peter said. "I've been watching him for years. He doesn't like us on his turf. He knows we're too big to fight, but maybe not too big to scare."

"So beautiful," Anna murmured, "such color and grace. I will never forget this moment, and I promise I will never again go to a zoo as long as I live."

Peter laughed. "Just seeing one makes you feel like you can fly, too, doesn't it?"

"Yes, yes!" Anna exclaimed, turning to him. "I just felt I could reach up and follow him along to the sky."

"They have more character than bald eagles, in my opinion. It's a real gift to be able to see one. I've seen the adults maybe only ten times over the years I've had this property. I'm glad you got to see it. . .with me."

Anna was subdued. "I can't explain the feeling of watching that bird, Peter. It has a special meaning for me. Just one more thing to think about, I guess."

Going down was nearly as difficult as going up, and Anna could feel the breeze stiffen and cool from minute to minute. Within fifteen minutes, the sky had darkened and in ten more, the first drops of rain fell.

"We'll take a little detour here and find some shelter," Peter said. "Sometimes these little cloudbursts bring lightning, too."

Anna's heart quickened. At the first peal of thunder, she felt a rising panic. She did not like storms. Peter seemed to think she was some sort of superwoman, but she knew her own secrets. In small things, like snakes and thunder, she was often afraid. Perhaps it was one reason she had chosen city living.

Soon Anna could hear the thunder rolling peal upon peal in the distance. On the horizon, the lightning flashed. She wanted to ask Peter to hurry, but he seemed rather unconcerned. *Maybe he's used to being out in the woods in the rain,* Anna thought, *but I'm not.*

"Peter, I think. . .I'd like. . ."

"This way," he said, and they left the game trail they had been following, crept through some laurel, and entered a small cave. Immediately the thunder was outside instead of all around, and Anna felt safe.

The serious rain began then, smacking the laurel leaves and running together down the slopes. The storm came hard and fast and the wind blew, but the cave opening was protected. Peter and Anna sat side by side, their knees drawn up to their chins, backs to the cave's interior wall, and catching glimpses of the lightning through the laurel bushes.

Peter did not ask Anna if she was afraid. He could feel that she was now relaxed, and if she was not enjoying being here, at least she was content to wait. He was disturbed by an overwhelming desire to draw her close, to tell her she was safe and that he would always protect her and help her through this kind of unsettling time in her life. But how could he, knowing himself as he did? He had nothing to offer her, despite his obvious boastful show of property. She did not need land or money. She needed a man, as he had said to her, who would be there for her when she needed him.

He thought back over the past few days and wondered when he had first begun to sense that he cared deeply for her. Was it seeing her in need or seeing her in control? Was it the fragrance of her hair in the heat of the sun as she cried against his chest? Was it the sincerity in her voice as she spoke of her relationship with God? Was it simply that she loved everyone she met? Or was it only this moment, sharing the wonder of the earth with her as the wind brought the aroma of rain and leaves to them? All he knew for sure was that he dared not look at her.

"You're very quiet," Anna said.

"When I don't have anything to say, I don't talk."

"I think that may not be entirely true. I think you have a lot to say that you've never said. Maybe nobody listens?" she asked, turning toward him.

"Maybe," he mumbled, resisting the urge to meet her eyes. He willed her to keep talking, to somehow say for him what he could not say himself, to discover his secrets without having to form the words in his own mouth. But she was quiet; the storm was over.

They left the cave and were greeted with showers from the laurel leaves as they passed through them. By the time they reached the hollow, they were thoroughly drenched.

"We might as well have walked in the rain," Anna said, wringing water from her sweatshirt. "Would you mind building a fire for me before you go? I don't have any heat in this vehicle." She was beginning to shiver. The sun had not returned, and she dreaded the prospect of a gray, cold afternoon.

"You grab some dry clothes," Peter said, "and come with me. We'll dry off at my place and get something to eat."

Anna was too uncomfortable to argue. She shoved a change of clothes into a plastic bag and climbed into Peter's truck. In minutes, they were pulling up to a log home, set in a small clearing. There was no lawn, only young trees planted around the house, apparently to replace those lost during construction.

"Peter, is this your house? It's lovely!"

"And I've got hot water."

"Hot water? I never realized how much I could miss it! I've got a shower in the motor home, but not enough fuel for the water heater."

Anna stayed in the shower so long that steam began to pour from under the bathroom door. Peter built a fire in the fireplace, and after Anna was dressed, she sat cross-legged on the floor in front of the fire, engulfed by the big cowl-necked sweater he had seen on her the other day.

Anna was pleasantly surprised by the interior of the cabin. She had half expected to see traps and flintlock rifles hanging on the walls, but the place was outfitted with strong, masculine furniture in good fabrics that were not too heavy for the room. There were no curtains, but the windows were made of double insulated glass, and there were louvered shutters that could be closed against the sun. A collection of portraits was grouped on the wall above the sofa, and a few knick-knacks, mostly small wooden carvings, softened the stark log walls.

Peter, now in a sweat suit and wool socks, put one more log on the fire then sat down beside Anna.

"Is that your family?" she asked, pointing to the portraits.

"Uh-huh. That's Mamma, her name's Audrey, that's my sister Rose, and Darron and Alysia, you know. Some other odds and ends of relatives."

She smiled. "I like your house."

"That makes two of us."

"Will you rent it out when you leave?"

Peter almost said, "Leave where?" then remembered that he had made the commitment. He shrugged. "I don't know. I guess I hadn't thought that far ahead. I don't think I'd like to have anybody else living here."

Anna spied a rocker, obviously of some age, with a quilt draped over the back. She got up and went toward it, then paused. "Is it all right if I sit in this chair, or is it just for looks?"

Peter smiled. "One thing I don't have is stuff that's just for looks. That's one of Alysia's quilts, by the way. The rocker was my granny's. Mamma gave it to me when I built the place."

Anna settled into the chair, pulling it closer to the fire and wrapping the quilt around her shoulders. She thought of Barry's expensive apartment, its white wool carpet immaculate, the windows offering a view of the city, the kitchen that was never used, the custom-made sofa. It was gorgeous and tasteful, but Anna knew you could never go there in wet boots. Of course, in her other life, wet boots were not a problem.

Gazing at the fire, she thought of a conversation she had had with Barry when she had been looking for a new apartment and suggested she might like a fireplace.

"A fireplace?" he had said, looking at her as though she were from outer space. "I'd have to redo the whole place if it had a fireplace in it. Besides, they're dirty. There's one at the club, and somebody's always running through with an ash can. You're such an impossible romantic sometimes. Be practical."

It was good advice, Anna knew, but sometimes hard to take. She had to make a conscious effort to remain independent. It was easy for her to give herself to others, even to Barry. She only hoped that when the right time came, she would be able to put aside her deliberate separateness and form the kind of working relationship she imagined love could build.

❦

"Anna? Anna?" Peter was gently shaking her shoulder. Her head was at an odd angle, her neck stiff. "You better wake up. You'll break your neck sleeping in that chair."

Anna willed herself awake. "It must have been the fire." Her voice sounded faraway. "How long have I been asleep?"

"About an hour. I hated to wake you, but I was afraid you'd suffer if you stayed in that position too long."

She rubbed her neck. "I think I already have, but it was worth it." She walked to the window and looked outside to see a steady drizzle blanketing the late afternoon sun. "What a day!" she said.

"I like a day like this once in a while," Peter said. "It puts things in perspective. And it's a good day to bake cookies." In the kitchen, separated from the living area only by a breakfast bar, he was pulling a sheet of chocolate chip cookies from the oven.

"I thought I smelled them," Anna said, joining him at the kitchen table for hot coffee and warm cookies, "but I thought it must be part of a dream."

"Ah, wait until you see what we're having for supper."

"What's it called?"

"Bologna *cordon bleu*."

After sandwiches and what Anna felt were far too many cookies, Peter made popcorn in a wire basket over the fire. Together they looked through a photo album filled with snapshots of mountain scenes, his friends, and his family. When Anna glanced at the window again, she saw stars shining in a clear sky.

"I'd better go, Peter," she said reluctantly.

"Why?"

"I. . .I don't know. Just because that's what one is supposed to say, I guess. Shouldn't I go?"

"Back to your old, dark, cold place?" His closeness to her as they shared the photo album was even more intense than in the cave. Could she possibly not know how much he wanted her?

Abruptly Anna closed the album and stood up. "Peter, take me back, please. I. . .I wouldn't want to do anything tonight that I might be sorry for tomorrow. I have so many decisions to make these next few days." She felt she was beginning to babble but couldn't stop herself. "I can't let the circumstances of the day keep me from thinking clearly. And there's work to do, and we hardly know each other. It's nothing you've done, but I have this idea about marriage, and I can't stay here, Peter, please."

On all the nights and afternoons and mornings when Barry had suggested she go to bed with him, she had never behaved so immaturely. She had always been ready with a witty remark and a clever dodge. Was it because those times had held no temptations for her?

Peter only said, "Well, have you got plenty of blankets? It will be cold tonight."

Anna nodded while she picked up her bag of wet clothing.

Peter took it from her hand. "I'll hang these out on the line for you. You can get them the next time you come over."

"Thank you," she whispered, for the kindness, and for the understanding shown by his open-ended invitation.

Peter drove her to the hollow and opened the motor home's door and looked inside before standing away and allowing her to enter. "I'll see you in the morning," he said, not waiting for an invitation this time.

Anna nodded. "I have an idea, Peter," she said. "I'm so pleased with the change that came over Granny's room when Alysia's quilt was laid out. I want to find some nice things to go in the house. . .a few pieces of furniture and some wall hangings. . .just so that, when I get ready to leave, it won't seem like I'm leaving behind an empty shell."

"Anna, is that sensible? If you leave the place unoccupied, it would be an invitation to vandals and thieves."

"No, it's ridiculous. It's the most foolish thing I've ever done in my life, but I want to do it anyway. While Alysia and I were at the library, I saw pictures of old houses like Granny's. . .like mine. Alysia said there are lots of antiques around here and that we might be able to find some things that would look right in the house without making too large of an investment."

"If that's what you want. Has Darron said anything to you yet about the contract work?"

"I'll see him tomorrow before he goes to work. I'm going to take Alysia shopping with me after the children leave for school."

"I'll find you there," Peter said.

"Don't tell me you like shopping," Anna said skeptically.

Peter wondered if he dared say he would do anything in order to spend time with her. No, she was not ready for it, and he knew in spite of his longing he could not make a commitment to her. He said good night and drove away, scolding himself for asking her to give more to him than he had a right to have and in despair because he knew he could never rightfully claim her as his own. Yet like a drugged man, he could not say no to spending time with her, talking to her, just looking at her.

❦

Alone in his own house, he wondered if Anna were as lonely as he was. The moonlight through the window in his bedroom fell like a beacon on the closet door, and in an impulsive moment, Peter threw the door wide open, dragged out a dusty leather case, and opened it. There might yet be a way to keep a part of her for himself.

Chapter 7

"Peter is coming here?" Darron asked as Anna joined him at his tiny kitchen table for coffee.

"That's what he said," replied Anna.

"Miracles still happen," he said as he got up and pulled on his cap. He picked up a large lunch box, and Anna tried not to invade their privacy as he and Alysia said good-bye at the door.

"This thing between you and Darron and Peter. . .just how bad is it?" Anna asked Alysia. "Or maybe it's none of my business."

Alysia looked uncomfortable. "I don't think it matters much, but I can't really explain it all, either. Darron and I knew that Peter would be mad when we started dating and then got married, but we thought he'd get over it, especially after we had little Wilford and then Emily. But it's like he avoids us more and more as the years go by. Darron has quit trying to mend the fence because it just seems to drive Peter further away. Darron loves him to pieces. It just breaks his heart that Peter won't visit."

"Well, all I know is he said he'd be here. Oh, there's his truck. Do you suppose he was just waiting for Darron to leave?"

"I wouldn't be surprised, though he barely speaks to me." She smiled broadly, a twinkle in her eye. "I just think he's crazy about you, Anna Giles, and he's going to do whatever he has to do to be with you. What about you? Do you like him?"

"Oh, Alysia, don't be silly. He's been wonderful to me, but I certainly didn't come here looking for romance."

"Nobody has to look for romance. It's everywhere. You've just got to reach out and grab it when it flits by." She went to the door to greet Peter and offer him breakfast.

❧

The three took Anna's car; Alysia insisted on sitting in the back. On the front seat between Anna and Peter lay a list of yard sales, flea markets, and gallery addresses.

"This is going to be a shopping spree to be remembered for years to come," Anna said, laughing. "The boost in Tennessee's economy this week will make headlines."

Alysia tapped Peter's shoulder. "What did you put in the trunk?" she asked.

"Camera equipment," he said curtly.

422

In the rearview mirror, Anna saw Alysia's startled expression. "Alysia? Are you all right?"

Alysia nodded, glanced quickly at Peter, then at Anna, but said nothing.

As the two women darted in and out of shops, turned over needlework pieces, and examined pottery and carved wood, Peter followed along like a puppy. Around his neck hung a camera that Anna knew was expensive and versatile. From time to time she watched him change lenses and filters and knew that he was at least a very good amateur, and probably more. Alysia was too caught up in the shopping to be aware of Peter's constant photographing of them and the scenes about them, but Anna knew. She also knew Peter did not want her to pose, and so she ignored him.

Anna found some furniture she liked and made arrangements to pick it up later with Peter's truck.

"I told you I'd come in handy," he said as they ate hot dogs at a roadside park.

"My mother used to say if you can't be decorative, be useful," Anna said.

"Oh, Anna, you're beautiful," Alysia said. "Isn't she, Peter?"

Peter smiled and took a big bite of his hot dog.

"Darron says the electrical contractor is going to start on the house early next week. Somebody's coming to dig a well the day after tomorrow, and then the plumbers will start. Darron thinks the old pantry off the kitchen will make a good bathroom, and that will save tearing up too much of the house."

The easy camaraderie of the group made Anna wonder what all the fuss had been about. This was a normal way for friends and family to behave. Alysia must be overreacting to Peter's moods, she reasoned. However, when they were alone in the ladies' room at a rest stop, Alysia said, "I've been dying to tell you! This is the first time Peter has had his camera out in the open for at least five years! I'm telling you, Anna, there's something going on here. You've changed him."

"Why would he not take pictures? He seems to be quite good at it."

"You will have to ask him that," Alysia said firmly. "I've probably blabbed too much already."

When Anna had finally made all the purchases for the house that she could possibly justify, plus a few things to take to friends in New York, they called it a day and drove back to Alysia's house. Anna received the biggest hug Alysia's expanding abdomen would allow, and Peter took his equipment and headed for his truck.

"When do we get to see the prints?" Anna asked.

"Maybe never," Peter said. "Mostly I shoot for my own enjoyment."

"A true artist," Anna said.

"You think photography is an art?"

"Of course!" she answered. "A good photographer is just as creative as a painter or sculptor. I've had photos done that, when I saw the finished product,

I could hardly believe it was me. A photographer can alter a whole situation by changing the angle of the shot a few degrees or by using a different light. I don't know how they do it, but I do appreciate it."

Anna saw the dust still clinging to the camera bag. "Alysia said you haven't done any photography for a long time. Why not?"

"Maybe there was nothing worth photographing. . .until today. Listen, it's early. Come to my place and have supper with me, or at least let me take you out."

"I need to go back to the motor home and deposit some of my treasure. Follow me, and we'll decide when we get there."

When Anna approached the hollow, she was startled to see another car there—one she recognized. It was Barry's white Ferrari. A hilarious image of the low-riding sports car, bumping along over the rough track, filled her mind. Barry would be fuming.

"I can't imagine how. . ." She got out of the car and went toward the motor home. Suddenly the door burst open, and Barry bounded to the ground in front of her.

"Darling, where have you been? I've been waiting here for hours, bored to death. How can you stand it?" He grabbed her and kissed her.

Peter watched from his truck, knowing at once that the man embracing Anna was Barry Carlson. He did, then, love her enough to follow her, and he would ask her to return to a life Peter could never be part of. Instead of shutting off the engine, Peter hit the accelerator and drove back the way he had come.

"Who's that?" Barry demanded.

"Peter McCulley. This is his land. He helped me when I first arrived and—"

"Great spot for a chalet, if the road were improved," Barry said, looking around. "Some trees would have to go, of course."

"Barry, how did you find me?"

"An odd set of coincidences, Anna. I stopped at that Sugarlands place to ask for directions to Memphis, and when they learned I was from New York, they said another New Yorker was staying in the neighborhood in a motor home. I knew it had to be you, especially when the guy said she had great legs."

"But how did you find your way here?" Anna tried to hide her disappointment at the fact that Barry had not actually been looking for her but had only been passing through town and bumped into her accidentally.

"Well, this guy said the New Yorker had been seen with a former employee and thought that you might be camped here on his property, so I gave it a shot. Just my luck! One chance in a thousand, and I come through. I tell you, I am truly amazing."

They went into the motor home, sat down, and Anna showed Barry some things she had bought during the day. "They're for the house, Barry. I found it. I found my granny's house. Would you like to see it?"

Barry waved the idea away with a slim hand. "Not especially. Are you going to sell?"

"I don't plan to. I just want to keep the place. It holds so many memories."

"Well, that's ridiculous. You know it isn't practical. It will degenerate in no time at all, sitting empty. . .or will you turn it into income property?"

Anna thought of Peter and remembered him saying he couldn't imagine anyone else living in his house. Who could live in Granny Huddlestone's home and do it justice?

"I don't have all the details worked out yet, but it will happen. How long can you stay? I've missed you."

"I was hoping to hear you say that," he said, "but I was also hoping to hear you say you'd be coming back to the big town. The question is, how long do you plan to stay here? I've got people clamoring for you, Anna. You're very popular in the district, you know."

"They'll be there when I get back. I need a little more time, Barry."

He sighed. "Time, Anna, time is what we have so little of. We don't get younger, now, do we, any of us. Have you decided on the partnership offer?"

Anna hesitated. "Barry, tell me exactly what you have in mind."

"A full partnership, dear, fifty-fifty, and you don't have to invest a cent."

"Why not?"

"Just think of it as a gift."

Anna watched his face, looking for some show of emotion. She had hoped for some indication that he had been considering marriage, that he would share the business with her as his wife.

"Do you love me, Barry?"

"Anna, of course I do!" he said, holding his arms wide. "I've always loved you. I've told you that hundreds of times."

"I mean, do you really love me? What if I couldn't work anymore, or if I weren't a model at all. What if I were a little shop girl with fat ankles? Would you love me?"

"Oh, don't be stupid. You are what you are, and I am what I am. This offer won't wait forever, Anna. I've tried to be gracious and understanding, but Phil Curtis is after me to get in, too. He's offered me a million five for what I'm offering you for free, Anna—free! I don't often give things away, you know. Give me an answer, and then I can get on with the paperwork."

"I. . .I just don't know." How could she make him understand she wanted more than a business partnership?

Barry babbled on. "Well, you've got to stop prowling around in the woods like some demented scout leader, ruining your skin with insect bites and too much sun. I saw Larry Tulloch the other day, and he said to get you back into town immediately, even begged me to tell him where you'd gone so he could come and see you personally. He has a marvelous contract waiting for you that involves the Bahamas in January. And Albert Haines was hanging over the bar at Sherry's party last night. He thinks he can get you into daytime television."

"I don't want to do television," Anna said flatly.

"You don't say no to Albert, dear. You can have the job on a plate. . .or you could have had it if you had been there last night. Opportunity is a temporary thing, love."

She nodded. "I agree." She felt cheated. Seeing Barry's car had given her so much hope. The experience was turning out to be something like buying a box of cereal to get the prize and finding it to be much smaller than the one pictured on the box.

"I'm exhausted, Anna. Why don't we go into town, have dinner, and find a room at one of those lovely hotels we tourists like so much?"

"I thought you were on your way to Memphis."

"Oh, Memphis, that can wait," he said, moving closer to her. "I have to get this buying trip out of the way as soon as possible. Can you believe I left Sherry's party half drunk and drove to Charlotte to make an appointment at a mill this morning?" He laughed uproariously. "Life is outrageous sometimes. Then I decided as long as I was on the road, I'd go over to Memphis and see Arlen, you know, the guy who does those shirts with the painted designs? We handled that spread for some magazine, I forget which. And here I am. Are we going out?"

"You didn't really come to see me, did you?"

"I'm here, aren't I? Don't pout; it's so teenage. Anna, isn't there anything to drink in this place? I've got to have something."

"Orange juice, bottled."

A look of disgust covered his face. "Here you are in the place where they make some of the finest whiskey in the world, and all you have is orange juice. Come on, come on," he begged. "Let's get out of here. I'm becoming claustrophobic."

"I think you'd better go ahead without me," Anna said. "If you have other offers on the partnership, then I think you should accept them. You accused me of being impractical, Barry, but you can't refuse a cash offer for half of the agency. I'll be happy to continue working for you, though."

Barry was growing impatient, something that didn't take long to happen. "I won't take no for an answer, Anna. You must come in with me." He pulled an envelope from his pocket and unfolded the paper inside. "Here's the contract. I had my attorney draw it up, but you had already left town by the time he delivered it to me. Just sign, and stop playing hard to get."

"What's the hurry?" Anna asked, irritated. "There's something you aren't telling me, Barry." She took the contract from his hand and began reading.

He rolled his eyes and sighed, "It's you, Anna. The reason I want you in the partnership is that with you comes a host of people who like you. Let's face it. Phil

Curtis has cash but nothing else. Everyone in New York. . .well, maybe not everyone. . .loves you. You'd bring a hundred times as much business my way as Curtis would. I could expand. We could expand, I mean. We could run the biggest agency in New York. No one could touch us."

"That is a monstrous exaggeration," Anna said. "I know I'm popular, but certainly not that popular." As she scanned the paper, she caught sight of the phrase "credible individual." She read a bit farther, then let the paper fall into her lap.

"Well, as usual, you've told half the truth. Why didn't you just tell me you needed someone with good credit to underwrite your debts, Barry? You've mortgaged the agency practically out of existence, haven't you? What's the matter? Wouldn't Phil Curtis settle for anything less than buying you out? Where are all your rich friends?" she asked, her voice rising. "Are you so near the edge that you have to come to me, nothing more than a working model, to bail you out?"

Barry jumped up. "You're missing out on something big, Anna. And remember, if you don't sign, it will be very tough for you once you get back to town. You think you can get by on your personality? Well, personality doesn't print. You're at the worst possible age for a model, dear, too old to do the glamour features and too young to pose for false teeth cleaners and vitamin supplements. The years ahead are going to be lean, and I can make them leaner than you imagine. Or you can go into business with me, and we'll both get along just fine."

"This is all I've ever been to you, isn't it Barry? I'm your safety net. You knew it the day you signed me up. I am New York's biggest fool. . .next to you."

Barry reached out to slap her, and she lunged against him, afraid, furious, and humiliated.

"I'm sick of your games, Anna," Barry said, grabbing her shoulders. "I haven't made this awful trip for nothing. I'll get some satisfaction, one way or another." He pushed her down, and she was amazed at how strong he was. She could not push him away, and the touch of his mustache against her cheek as he pulled her to him felt like wire.

🦋

Peter drove furiously along the dirt road, unsure whether to go home or just keep driving, out of Gatlinburg, out of Tennessee. This would be as good a time as any to leave. He had his camera with him, and trapped inside, the most beautiful day he could remember in many years.

If only I could tell her everything. He knew she would understand him and be conciliatory, but he also knew that it would change nothing. It was not her acceptance he wanted. That would only make the leaving harder.

The sight of her in Barry's arms had been like a bullet to his brain. Was he destined to spend all his life loving people who were beyond his reach? He braked to a halt, laid his head on the steering wheel, and fought the despair that rose in him like a sickness. *I have to try. I have to try just once more.* In a rush he wheeled the truck around and drove like a madman toward the hollow.

❧

"Barry, don't do this," Anna begged. "We've been friends for so long."

"You know you've led me on for years," he growled. "I won't take it anymore. You and your cleverness, always just out of reach. It could have been different between us, but you had to have your own way." He slapped her, and her scream pierced the thin walls of the motor home as Peter came walking up.

The movement of the vehicle told him she was struggling, and he bolted for the door. In a lightning-fast movement, he jumped inside, tore Barry away from Anna, and tossed him headlong out the door, then jumped outside himself.

"Stay there!" he ordered Anna, who now cowered on the sofa.

"Keep her!" Barry shouted as he pulled at his shirt and walked toward his car. "Where I come from, there's one like her on every corner."

The words were like a bomb in Peter's brain. He shot forward and wrenched Barry away from the car door, taking grim pleasure in the look of terror that crossed the perfectly shaven and moisturized face. Grabbing Barry by his designer tie, Peter punched him soundly in the nose and felt the satisfying gush of blood on his knuckles. Still holding the tie as Barry howled, he pulled out his bandanna-style handkerchief and shoved it in Barry's collar.

"Wipe your nose," he said, and opened the car door and pushed Barry inside.

Barry spewed profanity as he pulled away, but Peter wasn't listening. He went inside where Anna was wiping her eyes and holding the contract in her lap.

"Are you all right?"

She nodded. "I thought we were at least friends. He never wanted anything from me except what was of personal benefit to him." The sadness in her voice was so profound that Peter found tears in his own eyes. "I don't know what to do," she said, looking at Peter. "If you hadn't come. . .why did you come back?"

"I don't know exactly. Something in me just said, 'Go back and try to take her away from him.' I love you, Anna. I love you with all of me that there is, which isn't much, but I would do anything for you." Quietly Peter encircled her with his arms and let her rest there as she tried to make peace with the fact that the most significant relationship in her life was over, and that a man she had known for only a few days was declaring his love for her.

"Take me somewhere," Anna said at last, "anywhere, just away from the motor home. I want to open the doors and windows and let the place air out. I don't even know if I can sleep here tonight. Barry has just ruined everything."

"He's definitely a spoiler," Peter said, "but I did a little damage myself. He's not quite as pretty as he was when he came here."

Anna smiled in spite of her heavy heart. "You're better than a dose of medicine," she said.

"And easier to take. Come on out when you get changed, and we'll go out to eat."

In fresh clothing and with a hot meal inside her, Anna once again felt that she could carry on with her life, though the terror of Barry's attack continued to haunt her. The physical threat was less offensive to her than the betrayal, yet she chided herself for believing for so long that he could treat her differently than he treated everyone else. What was it her granny used to say? "The fruit doesn't fall far from the tree."

As they left the restaurant, Peter said, "Do you feel like going to a place I like, here in town? It's kind of quiet and different."

Anna nodded, wanting only to be cared for.

"It's sort of a tourist trap," Peter said as they parked in the lot of a place called Biblical Gardens, "but there's a part of it I like." They bypassed the tour of wax figurines illustrating scenes from scripture and went into a courtyard where pools and vegetation softened the patio area. Peter took Anna's hand and guided her to a small bench. The place was empty except for the two of them.

"I know you were surprised to see me in church, Anna, and I'm not sure exactly why I haven't been able to share with you my true feelings about my faith. I suppose it's pride. That is a problem for me sometimes."

"Only sometimes?"

He smiled at her, knowing she understood his hesitancy. He pointed across the courtyard toward a statue representing Jesus, placed against the far wall. "Look at that for a minute," he said. Then he got up, and taking Anna with him, they walked to another corner of the courtyard. When she looked at the statue, she saw that the gaze of the figure seemed to have followed them.

"It doesn't matter where you go," said Peter, "the statue is always looking at you. When I was little, we lived in a neighborhood just about like the one Darron and Alysia live in now. I used to run to the woods whenever I could, though. We went to church every Sunday, and I liked going. One day I got down on my knees beside the creek, and I promised God He could do whatever He wanted with me, and that I would always try to live by His rules. I said I believed what the preacher had said about Jesus dying for my sins. I was glad for that, I told God and said thanks a lot. I was looking forward to seeing Him in heaven someday. I think I was eight or nine then. First thing you know, my daddy died. Mamma said it wasn't God punishing us, that everybody dies and we weren't being singled out, but it was hard for me."

Anna listened, sensing how hard it was for Peter to speak. All the while his eyes met the eyes of the statue.

"I lived clean and right, Anna, all through high school and college, but I never felt like it was a two-way street. God didn't seem to be doing anything in return. I didn't understand. I knew I was forgiven and accepted, but where was He? After a few years, it just seemed like what had been so important when I was a kid wasn't that important anymore.

"Then one day I came here and found this place. I saw that statue and I thought, *'He's watching, there's no doubt about that. He always has been. The question is, is that a good thing or a bad thing? Is He pleased or not? He sees it all, but does it make Him happy? I don't know.'*

"When I heard you talk about your decision, I just wanted to feel that close and personal to God again. I think sometimes one reason I keep close to the creek banks is because I want to find that feeling that's gotten lost over the years."

"How lonely you must be," Anna whispered. "You don't think of that gaze as being a look of love and concern and approval?"

"It could be," Peter said. "I hope it is. I keep trying. But I keep thinking that maybe behind the look He's saying, 'Yes, Peter McCulley, don't think you've got Me fooled. I'm watching you. I know what you really are.' "

"And what is that, Peter? What are you?"

He shrugged. "I'm a not-so-young-anymore man with no visible means of support."

"That's not what I see." Anna waited until he was looking directly into her eyes, then said, "I see a man with character and principles. . .and pride. . .who is loved by many people, as well as by God."

"Do you love me, Anna?"

Now it was Anna who looked away, wanting to say yes and perhaps heal his pain but knowing that she could not say it with certainty.

Peter said simply, "Let's go," and in silence they walked back to the truck.

As they drove, Anna's mind raced over the events of the past few days, retracing her emotions as she thought of Peter's sudden involvement in her life. *Do I love him?* she asked herself. *Do I even know what love is?* She knew she needed time to put Barry completely out of her mind before she could begin to think of Peter as anything except a good friend.

Peter interrupted her thoughts. "If you don't want to go back to the motor home tonight, you could go to Darron and Alysia's or come to my place."

"Darron and Alysia hardly have room for their own family. I don't want to inconvenience them. Where are they ever going to put a baby?"

Peter shook his head. "Hang it on a hook, I guess. Darron just doesn't have the cash to get into a bigger place right now, though I know they've been saving. Don't worry. One thing you have to say for Darron and Alysia is that they make do with what they have."

"There's a lot that can be said for those two," Anna said. "Peter, there's more between you and Darron than his marriage to Alysia, isn't there? Alysia told me she realized shortly after her engagement to you that you were not right for each other. Surely you would have known it, too. You wouldn't have wanted her to be unhappy. What is it? What keeps you from enjoying the companionship of your own brother when he obviously worships you?"

"Worships me?" Peter questioned. "Maybe when we were kids, but that was a long time ago."

"Has he done something to you or taken something away from you? Why can't you be the brother to him he wants you to be?"

"I'll tell you why, Anna," Peter said. "It's because I am so jealous of him, I can hardly stand it, and it has nothing to do with Alysia. What I want is not her, but what they have together. Have you watched them? Have you heard the way they talk to each other? There's no place they would rather be than together. That little apartment's a sanctuary to them. They're so happy, and I would give anything, anything I have or ever will have, to find that kind of happiness."

Quietly Anna said, "And do you think I'm the one who will make you that happy? Is it a matter of finding the right person, or is there some other ingredient in their magic formula? I want to know, Peter, because I want the same thing."

"I know how I feel," Peter replied, "and right now, that's all I know."

"My parents had enough money to live as they wished, and they loved each other, but I think there was a restlessness about them. For years I've said I wouldn't settle for anything less than the kind of marriage that Granny Huddlestone used to talk about, and I was waiting for something. . .fate, I suppose, to make it happen. But now I wonder."

By the time they had reached the hollow, Anna had made up her mind to stay alone, despite Peter's protests.

"Don't worry," she said. "Barry is much more interested in making money than in hassling me. He's halfway to Memphis by now. Do you still have time to pick up the furniture?"

"I'll do it first thing in the morning," Peter said.

"Thank you. I'll meet you over at Granny's."

"I'll be there," he said.

"You always are," she answered.

Chapter 8

Anna was up early, and after a breakfast beverage and a swim in the freezing creek water, she drove to the house. The trunk of the car was already loaded with cleaning supplies, and Anna felt a sense of anticipation as she thought of the items she would place in the various rooms of the house.

She arrived at the house, and when Peter got there, she was beating the dust out of the cushions of a sofa and chair that were older than she was, but dry and still in good condition.

Anna waved as he came down the hill from the road. Her hair was tied back with a cheap scarf, but she wore a rose pink linen peasant blouse with an ankle-length batik print skirt. On her feet were sandals. Somehow the image of housemaid did not imprint on Peter's mind.

"Are you ready for your furniture?" he asked, pointing to the back of his truck.

"Oh, you have it already! I think I'm just about through with the cleaning. Frankly I'm not much good at it. Come to think of it, I've never kept house. I've lived in apartments and usually hired people to do the little that needed to be done. As a matter of fact, I guess I've never really lived in a home much. I suppose they get pretty dirty when you actually do all your cooking and eating and laundry and everything right there."

Peter laughed. "They do, and if you throw in a couple of kids, the dirt piles up like everything else."

"Come and see what I've done," Anna said, pulling Peter along with her into the house. She showed Peter the dishes she had found, now clean and displayed artfully on a sideboard in the kitchen. The shelves were simple oak slabs, smoothed with years of use and cleaning. In another room was a chest and inside it were half a dozen tablecloths and some crocheted doilies and lace curtains. Here and there were other remnants of her great-grandmother's life—a cotton dress hung on a hook in the bedroom where there were no closets; a metal washbasin on the porch used for rinsing bare feet covered with garden dust; an ax embedded in a stump overgrown with weeds.

"I wonder what my parents did with her personal things," Anna said as she and Peter walked through the house. "There must have been papers, photographs, things like that."

"Maybe that lawyer fella knows," Peter said. "If he's got the deed to this place, chances are he knows about the rest of the stuff."

"It hurts to know that my family is gone, Peter. We should have spent more time together. My parents should have saved Granny's things for me, or at least let me see them after she died. It's my fault, too. I was busy with my career and didn't stay as close to my parents as I should have."

"Anna, there's no good in blaming yourself. You did what you could. You did the right thing by coming back here and finding this place. You'll have another family someday, and you can share this with them." He took her hands in his and pulled her outside. "Look, I want to show you the pictures I took yesterday."

They scrambled up the hill, and Peter spread out about two dozen color snapshots of Anna and Alysia on their shopping spree. Anna laughed at the expressions of delight that Peter had captured, at the weary shoppers with bedraggled hair eating hot dogs in the park, and at the trunk of the car filled to overflowing with household items.

"Let's start taking things inside," Anna said. "I don't want to clean anymore. As long as the spiders are chased away and we aren't leaving footprints in the dirt on the floor, I'm ready to start playing house."

They lugged in wooden footstools, table lamps, kitchen chairs, and a table from Peter's truck, then started on the boxes of decorative things in the trunk of Anna's car. She scurried about the rooms, placing wooden carvings on an old corner shelf, a brass vase on a window ledge, an antique oval picture frame with bubble glass on a living room wall where a nail had been waiting, empty, for more than a dozen years.

"Maybe you'll find a photo of your granny, and you can put it in that frame," Peter said.

"Maybe. I wonder if there is a photo of her somewhere."

As they made one more trip to the road, Peter said, "Maybe you could use this other one, if you like it."

He opened the door of the pickup and took out an envelope. Inside was a black-and-white print of Anna sitting in a rocker, her hands together at her chin. She remembered sitting in the chair the day before, pleased with the feel of it, but not noticing that Peter had been busy with his camera.

The photo had a soft quality that emphasized the serene expression on Anna's face. The light in the shop where the rocker had been purchased had come through several four-paned rustic windows, one of which was captured in the photo. If Anna did not know where the picture had been taken, she would have assumed the setting was a real home.

Silently she looked at Peter, not knowing what to say. His expression showed his anxiety, and she remembered that Alysia had mentioned that Peter had stopped taking photographs years ago.

She was drawn back to the photograph again, pulled into the emotional aura it presented, even though she herself was the subject. This was truly art, Anna thought, a factual photo that created a timeless moment so much greater than the actual event.

Again she looked at Peter. "You printed this, didn't you?"

He nodded. "I've got a darkroom at the house."

Slowly she shook her head. "I. . .what can I say? I've been photographed by hundreds of people, but never anything like this. Can I really keep it?"

"Yes," he said. He had made the photo for himself, knowing the instant he had seen her relax in the rocker and raise her hands to her face in an unconscious gesture of pleasure, that it was a perfect setting for a perfect subject. He remembered the feeling of excitement as he had focused and shot at least a dozen frames before she became aware of his activities and laughed and waved him away.

"Why did you stop?" Anna asked quietly. "Alysia said you had given up photography, but she wouldn't say why. This is the best work of its kind I've ever seen, Peter, and I work with some very talented people."

"Talent doesn't count for much at the grocery checkout. I haven't had a lot of time for hobbies lately. It just seemed like a good day to get the stuff out."

"Oh, all right, don't tell me if you don't want to," Anna said, frustrated at his tendency to quickly cut off communication. She put the photo back into the envelope.

Peter walked over to her, and as she turned, he said, "I want to, Anna. I wish I could just tell you everything, but I can't."

She nodded. "I'm sorry. It's wrong for me to expect confidences from you. After all, we hardly know each other."

"I know you, Anna," Peter said. "I can't stop thinking about you. I thought for a long time that I was in love with Alysia, and in a way I do love her. She's a wonderful woman, but almost from the minute I met you, I felt for you what I've never felt for anyone else. Anna, how can I make you love me, too?"

"Make me love you? I don't think that can happen, Peter. You and Alysia were very close once, but you simply did not love each other. Love is either there or it isn't." She searched his face, wanting to be as honest as she could be without raising false hopes. "I know we're together for a reason. I believe God directed me here, and it's no accident that you've become a part of my life. You're everything a woman could ask for. There's just something that keeps me from saying the words you'd like to hear."

"Just don't say, 'Can we be friends?' That's one thing I don't want to hear."

Anna smiled. "We certainly are more than friends, Peter, much more. You've changed my life forever."

They were interrupted by the arrival of a utility truck. "This the place where we're supposed to bring power?" said the driver, checking a paper on a clipboard.

"Darron must have called them," Anna said. "He seems to be enjoying this project almost as much as I am."

"Darron is good at a lot of things," Peter said.

"Are you proud of him, or are you being sarcastic?"

"Both, I guess."

"Take my advice," Anna said. "Don't lose the ones who love you most. A memory. . .even a good photograph. . .is never as good as the real thing."

Peter took the last box from the trunk of Anna's car and carried it into the house and set it on the kitchen table. Then they stood on the porch and watched as the line workers established the connection to the house.

Suddenly the man on the ground yelled and jumped sideways. "There're snakes everywhere!" he declared. "You two gonna live in this dump, you better get yourself a pig."

"A pig?" Anna asked. "What's he talking about?"

"Pigs kill the snakes," Peter said, "but if you'd rather, we could get a goose. They kill snakes, too."

"Maybe I should try to get some more of the grass cut. I'd hate to have any of the workers who are going to be around here get bitten."

"Once people start working here, the snakes will catch on to what's happening and leave. If it makes you feel better, though, I'll get a gasoline-powered trimmer and mow the tall stuff."

"Would you? I'd feel much better about it. Promise me you'll be careful."

"I promise. Are you going to be here for the rest of the day?"

"I expect Darron will be by after work, so I'll stay at least until he gets here."

After Peter left, Anna went back into the house, trying to imagine how it would look when lighted. She remembered the kerosene lamps that had been there when she was very young and recalled the pungent odor of the fuel. Sometimes, as Granny lighted a lamp, she would sing a song like "This Little Light of Mine" or "Thy Word Is a Lamp to My Feet," which had no meaning whatsoever to Anna but were fun to listen to. Granny had once told her the story from the Bible of the foolish women who had no lamp oil when it was time to go to a wedding and admonished Anna to "Be ready, honey. When God gets ready to move, you be ready."

Anna looked out at the linemen and wished once more for her granny's companionship and wisdom. She also made a mental note to find that Bible story and read it again. Perhaps it would make sense now.

Anxious to see how the work was progressing, she pulled the chain on the single electric light that hung in the kitchen. Though she had replaced the bulb this morning, there was no light. She sighed and went outside to fill a flower box by the window with petunias, where Darron found her when he and Wilford arrived.

"Linemen still here?" he said, squinting into the sky. "Must be they had some problems. I'll go see what's taking so long."

"Have you got any jobs for me, Miss Anna?" Wilford asked. "Daddy said I could come along if I promised to help and not be a pest."

"If you could get some water from that old spring and bring it for these flowers, that would help me a lot." She handed him a small plastic pail, and he trotted off.

"Well, they're just about done," Darron reported when he came back. "Now we talked about not having a whole lot of wiring done. There's no problem with codes in a remodeling project like this, so you can pretty much get what you ask for. You want a light and an outlet in each room, right?"

Anna looked up from the flowers. "A light? I'm sorry, Darron, I guess I wasn't paying much attention."

"You got your mind on something more interesting than power lines," he said with a smile. "I passed Peter on the way over here. Alysia's determined to get you two together somehow."

Anna smiled. "Darron, your brother is a most unusual man. Come here. I want to show you something."

Together they went to the road where Anna's car was parked. She gingerly picked up the envelope containing the portrait Peter had made and handed it to Darron.

Darron slipped the photo out and gazed at it, offering a long, low whistle. "Well, he sure hasn't lost the touch, even after all these years."

"What happened, Darron? Why did he quit photography? He has so much talent, and he obviously loves the work."

Darron shook his head sadly. "Peter isn't an easy guy to get close to, Anna."

"I've found that out."

"Well, you've gotten closer than anybody else has in a long time. If he's going to tell anybody his secrets, it will be you. When he's ready, and I think he's almost ready, he'll tell you. Don't worry, it isn't anything so deep and dark as all that. In fact, when he does tell you, you'll probably wonder what all the fuss was about, but Peter. . .well, he feels things more than other people do. It's part of the reason he can do things like this," he said, handing the photo back to Anna.

As they went toward the house, Darron said, "Anna, I just have to say I'm awful pleased to see Peter working again. I don't know exactly what's between you two, but I'm hoping, praying, that he'll find himself soon. If you're one of the pieces of the puzzle in his life and God brought you here to fill up a certain spot, then I hope Peter doesn't do anything stupid to mess it all up. And maybe we can all be something special for you, too."

"You have been, Darron," Anna said. "I came looking for support, and I found it in you and Alysia and, in a way, in Peter, too. This old, worn-out house is sort of the glue holding us all together, I suppose. Isn't it funny how—"

A scream, followed by another that was higher and longer, stopped them on the porch, and Darron immediately bolted toward the spring.

"Wilford! Wilford! Where are you?" he shouted.

The linemen looked toward Darron, and the one on the pole began pointing and shouting. Darron saw the tall grass waving and barged through to where Wilford lay, rolling on the ground, clutching his ankle.

"A snake bit me, Daddy!" he howled. "My leg hurts!"

Darron lifted the boy in his arms and hurried toward the house, hearing as he went the lineman's words, "I kicked up some copperheads awhile back. Be careful."

"Anna, he's been bit," Darron said, his voice trembling. "I'm going to take him to the hospital. Is Peter coming back here?"

Anna nodded. "He just went to rent a grass trimmer."

"Wait here for him. Tell him what happened. Ask him to get Alysia and bring her to the hospital. He'll know where to go." He was on his way up to the road before Anna could answer.

Anna paced the front porch until Peter returned. "How serious could the bite be?" Anna asked as they drove toward Alysia's home.

Peter's shoulders hunched briefly. "Depends on the size of the snake and what it was. Darron doesn't even know for sure if it was a copperhead, does he?" Peter didn't want to mention rattlesnakes.

Anna stayed at the apartment with Emily while Alysia and Peter drove to the hospital. Darron was waiting for them and enfolded Alysia in his arms as soon as he saw her.

"He's hurt; it's a bad bite," he said. "They're doing what they can. The doctor says it isn't life threatening, but they have to try to prevent tissue damage right away or his leg might not be right again."

The three sat together in the waiting room, and soon Peter and Darron's mother, Audrey, and their sister, Rose, arrived.

"Poor little Wilford," said Rose. "What was he doing running around that old place, anyway?"

"Helping," Darron said defensively.

"I never should have let her start working there until the grass was cleared," Peter said. "I even teased her about the snakes. How could I have been so stupid?"

His mother sighed. "Oh, Peter, there you go again, thinking the whole world is on your shoulders. Darron told us exactly what happened, and it could have happened to anyone. It's nobody's fault. People get bit by snakes every year. I'll tell you something. I know in my heart Wilford is going to be all right. I've prayed and prayed that this family would be healed, and although my heart breaks for Wilford and I'm sorry he's the one to pay the price, I'm happy as I can be to see you two boys together again, talking face-to-face like two human beings. Now there, that's just how I feel."

"Never mind, Mamma," Darron said in his typically soft, conciliatory voice. "Peter and I never did have a quarrel, did we, Pete?"

Peter glanced briefly at Alysia and in her pleading look caught the full effect of her faithful acceptance of him and her absolute, unyielding love for Darron. As he looked at Darron and understood that the door to his return always had been and was even at this moment wide open, he knew that he no longer had the strength to be angry with them for their success.

"I never did have a quarrel with Darron, Mamma, except maybe when he wore my new jeans to the football game without asking."

"If I'd have asked, you would've said no," Darron said.

"Guess we'll never know," said Peter.

They returned to their silent waiting, each one knowing that at least one wound had already been healed. When a doctor finally came to give an update, the whole family crowded around him like a group of schoolchildren.

"I asked him what color the snake was," said the doctor, "and he said it was orange, which leads me to believe it was a copperhead, especially with the appearance of the wound. The swelling's stopped. He's in less pain now." He nodded at Darron and Alysia. "You two can go in for a few minutes, then you might as well all go home because he's going to be sleeping a lot."

Audrey said, "I'll go stay with Emily. Peter, you take me over there. We'll give your friend the news. She might want to come and visit tomorrow herself."

❦

Anna was amazed that the moment she was introduced to Peter's mother, the woman hugged her warmly and treated her like a long-lost friend.

"Thank you so much for helping," Audrey said, but Anna had no idea of just what she meant.

"Peter, I'm so surprised by your family. They are wonderful people!"

"Kind of makes you wonder how I got in, doesn't it?"

Anna laughed. "You know what I mean."

"Mamma is a wise woman," Peter said. "I told you the other day that I was jealous of Darron. I think I've finally been able to admit it to them, too, while we were all together. Mamma understands what's happening, and she knows you're a part of it. She's grateful. So am I."

"It could have happened without me."

"But it didn't," Peter said.

❦

When they arrived back at the motor home, Anna invited Peter in to eat. Anna made tuna sandwiches and warmed up some soup on the stove. Just as it reached serving temperature, the flames of the tiny gas burner flickered and went out.

"Well, I guess this is my last hot meal," she said. "I'm out of fuel."

"You can always get another tank of propane," Peter said.

Anna turned and asked, "Why, Peter? I won't be here that long."

Peter continued to eat. There was nothing he could say.

"And what about you? You've been reunited with your family. Can't you make a life for yourself here now? Do you still think you have to leave the only place that's ever going to be home to you?"

"Do you like Chinese food?" Peter asked.

Anna raised her hands in frustration. "What does that have to do with anything?"

"Sweet and sour, Anna," Peter said, leaning back in his chair. "You take a bite, and you can't decide. Is it sweet, or is it sour? The sour turns the sweet, and vice versa. That's how this place is to me."

"I know about the sweet. But what about the sour? What is it that's keeping you from your life and your work?"

He crossed his arms on his chest, partly to keep from reaching across the miniature motor home table to stroke Anna's hair or caress her hand. His crossed arms also shielded his heart and symbolically pressed away the ache that came from knowing that the same thing that kept him from his work also kept him from Anna.

Certainly she had a right to know about his past, but telling her, he knew, would only drive her further away. Things were going well now. They were friends. If she knew more, that would end. Not only would she not like him, he reasoned, she would certainly never love him. Yet how could he say he loved her when parts of his life were marked OFF LIMITS?

"Let's take a walk down by the creek," he said. "Maybe we can talk."

Chapter 9

It's a pretty place, isn't it?" Peter asked as he and Anna stood at the edge of the water and looked up and down the stream. Ragged pines hung over the bank where the stream widened and deepened, then farther down a series of short falls took the water around a curve and out of sight. Mosses were greening up for summer, and the leaves on the hardwoods were beginning to lose their brightness as their unfolding became complete. The mountainsides were shady with sunlight penetrating only in the clearings where rocky outcroppings soaked up the heat.

"Yes, Peter, it's lovely," Anna said, wondering what Peter was trying to say and why it was so hard for him.

"This is where I started doing serious photography," he said. "I got interested in cameras when I was in high school and took some pictures for the yearbook. Then when I went to college, I studied a bit more, but this is the place that made me want to do nothing except take pictures. This was the first land I bought. I was nineteen, and I used the money my daddy left me for college. That's one reason I went for only two years."

"Photography is expensive. How did you keep yourself in supplies?"

"I went to work, like everybody does. I sold a few pictures, but I had this idea that somehow I could take all of this"—he waved his hand toward the scene before them—"to the rest of the world through my work." He laughed briefly. "Pretty grand idea, wasn't it?"

"And worthwhile. After all, that was Ansel Adam's desire long before environmentalism was a buzzword. He did it, too."

"Well, I didn't do it. I opened a studio in order to make a living doing something I was reasonably good at. . .or thought I was good at." The image of the empty storefront in the strip mall came to Peter's mind. He could even see the old cars parked on the blacktop, the empty soft drink cups and hamburger wrappers lying around, and the sun beating on the treeless lot.

"A studio? You did portrait photography?" Anna thought of the photo he had given her.

"Portraits, weddings, graduations, little kids." He nodded. "In the first year I worked fifteen or eighteen hours a day sometimes, trying to get up and running. It just never did fly. People quit coming, but the bills didn't. Finally it came down to a choice. I could sell the studio, or I could sell this land. I decided to sell the studio."

"I don't understand. Your work is so good. Why did the business fail?"

Peter shrugged, then tossed a pebble into the creek. He shook his head and said, "I don't really know for sure. People were polite, but they just never came back, and they sure didn't bring their friends."

Anna waited for more, but Peter seemed to be finished with his revelation. She remembered Darron's statement that she might wonder what all the fuss was about.

"Peter," she began cautiously, "are you saying that because your business failed, you gave up on your life, your art, and your family? I don't understand. Businesses fail every day."

"Something just ended for me there, Anna. I walked out one day and locked the door. I wouldn't even go back for my equipment. Darron went over one day and collected everything before the new tenants moved in. If he hadn't dumped it on my doorstep, I wouldn't have it today."

"But surely you understand now that your engagement to Alysia didn't end because the photography studio went under."

"It was a good excuse at the time. I told Alysia I couldn't support a family and we couldn't get married, but she had already told me it was over between us. It sort of helped me keep my pride to think the breakup was my idea. Then she started dating Darron, so the studio was another reason to keep him at arm's length."

"What does the studio have to do with him?"

"He told me not to start it in the first place," Peter said.

"And you didn't want to hear him say, 'I told you so.'"

"No, especially not while he was walking down the aisle with my ex."

"And the look, Peter? What about the eyes of God? Did you think He was watching then?"

Peter turned toward Anna, not missing the earnestness in her voice. He did not want to damage her faith, but he knew he could not hold up his own as an example.

"I knew," he said. "But like I said, it didn't seem to make any difference."

"Did you ask for help?" Anna could almost feel the pain Peter must have experienced in his failure, and she suddenly understood that what seemed like just another step in life to Darron and Alysia was devastating to proud, sensitive, artistic Peter.

"Did you call to God for direction? I did, Peter. When I didn't know what else to do, I just put myself in His care, and He led me here, to you."

"Did He?" Peter smiled. "You don't love me, Anna. If He led you here, it was for your benefit, not mine. For me, knowing you and loving you is one more failure in my life."

Anna could hardly keep the tears from flowing, and she turned her pain to anger. "You and your stubborn pride!" she cried. "You have all these wonderful things in your life, and all you can see is an empty photo studio where you were probably wasting your talents trying to get spoiled brats to smile for the camera. You just thought you couldn't be the best, so you refused to try. How can you throw away your life like this?" She wanted to make him try again, demanding that he stop resisting God and making petty excuses for his own choices.

As she stood trembling with emotion before him, Peter forced himself not to take her into his arms. He would not take advantage of her sense of right in order to satisfy his own longings.

"Don't be angry," he whispered. "You're the only one who knows how much it hurts. . .and it still hurts. You're right, I'm proud. When Daddy died, I decided I would take over. I was the good student, the athlete, the leader in the family until I got old enough when it would really count for something. Then I lost my livelihood, my fiancée, my brother's respect. It's been downhill ever since."

"You never lost Darron's respect," Anna said. "He's always loved you and admired you. It happened in your own head and your own heart. You learned that today, didn't you? When a crisis brought you all together, you saw that the love is still there."

"Well, blood is thicker than water, you know. Family really can't disown you."

"I don't believe God has disowned you, either," Anna said. "I think He's just waiting for you, just like Darron and Alysia and your mother have been waiting all these years. Don't quit, Peter. Don't stop trying, please. You have so much to give."

Peter was quiet for a moment. He remembered the first day he had spent with Anna, and he realized that something about her made him want to go on, to reconstruct the dreams that for so long had been associated in his mind with pain. He had to acknowledge that, except for Anna, he would have packed his truck a week ago and gone in search of something to fill the hollowness in his own soul. He just didn't believe he could do what she was asking of him.

"Will you wait for me?" he asked.

In a moment, Anna knew that if she could not love Peter, she could never love anyone. She realized that in feeling his pain and loss, she had been joined to him in a way she never could have been even through all the good times they might share.

"I'll wait," she said, "if you'll work."

Silently they followed their shadows to the motor home. Anna said, "I'm going to go in to the hospital for a while. What should I take for Wilford?"

"He likes puzzles. He's a math whiz." At the door, he asked, "What about getting that propane?"

She searched his face, knowing he wanted her to stay.

"I'll see about it tomorrow." At least they both knew she wasn't going anywhere that night.

At the hospital, Anna found Alysia in the waiting room. "I'm so glad you came!"

Alysia said. "Darron had to get to bed; the poor man was exhausted with all that's happened. I wanted to stay awhile yet. They said Wilford would be awake before too long and I could see him before I go home for the night."

"I didn't really expect to see him," Anna said, sitting next to Alysia on the hard sofa. "You can give him this when he wakes up." She handed Alysia a pocket calculator and a book of games that were played using calculations.

"Oh, it's just perfect!" Alysia declared. "He'll be so excited. How did you know he likes this kind of thing?"

"Peter told me," Anna said and then smiled at Alysia's knowing grin. "Alysia, you're just like a schoolgirl. You have to get over the idea that Peter and I are going steady."

"I won't get over it. I'm hoping to get you as a sister yet."

"Well, you've got me as a sister one way or another," Anna said. "You know, Peter did finally tell me just this evening why he quit photography. You and Darron don't understand why he was so devastated by his failure, do you?"

Alysia shook her head. "No, he just gets so worked up over every little thing, bless his heart. At the beginning, Darron told him it was a bad idea because Darron had seen Peter's work. He didn't think Peter was going to be happy cooped up inside all day with runny-nosed kids in bow ties who didn't want their pictures taken, but Peter insisted he could make it work. The trouble was, Peter was too good. People wanted nice posed pictures that flattered them. Peter takes the kind of pictures that show people what they really are, if you know what I mean."

Her own portrait flashed in her mind. "Yes, I do know," she said slowly, trying to imagine the response of a self-promoting debutante to such a work. No, people would have responded badly to Peter's style of portraiture, and he would never have compromised his work to curry favor with customers.

"Another problem Peter had was that he's no accountant," Alysia said. "I offered to keep the books for him, but he didn't want that, especially after we broke up. By then it was too late, anyway. He didn't want to advertise, either. Said it made him feel like a prostitute. Can you imagine? The whole thing was a bad idea. But being Peter, he just used that old studio as proof that it was he, not the business, that was a failure."

Alysia turned on the calculator and pushed a few buttons. "Peter's not much good at taking help, and Darron's almost as bad. You saw how he was about the job offer. Why are men like that?"

"I don't know, Alysia. The men I've known in the fashion industry are always asking for help." Once again Anna's stomach churned at the thought of Barry's deceit. "For all the problems it causes, I think it's better for men to be like Peter and your husband."

Alysia put her arm around Anna and giggled. "They are awful nice to marry."

Chapter 10

Anna lay in the too-short motor home bed, watching the moon drift past the tops of the pines. The day had been exhausting. After her visit to the hospital, she had returned to the hollow and immediately gone to bed but had been unable to fall asleep.

Listening to the night sounds, she realized how comfortable she had become in this environment in only a few days. New York seemed so faraway, especially now that Barry was not waiting there for her. The trouble was, she had no plans for tomorrow. None of the reasons that drew her to Tennessee still remained.

Granny's house had been found and would be available to her if she ever wanted to go there. Anna now knew that the important thing was not living there, or even having the house, but having made peace with her own past by accepting the changes that had come with the death of her parents. The house was a monument to the love she had known in her life.

There was no more question about going into business with Barry; there was certainly no possibility of a continuing relationship with him. He would probably never even speak to her again, she thought, and she did not mind that at all. It was not the answer she had hoped and prayed for, but it was an answer just the same.

Watching the shadows in the sky, she knew that the faith in God that she had developed in New York would carry her anyplace in the world. Day by day she had become more comfortable with God's dealing in her life, more aware of it, and more trusting. Meeting Darron and Alysia had been a joyful part.

Once more she looked at the photographic portrait of herself that Peter had made. With some sadness she admitted that learning about his life also had helped her to cling more tightly to her own faith. Seeing his suffering and believing that it was largely a result of spiritual turmoil made her determined not to make the same mistakes.

She dared not think about the effect he had on her personally. There could be no future with Peter because he refused to return to the point of simple faith where he and Anna could begin a life together. Seeing Darron and Alysia and remembering her granny had shown Anna that a good marriage had to begin with that kind of mutual belief. She consciously erased the vision of Peter's face, knowing that their separation was coming soon.

Though it left her with a hollow feeling, Anna knew that there was no reason for her to stay in Tennessee. Tomorrow she would begin preparations to return to New York. A sense of urgency was gradually building in her. There was business that needed her attention. At the same time, she knew there were serious decisions ahead of her, because Peter's photo, as Alysia had said, had shown her the truth about herself. Barry was right—she was not getting any younger.

Once more she looked at the picture before slipping it back into the brown envelope. Though Peter had captured perfectly her feelings and even a part of her life, the facts were also there. She was getting too old for the work she was now doing. She thought about Barry's angry words. "You're at the worst possible age for a model," he had said.

The truth of those words was all the more bitter because it was Barry who had said them first. She would have to begin thinking about other work.

❦

The next day Anna got up early and went to see Darron before he left for work. On the way, she had an idea.

She sat with Darron and Alysia at their kitchen table with a cup of coffee, carefully planning her words.

"Anna, I just wish you'd stay awhile," Alysia was saying. "We're just getting to know you. At least promise me you'll visit when the baby comes."

"I wouldn't miss that for anything," said Anna. "You know, you two have done so much for me, I hesitate to even ask this, but I need the help. Granny Huddlestone's house is just sitting there. I did the few things necessary to satisfy myself, and now I have to leave. Would you two consider living out there as caretakers of the house? I'd pay you, of course. It would certainly ease my mind."

Darron blinked as Alysia squealed and tugged at his arm. "Darron, Darron, we could get out of town! The kids would just love it. Let's do it."

Anna interrupted, "Remember, it doesn't have the kind of conveniences you've been used to. There will only be the one small bathroom."

"That's all we've got now," Alysia said.

"There's no modern kitchen," Anna added, "although I wouldn't mind if you put in a range and sink."

"Say yes, Darron," Alysia pleaded. "I just love that old house. I have since the day Anna and I went out there to clean. I've been so jealous, I'm ashamed of myself."

Darron finally spoke. "I won't take any money, but I'll just tell you I've been worried about that old house since you two started filling the place up with stuff. I'd hate to see anything happen to it now that you know it's what you want. We could live there. We'd have some more room, and I'd be closer to work."

Alysia bounced on her chair like a child. "Thank you, Anna! Thank you, thank you." She made a final bounce up, took two steps to Anna's chair, and hugged her.

Anna laughed. "Don't thank me yet. You may be sorry once you get into the old place. It isn't exactly a palace, you know."

"It is to me," Alysia said. "Besides, knowing how special the place is to you makes it a home for me. And remember, the house is yours. You can have it back or come visit whenever you want."

Anna looked at her two friends, unlike any friends she had ever had before. How long until she would see them again? she wondered. "I'll be leaving in a day or two," she said. "I may not see you before I leave."

Alysia looked away. "I won't let go of you, Anna. I believe God brought you to us. . .to all of us. . .and somehow, it's going to work out."

"You'll always have me," Anna said, "just as I'll have you. Now don't fret. What do you think Wilford will say when you tell him about the move?"

"I think he'll say he wants a pair of high-top boots," Alysia said.

🦋

High-top boots were what Peter was wearing when Anna found him, cutting grass in a wide swath around the house. He had already mowed beyond the spring and was working at the back side of the house when Anna cautiously approached. The noise of the gasoline-powered trimmer was deafening, and Anna had to wait for Peter to turn in her direction in order to get his attention.

"I had breakfast with Darron and Alysia," she said. "Wilford had a restful night. He'll be coming home later today."

Beads of perspiration clung to Peter's skin just above his eyebrows, and he wiped them away on the back of a gloved hand. "Well, I don't think anybody will see any snakes close by here, as long as the grass is kept short through the summer. If it gets long, though, they'll come back."

"Darron will keep it cut, I'm sure," said Alysia. "They've decided to come here and live."

"No foolin'!" Peter's face brightened in a way that surprised Anna. She had half expected an argument from him. "That's real fine. Darron's kind of a mother hen. He isn't happy unless he's got a certain amount of things to take care of. He'll like the old place."

It occurred to Anna that she should tell Peter she was planning to leave, but the words woud not come. There was still time, of course.

"Come over here and see if you think this might have been your granny's garden," Peter said, leading Anna along the edge of the cleared area. The ground was level and had a softer feel under Anna's feet than the rocky yard. Peter pointed out the points of iris foliage.

"I think this is sage," he said, pointing to another plant, "and here's mint."

Anna turned and looked at the house. The place where they stood was directly in line with the kitchen window. "It's the garden all right," she said. She turned ninety degrees and pointed. "The hen house was over there." Through the bushes they could see a few remains of the old building.

"This was a wonderful spot. I didn't like the chickens, but I loved the garden. Every morning while I was visiting, Granny and I would walk out here and see what had changed since the day before. It was like visiting friends for her. 'Oh, look how the radishes have grown,' she'd say, or 'Why, would you look at that? While we were asleep, the mustard sprouted. It puts me to shame. It worked all night long while I rested.' "

"Have you ever had a garden of your own?" Peter asked.

"No, I don't even keep houseplants.

Suddenly Peter said, "Anna, let's go back to the mountain where we saw the eagle. Come with me, please. I want to take some pictures up there later this afternoon. Let's go about three o'clock."

Anna hesitated only a moment. "All right. Come over to the hollow when you get ready to go. I'll be there." She did not say she would be packing.

When Peter arrived at the motor home, Anna was sitting on the ground outside, in the shade, reading a book. "What have you got there?" he asked, taking her hand to help her up.

"T. S. Eliot," she said. "Do you like poetry?"

"Some, if it's the kind that doesn't paint everything as a disaster. After all, 'Humankind cannot bear very much reality.' "

"So you do like Eliot," Anna said. It was a good point of conversation and launched them on their hike on a wave of camaraderie that reminded Anna of other days during her stay. She was going to miss Peter. For all his prickliness and black despair, she liked spending time with him. For a moment, as they walked along, she wondered whether any of her old friends in New York were really friends at all. Was she returning to a void? The urge to simply accept Peter's love and stay with him was very tempting just then, but she made herself put the thoughts aside.

"Will you try to photograph the eagle?" Anna asked as they neared the place where they had seen the bird before.

"If we see it, and if the light is right, and if, if, if, yes." Peter said. "I spent almost a whole year tramping around here, taking pictures of the birds and their young. I don't have any pictures from this point, though. I'd like to have some for the collection."

They walked around examining the tiny wildflowers that grew in the sunlight of the summit. The blankets of green, which Anna had never taken time to look at before, now offered an almost infinite variety of shapes and hues, from tiny mosses on the rocks, to tall trees of half a dozen varieties.

"There's so much to see," said Anna. "In New York there are maple trees planted in rows and surrounded by cement. It's pleasant enough, but there isn't much variety."

"I knew a photographer in college who published a whole book on lichens that grew in the county where he lived," said Peter.

"What about you? Have you published any work?"

"Oh, half a dozen photos some years back. Nothing you can point to with much pride. Strictly illustrative stuff."

"Have you decided what you'll do now, where you'll go?"

"No."

Anna sat with her back against a tree and watched the blue haze above the mountains deepen and intensify as the sun inched along the horizon. Peter brought his camera and sat beside her. Silently they scanned the sky, waiting.

"Does the eagle come every day?" asked Anna.

"No. It hunts other places, too, but I was here yesterday and the day before, and I didn't see him. It's about time for him to make a pass through here." He raised his hands, forming blinders at his temples. "I think. . .looks like that could be him."

Anna could see just the smallest speck in the sky. Beside her, Peter raised his camera and focused the telephoto lens, changing it moment by moment as the speck came closer.

Suddenly Anna cried, "Look! There are two of them!"

Sailing through the air, slightly behind and to one side, came a second eagle.

"Well, he's brought his wife," said Peter softly. He stood up and moved quickly to a different position.

Anna heard the familiar *click* and *whir* of the motorized camera but knew this time she was not the focal point. She watched the birds in their path, realizing that they would not come directly toward the place where she and Peter stood watching as they had the other day. At first she sat very still, but as they came closer, she could not help but be drawn into their quest. Slowly she stood up, and it was as if they called to her, and even made eye contact, inviting her to rise above the common life she now knew, and fly.

The moment was poignant but brief. In only seconds, the sky was again empty as the pair vanished into the distant haze.

"Don't you just wish you could go with them?" Anna said quietly as Peter returned to her side.

"Every time I see them," Peter said. "In my collection I've got some pictures of one that was wounded. It made a dive for a young raccoon and smacked its wing against a rock. It stayed on the ground for a couple of days. Every time I tried to get near it, though, it would fly off, so I knew it could fly. You know what I think? I think it was afraid to fly. After about two weeks, I found it dead."

" 'Because these wings are no longer wings to fly, but merely fans to beat the air,' " Anna quoted T. S. Eliot. "We could all fly, I suppose, except that we're so afraid to fall." She looked directly at Peter. "And once wounded, it's very hard to trust, isn't it?"

When he did not reply, she said, "The eagle died, Peter. For an eagle, there are only two choices: fly or die. God has given you wings. He's the very air that holds us up. You have to believe."

Peter watched her face intently, revealing nothing of his own emotions. At last he said, "You're leaving, aren't you?"

Anna nodded ever so slightly. "It's time. I have to go."

"I thought you said you'd wait."

"I will, but not here, not being next to you while not really being with you."

Behind them, the sky, completely free of clouds, deepened to form a magenta curtain. In the shadow of the great pine, Peter slowly enfolded Anna in his arms, and she answered his embrace. Her eyes closed, she pressed her face against his sunburned neck and felt the heat of his skin against her cheek and the soft brush of his hair against her temple.

He held her for a long moment, sensing her heartbeat even as his own quickened. When he felt her gradual movement away from him, he held her just for one more moment and kissed her softly.

"Knowing you're right doesn't mean I can just do what you want," Peter whispered. "I am what I am."

Anna nodded, forcing herself to step away from him. "And I do what I have to do."

Chapter 11

Except for brief snatches of conversation about returning the rental car, finding the best route to the interstate, and preparing the motor home for the trip, the walk home for Peter and Anna was silent. Peter's terse goodbye left Anna sad and lonely.

For her last evening in the hollow, Anna went into the motor home but found the space too confining. Dressed warmly for the night, she took blankets and a pillow, a flashlight, and a book and found a place near the creek to spend the night. Although she was not afraid to sleep alone in the woods, the habits she had acquired in New York were strong; she took her handbag containing her money and identification and locked the door behind her.

She read by flashlight until the light began to dim, then settled down for the night, but the strangeness of the sounds and shadows made it hard to sleep. She lay awake thinking of Peter, wondering if he, too, had slept here and whether she would ever see him again.

She did not know she slept until she was awakened by some unknown sound. She lay still in the darkness, watching the woods, wondering if the slight movements she heard could be those of an animal. After a few minutes, she heard what she knew was the closing of a car door, and she realized that someone else was in the hollow.

Peter must have returned for some reason, she thought. He would be worried if she did not answer his knock at the door. *Why would he be here now?* she wondered. She estimated the time to be somewhere around 3:00 a.m.

She got up and walked along the creek, and as she peered through the trees, she caught a glimpse of a white car. It was Barry's car! She dropped down behind the bushes, waiting to see if he would go away, when he realized she was not in the motor home. Barry was not in sight, but soon he came around from the other side of the motor home. He did not knock or call for Anna. Instead Anna saw, to her horror, that he had in his hand a gasoline can and was splashing the liquid onto the sides of the vehicle. Calmly and silently he produced a flame on his cigarette lighter and ignited the fuel.

Quickly he stepped back, and in the light of the flames, Anna could see his smug expression. She pressed her hand hard against her mouth to keep from crying out as the flames leaped around the door. Had she been inside, it would have been impossible for her to get out.

Barry then walked to the rental car parked nearby, poured the rest of the fuel inside on the upholstery, and set it afire. He stood, watching the blaze.

"See if your Boy Scout can help you now," Anna heard him call. Then he got into his car and drove away.

Anna huddled at the edge of the woods until she was sure he would not see her. The flames danced higher and higher, roaring as they consumed everything in the motor home. The car exploded, sending a ball of flames into the sky, and Anna was suddenly afraid that the woods might also begin to burn.

She stood helplessly as the heat shriveled the ferns and melted the pine needles of the trees closest to the clearing. She could not decide whether to sit and wait or try to get help. Certainly there was nothing she could do about the fire. At last she began walking, knowing that many miles separated her from any other person.

Before she had rounded the first curve on the track that led out of the hollow, she heard a car engine. She stumbled off into the trees, afraid that Barry was returning to check on his work but ran out again when she saw that it was Peter in his truck.

She ran behind the truck as Peter drove to the clearing, jumped from his truck, and started toward the remains of the motor home. She heard him screaming her name, peering into the blaze.

"Peter! Peter! I'm all right!" she shrieked. Gasping for breath, she came within hearing range just as he was about to rush into the flames. "Don't! I'm here, Peter!"

He turned and saw her then, and ran to her and held her once again. "What happened? You could have been killed!"

"Barry came back. He set everything on fire. He. . .he actually tried to kill me, Peter. How did you know? How did you get here so quickly?"

"I guess I have to tell you I haven't been completely honest with you," Peter said. "Each time I drove up here with you, I took the old county road off the highway. The fact is, if you go on that old logging trail that runs off into the woods just beyond that bend, you come out at my house in about fifteen minutes. This is my backyard."

Anna stared, her mouth wide open. "You mean, all this time. . . ?"

"You haven't actually been alone. Did you think I'd let you stay here with no one else around? I was only about half asleep when I heard the explosion. I could see the flames from my place. Oh, Anna, I was so afraid. . . ." He clung to her as the flames poured their wrath into the night.

"Well, there's no sense calling the fire department. By the time they get here, it will all be over," he said. "Come and stay at my place, and in the morning we'll take care of the details."

❧

Anna slept late and awakened in Peter's spare bedroom to the smell of bacon and coffee. She showered and put on the same clothing, the only clothing she now had. After breakfast, she and Peter started toward Gatlinburg.

"This is going to be hard to explain to the insurance people," Anna said. "I suppose I should get a police report."

"They can confirm that the fires were set deliberately, but it might be hard to prove it was Barry who did it. You can't go back to New York," he said firmly. "You can't even think about it as long as that loony person is there."

Anna remembered the steely look on Barry's face as he watched the fire. *What could have happened to him?* she wondered. He was callous, but what would bring him to the point of murder?

As Peter and Anna came to a point where the road took a particularly sharp turn and the mountain dropped steeply into the river below, they came upon a police car. There was a break in the guardrail.

"Looks like somebody went over the side," Peter said. "I'll go speak to one of the officers about stopping up at the hollow to look at the fire damage."

He pulled the truck over to the side of the road and walked back to the place where the guardrail had been broken. One officer was helping another up from the bank.

Anna watched in the rearview mirror then saw Peter coming back toward the truck.

"Anna, can you come over here? I think maybe it's Barry's car down there."

Anna felt a wave of nausea and found it hard to catch her breath. She got out of the pickup and walked to the side of the road, afraid of what she might see hundreds of feet below. There, half submerged in the river and looking like a discarded toy, was the white Ferrari.

"Is he in there?" she whispered.

"The driver's body is in the car, ma'am," the officer said. "It's a white male, maybe about six feet tall, dark hair, thin mustache."

"That's Barry," she said, and her voice broke into sobs.

"There aren't any skid marks here at all," he continued. "After hearing what Mr. McCulley had to say, I believe the driver must have deliberately accelerated and slammed into the rail. He must have been doing close to sixty. The car practically flew more than halfway down. I'd say he did what he came to do and killed himself."

Anna sobbed quietly, thinking of the waste that characterized Barry's life and death. She would not see him flitting in and out of the modeling sets. She would not see him in his apartment or her own. His carefree, haughty smile was gone forever.

"He was on the verge of financial collapse," Anna said when she could speak. "He had been on his way to Memphis to see business acquaintances there. He. . . had asked me for money, but I refused. If they also refused in Memphis, it may have been too much for him."

And so, by the end of the day, Anna was on her way to Louisville to catch a plane to New York.

🦋

For days, Peter remained secluded. After the motor home and car rental companies had investigated, he worked at the hollow, clearing the debris caused by the fires. Photography was his only pleasure. He shot rolls and rolls of film at the creek and around his home, and stayed in his darkroom for hours at a time.

Three weeks after Anna left, Peter was sitting in a straight-backed chair on his porch when Darron drove up. Darron marched toward him, obviously resolved to accomplish a mission. Peter sighed, knowing he would have to deal with the man.

Darron tossed a magazine into Peter's lap. "Pete, I'm mighty tired of seeing stuff like this and knowing you could do better," he said. The open pages of the magazine showed photo illustrations of a deep-South family reunion—the food, the people, and the home.

"We've been all though this, Darron. Photography will never be a business for me. I can't make it work."

Darron's lips were set in a firm line, and he seemed like a schoolmaster about to berate an errant child.

"How much are you going to have to lose before you look up and pay attention to what God's trying to show you?" Darron demanded. "You were good to me all my life. When Daddy died, you were a father to me. I loved you like a daddy, but when I got old enough not to need one anymore, you felt like you'd failed somehow. You didn't. I just grew up, that's all. I wanted you for a brother then. But no, you wouldn't have it any way but yours. I wanted to help you in your business, and so did Alysia, but you were too stinkin' proud. You were willing to let all of us just disappear out of your life rather than admit you needed anybody else. Well, now look at you. You haven't even shaved in a week, holed up here like a hermit. You let the best thing that's come into your life slip away from you rather than get down on your knees and tell God you need His help. You know He's waitin', Pete. You know He's been knockin' the chucks out from under you for years in the hopes you'd give up and let Him do the work Himself. Instead, you just keep trying to find new props. You called the shots when we were growing up. Now I'm telling you something. You get yourself right with God and get to work using the talents He gave you, and if you got one single brain cell in that thick head of yours, you do anything you can to win Anna. So help me, if you throw your life away, I'll beat you myself."

"Anna doesn't love me, Darron. It takes two, you know."

Darron grabbed the magazine and slapped his brother on the side of the head with it. "Make her love you, Pete! All she's waitin' for is for you to give in and surrender to the Lord. I know you've been wrestlin' with Him, just like Jacob, for years now! You can't win unless you surrender. You've got to do it!" He smacked

Peter again then threw the magazine to the floor of the porch. "Anna can't commit her life to a man who's too proud and stubborn to take orders from God. Be the man you used to be when you were a kid."

"That doesn't make any sense," Peter said defensively, rubbing his ear.

"It's the only thing that makes sense. I'm through tryin', but Anna, God bless her, I think she'll pine for you 'til the day she dies. Not because she needs you, but because she wants you to enjoy the kind of spiritual life she knows you could have. It's what I want, too, you big fool." He spun around, strode off to his car, and drove away.

Peter sat on the porch, watching the dust clouds form behind Darron's car. He wondered how long Darron had been working on that speech and how he had worked up to its delivery. Something in the act had touched Peter deeply. Maybe it was that Darron would risk losing their newly discovered relationship in order to do what Darron thought was the best thing for his brother. Darron was wrong, of course. Anna's lack of love for him was just one of a series of failures in his life. He wanted to think of it in terms of fate, but somehow he could not.

He also could not dismiss Darron's accusations and challenges as easily as he wanted to. Though he busied himself as best he could, Darron's stern face kept coming back to him. Finally he walked across the porch and picked up the magazine and glanced at the photos. They were good photos and illustrated the story, but they gave no hint of the relationship of the people to the event. The people might all have been hired models, models like Anna. *No, even a poor photographer could not make Anna look as stiff as these people, as removed from their experiences as these laughing faces seemed to be.*

All his efforts to clear his mind of her face and presence had been useless. With each passing day he missed her more. When he drove past the Huddlestone property, he imagined her face at the window. Had she really come into his life, and then, taking part of him with her, gone away?

Peter left the porch and went into his house. He pulled from a drawer the color snapshots of Anna and Alysia on their shopping expedition and looked at each one. Would he ever have anything except her likeness on paper? If Darron were right—a possibility difficult for Peter to concede—there might be one chance left for him. It involved tremendous risk, however, and Peter once again felt the familiar sensation of fear. What would happen if he actually trusted God with his life?

❧

Later that evening, people walking through the courtyard at Biblical Gardens noticed an unshaven young man sitting on a bench and staring at the carved figure of Christ.

Chapter 12

Anna ignored the conversations around her in the restaurant, stared at her plate, and lined up the julienned carrots as she thought about Phil Curtis's offer.

"It's what you would have done for Barry," Phil was saying, "but with no strings. I know you'd make a good partner and a good manager. The younger models look up to you and respect you."

Phil's reference to younger models had nearly as much emotional impact on Anna as his reference to Barry. She had known for some time about Phil's changes in the management of the agency, which he had purchased when it had gone into receivership after Barry's death. Now he was offering Anna the job of manager.

While many people had been sympathetic to Anna after her return to New York, she found few jobs once her existing contracts were fulfilled. With fewer jobs came fewer friends, fewer nights away from the apartment, and more and more memories of Peter. Knowing she had made the right choice was little consolation. She had never been so lonely.

Phil Curtis had begun asking her out a few weeks previous to his offer to let her manage the agency. He was an old friend and a good businessman. Anna was glad to spend time with him, and she knew that his offer was sincere. If only it didn't seem so hollow! She could not help but remember that only about four months ago, a similar offer had helped take her away from New York to what now seemed like another world.

"I just don't know exactly what I want to do right now," Anna told Phil. "Can I take a week or two to decide? I'm not sure I want to give up modeling yet."

His attempt to conceal surprise was not missed by Anna. "Oh, well, sure, if you want to be in front of the camera awhile longer, that makes sense. You have a history of good work, after all. I'm sure the work's there for you. If you decide to handle the business, though, I'd love to have you."

He took Anna to her apartment, offered a friendly kiss on the cheek, and was gone. Anna went inside to finish a letter to Alysia that she had begun earlier.

I can hardly believe it is halfway through October, she wrote. *I suppose the mountains there are beautiful. I haven't even been out of the city since I returned in June.*

In addition to feeling torn in half when she had left Peter at the bus station in Gatlinburg, Anna returned to New York to find that funeral arrangements for Barry had fallen to her. He had left her plenty of responsibilities but no resources. His assets were all gone. She paid for the funeral herself and acted as hostess to the few who bothered to pay their respects. Then she got on with trying to put away the memories of both men.

The summer and early autumn had passed slowly for Anna. She had struggled with Barry's death, even though a call from his contact in Memphis helped her to understand that she had nothing to do with his suicide.

"He was as angry as I've ever seen anyone," the designer had said. "I told him I couldn't give him the money because I didn't have it, and he nearly went crazy. He said if he couldn't live well, he wouldn't live at all. He said you were the only person who had ever really loved him, and since you probably hated him now, he might as well go out in style."

"If he thought I loved him, why did he try to kill me?" Anna had asked.

"I'd say it was an illogical and crazy way to get back at your boyfriend. You know Barry. He had to blame somebody," the designer had replied.

Anna wrote,

> *I'm so glad you're all moved into Granny's house. I hope you'll be happy there. What am I saying? You and Darron will be happy anywhere. You'll never know what your friendship means to me. Be sure to tell me when you get the phone installed.*

What she could not write were questions about Peter, whether he had moved away from Gatlinburg, whether he had found a job, whether he ever spoke of her. He had not written or called. How real could his love have been? Anna could not answer that question, but since her separation from Peter, she had come to understand the reality of her love for him. Had she not physically torn herself away from him, she knew she would eventually have surrendered to him.

The letter continued,

> *Remember, you're supposed to be eating well now that you're in the last part of your pregnancy. You want to have a smart kid, don't you? Get lots of protein. I'll be there to see you as soon as you're ready for company after the baby is born. Have you picked out a name yet?*

Jonadab. Anna laughed to herself, thinking of Peter's joke about naming a baby after his grandfather. She wondered if that were really his grandfather's name. There was so much about Peter she didn't know, and now, probably would never know. She sealed the letter and dropped it in the mail slot in the hallway, then went to bed.

※

In a week, Phil called again and asked her to attend a show of new products with him. They looked over the booths one by one, comparing the techniques of the live models demonstrating various products and speculating on the possibilities for income from such events for the agency.

As they sat in the hotel lobby and sipped coffee from Styrofoam cups, Phil said, "Anna, I want you to know I care about you a great deal. I'd like to be more than a friend to you." He slipped his arm lightly around her shoulders and moved a bit closer on the sofa.

Anna stared at him, knowing from the change in his expression that he could read the doubt and surprise registering in her look.

"Don't think I'm trying to pull a Barry Carlson maneuver here," Phil said quickly. "My affection for you remains whether you want a job with the agency or not. I would have made serious efforts to win you long ago, but Barry seemed to be first in line." Anna started to protest, but Phil silenced her with a wave of his hand. "I understand, Anna. You need time to get over Barry. That's fine with me. I just want you to know where I stand. You and I are adults; we don't have to tiptoe around. I find you very attractive. I want to have a special relationship with you."

Anna's mind was whirling. If she could not have Peter and the kind of complete love she had dreamed of, perhaps it was best to settle for friendship and security, the kind of relationship she knew she could develop with Phil.

"Phil, do you have faith in God?" she asked.

Phil's expression softened. "Yes, I do, Anna. I heard the rumors about your decision, and it made me do some serious thinking. I've been reading and studying the Bible for months. I've come to believe in Jesus Christ as my Savior. I'm learning a lot about the Christian life."

※

That night Anna lay awake, wondering if a whole new part of her life was opening before her. Phil had always impressed her with his reliability and common sense, existing as he did in the midst of a crowd of frenzied socialites. He had always been a gentleman, and even before his conversion, she had never known him to be dishonest or even unkind to the models with whom he worked. As for love, she had heard that people were often surprised by it. Sometimes it just grew if the seeds were planted and nurtured.

She thought once again of her granny's wisdom. "There's no flavor like that of a wild strawberry," she had said as they bent over the hillsides, picking the stems laden with fruit. "A berry patch in the garden is handy, though, and makes life a lot simpler. You just have to decide what you're willing to give up."

Could she give up the dream of perfect love she had come so close to with

Peter and accept the kind of life she would have with Phil? She did not know, and it seemed unfair to have to make the choice.

Tears rolled from the corners of her eyes onto the pillow as she tried to understand why the God she had honored had brought such heartbreak into her life. It did not seem to her that He was managing things well. It was very confusing. Remembering the summer, however, reminded her that she really had no choice except to trust Him.

The next morning, when Anna collected her mail, there was a plain envelope, rather wrinkled, with no return address. Inside was a piece of lined paper, ripped from a small spiral-bound pad. On the paper was written, "What we call the beginning is often the end, and to make an end is to make a beginning. The end is where we start from."

"T. S. Eliot," she breathed. She knew it was from Peter, but what could it mean? Where was he? Did he just want her to know he was safe? Or was he ending it all?

She paced about the apartment, nervous energy driving her into mindless activity. At least twice she reached for the phone, then remembered that Darron and Alysia would not answer at their old number.

When the doorbell rang just before noon, she practically ran to answer, glad for any interruption of her wild imaginings.

Peter stood before her, smiling, a small portfolio at his side. His crisp, white shirt made his tan face seem even darker, and the suit he wore was obviously new.

Anna stared at him for a moment, then pointed to the suit. "J. C. Penney?" she asked in a voice barely audible.

"How did you know?"

"It's my business to know," she said and then backed away to let him into the room.

He looked about, saying nothing for a few minutes. "So this is where you live," he offered.

She nodded, gazing at his back until he turned and faced her.

"Anna, can we sit down? There's something I want to show you."

For a moment, Anna considered asking him to leave. She was tired of being hurt, tired of saying good-bye, tired of hoping and despairing. Simple courtesy, however, caused her to go and sit down at one end of the long sofa. She kept staring at him as though he were an apparition.

Peter saw the envelope and notebook paper lying on the coffee table. "You got my note. I didn't know what to say, so I thought I'd let a master speak for me." He laid the portfolio between them on the sofa cushion and unzipped it.

"I've been working," he said simply, and spread out before Anna both the original prints and the published counterparts that chronicled the progress on

Granny Huddlestone's house. The accompanying article was titled "When Love Comes First," and it detailed Anna's decision to fill the house with beautiful things before starting the improvements.

"This is a magazine published by a historical society in Tennessee," said Peter. "They liked my work. They want me to do three more features this year."

Anna's gaze was drawn back to the photos, which included shots of herself smoothing out Alysia's quilt on the bed and pouring water from an old chipped porcelain bucket onto the flower boxes.

"Did you write the article?" asked Anna.

"One of the society members wrote it. She had plenty of material after she got through interviewing Alysia."

Anna could not help but smile as she imagined Alysia's enthusiasm. Peter's work, however, crowned the story.

"I'm very happy for you," Anna said. "You've crossed a long bridge. Don't ever go back, Peter. The world would be a poorer place without your work. Just look! You've done what you always wanted to do. You've brought some of what's best from your home and shared it with. . .well, maybe not the world, but a lot of other appreciative people."

"Alysia's been doing my bookkeeping. You'd think she has enough to do with two kids, but she says she needs brain work once in a while. She does letters for me, too. I work from my house. No more storefronts."

Anna searched his face, hoping for a clue to the mystery, but finally had to ask. "What happened?"

Peter stretched against the back of the sofa, his hands behind his head. "You remember when you came to Tennessee last spring, you had a question. You knew there was a God, and you knew your life was influenced by Him. Your question was, so what? Does it make any difference? And maybe a bigger question was, could you trust Him to do the right thing? Anna, I had the same questions, exactly the same. Finally one day I had to start over, like the poem said and like I did that day down by the creek when I was little. I just promised God I'd quit looking for results and just do what He wanted me to do."

"I know it was hard for you. What made you do it?"

His hands still behind his head, Peter turned a few inches to catch sight of Anna. "Because Darron threatened to beat me if I didn't," he answered.

Their laughter was followed by a noticeable silence until Peter said simply, "I love you, Anna."

He replaced the items in the portfolio and carefully zipped it shut. He moved forward on the sofa, sitting with his elbows on his knees, his fingers loosely intertwined. "I couldn't come to you until I knew I could succeed in the work I wanted to do, and you wouldn't have me until I was ready to surrender to God. If you'll say you love me, there's nothing else in this world I would ever want."

"Nothing?"

"Well, one little thing, I guess. Marry me."

In an instant Anna was in his arms, wrapped in the strength of his healed life and cradled in the comfort of the knowledge that while more questions might come in the days ahead, there would always be an answer.

"I thought I might never see you again," she said. "I just about went crazy when your note came. I was afraid you had gone off somewhere all alone and were just brooding."

"Well, I did that for a while, I admit," Peter said, holding her close. "But I'm back. I'm not afraid anymore. I want you to come with me just as soon as you can and promise me you'll never rent a motor home or even go near a bus station again."

"You know what my granny used to say?" Anna asked. "I can still see her, sitting on the porch, soaking her feet, and saying, 'No matter where you are, if it isn't home, it's too far away.'"

"What was your granny's first name?" Peter asked.

"Evangeline. Why?"

"Just in case we have a girl. Otherwise—"

"I know, I know," Anna said. "It's Jonadab." She kissed him and thought she could taste wild strawberries.

CATHERINE RUNYON

Catherine makes her home in Michigan with her family. She is a news editor and columnist at the *Advance* newspaper. Catherine writes inspirational romance because she wants "to make a positive contribution" to the romance genre and to let her readers know that "though all hope seem lost, He [God] remains faithful."

A Letter to Our Readers

Dear Readers:

In order that we might better contribute to your reading enjoyment, we would appreciate your taking a few minutes to respond to the following questions. When completed, please return to the following: Fiction Editor, Barbour Publishing, Inc., P.O. Box 719, Uhrichsville, OH 44683.

1. Did you enjoy reading *Appalachia*?
   ❏ Very much—I would like to see more books like this.
   ❏ Moderately—I would have enjoyed it more if _____
   _____
   _____

2. What influenced your decision to purchase this book?
   (Check those that apply.)
   ❏ Cover   ❏ Back cover copy   ❏ Title   ❏ Price
   ❏ Friends   ❏ Publicity   ❏ Other

3. Which story was your favorite?
   ❏ *Afterglow*   ❏ *Eagles for Anna*
   ❏ *Come Home to My Heart*   ❏ *Still Waters*

4. Please check your age range:
   ❏ Under 18   ❏ 18–24   ❏ 25–34
   ❏ 35–45   ❏ 46–55   ❏ Over 55

5. How many hours per week do you read? _____

Name _____

Occupation _____

Address _____

City _____ State _____ Zip _____

E-mail _____